THROUGH THE VALLEY

By the Same Author

Fiction

NO ARMS, NO ARMOUR, 1939
CAPTAIN SMITH & CO., 1943
THE JOURNEY HOME 1944

Travel

DEATH BY MOONLIGHT, 1937

THROUGH the VALLEY

Robert Henriques

The Reprint Society London

FIRST PUBLISHED 1950
THIS EDITION PUBLISHED BY THE REPRINT SOCIETY LTD.
BY ARRANGEMENT WITH WM. COLLINS SONS & CO LTD.
1951

PRINTED IN GREAT BRITAIN BY
WILLIAM CLOWES AND SONS, LIMITED, LONDON AND BECCLES

To the Memory of
PHILIP AND EVAN

" Through the Valley " is a novel
and all the characters who appear in it
are entirely fictitious

CONTENTS

Song of the Century . . .

We march to the night and we plunder the century—
Nothing to loot, for we've looted the lot—
Our hearts are heavy, our hands are empty,
From too much getting and too little got.

We'll halt towards nightfall, and open the bottle—
" I'd sing you a song, boys, but what's it worth? "
For our hearts are cracked and our ears unhearing
From too much laughter and too little mirth.

I'll get out my chart and I'll get out my compass,
I'll kick out the camp-fire and search the night,
But my heart is broken, my eye unseeing
From too much burning and too little light.

I'll search for the hilltop that ought to be showing
A star of the morning somewhere above
" Don't know where I've got to, don't know where I'm going—
Through too much loving and too little love."

So we've had it, boys, befogged and benighted,
Bewitched and bewildered! Is there a plot?
Is there a pilot; a beacon sighted
Through the valley? Or what?

BOOK ONE

The Week Before Christmas, 1926

"GEOFF, what are you doing?"

Geoff's father was never quite asleep. At the first creak on the landing, caused by his son's shoeless feet, he heard his own voice, unnaturally thick and strained, calling from his semi-consciousness. And as the door now opened, he was already sitting up in bed, striking a match to light the bedside candle. With his elbow he must have struck the ledger and the pile of papers that had been on the table beside the candlestick, for all of them slid to the floor and scattered. There they lay, like the spread of catastrophe: the heavy account book of the Neapcaster Park Estate and the various bills, receipts, estimates and valuations which the tired mind of Geoff's father, old Mr. Richard Greenley, the Agent, never ceased to consider and lament. Since the death of his wife, at Geoff's birth, there had been no other subject that the Agent's thoughts and passions, sleeping or waking, had ever engaged but the affairs of the Meredith farms and the Meredith family which he served constantly. When he prayed, it was a hopeless prayer for their prosperity to be restored and a humble gratitude for their kindness. His friend and employer, General Meredith, for all his wilfulness, was scarcely separate, in the Agent's mind, from a higher Master.

And now Geoff, as soon as he entered his father's room, went down upon his knees to collect the scattered documents. Well might he do so, as a true servant; for the son, also, owed gratitude beyond repayment that he had been taken as an infant into the nurseries of Neapcaster Park, in the Cotswolds, to be brought up and later sent to school with the General's only child, young Ralph Meredith. "That's right, my boy!" the Agent said, as

Geoff, still on his knees, replaced the ledger and papers beside his father's bed. "You're sure there's none left?"

"That's all of them, Father."

Mr. Greenley had looked at his watch. "But it's not yet four o'clock!"

"No, Father. I was going with Adam Rogers, stopping the earths in Slender Ladies Covert."

"You must sleep *some* time, my boy."

"Yes, Father, I do . . . I always go stopping the earths when Adam does."

"Do you? I didn't know about that." So little the Agent knew about his son who, so recently, on his fifteenth birthday, had been returned to his father's home. "Don't get in Adam's way, will you? Don't bother him."

"No, Father; he wants me; I help."

*   *   *

Quietly Geoff closed his father's door and still continued to walk on his stockinged toes, as noiselessly as possible, as he went downstairs. The sort of conversation that he had just had, belonging almost to sleep and to a formula of father-and-son relationship which was only legendary between them, and had never properly been practised, took place in the tongue of a befogged frontier trodden by the just-awoken. Along this frontier, everything experienced went directly to that most distant of the memory's stores, where it could lie hidden for years and then be produced with tremendous emphasis; and familiar places became more familiar in a whole new set of proportions that were no more subject to measurement than the dreams they followed. The small house became big in its creaking darkness and candle shadows.

As Geoff sat on the immense sofa that faced the hall fireplace, and started to put on his boots, he knew that his father, unable to sleep, would be again busy with his ledger. His father's voice, coming faintly through the closed door of his bedroom and down the carved staircase that was incongruously graceful for so modest a building as the Lodge, reached the firelit hall. The words were inaudible but they would be solicitous, bidding Geoff to go carefully down the hill in the dark or to wrap up warmly on such a bitter night. And because, at this unreal or too real hour, it was possible to feel or imagine the deep, clinging love that ought, surely, to bind together father and son, Geoff returned upstairs in his boots to say: " I'm going now, Father. I'll be back for break-fast."

The old man, who looked even older than his age with his thin hair rumpled, his neck scraggy in the open collar of his pyjamas, and his face still drawn with sleep, kept a finger on a line of the ledger as he looked up. " Have you made yourself tea? "

" I hadn't thought, Father. I don't want any."

" You oughtn't to go out without a hot drink. The kettle will be almost on the boil."

" Would *you* like a cup, Father? "

The old man hesitated. " Not unless you're having one your-self."

" All right," Geoff said. He had a peculiar sensitivity that made him reproduce sympathetically, in his own lips and tongue, the old man's craving for the warmth, taste and sweetness of a cup of tea. But even when he had made the tea and taken his father a cup, he drank none of it himself. There was no time to let it cool, because Adam Rogers would never wait. The boy hurried from the room, glad to escape the slightly sour smell which belongs, in the nostrils of youth, to the beds of the aged.

*   *   *

When Geoff closed the front door behind him, the coldness and stillness of the night pushed against him like a headwind. The trees of the Park and the beeches along the road creaked in the Christmas frost, and the dead leaves made a pattering sound as if creatures were treading them. There was no light at all, no glimmer to be reflected in the frost; and yet the frost was visible on the few yards of garden path that led to the gate, and on the gravel of the drive beyond it. And the grass beyond the drive, crackling underfoot as he set a course across the Park, was a good deal paler than the surrounding trees. And so he had seen the shadow against the grass before he came to it. He had been aware of a shadow but had not put it to analysis. He had not been prepared to see it move.

It was a terrible thing when the shadow moved. He stopped and stood perfectly still and soundless, terrified. It was like a moment of falling—when a man has lost his balance on a height;

a moment of waiting for pain, when a man has been struck a blow which has not yet reached his nerve centres. It was fear. But the fear went as soon as the shadow became a person and the person spoke. "I say, Mister," the tramp said; "got anything to eat?"

"Afraid not," Geoff said.

"What about back in the house?"

"I'm sorry—I haven't time . . ." The unconsidered answer came quickly. "I'm not going back to the house."

"Aren't you?" The man spoke unpleasantly. "Listen, Mister!" He took hold of Geoff's wrist. "Just you listen!" Geoff pulled his wrist away and knew at once that he was stronger than the tramp. "You're only a young 'un," the tramp said. "Only a lad."

Geoff thought that the shadow extended itself into an arm raised for a blow. As a matter of fact, he scarcely thought at all, but he hit first, hitting the man bang in the middle of his stomach.

Having never hit any one before, except in a boxing ring, he was first astonished, and then excited, and then regretful and then frightened to find that a blow struck by himself had such effect. The shadow contracted itself, remaining apparently on its feet, but doubled up, gasping and groaning. "You're all right, aren't you?" Geoff asked, feeling for the shadow and getting hold of a shoulder that was thin and sharp. "You aren't hurt? You're all right?" His questions became increasingly anxious as his hands found their way about the man's figure and tried to lift it gently, to straighten it. "I didn't mean to hurt you. I'm sorry I hurt you. You're all right?"

Quite suddenly the man stopped his groaning and said: "Why d'you do that? You'd no call to do that, Mister."

"I thought you were going to hit me."

"*Me* hit *you*! *Me* hit *you*!"

"You raised your arm."

"You hurt me bad," the man said. "It's assault. It's damages in court." The man groaned again. "You hurt me very bad. I shall want your name and address."

It was a good thing that the situation had so quickly become ludicrous. "I live there, in the Lodge," Geoff said. And looking back, he could see the light in his father's window, a candle that burnt in another world altogether, another lifetime. "I've got to get on," he said; "I'm late. Are you coming?"

"That's my business," the man said. "You didn't have to hit me."

"You'd better come along to the road. You're trespassing here."

"That's not your business."

"In a way it is. My father's the Agent here."

"Lackey," the man said. "A bloody lackey." His violence started him coughing. "You ever been hungry?"

"Come on," Geoff said and put his hand on the man's arm.

"Don't you hit me again," the man said, in between the coughing. "Hit me again and you might get something different. Just you try it!"

"I'm not going to. Come on to the road!" And when Geoff moved towards the road, the man followed but kept his distance behind, refusing, when Geoff stopped, to draw level. "Where are you from? Where are you going?" Geoff asked him. But the man would not answer.

On the road it seemed to be a good deal lighter; and now that they could see each other, their relative sizes and proportions— and the proportions and sizes of the whole affair—appeared quite different. He was not much of a man, the tramp, undersized and ragged in a long, trailing coat. His miserable and formless shape was just visible, and he was shivering. He had no hat.

"Now I lost me hat!" the tramp said. "I had a hat an' now I lost it." As he raised his hand to his head, something fell on to the lane, tinkled and rolled towards Geoff who picked it up. It was a broken bolt. Again the proportions changed.

"You were going to hit me with that!" Geoff said.

"You couldn't hit any one with a thing like that, Mister. See for yourself!"

"You could hold it in your fist," Geoff said, trying it. "It would make a lot of difference. You could hurt a man that way."

"It's my bit of a bolt. That's all it is. You give it me back!"

"No," Geoff said, putting it in his pocket.

"It's mine, Mister. It belongs to me. You wouldn't take what's mine, Mister, would you?"

"I'm taking this."

"You're a lot bigger than me," the man said. "I wouldn't

hit any one. I wouldn't hit a man a lot bigger than me." He was
a pitiable creature. "You ever been hungry?" he asked for the
second time.

"No," Geoff answered. He felt very humble about it. "I
haven't ever had to be hungry."

"You wait till you're hungry. You wait till it's your turn,
Mister, your turn to be hungry. Then go hitting folk."

"Nobody has to go hungry in England," Geoff said.

"Don't they? Don't they then?" The tramp's voice rose.
"That's what they tell you, isn't it? That's what they teach you
in the schools. Nobody has to go hungry! Go to the workhouse
—that's it—go to the Institute!" The man's voice dropped again.
It rose and dropped dramatically like a piece of childish acting.
"Ever tried the muck they give you? Ever tried it? You can't
eat it, Mister; you can't keep it down." The man turned away,
became again a shadow. The shadow receded and was gone, but
the voice continued. "You wait, Mister. It's easy to talk. It's
easy to go hitting people. It's easy to talk, with a bloody great
place like this, with a bloody great house, with nothing to do but
live, nothing to do but live on your own fat, nothing to do but
live on the fat of others, with a bloody great house, a bloody great
place like this, it's easy to talk . . ." The voice had risen to its
climax and then diminished and become mixed with shuffling
footsteps. "You wait, Mister. You see what's coming. You
wait . . ." The footsteps died, but the voice completed the passage
with one final declaration. "I wasn't going to hit you, Mister.
I wouldn't have hit you . . ."

*   *   *

When the voice and the footsteps had gone, Geoff turned back
into the Park. He had come to the road only to lead the tramp
off the premises; and Adam's cottage—which was his destination
—lay in the opposite direction, southwards across the valley, down
and over the river and up again. The shortest way across the
valley to this cottage was straight down the gentle decline of the
drive and through the house or stables, on through the gardens,
and on down the lower and steeper slopes of the hill to Garden
Bridge. But if Geoff were to take this route, the dogs would bark
and the household be woken. He took, therefore, a long, slant-
wise cut across the Park, which would bring him to the first of

several cart-tracks, all of them by-passing the house to the east and converging on the river at Swain's Bridge. Until this track was reached, it was not an easy way to find in the dark. It was rough going and a strenuous passage. Direction was difficult to keep, and after a short while, Geoff was not at all sure that he was right. The seconds and minutes became elongated while he remained in doubt. Doubt in all things was his overwhelming affliction. There had to be faith. As if you were in church, there had to be faith that, if you continued on a south-easterly course, you were bound to strike the track.

There were no moon or stars, and no guiding marks except a vague, twisted familiarity about some of the groups of trees. The only aid was the lightest wind, which had been drawing from the north-east, bringing the frost, and so had to be kept on the left cheek. But if the wind was changing, backing to the west at the approach of dawn, even this aid would have vanished. And yet if the wind was *not* to change in this way, there would be no morning thaw, and the ground would remain hard, hard as concrete, too hard to hunt—and another prayer would have gone unanswered.

It was therefore a complicated faith that Geoff needed: faith in prayer, and faith in the particular prayer that he might get each one of the five days' hunting that could be fitted into the Christmas holidays on one pony; faith that the wind must, accordingly, be changing or about to change, so that it would bring a thaw; and faith that—in spite of a changing wind which left him with no aid to direction—he was able to find the way through this complete darkness. For those whose lives depended upon faith, life was difficult. But it was easy for people like Ralph who depended upon laughter and disbelief.

In spite of the tussocks and ant-hills in this part of the Park, Geoff started to run in order to get the act of faith completed as quickly as possible. He stumbled and was panting. But surely there was no sodden, swamp-like patch, ankle-deep, between the drive and the track? Yet the squelch of his boots was a wonderful thing to hear. It meant that, in spite of the cold, the frost was breaking; the thaw was starting; the ground would be soft enough for the feet of horses and hounds; and the Meet at Neapcaster Park would not be cancelled. They would hunt a fox. Prayer worked! And yet, and yet . . . the heart's desire was equally achieved by those like Ralph who didn't believe in prayer,

17

who didn't pray. He also would hunt. Geoff reached the track.

On the slippery track it was easy to fall and to suffer some injury which would prevent hunting. It was safer to go with caution. But Ralph Meredith went nowhere with caution. He knew that he would not be hurt; and when he was in fact hurt, he knew that it would be a negligible injury; and when the injury proved, in fact, to be serious, it was of no consequence. Hunting was the grandest thing in the world, but there was no grandeur sufficient to be worth the worrying and the caution. And if you were stopped from hunting, you could always work out mathematical puzzles from an American book got last Christmas and called *So You Think You Can Add?* Ralph knew that he could add. Geoff knew that he, personally, could not. It took a tremendous amount of work to get a place above Ralph in mathematics; and when this had been achieved, Ralph was unimpressed.

Ralph was always certain and often wrong, and he never cared much, one way or the other. But Geoff knew that his doubts were inescapable, declining to be stilled by reason, requiring constant faith, and inflicting constant hurt. The new doubt that had just started and was now growing inside him, like an indigestible lump in his stomach, threatened to be persistent. He was no longer sure that the tramp had been going to hit him. He was no longer sure that the tramp, when he said afterwards that he wouldn't have hit him, wasn't speaking the truth. So Geoff thrust his hand into his pocket and grasped the bolt.

Ralph would have stood no argument about the tramp. Of course he was going to hit you, with that bolt as a sort of knuckle-duster, a murderous blow. And even if he wasn't going to hit you, a smack in the stomach wouldn't hurt a chap like that. And even if, in fact, it did harm him, you couldn't take it back. It was too late now to worry. It was no good ever worrying: it was always too late.

Ralph never worried. Nor did he ever hesitate, as Geoff was now hesitating on the bridge across the stream. The left-hand track, circumventing the wood, was longer and more moderately sloped; the right-hand track, going up to the bottom of the cover which it followed along to the central ride, was shorter, rougher and steeper. To the left you could run; to the right you would have to walk. Geoff paused. Ralph would already have been half-way up the hill, one way or the other, probably the easier.

But Geoff, because he had hit the tramp undeservedly, took the shorter and steeper route up the hill—where it was only possible to walk—and made himself run along it. As he ran, he gasped for breath in the way that the tramp had gasped after the hit in the stomach. The gasps became words and phrases in the rhythm of his slow, painful running. " I wasn't going to hit you . . . you've never been hungry . . . this running is hell, hell, hell . . . I wasn't going to hit you . . . Ralph couldn't run up here . . . I'm actually tougher than Ralph . . . a bit tougher, a bit, a bit . . . I wasn't going to hit you . . . I wish I hadn't hit the tramp."

When he got to the top of the wood, with only a short field to cross, he could see the light in Adam's cottage. Old Adam, immensely old, wide, solid and squat, a most peculiar figure, peculiar at any time but less peculiar than usual at this hour of pre-dawn darkness when all life was subject to distortion, came out of his cottage at the sound of Geoff's approach. He carried a spade, an unlit lantern, a crowbar and a sack. The sack was unnecessary, but he always carried it, for there was always the chance that something would be found to be put into it. Geoff took the crowbar, the heavier of the implements. Neither of them spoke, and there was a grand and exciting feeling about this ritual of not speaking. In silence they walked back down the track by which Geoff had come, re-entered the ride through the wood, and turned off it along the steep hill-face to the badger earths. When they left the ride, they needed a light, and Geoff—still without a word spoken—lit the lantern.

*   *   *

Slender Ladies was a long, narrow covert, and the badger earths were at the end. Old Adam and Geoff spent at least an hour at the badger earths, all the time without speaking. The earths had many entrances and exits spaced along a steep, almost vertical bank for some fifty yards. The twisted and upthrown roots of trees girdled and intersected the mouths of these deep holes where the badgers lived and the foxes visited.

Much earlier that night the old man had started his operations on this subterranean city; and the smell of human urine, with which he had dressed the holes in order to drive out their occupants, still flavoured the wood. And now, at each hole, he put his ear and listened, he put his nose and sniffed, and knew then that there had been no returning. With spade and crowbar, he and Geoff filled in the entrances, to bar the foxes out.

When they had finished, there was some light in the sky; not a positive radiance, but a first suggestion that the darkness might seep away into the morning dusk. The old man blew out the lantern, and at once the light increased. He was old, old, old and grotesque. He was not the shape of a man at all. But in the first light of the day, like the first light of the world, his slow, semi-conscious, reptilian animation was natural to the swirl of mist.

Like a scaly thing, the old man moved through the trees and undergrowth. Following him, Geoff could scarcely hear his leader's footsteps, though his own were noisy. The two of them went up the ride to the gate at the top, through the gate and into the field, along the track at the edge of the field to the old man's cottage. Outside the cottage a girl, a granddaughter of Adam's, was waiting. At first they saw only the pallor of her frock against the dark wall; and then they saw the pallor of the stone wall against the dark trees, and the trees black against the first lemon tints above the crest. At last they saw the girl's young and lovely face, and the big belly, full of child. To this belly, Geoff's gaze was drawn and fastened.

" Her should ha' had it by now." Old Adam had broken his morning silence. " Her's more'n a week late."

" It's Judy!" Geoff said, making himself lift his eyes to the face of this girl who had once been a maid in the Merediths' house. " I didn't know . . . I hadn't heard . . ." His throat was too narrow for his voice. " I didn't know she was married," he said. But he knew that " married " was not the word that his voice had wanted.

" Her's never married. Her's not in the married state."

They had reached the gate to the cottage garden where the girl stood motionless. As if her ears were shut to their voices, and her eyes unseeing, her face was expressionless and strangely lifted; her gaze was above their heads. The beat of her heart, and her breathing, were drawn down into the belly which held all her own life, as well as her child's, within the throb of its compass. Apart from the belly, she was a tiny thing, scarcely existing.

" I didn't, I didn't know . . ." The spectacle caused a paralysis of thought. As if he was a bridled creature, Geoff had been led right up to the gate where he stood beside Adam; the two of them, side by side, were inspecting the girl. The saliva in Geoff's mouth was sour with fright.

The old man let a toothless grin spread like the ripples of a risen trout to crease the stretch of his face. " You're young, Mas'r Geoff! "

" I'm not! " The reply was a child's reaction. " I'm sixteen next birthday. She's not much more herself."

" The lad as gave her *that* . . ." the old man said, pointing at the belly, actually touching it, poking it with a finger that was thick and blunt and always reddish with dried blood, " he was the same, you see; he were sixteen, same as yourself."

" Who? Who was it? " Geoff could not prevent his speech. The girl had not moved, but stood like a domestic beast that knew the tone of a voice but not what it said.

" You doesn't know that, Mas'r Geoff! " The grin returned. " Not as she'll say herself—but you ha'n't heard them talk? " He spat directly at the girl's feet. " Best ask her, Mas'r Geoff! "

*　　　*　　　*

Belonging to the myth of these woods, where the silver birches grew in groves amongst the elms and oak, this creature called Adam sat by the badger earths while the whole company of the hunt made its way in procession to the track which Geoff had taken that morning, and down it as far as Swain's Bridge. Over the bridge, they took the alternative route, bearing to the left, and thus keeping clear of the covert, to reach the road above it. There the train halted, like an army in column, with the Master at its head.

The Master had received certain information and, looking round for a handy messenger, saw Geoff. Catching the boy's eye, the Master lifted his little finger and crooked it. And Geoff, blushing at the honour, kicked his cob in the ribs and drew level.

The Master, whose name was Guy Bredon and who was a big, bluff man, pleasant and shrewd, leant towards Geoff and spoke softly in his ear. " All right then," he concluded, " slip down the ride and tell Craddock! There's a good lad! "

Again kicking in the ribs the grey cob from Kildare, Geoff pressed his way through the crowd of horsemen. " Excuse me, sir . . . Please, Colonel Black . . . I'm sorry, Mrs. Bredon . . ."

As Geoff's cob bumped into the quarters of a hot little chestnut mare ridden by Colonel Black and slipped between him and Mrs. Bredon, the Master's wife, to reach the gate off the road by Adam's cottage and thence the track downhill to the covert, Colonel Black leant across to speak confidentially to Mrs. Bredon, and she advanced her horse a trifle to hear what he had to say. With a finger of the gloved hand that held her hunting-whip she touched the loop of grey-gold hair that drooped—contained in its net— from beneath her top hat, covering her ear; and in response, Colonel Black leant still farther towards her and, changing his reins, put his left hand upon the withers of her horse. But all he said into her ear, after this most careful preparation, was: " A very nice . . . cob, that; a very nice cob that young . . . Geoff Greenley's riding. Cost a packet, I gather." He had a habit of catching his breath as he spoke, cutting up his phrases into queer shapes between scarcely audible gasps.

Mrs. Bredon straightened her back, nodded, and pressed her lips together into an expression of general interest, an acknowledgment of significance, like the cocked ears of a horse; and the two heads converged again, as Colonel Black gave the slightest twitch of a beckon with one finger and whispered: " Harry Meredith got that cob from Ireland for the boy. I've heard as much as . . . a hundred and fifty quid mentioned! "

This time, as Mrs. Bredon straightened herself on her side-saddle and gave a little pat to the skirt of her habit, her lips were pressed into a downward curve that meant a mocking, a childish dismay, and that once had caused the flesh of her exquisite cheeks to flow into puckers and dimples. The memory of these fascinations still moved the unweary, unforgetting passions of Colonel Black, who leant towards her for a third time and now put his hand on her forearm as he said: " I gather that old Greenley begged . . . him not to do it, but Harry *would* have it . . . won't look at his overdraft—when it's anything to do with that lad."

And Mrs. Bredon, glancing upwards at the deep, rather distant eyes, blue and serenely folded in the tanned hide of Tommy Black's face, still exceedingly handsome, released her breath from a breast tightened with old recollections as she answered: " Old Greenley's a damned good agent and a damned good friend to the Merediths. But you and Harry—both of you—were always fools with your cheque-books. And . . ." she added with a little catch in her voice, a sort of squeak, "*and* it's brought poor Harry . . ." She shrugged her shoulders, twitched her lips comically and let it go at that.

* * *

Harry Meredith, the General, waiting twenty yards down the road on a big bay horse, watched Geoff swing open the gate off the road, noted with satisfaction that the gate—one of his own—was still well hung, noted with regret that Adam's cottage was again in need of repair, and said to the Master beside him: "Guy, we may be breaking up, the two of us, but that lad's coming along very nicely."

"Young Geoff?" The Master nodded. "How old is he now, Harry? The same age as your own boy—is it?"

"Not quite," said the General. "There's the best of a year between 'em—Geoff's the younger."

"But good friends, I take it?"

"Oh, inseparable, quite inseparable," the General said.

Behind his father—farther down the road and out of earshot—Ralph Meredith pushed his feet forward in his stirrups, tipped his bowler hat over his forehead and, with a casual and arrogant air, smacked his pony's neck with the shaft of his crop. "Wonder what old Geoff's on to?" he said to the girl beside him.

She swung her head round in an exaggerated movement, flipping her blonde pigtails over her shoulder, and said: "I rather like Geoff."

"He's all right," said Ralph.

"Do most of you like him at school?"

"Most chaps do, I think. He's a trifle dim, of course."

"Geoff dim? Well, perhaps he is, a bit."

"Not so much dim, but he never talks."

"I shouldn't call him a very *sensitive* person," said the girl with an air of wisdom. "I should call him *reliable* . . . very reliable, I should think. He wouldn't ever be worried, would he? So *solid* . . ."

"He's gone down to the covert," said Ralph, who was now standing in his stirrups to watch Geoff out of sight.

* * *

Geoff, cantering down the track to the wood, matched very well the comments made on him by those who watched. In his

23

physical equipment there was no clue to his capacity for doubt and pain. Square and strong on his cob, he appeared less overgrown and better balanced than when on foot. He was pleasantly ugly. He now approached Craddock, the huntsman, who was sitting his horse at the top of the ride, pulling at the peak of his huntsman's cap and talking to Flower, the Merediths' head-keeper.

"Well, young Geoff, what d'ye want with me?" the huntsman asked, turning his head quickly with a twist like the hop of a bird. His face, smooth, unaged, brown, honest but knowing, was a cross between that of a gypsy and a naval captain. He winked at Geoff, the boy being no more than the son of the Agent. "What d'ye want with me, my lad? I'm busy."

"The Master says . . ." Geoff began; but Craddock, twisting his neck with another muscular twitch, called to his first whipper-in: "Hey you, Fred! Look to Watcher and Wanderer, can't you?" He saw Fred wheeling his horse and cracking his whip at the two young hounds who had unearthed a rabbit's paunch and were tugging it between them. He heard the lovely, slow, lazy, echoing crack of the whip and the sharp yelps. "*Your* two pups," he said to Geoff. "They that Mrs. Meredith was walking up at the house."

"The Master says—will you draw the covert uphill, away from the lower bridge."

"So he hopes to run to the Vale," said Craddock bitterly, "and *I* hopes to kill my fox."

"It wasn't that . . ."

"Oh, wasn't it?" The huntsman interrupted. "They want a gallop, and so do I; but the hounds need blood."

"It's Sir Frederick's earths," said Geoff. "They aren't stopped."

"And why not?" The question was sharper than his whiplash.

"I don't know. They just aren't."

"Sir Frederick bloody Betts," said Craddock. "Do you hear that, Tom?" he said to Flower, the keeper. "Sir Frederick bloody Betts!" Then, speechless and defeated, he drew his horn from between the buttons of his pink coat. "All right," he said to Geoff. "You can slip down to the bottom end and wait by the track till we've got away at the top. Will ye please do that?"

"All right," Geoff answered, with pleasure at the importance of his mission.

"There's a merry lad!" said Craddock, and standing in his

stirrups he called to the first Whip: "I'll draw it from the bottom up." And then, as Fred's whip started to crack, the huntsman reined back his horse and said to Flower: "And what about *your* earths, Tom? Reckon they're stopped?"

"Stopped," the keeper answered. "I've had old Adam with his hams in the badger earths most of the night. I can't do more than that."

"You can't," said Craddock, and viciously kicked his horse.

*   *   *

A long time later—some seventy minutes—a long way over the hill, on the windy side of the uplands, a farmer, called Mr. Trant, was ploughing a stubble. Stopping his tractor, he rose to his feet and cried aloud: "There goes the little red bastard!" And as he ran across the field, he put his hand to his mouth, hollering a high and desperate shriek that tore at his throat. He left his work and hurried down the hill to get his horse.

Trant was fortunate, because hounds shortly checked.

"Have a fag?" Colonel Black said to Geoff, as they both dismounted to rest their horses. "No? I suppose you're too young yet. That's a grand little cob!"

And Mrs. Bredon, looking at her watch, said: "Seventy-six minutes of the very best! I should say a twelve-mile point!" Then, turning in her saddle: "Hallo, Ralph, so *you*'ve caught us up! And your mother too! My dear, dear Anne!"

Anne Meredith, a perfectly lovely woman, even more lovely in a veil than without, because more young, nodded her head like a doll, a mechanical toy, and said: "That was very, very, very nice!" She was a tiny and exquisite ornament on a large and superb horse. She stroked her habit smooth, and she sniffed at the violets in her coat. "Now *everyone's* going to catch up," she said with regret. "And look, Ralph, there's poor little David Levine . . . So frightened, poor boy . . . but, I think, so brave . . ."

"A very decent little chap," said Black. "He'll grow like his father."

"If he's got to grow like Daniel," said Mrs. Bredon, "he's got to grow a terrible lot. Dear Danny! I've never seen any one so big, outside a circus."

"Poor David's ever so small," said Anne, delicately touching the bun at the back of her hat. "Just a dark little wisp. And

25

Ralph . . . my horrid little Ralph—he's so perfectly beastly about him. But Geoff . . . That cob went well!" she said to Geoff. "You like him all right?"

"Who, Mrs. Meredith?"

"That poor little David Levine . . ."

"Stop your chatter," said Tommy Black. "They're off again!" He was listening intently, his eyes and all his senses directed at a long straggling covert of willow and ash. "The Levine boy's all right," he said. "Now both you . . . bitches, shut up!" His head was cocked, his lips pursed. He was listening, listening.

"Hey, little bitches!" called Craddock down in the cover. "Loo in, little bitches!" And he called them to him with his horn. "Put 'em to me, Fred," he shouted crossly. "Put 'em to me, can't you?" He knew he had lost his fox; that the fox from Slender Ladies had doubled back. "I'll find 'em another," he said. "*I'll* show 'em sport! *I'll* hoodwink the lot of them! *I'll* break their bloody necks before I've finished . . . Hey, little bitches! Hey, my darlings," he crooned to his pack, "find me a fox!" There was anger in his love.

"I think Craddock's wonderful," said Mrs. Meredith, listening to his glorious voice and his horn, and hearing hounds speak to the new scent.

"He's a rogue," said Black. "Plays to the gallery. Bet you . . . the earth—he's on to a fresh fox." As he spoke, he got smoothly and quickly back on to his horse; as his knees touched the saddle-flaps, he was riding off.

"Just look at Madge!" cried Anne. "I call that sly, if you like!"

For Mrs. Bredon, without a word, had trotted down the meadow, had half-jumped, half-scrambled her horse through a gap in the hedge and had disappeared down the bank. At the same instant a dozen, a score of hounds, and then the whole pack, were heard hunting the fresh fox, with Craddock sounding the "gone away" on his horn, and all those followers of the hunt who had been left behind but had now caught up pressing for gap or gate. Thundering past, the whole crowd of them followed the one or two who knew the way, or who had the courage to find it, and who jumped or scrambled first.

"Now we've got left behind," said Mrs. Meredith. "That comes of chattering. Come on, Ralph!" Smacking her horse on

the rump with her whip, she cantered him down the field and put
him at the nearest, the highest part of the hedge. A beautiful horse,
he stood back from the hedge, bunched himself—as Anne's
diminutive shoulders swung forward—then leapt, then flew, then
soared, then stretched himself in mid-air, with a great kick back
of his loins into space, as he saw the deep, steep drop on the farther
side. "Oh dear!" said Anne to her violets, "we've jumped
down a precipice!" And lying back in her saddle, she let the
reins slip through her fingers to give her horse his head. "Lovely!"
she said as her horse landed and galloped on. "But, goodness me,
how frightening!" She thought she had been frightened. She
thought that this was fear. "I *was* frightened!" she said.

* * *

So were two of the three boys whom she had left behind her.
They were both frightened. Not Ralph! Ralph responded to
danger not with the common sense of fear, but with laughter. He
was made like that. When his body became aware that it might
get hurt, the gamble of it, the doubt, sent an exquisite pleasure
into his belly and a laugh to his eyes and lips. And now he started
to laugh when his pony started to jump the hedge. Geoff saw him
laughing but, because of the steep drop, he could not see him fall,
roll over clinging to the reins, get dragged a few yards by his pony
scrambling up, and then re-mount and ride on, laughing and
laughing, fit to bust! And by then Geoff had pulled up his cob
and was trotting down the hedge in search of a gap.

Geoff knew fear too well—the liquefaction of his loins, the caught
breath and the awful dropping of his guts as power flowed out.
And now, cantering along the hedge, he was avoiding the fear that
chased him but had not yet caught him up. Finding a partial gap
in the hedge, he turned his cob towards it, laid his body flat along
the cob's neck, let go the reins altogether, and allowed that intelligent animal to crawl its way through with cautious steps. He
emerged from the hedge and set heels to his cob at the same moment
as Ralph regained his saddle.

He thought he heard David Levine's voice—David calling in
a curiously high key—but of course he did not stop. The wind
was in his face, hounds were running fast, and he was well up in
front.

David had fear in his blood, dominating everything that he

did: fear of danger, fear of people, fear of contempt, fear of fear, and fear of himself. It was rare that he yielded to any of these fears. Sometimes he thought he had done so, and his mind harboured, in that respect, a sense of guilt. Sometimes he fought the fear, with great, conjured dreams of valour that he tried to imitate. And sometimes he plunged right into the fear, like a man diving from a height, seeking and taking some quick, irrevocable decision, hurling his body into some foolhardy act to convince himself that fear was not dominant. Thus David, at this moment, although his brain told him the rashness, even the absurdity, of putting his own indifferent little mare at this particular hedge, chose a spot right out on his own, sat down in his saddle, and rode her at it.

Once committed, his brain was clear. But fear remained. Fear removed from his muscles and nerves a fraction of their purpose. In the place of purpose, fear flowed in. It ran through his loins, his thighs, his knees, his saddle, and thence to his horse. It ran through his arms, his wrists, his fingers to the reins and the bit, and thus to the heart of the horse by another route. The heart of the horse did not leap into space. It made a competent effort. The mare jumped cleanly enough; but when, in mid-air, she and her rider saw the vast drop, the gulf, on the other side of the hedge, they together surrendered.

The mare lay on her back and rolled on David's legs. For an immeasurable period of time that might have been an instant or a life, he knew nothing but abandonment. Everything abandoned him. Then, in the desperate choke of fear, he was struggling to rise and found himself caught by the legs; he found himself fast. The previous fear was nothing beside the vast, monstrous awfulness that now engulfed him. The mare rolled over him, as if to crush altogether his thighs, his genitals, his guts, his heart, his face. Shouting for help, his voice came out in a shrill, falsetto shriek, a scream of death.

The mare rolled away from him and got to her feet. He lay quite still while the scream, his own terrible scream, returned through his ears to the soul that ought to have fled. But the soul had not fled. And the sound of the scream, the mark of it, the scar, the blemish, was now on the soul for evermore, for the rest of his life.

As David lay on the ground, his eyes noted a castellated edge of cloud, with tower and spire, the fringe of it bright with sun.

He heard a voice that was not unfamiliar: "It's Mr. Levine, isn't it? Are you badly hurt?" A cheerful face came between him and the sunlit cloud. It was a neighbouring farmer, Mr. Trant. Mr. Trant must have heard the shameful, indelible scream. "Mr. Levine—are you hurt?"

"I suppose so," David said. "I don't know, Mr. Trant." He tried to twitch one knee. It moved. He flexed the other, then moved his arms, then breathed deeply. There was no pain to any of these movements, no pain at all. The absence of pain made his scream more shameful. He yearned for pain. "I don't think I *am* hurt, Mr. Trant," he said; "not much, at least."

"That's right," said Trant. "You're a lucky lad. 'Twas a very nasty tumble, a terrible spill."

"The mare was on top . . ."

"Aye, she was. Let's get you up . . ." The farmer put out a hand, but the boy got quickly to his feet. They caught the horse, which was peacefully grazing the grass at the foot of the hedge. "I'll give you a leg up," said Mr. Trant, helping him into the saddle. They broke into an easy canter and went on together in pursuit of the hunt.

*   *   *

The scent had been good on the hills but was better still in the Vale. They were out of the Cotswolds now, with the steep escarpment behind them, on the very edge of the country that was hunted by the Neapcaster pack. Hounds ran on fast for another thirty minutes without a check. When at last they lost their fox, it was in a bed of withies on the banks of the River Eve. Then Craddock dismounted, handed his horse to the second Whip, and entered the withies on foot. In the water meadows outside, the followers who had remained with the hunt—perhaps some fifty out of the couple of hundred who had been at the meet—collected gradually, sorted themselves into their accustomed groups, and either resumed their gossip or, by carefully turned comments, drew oblique attention to their feats during the gallop.

"I thought I'd bought a packet of trouble," said Sir Frederick Betts. "I thought I'd steal a march on you all . . ."

"Tommy!" Mrs. Meredith called. "If I get down, can I count on you to help me up?"

"With more pleasure than you can . . . guess at, Anne, my sweet!"

"When all of you went left-handed," Sir Frederick persisted, "I went right, and . . ."

"Or will you," Mrs. Meredith continued, "go galloping into the blue—all sly like Madge?"

"I will not," said Tommy Black. As he spoke, his eyes seemed to penetrate her figure and her face with the same casual speculation that he addressed naturally to every woman: in a few hours, or in twenty years, each in turn needed him.

"If you go right," Sir Frederick went on, "there's a whacking great post and rails and then . . ."

"Does this go on long?" Mrs. Bredon asked him. "Because, really, I rather want to vanish behind a bush."

Sir Frederick knew too well that he lacked the artistry to deflect rudeness and to hide his discomfort. He knew that his red face was becoming redder, that the process was noticed with satisfaction by those who caused it. But he did what he could. "Please allow me," he said to Mrs. Bredon, "to hold your horse."

"No, thank you very much," Mrs. Bredon answered. "For so many years now—except for the war—Colonel Black has had to do that for me. Tommy!" she called, beckoning him with her finger.

Tommy strolled over with a good-natured wink to Sir Frederick Betts; but the man, turning his horse, rode slowly out of sight.

"Poor man!" said Anne Meredith. "We never do let him tell his stories . . . You *were* unkind to him, Madge."

"He brings out the worst in me," Mrs. Bredon answered. "And such a horrid worst it is!"

"So foul you were about the war! He *did* do something or other that somebody had to."

"He made poison gases," said Tommy. "The wind changed and they . . . choked us."

"I'm not in the least surprised," Anne said. "No doubt it's the very same stuff that he puts on his fields. I'm told it ruins scent."

"But it certainly . . . grows big crops!"

"And well it might! You should hear Mr. Greenley tell you what it does to the earth."

"Old Greenley is just too . . . conservative for his job."

"You should hear Harry, then," said Anne. "He says that Betts just buys up everybody's land when they're hard up. And

30

as working swiftly, tightening girths and changing
Master Ralph had a tumble, I see." He spoke with
the girth between his teeth as he hauled it tight. He
grey mare in the belly. "She blows herself out," he said
ss. " I see the back of his coat," he said, referring again
But he doesn't hurt himself! I reckon he bounces."
unces," Mrs. Meredith murmured, thinking how true
ll the Meredith men in history.
e covert Harry Meredith was saying: "You know,
nt to think a minute. If we let him across the river,
bridge between here and Medlicote."
ning his back from the hole which he had been in-
th Craddock, the Master nodded. He took off his
and scratched his head. Without his cap, his face
ier and older, even pompous, and his hair was seen
and turning grey. "We *shall* have to think a bit," he
"What about it, Craddock? The General says . . ."
you worry about that," said the huntsman. He had
intention of letting the fox run anywhere at all. He
l that his hounds should have it.
t much use to argue with a huntsman at these moments,
ster did say: "He's a good fox. He's been a good
Craddock. Give him grace, won't you? Give him a
start of us."
addock, with a black heart, shouted to his Whip:
dogs back, can't ye, Fred? We don't want 'em a' top
n he turned his attention to Will, who was unbuckling
h from her haversack.
go down deep as the night," Will said to the huntsman.
you your fox."
she will," said Craddock.
l the second whipper-in were herding hounds to the
thicket; and the Master and Harry Meredith were
eir way through the pack, returning to their horses.
to the wall outside the wood, the General saw his wife,
at Grant had finished working on her saddle. The
Jimmy, would be busy with his own. As he climbed
er the wall, the General watched his wife with love.
ack's cupped hands were held for her tiny foot, and he
upwards tip, so that she seemed to float, to hover and

then—if you'd believe it—he just makes his farms into factories
and runs them with his fertiliser factories *and*, so Harry says, just
drags corn out of it, so that it all gets poorer and poorer—or one
day it will do—while he gets richer and richer . . . At least, that's
what Harry says."

" Harry," said Tommy Black, " is just too . . . conservative to
live."

" Anyway, he says that Betts is a crook."

" I very . . . much doubt, Anne dear, if he really did."

" He says it's criminal the things he does."

" Ah!" said Tommy, " that's a different story!"

" Did he say even that? " Madge asked. " It's very surprising.
I've never known Harry have a bad word for any one all his life."

" Nor me," said Anne; " and sometimes it gets very boring
indeed only to hear nice things said about every one. *But*," she
added, " he does say sinister things about Freddy Betts."

" Even that surprises me."

" What he minds," Anne said, " is the way Betts behaved to
Mr. Trant, turning him out, like he did. We sold him Swire's, as
one does, and he promised Harry that Mr. Trant should stay, and
then . . ."

" Did Harry get it in writing? " Tommy asked.

" I dare say he didn't, but I'm sure Betts said . . ."

" A different story," Tommy said again. " You should write
things down with . . . chaps like me an' Betts."

" What Guy minds," said Madge, " is Betts getting so rich, and
every one else . . ."

" Bless me!" said Tommy. " Guy Bredon's a nice one to
mind about a thing like that! A feller who owns a bank . . ."

" It isn't really a bank," Madge said vaguely. She had twisted
her body to look behind her and now had one hand on her horse's
rump and the other on its withers. Across the water meadows she
could just see a glimpse of scarlet through the untidy straggle of
thorns towards which Sir Frederick had been making. " He's
found just the place," said Madge. " He would!"

* * *

Later David joined Geoff. It was the one person to whom he
could talk unguardedly. "I felt an awful fool . . . I honestly
thought I was dead. I meant to shout for help, and it came out

like a shriek; and when Trant asked if I was badly hurt, and I found I wasn't, and after that awful scream had come when I tried to shout . . ." He just couldn't help telling Geoff the whole story. To display his shame seemed to be some sort of redemption.

"You know, Dave," Geoff interrupted him, "you really are the biggest bloody fool on earth. Why talk about it? If *you* didn't say anything, nobody else would. Only Trant knows, and he doesn't talk."

At this affectionate reproof, David felt an immense swelling of the heart which burnt with gratitude and love for Geoff. But he saw now that Trant had walked up to Ralph and that the two were chatting together.

Following his glance, Geoff said: "You don't think that Trant would tell Ralph?" He laughed. "Of course he wouldn't; he wouldn't trouble to. But *I* might, you know . . . But I won't."

Trant was in fact saying: "You weren't the only one, Master Ralph, to jump that fence. By a long chalk, you weren't. There was Craddock himself and Fred, and the Master and Colonel Black, and Mrs. Bredon and your own mother, and there was Geoff . . ."

"He crawled and creeped, I expect."

"He got there as soon as yourself. And young David Levine —he took it on your left."

"He never got his horse over that!"

"Oh, yes, he did. He had a bit of a tumble, same as yourself, but he was soon up and on again."

"I don't believe it," Ralph said. He meant merely to express his contempt—a mild sentiment—for the young Jew who was at school with him. "Anyway, the fence is lower on the left."

"Oh, no, it isn't, Master Ralph. If anything, 'tis steeper. And he's younger'n you, and his horse isn't half so good." Trant nodded. "But you don't like him much, do you?"

"I don't bother to dislike him. He isn't worth it."

"If he grows to be like his father, he'll be worth plenty. His father's as good a man as we've had."

"He doesn't hunt."

"Nor would you," Trant said, "with a shrapnel lodged in your chest. He used to go with the best of us. He was as keen a man as your father himself, or as Colonel Black. You should ha' seen the three of them when there was a real, tearing scent!"

32

Ralph was too uninterested t[...] dock's gone and lost our fox," h[...]

"Oh, no, he hasn't, Master [...] right enough. Fox has gone to gr[...] if you trouble to hearken."

*   *   *

"He's been a good fox to us,['] Meredith as they stood together [...] Craddock will want to dig him o[...]

"He will, Guy. I dare say h[...] hated this part of the day's hunti[...] had to be given their blood.

"Here's old Will," said the M[...]

Pushing his bicycle, Will came [...] ageless little creature, brown, bris[...] his shoulders there was slung a ha[...] a terrier was buckled, their heads [...] and daughter. The young one wa[...] but the old lady, more philosophi[...] of pink tongue showed itself whe[...] placed or missing. "That's a rare o[...]

Will's own face, ancient but scar[...] as he passed and acknowledged th[...] of the hunt. To each he touched [...] wore together with a coat that had [...] Mrs. Bredon, 'morning, your Lady[...] ning, General, 'morning, Mrs. Mer[...] could be counted to earn him a qu[...] he looked in the other direction as [...] Propping his bicycle against the wa[...] climbed inside with his terriers and [...] and Harry Meredith.

Everything then happened very [...] train of grooms had arrived by road[...]

Grant, a groom from Neapcaste[...] and had slipped from the back of t[...] her. "A good hunt, Madam?" he a[...]

"Simply lovely," Mrs. Meredith [...] swallow."

Grant [...] leathers. [...] the end o[...] punched t[...] to his mist[...] to Ralph. [...]

"He [...] this was o[...]

Inside [...] Guy, we [...] there isn'[...]

Straig[...] specting [...] peaked c[...] looked h[...] to be sca[...] answered [...]

"Dor[...] not the l[...] was resol[...]

It was [...] but the [...] fox to us[...] gentlema[...]

And [...] "Get th[...] of us." [...] the old b[...]

"She[...] "She'll [...] "I k[...]

Fred [...] edge of [...] threadin[...]

Com[...] and saw [...] young la[...] painfully [...] Tommy [...] gave her [...]

then—if you'd believe it—he just makes his farms into factories and runs them with his fertiliser factories *and*, so Harry says, just *drags* corn out of it, so that it all gets poorer and poorer—or one day it will do—while he gets richer and richer . . . At least, that's what Harry says."

"Harry," said Tommy Black, "is just too . . . conservative to live."

"Anyway, he says that Betts is a crook."

"I very . . . much doubt, Anne dear, if he really did."

"He says it's criminal the things he does."

"Ah!" said Tommy, "that's a different story!"

"Did he say even that?" Madge asked. "It's very surprising. I've never known Harry have a bad word for any one all his life."

"Nor me," said Anne; "and sometimes it gets very boring indeed only to hear nice things said about every one. *But*," she added, "he does say sinister things about Freddy Betts."

"Even that surprises me."

"What he minds," Anne said, "is the way Betts behaved to Mr. Trant, turning him out, like he did. We sold him Swire's, as one does, and he promised Harry that Mr. Trant should stay, and then . . ."

"Did Harry get it in writing?" Tommy asked.

"I dare say he didn't, but I'm sure Betts said . . ."

"A different story," Tommy said again. "You should write things down with . . . chaps like me an' Betts."

"What Guy minds," said Madge, "is Betts getting so rich, and every one else . . ."

"Bless me!" said Tommy. "Guy Bredon's a nice one to mind about a thing like that! A feller who owns a bank . . ."

"It isn't really a bank," Madge said vaguely. She had twisted her body to look behind her and now had one hand on her horse's rump and the other on its withers. Across the water meadows she could just see a glimpse of scarlet through the untidy straggle of thorns towards which Sir Frederick had been making. "He's found just the place," said Madge. "He would!"

*   *   *

Later David joined Geoff. It was the one person to whom he could talk unguardedly. "I felt an awful fool . . . I honestly thought I was dead. I meant to shout for help, and it came out

31

like a shriek; and when Trant asked if I was badly hurt, and I found I wasn't, and after that awful scream had come when I tried to shout . . ." He just couldn't help telling Geoff the whole story. To display his shame seemed to be some sort of redemption.

"You know, Dave," Geoff interrupted him, "you really are the biggest bloody fool on earth. Why talk about it? If *you* didn't say anything, nobody else would. Only Trant knows, and he doesn't talk."

At this affectionate reproof, David felt an immense swelling of the heart which burnt with gratitude and love for Geoff. But he saw now that Trant had walked up to Ralph and that the two were chatting together.

Following his glance, Geoff said: "You don't think that Trant would tell Ralph?" He laughed. "Of course he wouldn't; he wouldn't trouble to. But *I* might, you know . . . But I won't."

Trant was in fact saying: "You weren't the only one, Master Ralph, to jump that fence. By a long chalk, you weren't. There was Craddock himself and Fred, and the Master and Colonel Black, and Mrs. Bredon and your own mother, and there was Geoff . . ."

"He crawled and creeped, I expect."

"He got there as soon as yourself. And young David Levine —he took it on your left."

"He never got his horse over that!"

"Oh, yes, he did. He had a bit of a tumble, same as yourself, but he was soon up and on again."

"I don't believe it," Ralph said. He meant merely to express his contempt—a mild sentiment—for the young Jew who was at school with him. "Anyway, the fence is lower on the left."

"Oh, no, it isn't, Master Ralph. If anything, 'tis steeper. And he's younger'n you, and his horse isn't half so good." Trant nodded. "But you don't like him much, do you?"

"I don't bother to dislike him. He isn't worth it."

"If he grows to be like his father, he'll be worth plenty. His father's as good a man as we've had."

"He doesn't hunt."

"Nor would you," Trant said, "with a shrapnel lodged in your chest. He used to go with the best of us. He was as keen a man as your father himself, or as Colonel Black. You should ha' seen the three of them when there was a real, tearing scent!"

32

Ralph was too uninterested to continue the argument. "Craddock's gone and lost our fox," he said.

"Oh, no, he hasn't, Master Ralph! He knows where he is right enough. Fox has gone to ground, and you can hear huntsman if you trouble to hearken."

* * *

"He's been a good fox to us," the Master was saying to Harry Meredith as they stood together outside the covert. "I suppose Craddock will want to dig him out."

"He will, Guy. I dare say he's right." They both of them hated this part of the day's hunting, but hounds, now and again, had to be given their blood.

"Here's old Will," said the Master.

Pushing his bicycle, Will came across the meadow, a diminutive, ageless little creature, brown, brisk and important. On each of his shoulders there was slung a haversack; and in each haversack a terrier was buckled, their heads protruding. They were mother and daughter. The young one was whimpering with excitement, but the old lady, more philosophical, was just grinning. A slip of pink tongue showed itself where some of her teeth were displaced or missing. "That's a rare old bitch!" said Harry Meredith.

Will's own face, ancient but scarcely creased, shone with delight as he passed and acknowledged the more distinguished members of the hunt. To each he touched his huntsman's cap which he wore together with a coat that had once been pink. "'Morning, Mrs. Bredon, 'morning, your Ladyship, 'morning, Colonel, 'morning, General, 'morning, Mrs. Meredith . . ." A touch of the cap could be counted to earn him a quid at Christmas. Nevertheless, he looked in the other direction as he passed Sir Frederick Betts. Propping his bicycle against the wall that confined the covert, he climbed inside with his terriers and was followed by the Master and Harry Meredith.

Everything then happened very quickly, just when the long train of grooms had arrived by road with the second horses.

Grant, a groom from Neapcaster Park, had found his mistress and had slipped from the back of the grey mare he had brought her. "A good hunt, Madam?" he asked her.

"Simply lovely," Mrs. Meredith answered. "She went like a swallow."

Grant was working swiftly, tightening girths and changing leathers. "Master Ralph had a tumble, I see." He spoke with the end of the girth between his teeth as he hauled it tight. He punched the grey mare in the belly. "She blows herself out," he said to his mistress. "I see the back of his coat," he said, referring again to Ralph. "But he doesn't hurt himself! I reckon he bounces."

"He bounces," Mrs. Meredith murmured, thinking how true this was of all the Meredith men in history.

Inside the covert Harry Meredith was saying: "You know, Guy, we want to think a minute. If we let him across the river, there isn't a bridge between here and Medlicote."

Straightening his back from the hole which he had been inspecting with Craddock, the Master nodded. He took off his peaked cap and scratched his head. Without his cap, his face looked heavier and older, even pompous, and his hair was seen to be scant and turning grey. "We *shall* have to think a bit," he answered. "What about it, Craddock? The General says . . ."

"Don't you worry about that," said the huntsman. He had not the least intention of letting the fox run anywhere at all. He was resolved that his hounds should have it.

It was not much use to argue with a huntsman at these moments, but the Master did say: "He's a good fox. He's been a good fox to us, Craddock. Give him grace, won't you? Give him a gentleman's start of us."

And Craddock, with a black heart, shouted to his Whip: "Get those dogs back, can't ye, Fred? We don't want 'em a' top of us." Then he turned his attention to Will, who was unbuckling the old bitch from her haversack.

"She'll go down deep as the night," Will said to the huntsman. "She'll get you your fox."

"I know she will," said Craddock.

Fred and the second whipper-in were herding hounds to the edge of the thicket; and the Master and Harry Meredith were threading their way through the pack, returning to their horses.

Coming to the wall outside the wood, the General saw his wife, and saw that Grant had finished working on her saddle. The young lad, Jimmy, would be busy with his own. As he climbed painfully over the wall, the General watched his wife with love. Tommy Black's cupped hands were held for her tiny foot, and he gave her an upwards tip, so that she seemed to float, to hover and

34

to alight with such ease astride the pommels, and there to adjust the skirt of her habit with such grace, slipping the elastic over her instep, patting the heavy cloth into place, sniffing again at the violets, patting the neck of her horse—all so sweetly that the General's heart, tired as it was, said again: "What a lovely thing, thank God!"

Then he was struck to his knees. Several men were shouting behind him—one with a falsetto voice—and a whip cracked. The General fell flat. A hound struggled clear of his legs, and a dozen more streamed over him. Geoff had somehow come to him and was helping him up. The Master, hastening to his horse, stopped to call: "Are you all right, Harry? Fox wouldn't wait for us. Thought he'd do a bolt."

"He nearly bit me!" said Black, testing his girths.

"Craddock must be out of his mind," Anne said, "letting the fox do a thing like that."

"Now stop being funny," said Madge Bredon: "we've got to think . . . There he goes across!" She pointed with her whip to the fox, who was swimming the river.

"There's not a bridge for a mile," said Tommy.

Anne walked her horse to the river's edge. "What are *you* going to do, Mr. Trant?" she called, as the farmer bustled past and drove his horse down the bank. That cautious animal skidded grudgingly into the water and stood there hock-deep.

"I believe there used to be a ford hereabouts," the farmer called over his shoulder, beating his horse on the rump.

"I reckon you're right, Mr. Trant," said Craddock, driving his horse into the stream.

"I hope so," Anne said. She struck her mare with her heel and disappeared demurely into the river.

David Levine, looking at her miserably, shut his eyes and hit his horse with all his skinny might. He, too, followed the farmer, the huntsman and Mrs. Meredith. But as the water closed over his head, he saw, scrambling with his pony up the far bank, Ralph Meredith.

Only Ralph, the huntsman and Tommy Black were seen somehow to get across and to be galloping on together over the far meadow. The sound of hounds grew faint, as the remainder of the hunt hurried away in search of a bridge. A few friends stayed with the grooms to help Trant and David in their struggle to get back. Then Geoff was seen, some way downstream, crawling out of the river on the far bank and followed by his cob.

"Oh, well done, Geoff!" cried Mrs. Bredon.

"Good God—look at Anne!" the General said. "Geoff, Geoff!" he shouted to the boy with great anxiety, as he saw his wife emerging from the river, hatless, her long hair about her shoulders and a cascade of water down the channel of her back and her skirt.

"My hat!" Anne shrieked. "Somebody save my hat!"

It floated daintily past. It was a lovely, shiny silk top hat, bobbing upright in the current like a child's boat. Geoff was fishing for it with his whip.

"Don't bother about her hat," the General shouted. "Where's her horse?"

"_I've_ got my horse," Anne shouted back. "I want my hat." She pulled the sodden mass of violets from her coat and threw them on the grass.

They could see then, across the river, that she still had her reins looped about her wrist, but that the animal was submerged in the water and rushes, except for its head. It had ceased plunging and now lay winded, resigned and still.

"You'd much better come out," Mrs. Meredith said to it. "Oh, Geoff—I _am_ glad to see you!"

The boy had come to her along the bank, and together they pulled at the horse's head and struck at the water with their whips. From the other side, Mrs. Bredon, the General and the groom, Grant, were shouting advice.

"Send Geoff to get brushwood," Mrs. Bredon called.

"My dear Madge, from where?" Anne asked, for on her side of the river the meadow was bare and woodless.

"What you want is a rope," the General shouted.

"Stop that!" Mrs. Meredith said very sharply to Grant, who was throwing substantial clods at the tail of her horse. But something had happened, and the animal, with a great plunge, came scrambling up the bank. Geoff ran backwards, pulling at the reins, and Mrs. Meredith hit the horse quickly with her whip. The mare stood quietly beside her. "You must give me a leg up," she said to Geoff.

"You're not going to ride home like that!" the General shouted.

36

"I shall certainly get pneumonia if I don't," his wife answered.

"Do let Geoff telephone for Victor."

"I was going to, of course."

"Do keep moving till you get to your car," Mrs. Bredon shouted. "Try to keep warm . . ."

"My dear Madge, do you take me for an idiot?"

*　　　*　　　*

Half an hour later, the alarm went, unexpectedly, in the pantry of Neapcaster Park.

On these afternoons, when every one was out hunting, it was a restful time on the sunless side of the baize doors where the carpeted floors changed to stone and linoleum. The butler took his after-lunch tea with the cook in a room that used to be called "the Upper Servants' Hall" but was now, in the new democracy, renamed "the Upper Staff Rest Room."

"He's a queer little thing," the cook was saying. She was talking about the butler's pantry-boy, Walter Wallis. "All the Wallis's are queer. They're religious."

"He's spry when it suits him," the butler answered.

"Spry! He's never awake."

"He's only a kid. They're all dreamers."

"What's he got to dream about in your pantry?" She started to laugh, slowly and quietly. "Dreaming at his age! Dreaming in your pantry!" Her massive elbows on the table were the channels through which her laughter made the room shake and the china tinkle. Otherwise her mirth had no sound in it. "You're laughing yourself, Mr. Draper!"

"Indeed I'm not, Mrs. Carr."

"All I can hope is he doesn't choose one of my girls for one of his dreams. With that spotty face . . . You'd better stop laughing, Mr. Draper, or put down that cup . . ."

"There's someone at the door, Mrs. Carr."

"Come in, come in, come in! Well," she said to the boy, "are your ears burning?"

"What is it, son?" the butler asked; "the telephone? I'll come directly."

"Let's get this straight," the butler said as he strode down the stone corridor with the boy, young Walter, pattering behind him. "The telephone rang—and where's Frank?"

"Mr. Timlake went to the post, Mr. Draper."

"So you answered yourself? And it was Master Geoff?"

"He wanted to speak to his dad, Mr. Draper. It was urgent."

"You tried the office?"

"I pushed the key and I rang four times, but there wasn't any one there, Mr. Draper, so I came for you."

"That's right," the butler said. They had come to the pantry, the first room on the servants' side of the bottom baize door. The butler took a look at the cedar tank where the boy had been at work on the silver—too ancient and precious to be treated with powder and polish. "Not that pink soap," he said, "that's no use."

"The other was all used up, Mr. Draper."

"I'll give you some more directly." The butler rinsed and dried his hands under the other sink and then went to the house exchange. It was in an alcove off the pantry, next to the silver room. Down the telephone, he said: "Yes, Master Geoff?"

Poor Geoff, dripping and shivering in the hall of Mr. Trant's house, where he had got the use of the telephone, explained what had happened.

"You don't want your dad," the butler said; "you want Victor." He snapped his fingers at Walter. "Pencil, sonny!" Then, in the margin of the pink-coloured *Sporting Times*, he wrote down the route that the car was to take. "Shipford—Neap St. Andrews—Faircote—Medlicote—Everbridge . . . All right, Master Geoff, I'll see to it. You'd best get dry yourself; I can hear you chattering."

This was a job of work that had to be done to a turn, as neat as a steak. He got the garage. "Mrs. Green, I wanted to speak to Victor . . . Here's a nice one, Vic," he said when the chauffeur came to the phone. "Mrs. Meredith's fallen into the river!" They were friends of very long standing. "The big car, I should think, and you'll call at the stables? I'll warn them." He read out the route and added: "If you'd like to pick up a flask, I'll have one ready."

There was no answer from the stable telephone, so he sent young Walter with a message for the stud groom, Mr. Ogden.

Frank Timlake soon strolled into the pantry and put each foot in turn on the table to take off his bicycle clips. Ten minutes ago, having a few words on the side of the road with Bessie Rogers—

the sister of the girl who was pregnant—he had been a man. Except for his thick, black livery trousers, his white bow tie, and the strip of yellow-and-white striped waistcoat showing from beneath his tweed coat, he was a man. Back in the pantry, he was a footman, getting it hot from the butler, who was filling a pigskin and silver flask as he spoke. "If you don't want the job, there's plenty of likely lads who do. You'll see 'em in queues where you come from—looking for work. It's no trouble for me to train 'em." So as not to meet the butler's eye, Frank polished the buttons of his livery coat. "If you want to sniff around Bessie Adams," Mr. Draper continued, "it's no concern of mine on your afternoon off. You get your afternoons off, and this isn't one of them."

"I went to the post, Mr. Draper . . ."

"Get on with that silver."

Frank tied on his baize apron and went to the cedar sink.

"There'll be a lunch tray wanted for the mistress in half an hour."

"Yes, Mr. Draper."

The butler went through to the front hall where he left the flask for Victor to collect. As soon as the baize door swung shut behind him, and his footsteps were muffled by the deep carpet, his bearing changed, his shoulders drooped but his back straightened, and his pace, although brisk, became solemn. As soon as his feet were back on the stone flags of the servants' corridor, he started humming and slouching, but his shoulders were drawn erect. He went to the kitchen, tapped on the door which stood open, but waited outside it. He could see Mrs. Carr inside, but it was one of the girls who came to him. "I'd like a word with Mrs. Carr, please, Lizzie." The cook was in fact a spinster, but her office carried the title of a married woman. She came to the door to speak to him, and he told her what was happening.

"So she's been swimming, Mr. Draper, and she'll want lunch!" The cook was hugely delighted, but she stood firm in the doorway. "Does she think of the trouble it's causing?"

"I dare say she does," the butler answered. He had been with the family a very long time—since he had come as a boy in the early 'nineties—but the cook was comparatively new. She had come some seven years previously, at the end of the war, when the house was transformed from a hospital back to its proper uses.

"Six in the morning till ten at night isn't good for young girls, Mr. Draper. There's two of them having a lie down at this moment."

"Just a poached egg, Mrs. Carr."

"It won't be a poached egg, Mr. Draper; I can't afford to have a poached egg held over me for the rest of my life in this house . . . Lizz!" she shouted, "leave those things and fetch down Millie and Kate."

"And I wanted to warn Miss May," the butler said, as the girl scampered off.

"Lizz!" the cook shrieked after her; "come back! She'll fetch Miss May for you, Mr. Draper; that'll save your legs."

*   *   *

When Lizzie had climbed the three flights of narrow, uncarpeted stairs to the attic wing where the women servants slept, she tapped on the door of the end room and heard a sort of groan as Miss May woke up. Miss May was strewn about her bed in crumpled abandon. The room looked like the wreckage of a gust of passion; but the only passionate surrender she had made was the relief of her feet. She had thrown off her clothes and thrown herself down because she was tired, and her feet hurt her.

Miss May's surname was not used, and not known, in this house. Having too many syllables it was inappropriate for the station of lady's maid to Mrs. Meredith. But in all other respects she was, in public, a perfect servant, being neat and quick, bearing herself demurely, and having a sweet expression and a fair, creamy complexion.

Up in the attic bedroom the world was different, with a different climate and a different tongue. She wasn't the best thing in the room, and the room was awful. Upon the varnished floor there lay askew a square of threadbare rug with carmine roses. And upon the rug, Miss May's corsets were telescoped around one shoe. The other shoe was under the bed with the chipped chamber pot; and since the windows of the room were shut and cobwebbed, the smell was stale and unpleasant. A black dress had been thrown across the open door of a yellow-stained wardrobe with a cracked glass. A chest of drawers, a single chair and a washstand—all of the same horrible colour as the wardrobe—practically filled the room; but on all these articles of furniture, odd garments were strewn. Slops had been emptied, by one of the girls, from the flowered china of the washstand; but the basin had not been cleaned, and a line of dirt ran round the inside of the circumference. Powder had been spilt on the bedspread, which had an ill-matched patch in it. This bedspread had not been removed by Miss May and it lay crumpled beneath her. Although she was twenty-four years old and fully adult, she still had a girl's joys and sorrows retained in the preservative of domestic service.

With the appointments of the room, and with its general condition, Miss May was very well satisfied. The neatness, softness, harmony and fragrance of those parts of the house in which she worked, and especially of her mistress's bedroom, were cleanly divorced in her mind and her senses from this place that was her own and in which she slept. On the other side of the baize door, she would have noticed immediately the first trace of an unpleasant odour. But this room of hers, in *her* nostrils, smelt all right.

The closed window of this bedroom looked out upon a slope of stone-tiled roof, with dead leaves and other refuse blocking the guttering. The iron bedstead, on which Miss May was abandoned, stood beneath the window. She lay with her arms and legs widespread, knees bent, stockings slipped about her ankles, pink petticoat rucked up about her belly and blue bloomers underneath. "Oh, holy saints!" she cried, when Lizz said that she was wanted. She tumbled up, scratched herself under the armpits and set about herself with her mistress's powder and lipstick. "Lizz," she called after the girl, wanting a fuller account of the news, "Lizz, dear, come back!"

But Lizz was at the other end of the passage, setting upon Millie and Kate, who lay intertwined on one of their twin beds. Millie she smacked on the bare buttocks, and Kate she tickled in the ribs, and both girls responded until all three of them were squirming and squealing about this tiny room where the windows had not been opened, nor the beds made, for a good many months. They were fourteen, fifteen and nearly eighteen years old, respectively, these three girls—Lizzie, Kate and Millie—whose mothers had sent them into service at the Park where they would be well fed, well cared for, and taught nice ways. Millie, the youngest, was earning five shillings a week as well as her keep. "*I'll* wallop *you*," she shrieked, throwing herself at Lizz.

Thrown violently into the passage, Lizz ran backwards towards the stairs, coming sharply against Miss May, now pink and white, smart and haughty, in her neat black dress. "I'm ever so sorry, Miss May!" Lizz said. With her hand to her mouth, she ran back to Millie and Kate. "She just give me a look, and on she went, as if I wasn't so much as dirt."

"Who was it?" Millie asked from the floor, where she was held securely by Kate's legs about her neck.

"Maisie," Lizz said. "And if you don't hurry, it's me who'll get it."

When she reached the foot of the stairs, Lizz, prim and modest, slipped past Miss May and Mr. Draper, who were talking together half-way between kitchen and pantry. In the kitchen Mrs. Carr said: "Those girls are taking their time," but she was too busy to ask for excuses. "It's soup from the stock," she said, "a cutlet, creamed taters, and I'll make her a sweet *soufflé*. And open a bottle of peas."

"Yes, Mrs. Carr."

"And hurry yourself. She'll be back any moment."

*   *   *

The car swept past the school at Neap St. George, five miles from home. The schoolmaster's letter, received five days ago, was still unanswered.

Anne lay back and shivered. No matter how warm and costly the car, the clothes, the rugs, the furs, when the waters of the river had reached the skin, they touched a shivering woman. The cold, imprisoned by the wet clothes that pressed against her flesh, could escape only inwards, into the spaces of her body; an agony so keen that her brain, in flight from its recognition, sought refuge somewhere, anywhere, anywhere external to herself. The letter from the schoolmaster, whose school and house they had recently passed, had got to be answered. "Mr. Robbins . . . a funny little man with such an aggressive face . . ." They all had aggressive faces, all his sort; like the new doctor, the new little red-headed doctor who was coming to dinner that night . . . *à la lanterne*, they all meant, she was sure of that . . . "and they may well be right," she said.

"A decent little man, Mr. Robbins. I dare say he's even a *clever* little man." And because he had asked her, she had taken

42

that boy, Walter Wallis, into her house. There were other more suitable applicants, but Mr. Robbins had said: " Mrs. Meredith, will you please, *please* give him a chance?" And a chance the boy had got. But there was no end to it; and now Mr. Robbins had written her a letter. The position of pantry-boy, he seemed to think, offered scarcely adequate prospects for the talents, the very genuine and very remarkable talents, the maybe hidden talents . . . Mr. Robbins had written such a lot, page after page of his close script, as if one had nothing to do, no other worries, but to sit down and read it.

" With the very best will in the world . . ." She shook her head —part thought, part tremor of cold—" I can't for the life of me think . . ." The boy could be footman. The boy might even be butler. The boy had circles under the eyes and pimples on his cheeks, and a most ungainly action. " Now if he were only a horse, one could have him fired to straighten those hocks . . ." She managed to giggle to herself at that. But even this remedy would be unlikely to cure him of the trance-like way in which he ambled about his work, or else scampered madly around the house, as if inspired by some secret purpose, impelled by some hidden force. He was just another child, of course.

" How young . . . how terribly young," she thought, as the cold flowed up her limbs in a new onrush that almost reached her heart, " how young they all are!" How onerous—when one felt old, and the heart flinched—all these young people, all dependent, all rebellious against their dependence, and all irresponsible.

The car had entered the drive gates. On her right was the lodge, with another of them there, another of the children, little Geoff: the arms round her neck in the firelight, the tears, the sobs. " What is it? What is it, Geoff dear? What is it?" But it wasn't anything. It was just tears on the neck of her evening frock. It was just sobs and shaking tears upon her breast; and Ralph, sitting upright in the next-door cot, was saying: " Mum . . . Mum . . . Mum . . ." until she turned to him. And then: " Geoff hasn't been very good. That's what it is! He hasn't been good."

" You horrid little sneak," she said; but Ralph only laughed, bouncing about in his cot, and Geoff didn't seem to mind; indeed, he had stopped sobbing and was almost asleep.

43

The car slid between the stone gateposts with the ancient heraldic ornaments, moss-grown and defaced. The long decline of the drive suddenly steepened; and there—below and ahead—certain haphazard windows along the whole length of the house were already alight! Breaking the formal façade, they gave to the place the casual cheerfulness of a city at dusk. The car swept crunching round the courtyard, with Victor sounding his horn, the lowest and deepest of his horns, the *long . . . short, short* which was his habitual warning. She was home.

" So Walter has to go to school! " she said almost bitterly as the car, circling the courtyard, took her past the lights of the servants' corridor. " And now, no doubt, he'll be scampering, scampering madly to get to his post before I get to mine, before I enter the house! " And Victor repeated the warning on the horn before he pulled up the car alongside the steps beneath the portico.

*   *   *

The horn saved Frank, the footman.

All preparations had been made for the reception of casualties; and in the house, there was one of those lulls, periods of unnatural quiet, which are common on any battlefield. Every one was ready and waiting; there would be at least twenty minutes of idleness; and the boy, Walter, had put on his steel spectacles and had sat himself upon a high stool at a corner of the dresser. He was studying.

This studying of Walter's was one of the features of the house of which Mr. Draper was most proud. " *If* you've got it *there*, young Walter," he used to say, tapping his forehead, " you want to let it out . . . You may end up like Dick Whittington." He had cleared a short span of the dresser. " You can do your bookwork here in your off-moments. You can leave your books here, so long as they're neat and tidy. And nobody's going to touch them. Do you hear that, Frank? "

" If *you* think he's got it there, Mr. Draper . . ."

" Maybe he has, Frank, maybe he hasn't." The butler was anxious to avoid squabbles and jealousies in his pantry. Seeing Frank's face, and seeking for a means of putting things right for the lad, he picked up a newly-cleaned salver, impeccably bright, and whipped round on Walter. " And maybe *you* haven't made much of a job of *this* . . . Give it another rub! "

" See here, Frank," the butler said later, when Walter was out of the room, " *you* may think the kid's a weed; but he's the only runner we've got in *this* stable." It was a paternal inspiration to choose a metaphor that would find its way to the sharp but unwilling brain of the footman. " It's a credit to both of us if he gets in the money."

" Not much chance of that, Mr. Draper."

For once, the butler persisted. Frank was the elder of the two boys by nearly three years, being past eighteen; and since he seemed to have few talents and very limited prospects, was himself in need of encouragement. " He's a square peg in the pantry, that kid," the butler said to his footman. " You've got to consider him, Frank. One of these days, you'll have a pantry of your own, with a staff of your own to think of. And good lads won't come to you, Frank, never in the world, if you don't look after them. So *you* look after young Walter! "

Frank was doing so now, while the house was awaiting its mistress's return. He had worked out his week-end bets and had looked at the pictures in the daily papers. With the butler out of the room, he now pulled Walter's book away from him and looked at its title. " *A Short Economic and Social History*," he read aloud. " You must have a heap of economic worries on seven-an'-six a week, Walter boy! "

The boy went white. It was less the loss of the book than the turmoil, the black and potent wave engulfing him, which stole his power of thought. He could no longer think. While he was at his book, facts seemed to be clear objects, having a shape, a weight, an order, a succession; and as soon as he had sat upon his high stool, put on his spectacles and found his place in a book, all the printed words shone with distinction, and he achieved new stature amongst them. But when the book was snatched from him, all the facts in the world were swept away in a flood, carrying his stature with them, and he found himself tumbled over in the darkness, defenceless. " Please, please, Mr. Timlake . . ."

" You can call me Frank, Walter boy, because I want your help."

" Please, please, Frank . . ."

" It's an economic problem of my own, Walter boy. It's forty-eight pounds a year, Walter boy, less sevenpence a week insurance. It's three bob a week backing my fancy, and an extra two-an'-a-tanner on the Derby, the Oaks and the Lincoln . . . You aren't

45

paying a bit of attention!" Frank said. "I don't reckon you're taking your book-learning as you should. Give us that pencil!"

Walter, unaware of his actions, unaware of anything except a quaking fog of apprehension, gripped the pencil, held it against his chest and turned his back to the footman.

"Let's have it!" said Frank, spinning the boy round and taking the pencil by force. He started to write laboriously on a fresh page of Walter's exercise book. "Now," he said as he wrote, "if none of them horses come in worse than second nor better than seven to two . . . That's not got it either," he said, tearing out the sheet; "better'n five to four, it should be . . . And what's the matter now?"

For the boy had uttered a curious cry, like the last squawk of a hen before its neck is wrung. "My book!" he cried, throwing himself at Frank.

"Your book's all right," the footman said, holding it out of reach. "It's only a page I want, to light a fag." He twisted it up and went towards the fire.

From Walter's throat there came a sound that had started as a shout but had lost its pitch, had sped up the scale and ended as a shriek. It was not unlike the scream of David Levine when he lay with the pony on top of him, out hunting. He was quite unaware of the thing that he had in his hand—a "steel" that was used for sharpening knives—with which he attacked Frank. A chair crashed, and the boy found himself held in the air by hands that had gripped him from behind, under the armpits. He saw Frank's face change swiftly, like a light gone out. Certain muscles collapsed; the lower part of the cheek went flabby; the mouth fell ajar.

"Hop it outside!" said Mr. Draper to Walter, putting him down in the doorway. "Hop it, quick!" The door of the pantry was shut, excluding him; and he found himself gasping for breath, standing on the scrubbed linoleum of the corridor, with tears falling so freely that they dropped with distinctive plops at his feet. Their very sound made them increase.

"What's the matter, Wallie?"

The use of this familiar name which belonged only to his home, a respectable cottage on the outskirts of Neapcaster town, drew Walter's attention to his own heaving belly, tight throat and wet, salt lips. Trying very hard to control himself, he drew a great breath that turned itself into a sawing sob.

"Get a hold of yourself, Wallie," she said, and put a hand on each of his shoulders, un-bowing them, so that his eyes travelled up her skirt, her bodice, to her bent head.

"I'm very . . . sorry . . . Miss May," he managed to gasp from his belly.

"Your Mum wouldn't like to see you like this."

"No, Miss May."

"It's like you was a baby again," she said tenderly, for she had known him since he was newly born, and she a schoolgirl, with only a few more years before she'd be going into service. "Why!" she thought, exaggerating slightly, exaggerating by perhaps six or seven years, "why, he might almost have been my own kid, if I'd started as young as Judy Rogers." So she asked: "What is it then, Wallie? What is it?"

Before the boy could manage to speak, the question was answered by the sound, even through the closed door of the pantry —thick and burglar-proof—of the butler's voice. Then Frank, it seemed, started to speak but was quickly interrupted. It was rare indeed for Mr. Draper to be talking in such a way, loud and angry.

"Come on, Wallie!" she said. She had been speaking in the soft natural tones of their home; a speech which she usually managed to prohibit as unseemly to her status. "You'll be right as anything now! 'Tis all over; 'tis all over now, isn't it, Wallie?"

The boy nodded, and Miss May turned and walked down the passage. She looked back over her shoulder and smiled maternally. She liked kids.

By some curious reaction, Walter, left alone in the corridor, felt excited. He felt even joyful. Taking a pace or two, he came to a window that was opposite the lowest turn of the back staircase, giving it light. Through this window, he looked upon the broad gravel courtyard that lay in the dusk like a pale pool, enclosed by the L-shaped wings of the house and by a high wall. Out of this pool, as if feeding it from above, the drive rose sharply to nick the nearby crest at a point where the ancient avenue of elms, seen from the window in perspective, and thus telescoped together, looked like a wood contained by the walls of the hill. At this moment, these walls sloped inwards to a point, a beacon of wild sky alight with orange splendour.

It was not yet evening; but the day had gone into the gloom

of a stormy afternoon, with the rain swept away by a rising wind and the last of the sun piercing the rainclouds at this one spot. From the windows of the corridor, there would be no direct view of the sunset. But there was this foretaste of reflection in the northern sky, a thing of crimson and ochre, gleaming for a few seconds like a blade twisted in salute, like a trumpet raised for a fanfare.

A hard wind from a very great distance was bending the trees around the house. Their creaking, and the breath of the wind, with all its subsidiary noises, could be heard, even through the shut window. The wind swept the gravel, almost moving it, swept a few fallen leaves below the window, and swept the roofs. And Walter, whose hands were clenched and twisted about his wet handkerchief, who was standing upon his toes, and whose face was lifted to the window, was seized by the certainty of greatness; and that somewhere, even within himself, there was a great irrepressible power, a great loveliness. Through the last moisture on his lashes, he saw a passing glory that was his own glory. He thought he saw God.

There—above the treetops of the drive—was the distant light! Beautifully, it touched the crest, running its finger along the hilltop. Then, as the car turned into the drive, the light broadened, became a fan-shaped aurora, and approached. Watching this wonder, Walter forgot altogether his duty until Victor, sounding on his deepest horn his customary warning to the indoor staff, caused the boy to tear himself from the window, to tear up the corridor and to hurl open the pantry door with a crash, shouting: "Horn, horn, Mr. Draper! It's the horn, the horn!"

It was not until long afterwards that Walter acknowledged pictorially the relaxed, whitened face of Frank, with his miserable eyes, his long body somehow unfastened and made skinny, and his fingers twisting beneath the grave reproach of Mr. Draper, hard and patriarchal. Afterwards, also, the boy seemed to recall the words that were being said: "I'd like to give you the chance, mind you, I'd like to . . . but I have to think . . ." Then both heads were swung round, startled, and both faces changed instantly, as if a window blind had been snapped up, at Walter's exultant shout: "Horn! Horn!"

"Lively, Frank!" said the butler, reaching for his coat. " Get dressed up, Walter!" And the call of the horn was repeated.

Frank, half into his livery jacket, was already out of the pantry and through the baize door. It was still swinging when Mr. Draper, correctly dressed, also reached it. Walter scurried past along the noiseless carpet. " Steady, steady," whispered the butler. " Time enough."

As the car pulled up beside the steps, at the very moment when it came to a halt, the door was opened by Frank. And Draper, standing a little behind him, switched on the lights of the hall, relieving the dark afternoon. Walter stood opposite, facing him.

Anne, lying back in the car, saw the lovely gleam of welcome and her servants awaiting her. " How they manage it," she thought, " I really don't know! But always, always they seem to be hanging about the front door, waiting, just waiting . . . And I must say," she concluded her thought—cold, shivery and sleepy as she was— " it's really very pleasant and comforting."

*   *   *

" Draper—I don't think I can move."

" What a terrible thing, Madam. Anything might have come of it." Draper was stooping inside the car, unpeeling the rugs and handling them behind him to Frank. Mrs. Meredith's hand clutched his forearm while she pulled herself up from the low seat. He raised his forearm, to take more of her weight, as she stepped out.

" I'm getting very old, Draper; very stiff."

" So I should think, Madam, after such an experience."

" Yes, oh yes . . ." she said vaguely. That part of her mind which made observations was lagging a long way behind. Now, as she climbed the steps into the hall, she was recalling the sight of Draper descending them. He had a broad, pink face which shone with sympathy. He was really quite a tall, lithe, athletic person—a good cricketer, they said—but he came down the steps with a sort of professional daintiness, head thrown back and to one side, feet tripping like a girl's. When she let go of his forearm to mount the steps, he put his fingers under her elbow. He came up the steps at her side, one step behind her. He was scarcely ten years older than herself.

She entered her house. " Good evening, Frank. It *is* a dark afternoon, isn't it?" Frank held open the glass doors that led from the front hall, a sort of lobby, into the main hall which was the central chamber of the house and which stretched its full width, from the drive to the garden front. " Good evening, Walter. What a horrible, horrible day! So nice and warm inside." The boy caught his breath, as if he had forgotten something, tried to smile at her, and hurried past Frank and down the steps to the car. " Our genius! " she thought. " I suppose he has to bring in the flask." And as she reached the centre of the hall and the foot of the great staircase, she seemed to remember that Frank had been making signs and signals to the boy as he held open the glass door. " Oh dear! " she sighed, as she stood in the hall, feeling the full weight of her wet clothes. She raised her eyes up the staircase, and May was at the top waiting to meet her. " Oh, Draper, I'm so old . . ."

Draper gave a little laugh, almost a giggle. " What a thing to say, Madam! "

She was climbing the stairs and she thought how pleasant the house had smelt as she entered it; how the sweetish smell—of heliotrope and furniture polish and pot-pourri, a very ancient and beautiful odour—had lapped her face as the inner door was opened. The lights of the hall were reflected, all the way up to the roof, on the varnished surfaces of the pictures. They almost excluded the daylight; and yet, from the foot of the staircase, she had been able to see, across the hall and through the french window which led on to the terrace, the grey landscape, itself like a framed painting, falling to the river and up again to the russet mists of Slender Ladies Covert. May was waiting at the top of the staircase, Draper at the bottom. Draper said: " There will be a tray ready, Madam, whenever you want it."

She clung to the staircase and managed to turn her head and smile. " Now you mention it, Draper, I'm really quite, quite hungry. Just a poached egg and some tea."

" I think Mrs. Carr has got you a little lunch, a cutlet . . ."

" Oh dear," she said as she went upstairs, so that most of her words were inaudible, " *that* means that two of those girls, if not three, have missed their afternoon nap. They've been dragged downstairs to peel potatoes . . . Oh, May! " she cried, " I've been so silly and I feel so old . . ." For the girl had come down a few of the stairs to meet her.

From the head of the staircase she could see right down the passage to the open door of her bedroom at the end of it. The pink-shaded lights were still further softened by the tremble of flames in the grate.

*　　*　　*

Miss May took a whole heap of wet clothes, wringing wet and occasionally dripping, all the way down to the drying-room, beyond the kitchen and the Lower Servants' Hall and next to the boiler-room. What a weight the things were! No wonder that the child could scarcely stand up! No wonder that she lay in her bath and scarcely knew what she was doing or saying. She was a queer one —if ever there was.

All the way along the upstairs passage, Miss May thought of her mistress as "a child . . . a queer kid." It was not until she reached the baize door at the end, that the child grew up, becoming an adult, impersonal "she."

Beyond the baize door, Nanny lived in retirement and seclusion. There was always a light under her door; it was thought that she slept with her light on, but nobody knew; and the light was only a symbol that Nanny was there, for ever and ever, unseen and unheard but watchful, waiting; waiting for somebody to fall ill, so that she could come out of her hiding to creep about the house, surly and secret, until they were well again. At other times, it was only the girls who saw Nanny when they took up her meals; although, on a sunny afternoon one sometimes got a sight of a broad, squat back, rolling like a sailor across the Park.

Miss May's step became much less brisk as she passed through the baize door. The act of letting it swing shut behind her completed the change. And then Nanny's door opened. It was a remarkable thing, but it swung open quite silently, just as Miss May reached it. The grey hair was done up in curlers, and in the poor light of this part of the house, the face looked quite red and cheerful, not at all malignant, not at all old, not even middle-aged, but young, quite young, or perhaps ageless. "Very wet," Nanny said, looking at the drips on the lino floor.

"She's had a ducking," Miss May answered. "Fell in a river."

"None the worse?" The question sounded doleful, rather than anxious, as if it was a sad thing, the way so many of these accidents passed off so lightly nowadays.

"Oh, _she's_ all right," Miss May said. "Trust _her_!"

The door closed again silently, and Miss May passed on, her

51

feet clattering, until she got up on to her toes with prettier, tripping footsteps. When she came to the servants' staircase, it was so narrow, and her arms were so full of clothes, that she had to go down sideways and ran into Mr. Draper at the bottom.

"Hallo! Hallo, Miss May," said the butler. "What an armful of things! What a to-do!" He spoke pleasantly and warmly. It was a pity—she thought—that he was supposed, by some, to be a nancy. She doubted—she doubted very much—if it were true.

As usual, Mrs. Carr's voice was strident through the kitchen doorway; and as usual, one of the girls—Lizzie, she thought—was making excuses. And the odd-man, Noel, with his limp and his twisted back, passed her, as usual, without a word spoken. Everything was as usual, except that the door of the drying-room was already half-open, and the hot air met her in the passage. Frank was inside, hanging up the rugs from the car. Frank was a long way beneath her and five or six years younger. She and Frank scarcely ever spoke. They rarely had the chance.

*   *   *

Frank was without his apron and without his livery coat. His sleeves were rolled up, and there were ginger hairs on his arms which caught the light from the unshaded, central lamp. He turned, quite startled, when the door was pushed wide, and the whole heap of clothes appeared suddenly, with Miss May's head above them, and Miss May's legs beneath.

"Oh, it's you, Miss May," he said stupidly.

"Of course it's me. Give us a hand, can't you?"

He put out his two great big, ginger-haired hands and touched the topmost of the garments. Seeing what they were, he dropped them quickly.

"They aren't hot!" Miss May said.

Afterwards—immediately afterwards—he thought of all sorts of wonderful things to say, and all sorts of wonderful things to do with his hands. He had talked enough about it; he had read enough about it in the threepenny books; he had heard enough about it; he had seen enough of it to know the rules by heart and to fall into the ways of it—he, himself, would have thought—almost by instinct. But he just grinned unhappily and went red.

"Go on," Miss May said. "They don't bite!"

Together they piled the clothes on the big bare table that stood in the middle of the room, under the lamp. Then she started humming while she hung them up, garment by garment, but very swiftly and neatly, on the rails above the pipes. He watched her silently. It was, of course, hot, very hot, in the drying-room, but his limbs felt cold and weak. Suddenly, just as she had finished and had her back to him, he made a great effort and put his hands, clumsily enough, upon her hips.

"No thanks!" she said, and just twisted herself clear.

"I'm sorry, Miss May," he began, "I'm ever so sorry . . ."

But she had gone out and closed the door behind her with a bang. He was left alone, shut up in the hot, steamy room, with sweat streaming down his forehead and down his arms which still felt cold as ice. Thinking it over, he could have sworn she was laughing. All the time, she was laughing. Right at the end, when she ran out and slammed the door behind her, she was not angry at all—but laughing.

With his arm he wiped the sweat off his forehead, and it dripped from his arm on to the stone floor of the drying-room. "There must be something wrong with me," he said. "According to what they say, I can't be half a man, not half. According to what they say, they just fall into your arms, throw themselves at you— and there it is. But with me . . . with me," he said, in the steamy prison of the drying-room, where he stood flushed and red and contemptuous of himself, "with me, it isn't like that. It isn't like that with Bessie Rogers, and it isn't like that with Miss May. Because . . . because . . . how do you start on it?"

He spent a long time hanging up the rugs, sweating in the heat and sweating from the encounter, and all the time he was trying to work out what he ought to have done, both with Bessie Rogers up on the road, and with Miss May down here. At last he thought he knew, and he walked slowly down the kitchen passage, on his way back to the pantry, working out just how it should have happened, just what he should have said and done, and what would have come of it. He was excited by the time he reached the end and then, when he turned into the pantry door, he heard her voice again. And he saw her pink legs, beneath her black skirt, as she stood with her back to him.

He didn't hear what she was saying. Afterwards, when he recollected the moment and the tremendous impact upon his guts of the pink legs beneath the black skirt, he thought she had said something like: "I don't believe you would, Mr. Draper. Not for a moment, I don't . . ." And then Mr. Draper was laughing in a throaty sort of way, and she was laughing high up the scale, so that they were both laughing together, closely and secretly. It made him wild and rather disgusted that this girl and this old man of over forty should be laughing together like that, standing close together, their shoulders touching, and sharing some kind of a secret. They were putting the final touches to the tray for the bedroom.

"I'll send it up for you," Mr. Draper said. "There's no call at all for you to carry it yourself."

"*I'll* take it up for you, Miss May," Frank said, his voice coming much louder than he had expected.

They both stopped laughing and turned round. Mr. Draper just looked at him. He gave him one of those haughty looks with his head raised and tilted in that pansy way of his. It was one of those looks that made the chap at the other end of them feel like dirt. But Miss May laughed again, a little, chuckling laugh, musical and happy.

"Condiments, Frank," Mr. Draper said. "Where's the cruet?"

"Condiments, Mr. Draper!" Miss May said, and laughed again, as if there was some hidden meaning to the word. "She never takes them."

"A tray's not right without them, Miss May," the butler said; and he sounded really pompous about it, but she went on treating it as a joke, still laughing. And as she laughed, she looked past the butler, straight at Frank. He got the cruet and was going to put it on the tray, but she stretched out her hand and took it from him. Her fingers were cool and tiny. The laugh went out of her face, but her eyes were still smiling. And then they heard the horn again.

"Horn!" Mr. Draper said. "Jump to it!"

Miss May whipped up the tray and scampered out of the room, while Frank grabbed his long-tailed livery jacket.

"Roll down your sleeves," the butler said. "Now look slippy!"

Frank was through the baize door and half-way down the carpeted corridor before Victor gave him his second warning. It was just as well, because the General, who was now returning, was very particular.

★   ★   ★

The General did not move, nor consider moving, until the rug had been taken from his knees. Then, emerging from the car with dignity and friendliness, he entered his home. His face never gave any indication of his feelings, but his eyes moved in a calm, contented and approving way from one to the other of the people gathered about him. He nodded dismissal to Victor, nodded a greeting to Frank. "Everything all right?"

"Yes, sir. Thank you, sir," Frank answered.

"How's your mistress?" he asked Draper.

"None the worse, sir—so May tells me."

"That's it, that's it," the General said vaguely. And turning to Walter, he asked: "Well, young feller, going to take my red coat, are you?"

None of the things that the General said at such times meant very much. Certain words came from his lips because, otherwise, his silence would have some sort of special significance for those who were serving him. And none was intended. The significance of these occasions was their ordinary nature and their invariability.

The short, square and immensely solid figure of the General stood in the outer hall, a chamber which was reserved for the reception of those visitors who were not quite lowly enough to go to the servants' entrance, but who did not entirely qualify for the morning-room, the library, or even the main hall on the other side of the glass doors. "The boys are not back, I suppose?"

"Oh no, sir," Draper answered and held open a door on the left which led to a whole series of stone-floored rooms—store-rooms, washing-rooms and lavatories—extending all the way along to the kitchen quarters and ending with the gunroom. The gunroom had a second doorway, opposite to the first, which opened into the kitchen corridor, directly opposite the pantry. By this route, as an alternative to either of the baize doors on either of the main floors, one could pass from one to the other of the two utterly different worlds which existed, and were complementary to each other, within this building.

The gunroom itself, a large place, was a neutral state. It was here that one interviewed the senior officers of the estate—the head-keeper, the stud-groom, the head-gardener, the foreman of the Home Farm. It was here, also, that the Meredith boys graduated when they left the schoolroom. And it was between here and the billiard room that the exclusively manly part of Meredith life was centred. No women entered; and a man could take off his dripping clothes and stand naked as safely as if he were behind a door sacredly printed " Gentlemen." Once in here, a man could be reached by the feminine world only through the agency or butler or footman.

With extreme contentment—in spite of his damp attire—the General now stood before the glass doors of the gun cupboard which was built into the whole of the wall opposite the window and which contained some thirty shotguns and rifles. Their oiled surfaces shone with happy memories from his earliest childhood.

Below the gun cupboard, and part of it, there was an ordinary cupboard which stood hip-high. This had many doors and, being considerably deeper than the glass section above it, was topped by a convenient ledge on which the head-keeper could clean the guns after a day's shooting. At other times, no object whatsoever might be left on this ledge except the hunting, shooting and fishing diaries, a threepenny bottle of ink and a penny penholder. The General opened the hunting diary, as big and heavy as a ledger. With his firm but uneasy calligraphy he wrote in the date, the place of the meet, the horses that had gone out from the stables and the persons who had ridden them. The remaining space, left for a description of the day's sport, would be filled in later by Geoff, either in his own handwriting or with a cutting from the local newspaper.

The General wrote very slowly but he was not the least embarrassed by the attendance in idleness of the butler, the footman and the boy while he did so. It was as right and proper as the ritual of a Regimental orderly room. Times had sadly changed, but something still remained and was preserved properly. Very carefully the General blotted his entry. Frank had seen that there was a clean slip of blotting-paper, cut to the right size, inside the diary.

The General now moved past the central table, with its orderly litter of objects connected with farming or sport, past the racks of fishing rods, the pegs supporting macintoshes, creels, landing nets, cartridge bags, and below them the rows of gumboots and waders, to the area of the window. Here, into an upright arm-chair which had a worn leather seat, the General lowered himself. Walter knelt.

While Walter unfastened the garter straps which connected the General's top-boots to the third button of his white breeches, the General asked: " Is Mr. Greenley still here?"

"In the office," Draper answered, "waiting to see you, sir, I gather."

It was now Frank's turn to serve his master with the same office that May had performed for her mistress. Parting the tails of his livery coat, he presented his backside to receive the sole of the General's boot. The other boot he grasped between his thighs and tugged. As it came free, he was propelled a few paces across the stone floor. "Made ye a bit muddy, I'm afraid," the General said, "but no doubt young Walter'll brush it off." While they dealt with the second boot, he said to the butler: "Ask Mr. Greenley to come to the library."

"Shall I serve tea in there?" the butler asked, speaking over his shoulder because he had gone to one of the lower cupboards where, warmed by the water pipes, stockings and slippers were ready for the General's feet.

"Please," said the General; "two eggs."

The number of eggs to be poached for tea was one of the few variations that could still be played on this traditional theme. The butler looked at Frank and gave a little jerk of his head. Frank's part in the ritual was now finished. His only jobs were to tell Mrs. Carr about the eggs and to carry the mudstained boots to Noel, the odd-man, who was waiting outside the pantry to take them and to put them at once into a bucket of tepid water. Walter remained with Draper, waiting for the pink coat. Again he knelt and unbuttoned the breeches at the knees and drew off the long silk stockings. These had been Anne's, and they were issued to Draper by May, as and when they became laddered and useless for their original purpose. While Walter stripped off the stockings, the butler remained stooped at the cupboard. Here there was an assortment of fresh clothing to meet any exigency of the day's sport—from the effects of total immersion to those of a slight mist.

"Breeches, sir?"

"They're all right, thank 'ee, Draper." The General pulled on the woollen shooting stockings and the slippers. He stood up and let the butler strip off the long pink coat and substitute an old tweed jacket. The pink coat was handed to Walter. The boy made his exit. The ritual was almost finished.

"I gather, sir, that you had an exciting day's sport?" At this point it was customary for the butler to ask some such question, and to note as omens the tone and nature of the reply. Thus, when the General answered: " Capital sport, Draper, quite capital," word could be passed that when Lizzie later requested an increase of salary from £26 a year to £32 10s., it would be graciously granted.

The General now moved off. His feet in their slippers shuffled on the stone floor while Draper opened in turn the various doors that led from the gunroom back to the front hall, and thence to the main hall and the library. The butler waited while the General paused in the lavatory to wash his hands and to brush the fluffs of grey hair that remained above his ears. Then, with a damp towel, he smoothed his scrubby moustache and wiped the red rim left on his forehead by his hard hat. He leant for a moment on the wash-basin and straightened himself slowly, with an appearance of some pain. He shuffled on. Draper saw him as far as the hall.

" Nothing else, sir ? "

" Ask Mr. Greenley . . ."

" To come to the library, sir. Directly."

The General shuffled across the parquet floor towards the carpeted corridor and towards the library doorway.

" Waddling away like an old duck," was Mr. Draper's first mental comment as he watched his master go. But he withdrew it at once because he felt warmth, sympathy and even tenderness for the ageing gentleman whom he was privileged to serve. And he knew very well how the General screwed up his old body and his tired spirit for his public appearances, and how he unwound himself slowly and painfully on his return home. All the tiresome procedure in the gunroom was a form of comfort and reassurance. When it was over, the General could continue, renewed, fortified. Nobody in the world could understand this as well as Draper.

" What a splendid feller he is, what a good friend he is," the General thought as he entered the library. " And a very passable wicket-keeper." He was referring, of course, to Draper.

Thinking of the Neapcaster Park cricket team, and of all the good men who played for it, the General went to the library fire and stood there warming his back and again deeming himself fortunate. One couldn't carry on, these days, one simply couldn't carry on, if it were not for the splendid lot of fellows who served him so faithfully.

The General raised his head. " Come in ! " he called, and he turned with a certain gallantry to face the door. There was a bad time coming, and he was ready for it. " Ah, Richard," he said with great affection as Mr. Greenley, his agent, entered. " Young Geoff went splendidly to-day. You should be proud of him."

* * *

In the kitchen corridor, Frank was taking a breather. He was standing by the window at which Walter had been granted his vision; the window which gave light, by day, to the servants' staircase. The day had almost gone, and the black panes gave nothing, now, except the reflections of unshaded lamp bulbs hanging at wide intervals about these stone quarters. Frank advanced to the window and pressed his face against it. Then he could see that the day had not altogether departed but had left the faintest memorial on the hill's crest. He suffered an instant of wild, undecipherable longing that matched the wild, wild night whose winds were pouring along the hillside into the courtyard.

There was a half reflection, a twist of black skirts and pink legs from the turn of the staircase behind him. But at the same moment, the baize door, some twenty paces away to his left, creaked and swung open and shut. The butler had returned. He let his voice ring like a trumpet through the stone precincts. " Tea in the library!" The call conflicted with the rustle of skirts and the trip of light feet. " Tea, Frank!"

Whistling between his teeth a few mutinous bars, the footman strolled towards the pantry door. He was airing his manliness. But the call, disallowing manliness, was repeated. " I said tea in the library!"

" All right, all right, all right . . ."

" What's that, me lad ? "

" I said ' All right, Mr. Draper.' "

The light feet on the lino floor were coming up behind, overtaking him. There was also a clink and tinkle of glass and silver. She said: " If you haven't got a pair of hands, I have."

He turned and answered: " Oh, I'm sorry, Miss May." And he stretched out his big, red hands to take the tray from her. He was made suddenly aware of his own hands, that they were big and red, hers being tiny and white, with the nails polished.

They had together reached the pantry door, and she looked right past him to say to the butler: " She never wanted it. She never wanted a mouthful." It was the butler who took the tray from her. "Do you know what she did with it?" Miss May asked. She made the gesture of pulling a lavatory plug. It was a very daring act, a very improper attitude, for the servants' quarters, but the butler laughed. "Ho . . . ho . . ." he said. "That's it, is it?"

She nodded. She finished her nod with her chin a little in the air; and she ignored Frank. She gave a wink to Mr. Draper.

"She all right?" the butler asked, jerking his head upwards.

"Sleeping like a baby. I've a mind to finish off what I missed myself."

"Forty winks, was it?"

"Fifty," she said, looking at the pantry clock.

"Tea in the library, Frank!"

The tray was all ready except for the silver teapot, the silver kettle, the silver milk jug, and the two hot-water dishes, the one for the buttered toast, and the other for the poached eggs. Frank went out of the pantry and down the passage towards the kitchen, but Kate met him carrying what he wanted. Behind him he heard a ripple of high-pitched but soft laughter, and the butler joined in. Their voices became joined together; and the junction caused in Frank an upheaval as vast, and with as vast consequences, as the eruption of an ocean's bed. The queerest unknowns were loosed beneath the surface. He quivered.

With a shaking hand, Frank took the tin tray from Kate. He bent his head and whispered.

"Oh, I couldn't," she said.

"'Course you could, Katie."

"What is it you said?"

He repeated it into her ear. She screamed with laughter. "Not on your life," she said. "Not on your life, I wouldn't."

"Go on, Katie."

"What was it, Frank? Say it another time."

For the third time he repeated it.

Suppressing her laughter, she said: "You think I could do a thing like that?"

"'Course you could. It's nothing."

"I dursen't."

"Frank!" The voice smacked you in the side of the ear.

"Coming, Mr. Draper!" As he turned, he had a last whisper to the girl, a last appeal. "Be a sport, Katie!"

* * *

The General had been behaving badly. After his day's hunting he felt like a privileged warrior come back to those who had waited by the hearth. And now with Richard Greenley, his very old friend and Agent, the one person to whom his grey and rugged face might sometimes disclose a trace of feeling, he was being pleasurably difficult.

"Well now," said the Agent, "this thing—I spoke of it yesterday . . ."

"I dare say you did, Richard."

"And we talked it pretty well out, a few weeks back."

"One lump, isn't it? And the milk in first?"

"Please . . . And now if you'll please listen to this letter . . ."

"Is it rather strong for you? Your heart?"

"Just fill it up with water . . . This latest offer . . ."

"It looks pretty filthy," said the General, pushing the teacup to his Agent, who sat beside him on the sofa.

They were both very sturdily built, they might have been twins, or at least brothers, with the Agent slightly the shorter and the less solid. It was true that the General's remarkable strength had gone at last a little portly, while the Agent's muscles had shrunk; that the General's blue eyes had lost more of their colour, and were further withdrawn beneath eyebrows that overhung and bristled, than those of his friend; and that the General had his family's nose, snub and impertinent, which Greenley had not. But they had both, obviously, been strong, athletic, outdoor men of character and tenacity; tenacity being the dominant feature that they had in common.

Yet there was one very interesting thing about these two men: if you had wanted to reconstruct them in their youths, you could have taken their two sons, respectively, as very faithful copies. Yet their sons were not in the least alike—Geoff being tall, strong, blunt and awkward, while Ralph was short, strong, quick and subtle—so that it was only in age that the two fathers had grown so similar.

The General filled his mouth with toast and honey. "A sharpish appetite," he said.

But Greenley, taking from a file the sheets of thick paper with the Lincoln's Inn address, started to read: "*With regard to the offer of Sir Frederick Betts to purchase all or part of the outlying farms of the Neapcaster Park Estate, that is: the Wold, the Dumbles, Hatherfield, the Sherriton Brook farms . . .*"

"Don't read that damn thing," the General interrupted. "Tell me the gist of it."

"In the long run it's probably shorter to read it."

"I can't stand their roundabout talk."

"Well," said Greenley with a sigh, turning the pages and deciding that he must, nevertheless, start at the beginning, "they first of all say that they think the offer highly satisfactory . . ."

"Of course they do!" The General took more toast. "From our point of view—it's generous to the edge of absurdity. From Betts' point of view—he wants the farms regardless."

"He hardly says that . . ."

"Well, I ain't selling 'em, anyway," said the General, gulping toast. He pulled from his pocket a large handkerchief, blue and red, and carefully wiped his moustache which was still almost silken. "I ain't!" he repeated.

"Well, that saves me a couple of pages," said Greenley. "And it brings me to the second alternative." He was still referring to the letter. "To let the House and Park," he read, "and to live in one of the farms, and from there to manage the Estate . . ."

"Would any one take this place?"

"With the shooting and fishing . . ."

"Do I hear you right?" The General had risen abruptly and walked to the fire. His words came in a gulp, a choke. "Do I understand you correctly?"

"I expect so," Greenley replied. "I expected you to find that suggestion particularly distasteful."

"*Unthinkable* is the better word for it . . . Heaven knows! We've cut our expenses to the limit—beyond it. We've twisted ourselves inside out with economies . . ." The General was in earnest. He meant precisely what he said, yet there was a touch, a *soupçon*, of conscious humour about it—the shaving of lemon peel. "But to let go the shooting!"

"Well," the Agent continued, "there is still another alternative mentioned."

62

"If it's as damn silly as the others, I shouldn't trouble with it, Richard."

"They suggest," said the Agent, referring to the penultimate page of the letter, " that we might get the Trustees' permission to sell a number of the heirlooms . . ."

The General gave a grunt that might have meant anything. He walked to the big desk beneath the windows that looked by day across the terrace—southwards across the valley, to Slender Ladies and the road beyond—but now were covered with maroon curtains. The General sat down at his desk. It was an omen of serious intention.

But he could not really understand that this desk was his, his own, and that he was not still the small boy, brought to the door by Nanny, and left to cross the big room by himself, to say "goodnight" to his grandpapa and to receive, from the top drawer on the right, an oblong of chocolate done up in an inner covering of silver paper and an outer covering of red. Or if not that, he must be the schoolboy, come on the last evening of holidays to receive his three pound notes. Or the Cavalry subaltern getting his birthday cheque for a new horse. Or if not that . . . or . . . or . . . Nothing was certain except that here, at this desk whose appointments were unchanged and unchangeable, here in this room whose furniture and hangings and books had long been unalterably established—here, there had to be some one whose name, features, outlook and principles—above all, principles—were unmistakably Meredith. "Come over here, Richard."

But the Agent was already on his way from the fireplace. He drew up his own chair beside that of the General. There was no pigeon-hole for his legs, and he was uncomfortable.

"So what's the proposal, Richard?"

"The pictures are worth a great deal of money, and prices are good. The furniture, the silver—especially the silver . . . they also are worth, are worth . . ."

"A lot!" said the General. "Go on, Richard! You're a soft-hearted chap, aren't ye!" He grinned: a movement of the features that started with a twitch of the bushy eyebrows and ended around the lips; an expression that had once been famous and imitated throughout the regiments of his Cavalry Brigade. It meant a sort of childish wickedness. "We could get in camp-beds," he said, still grinning and twitching his head as he spoke;

" we could draw our blankets from the Quartermaster; we could settle in here, snug as a trooper . . ."

The Agent half-raised his hands in a hopeless gesture. He referred again to his letter. " Quite seriously they suggest . . ."

" And quite seriously," said the General, " I'd rather go down with me flag flying and the Van Dyck still on the stairs." He liked the metaphor. He grinned again and repeated it. " Flag flying and guns firing—by Slender Ladies Covert."

" Well," said Greenley, " since that disposes of all the suggestions, I suppose we're back at the first."

" Freddy Betts?" The General fingered the appointments of his desk: the inkwell, the snuffbox, the candlesticks, the clock, and all the things that had been there for as long as he could remember. And he thought: " Why should this happen to me? To *me*, Harry? My family were never spendthrift folk, never gambled, nor excessively drank, nor neglected their duty . . . They looked after their tenants, good times and bad, looked after their land, preserved their trust . . . They lived the life they were born to, and lived it steadfastly . . . How had it come about?"

" Taxes," said the Agent. " Rising wages, the cost of labour, the cost of mending a barn, mending even a stone wall . . . used to be a few shillings, now it's a hundred pounds . . ." For his own conviction, the Agent explored their state. Sometimes his thoughts were aloud; sometimes they ran without speech. " And death duties," he thought—" they took the capital needed on the farms . . . And the fall of agricultural prices—so that the farmers couldn't pay a proper rent . . ." It all mounted up, measure by measure, straw by straw, to the broken back. " Cheap food!" said the Agent, thinking of the shiploads of wheat from the American Continent, grown at a loss, subsidised by foreign Governments, sold to the British millers at a price below the British costs of production. " Nobody cared; nobody, except the British farmers and the British landowners. And they didn't count . . . Nothing counted, provided a Government made food cheap for an urban population, and so kept office. The land didn't count . . ."

But the thought, the speech—what had been said and what had been silent—seemed to have gone astray. " What had these things got to do with this house, this room, this desk? What should a Government care for a Meredith? What should any one

64

care? Who should care—who, who, except . . ." The Agent's passion erupted and his heart cried: "Who should care except me, Greenley, the boy who stood with his feet in a trickle of blood, the man who knelt by the coffin of his wife?"

"You know," said the Agent suddenly, surprising himself, "you know that I love this house, this property and . . . this family . . . as much as you do yourself . . ." He found that he had risen and had gone round behind the General, putting a hand on his shoulder. Without knowing which of his thoughts had flowed into speech, and which had been unexpressed, he felt that his own heart was now open, and the General's receptive. "You know what I owe to you and yours. You know that your father, when mine . . . when mine . . ." It was not embarrassment but decency that had to be overcome before he could add: "Shot himself at Swire's and you, your father, that is, he finished my schooling, then took me into the office, then made me Agent. And you, you yourself . . ."

No part of the General had moved, not even the muscles of his neck on which the Agent's eyes were directed. Yet it seemed that their hands were clasped. "You gave me the Lodge to live in—me and my wife. And when she died . . . didn't you take my son, didn't you take Geoff . . ."

"For God's sake be seated, Richard!" the General said. "Don't stand fidgeting behind me like a damned footman!"

The General knew no other way of stating his own love. And as Greenley resumed his chair, the stream of joy, sorrow and love ran freely between the two of them, as if they were both weeping. "God bless you, Richard."

They sat so still, so silent and contented that it seemed like the end of existence. "Your family and mine," said the Agent's heart in the long silence, "have always belonged to the same place, the same fields, the same particular earth; have lived the same life, were born to it, died in it; christened, wedded, buried in the same church, lying, to this day, scarcely apart . . ."

There was no need to speak, not yet. "What was the difference between us? Only our station. A difference so small beside what we had in common. You know . . ." The words seemed loud and faithful, though nothing was said; the voice was their common belief. "God makes men equal in His sight, but stations them differently in the sight of each other. That difference we cherished;

all of us, from the labourer in the field to the master of this house, we cherished it. We lived without envy . . ."

The General had moved in his chair, slewing himself so that now he had his hands clasped on his stomach and his eyes on his friend's face. " Richard—my family had privilege and duty. They tried to enjoy the one and discharge the other. They must have failed sadly."

" But they didn't, they didn't!"

" Then why . . . why, in God's name, Richard . . ."

It was the nearest to despair that the General had ever allowed into speech. Returning his direct regard, the Agent said: " It's not what happened here . . . it's not here that it went wrong. No, no, it could never be that!" But speech demanded thought, silencing the heart. And a tired mind, so much less coherent than a loving heart, could collect so little of the truth. " It's in other places, you see, not here . . . it's elsewhere that the privilege and the duty, they no longer went together . . . that privilege was bought; duty forgotten. It happened like that . . ."

" Did it, Richard? Has it?" The question was a genuine inquiry. " Even supposin' that you're right . . . can I help it?"

" No, sir, you can't."

" Well?"

Suddenly they heard the clocks ticking: two clocks in the room beating time in syncopation.

" Nor, sir, can you help the consequences. Nor can you escape them."

From the General there came a soft grunt, as if he had been struck in the ribs. But in his face, and in the words that followed, there was no corresponding acknowledgment. " What happens elsewhere, Richard, is no concern of mine. I still have my duty to discharge. I shall continue to discharge it."

" But you see you can't."

" Why can't I?" The question came sharply. " Why not?"

" Because the State has removed from you the means of doing so." There was a silence. Then the Agent repeated his words precisely. The silence continued.

At last the reply. " The State has relieved me," the General said, and there was no expression whatsoever in his voice. It was quite colourless. "I am relieved of my responsibility. I am dismissed. That's what you're telling me."

*   *   *

Richard Greenley watched his friend closely, but learnt nothing. The General's face was a complete concealment. The General's thought was a long way beyond his friend's guesswork.

The General's thought was two stages distant from the present realities. The last time that he had been dismissed, when the Corps Commander had said to him: "I'm sorry, Harry, not to give you the Division, but I think . . . to be honest, I think . . . a brigade's your limit," the words had seized his mind and carried it on dark wings to the most appropriate recollection, to the most apt situation that had pictorial symbols. It was a cellar near Ypres. A signaller was asleep in the corner. The signaller had to wake when the buzzer became insistent.

"We're all right where we are, sir," the General said over the telephone. The shelling was heavy overhead, the line bad and the voice indistinct. "Thanks all the same, but we're all right. Yes, I'm tolerably certain . . ." And the line went dead on them. As soon as the line had gone, the shelling got worse. There was an uneasy feeling in the headquarters of the Yeomanry Brigade. Turning himself round on the packing-case, the General said: "I say, Danny, this sandwich is pretty beastly. Can't that fellow think up anything more original?"

The shelling stopped, but there was no relief, only a tense, heavy uneasiness. When Guy Bredon came down those steps, he was pretty rattled. "They're right through us, Harry. It's bloody chaos."

"Have you had lunch, Guy?"

"We ought to do something, sir. We ought to do something pretty drastic."

"Sit down a minute, Guy. Have a rather nasty sandwich?"

"Time to move?" suggested the Brigade Major. He was Daniel Levine.

"No thanks, Danny. I like it very well where we are."

"Don't you think, sir . . ."

"No, Danny, I don't. Have a sandwich?"

When General Roy, the Corps Commander, said, "I'm sorry, Harry . . ." the General didn't argue. Anyway he wouldn't have

67

argued, but now he knew there was no cause for argument. He had been wrong. Roy never had to say: "You lost the half of your Brigade . . ."

"I see, sir," Harry had said. "I'm sure it's a wise decision."

That corner of the cellar, with the dust and the yellow light in the upwards slant of the steps, was clear in the quiet library. It was there, just there, by the maroon curtains. And Richard had said: "The State removes from you the means of discharging your duty." The General grinned. "And gives it," he said aloud, "to that man Betts."

"Gives what to Betts?" The Agent was startled after so long a silence.

"The means of discharging my responsibility, my duty."

The Agent considered this a while. "I think that's right," he said.

"And so," the General continued, "having got the means, he now wants the duty with it? Is that it, Richard?"

"It may be—but I doubt it. He wants the farms. He wants them for his business. He wants to have money in land. He wants . . ."

"And I'm to oblige him?"

"To your own advantage," Greenley said, and realised at once how foolish was his answer.

The General's face at last showed feeling. The features remained unmoved, but their colour that had long been lost, the colour of his youth, the deep, hot red, was slowly returning.

"Ralph!" the Agent said quickly. "It's Ralph we have to consider."

The silence continued.

"Not only Ralph," said the Agent, "but the tenants. You've got to think of the tenants. You've got to think of a fellow like Trant. You've got to think of the farms. There's so much that needs doing; there's so much overdue, years overdue. And *we* can't do it. There's the Wold barn, the water at Sherriton's, there's the sheds up at Dumbles . . ."

But the General had given a twist of the wrist, had raised a finger, meaning that he wanted silence. It was a long time before his head started a slight pendulum movement as he nodded assent. It was a little like a doll, a mechanical toy. The decision was terrible, but the gesture almost comic.

"Calculation, decision, execution," the General would have said if he had bothered to put into words the long silence. "All right—get on with the thing—the decision is taken," he would have said if the nodding of his head had not been sufficient for Greenley to interpret. It was not necessary, by word or signal, to indicate that there would be no subsequent wavering, no reconsideration. The Agent knew his employer too well to doubt that the matter was settled, once and for all, by this mechanical nodding of the head—doll-like and ridiculous.

*　　*　　*

Millie gave a scream of laughter, half stifled, and Kate giggled. They were whispering and scuffling outside Miss May's bedroom in the forbidden corridor that belonged to the upper servants.

"Go on, Katie! Go on—knock."

"I don't think I will."

"Why not, Katie?"

"It wouldn't be nice." Kate was nearly two years older than Millie, getting towards her sixteenth birthday, and was beginning to acquire new standards of seemliness.

"You daren't," Millie whispered, poking her in the back.

"There isn't any reason to give. You think of a reason."

"Tell her it's a message from Frank. It is too, isn't it?"

"What's the message to be?"

"What he said of course."

"Oh, Millie!" Kate clung to the younger girl and bowed her head with laughter, the two of them giggling and gasping in each other's arms until they were almost hysterical. "Oh, Millie, you are awful!"

"Go on . . ." Millie squealed, not sure why she was laughing, but enjoying herself immensely.

"Be *quiet*, Millie!"

But the door had opened, and Miss May, cross and dishevelled, stood pulling at her skirts, smoothing her elastics. "What are you kids doing out here?"

Kate, frightened but still shaken stupid by the memory of her own laughter, only shook her head. Millie, equally fearful now, had forgotten altogether the source of their joke and stood with her mouth open and her eyes fixed on the floor.

"What is it, Millie?" Miss May asked quite kindly; and when

the child didn't answer, put a finger under her chin and raised her head. "Come on—what is it?"

"I don't know, Miss May."

"You must know what you were giggling about."

"Honest, I don't, Miss May." And it was quite clear that she didn't.

"You, Katie? You're old enough not to be so stupid."

Katie, also, shook her head in despair and stupefaction.

"Anyway, you know you're not allowed in this passage, not unless you're sent . . . Oh, you're hopeless kids."

"We *was* sent," Millie whispered, remembering all about it.

"Who sent you, then?" When there was no answer May had had enough of it. She was about to abandon her inquiry when Kate, white-faced, hands clenched, said in a low voice: "It was a message, Miss May."

"A message? Well, you'd better give it me."

Kate shook her head.

"Come on, you silly little fool," Miss May said, and took her by the shoulders. "What . . . was . . . the . . . message?"

"It was about you going to the drying-room," Millie said quite calmly, remembering now. "Go whensoever you like it."

"Of course I'll go to the drying-room when I want. Whoever told you to tell me that?"

"It wasn't that," Kate now managed to say, while Millie, her recollection spent, let her mouth fall open again and her eyes drop. "It was to tell you that when so be you feel like going to the drying-room, you're to tell *him* first." She started to weep, tumbling into her tears for security.

"Tell who?"

But Kate was too heavily committed to her sobbing, and Millie to her immobility, for either to be able to answer.

"Tell who?"

Both girls now wept.

"Very well," said Miss May. "I shall take you both to Mrs. Carr."

"No!" Kate gasped, terrified. "No . . . No, Miss May."

"Then who was it?"

"Mr. Timlake," Millie cried and resumed her sobbing.

"Mr. Timlake? You mean Frank? Frank!"

Both girls nodded.

70

"Frank, was it?" said Miss May, with fury in her voice. "Of all the . . ." But interrupting herself, she stooped to say gently to the children: "All right, then. Go on off and wash your faces, both of you." And withdrawing into her room, she shut the door on them. "Frank, my God!" While she refastened her stockings and rehooked her skirt, she looked into the cracked glass. "Of all the pimply town-bred louts that we've had in this house . . ." In a couple of shakes she'd be telling the whole disgraceful story to Mr. Draper.

* * *

"Can I have a word with you, Mr. Draper—private?"

The butler at once observed a note of strain, almost of excitement, in Miss May's voice and, later, the increased colour of her cheeks. She was obviously upset, and this condition was most becoming. It gave a quickness and poise to her body, which was apt at other times to be dumpy, and it drew together the features of her face which often seemed stodgy and pudding-shaped. Miss May was a very changeable girl altogether, and both her mood and her appearance could be transformed as quickly as an April landscape.

Pushing past Frank, Mr. Draper came into the passage and closed the pantry door behind him. "We can't talk in there," he said. "And I can't very well turn them out. They've a heap of things to get on with."

They walked down the passage together and stood at the foot of the staircase, facing the black, uncurtained window through which young Walter had been granted his glimpse of godliness, and through which the footman had been provoked by the wildness of the night. It was here that she told him the story. While she spoke, her eyes looked modestly into the darkness of the drive; and Mr. Draper's eyes, as she was aware, dwelt upon the lights in her hair, the back of her neck and the backward profile of her cheeks. His gaze, she felt, was essentially paternal, benevolent, protective, but not altogether without a decent excitement, decently suppressed, entirely respectable.

Her voice carried her indignation; but all the time she was saying these terrible things about the footman, she could not quite discard a pleasant impression of Frank, tall and strong, his pale face slightly freckled, his hair curly and touched with red. Although she was fully convinced of her propriety, she felt a touch of shame, distantly experienced. She enjoyed the knowledge that she was hurting Frank; and this enjoyment came not because she thought him abhorrent—as indeed she did—but because, somewhere over the hill, somewhere deep inside herself, she found him not unattractive. This dim awareness—that she took pleasure in hurting a creature that shamefully attracted her—was itself shameful. Its very shamefulness made it still more pleasant.

"That settles Master Frank's goose," the butler said when he had heard the end of it. "Leave it entirely to me, Miss May. I can promise you satisfaction."

Miss May had a prick of regret. She turned her head and parted her lips to speak, but her mistress had awoken. The third housemaid was calling from the top of the stairs. "Miss May—your bell, your bell! It's rung twice."

The double ring meant that May, personally, was wanted and that a substitute was not acceptable.

*   *   *

At the moment of waking up, Anne Meredith spoke aloud. A name, coming out of a dream's wildness, escaped. Hearing her own voice, she pulled herself sharply out of sleep.

The heat of her bath had made her silly.

"Will you get out now," May had asked, "or will I fetch your lunch?"

"I don't really want any lunch."

"You'd better . . ." They both sniggered, because it was not quite correct to be explicit about Mrs. Carr's temperament.

But when May had gone to fetch the tray, the prolonged effect of the hot water had become intolerable. It was absurd to remain in the bath any longer. "At least I can get out of the bath by myself!" she said—she said aloud—but she made no move to do so. She was frightened.

Her fear was not reasonable. It belonged to the body. She feared motion and she feared stillness. "I dare not be still. I dare not surrender motion. And even if I dare, I cannot." She was caught in her orbit and held revolving on her course as surely as any planet. "If I cease to move, my light is extinguished. If I continue in movement, I am imprisoned faster and faster." This way or that, in stillness or in motion, escape was impossible.

72

It made no sense, and she knew that it made no sense, but there were things that were truer than sense. These things were her body.

When you were young, there was no fear of extinction and no fear of stillness. Your body was your reassurance. It exulted, and you were assured of yourself and of your purpose. Your body was your purpose. And it had had one child, one curious and painful act of duplication. Then it was finished. But when she looked through the scented steam, looking along the length of her body, there was no crease or wrinkle, no sagging skin nor lack of firmness, but only the fearful knowledge, exquisitely hidden, that the loss of her body had already started. And never could be stopped; never, until it was worms and dust! "So little time!" she cried, speaking aloud in the terrible loneliness of her bathroom.

So easy, it was, to remember when Harry could stand naked and exultant! But now—but now he had to hide his flesh, hiding its pains and distortions. And her own flesh had to follow the same course of dissolution; to gather itself into folds, to bulge, sag, hang loose, parch, wrinkle, dissolve at last. The dissolution began so soon. As soon as your youth was lost, the dissolution started. There was no pause, but only this mad, elliptical movement on your terrible orbit: so slowly out of your youth; to the time of exultation; then back again, faster, faster, faster into your dissolution, your end. There was so little time! But her body had not yet rounded the elliptical corner. It was only that now it was unused, unwanted.

Without the usage of her body, there was no motion. Without motion, the light died, and there was extinction. Yet without stillness there was no peace and no freedom. There were peace and freedom only when the body rejoiced in its usage. Or there might be peace and freedom in extinction. This didn't go into words. None of it went into words or came out of reason. It belonged to the body.

May had now returned and wrapped her in the long towel, warm from the pipes and rough. "You've been in too long," the girl had said. "It's made you dizzy."

May had led her into the bedroom; and while they joked together and giggled together about the tray of food, disposing its contents into the fire and down the lavatory, that terrible fear persisted. "Lights! Music! Movement!" she wanted to shout, to

73

scream, to hear echoed. She wanted movement, but she wanted to escape the movement that was prescribed for her, the movement towards dissolution along the prescribed course, the prescribed orbit. She wanted to escape from the imprisonment of her orbit; from the whole order, the whole constellation, of which her orbit was a part.

" A nice sleep is what you want."

" I think it is."

May had put her to bed and switched off the lights. Only from the fireplace were cast the gentlest shadows and reflections. The door had closed softly.

There ought, then, to have been release. The conscious mind should at once have taken flight. But instead, it had first to suffer, like a drunken man shut in the dark, that monstrous and sickening sense of vast rotation.

In the library below her bedroom, her husband learnt by degrees that his whole constellation was exploded. And yet, while he came to acknowledge that his order was thus broken, she lay and suffered its imprisonment. That same order had got her as a captive. That order would let her go only when her movement ceased, and her light was extinguished, and she had gone the round of her orbit, and had reached dissolution. Until that hour she was a Meredith woman, caught in the unbreakable order of this house, its lands, its masteries, its burdens; caught, ornamented, administered, enfolded with comforts, adorned with dignities, traditions, conventions that entangled her, dictated to her, and demanded from her a procession of words, deeds and postures that had no purpose except to drag her on, in her inescapable course that led without pause, faster and faster, to her last dissolution!

In the room below, her husband accepted the sentence that the order was broken. In the room above, the woman wept for the liberties that the order had stolen. She wept for her youth before it was altogether lost. Then she slept.

* * *

When Anne awoke, there was this word, this name, in her mouth. As she lay almost asleep, almost awake—between the two states of freedom and captivity, youth and dissolution—her lips parted, and the name escaped them. She called it twice: " Tommy! Tommy! " She called it aloud, and the sound of her own voice pulled her more nearly awake, so that she sat up quickly, happy and excited. She was young, she was free. Seeking to fasten at their source her youth and her freedom, she explored her recent sleep. It was then that the cry which she had uttered from the needs, the longings of her limbs and body seemed to echo down the long vault of herself and return to her shamefully. She made an effort, a great physical effort to escape it: she stretched out a hand from the edge of sleep, groped for the switch and turned on the light. To her surprise the room was empty.

Yet the echo of her cry remained, faintly repeating itself even when she rang the bell for her maid, even when she felt the slight tremor of her maid's approach, even when May opened the door and entered. And though she felt shame at these echoes—because they were a command that could be obeyed only shamefully—that shame was exciting and pleasant. It was even more than that—a promise, a decision.

When May entered the bedroom—straight from her words with Mr. Draper, and with her own sense of shame as an easy burden—and when she stood beside the bed of her mistress, there were thus two women together, each with a secret shame, a pleasing sense of shame, and each secretly exultant. In neither case was the shame or the pleasure or the exultation consciously acknowledged.

May said: " I was just wondering whether I shouldn't wake you."

" What shall I wear to-night? " Anne asked her. " I suppose black? "

" Which black? " May opened the long cupboard where the evening frocks hung in a noble rank.

Anne lay back on her pillows and stretched. " The Worth," she said, " the one with the gold belt."

" This one? " May held it up. " You haven't worn it yet."

" I don't think I have."

" You're never going to put on a new frock; not just for to-night? "

" Perhaps not. But perhaps . . . Yes, perhaps."

Then the telephone rang.

" I'll answer it," Anne said quickly. The instrument stood by her bed. She knew, yes she knew, that the voice that was coming was Tommy Black.

May, watching her before she spoke into the thing, while she

75

was curling her legs beneath her and stretching out her hand to take it up, was aware of a change of key. Magnetically the room recorded it.

"Hallo!" Anne was saying in quite an ordinary voice, but slowly and with a sort of laugh behind it. Then the voice changed, and the magnetic field was cut off, sharp. "Who is it? *Who*? Oh—Mr. Levine . . . Danny, is that really you? It doesn't sound like you in the least." The room had gone dead. "I don't really know, Danny. I forgot to ask Harry, and I'm in bed at the moment, just woken up . . . Oh, no, *no*—it was high time I did. And I don't think it matters *what* you wear. Guy, I suppose, will put on his pink coat, and Harry. But there's a little doctor coming, and *he* won't have one . . ." She listened for a few moments and then said: "See you at half-past eight. So looking forward . . ." and cut herself off while she was still speaking. "So tiresome!" she said to May, and like a child, leapt from her bed.

In her pink quilted dressing-gown, long-skirted to the floor, hanging open but still tight at the waist, she stood in front of the fire which May had stirred to flame. "If the men could see her like that," May thought, "they'd be knocked flat. Younger than me, she looks . . ."

"My jewel-case, May! It's going to be emeralds to-night!"

"Ear-rings and all?" May asked.

"Well, why shouldn't I?" Her mistress sounded quite defiant about it, and then the telephone rang again. "That bloody thing!" she cried. "I can't think why Draper doesn't answer it. May, dear, if you wouldn't mind . . ."

Taking up the instrument, May recognised the voice. "It's her maid, sir," she said. "I'll just find out . . ." And covering the mouthpiece, she asked: "You don't want to speak to Colonel Black?"

At once, that tingling feeling about the room was restored. "So *that's* what it is!" May thought.

Anne had scampered across the room, all legs and loins, and jumped on to the bed like a pink kid. May felt like spanking her as she went past. "It isn't a question," she thought, "of her being younger'n me. It's whether she's Millie or Kate!"

Sitting with her legs doubled beneath her, Anne cuddled the telephone as if it was a teddy-bear. "Tommy!" she cried with a sort of reproach, a laugh. "No, I wasn't in my bath, but I haven't a stitch . . ." She chuckled low down in her chest. " No, Tommy dear, that's *not* an original remark. Rather adolescent, I think . . . Anyway what . . ." It was evidently the same question as before. " I don't care a rap what you wear, not one rap . . . *Personally* . . ."

Busied over the drawer of stockings, by which she was kneeling, May thought: " And all that for an old gentleman like Colonel Black! " Now he must be asking about the ducking her mistress had got, because she answered: " Oh, I swam and I swam, and *eventually* I came out the other side—with Geoff . . . Of course, my dear Tommy, I'm quite sure *you* got across. You *would!* "

What a time they took, the two of them, saying what they meant! May held up a stocking to the light and gave up listening altogether, busying herself with her mistress's clothes, until she heard her say in a guarded sort of voice: " No . . . no, I'm not." And she knew at once that Anne had been asked if she was alone in the room. " Yes, that's all," Anne said. And May knew that it meant herself. " That's all " . . . Only May—only herself. She listened, then, intently.

" Where? " Anne was saying. " *Where?* The South of France, the Esterelle? Oh, Edith's place! But I thought she was selling it . . . Well, that's very nice. But when? *When?* In a few weeks! In the middle of the season! My dear Tommy, you must be mad! "

" Look at that kid! " May thought. " Wriggling about on the bed, as if, as if . . ."

" Fed up with hunting! " Anne cried; " after the best day, the very best day we've had for years and years . . ." There was a long pause while Colonel Black was talking, and May thought that she could almost hear his voice. " Don't talk to *me* about the law of averages! " Anne said. And then, in a more hesitant voice: " No, I don't think we get the *Sunday Express* . . . But, of course, if Professor Thingummy is right, and there's going to be a frost for weeks and weeks . . ." And after a pause, after a long, long sigh: " Of course I remember the mimosa is out. Of course I remember the champagne before lunch, and the lights of Cannes, and it's sunny three days out of four . . . Oh, Tommy, *shut up!* " And finally, in a very practical voice, quite curt: " How many spare bedrooms do you think Edith has got? "

There was a thunderous banging on the door, and May hurried

across. Holding the door half open, she said to her mistress: "It's Master Ralph."

"It's Ralph," said Anne down the telephone. "He's just got back. He's coming in now." She drew her dressing-gown about her and groped for the clips that fastened it. "Oh, yes—I'm quite sure *he* got across all right. He's like you; he always does . . ." She said good-bye and rang off. "Come in, Ralph dear. I'm only very slightly indecent . . ."

*   *   *

Ralph had just got in. Having ridden through a wild night and won his home, he felt valiant.

All the horses and all their riders and all their grooms were back at last, after assembling as a company at the Bull Inn of Neap St. Andrews, a dozen miles from Neapcaster Park. "Those hosses could do with a pint of beer and a bucket apiece," said Watts. "They've a long road ahead."

"You could do with one yourself, couldn't you, Watts?"

"So I could, Master Ralph."

The lights flowed out from the windows of the inn barring the road. The wind was unkind, and though the actual rain had stopped some time ago, it was a dirty night to be riding with a wet coat on your back and wet knees to your breeches on a slimy saddle-flap.

"What about you, Master Geoff? You and your horse have had their sup."

"I ought to push on home."

"You ought, Master Geoff."

"Well—I'll see you in the stables."

"You keep with us," said Watts. "It's a lonely way in the dark. It won't hurt that cob to wait."

So the three horsemen turned into the beamed archway whence the long, triangular slip of light was pushed into the road. "You're soft, you're *bloody* soft," Ralph said to Geoff.

In the yard they found Ted Foster, the strapper. He and his horse had had their drink and were getting themselves straight for the road. "You've taken your time, haven't you, Ted? A hoss likes his home, same as you do yourself."

"Yes, Mr. Watts." The young strapper gathered his reins and put his foot in the stirrup.

"Seeing you've taken your time, you'd best stay along of us."

"Yes, Mr. Watts."

"You're soft as Foster," Ralph said to Geoff. "Soft!"

Watts slipped from his saddle and went to the horses' heads. All his movements were quick and gentle. He handed his reins to Ted. "Take out them bits and loose them girths, while I rouse 'em within."

The horse and the pony—for the others had already drunk—butted at your chest and stamped. When you freed their bits, they shook their heads out of reach. You had to wrestle and coax and stretch to get the head-straps refastened under their chins.

"Watch out for that pony, Master Ralph," Ted said. "Her's a bit of a bastard now an' again. She'll likely give us a nip."

But instead, when her girths were loosened, she gave a glorious shake, quivering all down the spine and ribs so that you, yourself, could feel the relief. She plunged with her hoof on the cobbles, stamping her pleasure, regardless of your foot.

Watts had opened the side door into the inn, and a girl had come from the kitchen to switch on the passage light. Shading his eyes, Watts asked: "Is old Joe Trinder about?"

"I'll send him out to you, Mr. Watts."

Back with his horses, the old groom ran his hand down the neck of each, feeling that they were dry, fingering the harsh, white sweat-marks left by the reins and neck-straps, the saddle, the girths. He ran his hand down their legs, searching for thorns or cuts. When he came to the old grey mare, he stooped to examine the bandages that he'd stitched to her forelegs that morning. "Reckon I'll have these off," he said; "she'll be easier without."

You wouldn't ever forget the sight of the short, spindly figure standing under the lamp, bowler hat on the back of his grey head, whip under his arm, legs apart, as he stretched and fumbled for his breeches pocket beneath the wide skirt of his coat. With his knife unclasped and held between his teeth, he stooped once more amongst the horses' legs. The steam from the horses hung around the lamp. There was nothing happier than this.

"Now then, Master Ralph!" Watts said sharply. All the horses wore kneecaps, fitted at the start of their ride home, in case they slipped. "Take a look at 'em," said Watts; "see they don't rub . . ."

Ralph's pony stretched out her head, ears pricked. She whispered, she whinnied beneath her breath, a purr of impatience, as

79

an old man, unshaven, limped from the bright doorway. On the back of his bald head he wore a cap, and in each hand he carried a bucket whose surplus slopped on to the cobbled yard. " I've put a pint of brown in each," he said to Watts.

The groom put his hand into the tepid mixture, testing it. " It's chilled all right," Joe said crossly. " What do you think? " He had once been a family groom and afterwards an ostler. Now it was mostly motors that he had to wash.

" Always see for yourself," Watts answered, with a wink at Joe and a slight gesture of his head towards the two boys. " 'Twouldn't matter if a 'oss could speak. Feel it yourself, Master Ralph! "

The horse and the pony, jealous, threw their heads at each other, threatening to entangle the loose-hanging bits. As soon as a bucket was put at their feet, the two noses were thrust into it. " Thirsty—the darlings," Joe said.

The horses, their necks down-stretched and outstretched, drank long and quietly. Their nostrils were opened wide, and the passage of water between their soft lips was marked by the throb and undulation of the muscles along their throats. When their first thirst was assuaged, they became more playful, sucking and sniffling, raising their muzzles a few inches above and beyond their buckets, spilling, slopping and dribbling the liquid on to the cobbles, stretching and curling their lips, pausing to dream with distant gaze, then lowering their heads again, again to drink. What happiness was this!

Joe came back with five tankards.

" Nobody else couldn't balance 'em like that," said Ted.

Ralph took long draughts of beer, uninterrupted, like a grown man.

" Luck to you, Dickie Watts! " said Joe over the rim of his tankard. " I'd be glad to see more'n 'em here," he said, looking with joy at the horses. " Parsons and one o' their lads were in here to-night . . . I don't like that lot! " Parsons was one of the grooms to Sir Frederick Betts.

" I don't like 'em neither," said Watts.

" I don't like that Betts nor all his works."

Watts remained silent with a sideways glance at the boys. Ralph knew that he wouldn't discuss their neighbour in front of them, but only their neighbour's men.

"He'll keep on spreading and spreading," Joe said. "He'll keep on buying up. He hasn't finished by half." He looked into his empty tankard. "Got his eye *your* way, I hear," he said to Watts. He limped off a few paces and then turned back. "Looking your way again, I've heard said."

"What's that?" Ted asked him.

"Get them bits back," said Watts sharply. Feeling in his breeches pocket he got a handful of small silver. "I'll settle with Joe, and we'll be on our road. It's a fairish step."

They tightened their girths and mounted stiffly, reluctant to lower themselves into the wet saddles. "Twelve bloody miles," said Ted.

As they rode through the archway, headlamps hit them, a horn shrieked and a car sped past. Ralph, speaking for the first time, said: "I bet that's bloody Betts!"

The wind, even in the valley, tore into their faces. They pressed down their hats. "That bloody Jew, Betts!" said Ralph. He was riding a bit ahead, and the wind carried his words to Geoff. In reply, Geoff had to shout. "He isn't a Jew," he shouted.

"What's that?"

"Betts isn't a Jew."

"Of course he is. He must be—else he couldn't have made all that money; he couldn't be such a crook."

"He . . . is . . . not," Geoff shouted against the wind.

"He must be, or he wouldn't go buying chaps up. He's as much a Jew as that tick Levine."

"*I* don't think Levine's a tick," Geoff shouted. He had to repeat it against the wind; "Levine . . . not . . . not a tick."

"He must be a tick," Ralph said. "The same as that Jew, Betts."

After a few minutes they came, for a brief while, into the half shelter of a group of cottages. Ralph, riding level with Watts, asked: "What did Joe mean about Betts? 'Looking our way,' was what he said."

"I dunno, Master Ralph; it's just talk."

"I bet you *do* know, Watts."

"I don't know at all, Master Ralph."

Ralph's pony stumbled, and the boy jerked at the reins. "Git up, you bastard," he growled, copying the young strappers.

"The fault's yourn," Watts said, "if you leave hold of her head."

"Git up, you bastard," Ralph repeated. "Git up!"

"If you think she's a bastard, Master Ralph, you should leave her home in the stable. She's done you fair, hasn't she, that little 'oss?"

They drew clear of the village along the lonely road, and the wind again increased. "We'll jog on," said Watts, and he pressed the General's bay into a slow trot.

*   *   *

The road followed the river, crossing and recrossing it within the steep valley. It rose and dropped with the lateral undulations of the hill, sometimes taking a cut across a shoulder, a thigh, a breast, but always returning again to the river's course. Even in the shelter of the valley, it was a wild and lonely ride in the high wind which cut off each man from his neighbour. The wind had an opaque quality, as if it was itself darkness, reducing a horseman a few yards ahead into a thickened shadow.

After Neap St. Mary they had a choice of routes: to follow the road that ran through the valley all the way to Neapcaster Park, or to cut up through Broadlands Wood on to the Wold above. The latter was the shorter course by a mile and a half, but rough and tricky in the dark.

"We'll keep to the road," Watts said.

Ralph said: "It's shorter over the hill."

"But rough, Master Ralph."

"I'm going over the Wold."

"I can't stop you, Master Ralph."

"I know you can't," Ralph said.

"'Twon't benefit you," the old groom said, and his voice was quiet but very angry. "'Twill be no good for the 'osses; an' after it all, we'll be home the first."

"What'll you bet? Are you coming, Geoff?"

"You stay along of us, Master Geoff."

Geoff hesitated, wanting to stay with the grooms.

"Are you coming over the hill or are you soft? Are you coming the quick way home, or are you soft like Watts?"

"This is the quick way home," Watts said.

"Oh no, it isn't. Are you soft, Geoff?"

"I'd better go with him," Geoff said.

"Please yourself, Master Geoff. It's your own little hoss. If 'twere mine, I'd stick to the road. But please yourself."

"You're soft, Geoff!"

But it wasn't that he minded being called soft. He wasn't as soft as that! He wasn't so soft that he'd do a thing for fear of what Ralph would say or think.

"Are you coming or not? I can't hang about all night."

There was some deep impulse, an unconsidered loyalty, that bade him follow Ralph. Where Ralph went, he had to follow. He had to follow him for no reason at all—except that he was Ralph.

"I'd better go with him," he said.

"We'll be home afore you," Watts repeated.

"You bloody well won't," Ralph said, as Geoff joined him on the cart-track up the hill.

The old groom's voice was torn by the wind. But now he let them hear his anger. It was no longer hidden. "You go easy . . . take it easy . . . no way to serve a hoss . . ." The wind stole his words. "Sweating hot . . . muck sweat . . ." The voice pursued them in its shreds. And then, a final shout: "You bring them ponies in dry, dry . . . dry, Master Ralph."

"If we bring 'em in hot and sweating," Ralph said to Geoff, "we'll never hear the end of it, never."

"I should think we wouldn't!"

"But we *must* get in first."

*   *   *

The cart-track led up from the river in a long slant across one face of the valley, up through the woods above Neap St. Mary, while the river and the road below swung off in a broad, wasteful circuit.

Leading the way, Ralph's pony swung steadily up the hill. This uphill movement was more joyful than any other, for it threw the thighs of a man deep into the saddle, deep into the horse. It seemed to join together the man and the horse, as if one web of muscle, one circuit of nerves, one course of blood, ran through them both. Ralph rubbed the knuckles of his free hand along the roughness of the clipped mane at the base of his pony's neck. He kneaded the withers, feeling the hard muscles moving between his cold fingers. Opening his hand, he laid it along the flat planes of the neck where the muscles moved in rhythm at each step. Through the dark, he could just see the ears prick forward.

He could hear the wind made softer in the bare treetops. Even in the naked winter, he could smell the woods, after rain, and the sodden mast.

When they reached the crest the wind was their master. Its full force came across the uplands, barring the way, stealing their breath, tearing the breath from their lips. The pony stumbled, and it was a mortal conflict with the wind to clamp the muscle between your legs, to lift the horse and press it onwards along the rough, invisible track. They went on like this for several miles across the top of the world, the wind making time and space meaningless. Into the wind Ralph sang and shouted his joy, unable to hear any sound at all from his own voice.

He was still singing as he fell, without any knowledge that his pony had again stumbled, except that, as he lay on the wet tussocks, the muscles of his thighs and legs recalled their urgent stiffening as they tried to recover and recollect the safety that was suddenly lost. Then pain struck his shoulder, and Geoff, leaning over him, seemed to be shouting from an old world that had been shed, as a horse sheds its coat.

"Is your pony all right?" Geoff was shouting.

"How the hell should I know?" Ralph answered. "She fell; I didn't."

When they had got hold of the pony which had risen but was cropping, unalarmed, the coarse grass, they found that the saddle had slipped right round underneath her belly. Geoff said: "You didn't properly tighten those girths."

"You bloody well shut up!" Ralph said. "My shoulder hurts."

"Is it bad?"

"I dare say it's broken a bit."

"I bet it isn't," Geoff said. "I reckon we're off the track."

Getting to his feet, feeling the pain sharp in his shoulder, Ralph said: "That's the sort of fool thing I'd expect you to reckon. We're still heading right. The wind's still in the same place."

They took some time getting the saddle straight and the girths tightened. "We *must* get in first," Ralph said. "Catch hold of her head, can't you?" And as soon as he had remounted, while Geoff held the pony, he pressed on again into the darkness, with the wind full in his face. Faintly he heard Geoff shout, and he answered with the wind: "You don't need any one to hold a quiet old cow like that cob." Grinning like his father, as he thought of Geoff hopping around with his foot in the stirrup, trying to get on to his cob's back, he shouted again: "*Must* get ahead of them! Can't wait." He hoped, he prayed, that they were heading right.

Soon the cob, not Geoff, caught up. Geoff had only to sit on the cob's back, like an old sack, and that cowlike animal would carry him along all right. As soon as he heard Geoff's voice, Ralph knew that he had, for some time, been aware of a light ahead. It was at first a star, but now too low for a star, too big, too bright.

"Adam Rogers!" Geoff was shouting. "Adam's cottage! Slender Ladies!"

"Do you think I didn't know that?" Ralph said and increased his pace to a sharp trot.

When they came to the road by Adam's cottage, they were over the top of the hill, and the wind, caught by the crest opposite and by the curve of the valley to which they were returning, was at once more moderate. Ralph's pony fussicked at the gate, and Geoff had to open it. Through the uncurtained window of Adam's cottage, they saw the girl, Judy, sitting by herself and looking into the night. Her gaze was directly upon them; and, except that she made no sign or movement, it was hard to believe that they were invisible. Her hands were clasped tightly about her enormous belly, as if it pained her.

As soon as they had ridden down the track into Slender Ladies Covert, it became suddenly quiet. The quiet was as startling as the first, tremendous onslaught of the wind when they topped the Wold. In too loud a voice Geoff started to ask: "Did you see . . ."

"Yes," Ralph said. He spoke in a curt voice.

"She's going to whelp, isn't she?"

"What do you think?"

"Do you think to-night?"

"How the hell should I know?" Ralph said. In silence they rode down the track through the wood. Then he asked: "Is that cob of yours sweating?"

"Not in the least. But I bet yours is."

"She is a bit, as a matter of fact. She's a blood animal, not a cob."

"The fall would have started her off," Geoff said. "If we don't get her dry, we can't ever face Watts."

"Don't you tell him we had a fall! He'd laugh like a drain if he knew we came down up top . . . After that, we *must* get in first."

"All right." Ralph slipped off his pony and started to lead her down the track. It was not easy in the dark. "My shoulder hurts," he said. But he walked in front of his pony, leading her, all the way down to the river at Swain's Bridge, and up the far side along the track that Geoff had taken that morning before sunrise. Half-way up the hill, they took a lateral track to the left, a wide and easy way that led, in a very short distance, to the stables. Behind the stables, the house loomed high and full of light.

As they came into the stableyard, Grant came out to meet them with the youngest strapper, Jimmy. It was Jimmy who took the cob.

"He's quite dry," Geoff said. "He's all right."

"The pony's dry," Ralph said, handing her over to Grant. "I suppose the others aren't back?"

"Not yet, Master Ralph."

The boys slipped into the house by the servants' door and went along the kitchen passage to the gunroom. They pulled off their boots and left them lying on the stone floor for Frank or Walter to fetch later. Geoff put on gumboots and went to get his bike, to ride home to the Lodge and change for dinner. Ralph put on slippers and went up to see his mother. The door was opened by May, a creamy, springy sort of girl, a woman really, but not bad. Through the half-open door he heard his mother talking on the telephone and then calling to him to come in. "I'm only very slightly indecent," she said.

*　　*　　*

When Ralph went to give his mother a formal kiss, she held him off with her hand, saying: "I love you very dearly but—look at yourself in the glass!"

"Oh, Master Ralph!" May cried as he sat down on the bed. "You'll make everything that filthy!" For he was smeared and spattered with mud from forehead to breeches. All over his buff breeches, yellow waistcoat, tweed coat (for he was not yet old enough to wear white breeches and a long-skirted coat of black or pink), white stock and deep red, russet, gypsy face, he had specks and spatters of mud clinging like scab. He was clean only from the red rim on his forehead, left by his bowler hat, upwards through his short, mouse-coloured hair. This hair was fine and silky, his only inheritance from Anne, for the General's had been coarse and tough.

"And you're wet!" Anne cried, feeling his coat.

"Of course I am. It's been raining."

"I suppose it has," Anne said vaguely, for the room, by night, was insulated from any knowledge of the weather outside. "Is it raining still?"

"It stopped hours ago—there was too much wind; the hell of a wind. Now it's going to freeze, and the wind will drop."

"So it's freezing," Anne said thoughtfully, lazily, as if referring to a dream. "There's a man in the *Sunday Express*, I'm told, a Professor . . . he says it's going to freeze now for weeks and weeks."

"I bet it doesn't. I've got to have four more hunts before I go back."

He lolled on the bed and watched May hanging up the long black frock. "It's all ready," she said. "Will you ring, Mam, when you want me?" He watched her cross the room, come past the bed and go out. When the door had closed, his mother said: "You *mustn't* watch girls like that. It's rude. At least . . . at least, you're not old enough." He did not answer, and there was no expression on his face, but behind the unmoving features there was that smug, lazy, secret satisfaction. "You're wet," his mother said again. "And you haven't got too much time before dinner . . ." While she spoke, she rose and went across to the dressing-table where the emeralds were laid out.

Getting up from the bed, moving with his quick, sleek action, Ralph followed her across. "I say!" he cried, looking at the jewellery, "you're not going to plaster yourself with all that?"

"Most certainly I am!" She had sat down at the dressing-table and was starting to do her face. Her long fingers played amongst the rows of pink jars and the tubes of cosmetics. "Your old mother . . ." she said, unscrewing a pot, sniffing it and screwing it up again. "Can't she do her best, can't she be pretty, pretty as she can, when . . . when her friends are coming to dinner?"

"Oh hell!" he said. "There isn't a party?"

"You know quite well there is."

"I didn't. I forgot."

"How absurd!" she thought. "How fantastic it is! How old, how old I have to feel!" For the things she found that she said, and the answers he gave her, came from the past; word for word from the past, from the very beginning. "He might be Harry! He *is* Harry!" So there she was—sandwiched between

87

the two Meredith men, who were only *one* man, sixteen and sixty!
And there she was—back where she started!

"Who's coming?" he asked.

"Nobody very much. Nobody very alarming. Just the Bredons,
and Tommy Black."

"*He* got across the river. He still goes like stink."

"Why ' still '? You horrid little boy! He's no older than me,
not much." She played with the tubes, she played with the brushes,
the bottles, the pots. "Your poor old mother . . ." she said.

"Who else?" he asked.

"That new doctor and his wife: the little Scotch person who
came last month. And there's Danny Levine and David . . ."

"Oh, God!"

"That's just stupid," she said sharply. "Really it makes me
quite cross. He's your age, your school, your house . . ."

"Awful little tick!"

"You boys!" she cried. "You boys are just swine . . . swine
. . ." She swung round on her stool, turning from the looking-
glass in real anger. "You'll see!" she said. "You just wait and
see! He'll be worth the lot of you."

"I doubt it," Ralph said.

She thumped her knees with her clenched fists. "You wait!
You wait till you're all men—not horrid, filthy, dirty little school-
boys! You wait! You'll see . . ."

"He's a dirty little Jew," said Ralph.

"How dare you!"

Ralph raised his arm in time and took on his wrist the tube
of cream that his mother had flung at him. "You filthy, filthy
little boy!" Her voice was raised, as if she were scolding a dog
that had made a mess on a rug. "I *won't* have that said in this
house! I won't, I won't!" She was standing in front of him
now. She had to look up at him, for although he was short, her
eyes scarcely reached his chin. "How dare you . . . *dare* you talk
like that!"

"Well, he *is* dirty, Mum. He doesn't wash." Ralph spoke
quite evenly and in good humour. He had no fear of his mother.
He stooped to pick up the tube that she had thrown at him. "Here's
your thing," he said.

"Oh, you make me so sick!" But she had turned towards
the curtain which, facing the bathroom door on the opposite wall,

hid the entrance to her husband's room. Harry, hearing their voices, had come in without his usual knock. She saw him, ready for his bath, wearing a long silk dressing-gown drawn tightly about him. It made him look scraggy about the neck, and elsewhere fat: another generation, another race, another species altogether, from herself.

"I have it from Draper, who has it from May, that you are none the worse," he said to his wife. He spoke in that particularly irritating voice, paternal, patriarchal, that he used when his wife and his son, both of them, were alone with him. "I also heard," he added, "what appeared to be a brisk argument. Can one join it?"

"Certainly," Anne answered. "Oh, certainly. Ralph calls David Levine 'a dirty little Jew.'"

"Well, one does rather, doesn't one?" said Harry.

"And Danny's been a friend all your life!"

"Oh yes—very much so. He's a very good chap."

"Yet you still call him . . ."

"I don't, as a matter of fact," the General said. "But it might slip out about any one else."

"But . . . do you *feel* it?" she asked, touching her heart. "When you think of a Jew, do you *feel* that he's dirty or stinking or bloody or a crook?"

Her husband hesitated. He rarely, if ever, gave an altogether flippant answer. There was always truth in it. He was too honest a man for easy appeasement.

"Harry!" she cried. "*Do* you?"

"No, no," he said. "So many of my friends, so many of my very best friends . . ."

"Oh, don't, don't, *don't* . . ." she cried, "don't you *dare* give me *that*! And it goes on 'but, but, *but* . . .'"

"Well," he said, "but it's true. Danny now . . . Danny's all right. But he's one of the few, one of the specials; family been here for centuries—or something of the sort . . . My own regiment, my Brigade Major once—a very interesting chap, a *fine* chap . . ."

"All the same," said Ralph, "his son does *not* wash."

"You horrid little boy!" said Anne, laughing. "Get out of my room and let me dress."

* * *

89

Left alone with her, and wanting to put his arm about her, to kiss her neck—for he still found her enchanting—the General approached the stool on which his wife sat. She did not look up; and he, unhappily aware that his touch displeased her, kept his hands in his pockets. Beneath her dressing-gown, she was pulling on her stockings. As he came near, she drew her dressing-gown close.

He started to say: "I had a long session with Greenley." But then he decided not to worry her, not yet. "A somewhat dreary affair," he concluded.

"And I . . ." she said, "this schoolmaster man . . ." And she touched the pile of letters that lay on her dressing-table. "He'll have to be answered."

"Young Walter?" her husband said. "That scrap of a lad. You'd never think it."

"It's very tiresome. Tiresome that he can't pass examinations, like anybody else."

"I never could myself."

"Of course not," she said. "Nor Ralph."

"Yet a genius," said the General. "A genius, isn't it? Dear me—a genius in our pantry! Well," he said, "I suppose we shall have to do it. We shall have to find him a school—a school somewhere or other, a school of sorts."

"Can we afford it?" she asked.

"Oh no, we certainly can't! But somehow one does it." In the pocket of his dressing-gown he felt an envelope. He drew it out. And there it was—the big, mauve thing that had been at the back of his mind all day, unknown, unacknowledged. "And this!" he said to his wife. "What do you think of this?" He laid it in front of her.

"What a thing!" she cried. "What a horrible-looking thing!"

"It's a skeleton," he said; "a real skeleton in our cupboard. A long way back . . . my grandfather . . ."

"Again? That old man again?"

"Again and again," the General said. "This time there's a feller called Seytoun . . . he may be a tiresome chap. He's living at Cannes . . ."

"Cannes!" she cried. "Near Edith!" And it seemed a coincidence, a wild and wonderful coincidence, full of guilt and excitement. She took up an emerald ear-ring and held it against her hair, her neck, as she looked in the glass.

"There's a girl, a daughter. He's sent her photograph."

"Oh, has he?" she said absently, for she was fastening her jewels. "What's she like? Is she anything much?"

"From her picture," the General said, "she's a lovely thing. Her name's Alex."

"Oh, yes?" his wife said. "Alex . . . Alex . . . a pretty name, a curious name . . . I rather like it . . ." But he had lost her attention. Her thoughts were distant. "Cannes," she said; "mimosa," she murmured; "champagne before lunch."

"It's going to cost us a bit," the General said. "I can see that coming. I can see it ten miles off."

"Oh dear," she answered, "how tiresome, how very tiresome . . ." But the words, trailing into the scent which she was now spraying upon her neck and hair, meant nothing, absolutely nothing. So he took up the envelope and replaced it in his pocket.

"Oh," he said, "there's another thing. I had a sharp encounter with Draper on my way upstairs. There's some sort of trouble between May and Frank."

"There *would* be!" she said. "There just *would* be!"

And he rather agreed with her. This was marriage, this was love! A long session with Greenley; a tiresome letter from a schoolmaster; the boy, Walter, to be sent to school at Meredith expense; a mauve envelope and another liability, still one more liability, left from the past; a girl, a lovely little girl called Alex; and now some trouble of sorts between a maid·and a footman. *This* was left of love! All of it; all that was left. And his wife, enchanting, was twisting herself about; her tiny, exquisite body posing itself before the glass. He wanted to kiss the back of her neck as she sat in front of the mirror. He wanted more than that. He stooped.

"Yes, dear," she said to her husband, whose breath was in her hair, "*what* about May and Frank?"

Disappointed, he straightened himself. "A message," he said. "He sent her a message that he'd like to meet her. In the drying-room, he said."

"Why ever the drying-room?"

"I can't think."

"I suppose," Anne said, "there's awfully few places in this house . . . it's not designed for it."

"May, it seems, is furious."

"Really!" Anne cried. "It's quite ridiculous! The girl ought to be flattered."

"But she isn't," the General said. "And Draper . . ."

"He's jealous of course."

"Quite likely he is. But he's very insistent that Frank must be sacked."

"Sack Frank! And he's just getting good!"

"That's what I said. And there's no one to take his place. It means starting afresh and making allowances for this and that. Whenever there's anything amiss, forgotten, gone wrong—it can always be the new footman."

"There's Walter, of course. But he hasn't the figure."

"Too small. Too young altogether. And you forget . . ."

"Of course—he's a genius!"

"Well," said the General, looking at her clock. "It's late. I've scarcely time for a bath. But I shall have it. I shall have it!"

He left her alone, and she stood up and walked the length of her room towards the long mirror at the end of it. Swinging her skirt, she watched herself advance. Turning and looking back over her shoulder, she saw the movement of her hips. "Well!" she said to herself. "Well—if *that* doesn't suit you, Tommy Black!"

"I say!" said the General, returning, and she whipped round guiltily, with a fall in her belly, as if she had spoken aloud.

"You gave me a start."

"Sorry, sorry," her husband said. "This business with Frank. Will you have a word with that girl of yours?"

"I just couldn't bear it to-night. To-morrow, perhaps."

"Well," said Harry, before closing the door behind him, "I'll see what I can do with Draper. I only hope he'll relent."

*   *   *

In the dressing-room upstairs, the General was finding for Frank's conduct an excuse, or at least an explanation. "He just forgot himself," he said, standing at his glass and straining at his stiff collar until he got it over the stud. "He's only a panicky sort of lad," he said to Draper, "they all are, at that age—like a young horse . . ." During his military career, the General had made so many of these appeals for leniency that he sometimes forgot that it was not a cavalry Commanding Officer, nor the Riding Master, nor the Farrier Sergeant-Major to whom he was speaking. And the metaphor of the young horse seemed so appropriate that he let it run on while he struggled with a white tie, spoilt one of them, threw it away and started on another. "They don't want all stick an' spur," he said. "These lads—they want easy hands, they want gentling, they want . . ." He seemed to be off the point, and he stretched out his arms backwards for the pink tail-coat with the buff lacings that Draper was holding. "They want," he said, "forgiveness."

Without a word, with no sign of relentment, the butler eased the pink coat over his master's shoulders.

"He just forgot himself," the General said weakly.

"If I may say so, sir, he forgets himself too often."

"He's young, Draper."

"I doubt, sir, if he's really our type of lad."

The General considered this proposition and had to admit its validity. "The boy comes from a rough home," he said.

"So I should suppose, sir."

The General sighed audibly, intending Draper to hear him. "I know it's asking a lot of you," he said, paying respect to the stubbornness of Draper's defence. "But I'd like to give him a chance . . . *Another* chance," he added hastily. "Do you know about his father?"

"I can't say I do, sir."

But the General persisted. "The best squadron sergeant-major I ever knew," he said. "Had an arm shot off. Learnt a trade, got a job—and lost it. He married a slut—five children . . . this lad, Frank, the eldest . . . brought up in a slum tenement . . ." He let his voice trail away. He paused, hoping for help from Draper, for some signal of understanding.

"It's not me so much, sir," said the butler, taking the soft clothes-brush for a final touch to the General's shoulders, "as Miss May. I had to promise her satisfaction."

"I'll get Mrs. Meredith to talk to her in the morning."

The General walked across to the long mirror. In these clothes he was still tolerably satisfied with his showing. He examined his nails. He wanted the willing assent of the butler and he was sure that there was some way of winning it. It was a question of humour. Picking up his ivory brushes with the crested backs, he gave a touch to his grey moustache. His eyebrows twitched; he grinned. "Tell you what, Draper," he said. "The feller's a very useful bowler. If you ask me . . ." He put just a drop of eau-de-Cologne on the handkerchief that lay ready. "You don't like keeping wicket for him. He's too fast for you!" He gave the butler an enormous wink. He started to fill his pockets with the things that always went with him—cigar-case and cutter, notecase, a gold pencil. "As a personal favour to me, eh, Draper? Give him another chance."

"Very good, sir," the butler said. And being a kind and a just man, he went straight downstairs to tell Frank that the General had been persuaded to relent.

*　　*　　*

"Hallo, Draper!"

"Do you want anything, Master Ralph?" This young man spent too much time in the servants' quarters. The baize door was supposed to be a two-way obstacle.

"Dad down yet?"

"He will be, very shortly."

"Geoff clocked in?"

"Master Geoff was here twenty minutes ago. He went out again to the stables."

"I've just got time, haven't I?"

"No, Master Ralph."

In his dinner-jacket, Ralph ran down the kitchen passage and out by the servants' door, across the courtyard to the stables. The wind had dropped completely, and it was freezing hard beneath a clear sky of many stars. Watts was in the box with the General's bay, refastening the rugs.

"So you did get back?" Ralph said.

Watts did not answer.

"Were you a long time behind us?"

Watts maintained his silence. Ralph went along to the cob's box and found Geoff just finishing the bandages. He had an old raincoat, used as an overall, over his dinner-jacket. "Is he all right?" Ralph asked.

"This cob's right enough. Have you seen your pony?"

"Anything wrong with her?"

"See for yourself."

But when Ralph got to his pony, Watts was already there and had turned back the rug from the chestnut quarters. They shone

with rimes of white, dried sweat and dark edges of fresh moisture.
"Hey you, Ted, come here!"

"What's the matter, Mr. Watts?"

"Come here, you! Why didn't you tell me she'd broken out?"

"She hadn't a while ago," the boy said sulkily. But now he
had only to run his hand up the pony's neck to find that the base
of her ears were soaking wet. "She's still sweating bad."

Ralph said: "And I led her home from Slender Ladies!"

Turning his back on Ralph, Watts said to Foster: "She's a
blood mare, that little hoss. She wants bringing home very quietly
along the roads—not galloping about the Wold. You know what
you got to do?"

"Yes, Mr. Watts."

"Take her on the dairy track."

"Yes, Mr. Watts." The boy looked hopelessly at the stable
clock lit up in its tower above the archway. It was close on half-
past eight, and he'd been at work since six in the morning. On
the level stretch of track behind the stables and alongside the dairy,
it would be dark and lonely. But he slipped a head-collar on the
pony and led her out of the box and out of the yard, to walk her
up and down until she dried off.

"It's freezing," Ralph said; "freezing hard; going to freeze
for a month. Oh hell!" He walked away from the box, with
Geoff following. "We'd better get back. It's perishing cold."
Over his shoulder he called good night to Watts but got no answer.
"My shoulder hurts like hell," he said to Geoff. But Geoff did
not answer either.

* * *

The first of the cars must have turned into the drive, for its
lights were fringing the crest above the courtyard. Ted Foster
could see them as he led Ralph's pony up and down the track by
the dairy. All the house seemed to be alight, and even the curtained windows let shafts escape across the stable roofs.

Oh, but the night was cold! And the world had never been
turning more certainly than now through the star-filled sky in
which a mountain of cloud climbed up and up until you cricked
your neck to see its peak.

The chestnut pony wouldn't walk. She fretted and jogged and
jiggled along the track. He tried to soothe her, with a hand on the

neck and soft words: " Ah, give over, you silly, give over . . . d'ye want to be here all night ? " But it seemed she did.

The lights of a car rose like a great aurora behind the spinney that sheltered the dairy. Up in the branches he could see a black bundle, an old cock pheasant at roost. " I wish I was Adam Rogers —with pheasant for dinner every night."

He heard slow footsteps upon the fallen leaves, and Grant came past on his homeward way. " 'Night, Ted," he said, " won't she cool off ? She's a bad 'un, she is, for sweating." He didn't stop, but there was enough light from the stars to see the hump on his back.

" Wish I was Charlie Grant with a home an' kids—pinching a sack of stable oats for my fowl-house."

" Wish I was any of those chaps with their pickings. A sack of taters for the pig . . ."

" Wish I was even Frank, in his flunkey togs, with pickings in plenty up at the house."

The cold in his toes and fingers crept inwards like death. He slipped his hand under the rugs, alongside the warm flanks. " Jesus —still sweating ! " he said. Nervously the pony plunged to the side of the track.

" 'Lo, Ted ! " she called, she laughed. " Talking to yourself ? Ha'n't you none better ? " He hadn't heard her footsteps, and only the pony had seen the twist of her light skirt.

" 'Lo, Bessie Rogers," he said. " Bin havin' a word with Frank ? "

" Frank ! " she said. " Him ! *Him !* "

" There's better lads than Frank."

" I should hope there was ! " she said.

" Judy's big."

" She's over big," her sister said. " 'Twill maybe come to-night. She's fretting overmuch. 'Twon't come if you fret."

" *He* isn't fretting, you can bet your life."

" What's *he* got to fret about ! " she said.

" That's right."

" I must be getting along . . . 'Night, Ted."

He put his arm round her waist, but she wriggled away. " Look out, can't you ! " she cried.

" What's the matter ? " he asked, surprised. But his fingers had touched her bosom. " Oho . . ." he said, " aren't your chickens laying enough eggs? Wish I had the key of the dairy meself."

"I work there, don't I?" she said, whisking herself past the pony. "'Night, Ted."

When she had gone the track became very lonely. His own girl was Lizzie, in the kitchen close at hand; always close at hand, but he could rarely get to her.

The last of the cars seemed to have arrived a long time ago, and the lights of the house had become more distant. The night was very cold—colder and colder. The heap of clouds had slid down the sky behind the wood.

"They stars are terrible bright . . ."

It was old Watts who had come quietly down the path. The boy had heard his footsteps. "Is she still fretting?" the groom asked.

"Still breaking out, Mr. Watts."

"Ah," he said. "It's her blood. I've known they blood 'uns carry on like this for half the night." He stood looking up at the stars. "I'll take her," he said. "You can be getting along. Slip in, on your way, an' tell Mrs. Watts I'll be a while yet."

The boy handed over the pony. He didn't know how to say "thank you," so he just nodded and said "'Night, Mr. Watts," and went back up the track. Behind him, he could hear the old groom talking to the pony: "You silly, flipperty gal . . . flipperty lass . . . be easy, can't ye?" Soon he could hear neither the footsteps nor the voice.

He went into the yard to get his bike. As he did so, a last car came crunching the gravel in a broad, rustling sweep, the wheels sweeping the drive, and the lights sweeping the house. It was not one of the guests, but Victor and the Rolls Royce.

*   *   *

In the end they had to send Victor and the Rolls Royce for Tommy Black. The news of his delay, and later the impact of his arrival, caused two noticeable conclusions in the affair of the evening; like two punctuation marks; like the endings of two movements of a symphony which had started with the command "Door!" issued by Draper to Frank as the first of the headlights lit the courtyard.

In the Oak Room, Anne was waiting, scarcely aware of her son, of Geoff, of her husband. Yet her awareness was acute. It was the awareness of an animal in a cage, a pen, waiting for the door of release to be opened, hearing invisible footsteps, and then others, and then more, and relating them, each time, to its own predicament.

"*Door!*" said Draper to Frank, as the two servants waiting in the outer hall saw the first headlights. And as the car drew up, the door of the house swung open.

"'Evenin', Draper." Guy Bredon was out of the car before the chauffeur could leave his seat; he had greeted Draper and had turned to help his wife before butler or footman could get to her. It was a bustle and a clatter when the Bredons arrived for dinner. "How's Mrs. Meredith? None the worse for her ducking?"

"Remarkably well, sir."

Within the Hunt boundaries, Guy entered any house with legitimate familiarity. His role was *enfant terrible*, beneath which play, recognised for what it was by those who knew him well—masters and servants alike—his competence, shrewdness and even wisdom, as well as his vast generosity, could exercise themselves without embarrassment. By a sort of buffoonery, deliberate tactlessness and schoolboyish rudeness, he made a show of hiding both the ability which maintained and increased his wealth, and the philanthropy which that wealth supported. "I found you the name of that book," he said to Draper, and got from the pocket of his pink tail-coat a slip of paper typed by his secretary. "But leave the General a drop or two, won't you?" It was a book on wines and vineyards, in which subject the butler took much technical interest. "I'm having it sent to you."

"That will be most useful, sir."

"I don't know that the General will agree with you! And you . . ." he turned to Frank, who had taken his overcoat, "there's another four months, is it, another five months, before you next send my leg-stump spinning over Draper's head?"

"Yes, sir," Frank answered guardedly, with Draper's eye on him.

"Eh? What's that?" Guy asked sharply, dissatisfied with the footman's answer.

"You should wait for the loose ones," Frank said with great daring. "You shouldn't swipe a good length."

This pleased the Master immensely; and although Draper grunted "Watch it!" into Frank's ear, the Bredons broke into laughter which travelled through the house and arrived faintly in the Oak Room. Anne's expectancy diminished, but the pain of waiting increased. She could hear the noisy and leisurely approach of Guy and Madge; he coming slowly ahead with his powerful and heavy body, his rolling step, his red face and dark-grey hair —where he wasn't bald—and his loud voice; and she lagging behind to glance at the familiar pictures, with her body still slim, her eyes still wide and bright—though her prettiness had collapsed —and her grey hair still touched with yellow. Anne had to suffer their entrance as a phase in her ordeal of waiting.

"Still alive, my dear, after all that swimming?"

"You must have the gills of a fish."

"Who's coming to-night?"

"Only Danny," Anne answered, "and a new little doctor and his wife."

"Really you might have warned me!" Madge said. "I should have had a headache. Nothing would have got me here."

"What's wrong with him?" Harry asked. "He's only Scottish."

"He's red," said Guy; "red head, red politics."

"Old Blunt was getting past it without a partner."

"But what a partner to choose!" Madge cried. "I had him last week when Blunt couldn't come. He told me . . . he told me . . . I can't bring myself to repeat it."

"They tell me he's able enough," said Harry. "They say he's here for his wife's health, and she . . . and she . . . What was it, Anne—something peculiar?"

"Daughter of an Oxford don," said Guy.

"Guy always knows," said Harry.

"You see?" Madge said. "A professor's daughter!"

"She was trained as a nurse," Guy continued, "though I can't think why. And now she's a publisher's reader—whatever that may be."

"Reads the proofs," said the General.

"Nonsense, Harry—you don't know a thing about it."

"Anyway," said Madge, "it's all very regrettable."

Rolling alongside Geoff, for whom he had always shown a very special affection, Guy took the boy's arm and kneaded it, repeating, "Well, young feller, how goes it, how goes it?"

*   *   *

99

"Door!" said Draper in the outer hall; and as Frank went down the steps, a small blue car drew up.

The young doctor stuck out his ginger head. "Where shall I put her?" he asked.

"Just draw it clear of the door," Frank answered. "It'll be fetched." For Victor was waiting in the pantry for this purpose.

The doctor parked his car. "Can't it stay here?" he asked, getting out before Frank could open the door for him, pulling the rug off his wife's knees and slinging it over the bonnet. "I may want it in a hurry. Won't it do where it is?"

"They're always fetched, sir."

"Oh, all right," he said, as his wife prodded him. Resentful and nervous, he hustled her out of the car and into the house. "Good evening," he said to Draper, pushing his wife in front of him and getting out of his overcoat before the butler could help him take it off.

"Would you care to go upstairs, madam?" the butler asked. He lifted his head very slightly towards the half-landing where a housemaid waited for this contingency.

"No, no—you don't want that," the doctor answered. And his wife slipped off her coat and handed it gracefully to Frank. She was a fine and beautiful woman, a contrast to her short, slight, nondescript, reddish husband. She moved with dignity in a bright green velvet dress which was very becoming but out of fashion; for the fashions put waists round the loins and flattened the breasts, while she had her figure unmistakably and naturally proportioned.

"This way, please," said Draper. He spoke with faint distaste —for this young man and his wife were already known for their unpleasant politics—and with the hauteur permitted towards any one who rendered paid, personal service. He could well remember the time when doctors, solicitors, schoolmasters, practising or working in the county, rarely got into this house except to exercise their professions. It was at least to be noted with satisfaction that he was uneasy—as a country doctor in such surroundings *should* be uneasy—that he walked across the hall quickly and aggressively, with his chin up, and that when his wife stopped to say: "Look, that's the Van Dyck!" he gave her an impatient push.

But now she was not to be hurried. "And *that's* the one there's all the argument about!" she said. "I'm sure it *is* a Constable." Her low voice was resonant and musical. It matched very well a certain nobility in her carriage, her pale or creamy skin, and her very dark hair. And as the voice was caught in the Oak Room by Anne's anxious ears, again the tension was released while the suspense, the pain continued. But the doctor and his wife had scarcely entered and been introduced before Anne was aware—through faint tremors that were caught by her tightened perceptions—of new arrivals.

*   *   *

"Door!" said Draper to Frank.

It was a very long black car of foreign make from which Daniel Levine drew himself with Frank's help. He was an immense man with a powerful but pleasant voice. "Freezing—going to freeze harder," he said to Frank. He stood with a leopard-skin rug over his arm, one hand on the bonnet of his car, and his great black head lifted to the stars. "I'll cover her up, but I suppose . . ."

"Yes, sir," Frank said. "Victor will be fetching her."

Frank and the butler were both smiling, for they liked Levine, whom Draper had known since they were both boys on the village cricket field. "It's a long time, sir, since you've been to see us," Draper said.

"It is, Draper. I've been abroad—in the South of France."

"And all last summer . . . you didn't come once for the cricket."

"I daren't play nowadays, Draper. It makes me cough."

"You heard about Master David's catch? We shan't forget that in a hurry," said Draper kindly, for he liked the boy and knew him to be nervous.

Levine had thrown off his coat and was striding across the hall towards the morning-room, with David some way behind. "Not there, sir," Draper had to call after him. "We're back in the Oak Room to-night."

"The pictures, then?"

"Back from the exhibition, sir."

"Oh, good . . . good . . ." said Levine absently, wheeling across the hall with his great shoulders bowed and his chin thrust forward. Even this ancient and solid house shook under his tread.

"This can only be Danny!" said Madge.

And Anne's suspense broke into great anger. While she greeted Daniel Levine, her heart was enraged with Tommy. "Why must

101

he always be late? Why must he always be the last? How *dare* he be late to-night!"

*   *   *

"How nice to have the Dutch back with us!" said Danny, beaming round the room at the pictures. "And how well they looked in Paris!"

"You went to see them?" the General asked.

"Of course . . . on my way down South, to Edith's."

"Edith's! You've been to Edith's?"

"Didn't you know, Anne?"

"Yes, yes," she said. "Of course I did. Of course I knew . . . I suppose I'd forgotten . . ."

There was nothing positively remarkable about her words, or the way she said them; yet Levine's quick senses missed something, some lustre or transparency, in her response. He found himself watching her, as he said: "I've only just got back. Edith sent you all nice messages. She was saying she hoped . . ." But some look in her eyes, as if he were causing her not pain or distress or even discomfort, but a sort of unwilling excitement, made him interrupt himself and turn away quickly. Facing the doctor's wife, whom he recognised without introduction, he said: "You must be Mrs. Macdonald. I know all about you. I know your father, of course . . ." But again he had to turn—reluctantly to turn from the doctor's wife—because Anne was calling to him in a voice which, this time, was positively unusual in its sharp undertone: "*Please*, Danny . . . what was it Edith was hoping?"

"Oh, only the usual," Levine answered carelessly. "Only that some of you—that you, Anne, in particular—would go down and relieve her loneliness."

"I wish she would," said Harry, who was talking to Madge. "Anne needs a rest."

"A rest!" Madge cried. "A rest from what?"

"From all my duties, of course," Anne said with a weak giggle. And now she was frightened of her voice. It was not her own; it must be evident that it was not her own. For her ears, her senses, the whole of her body, were too busy listening and waiting for her lips to be able to speak. And so, since she dared not withdraw her voice from the orchestra, she turned to David. "Why, David!" she cried, "I scarcely noticed you. You crept into the room like a little mouse!"

The boy managed to work a smile into his lips; but his eyes, while directed politely at Mrs. Meredith's face, glanced miserably sideways, drawn to the corner of the room where Ralph stood. Ralph and Geoff were together; and while Geoff was smiling a mild greeting, Ralph's gaze was hard and was launched at the wall behind David's back. It was a blank and deliberate gaze. To David it was very familiar.

Across the beam of Ralph's steady contemplation, the chatter and the laughter ran, fused and redispersed itself like blobs of mercury. There was warmth and intimacy in the inquiries and allusions, some of which had their source in the far past, even in a past generation. The Bredons, the Merediths and Daniel Levine—they could not remember any year—or at least any sequence of years, other than the war—when there had not been friends, in red and black tail-coats and lovely frocks, sipping their sherry just here, in this room, lit no less by the bright fire than by the hooded lights above the Dutch and Flemish pictures; friends laughing beside the marquetry table on which were set out the sherry decanters and glasses, while more distantly, in gentle shadow, or rather in an absence of direct light, there stood the tall Ming vase, the Tang horse and, not in the least incongruous, the Rodin lady.

Upon the polished floor there lay Chinese rugs of blue and white; upon the Chinese rugs, men's feet in patent-leather shoes paced and paused, shuffled and pointed gracefully, as if this encounter, at the start of an evening, was a formal measure danced to a traditional air. Friendship ran like a stream with bright reflections. Yet the uncertainty in Anne's heart grew like thunder, and the apprehension increased, so that, very soon, she was forcing her lips to chatter and laugh with even more fever than usual. Nobody noticed it; every one else was at ease and happy. Every one else, that is, except David, who quivered inwardly from Ralph's examination, except Ralph whose silent distaste was mounting, except Geoff who was indifferent, and except the doctor who felt himself altogether in a foreign land amongst foreign people. This feeling he purposely engendered within himself and continued to feed with his private observations.

The four or five people who were left by these exceptions quite easily maintained the atmosphere of universal ease, friendship and merriment.

"Isn't this room enchanting?" Mrs. Bredon asked the doctor's wife.

"Quite enchanting," she answered; "of course, I'd seen photographs . . ."

"I always think," said Anne, "that it's *much* too much of a museum piece . . . Do *you*," she asked the doctor, "do *you* like drinking sherry in a museum piece?"

The doctor moved his feet uncomfortably. "I'd hardly thought of it," he answered.

"The doctor," Levine said, "may think we're all a museum piece, all antiques—or at least all obsolete."

To this accurate proposition the doctor returned a malevolent glance. His discomfort was becoming generally perceptible.

For the doctor, like Anne, was waiting; actively and impatiently waiting, as if nothing that was happening at the moment was of the least consequence compared with what was to happen hereafter. But whereas Anne's expectancy was for the door of the Oak Room to open, the doctor awaited some great and glorious upheaval out of which should emerge the dignity of a new mankind in a world of logic.

"I'm devilish hungry," Guy said. "What are we waiting for?"

"We were waiting for Tommy," the General answered.

"That horrid little man!" Anne cried. "Always late! You'll see—he'll have lost his collar stud, or his car will have broken down, or . . . or . . . anyway, there'll come a telephone message . . . Yes, Draper?"

"A telephone call, madam, from Colonel Black."

Every one laughed. "You fixed it, Anne," Guy cried. "You know you fixed it!"

"His car has broken down, madam, and he is now at Mr. Trant's house."

"With a good twelve miles to walk," said Guy.

"Fourteen," said Ralph, "unless he cuts across the Wold."

The joke was splendid. "Well said, young Ralph!" Guy cried amidst the laughter. Even Draper smiled.

"I suppose we shall have to send the car," the General said to his butler. "Will you tell Victor?"

"I hope we shan't have to wait dinner," said Levine. He spoke to the doctor's wife.

"I shouldn't care to have to face Mrs. Carr if we do," said Guy Bredon.

On a wave of laughter the company swept down the passage, across the hall and past the morning-room door to the dining-room.

"What a cook!" said Guy to the doctor's wife. "You don't yet know Mrs. Carr? You will to-night. By her deeds you will know her . . ."

* * *

"All right, Frank," Mrs. Carr called cheerfully.

The footman was tapping discreetly at the hatch which led from the kitchen to the corridor. He was even more afraid of the cook than of the butler, but now that dinner was starting—action was joined—she was a jovial captain. "Open up, Lizz!" she ordered.

Lizzie flipped up the hatch, winked at Frank and ran across to the range to whip the silver tureen out of the hot-plate. It was a fair weight. "More haste, less speed," said Mrs. Carr, and pushing to one side the saucepan in which she was mixing a white sauce for the fish, she grasped the soup pot. "Give me a spoon, girl!" She tasted the soup, added a last touch of pepper and parsley. "Now the ladle . . ." Scooping to the bottom of the huge iron pot, she filled the tureen. "Careful—it's a weight!" And while Lizz carried it across to the hatch, Mrs. Carr got the white wine from the dresser and returned to her sauce. "Get me the cream— the thick!" she called. "And take a look at that roast . . ."

Opening the oven door and basting the pheasants, Lizz asked: "Shall I start on the gravy?" The question had to be repeated, because the cook, having seen the soup on its journey, the fish all but ready, and the white sauce made, was standing in thought, kneading the palm of one great hand with the fist of the other. "Mrs. Carr—should I start . . ."

"Yes, you can start . . . I've a mind, I've a very good mind . . ." And she looked at the girl, whose mother had led her into the kitchen by the hand, leaving her so trustingly with the cook for care and education. "I've a very good mind to-night to give you your chance."

"Oh, Mrs. Carr, not . . ." But the girl could not bring herself to complete the expression of such extravagant hopes.

"Well—we'll see in a minute," the cook said.

* * *

The dinner was going like a tune; the dinner was running like a river. Up and down the long table, the talk rippled. No one was silent.

"I thought we should be late," the doctor was saying. "I thought at least we should be the last to get here. They brought me in a tramp, bitten by a dog."

"Was he much hurt?" somebody asked politely, but there was no pause for an answer.

"The bite was nothing . . ." But nobody was listening. "Six families!" the doctor thought. The meal that was being set before them would keep six families for a week, if justly distributed. He started to count the people at the table.

"The tramp, sir . . ."

One of the boys—the silent, overgrown, pleasant-faced boy— was asking a question. "Is the tramp . . ."

"The bite was superficial," the doctor answered. "But he had a distressing story. He was suffering mostly from general misery —and of course a touch of starvation."

The remark, striking a pause in the general talk, attracted the company.

"Not a bad life, a tramp's . . ."

"But so prickly a haystack . . ."

"And all those creepy-crawlies!"

"But not a worry in the world . . ."

"Nobody has to starve," said Guy Bredon loudly. "Nobody has to be a tramp if he doesn't want to."

"Nor a Master of Foxhounds," said Daniel Levine.

The laughter swept up the table, surging around the tramp and lapping his various aspects, as if he were a submerged rock. When it receded, Levine was saying: ". . . but even a tramp has his purpose."

"I doubt if he knows it," the doctor said.

"That is his tragedy."

"And his purpose?"

"To serve our conscience, Doctor; to prick it."

"Ah, yes!" said the doctor's wife from across the table. She had a beautiful, low voice, a sweet voice. She had wit. She had an obvious intelligence and a quick, sensitive, friendly response. But these of her features which matched those of Levine himself— being the feminine and more graceful counterparts of his own—

were only the surface of her personality. Underneath she had a contrary quality, a kind of deep immobility like a pool, which his restlessness detected and desired. It made her his complement. It made him feel as if the disquietudes of his own depths could flow into her peacefulness and let him rest.

The talk at table ran in eddies and ripples, diverted often to catch at a casual phrase and carry it on for a while until it got stuck somewhere and was left. Then later, some other twist in the current would take up the theme again, tow it a few yards farther, and dump it back upon the mud. The soup was excellent. The soup was finished and gone. And underneath the surface flow of the talk and laughter, a current ran between Daniel Levine and the doctor's wife.

"D'ye know," said Guy to Anne, " they're *still* talking about that tramp!"

"Danny is very persistent."

"Danny is too far-fetched . . ."

"Mrs. Carr's fish always has *something*," said Guy. "Undefinable, of course, but you know what I mean?"

"The tramp . . ." the doctor's wife was saying. "Oh yes . . ." But she was not yet sure of Daniel Levine. Was he with them, or against them? Politically, she meant; for she was too overwhelmed by the sheer size and pressure of the man to admit, so soon, an emotional relationship; and equally, she was too much aware, without admission, of his impact upon her own emotions to apply her logical mind to the things he said—some this way, some that. It was her heart that wanted a chance to breathe, so that she could balance the one side against the other and reach a reckoning. Her level voice hid an inward breathlessness as she leant across the table and said: "The tramp . . . You mean that he does rather give it away, doesn't he? He does rather show it up . . . the order, the whole order, the whole system . . ."

"Undoubtedly, Mrs. Macdonald." Daniel Levine's voice, like a wind canalised and contained, was too often too loud for the room. "Oh, yes! He shows up the system, right enough!"

His words were overheard at the other end of the table and were thrown up and down the length of it.

"Danny has a system!" somebody cried. "Back from the Casino at Cannes—with a system!"

"I know," said Guy, "*impaire* and *rouge*."

"Or just *rouge*," said Madge from the other end, from the seat next to the General

In the tide of laughter Anne cried: "My word, but we're all being witty!"

Under the cloak of laughter, in which he joined, Levine sought to continue. "What other system?" he asked the doctor's wife, "what other order would be better? If you shake up the lot and start afresh—if you shake the bottle and let it settle, won't you get . . ." Without raising his head, he let his eyes, from underneath his heavy brows, glance up the table towards Guy Bredon. They drew with them the eyes of the doctor's wife. And then the two pairs of eyes were again connected across the table, while Levine smiled and asked: "Won't the ablest always come out uppermost? And the tramps underneath?"

"The ablest? As at present, Mr. Levine?" She smiled, and so charmingly she raised her eyebrows, but the sarcasm directed at Guy was apparent.

"All right!" he said. "You don't yet know him. Till then —call it the most acquisitive."

"At first," she said, agreeing with him, "yes at first—the acquisitive will be first. But later . . ."

"Will there *be* a 'later'?"

"*You* ask me that!" she said almost beneath her breath. "*You*, Mr. Levine!" It was as if she had thrown across the table a thread, and he had caught it, and they had drawn it tight between them. Now they could play upon it. It ran untroubled through the chatter and laughter but trembled at the least touch of their intimate communications. In effect she had said: "A Jew can ask me that!"

"Ah, yes," he said sadly. "How fair that is! If we *have* a mission—it is to believe."

"But to believe what, Mr. Levine?" She was determined to make him say it.

He drew in his breath. He sent a whisper across the table: "And every man shall sit under his vine and his fig tree."

"And none," she concluded, "none shall make him afraid."

"But," said Levine more loudly, "the prophecy says—*his* vine, *his* fig tree! It's not to be a public park."

"Nor a private park either," said the doctor brusquely, joining the conversation, " with a notice saying—*Trespassers, keep out!* "

Levine laughed. " So the first stage of revolution . . ." And again the wind of his voice rustled the table.

" Oh lord ! " said Guy. " Danny's starting a revolution."

" First a system, now a revolution . . ."

" Danny a bolshie ! "

" Danny a red ! "

Everybody laughed gloriously. Everybody was happy. But David remained miserable. The intensity of Ralph's gaze across the table had notably increased.

" Now the fish," said Guy. " Now what is in store for us ? Now what miracle has Mrs. Carr been working with the fish ? "

Watching Mrs. Macdonald, who was watching Guy, Levine thought: and she's saying: " What a gross fellow he is, sitting at table, smacking his lips, stuffing food into his mouth and letting escape only adolescent comments and ribald, irrelevant jokes ! "

" The trouble with you, Danny," Guy boomed down the table, as if he was sitting at the head of it, and not merely one of the guests, and as if he had heard the whole argument and was in a position to sum it up, " your trouble is your warm heart. You don't see the obvious fallacy."

" Thank you very much," Levine said.

" You start with a tramp. *That's* wrong for a start; because the tramp's the exception; he isn't a part of any society. Everybody else is part of some sort of society, except the tramp. There's nobody else like the tramp."

He stuffed his mouth with fish and swallowed sufficient to be able to continue. " The tramp, same as the criminal . . . puts himself outside society; that's to say, outside our law and order . . ." Guy had changed his target and was speaking now in an offensive, overbearing manner directly at the doctor, without ceasing to eat all the time. " You'd hardly disagree, Doctor, that without law and order, without society, man becomes an animal ? Like the tramp . . . the tramp's more animal than man."

The doctor started to reply, speaking in a controlled voice that was obviously angry. " You'd hardly say, Major Bredon, that misfortune confers the status . . ."

" No, Doctor ! " said Guy, with a great swallow. " Please let me go on. Let *me* give *you* your answer . . ." When he was in this sort of mood, he had a trick of pointing his chin at the person to whom he was speaking, of jerking his chin to indicate punctuation and emphasis. This mannerism, combined with the extraordinary technique by which he managed to eat and talk at the same time, without committing any gross impoliteness over his food, and without losing the silence of the table, might have been calculated to provoke those who disagreed with him. They could scarcely fail to be enraged by the successive jerks of his chin, planted like banderillos in a bull. They could avoid anger only by laughter; and Daniel Levine and the doctor's wife were both almost laughing. But the doctor was not.

"You'd say, Doctor, I take it . . . that *our* society, our law and order, is a wicked affair? An arrangement of the privileged few, the acquisitive few, to protect their privilege and their acquisitions? To make sure that the rest of the world serves them and keeps them in luxury? That'd be your line, I take it?"

"I'd rather say . . ." the doctor began.

"Never mind, Doctor; I'm near enough . . ." He pointed with his fish-knife to retain the doctor's attention. "And if you could upset our arrangement, then there's some funny little creature called . . . the little man, isn't it . . . the common man, perhaps . . . the man in the street . . . who's going to pop up and be happy and free for ever afterwards? Isn't that the argument?"

"Personally, I would put it . . ."

"Quite, Doctor! I know it all. Each according to his needs, isn't it, and all men equal . . . Rubbish!"

Daniel Levine and the doctor's wife looked directly at each other. Each felt that overwhelming excitement, as if a match had been put to all the inflammable stuff of their hearts, of knowing without doubt what the other was thinking and feeling. The flames were joined in one combustion. It was a curious elation, without guilt, that was inspired in both of them, and between them, by Guy's attack.

"But I would answer you," Guy was saying, "that we're all inside one or other of the thousand little societies that make up Society—the world of Neapcaster, or the world of a factory, or of my bank, or of my old regiment, or of your profession . . . And as I see it . . ." And he saw it through his wine-glass, which he now held to his eyes before sipping and continuing: "in each of those societies, men have shuffled themselves into place with a rough but reasonable justice." He liked that phrase; he repeated it.

"They've got for themselves," Guy continued, "a law that protects each man's property, great or small, and each man's position, great or small . . . And that law works! It works, Doctor! It works because it's accepted. It's accepted, Doctor! It's accepted because it seems fair enough and because, in return for obedience, the fellers inside those societies get about as much freedom as they're capable of enjoying . . ." He interrupted himself to taste his wine more carefully and to remark: "If I may say so, Harry, this is devilish nice Chablis we're drinking!"

And still nobody interrupted him. The doctor no longer attempted to reply. He was not laughing, like his wife and Levine, but had dropped his eyes sullenly to his plate. Now and again those eyes were drawn upwards and sideways towards Guy, so that although the doctor's head did not move, except for the purposes of eating, he slid angry and malevolent glances along the table. But his wife looked up the table, and then looked back across the table to Levine, her eyes and Levine's being joined together, laughing at each other, laughing together; but this laughter was only in the eyes, and the other features of the two faces had no distinguishable expression.

"I'm not saying," Guy had continued, "that Society and its law isn't harsh and unjust. Very often it is. But a harsh and unjust law that's accepted is a lot better than a smug little law, a righteous and fussy little law, that nobody keeps. And anyway, dammit . . ." he raised his voice into a weary, exasperated drawl, "aren't we bettering the thing the whole time? Of course we are! We're making it softer and fussier; we're making what *you* call progress."

Now he had finished his fish. Laying down his knife and fork, he pointed his broad finger down the table, poking it into the air, stabbing at them. "You can take it from me," he said, "that if you try to speed the thing up, if you *do* get your revolution . . . there'll only be a new set of fellers on top, more acquisitive and more privileged than the old, less efficient because they're less experienced—and crooks!"

He smacked his hand down on the table as if they were all children sitting round him. He made the glass and the silver jingle. "Mark my words," he said, "you'll get crooks on top! That's all! *Because* . . ." He drew out the word like a final challenge. "Because, if you go upsetting the old law and the old social order —tipping it up like a spoilt child misbehaving at table—you'll only get a new law that won't protect *any one's* property or *any one's* position—so that it won't make a ha'porth of sense—not a ha'porth—and nobody'll keep it . . . *And*, Doctor, your Utopia will be a Utopia for the lawless, and for nobody else . . . *And*, Doctor, instead of the odd tramp and criminal putting themselves outside the law, outside Society, and turning themselves back into animals—you'll have the half of us doing it. The half of us'll be tramps . . . and lawbreakers . . ." He took a great draught of wine, emptying his glass before he rapped out: "Is that what you want?"

"Well, well . . ." said the General, breaking the silence that was bound to follow these not-uncommon outbursts of Guy Bredon.

"You mustn't be so cross with us," Anne said; "we're not foxhounds."

"Nor," said Madge, "a shareholders' meeting."

"Oh, yes," Levine said to the doctor's wife, "Guy gets like that sometimes . . . Oh, no," he said, as if he were answering the question that she was about to put, "it's by no means all nonsense, and it's certainly sincere. And he's a wise old bird when it suits him. I only wonder . . ." He paused, because he was thinking carefully. Sometimes he felt like Guy, and sometimes like the doctor. And often he felt that there was no complete truth, but only contradictions, within the laws and orders of man. "Is he right," he asked, "that you can't have a revolution, even a bloodless revolution, without lawlessness at the end of it?"

"You've got to make new laws, of course," she said briskly.

"Any one can make laws. But will they work? Will they be kept? Will they seem to be reasonable enough to be observed?"

"I should hope so," she answered. "Why not?" She was almost cross with him.

"I don't exactly know . . ." he said slowly, humbly. He searched his thoughts and his knowledge of history. And behind his thoughts, stirring but unrecognised, there was a joy that made her briskness and reproof not antagonistic, but a leap forward through acquaintanceship and friendship to the ease and trust of love. It was the briskness of an utmost familiarity, the rejoinder of a wife. Through his joy, he said: "I only know that Guy was most right when he was most brutal."

"About the tramp?"

"Ah—you thought that too?"

"Of course I did."

"Reduce a man to a tramp," he said, "and you reduce him to a beast."

"That's the real crime of it, Mr. Levine, isn't it? When he hasn't got food and work and clothes and shelter—let alone what Major Bredon means by property and position—what possible room is left for anything but beastliness?"

"It may be that, Mrs. Macdonald . . ." The sweetness of her voice and the gentleness of her manner, even when she spoke with asperity, made him increasingly humble. He paid her respect and admiration. "But I wonder if it isn't something more . . . If it isn't, perhaps, that we're all put in a cage by Society . . . If it isn't only Society that restrains the animal in us . . . If Society really does any more than just *that*."

"Don't you," she asked, leaning across the table, with her eyes wide and searching, "don't you over-rate the animal in man? Is it really so uncontrollable, so predominant?"

"And *you* ask *that*?" he said, circling back through the evening to their earlier conversation. "*You*—a trained nurse and the wife of a doctor . . . *you* who look at man through the limitations of his body—*you* can ask that question?"

"That's fair!" she answered. "If *we* have a mission . . ."

"I think so," he said. "And I think . . ." He shook his head. The pressure of the room had been mounting, and had suddenly become remarkable . . . Suddenly one says: "There is thunder in the air." Suddenly one says: "I love this woman." But it was more than that. So many questions had been asked and nearly answered, that an answer must be imminent. Daniel Levine, with this sense of pressure disturbing him, broke off the argument and concluded: "A very dangerous, very cunning, very relentless, very greedy, very frightened animal is Man—when he's out of his cage."

"When he's without law and order? When the cage is opened?"

"And he starts to live by his wits."

Frank the footman's voice came from the doorway: "Colonel Black, madam!"

*　　　*　　　*

To Levine, the entrance of Tommy Black at this moment was an absurdity. "These things are not reasonable," he would have said; "there are changes of atmosphere which are not revealed by barometrical measurement." And the room, before the door opened, had become so overburdened with omens—that were built like a wall enclosing himself and the doctor's wife, and excluding the rest of the company—and so strung with apprehension, that the entrance of the devil or the saint would have been less astonishing than that of the one person they were all expecting. For Levine had expected an answer: what would escape when the cage was opened? And by way of an answer, there had come Frank the footman and this quiet little man with the spindly legs and the poise of a horseman, with the subtle smile hidden behind his innocent eyes, and with the slight catch in his speech, the scarcely perceptible affectation—something between a touch of asthma and a negligible stammer—that gave his soft words a peculiar phrasing and impressed them with irresponsibility. Nothing he said could be of any consequence; yet his voice made you listen. Everything that he did was irresponsible and slightly humorous; but it was in earnest. He carried his head a little on one side. He moved with exquisite ease and balance. And any one could see how his quietness and humour, his hidden smile, his understanding and his irresponsibility, must attract a horse or a woman.

When Tommy Black entered that room, the atmosphere collapsed. The private threads that had been spun between person and person—as between Daniel Levine and the doctor's wife—were cut. Thus released, Levine was made aware—by intuition, rather than by anything done or said—of a new relationship. Certainly Anne gave no sign of it, unless it was a negative sign, an inner withdrawal, as if something had been satisfied. And by comparison with her normal habits, she was very quiet.

"It's all very . . . well to laugh," Tommy said, in his lazy, breathless voice, "but how would you . . . like it? Have you ever seen the . . . wheel of your car spinning down the road in front of you?"

They made the usual jokes.

"Naturally," he answered, "I've had one or two with Trant. But not before . . . I hadn't. Not a drink all day, as a matter of fact—not since a little glass of wine in this . . . very house, at this morning's Meet."

"Anyway," Madge said down the length of the table, "*anyway*, Tommy, what were you doing at Trant's, when you should have been dining here?"

It was curious, thought Levine, to remember that Madge and Tommy, so long ago—when she had been quite young and very beautiful, and he had been much the same as he was now—had gone off together for several months. "Trant's!" Madge repeated. "Suspicious, I call it."

It was still more curious that Guy had not minded, and still did not mind, and indeed treated Tommy as if he owed him gratitude instead of rancour. That was the great charm of Tommy Black: whatever he did, even if he sold you a useless horse—and the buying, training and selling of horses was the way he lived— he made you feel grateful.

"Yes," Guy said, repeating his wife's question, "what *were* you doing at Trant's?"

"As a matter of fact, I was . . . selling a horse."

"To Trant? Get on with you, Tommy!"

"On my way *home* from selling a horse. I say, Guy . . ." Draper had brought him the soup . . . "is this soup all right?" He sipped it. "Yes—it's all right. And that pheasant looks . . . pretty decent."

"There's fish in between," Anne said. "You must hurry, Tommy, if you want to catch up."

"I will, I will." But he put down his spoon and turned to face her. "My dear Anne! I scarcely noticed you. You were so . . . quiet. And all these people asking rude questions." He got up, walked behind her chair, put his hands on her shoulders, and stooped to whisper in her ear. He kissed her cheek.

"How he gets away with it!" Levine marvelled. It was like a Frenchman making love to his girl in a restaurant, and nobody minded. Harry watched it benevolently. And Madge, leaning back, said: "What about *me*, Tommy?"

"You next, Madge. But Anne's my . . . hostess." And he walked right down the table to kiss Madge Bredon. Then, on his way back, he stopped opposite Levine, to take the hand of the doctor's wife.

"How he gets away with it!" And then Levine had a terrible moment of revelation. Was it, perhaps, that the husband remained ignorant? That there was some extraordinary property in the man—a protective colouring, a power of natural deception—so that all those curious coincidents, bringing Tommy and *this* girl together at Aintree or Goodwood, and Tommy and *that* girl together at Edith's villa, those coincidents remarked and correctly interpreted by every one else, were unnoticed by the man peculiarly affected?

Levine was too honest a person not to pursue a thought that had once struck him but had turned and fled. The whole pursuit and capture was an instant's flash, a thrust of flame. Its horror faced him now, at this moment, like the nauseous fear that followed a nearby explosion, a miraculous escape. He, also, had his unacknowledged coincidence. His own wife, Ruth, shortly before her last collapse . . . The recollection drew to itself incident after incident—phrases, allusions, glances—like a magnet amongst steel filings. The cluster composed an obvious truth.

Once the truth was obvious, the horror increased. But the horror belonged not to the painfulness of the truth and its moment, but to its painlessness and its triviality. He didn't mind; he wasn't angry; he felt no grievance: *that* was the horror of the truth. He, also . . . He, also, like the rest of them, didn't mind about it. He, also . . . If Tommy had made her happy, what harm . . . " Now, Tommy," he heard his own voice saying, " your tall story about a horse . . ."

" My dear Danny," he answered, and he was still standing behind the doctor's wife, so that she was looking back at him and laughing, " do you think my . . . stories are all tall?"

" Well, Tommy," he said, " you do rather live on tall stories, don't you?" And even while he was still speaking, with such ease and flippancy, he made himself say to himself—as a way of escape from more painful thoughts—" All the training of a lifetime, from my first schooldays, might usefully have done nothing else but teach me to hide my heart behind such remarks."

Every one laughed. And out of the laughter came Tommy's voice: " That's too unkind of you, Danny. An old bosom of . . . mine, like yourself." And he put both hands on the back of the chair where the doctor's wife was sitting and leant over her shoulder towards Levine.

Were all the men round these tables in all the houses of the County bound in this secret union? Were they all the providers of Tommy Black? Levine looked at Guy; he looked at Harry; then he looked at the doctor. The doctor, for the first time that evening, was smiling. Like a cat that is stroked he was arching his back, purring, smirking, as if he had received some great and well-earned compliment. And Tommy, laughing as he leant over the shoulder of the doctor's wife, was looking into her eyes until her eyes were caught, and then letting his eyes travel about her splendid figure as if she were a horse, and then returning to her own eyes—while his sensitive hand rested upon her shoulder—and saying: "My word! But do y'know—this County has had a stroke of luck at last!"

Anne was watching the doctor's wife. And Anne was laughing and radiant. She was made vicariously happy by Tommy's new attentions. The doctor was happy; Guy and Harry were happy; Madge was happy; and Levine himself was happy. The degradation was complete.

"Now about this horse!" said Guy, as Tommy went back to his seat; "I want to get to the bottom of this story about a horse."

"He's told you," said Anne, "he was selling a horse in the dark to Mr. Trant."

So they all laughed again, and Tommy, when his eyes had travelled to Anne, to the doctor's wife, to Anne, returned to his fish.

"Not to Trant. He wasn't selling the horse to Trant. He was coming *back* from selling a horse to somebody else."

"And I bet I know who it was!"

"I should think it was Freddy Betts."

"Oh, Tommy! Look, he's blushing! It *was* Freddy Betts! I bet he sold him a stinker."

Tommy, without looking up from his plate, said: "It was a very, very . . . good horse."

"And I bet it was a very, very good price!"

With Tommy in the room, with Tommy the centre of the conversation, each man lost his individuality. He lost himself. And they all found themselves talking to a pattern, all the same, in the same sort of voice.

"It was a very fair price," Tommy said.

"And I bet I know the horse!"

"That chestnut screw he got from Springer."

"That's it—for sixteen quid."

"And he's sold it to Betts for five hundred!"

"Hasn't he got to live?"

While they all laughed, Tommy laid down his knife and fork. He had anyway finished his fish. "You're all being simply . . . horrid to me," he said. "You're all being so beastly to me—you

117

all always are—that I think I . . . shall clear out and live somewhere else. Somewhere sunny and warm and . . . bright. With
mimosa and champagne instead of all you . . . horsy people." He
sipped his wine. He sat back so that Frank could take his plate.
He was always so open about everything. "Who's coming with
me?" he asked. "What about Anne? Will you come and . . .
live with me in the South of France? What about you, Mrs.
Macdonald? What about Anne?"

"Oh, they'll all come," said Guy, "the whole bitch pack."

"We've had to tell you before," said Anne, "that we are *not*
all foxhounds."

"May I ask, Tommy," said Levine, "how you propose to
live?"

"Certainly, Danny. By my wits!"

The thing was so true and just that the laughter was uproarious.
Draper had to turn aside to hide his titter. Frank had to double
himself over the sideboard.

"By my wits, of course," said Tommy Black.

At the other end of the table, Guy raised his head quickly.
"Now this," he said, "this is why we really came! This is Mrs.
Carr's supreme accomplishment!" Frank was handing him the
other dish. Reverently Guy helped himself and dreamily tasted
it. "Superb!" he said. "A really unique experience! A great
cook at her greatest; the last of a great art, no doubt; the last
generation of great artists . . ."

The news was conveyed by Frank to the kitchen. "The
savoury?" said Mrs. Carr. "So soon as that? Can you give us
a jiffy?"

"I should think I could!" said the footman. "That *soufflé*'ll
go round again and again—what's left of it. To hear them talk,
you'd think it was the golden trump."

"There!" said the cook to Lizz. And she was so delighted
that she even turned to the hatch, in order to explain to Frank:
"It was Lizz that made it. I reckoned she'd earned the chance."

Lizz glowed and blushed. She had to turn away, and to clasp
her hands about her plump breasts, to hide her exultation. "And
I've news for you, too," Mrs. Carr continued, improving the hour.
"Miss May says the Mistress agrees, and she'll tell you herself in
the morning. You're to get your rise!"

"How much?" Frank asked. And Mrs. Carr, permitting this impertinence, said: "Half a crown a week!"—as if it were a king's fortune. "And a heap more," she added, "than I was getting at her age. But times are changing—and so they should."

A sort of chuckle of pleasure came from Lizz, whose tight, apple cheeks seemed to rise as if they might meet her forehead. Frank, catching her glance, winked and made her laugh outright.

"It's no laughing matter," said the cook. "Money's a serious thing. Nothing more so." Then she laughed too, and so did Frank. "You're a silly girl!" she said. "And to-morrow, *if* you behave yourself, you can slip down to the stables for ten minutes and tell Ted Foster all about it."

"Ted Foster!" said Frank scornfully, while Lizzie went very red.

"Ted's a good enough lad," said the cook loyally. "As good as a girl could want." She whipped open the oven door. "It's ready!" she said.

And just at that moment, Draper got a chance for a word with young Walter outside the dining-room door. "It's all right," he said.

The boy looked up at the butler, not daring to believe what the news might mean. From his station outside the dining-room door, whence it was his duty to carry the dirty crockery to the kitchen, he heard only those fragments of conversation that were loudly uttered or that happened to catch a silence. Levine's resonance often reached him—even when that great voice was lowered to a whisper—and Walter had heard him talk about the Prophets, and the doctor's reply about the vineyard and the private park. Such great sayings as these got lodged in his heart, and his ears sought constantly for similar treasures to add to them. But they had caught no mention of himself.

"You're to be sent to school," the butler added.

The boy drew in his breath so hard and so far that his whole body shook. He saw a row of coloured bottles, containing knowledge, and a bearded man mixing him a prescription. When the prescription was taken, the drinker grew great, mighty and noble. He would talk like the doctor, like Colonel Levine himself.

"You like school?" the doctor's wife asked David Levine. It was a very common question which he hated to have to answer. He knew that she only meant to be kind—to admit one of the children into the conversation. He prepared his answer.

"Frank, Frank! I'm to be sent to school!" Walter cried, following the footman through the baize door into the pantry. "School, school! I'm to go there!"

The footman grinned and ruffled the child's hair. "Well, Walter boy," he said, "I hope you like it."

And the doctor's wife was persistent. "You *do* like school? You do like it?" she continued to ask David.

* * *

"Do you like school, David?"

"What about you, Geoff, do you like school?"

"Did *you* like school, Doctor; did *you*, Madge; or Guy?"

"I didn't care for it a lot," Guy said. "I was always getting beaten."

"Much good it did you, Guy!"

"Do you like school, David?"

"Anne, did they . . . beat you at school?" asked Tommy.

"Not exactly beaten, Tommy. I got order marks. One order mark for running *up*stairs; two order marks for running *down*-stairs; three order marks for shouting on the stairs . . ."

"That staircase must have been a terrible place," Guy said.

"Not as bad as the dorm," Anne said, "or the bathroom. The bathroom—that was the worst! If you so much as whispered . . . And when you got ten order marks, you had to learn a poem."

"You must know a lot of poetry!"

"Well . . . yes! But I was rather a *sly* little girl. I nearly always managed to learn the *same* poem." She shut her eyes. "*In Xanadu did Kubla Khan a stately pleasure-dome decree: where Alph, the sacred river, ran through caverns measureless to man down to . . .*"

"They got so tired of beating me," said Tommy, "that I once had to write out a bit of German a hundred times. I'll never . . . forget it. Most useful, it was."

"Now you've upset me," Anne said, shutting her eyes again. "*In Xanadu did Kubla Khan a stately pleasure-dome decree where . . .*"

"It's amazing," Tommy said, "how far you can get on one sentence of German. After the war, in Germany . . ."

"*. . . Alph, the sacred river, ran through caverns measureless . . .*"

"I want to say my bit of German."

"I want to say my poem. It's only one verse that I remember."

"Let him say his German first. I'm sure it's shorter."

"Very well," said Tommy. He also shut his eyes. "*Entschuldigen sie, gnädige Frau, sie haben ihr Taschentuch fallen lassen.*"

"What does it mean, Tommy?"

"I think it's a sort of . . . rude whistle, when you see a taking skirt."

"I don't think it's that at all."

"Do *you* know what it means, David?" The doctor's wife was determined to make him look less miserable.

David shook his head.

"It only means 'Pardon me, gracious lady, you've dropped your handkerchief!' And I don't really see," she continued, "what use it was to him."

"Oh, Mrs. Macdonald!" said Guy.

"Gracious ladies don't so often drop their handkerchiefs."

"They do when Tommy's around."

"The whole street," said Madge, "is one long paper-chase of dropped handkerchiefs."

And Frank, as he brought in the warm plates for the savoury and heard the renewed laughter, whispered: "They're being very comical to-night, Walter boy." But the boy was still dumb with happiness. Very, very carefully he carried his load of dirty plates, as if the glorious future, the opening of the great door—as it seemed to him—the offering of the coloured bottles, depended upon the success of to-night's duties.

"Now!" Anne said firmly. "I will. I really will!" And shutting her eyes she got through several lines of the poem. "*. . . through caverns measureless to man, down to a sunless sea. So twice five miles of fertile ground with walls and towers were girded round: and there were gardens, bright with sinuous rills . . .*"

"Sounds a bit like this place," Tommy said.

"Twice five miles," said Guy. "That must be about it, isn't it, Harry?"

The General sat forward in his chair, but he did not answer.

"If you walked all the way round the outside, Harry . . . It'd be around ten miles, wouldn't it?"

Somehow, every one looked towards the General, expecting an answer. The effect was remarkable: the laughter was so suddenly replaced by this curious, ominous feeling of attention, of imminence, while the General watched the door, waiting for one of those brief interludes in a dinner-party when the room would be empty of servants. "How much, how much did you say?" he finally asked.

"Twice five miles of fertile ground," said Anne brightly, "with walls and towers were girdled round . . . *Fertile* ground, mind you! The Wold can't count."

"Fertile or not," the General said, "I wouldn't count the Wold anyway." There was very little expression in his face. But every one in the room listened to him. The *soufflé* had been cleared away, and both Draper and Frank were, for the moment, absent. "Not the Wold," said the General, "nor Trant's as it now is, nor the Dumbles, nor the Sherriton Brook farms, nor Hatherfield . . . I'm selling the lot. I've got to!"

"I know," said Ralph cheerfully; "I heard it in the pub to-night. We're selling to that . . ." He checked himself. "We're selling to Freddy Betts." His father looked at him sternly, and Ralph turned his head, not in any abasement, but to renew his steady regard of David Levine.

Nobody else spoke, and there was scarcely a movement. The General looked straight down the table at his wife, who dropped her eyes to her plate. She felt a great excitement. Without raising her head she looked at Tommy Black, confirming what she had known before—that he was watching her.

Guy Bredon had gone very red with anger, sorrow, shame and astonishment at this declaration made in public, and in so extraordinary a manner, by his oldest friend, and at its tragic content. About to speak, he saw Draper and Frank enter with a new set of plates and the savoury. Then, swallowing the words that had almost been uttered, he made his greatest effort. "Good God!" he cried, seeing the legs of partridges, grilled, rolled in bacon and mounted on toast, "this is too much, too much . . ." It was not a really remarkable savoury—*jambes de perdrix farcies*, a variation of a common dish, but he raised his glass to it. "Anne—is Draper to be my deputy, or may I, in person, attend Mrs. Carr in the kitchen to give her my warmest, most admiring, most affectionate embrace?"

*   *   *

Gratefully they let the laughter catch them up and toss them about. But Tommy continued to gaze so steadily at Anne's face that the doctor's wife leant towards him and whispered in a perfect accent: "*Entschuldigen sie, gnädige Frau* . . ."

Not in the least confused, Tommy looked round, smiled into her eyes, as if he was only too pleased to share with her a secret, and turned back again to Anne.

"That was malicious!" Levine said softly to the doctor's wife. She nodded. "I simply can't think what made me do it."

Although he was silent, she knew by his smile that he was saying sadly: "But I know only too well how women, all women, behave in such ways with Tommy Black!" And the thread of understanding, that had been spun between them earlier in the evening and broken by Tommy's entrance, was re-established and made to tremble with such common emotion that she had to turn again to David and again to ask: "But you've never told me. *Do* you like school, David?"

Outside the door, Frank, in passing, tweaked young Walter's ear. "Going to be a schoolboy, Wallie, in a funny little cap?"

David, beneath Ralph's unmoving stare, answered the doctor's wife. "Yes—I do like it."

"I knew he was a liar," Ralph was thinking, "and here's more proof! A liar, a bolshie, a red and—whatever they say—he does *not* wash. He was even beaten for not washing. He was beaten for cutting ' tubs.' "

*　　*　　*

There would be some sixty boys between the ages of eighteen and thirteen returning together, on a winter afternoon, from compulsory football. Following the general throng, whose bass and treble voices mixed and echoed under the archway as the boys turned from the street into the quadrangle of the House, came Ralph. On the back of his head was the gold-tasselled skull-cap of blue velvet, worn by members of the school team. He had no need to hurry; for, by one of the rights and privileges of his position as a prefect, he could saunter into the bathroom at the end of the homeward procession and claim an immediate tub. "Denham played a decent sort of game," he said to Bolton, the House Captain, as together they crossed the Quad.

"He's a little small as yet," Bolton answered; "but I've got my eye on Rice."

"They've both got guts."

"Oh, they're both gutful enough."

"All right, Denham, you needn't budge," Ralph said to the

small boy who stood respectfully aside from the House notice-board. " But, I say, you seem to have changed a bit quick ! "

" I ran back," Denham said. " My people are coming to-night."

Ralph nodded. " Hope they give you an adequate repast."

" Decent little chap," said Bolton, as Denham scuttled off. " And decent of you to tell him he needn't budge."

" Personally, I never make 'em budge—unless their manners want smartening up."

Keeping both their hands in their pockets—which was one of the privileges of their eminence—Ralph and Bolton entered the changing-room, a small place whose seating accommodation was insufficient, although the parallel rows of benches had super-structures carrying pegs, numbered, one for each boy, to take his towel and clothes. Here, in the press and scrimmage of bodies, the boys stripped naked and then, taking their towels, entered the adjoining bathroom to wait their turns for a tub. Some of these naked bodies were large and hairy, smelling of sweat; some were young, smooth and odourless; and a few, like David Levine's, were sallow, skinny and contemptible.

As usual, David was desperately hoping to have removed his clothes and boots, and to have got into the bathroom, before he was evicted from his seat. Abnormally squeamish to the smell of maturity which disturbed his stomach and deprived his limbs of their small dexterity and his brain of contrivance, he wanted only to be left unnoticed. A miserable and quaking creature, when he heard the voices of Bolton and Ralph, he abandoned at once his wits.

" All right, Galloway," Ralph was saying. " You've nearly done. I don't mind waiting."

But Bolton, finding beneath his peg a boy in the House Fifteen, immune from eviction, turned to David nearby. " You, Levine—budge ! "

Hastily rising, David hung up on his own peg—beneath which he had been sitting—the sweater and vest that he had already discarded. " Buck up ! " said Bolton, and taking the empty seat, started slowly to unlace his boots. David, kneeling on the floor in the full flow, the current of passing boys—for his peg was near the door into the bathroom—started to do the same with the utmost speed. Soon he was standing naked, holding his shorts, stockings and boots, waiting in front of Bolton to get to his peg. Patiently he waited, trying to keep his feet in the press, sometimes staggering as a passing boy gave him a push, either deliberate or unintentional.

While he waited, the only part of David's mind which remained active got itself divorced from his physical distress and committed to prayer. Because prayer had recently proved so fruitless, David, anxious to give God the utmost chance of granting his request, made it as modest and distant as possible. " O God and God of my fathers—next term give me a peg that isn't near Bolton and isn't near the bathroom door."

" Don't, for God's sake, stand staring at me with that dopey face! " Not meaning to be unkind, Bolton could not help himself.

" No, Bolton." David turned about.

" Do you think I want that disgusting bum under my nose? "

" No, Bolton."

" Then for God's sake, get out! "

" Yes, Bolton." Clasping his things, David shuffled away. Much as he hated his peg, it had the quality of home. Now that he was made homeless, he became still more furtive and, as a spectacle, still more repulsive. But it was quite unintentionally that a passing boy pushed him against Waite, who was seated on his bench. " For God's sake! " Waite said, not unkindly, and gave David the mildest piston-kick which sent him across the room to a very decent chap called Meadows. Meadows raised a purely defensive knee, and David was deflected to Selby, who tripped him up. His clothes were scattered, and a boot landed in Barker's lap.

Barker's voice alone could turn fear into panic. " Don't you throw your bloody boot at me," he said, and he slung it across the room towards the door, which opened at that moment. The boy who was entering automatically heeled the boot into the passage.

In this way, David had soon lost all his clothes, and the situation was now so desperate, although common enough, that his prayer became quite ambitious. " O God and God of my fathers—don't let it be Bolton! " For, of course, he was certain to be beaten that night, either for losing his clothes, or for leaving them about, or for coming back to look for them after " Bell " had sounded; and thus he prayed: " Please God, don't let it be Bolton who beats me, but one or other of Thy servants, the other prefects, Ralph or Noakes, for instance, who doesn't enjoy doing it and won't so much hurt . . ."

Bolton had at last left the bench, so that David could now get his towel and creep into the bathroom. Already seated in the round tub opposite the door, Ralph was soaping his legs; and his eyes—the General's eyes, blue and distant—were directed, but not focused, on David's entrance. "Snockie," he said to the boy in the next-door tub, "you were bloody lucky to get that 'try.' You never touched it down."

"Rot, Merry, I certainly did!"

There was a long silence while Ralph considered the question and examined a bruise on his knee. "No, Snock," he said, "I don't think so."

At the same end of the room, David had taken his place, fourth in succession, in the line for a tub. There were other available places which would have got him a bath more quickly; but this one offered a flanking wall and, furthermore, was already awaited by three boys who were comparatively pleasant. First in the line of succession was Geoff. He looked round at David, and he smiled at him. And the whole grey world was, for that brief instant, burst with sunlight. It had not been a hidden smile but an open, if silent, greeting. From the great source of warmth in David's heart, a beam of gratitude broke through the membranes of fear. It lit upon this act of kindness and courage and credited it to God. A prayer which had never been uttered had been granted with grace.

"Jesus!" said Platt from the middle of the room, "it's running cold again! That sod Timmins is jewing us out of coke."

"Another cold bath for us!" said Meadows to David. But to this kindliness David stayed silent. For all words were dangerous; and the voices of Barker and Platt, their presence alone, the odour of their hairy bodies, were the source of menace.

"That bloody Jew, Timmins," said Barker; "I bet the Jew sells it."

"Timmins?" said Waite. "He isn't even a Jew. He hasn't even got that much excuse. He's just a crook." Waite was decent enough.

But the voices of Platt and Barker, when joined together, ground the whole world into small pieces. "'Course he's a Jew! Isn't he jewing us out of coke?" The grindings of the world submerged David, as if they were the ash of volcanic eruption. He was lost. "Must be a Jew if he's jewing us out of coke. Ask Levine! Levine would know. You—Levine—isn't Timmins a Jew, a Jew, a dirty

126

Jew, a dirty, lying, stinking Jew, a Jew like yourself . . ." In the ashes and dust of the world, the heart was punctured and collapsed; the mind fled.

A very reasonable voice, the voice of Platt, said quite gently: "Now don't get flustered, Levine. Just answer the question. Are you a dirty Jew or are you not? Before you answer—just think!"

"Oh, God," said Ralph, "they're at it again! It's so bloody unoriginal."

The voices joined and swelled, vibrating, like the chapel organ, like the wrath of God. The head of David turned this way and that. The eyes of David saw the eyes of Geoff, like a vision of God, a vision of hope itself. But the vision remained unlit. And the eyes of Geoff turned slowly away, as the voice of Geoff was distantly saying: "That wasn't a try of Snockie's, Phil, not ever on your life!"

"Can't you kindly answer the question?" asked Barker's voice.

"Can't you leave it alone?" asked Ralph.

"We could. But we can't, can we, have lying in this House?"

"It hasn't been lying again!"

"Indeed it has! It says it isn't a dirty Jew."

"Does it *still* say that?" Ralph asked in amazement.

"It won't answer."

Ralph looked at the quivering and heaving thing and at the open mouth. Controlling disgust, he asked quite gently: "Levine —are you a dirty Jew, or are you not?" The mouth shut and opened again, without a word spoken, but Levine seemed to shake his head.

"See for yourself!" said Platt. "He's incapable of the truth."

"Let's take this quietly, let's take it in stages," said Ralph. "The trouble with you, Platt, is you get him rattled . . . Now, Levine—are you a Jew, for a start?"

The Jew seemed to nod his head.

"There!" said Ralph with pride and relief. "I've got him to admit it! And since we all know that he doesn't wash, seeing he got beaten for cutting tubs . . ."

"He ought to speak the *whole* truth," Barker said.

"He just can't," said Ralph. "Leave it alone, can't you? It's become such a stale joke."

In the bowels and throat of David, quivering naked before Ralph, there was an uprush of gratitude. And at last there were tears, sobs.

In his prayers that night, in a liturgy compounded from that of his home and that of the School chapel, David gave thanks to God for the intervention of Ralph. "Praised and glorified be Thy holy name for the sake of Thy servant, Ralph, who is decent and just inasmuch as he said I didn't wash . . ." The fervour of his prayer shook David's bed.

"You aren't still blubbing?" Meadows whispered from the bed next door. "Honestly, Levine, they aren't worth blubbing about."

"O God of my fathers—I erred and strayed from Thy ways when I cut tubs, thinking not to go into the changing-room at all, but going straightways from the Quad to my study, and there being caught by Bolton spitting on my handkerchief to wipe the mud off my face . . ."

Sunk in prayer, David buried his face in his pillow; a posture which, anyway, relieved his sore buttocks. But the beating at bedtime had been inflicted not by Bolton, but by Noakes, the most lenient of all the prefects; and David's prayers, therefore, continued with thanks for the lenience of his punishment. And David was happy. He had prayed that it should not be Bolton, and it had been Noakes. Prayer worked! Faith was restored, strengthened. This was happiness.

But on the other side of the same dormitory, Geoff also had his head buried in his pillow. "O God, forgive me," he prayed. "O Jesus, let David forgive me for the sin of betrayal . . ." His pillow was wet with his silent tears. "O Lamb of God, forgive me for the sin of cowardice. I didn't, I didn't mean to turn away my head . . ."

David was soon asleep. But Geoff wept and prayed for forgiveness for a minute or so longer.

★   ★   ★

His encounter with the tramp, together with a number of his other sins which seemed to him to be distinctly if undefinably related, continued to trouble Geoff very deeply. To-night he was suffering a dreadful sense of sin, as if a dam had been erected and all the waters of his guilt had piled themselves up to an intolerable pressure. He recalled, for instance—as he noted the miserable eyes of David—his sin against a friend: by a sin of omission he had struck David at the edge of the bath-tub. By a sin of commission he had struck the tramp who had asked for food. By another sin of omission he had struck the girl, Judy, as she stood by the cottage gate with her hand clasped about the child in her belly. By sin and by sin and by sin, he failed daily and hourly to fulfil his purpose.

A sense of failure seemed to be prevalent in the room by now. When the ladies had left, the General had moved to the other end of the table, taking Anne's seat between Guy Bredon and Tommy Black. And now, to his two closest friends, he was talking more freely and confidentially than usual. Their voices were lowered, but Geoff heard the General say: " Well, Tommy, it's best to admit failure and have done with it."

" Nonsense, Harry!" Guy answered. " There's no failure about selling property these days. But why, in heaven, blurt it out like that?"

" I have to admit," the General said, " I surprised myself."

" An astonishing thing to do," Guy insisted.

" Well, Guy, it had to be told . . . Better the hour—you know."

Rising to conclude the conversation, the General walked to the doorway and turned out the lights, leaving the room lit only by the candles on the polished table. In his absence, Tommy's eyes met Guy's, and their heads made the slightest sideways gesture towards the doctor, expressing surprise and even censure that such things should have been said in front of him. And the doctor, seeing or sensing these scarcely perceptible signals, and interpreting them correctly, said to Levine: " Well . . . it's sad. But I suppose it has to come, hasn't it?"

" What, Doctor? What has to come?" It was Guy who asked the question.

" These changes," the doctor answered, trying to put it as politely as possible. " Social changes, you know. The redistribution of wealth."

" I suppose so," the General said, returning to the table. " But will anybody tell me . . .." and he looked around him with half a grin, as if he were positively enjoying the situation, " what social changes are involved by the redistribution of wealth from me to Freddy Betts?" He wanted an answer. His head scarcely moved as he looked in turn at every one round the table, every one just in the shadows, just beyond the gentle glow of the candles, shaded in pink, reflected in the polished wood and in the port and brandy glasses and decanters. Everything else had been cleared from the table by Draper and Frank, and the door shut behind them. The room was very quiet and intimate. "You, Doctor?" the General asked, as if he were testing his officers. "You, Guy? You, Tommy?" He came at last to Levine. "Ah, Danny, *you'll* know!" And they all smiled gently. "Danny will know . . ." And there was a long, long pause while the blood flowed through the common veins of friendship with a sensible pulse.

Levine shook his head. "You ought to be answered by an economist or a politician," he said, without looking up. But they still waited. When he raised his head, his eyes were sad. At last he said awkwardly: "But if they did answer you, I don't believe they'd be right. Because . . . I don't believe that our failure—our failure as a class—has got much to do with economics. I think we've failed with people . . . I think we've made a world that turns people inside out." Then he was silent. He had said more than he wanted to say. But these others, his friends, made his silence into a pause. He had to continue. By their silence and their expectation, they had drained the room empty; you could have filled it with what you liked.

"We have failed," he said. "We have made a world in which people act with so much fear and so much greed, so much envy and so little love, that they don't act . . . like people." He spoke quietly, humbly and hopelessly, with an unusual embarrassment. "Harry has to pay," he said, "for the failure of Christianity." Then he let his voice escape to its natural proportions, so that it filled the room. "Having made the man Jesus into a God," he cried, "why, oh why couldn't you worship Him? Why couldn't you even worship the God in man? Why did you have to worship man's contrivance?" He dropped his head again; he was silent. But one last sentence escaped with his sigh. "Why did we have to be afraid of man, so that . . . our fear could destroy us?"

He seemed to have no more to say. He had not answered them, yet the answer was there. In the silence that followed, each one of them, for himself, touched the hem, the fringe of an answer.

"And so," said the doctor, "for lack of trust, lack of faith, lack of love, a society disintegrates . . ." He spoke, without sarcasm, neither to endorse nor refute, but as if he was testing the analysis. In the manner that Bredon had handled his claret, the doctor now held to the light the things that Levine had said; and thus, observing their colour, sniffing their odour, searching their taste, he derived the verdict. "That's us!"

"Us?" said Tommy. Did he mean to resent the doctor's use of a pronoun including himself?

"Us!" said Guy. For at this table, in this room, within this massive house and great estate, disintegration was scarcely imminent. "So we're breaking up, Doctor, are we? And you and your socialist friends are helping us?"

"No, no," said the doctor quickly. "We're doing nothing of the kind. We're not destructive. Our work is positive . . ."

"Then what, if I may ask, *are* you up to?"

"Me?" said the doctor in astonishment. "I'm trying to cure the sick."

They all laughed then. They were, at least, a generous lot.

"Well done, Doctor!" somebody said.

And the doctor, taking advantage of the easier air, made a request that had been on his mind for some time. "Excuse me, General," he said, "but I may have a rather tricky case to-night. There might be a call for me. They know where I am, so I suppose . . ."

"Of course, my dear fellow," said the General. "But we'll make sure. We'll tell Draper." He rang the bell.

* * *

While they were waiting for the bell to be answered, the General, seeing his son watching him with the air of a dog expecting a sortie, nodded the required permission. "All right, you boys!" he said. "Get along with you!"

As the three boys went past his chair on their way out of the dining-room, the General beckoned to Geoff. "I wonder if you'd mind . . ."

Geoff bent his head to hear the command. It was always he who was chosen as messenger, for he had that special, unenviable quality which made people feel not only that he was a willing servant, but also that his service was dependable. To-night he was glad of the command. An act of service, he felt, would in some way be an act of atonement: by service, the load of guilt would be lightened. "There's an envelope," the General said, "in my dressing-room, I think . . ."

Keeping Geoff beside him by the elevation of a finger, the General turned to Guy Bredon. "I'm right in thinking, Guy, that your father and a feller called Seytoun . . ."

"That reprobate!" said Guy. "Your illegitimate cousin . . ."

"Not mine, but my father's . . . And now there's his son . . . and a girl, to boot, a granddaughter . . ."

"He was a hot 'un!" said Guy, happily afloat on recollection. "He an' my father were regular cronies . . . he lived at Cannes." And the mention of this town was enough to set him laughing; for in the old days there had been an alliance—a sort of one-way, favoured-nation status—between the society of Neapcaster and those parts of the French Riviera where all kinds of odd vices were somehow made respectable. "My father, I remember, every Easter . . ."

"That's as I thought," said the General. And he turned back to Geoff to describe the letter which he wanted fetched from his dressing-room. "A big, mauve sort of thing . . . revolting colour . . . stinks of scent . . . D'ye mind, Geoff?"

Accordingly, while Ralph led David to the gunroom, Geoff went upstairs at a leisurely pace.

*   *   *

A few moments earlier, Draper, hearing the bell, had sent young Walter to the same room of the house but on a different mission. The butler had seen that the boy was yawning tired; that he was past even that; and that he sat dumb and collapsed, with his eyes held forcefully open. The very moment that Frank returned to the pantry, Walter would become dispensable and would be sent to bed.

It was the best part of twenty minutes since Frank had been sent upstairs to tidy up the General's room, to put away the clothes that the General had taken off, and to put out the things that he would need for the night. These tasks should have taken the foot-man five minutes—say ten at the most—but he was not yet back.

The bell went in the pantry, and the indicator said "Dining-Room."

Draper said: "I shall have to go myself, seeing that Frank . . ." But he realised that he was talking to ears which heard nothing. "Wake up, Walter!" he said, shaking the boy gently by the shoulder; for the child, if he could not go to bed, had better be

properly awake than in this semi-conscious trance. " Slip upstairs,"
he said, speaking very distinctly into Walter's ear, " and tell Frank
to get a move on. Tell him he's wanted." And while the butler
went through to the dining-room in response to the bell, he saw
the boy Walter, still in his sort of trance, moving like one asleep,
wander uncertainly towards the back stairs, in search of Frank.

Walter came suddenly awake. The world which he entered
after this metamorphosis was not the normal, bodily woken-ness
of human beings, but a state of mental and emotional urgency.
Two things only were lodged in his consciousness: the glorious
promise of school—which had been in the pattern of his trance—
and his mission to find Frank. These two features of his life had
got themselves joined together in his brain, the one being con-
ditional on the other: if he wanted to go to school, he must find
Frank; if he failed to find Frank, he wouldn't go to school. He
entered a panic in which the discovery of Frank forthwith became
his only salvation. He broke into a gallop.

Accordingly, Geoff, starting later and going by the carpeted
route, performing his service, his act of atonement, reached the head
of the staircase a minute or so astern of the pantry boy. Indeed, he
met the boy not going into the General's dressing-room, but coming
out of it. And the boy was reeling about the corridor, white and
sobbing, and gasping again and again: " Frank! Frank! "

Walter was in a terrible state. Geoff had never before seen
a human being so utterly abandoned by his wits. There was a
reminder of David Levine, gasping, awash with fear, in the school
bathroom. There was also a reminder of the tramp, after he had
been hit in the stomach. But neither of these equalled—or anything like it—the state into which Walter had now collapsed. He
was struck by some terrible horror. The sobs that started in his
chest were unable to reach his throat. They turned into the gasps
that at length escaped his lips. Geoff took him gently by the shoulders, straightened him out, and asked what was the matter.

But the queer sounds that came in reply could be interpreted
only as " Frank! Frank! " and then a sort of howl, a wail of babbled
phrases enclosing the word " school " and linking together these
two words " school " and " Frank." The boy's quivering finger
pointed down the passage towards Mrs. Meredith's bedroom.

*   *   *

133

Frank, when he reached the General's dressing-room, was still humble, penitent and regretful about the message which he had sent to Miss May by the word of Kate and Millie. He could still find no excuse or explanation for his behaviour, except that he had gone temporarily into a panic, had gone daft. But the recollection of this daftness, in spite of its embarrassment, did not in the least diminish the stimulus, the state of wildness, provoked by the flicker of Miss May's pink legs beneath the black skirt, and by Miss May's laughter. It was the laughter that had done it. Her laugh had a deep, husky source which nobody, no real man, could ignore. And to-night Frank's maturity had opened as swiftly as a bud after an hour of spring sunshine.

Whistling very softly, Frank walked down the long, soundless corridor that led from the head of the stairs to Mrs. Meredith's bedroom at the end of the house. His destination was the adjoining room, the last on the left; but he could see that the end-room door was open and that the lights inside were lit. Miss May must be there, engaged on duties similar to his own.

Before he switched on the lights of the dressing-room, Frank stood for a moment in the doorway, in darkness. Knowing the General's habits, one could follow his tracks: the curtains across the window opposite were drawn a little apart where, after dressing for dinner, he had paused to look at the frosty night before going in to his wife; the door by which he had entered her room—at right angles to the window and close beside it—stood ajar; and the curtain which could conceal that door from Mrs. Meredith's side was only partly drawn. And now a shaft of light fell through this door and across the dressing-room carpet.

Advancing across the darkness to stand at the tip of this shaft, Frank imagined that he could hear and feel the fall of footsteps in the adjoining room, the movement and then the pause and rustle as if flimsy things, such as those Miss May had carried to the drying-room, were being handled. And looking out of the window, he could see the sharp starlight, the luminous whiteness of the frost and, far across the valley, the brightest star of Adam's cottage.

Within that star across the valley was Frank's girl, Bessie Rogers, now of little account beneath the overpowering impact of Miss May's legs and laughter. There was also her sister, Judy, whose pregnancy was—in some queer, unspeakable and splendid way— an expression of his own masculine inflation: there was something right and even wonderful in the mental connection. But the training of his childhood and adolescence made him at once put any such complicated feelings aside and transpose them with the simpler thought that some chaps had all the luck, and that the chap in question, having all the luck anyway, didn't have to worry. The worry was all on the other side of the valley within that star. The thought produced in him a sort of masculine leer. That was the way it was; that was the way of the world; the world of men.

Then, quite suddenly, as if his livery had asserted itself over his masculinity, he had gone to the door and switched on all the lights. At once, he had the sight of himself in his green uniform coat reflected in three mirrors. He had a number of tasks to perform up here, and a great many more awaiting him below. Going briskly to the window, he drew the curtains close. On the dressing-table he put straight the ivory brushes, shoe-horn, stud-box and cut-glass bottles. Into the top drawer he put the spare collar and white tie that had not been used. From the floor he gathered a further tie that had been crumpled and thrown away, evidently a failure. And only then he detected the envelope, a big mauve thing, lying half underneath the dressing-table. He fished it out.

" What you got there, Frank ? "

" Just picked it up," he answered defensively. And his words had slipped out before he was able to realise the astonishing thing that had happened: in spite of all his foolishness, Miss May, the unapproachable creature of his longing, had come to the door from her mistress's bedroom, was standing there now, and had asked him a question. And he had answered! Words were established between them.

" Let's see ! " She held out her hand for the envelope. " There's an awful lot of it," she said, pulling out the sheets and letting the photograph fall to the floor. " See what it is, Frankie ! "

When he stooped to pick it up, her skirts touched his cheek. " It's a picture of a girl," he said, " and she's all right ! "

But Miss May was absorbed in the letter. " It's written all over the page, crosswise and everything . . . And it ends up ' Your affect. cousin ' . . . with a funny little ' t.' Seytoun's the name, too, but I never heard it before . . . not spoken in this house." She sniffed the scented sheets. " I'll tell you what ! This is another of them wanting money. They make me sick ! Really . . ." She shook back her hair. " Every one in the world seems to come to us for

135

money. They think we're made of it." She folded up the letter "An' I dare say we are, too!"

Frank pushed the photograph in front of her, as a sort of humble offering. "It's a girl, Miss May."

"I didn't think it was a rabbit." But she took it and said: "Pretty, isn't she?"

No sort of word got anywhere near his lips.

"Go on! Say she's pretty!"

"Not as pretty as some," he managed to mumble.

"Not as pretty as who?" But when he remained silent, continuing to look at her with the same miserable appeal, she said: "Oh, you're no good! Here, give it to me!" And she took the photograph and slipped it, together with the letter, back into the envelope. With her neat fingers she smoothed it and put it straight and examined it carefully to make sure they had left no traces of their investigations. "Keep your fingers off it!" she said, as he held out his hand. "Where shall we put it?" She came right into the dressing-room and looked around. "Here!" she said, propping it against the mirror which stood on the dressing-table. "They'll find it when they want it."

Miss May cast a glance round the dressing-room. She had her chin up and she moved her head round quite slowly, looking at everything, with her eyes laughing. "He doesn't leave you a lot to do," she said.

He managed to answer: "No—I got to admit he's a tidy chap."

She let her eyes complete the circuit and come back to him and then slide down him to the floor. "Those housemaids!" she said, clicking her tongue. And she stopped right underneath him and started to flick at his knee, the knee of his black livery trousers where it had a patch of dust, a whiteness that it must have picked up from the carpet when he knelt to get the photograph. "'Twants a brush," she said. "I got one in here." And she straightened herself and flicked round on her heel and toe, as if it was a step of a dance. She seemed to expect him to follow her into the bedroom, for when she had gone out of sight, he heard her voice repeating: "I got one just here."

When he took those few steps through into the bedroom, following her, it was as much a physical effort, and as courageous, as anything he had ever done in his life. He cheered himself on by repeating his last remark, as if it was some sort of war-cry, and he heard his voice saying more than once: "I got to admit he's a tidy chap, I got to admit it." And then, by some curious sequence of subconscious thoughts, which may have retraced their way across the valley to the star of old Adam's cottage, to Judy, to his last positive reflection that some chaps had all the luck, to the lucky chap himself and thence, finally, to those other duties of his which required him to tidy Ralph's clothes in Ralph's bedroom, he found himself adding: "Not like young Ralph. He's a terrible untidy chap—young Ralph!"

The remark seemed to startle her. She was getting the brush from the dressing-table and she turned round quickly, knocking the brush as she did so and sending it under the arm-chair by the fire. "Don't you talk to me about young Ralph!" she said. "He's a young devil—that kid!" Then she added: "I'm all fingers and thumbs!" And turning her back to him, she bent down to retrieve the brush. She didn't straighten herself at once but stayed half bent, with her hands on her knees, and her head a bit on one side. In that position she looked backwards and upwards at him, and she was laughing. "Did I say 'kid'?" she cried. "*Some* kid! You're not much older yourself."

"Near two years," he said. And he was still surprised to hear his own voice.

"You don't act like it!" she answered. And this she said rather crossly, impatiently, getting up and swinging herself round again but, this time, coming back to him.

"Miss May!" he cried in a desperate sort of choke, not knowing what it was that had to be said to her so urgently.

"Well!" she said sharply. "Well, *what* is it?" But there was a laugh—half a laugh—in her impatient question. Letting herself swing back on her heels, she leant against one of the bed-posts. She put her hands behind her, clasping the clothes-brush behind the back of the bedpost, and throwing back her head, so that she was squinting at him past the tip of her nose, and laughing. "Want to say you're sorry—sorry for acting like a silly kid?"

He felt that his Adam's apple was working, and that his mouth gave a twitch, before he violently nodded his head. "You're not a bad chap, Frankie," she said. "You don't think enough of yourself, do you? You're big an' strong, aren't you?" She was teasing him, of course; he knew that. "An' I like them fresh freckles, and all that curly red hair . . ." Then suddenly she seemed to become shy and modest, leaving her head where it was, tilted back, but dropping her glance to his feet or his hands, so that her eyelids appeared to be shut. "Go on, then!" he heard her mutter. "Say it!"

So he said: "Sorry, Miss May!" and tried to explain. "I didn't mean it, Miss May. Really I didn't mean it . . . I don't know why . . . I don't know how . . ."

She burst out laughing again, with her head thrown right back. "You *are* a silly kid!"

Letting his hands fall, he found they were met by her soft forearms, which his fingers gripped. For the rest of his life he remembered hearing the clothes-brush go clattering against a chair. She must have thrown herself backwards on to the bed, pulling him on top of her; but as she rubbed her cheek against his chin, she was laughing so hard she could hardly splutter, "You silly kid . . . you silly daft kid . . . I'll laugh myself to death . . ." It was she who started kissing him, while she pulled his hair, pulled his ears and rubbed her knuckles down his shoulders and ribs. She interrupted her kissing, her fondling and her laughing to ask, in an astonished voice: "You never done this before, Frankie? My! You are late a' starting!"

*   *   *

In the gunroom, Ralph said sharply to David: "Where did you find that?"

"This?" It was a circlet of crimson elastic sewn with frills. "It was on the table. I just picked it up . . ."

"Nobody's supposed to take anything off that table unless it belongs to them."

"Sorry, Meredith!" David had been playing with it in an idle way, while some sort of desultory exchange of words had been kept up between the two boys. They were waiting for Geoff, and Ralph did accept certain courtesy duties with a guest in his house —even with David Levine.

"Give it us, will you?" David threw the thing across, and Ralph caught it. "It's that sod, Frank," Ralph said. "He delves in our pockets and finds things that aren't lost and puts them there. You know what it is?"

"No."

138

"It's a garter—a girl's garter. In the old days all girls had them. Now it's mostly only skivvies and the country bits. You know Platt and Barker—the chaps in our house?"

"Yes."

"They've got collections of these things. Platt has the best. He's got nine. I bet he cheats. You're only supposed to have them when you've poked the girl. I bet he hasn't poked nine girls." Ralph flicked the garter across the gunroom and went to fetch it. "You ever poked a girl?" he asked.

"No . . ." David had done terrible things with girls in dark visions, but he had never physically touched one, except to shake her hand or to dance with her awkwardly in public. His ideas of physiology and of the physiological details of sex were fogged and wildly inaccurate.

"You ought to try it some time," Ralph said kindly. "It broadens a chap's outlook. You ought to ask Platt to show you his collection." He grinned at the thought of Levine doing so. "*He'd* tell you a thing or two—mostly lies." He put the garter back in his pocket. "It isn't done, you know, to talk about the actual girls you've poked. Platt does it. He's rather a swine, Platt —don't you think?"

"Perhaps he is."

"Have you seen this?" Ralph asked. It was a large-scale plan of the house and stable, with a number of lines marked upon it in various colours, and with a title, inexpertly drawn in Gothic letters: "CLIMBING MAP."

"We go climbing from time to time," Ralph said. "On the roofs, that is. It's rather good sport. Would you care to have a go to-night?"

"All right," David said. The worst of all the indignities that he had to suffer was his own desire for esteem. He could not, in any event, have declined Ralph's suggestion; but he accepted it eagerly because, at the moment of acceptance, he was fired with the wild hallucination that here was a chance, perhaps, for some display of skill or courage that would lift him out of contempt. The fact that he had neither skill nor courage at his command was irrelevant. "I'd like it very much," he added.

"Good chap!" said Ralph, and the casual comment uplifted David's heart. "Here's Geoff!"

Geoff walked in by the door opposite the pantry. He walked

straight across the gunroom to the other door and into the adjoining lavatories. In a few moments Ralph and David heard him being very sick. It had been an effort of supreme control by Geoff that he had contained himself so long, and that he had kept back, until now, the vomit which had risen at the sight in Mrs. Meredith's bedroom.

*　　*　　*

After he had left Walter in the passage, Geoff had first followed his mission into the dressing-room and had found the mauve envelope. It was then that he had heard the sounds next door and had seen the lights from the bedroom through the open doorway. When he went through that doorway, carrying the envelope, he could not at first identify what it was that was happening upon the bed. Even the terrible state of young Walter in the passage outside had not prepared him for anything so loathsome as this.

It was a curious reaction that he suffered. He had seen and assisted the matings of all kinds of farm animals, and he had done so from a very early age without finding in these processes the least obscenity. But in spite of all the efforts of his elders, especially his schoolmasters, to establish in his mind a connection between the matings of plants, animals and humans, and to imbue that connection with mystical and religious properties, it was the lewd talk, the boasts, jokes and stories of other boys, that had easily prevailed. Indeed the schoolmasters—especially the headmaster during the talks that he gave to boys when preparing them for confirmation—had prevented the establishment of reasonable notions. They had spoken of the " God-given gifts of sex " and had suggested that mankind, even in the acts of reproduction, and perhaps especially in the acts of reproduction, was divorced from the animal world and made, in some way, beautiful and Godlike.

There was nothing beautiful or Godlike about Frank and Miss May on Mrs. Meredith's bed. The conflict between Platt's collection of garters and the clergyman's talk of joy, love and godliness, between the disease, allegedly sinful, of his own adolescence, and the lofty tributes to male chastity, and between sin that was black, and godliness that was chastity that was white—these various conflicts had produced in him a mental blank. This blank was in the very centre of his consciousness. The blank was now filled by this display upon the bed. For the next twenty-two years of his life the shock persisted.

There had been a single moment when he had lost control and had uttered, with a strange, hoarse cry, the footman's name. All sound and movement had thereupon ceased; and he had turned on his heel, with a military sort of movement, and had retraced his steps through the dressing-room into the passage. Because the thing which he had seen in the bedroom was so unforgettable, and had shaken and disgusted him so profoundly, he could allow no record of the shock to be apparent in his face, bearing or behaviour. Finding young Walter still quivering, gasping and sobbing in the corridor, Geoff took him by the shoulders and marched him all the way along to the servants' quarters, up the back staircase to the attic landing and into his tiny bedroom.

"You've had a sort of nightmare," Geoff said to him firmly. "Now you're to get to bed."

"But Mr. Draper . . ." the child gasped, as some sort of awareness of duty struck through the monstrous horror that engulfed him.

"Mr. Draper says you're to get to bed at once."

"But . . . but . . ." the boy choked.

"But what?" Geoff asked him gently.

"Will I . . . will I still go to school?"

"Go to school?" Geoff couldn't understand the question.

"I was to go to school if . . . if I found Frank."

"Oh, yes—you'll go to school all right."

The boy smiled and started dreamily to unbutton his clothes. Indeed he was already almost asleep. The gasping and the sobs stopped at once.

Then Geoff went briskly downstairs and into the dining-room —where the men were still seated with the port and the brandy— and gave the General the mauve envelope. "Thank ee, thank ee," the General said absently. "You're a good lad." And as Geoff left the room, the General was turning to Guy Bredon and drawing his attention. And Guy was saying, "What a real good sort that lad is, Harry! A dear good fellow!"

In the pantry, Geoff said to Draper: "I found young Walter nearly dead asleep. I sent him to bed."

"Did you indeed, Master Geoff," the butler answered. He would have been extremely angry if it had been any one else in the household who had given him this information.

"I hope it's all right. He wouldn't have been any use to you."

"I can scarcely do without him, Master Geoff, till Frank gets down again. He's taking his time upstairs."

"He'll be down in a moment," Geoff said, though he had no idea whether or not this statement was truthful.

"All right, Master Geoff. We'll manage somehow."

And then Geoff had gone through the gunroom, just noticing Ralph and David through a yellow mist which was forming before his eyes, and just able to reach the lavatory next door before the whole of his innards erupted.

*　　　*　　　*

In a minute or two, Geoff was able to join Ralph and David.

"You were catting, weren't you?" Ralph asked.

"Yes, a bit."

"I thought I heard you. What've you been eating?"

"The same as you, I suppose."

"You must have a lousy stomach . . . We thought we'd go climbing."

"There's a hell of a frost," Geoff said. "It'll be slippery."

"Levine wants to go climbing," Ralph said. "He doesn't mind a bit of slipperiness. We thought of trying the ballroom roof."

"That's crazy," Geoff said, "we've never even done it by daylight."

The ballroom had the full height of the house, and was a separate wing, beyond the library, at right angles to the rest. It was prolonged by the very high wall which contained that side of the courtyard.

"There's nothing to it," Ralph said.

"It's a good ten-foot drop on to the wall."

"What's ten foot?"

"It's plenty." Geoff turned to David. "Look, Dave!" he said, pointing to the plan. "We get on to the ballroom roof—that's easy. We go along the ballroom parapet—there's nothing in that. But it's the getting down."

"We just drop on to the wall," Ralph said. "Ten feet."

"The wall's not very wide. You've got to land on your feet." Geoff was very dogged about it. "If you don't land on your feet, you'll over-balance."

142

" And then what? " said Ralph scornfully.

" You'll fall into the courtyard."

" That's nothing much."

" It's fifteen feet."

" Look! " said Ralph patiently. " I'll go first. If I fall, you can go back. If I don't fall, I'll wait on the wall and steady you. Then you *can't* over-balance."

" If you'll wait on the wall . . ." Geoff said doubtfully.

" I've just said I'll wait on the wall."

Geoff said: " I still think it's crazy."

" Of course if you funk it . . ."

" I'm not going to do something I think's crazy just because *you* say I funk it."

" All right, then, Levine and I'll do it."

Geoff looked at David. " You don't want to do it either," he said.

" Listen! " Ralph said, with an air of great suffering and patience. " I've just told you . . . It's Levine who *does* want to do it. He's the guest."

" Do you? " Geoff asked.

And David said: " Yes."

" There you are! " said Ralph. " Levine's the guest. It's his option." He went to one of the cupboards and pulled out an armful of rubber-soled gym shoes, and each of the boys found a pair that fitted. When they had laced them on, they went through the baize door and into the billiard-room opposite, and then out of the billiard-room window on to the terrace. " We want to go quietly," Ralph said. " We don't want interference and explanations."

The terrace ran the full length of the house and it faced across the valley. On this sparkling night in the week before Christmas, there was no wind and so the cold was not evident. There was no moon, but a great height of stars, and as soon as the eye had got accustomed to the darkness, the features of the house could be quite easily distinguished.

" We get on to the roof by the library creeper," Ralph said to David. " It's almost a staircase."

" *That* part's easy," Geoff repeated.

They could see through a crack in the curtains that the dining-room was empty. Farther along the terrace, they could see that every one was gathering in the morning-room. It was a warm and comfortable scene. "Look at them guffing in there!" Ralph said. "Don't you pity 'em!"

* * *

Danny Levine came in first, striding ahead of the others, so that Madge thought: "What a restless fellow he is! Incapable of strolling in a leisurely way; incapable of leisure!" And, as she was expecting, he went straight to the chair he wanted, walking purposefully with his big stoop, his head thrust forward, his hands clasped, and he plumped himself down beside the doctor's wife.

"I shudder for my chairs every time that Danny sits down on them," Anne said. But her words were only cover, and her eyes were on the door.

"Well . . ." Danny said. "Well . . ." He rubbed his hands together but, after all that purpose, he seemed to have nothing to add.

Guy and Harry followed slowly, ignoring their wives, and taking the two most convenient chairs, one on either side of Madge, and continuing their conversation across her. "I shouldn't give him a penny," Guy was saying; "not if I were you." They were talking about Raoul Seytoun.

"I don't see that I can very well refuse altogether," said Harry, tapping his knee with the mauve envelope.

"Look!" said Guy patiently. "Listen!" he said. "Your grandfather did the handsome on this feller's grandmother. And now the fifty years is up, he hasn't the least call on you. And what's more, Harry . . ." Guy started to relight his cigar. "May I, Anne?" he asked conventionally.

"She likes it," Harry answered.

"And what's more," Guy continued, "neither you nor I, these days, have got the odd thousand a year to throw around so lightly."

"One has an obligation."

"Not a penny!" said Guy firmly, but he knew that it was useless.

"What," said Madge, "what, may I ask, is this thing you're waving under my nose?"

"Horrid colour, isn't it?" said Harry, taking out the sheets of paper and the photograph. "One of my grandfather's indiscretions." And he showed her the picture of the girl. "That's my

144

grandfather's great-granddaughter, I gather . . . Name of Alex."

Madge took the picture and held it at various distances from her face, trying to see it distinctly. "Anne!" she called. "Anne . . ."

But Anne had risen suddenly and walked down the room. Although she heard Madge calling to her, asking something about the picture of the girl—the Meredith nose, perhaps—she took no notice. She knew that she was behaving unguardedly and foolishly, and it was almost deliberate. She threw down her defences in the savage and careless way that she might have stripped off her clothes, and she was going straight to the little man, the horrid little man, who wouldn't come down the room to her but had stopped in the alcove by the doorway, pretending to look at the pictures and knowing very well that he had only to wait and she would have to come to him.

With his hands in his pockets he was jingling coins. He was rocking gently from his heels to his toes, and his head was pushed forward as he closely examined a painting. Making no acknowledgment of her arrival beside him, and without looking round, he continued that slight rocking movement, backwards and forwards, in an almost insolent way like a bad-mannered boy. Anne said nothing, determined that at least he should be the first to speak.

"Y'know . . ." he said with close attention to the picture, "they put a lot of . . . work in a thing like that. Somebody did." He took a sideways pace away from her, so as to confront the next picture in the row along the wall. She had to follow. "Just you look at those trees, Anne! They took no . . . end of trouble." Like an urchin, he whistled between his teeth, a single bar of some tune. "Freezing like stink outside," he said. "Real Christmas stuff, it's going to be. . . . Makes Edith's villa sound . . . pretty good." And he moved on yet again, to yet another painting. "Now that woman never breathed, did she? But it's a . . . devilish pretty frock you've got on to-night." Nevertheless he would not look at her, and she wanted very badly to pull his face round by the ear and slap it. And at the same time, she knew very well that he was perfectly aware of her feelings.

The little doctor came bustling into the room with an air of annoyance and slight urgency. He had been on the telephone in the library. "I was just talking to the district nurse," he said,

" when a voice interrupted and asked me to take a foreign call. I said would they wait till I'd finished—but they wouldn't."

" Oh dear!" Anne said. " How tiresome! I'm so sorry."

" She's on the phone now," said the doctor, " in the library."

" Oh, who?" Anne asked vaguely.

" I think she said Lady Parkes."

" Edith!" said Tommy. " What a coincidence!" And he looked at Anne at last. In front of the doctor, he let the laughter come from right behind those blue eyes of his, lighting them up, but without any corresponding movement of the thin lips. Nor was his glance decently directed at her face. It seemed to strike by accident the middle of her body, to penetrate it, and to come to rest somewhere inside.

" Edith . . ." Anne said, " I suppose I must speak to her—from all that distance." She went briskly out of the room, putting up the pretence of some irritation, hiding the turbulence that she had to suffer with a renewed attack of indecision.

Tommy, however, had no doubt at all about the outcome of her conversation. He resumed his whistling and his examination of the pictures.

✳   ✳   ✳

" It's really most irritating," the doctor said, " so inconsiderate." Standing beside Tommy Black, he also was pretending to look at the water-colour pictures.

" They *are* an inconsiderate lot, these . . . telephone people. But she won't be long; it's too expensive."

" It isn't the time," the doctor said, as if he were determined not to be too easily appeased. " But I don't know how I shall get on to Nurse again. I don't know where she was speaking."

" That's bad," said Tommy, as if it mattered to him immensely, for he would always take the trouble to charm, to win to himself, any one of either sex. " You didn't get the name of the patient?"

" Of course I did," the doctor said. " But they haven't yet put telephones into these agricultural cottages." He spoke sarcastically.

" Quite," said Tommy; " but I dare say the exchange'll tell you where the call was from. And anyway I dare say . . . we could work it out. The nurse can't have had a . . . lot of choice."

" She'd come from that cottage across the valley. I don't suppose you'd know it—above the wood."

146

"D'you mean Slender Ladies, I wonder?"

"Rogers is the name."

"Oh, old Adam! . . . The little girl, I suppose. Will she . . . have her baby to-night?"

"I hope so," the doctor said stiffly. He was not prepared to discuss his patients, and being unused to a country practice, was annoyed to discover that so much was generally known about his business.

"Straightforward, I hope?" asked Tommy.

"That's just what I was about to find out."

"It slips out pretty easily, doesn't it, with . . . most of these girls?"

"I wouldn't say that."

"It's her first baby, of course," Tommy continued, still further annoying the doctor. "I suppose they like to . . . have their little fuss?"

"This was the nurse," the doctor said curtly. "She does *not* like a fuss."

"Nor would I, Doctor, if I was a nurse." He laughed, still making an effort at appeasement. It was a hobby of his to be friendly with every one. "But it's a pretty safe bet that you'll find her . . . having a quick one at the Hare and Hounds. That's the nearest telephone by the best part of a mile—unless she'd come across country and come here."

It was then that Anne came back, saying that the nurse was again on the telephone, and the doctor hurried away.

*　　*　　*

"Poor little feller," said Tommy, when the doctor had gone to the telephone, "he's so important about it all, and so resentful. And how . . . was Edith?"

"Very well, thank you."

"That's good," he said. He knew she was angry, and he liked her anger. Still with his hands in his pockets, still jingling coins, and still whistling an occasional snatch of a tune, he continued to move along the pictures.

"Oh, stop looking at those stupid things!" she said beneath her breath.

"But they fascinate me, Anne. Just see this horse! The feller that painted it couldn't ever . . . have looked at the beast . . . sickle-

147

hocked, goose-rumped, ewe neck. . . ." Then he turned to her again, and this time he did look at her face. But once more his eyes were focused inside her, somewhere behind her own eyes. "Y'know you're just lovely to-night," he said in the softest whisper.

"Oh, go to hell!" she answered. Her words could only just be heard but they were savagely uttered. "I don't know how you had the nerve . . ."

"Did you . . . say you'd go to Edith's?"

"You rang her up yourself, didn't you? You got her to ring me back."

"Why not? Did you . . . say you'd go?"

"I didn't say one way or another," she answered with a coldness that ought to have been destructive, contemptuous. "I haven't yet made up my mind."

Knowing that she was lying, he said: "That's right! You don't want to . . . rush into these things." But he was still looking at her face, looking straight through her eyes and expressing his desire and his admiration. His eyes seemed to melt, almost to fill with tears, as if he had an unbearable longing, an unbearable loneliness that only she could assuage. With his eyes he was now entreating her. He said: "It's no light matter to bet on a fortnight's frost in the middle of the season."

The door was thrown open, but then Geoff collected himself, and although he was panting, managed to say calmly but urgently: "The doctor—David's hurt . . . the doctor!"

"What is it? What is it?" It was Daniel Levine's voice booming down the room. He and the doctor's wife had both risen at the sound of Geoff's voice.

"He's hurt," Geoff said, "it's David, David . . ." He could no longer hide the tragedy. "Oh where, oh where is the doctor?"

Tommy got hold of Geoff's arm. He was only about the same size as the boy, but he spun him round and held him. "Where is David?" he asked.

"In the courtyard. Lying on the ground by the ballroom . . ."

"Will you get the doctor?" Tommy said to Anne. He kept hold of Geoff's arm. "Come on, Geoff, show me! There's a good feller!"

Danny followed them out. The General walked to the fireplace and put his thumb on the bell-push and held it there. "It's no good the lot of us gettin' in the way," he said. " But one thing's sure as fate—we shall want Draper."

*   *   *

" I'm not too happy about her, Doctor," the nurse was saying on the telephone; " I'm afraid she's not advancing."

" Is she fully dilated ? "

" Yes—and the foetal heart's rising."

The doctor paused for a moment. He let the facts, the implications, the consequences, fall into place in his mind—the clicks of a combination lock. Sitting at the telephone in this spacious, tranquil room, within range of the bright fire, his mind prospected the night. It discovered the rigours of the cottage that was to be his battlefield; it predicted the battle itself. And he was just about ready for bed. " Oh, she's a posterior," he said at last, unable to escape the diagnosis. " I was half expecting it."

" You were right this morning," the nurse said admiringly. " It *must* have been the shoulder you felt."

" Yes, Nurse, I'm afraid so . . . It looks like the forks." He sighed. The chair in which he was sitting was too solid; the fire was too warm; the lights too soft. " Where are you speaking from ? "

" The Hare and Hounds, Doctor. I ran up here on my bike."

" Is she much distressed ? "

" She is rather."

It was then that Anne came quickly into the room. " I'm so sorry . . ." she said softly and without interrupting him. She conveyed emergency, she breathed the word " accident." He knew the approach so well.

" An ounce of chloral," the doctor said down the telephone. " I'll be with you as soon as I can." He hung up the instrument and turned to his hostess. " An accident, Mrs. Meredith ? " He had assumed a tremendous stature. The rest of the world had been shrunk to proportions in which he was a giant. " An accident ? "

" One of the boys, I think; in the courtyard."

" I shall want my bag, I expect. They insisted on taking my car. Would you kindly . . ." But she was already pressing the bell.

*   *   *

149

" What's up now? " said Frank, looking at the pantry indicator.
" Morning-room, Mr. Draper! They're ringing it fit to break."
He was still glad of diversions.

" You can go, Frank," said the butler, " and make it slippy."
But when the bell continued to ring, and he heard the faint click
which drew his eyes again to the indicator, and he saw that the
library had also joined in, he followed along himself. He had not
got very far before he met the footman running back.

" The doctor's car, Mr. Draper—his bag's in it. Master David's
hurt."

" Ring up Victor," the butler said. " I'd best go along myself."

" I'll bet it's young Ralph behind it! " Frank said, as he hurried
to the pantry switchboard.

The butler suffered a flush of annoyance. " Keep your bets to
yourself! " he said, unheard, as he moved like a warship towards
the hall. By wide repute he was unequalled in a real emergency.
He hastened with composure, with a mien brisk but steadfast.
" All the same," he thought, " young Master Ralph isn't so bad a
guess."

And Ralph, standing in the black drive, was regarding the
crumpled form of David with distaste. " Well, then, what *is* the
matter? " he was asking.

" Nothing . . ." David's breath drew the word into the faintest
cry, scarcely a groan. " I tell you . . . nothing's the matter."

" Then why don't you get up? "

" I can't."

" Then something *must* be the matter," Ralph said patiently;
" perhaps you've broken your neck? " He had his hands in his
pockets and he could see the white shirt-front at his feet, a splash
of paleness that might be the face, and the rest was a dark huddle
with the white gym shoes plainly at the end of it.

" I think . . . it's my leg." David's voice trembled only slightly.

" Then you've broken that . . . I say, Doctor! " he called.
" There's a chap here has broken his leg." The light had gone up
outside the porch; it could scarcely reach David, but it showed
the group of people approaching, the doctor amongst them.

" What is it, sonny? " the doctor asked, stooping over David
and switching on to his face the beam of a pocket flashlight. " No
—just stay as you are; just for the moment." He looked over his
shoulder at Ralph. " How did this happen? "

"Fell off that wall, Doctor."

"That wall!"

"Just up there."

The wall which enclosed the courtyard, running along in extension of the ballroom, seemed very high. Its top was visible against the stars of this frosty night.

"How did he get there?" Levine asked sharply. He was kneeling on the gravel now, and was holding his son's hand.

"We dropped on to it, sir," Ralph said. And Geoff added: "From the ballroom roof."

"If you'd just allow me . . . " the doctor said, speaking very gently to Levine and urging him out of the way.

"I'm sorry, Doctor." The big man got to his feet.

There was a sudden fall of light upon the gravel as Draper, assessing the emergency, moved into the ballroom, lit it up, and started to unshutter those of its tall windows that opened on to the courtyard. Over all the dressed-stone mullions of the house there was glittering frost.

Levine kicked Ralph's foot. "Gym shoes!" he said contemptuously. "On stone like this! Climb in your socks, you little fool!"

"Now we can see something," said the doctor, busy with a penknife.

David gave a short, quick cry.

"Yes," the doctor said; "I won't do it again." Rising to his feet, he said sharply: "You two boys . . . coats and rugs, and something for his head!" He saw the two of them gallop gladly towards the porch, and he drew Levine aside.

"I'm quite all right, Father," David was calling. "I'm quite all right really. I've just hurt my leg. . . ." He was insistent and he was laughing. "Nothing's the matter; honestly there isn't."

"That's all right, old chap," Levine answered—and he knew so well, so precisely, from his own similar experience, the struggles within his son's brain—"but stay as you are for the moment."

"Don't try to move, not yet," said the doctor, quite sharply. And then, in an undertone to Levine: "Compound fracture of the tibia and fibula. The bone's just pierced the skin." From professional habit he put his hand on Levine's arm. "And undoubtedly some concussion," he added; "all the symptoms. But . . ." And he looked up to the height of Levine's face, where he caught a glance of unguarded fear, "but there's no reason in the world why he shouldn't be quite all right in—shall we say—six months."

David's ears, quickened by concussion, caught the last remark. "Six months!" he cried.

"That's just a guess," the doctor said quickly, annoyed with himself that he had been overheard. "It mayn't be as long as that; it probably won't be . . ." For he could not know that David's heart had leapt joyfully and, even through the troubled mind, was already giving thanks to God that there would be no return to school for a period that was scarcely measurable.

Draper moved into the courtyard from the ballroom window. "Is there anything you wish, sir?"

"My bag as soon as you can," the doctor said. "And a plank we can use as a splint . . . and plenty of rugs if those boys aren't getting them . . . and if you see my wife . . ."

"I'm here," she said, coming forward. She had been standing discreetly aside with Tommy Black. And as she knelt beside David, the father felt in his heart a wave of relief and then of mourning, as if his own wife had been returned to him for a brief remembrance, a vision, of his loss. The doctor whispered in her ear, and she held out her hand for his penknife and flashlight. While she cut the stitches, she whispered to the boy some sort of reassurance. And though her words were inaudible to Levine, he caught their maternal nature, and he nearly wept.

The boys had come back with the rugs and pillows, and the doctor's wife had taken them. "She trained as a nurse," her husband said to Levine.

It was then that a curious figure, ancient, short and square, appeared out of the shadows. It was first seen as a squat bundle crouching beside the doctor's wife. A sort of crooning noise came from its lips, and the light shone on its white hair. From her seclusion in the East Wing, Nanny had smelt an accident.

Then Draper returned, escorting Frank and the odd-job man, who were carrying between them a weight of timber. "What sort of plank did you want, sir?" the butler asked.

Taking a look, the doctor gave a short laugh. "I'm afraid that's all rather too big. I just want to fasten his legs together. . . ."

"I know the form," said Tommy. "Come on, Draper, I'll show you."

"Good of you, Tommy," Levine said.

"Your car will be here directly," the butler said; and it was driven into the courtyard at that moment. On his way into the house, Tommy spoke to Victor, and the chauffeur drew up the doctor's car so that its headlights gave further illumination where it was wanted.

"Your bag, sir," said Victor, handing it to the doctor, and then he looked inquiringly at Levine.

"Please!" Levine said. "I shall want my own car shortly, I expect."

"I'm so sorry, sir, that this has happened."

"Thank you, Victor."

"I'm quite all right, Victor," David called to him.

"I'm sure you are, Master David."

"Now you be quiet, Master David," said Nanny. "You let *them* do the talking."

The doctor and his wife had the bag between them. "A quarter," he said to her, "I'll leave it to you."

Levine heard her say: "Now this will stop it hurting . . . perhaps there'll be a tiny prick." Her voice was beautiful, inflating his heart with sorrow. All sensitivity was heightened by this scene in the frosted courtyard; the slashes of light, the doctor and his wife beside the boy, and the larger group of people murmuring in the shadows behind. The thing was suspended like a lit picture in a room that was otherwise dark. Daniel Levine looked at the picture and he saw himself as one of its features.

The General entered, and the General's voice said: "I'm devilish sorry about this, Danny." And Levine's own voice answered: "Thanks so much, Harry. It's quite all right." People came into the light and were redissolved into the darkness, their voices distinct but distant. It might have been he, and not his son, who had been given the opiate. Draper had returned; and the scene was more calm and more substantial, with that commanding presence, as if a play was working to its climax. Nanny was kneeling with the doctor and the doctor's wife, all working deftly with the plank and bandages. "Far too many people . . ." said the doctor's voice. And Tommy also was there, somewhere behind them, for his voice replied: "I'll clear out of it, Doctor; I'm only in the way." Then Tommy came close, saying: "You're not worrying, Danny? I've been through it all myself, and *I'm* all right." He laughed and faded. Madge said: "Danny dear . . ." Anne said: "Danny, but I'm so, so sorry . . ." and he smelt her warmth and her perfume. It was Guy who was clearing his throat noisily, disgustingly, as if he were going to spit, but no spit followed.

Then Daniel Levine was himself taking part in an argument of time and distance. "We can too easily drop your wife," he was saying to the doctor.

"But *she* can drop *me* at the cottage."

"Then how will you get home?"

"But we can send Victor," Anne said. "Because, anyway, there's Tommy to be taken back . . ."

And Levine was insisting: "No, no . . . it's too obvious; it's practically on our way; it'd be a pleasure . . ."

"You can't take that boy home," said Nanny; "oh, no— you can't take him home to-night."

"He'll be better in his own bed," Levine said gently.

"But not to-night, Mr. Danny? Not to-night, Doctor?"

"I should get him home," the doctor said curtly. "Better to-night than later." Then he turned away.

"Yes," Levine said, "and we'll give your wife a lift."

"All right," the doctor agreed.

Groups of people, individual people, motor cars and lights were moved about the darkness like pieces in a game. Voices were released, swollen and extinguished. His own voice was as distant as the rest, as impartial. "Don't you worry, Danny . . ."

"Thanks, Guy."

"Good night, Danny; we'll ring you in the morning."

"Good night, Madge . . . good night, Guy."

He took the weight of his son's shoulders. It was nothing of a weight; the boy, like his mother, was such a shrimp of a thing. But they said he had huge feet and hands and would grow to his father's stature. "Easy, sir," said Victor.

"I'm quite all right, Victor," said the boy drowsily.

"Right as rain, Master David."

Between them, they laid the boy on the back seat of the long black car. Victor shut the door softly, solicitously. Draper held the door open for the doctor's wife and tucked the rug about her knees. Frank held Levine's heavy, fur-lined overcoat.

"I really am devilish sorry, Danny."

"Thanks, Harry."

"Good night, Danny—ring us if there's anything, the least thing, we can do."

"Thanks so much, Anne."

"Don't you worry, old chap."

"Good night, Tommy."

"I'm very sorry this has happened, sir . . ."

Everything happened again and again, events, voices and words repeating and rotating like the world itself.

"Good night, Draper, good night, Victor, good night, Frank . . . Thank you all so much for all your help."

"He's a fine gentleman," said Draper as the long car drove into the night. Its headlights painted a fan beyond the hill. The fan was laid upon the treetops; it dissolved into an aurora and slowly died. The horn distantly sounded.

"You should have seen him with his squadron," Victor said to the butler. "He was hot stuff."

"They'll want whisky in the hall," the butler said to Frank.

*   *   *

It was as bright as they could make it—with every lamp and candle that they could borrow crowded into that tiny upper room of Adam's cottage—and very quiet. Each individual sound was distinct with its own particular weight and value. Against the steady snoring of the girl, Nurse Mudie could hear the tick of her own wrist-watch. She sat at the head of the bed and dripped anæsthetic on to a gauze pad.

The doctor grunted as he struggled between the thighs of the figure that was laid, in her webbing harness, transversely across the wide bed. The nurse heard his forceps clank as he locked them home. "That's got it," he said. The nurse heard the crackle of the macintosh apron that he wore beneath his sterile gown. Whenever either she or the doctor moved, newspapers rustled.

There were newspapers everywhere, most of them bloodstained. They were spread all over the floor, the furniture and the bed. If you so much as moved your weight from one foot to the other, a newspaper rustled and ripped.

Through the thin floor Nurse Mudie could hear low voices in the room below. The people down there moved softly. They were putting coal on the fire. A bucket clanked, and water slopped on to the stone floor. When the old man coughed and spat, little

Bessie whispered to him. In the upstairs room they could hear it all. In the downstairs room they could hear the steady snoring of the girl, and the creak of a loose board under the doctor's feet.

The smell of carbolic filled the house. It defeated the smell of the old man's pipe, the smell of a rabbit paunched in the wash-house, the smell of onions hanging in the lean-to shed at the back. But in the upper room itself, it was tainted with the smell of anæs-thetic.

The doctor grunted again and stood up from the low chair on which he had been squatting. He stood between the girl's thighs. Nurse Mudie heard the metallic splash as he dropped another reddened swab into the bucket at his feet. There were fresh splashes of blood on the surrounding newspapers and on the doctor's gown. "Hang on, Nurse!" he said. "I'm pulling now."

Nurse Mudie, her sleeves rolled up, crooked an arm round the girl's neck and clamped her hand under the girl's armpit. She laid the palm of her other hand on the tight belly. The doctor waited. "There's a pain *now*," the nurse said.

"*Now!*" the doctor answered, and with all his strength he heaved at the forceps. The sweat streamed down his face beneath its mask. It was very hot in the small room, and very bright.

*   *   *

"Remarkably bright!" the General said to Geoff as they stood together at the french window, looking across the valley at Adam's cottage. He had watched his wife go slowly upstairs to her bed and then had caught Geoff on his way through the hall. He had beckoned the boy to his side, and now wanted to convey to him the miracle and mystery of new life.

When the General considered human birth, he heard the church organ, the carols that were sung in the snow which fell at Christmas about once in ten years at Neapcaster, and the solemn voice of the preacher declaring the significance of that festival. In all his years the General had never been near to a human birth. He had never heard the cry of a hurt animal issue from the mouth of a woman. He had seen plenty of battle casualties and a great number of swollen and stinking corpses, but never a woman's blood in any greater quantity than could be staunched with a pocket handkerchief.

"That light," the General said to Geoff, as he pointed across the valley, "they've got it lit up all right . . ." He felt in his heart that there was some lovely relationship between the lit cottage and the holy star. "That's where that poor little thing is having her baby. And that doctor—I should say he's a competent chap . . ."

The General sighed at his own inadequacy. "The father," he said; "it's a pity, a thousand pities, the fellow—whoever he is—won't marry her. You see . . ." He was breathing heavily from the dual efforts of thought and speech, scarcely co-ordinated. "You see, there's a child being born over there . . . a child with . . . with no great prospects."

The General took Geoff's arm and for some time kneaded the muscles with his fingers. He felt that physical touch might, better than speech, explain to the boy this whole tremendous business of the way of mankind. "Well run along, old chap," he said at last. "Time you were in bed. Good night to ye!" As an afterthought he added: "I'm sorry about that little feller, David Levine. A nasty business! All the same, it was devilish stupid of him to go climbing about the house in the middle of the night. . . ." As Geoff walked away, the General wondered how far he had succeeded in initiating the boy into the facts of human existence, the human mystery.

He need not have worried, for Geoff's heart, overloaded with guilt, was over-sensitive to realities. This day, the human way had been made apparent to him on its course through cruelty and degradation. He had no technical knowledge of human birth, but whatever was going on within the star of that brightly lit cottage was now, at last, joined in his troubled mind with Adam's ancient and stubby finger prodding the strained frock, with the girl's silent misery, with the way she had stood at the gate trapped by their eyes, with the gasping of the tramp in the black morning, with the sight of David caught like a rabbit by Ralph's regard, with the convulsions upon the bed and their sudden cessation at his cry of "Frank," and finally with the cry of David, half stifled and the soft crunch as his body hit the gravel. All these imperishable scenes and sounds were together wound about by a continuous coil that found its fastening in the star of Adam's cottage. The brightness of that star, making insignificant the million other stars of a frosty night, was the measure of his guilt. All the cruelty, pain and obscenity of the day was Geoff's burden.

★　　　★　　　★

Geoff went upstairs with a purposeful tread and marched into Ralph's bedroom. Ralph, like his father downstairs, had drawn the curtains and was standing by the window, looking across the valley. His fingers were playing with the crimson garter. At Geoff's entrance, he turned his head but not his body. "Hallo!" he said, "I thought you'd gone off on your bike. About time, isn't it?"

"I came back to see *you*," Geoff said solemnly.

Ralph flicked the garter across the room. "That's a pretty thing," he said. "Know whose it is?"

Geoff remained silent.

"Well, *I'm* not going to tell you," Ralph said smugly, "it's not done, you know." Ralph yawned. "I'm about ready for bed. It's a pity that tick Levine had to spoil a pretty decent day."

"That's what I came about," Geoff said. His face was, as usual, impassive; but Ralph was made aware that some great effort was being generated behind it.

Ralph yawned again. "Well—what?" he asked.

"You were a bloody swine!" Geoff said. It was probably the most violent remark that he had uttered since the end of his infancy.

Ralph hid his astonishment. "Well, the little tick insisted on climbing," he said. "He had the option."

"That's not what I mean."

"Well, what?"

"You know well enough. Why did you let him fall?"

"He looked so damn silly dancing about on the wall . . ."

"Trying to get his balance."

"I couldn't do a thing for laughing."

"You'd only got to put out a hand."

"If it comes to that, why did you let him drop? You could have pulled him back. You could see he was pissing with fright."

"You said you'd catch him."

"Well, anyway," said Ralph with a third yawn, "we shan't have him hanging about the house for another six months."

Very quietly Geoff said: "I'm going to hit you as hard as I can in the face."

Ralph knew that he meant it. "You bloody well couldn't," he said.

"You know I can."

"Not if I had two good arms, you couldn't." With his right

hand he touched his left shoulder. "This one won't move above my head. It's broken or cracked or something."

"You never said much about it."

"Do you think I want to give Watts a laugh?"

Geoff knew that Ralph, his closest friend, was speaking the truth. The two boys looked steadily at each other while Geoff tried to sort and reassemble the incidents of the evening and the sequence of cause and effect. "So that's why you couldn't catch hold of Levine!" he said.

"Why?"

"Because your arm wouldn't go up."

Very slowly Ralph's face showed indications of embarrassment, an increase of colour. He said: "I had the other arm, hadn't I?"

"You were holding on to the drain pipe."

Ralph turned away and went back to the window. In the quiet of the room they could hear the river. They could hear an owl hooting close to the house and an answer from Slender Ladies, right across the valley, close to Adam's cottage. Ralph said: "If I'd wanted to catch hold of Levine, do you think I couldn't have *made* my arm go up?" Geoff was unable to answer, and after some moments of silence, Ralph added: "Well . . . aren't you ever going to bed?"

Without any reply Geoff left the room and went downstairs and out of the house. Taking his bicycle that was propped against the stable wall, he rode slowly up the drive to the Lodge. Now he felt desperately tired; and as he went, he calculated that he had had a very long day indeed—twenty hours of it. When he reached the Lodge, he saw that his father's light was still burning, and although he had the greatest longing to go straight to his bed and fall asleep, and to avoid a long and complicated explanation at this hour of the night, he dutifully went into his father's bedroom. In any event, he could not have reached his own room unheard and would undoubtedly have been summoned as he crossed the landing.

"But there's nothing to be done, Father," he said at the end of his long narrative and examination. "There's nothing that *you* can do now, because, you see, they'll all be in bed and asleep."

But, as a matter of fact, he was not correct.

*　　*　　*

The doctor's wife went into the kitchen of her small house to get a little food ready for her husband's return. He would be very tired, and he had a full day to-morrow. Would he have to go out again to-night, to set that little boy's leg?

She had not left Levine's house until David had fallen into a sudden, deep sleep. The moment he was put between the sheets, the boy became newly conscious of his pain and very widely awake. " Now if you drink this . . ." she said, giving him a strong dose of bromide and aspirin, the only suitable medicines to be found in Levine's bathroom, " it won't hurt nearly so much."

" I'm terribly, terribly sorry for all the trouble I'm giving you," the boy kept on saying.

" You *must* understand," she replied at last, " that it isn't a trouble. I'm a trained nurse. This is what I was trained to do. This is much more important to me, really, than being somebody's wife. Besides," she added, " it's a pleasure to nurse such a brave little patient. You're a very brave boy, you know."

A lovely smile appeared on David's face. It might have been all his life that he had been waiting to have this said to him. In his mind—or perhaps it was his heart—there was a sudden and beautiful quiet, as if a gramophone that had been playing for a long time in some distant room had at last been stopped. The silence was heavenly. He scarcely realised that the sound of his cry, his scream, that he had uttered out hunting when the pony rolled on him—the terrible noise whose resounding and persistent echoes in his own ears had been increased by this latter accident—was at last stilled. By her remark, the doctor's wife had remitted the punishment of shame. The boy fell immediately asleep.

Then Levine had taken her home, while an old servant, roused from bed, sat and sewed within call of the sleeping boy. When they reached the small house which the doctor had recently leased, they could see from the black windows and the empty garage that he was not yet back. Rather doubtfully, she asked Levine if he would like to come in. She hoped he would refuse, because she felt that she could not yet bear to have his immense vibrations sent through her own home, remaining there after his departure.

" No, no," he said. " You don't want that." So they stood together in the drive of her house, and neither of them felt quite ready to part. " You know . . ." He looked up at the sky, and she saw the outline of his great, beaked face against the stars. His size made her feel too small; and when, as now, he bowed himself over her, she felt devoured. "This evening seems terribly incomplete," he said. "Don't you feel that yourself?"

"Well, perhaps . . ." she cautiously answered.

But he only said: "At dinner we talked so much and we said so little. And all we needed to do was to ask one question—' What is a man?'"

It was a pretty ordinary remark. But because he made it from his great height, with his head against the stars, and because the night was so cold and still, she looked up at him and answered breathlessly: "Oh yes, yes . . ." And only when she had been able to get the breath to think for herself could she add: "And all we talked about was society, wasn't it?"

"What we've made of society!" he said with terrible scorn. "A packet of petty little laws, with their ethics buried under regulations! A law, don't you think, that daren't take account of the soul at one end of man, and the reproductive organs at the other?"

"But only," she managed to say, "of all the middle stretches that aren't of the least consequence."

"A law that has everything to do with the regulation of men, but nothing to do with a mammal made in the image of God."

Feeling herself adrift, blown in his breeze, she seized hold of herself and made herself say, with astringent calmness: "I quite see your point."

And it made him roar with laughter, as if he was blowing down the house. "Well done!" he cried. "How right of you to turn off the tap, when all we want is a little more humour and a little less laughter . . . A little less shouting and a little more praise. A little less loving, and a lot more love."

"Psychologically speaking . . ." she said, caught once more in the current, clinging to the bank.

"We've had enough of that!" he said sharply, as if she were a schoolgirl, and he her master. "Enough! Too much! Too much of the magnifying-glass in the wrong places. Too much psychology! Too many excuses, explanations, threats . . . environment, influence and all the rest . . ."

"But . . . but . . ." She drew in her breath. To herself she said: "But I *will* speak!" and to him: "*That's* inconsistent! Now you've turned round on yourself."

"Certainly I have," he said. "But then I saw a star fall, right behind your house, right behind your chimneys. Didn't *you* see it?"

"No . . . I don't think so. . . ." She didn't quite know what he meant.

"Oh, it fell all right," he said; "honestly it did. And then I thought of your fellow Paul, your Saint . . . When *he* saw that great light, did it really matter in the least what happened to him at his mother's knee? Did it matter what school he went to? Did it matter whether his childhood was happy or sad? How he got his first girl? How he learnt about sex?"

"But we aren't all saints," she said.

"Aren't we? Aren't we?" he asked with real surprise. "What an astonishing declaration!" Then he went to his car. "At least," he said, "we can all go to bed."

When he was in the driving-seat and had started the engine, she came up to the car and asked, almost desperately: "And after all that . . . where have we got to?"

"God knows!" he answered. "Am I backing into anything?" He missed the shrubbery and got safely headed for the gate. "God bless you," he called and drove away. She went into her house and through into the kitchen.

* * *

Very soon the doctor got back home. And very soon now Nurse Mudie would have picked up all the newspapers and blown out every lamp and candle in the cottage bedroom.

The doctor was so tired that he could scarcely be bothered to put his car in the garage. But he did so. He was so tired that he could scarcely be bothered to rug-up the bonnet against the frost, or to light and fix the lamp under the bonnet to stop the cylinders from freezing, or to close the door of the garage after him. But he did all these things.

"Darling," he said to his wife, "you oughtn't to have waited up."

"Try to eat something."

"No."

"Whisky?"

"You haven't any cocoa?"

162

" Oh yes. The milk's almost on the boil." She knew what had happened when he came in like this. She pushed him down into the chair. " Which was it? " she asked.

" The baby's all right." He had his head in his hands. " Dear God—what a hope it's got! "

" The girl? " she asked very softly.

" A posterior. Then a hæmorrhage."

" No chance of a transfusion? "

" No chance of anything in a place like that."

She had got the cocoa, and it stood on the table, too hot to drink. She made herself put her hand on the thick ginger hair, cut close and very slightly curling.

" That girl," he said, " she hadn't anything to give that baby except its life."

His wife made herself finger the curls and stroke the head.

" Dear God! " he said. " I wish I believed in God. I'd pray for that baby."

" I'll pray for the baby," she answered.

" I wish I believed it could do any good."

*   *   *

The General, from the window of his dressing-room, could get a fair reminder of his property. " How," he asked, " how could this great estate—having as equal parts its stone, its lands, its Merediths—crumble and pass? It could no more do so than a regiment." And as he looked sideways from his window at the brave face of his house, and at the night whose glitter lay upon mullion and pediment, it was as if the Regimental band was playing the slow march of the King's review: men pass away, but not regiments. How, then, could the Agent's figures cause stone to crumble and building to be undone?

The General lay upon his bed and turned out the light. He was a very long way from sleep. Then he wished that he had taken a last look across the valley to see whether or not old Adam's cottage was still lit so brightly, whether that girl's affair was yet settled one way or another, whether that little doctor had finished his job. His curiosity was not sufficient to entice him out of bed. " But I bet that little doctor sleeps like a log! "

He lay with his eyes open as if he were already dead. " If Richard happens to be right," he thought, " I've not got a precious lot left to live for." Remembering the picture of the girl, he wished that he had not left it on the other side of the room. He wished, he wished . . . He wished that he could go in to see his wife, and that she were not so soundly asleep—as she always was—without the least regard for him. He wished that he could stop wishing. He wished, as he turned and turned upon his bed, that he could be tranquil and still. It was too much, of course, to wish that he might sleep.

The rest of the household slept. Anne, in the room next door, breathed steadily and sweetly in all her innocence, as if the fires of her body were already stilled by foretaste.

Frank lay, face downwards, on the trestle bed that had to be drawn, each night, across the strong-room door where the silver was kept. A mild resentment had followed him—with the memory of Geoff's startled voice—into a heavy sleep; and at six o'clock precisely, when the alarm clock went off, he would wake saying: "I never thought Master Geoff would do a thing like that." In the meanwhile, he was unaware of the cockroaches that crawled in great numbers around and under his bed.

In her dreams, Lizzie giggled. Next door, Kate and Millie lay intertwined in one of their two beds, leaving the other empty. From Miss May's room, in the other corridor, the short rasp of a snore was as steady and rapid as the beat of a small clock. Fully submerged in sleep, the girl's face was red and childish, and her mouth was open. Then she turned abruptly, violently on to her side, throwing an arm across her face. The snoring stopped at once, but was at once replaced in the silence by the ticking of somebody's clock.

"What, what, what," thought the General, as he creaked wearily from one side to the other, "what will happen to all these people of mine—on the farm, in the woods, the gardens, the stables, the kitchen—if I'm to go under as they say? What have they to depend upon, but me?" His burden was heavy.

★   ★   ★

"And thou shalt love the Lord thy God with all thy heart and with all thy soul and with all thy might." Daniel Levine was making his declaration aloud and in Hebrew. "And these words which I command thee this day shall be in thy heart. And thou shalt teach them diligently unto thy children . . ."

Levine interrupted his prayers to go into his son's room next door. The boy breathed deeply in his drugged sleep. There was a hump of blankets, erected over a framework, making a sort of tent above the broken leg. "What can I give you?" the father thought. "What can you get from me of all that I have—my knowledge and ignorance, experience and innocence, strength and weakness, hope and despair, faith and disbelief?"

Fearing that he could give his son nothing, Levine returned to his own bedside. He continued the ancient practice: "For Thy salvation I hope, O Lord . . . I hope, O Lord, for Thy salvation . . . O Lord, for Thy salvation I hope." These three sentences had to be repeated thrice.

Levine lowered his huge body on to the outsize bed that had been specially made for him. "I never do this," he thought, "without wondering whether the thing's going to stand up to it." Sitting upon the bed, his lips moved in the Hebrew words: "Be still, and sin not!" But the thought and the image of the doctor's wife, of the woman in the green dress, would not altogether vanish. Nor could the demands of his big body be altogether ignored. It was hypocrisy to pretend such ignorance. Man could not deny the body by thinking of the soul; nor was it sinful to think duly of the body; it was sinful only to think of the body without the soul; or to think of man without the body as well as the soul; or to conceive human life without the living changes, chances, demands, torments and temptations of the human body, the breast-plate of the soul; or to imagine that the human design might be otherwise than it was.

And again, quite suddenly, quite distinct, the image of a star falling behind the roof of the doctor's house dominated his thoughts. "The fallacy," he said. "Where is the real fallacy?" And the wave of the evening that had built itself up with the thought, emotion and experience of the evening, until its crest curled over, as now, to draw him into sleep, seemed to carry him on its way to one conclusion. "We talked about Man, about how we can change Man . . . What nonsense! What rubbish! Only God can change Man. Only a man can change himself . . . And all that we, a community of men, can do is to give man the chance . . . the chance . . ." Levine sighed deeply but not unhappily. "So we've got back, after all, to politics, economics . . . how tiresome!" He sighed again. "How tedious!"

Aloud, Levine said: "Stand in awe and sin not: commune with your own heart upon your bed, and be still!" This command also had to be thrice repeated before he could lay himself down slowly and carefully and stretch himself between the sheets. "It's only a matter of time," he thought as the bed creaked again, "before this thing really does collapse." But a curious peace, a feeling of design, was creeping upon him, as if it was of real moment that the night had folded itself with finality upon one day, while the sun would soon rise upon another. Drowsily he stretched out an arm and switched off the lamp.

BOOK TWO

September-October, 1932

NO longer a tramp in the early autumn of 1932, but now a respectable working man with a name, Ben rested his wheel-barrow in the drive of Daniel Levine's house and moved over towards the gate. " Wanting anything? " he asked.

The man on the other side of the open gateway turned his unshaven face and moved his jaws and cheeks as if about to spit, but instead swallowed.

" Well? " Ben said.

" Chance of work, chum? " the man asked.

" Bit late, aren't you? We wanted men around harvest."

" I was working around harvest."

" We've nothing now."

The man nodded and then looked around him, moving his head as little as possible but letting his bloodshot eyes turn and twitch and blink with a nervous reaction to the September sun-light. He was a young chap, and his bristles were reddish or golden.

" This a farm? " he asked.

" Sort of a farm," Ben said. " It's a gen'leman's house."

" I c'n see it's a gen'leman's house. Got your spuds up? "

" We don't grow 'em much around here."

" Some does. I see 'em." He moved closer to the gate, trying to increase his vision round the bit of shrubbery that enclosed the short and modest drive. " Is the boss a gen'leman farmer? One o' them? " There was a slight and tentative contempt in his ques-tion.

Ben spat. It was almost a reflex action, instinctive and in-eradicable by environment, to the word " boss." Then he thought: " Ah, he's a sly one, this "; and out of a selection of possible replies that occurred to him, said: "He's a bit of an invalid these days. A big chap."

The man's glance continued to flicker about his surroundings, as if he was seeking ideas. "I c'n milk a bit?" he said, as if he was asking a question. "I c'n look arter a boiler? I once worked in a livery stables? Did a bit o' gardening . . ."

"There's nothing here, I tell you. You'd best move on." Ben stood where he was, looking steadily at the tramp, and the tramp looked steadily back, eye to eye. Like two unacquainted and suspicious animals, the men on either side of the gateway let themselves harden against each other, building up, in place of the human understanding that had been almost spun between them, a sort of motionless hostility. They challenged each other until, after a few seconds, the weaker of the two, the one who was defenceless, let his head slowly sink. At this gesture of submission, Ben advanced to the gatepost and leant against it. "Well?" he said unpleasantly.

The tramp turned slowly and walked off. The sound of his shuffling along the road was soon dissolved in the slow approach of Levine's footsteps. Turning towards the house, Ben touched his cap.

* * *

"Nice afternoon, sir," Ben said crisply. He returned to his wheelbarrow, and guessing that he had been overheard, jerked his head in the direction of the tramp's departure. "Soon sent *him* packing!"

"Who was he?"

"Him?" Levine's head was nowadays bowed, and his shoulders humped, but he was still a very tall man; and Ben had still to squint upwards to look at his employer's face. It was a face that had fallen into valleys of sadness and perhaps some pain, but it still required an answer. "Him?" Ben said. "A chap making out he wanted work."

"Perhaps he did want work. Some people do, you know." The big man's eyes were looking above Ben's head, across the gateway, across the road and up the hill. Ben supposed that he was secretly laughing; but now the barrow had to be moved, to make way for the doctor's car that had turned slowly into the drive. As it crept past, the doctor waved to Levine, too casually, too carefree perhaps, for deception was now pointless. Levine, moving slowly, followed the car round the bend of the shrubbery to the door of his house, and the doctor was waiting there, standing by his car, with the sun in his face and the breeze lifting his ginger hair. "I was passing. I called in for my glass of sherry." The two men smiled at each other, like children with a secret.

"Nice afternoon," Levine said, wondering what loop or knot of their curious relationship—the three-threaded twine that each had hold of—would entangle them to-day. "Is he my doctor? Is he my friend? I cannot regard him emotionally as the husband of Dorothy." Their silence was peaceful. With the sun in their faces, they smiled. "Are you my doctor to-day?" Levine asked.

"I shan't charge you for this visit! How do you find yourself?"

"Autumn is sad. But I suppose it was always sad. Shall we go inside?"

The doctor kept quiet. Everything that Levine said—even the most casual remark or invitation—had now its special significance. It was difficult to talk with him. "I'm going away," Levine said.

"Where to?" It was a relief to be able to ask a simple question.

"The Riviera. My old solaces."

The doctor hesitated, puzzled. "Why exactly?" he asked.

"It's a place of unreality, isn't it? A sort of half-way house, don't you think?" Levine was walking heavily across the room, bringing the doctor his glass of sherry. "It's a stepping-stone, if you like." Now they were standing together by the window that looked southwards, away from the road, down the slope of the garden and across the invisible valley. Angrily, nervously, Levine turned his back to the bank of dahlias and Michaelmas daisies, the long flow of lawn between the beeches, and the fields beyond the sunken fence at the end of the lawn. "This is no place for saying good-byes," he said crossly, half humorously, looking over his shoulder, his eyes returning to the landscape. In the afternoon light the fields had fallen gently into the shapes and folds of bed-clothes around a sleeper. Almost they moved with the slow breathing of sleep. "One doesn't mind leaving the Riviera," Levine said. "One loves it; but one leaves it cheerfully, gracefully . . ."

"Danny . . . one can never be sure, never certain about these things." The doctor seemed to be appealing to his friend. "There are always chances . . ."

Levine laughed at him with kindness. "You're doing your duty," he said. "And I'm doing mine." He held up his sherry glass. " My first drink to-day—and it was only half full. And no cigarette."

" I shouldn't make a burden of it."

" I don't. I shan't. When I get to Cannes, I shall drink myself to death." He had not intended the joke, and it made him chuckle. As he tried to arrest his laughter and choke back the consequent coughing, his face went red. The root of the trouble had, of course, been his lungs and the inoperable fragment of shrapnel. They said that the weakness of the lungs had strained the heart. In a moment or two he had regained control. " That's better," he said to himself, as if he were talking to a child.

" When are you going ? " the doctor asked him.

" The day after to-morrow."

The silence was too overcharged to be supportable; too full of warring thoughts, pictures, suspicions. There was something more that had to be said—that Levine had to add—one way or another. But he did not speak. At last the doctor had to ask the question. " Are you going alone ? "

" Yes, alone." Levine turned quickly towards his friend, towards Dorothy's husband. He had something else to say, probably a protestation, probably the thing that the doctor wanted to be told. But their shyness or the perversity of their natures obstructed his words. It was the doctor who moved. He said that he had a patient to visit. He was on his way to the door.

" Mac ! "

The doctor turned back. The strain of his friend's face was distressing.

" When I get there," Levine said, " I shan't be alone. I shall stay for a bit with Anne Meredith."

That altered it. That shifted the whole emphasis of the word " alone," reducing its impact. The doctor was not yet sure what it meant either to him or to his wife, or to his friend—this rearranged relationship. " Mrs. Meredith ? " he said, with very little expression in his voice. " It's years since I last saw her."

" I'm very . . . fond of her." Levine spoke with difficulty, as if the words, which were more or less meaningless in fact, were of great moment. He was still standing with his back to the window, and he added casually: " I won't see you out, Mac."

" I won't say good-bye."

" No, don't."

"Shall I tell Dorothy?" The doctor spoke from the door. He felt that he had to force his words against the pressure of the room.

"Please tell her."

The doctor nodded. It was an awkward, nervous gesture. Going quickly out of the room, and closing the door, he heard Levine's voice raised: "I shan't be seeing her before I go. I shan't be ringing her up." Through the closed door the doctor heard these words repeated and could imagine that they were a cry of pain. He got to his car, grateful that the study windows looked out on to the garden at the back, and not on to the drive.

Ben had worked his way back along the drive, and his wheelbarrow was now close to the doctor's car. "Does she start all right now?" he asked.

"She starts all right," the doctor said, surprised at the question.

"We had a time with her the other night. It were three in the morning when the Colonel woke me to come and swing her."

"You mean my wife's car?"

"It were the same make as that; same colour an' all."

"Yes."

"It were Mrs. Macdonald trying to start her. It struck three o'clock . . ."

"You know," the doctor said, "the first time I ever saw you, you'd been bitten by a dog. And you were hungry." He got into his car and drove away quickly.

*   *   *

It was late in the evening when the doctor returned to his wife. Tired, he came into his plain little house, tastelessly furnished, where Dorothy, herself so decorative, sat amongst things unlikely and unworthy, as if they were a penance. By the window, now, she was darning his socks; and when he entered she lifted her head, smiled and went to get his meal from the kitchen. They scarcely spoke; and while he was eating she returned to her work, sitting against the evening, interposed between himself and the glow of the shrubs outside. Sometimes she looked towards him with remote affection. When she saw him pour out his second cup of tea, she went to refill the teapot. Then she refilled his cup, standing beside him and behind his chair, but not touching him. "Has it been a horrible day?"

"It has rather." His eyes remained downcast, and he did not dare look round. Feeling the breath of her affection, he could have responded only in the way which she found repulsive.

"Any one specially?"

"Danny Levine," he answered—long before he had meant to speak of him. And now that the movement was started, slow and full of agony, it had to proceed along its own measure.

"Is he worse?" she asked.

"He's very ill."

"He'll recover?"

"I'm not a prophet, my dear; only a doctor."

"I'm not a patient . . ." She said it not crossly, but with a private reproof that he perfectly understood. "Please!" She might have been speaking insistently to a child. "Please!"

There was a long space of silence between the questions and their answers. Neither the words nor the waiting for the words could release them from a stillness in which they were queerly stationed, fixed, as if posed by a photographer. Although he had finished his meal, he sat squarely at the table, looking at his empty plate. After touching his knife and fork, putting them straight, and then the salt cellar and the pepper pot, he rested his hands, palm downwards, on the tablecloth. And still she stood behind him, asking again: "He'll recover?"

"Haven't you seen him lately?" At once he despised and condemned himself for the question.

"A few days ago," she answered. "I was with him for half the night."

He had nothing to say to this reply. Whatever it meant, there was no guilt to be admitted, for the understanding between them was not restrictive. She could do what she liked, and so could he. But his lips failed to acknowledge the covenant. "Which night was it?"

"The night of the Carters' baby."

"Did you *have* to wait till I got called out on a case?"

"Wait for what?" She spoke very gently.

"To sneak away to him." None of these words were his own. He did not think that way, nor even feel that way. It was the pain of his wound that issued words, anger and hatred which came neither from his mind nor his heart. Beneath its wound, his heart loved her. "Sneaking away in the night!"

172

"We didn't make love together," she said.

"It would probably have killed him if you had." He was surprised to have said this, but more surprised that the words came so softly, reflectively, and therefore more cruelly.

"We haven't ever made love together."

"Why not?"

"I don't know. He never suggested it."

This made him laugh, and his laughter increased as he rocked himself over the table. The room was getting dark, and she also had to start laughing, putting her hands on his shoulders, so that they rocked to and fro together in the dusky room. "But he loves you?" he asked suddenly. And this arrested their laughter in the middle of its swing, with his chest resting on the edge of the table, and her hands on his shoulders slowly taking the weight of her overbalanced body.

"Oh . . . we love each other." It was a sort of cry carried on all her breath. Yet he remained crouched over the table; and she could not, or did not, disengage herself.

"Don't you want him to make love to you?"

"I dare say I do," she said, evidently considering her answer very carefully. "I hardly know."

"But you don't mind him touching you, kissing you, holding you?"

"Oh no."

"He does all that?"

"A little, I suppose . . . Not much. Not often . . . Only when it happens." He could not deny how hard she was trying to be truthful. "Only . . . when it means something else."

He lowered his head until his forehead was resting on the table and her hand was in his hair. "Why did you marry me?" he cried.

"I thought . . . I thought I was made that way . . . to hate all men touching me."

"Then why marry?"

"Medically speaking," she answered primly, "I ought to have got over it."

"But why *me*?" he asked miserably.

"Because I loved you."

Before he was aware of any intention to move, he had got up abruptly, almost knocking her over. He found that his hand was

173

on her elbow, holding it until she had got her balance. "Every month," he said, "I deliver babies conceived without love. Any other woman—any woman—seems able to make love without loving. But not you! Not you, dear . . . my dear . . ." He was aware that his love for her was a true and pure emotion. "You have to do it the other way round. To love, but not to make love . . . Only to love."

"I know," she said submissively. "If you know any way to make me different . . ."

"My dear, I'm not the Creator."

"You're a doctor."

"Why didn't you marry *him*?" he asked, "when Ruth died . . . when he was free? You could have gone then."

"I wasn't a Jewess."

"You could have become a Jewess—if he really minded."

"They won't let you."

"Rubbish!"

"Not if it's just because you want to marry. Not if you don't believe in God."

"Do *they* all believe in God?" He laughed; he almost spat.

"If you want to become one of them," she said, "it's different. I don't know why. But it is."

He turned on her then, having taken all that he was going to stand. "So you've found out all about it?"

She nodded. In the dark room, he knew that she nodded.

"Well, *I'll* tell *you* something," he said. "He gave me a message for you." Now it was too far gone to be put tenderly. "He's going away. Very soon he's going."

"When?" The question was whispered out of the darkness.

"The day after to-morrow . . . to the South of France. I was to tell you."

"For long?"

"Yes."

"For ever?"

He knew that his silence must be more terrible than any answer. And while he was glad of his own cruelty, he shared the pain that it was causing her. Neither the gladness nor the pain was escapable.

"Andy—when will he be back?" Her voice was normal—but more than normally expressionless. And she had used his name, which she did rarely. "Please, Andy . . ." It was not a plea, but the sort of cold reproof that she had used earlier in this conversation, as if it was said to a child refusing obedience. "Please!"

So he said outright: "He can't live very long. Didn't he tell you?"

She was quite invisible, but her voice said: "I suppose I almost guessed it." Then he could see and hear movement, as if she was searching about the room for a bag or coat. She said—in a vague, almost irritated voice: "I suppose I'd better go and see him."

"He doesn't want you to."

"Oh, I dare say . . ."

"I was to tell you that he wouldn't be seeing you before he went; that he wouldn't be ringing you up."

Without speaking, and apparently without finding her bag or coat, she went out of the room, out of the house. In a moment he heard the grate of the garage doors on the gravel, and then the starter of one of the cars. At first it failed to start, but later it was driven on to the drive, close to the open window of the room where he waited. Leaning out, she called: "Mine won't start. I'm taking yours."

"*Must* you?"

"I put your bag in the garage . . . and a roll of lint from the back seat . . ." She drove away.

When she had gone, he turned on the lights and started to read *The Times*. Very carefully, he followed and mentally disputed the first two leading articles. Then the telephone rang: as usual, it was the district nurse, and urgent. "I'll be with you in half an hour," he told her. Although he was pretty sure that he could start his wife's car, he made allowance for the delay it might cause him.

When he had unscrewed the feed-pipe sufficiently to see that the petrol was coming through, he started to check the ignition. It was getting late when headlights lit the tops of the shrubbery outside the garage. His wife was returning.

"Thank God!" he said, opening the door for her. "It's the Barrett girl—a bad hæmorrhage." As she got out, he took her place in the driving-seat.

She stood in the drive, dazed, saying: "He's gone. He's gone already. He went this evening."

"So soon? He said the day after to-morrow." With his foot

on the clutch, and the car in gear, the doctor waited for just a moment. " He said he was going to stay with Mrs. Meredith."

" Why? Why *her*? "

" I really don't know, my dear. I daren't wait now." As he drove off, he called: " Don't worry . . . don't worry, dear. I'll be back soon."

The moment he had gone, she remembered his bag. She called after him, but the car had turned out of the drive and was accelerating down the lane. Getting the bag from the garage, she ran after him down the lane in a futile, ungainly gallop. " Andy, Andy, Andy . . ." she called in the darkness, her voice high and breathless. " Oh . . . Andy, Andy! " Her voice shuddered.

Soon she stopped running and turned back, carrying the bag in her arms as if she were holding a baby. " Where is he, where is he, where is he? " she cried aloud, as she stumbled into her home.

*   *   *

Levine was at his club in London. It was after the doctor had gone that the house near Neapcaster, and all the solaces of that countryside, had at last seemed outworn and of no more use to Levine's limited existence. The anachronisms had become intolerably apparent to one who was about to depart and who had entered a different world—of different hearts and tongues—from those who were staying behind. The words, the gestures, the visions of those others were archaic, and their sufferings scarcely comprehensible. The things that mattered to them had become comic, like primitive taboos—a scandal, a fashion, a debt, a credit, a social distinction. Levine was free of the lot of them. He rang the bell.

The man who answered was unlikeable but competent. He entered the room softly, carrying a silver salver on which were set a medicine bottle and glass, a Waterford jug of water, a box of pills, a spoon. Why the spoon? He walked all the way to the table by the window, to put down the salver.

" You've been a long time, Hicks." What a thing to say to a man whom you would see for the last time within an hour!

" I'm very sorry, sir. I was upstairs packing."

" I'm going to drive to London to-night."

" Ought you to do that, sir? "

" I want to leave in half an hour—the big car. Please tell Victor."

"Your luggage . . ."

"Oh, don't fuss!" Levine said. "I'll just take a suitcase to-night. You can bring up the rest to-morrow."

The man went to the door but turned back to ask: "Will Victor be away for the night, sir?"

"For two nights at least," Levine said impatiently, watching the man withdraw in his leisurely manner, watching the door so slowly closing until, at last, the room was empty. But there was no longer any use to be made of this emptiness; it was only by habit that solitude was desired in this room where Levine had worked. He crossed to the door and called to Hicks loudly until the man, coming from the upstairs room to the head of the staircase, answered him soothingly. "It's all right, sir. I'm coming."

"Quickly!" Levine said. "I want to go quickly."

"I understand, sir."

Levine returned to the study. There was so much to be done, but no way of knowing what it was; so much to do, presumably, but nothing to be done with an hour. He could cross the room to the window, recross it to the door, to the desk, to the cupboard beside the fireplace, to the window again, to the chair! An hour had to be consumed. "Creator of time—take away this hour!" Levine looked at his watch and looked at the clock on the mantelpiece.

From his window he looked upon the small but lovely garden with its long strip of lawn running like a river into the pastures; the pastures running more swiftly down the steepening hill. There the heifers grazed, the yearlings, a likely bunch to be brought to the bull after Christmas, to calve-down and go into the milking herd, starting their useful lives, in almost exactly a year's time. . . . Was there no prospect that was painless? Even the elms had next year's buds already formed beneath the dying foliage. Where could a man's thoughts dwell in peace? "Thou leadest me by the still waters . . . Yea, though I walk through the valley . . ."

Levine looked at his watch and checked it again with the clock. The Lord had taken away nearly ninety seconds. Levine laughed aloud. "I can laugh. I can still laugh. While the heart beats and the lungs breathe, air can be expelled in laughter. I will lift up mine eyes unto the hills . . ." But he did not dare to pray, because to pray might be to weep. And soon that man would return to ask questions. He, or somebody else of the staff—Ben or Victor or the cook or the housemaid—would want their orders. How futile and irrelevant his answers would have to be! Levine clenched his fists and raised his arms, feeling the muscles, all the way through to his chest, still powerful. How brilliantly drawn, how mechanically brilliant while it lasted, was a man's body! "What can I do?" The clocks stood still. "What can I do?" He was a child with tears in his eyelids. He was a Man, made in the image of God, with courage in his heart.

"Excuse me, sir, will you want a dinner-jacket to-night?"

"Not to-night, thank you, Hicks. But would you please ring up the club and say that I want a bedroom?"

The man withdrew towards the door, but he did not go. "Excuse me, sir . . . I don't want to disturb you . . ."

"What is it, Hicks?"

"How long will you be away, sir?"

"I can't say at all."

"And while you *are* away, sir . . . what orders. . . ."

A man, of course, could not just walk out of his household, out of a life, an entity, that had been built around his needs and whims, leaving it suspended in space, without direction or impulse, until at last its momentum was expended and it fell disintegrated. "Master David," Levine said. "Mr. David," he corrected himself.

"He will be giving us orders?"

Levine nodded. "He'll be back in a couple of weeks."

"There, in my son," Levine thought, as Hicks withdrew, "there is my only perpetuity; there, and perhaps in some of the things that I have written . . . perhaps." But, like any beast of the field or forest, his certain perpetuity, his only certainty, was his son.

He found he was sitting at his desk where, in spite of a general clearance, a spiritual disinfection of the room and of his dead life, there was still a pile of clean foolscap and a fountain pen. He found that he had unscrewed the pen and had written: "*My dear Dave* . . ."

He breathed deeply as he felt that uplifting of himself—as if a current of air had caught the wings of a kestrel—and felt that power of his kind beating within himself so that, as a pig rooted in the earth and a cow cleansed her calf, his heart had vision. He wrote quickly, but not easily, and not without many corrections. The corrections gave him especial pleasure, as each phrase, each

178

sentence, and at last each paragraph, got its weight and shape and impact.

"Excuse me, sir . . . Victor is ready."

"Is the car at the door?"

"Yes, sir."

Leaving a sentence uncompleted, he wrote at the bottom of the page: "The car is here, and I must go." Then he signed the sheet: "*Your loving father, Daniel Levine.*" And he added the date. "I'm coming, Hicks," he said.

Before he had got to the door, he turned back. Taking up the sheets that he had written, he put them in the top drawer of his desk; and before shutting and locking the drawer, he let his eye cover the top page. "Did I write *that*! What a humbug I am with a pen!"

"I'm just coming, Hicks."

"There's no hurry, sir." It was another of the man's soothing remarks. Haste was the master's prerogative.

Levine reread the paragraphs. "*Very well! Now that little Mac has named the day, or very nearly, putting a limit on my life, drawing its frontier, I am free to choose between faith and disbelief as between two practical propositions.*

"*If I choose disbelief, I may indulge in any form of gratification that my body permits ('Eat, drink and be merry,' etc.), for the only remaining prohibitions will be physical. I may become a beast. But the prospect of dying as a beast is the source of all human fear—the fear which drives one to faith. And yet, because one is driven towards faith in this way, faith becomes terribly suspect: it is too easy. It is much less easy to be a beast and to turn round at the end, to face the fear like a tired fox. It is braver to be a beast.*

"*Beastliness, however, seems not only unattractive, but palpably a false state for whatever creature I am. By the very circumstance that, sitting in the shadow of death, I can see the frontier of life—and not merely guess it—and that I can see it as a frontier—and not as a wall of animal fear, like a wall of mist—I must assume that I am something more than a man-beast; that Man has to be written with a capital 'M'; and that my lifelong lip-service to Man, as a creature made in the image of God, is founded on truth. That is the total of my faith—that little knowledge.*"

He turned over the page.

"*This little knowledge is enough to make my past and present life look ridiculous. How have I been able to direct eighty or ninety per cent of my interest and effort to such irrelevancies as personal power, owner-ship, gain—instead of personal fulfilment? I just can't think! I have spent all my life declaring the Law and at the same time breaking it.*

"*The Law of life—if man is above beast—must be personal fulfil-ment. Jesus the Jew reduced it to a single command: 'Give away all, and follow Me.' But Christianity has spent the last two thousand years shuffling and twisting that order into a pack of rules, regulations, habits, traditions which make obedience to the Law itself quite impossible. Look at them! Look at the civilisation which is called 'Christian'! Look how it has stood the law on its head so that 'thou shalt not steal' has become 'thou shalt not eat'; 'thou shalt not covet' has become 'trespassers will be prosecuted'; 'thou shalt not bear false witness' has become 'the greater the truth, the greater the slander'; etc., etc.!*

"*I cannot myself obey the command of Jesus the Jew, because any-thing that I give away now is no longer mine to give. The doctor's verdict has already given it to you. All I can do is to go away, to get clear of the entanglement of personal property and to hope, in that freedom, for some last-minute chance before death of entering the Law of life.*

"*The Law of life that is the law of personal fulfilment is, of course, love. And the rules by which I have lived until now prohibit love, and even invest the word 'love' with meanings contrary to the truth. Seen from the shadow, Love looks like a breaking away from Self, in the same sort of way as a butterfly breaks out of its chrysalis. One feels that, if one could only comprehend the human chrysalis, earthbound life and Self would appear to be one human state, and Love another. And as soon as one thinks of it in this way, the choice between disbelief and faith, between being a beast and being a man, is nothing more than a choice of motives—greed or love.*

"*And if only it was a normal function of man that he could know from his childhood (say) the hour of his death, just think how easy his choice! He would lift up his eyes to the hills because elsewhere they would meet with too little love . . .*"

He left it and looked at the last page—at the very conclusion:

"*I know that I have written in this only trite, outworn things that are said constantly by every professional preacher, and are believed periodi-cally by almost every man and woman in the course of their lives. I do not suppose that it has been given to me to think one new thought, or to write one original phrase, worthy of perpetuity. But the point of the letter is this. When one can actually see the frontier, the physical end, and is driven by fear to faith—or freed from flight for faith—one becomes aware,*

*without doubt, that these trite things are verities. And one is able, I
hope . . . "*

Levine had come to the end of his interest. He wanted to read
no more. Closing the drawer and locking it, he went to the door
and found Hicks waiting outside it, discreetly invisible. " Would
you give this key to Mr. David? " Levine asked him.

The man would, of course, open the drawer and look and
perhaps even read what was written—or a few lines of it. " And
that odd chance," Levine thought, " may, by some queer chain of
consequence, perpetuate myself! " The man might act on what
he read, or react against it, or in some way alter, vary, allow to be
influenced . . .

Outside the door of his study, Levine turned back for a second
time. Going to his desk, he put the cap on his fountain pen, so
that dried ink would not encrust the nib, so that it would be ready
for writing when next . . . " I must really throw away habit," he
said. " I must, I *must* throw away a lifetime! "

In the hall, Hicks helped him on with a light overcoat. " It's
a warm evening, sir."

The big car was waiting by the front door. As they drove off,
Levine said to Victor: " Drive me to London quickly."

" You're always in a hurry, aren't you? " Victor said. " Always
the same." He was grinning and he shook his head.

* * *

From habit, Levine entered the club too quickly. Habitually—
but a long time ago—he had come here for shelter from the storms
which he himself generated, and to escape from the state of volcanic
crisis created by his own urgency that made, so it seemed, all under-
takings too big and all time too little, for human capacities. Therefore he had always stretched his purpose, straining for unnatural
achievement, yet always advancing his destination as he advanced
himself, so that his destination could never be reached and he
could never rest. It was only when he had hastened into the club,
parting the two swing-doors with both hands, striding up the
broad steps towards the hall, plunging into the dimness of panelled
walls and discreet chambers, that he felt the pressure that had got
built up inside himself immediately diminished.

That past was indelible but dead. There was no haste, no need
for refuge now. But by habit, and forgetting his weakness, he

scrambled out of his car as soon as it halted and entered his club with usual urgency. At the second stair he had to halt, to calm his breath. It was even an effort to step aside so that a grey cripple could pull himself up by the handrail. Of the many old men in the club—Levine thought as he waited—none could have long to live, but few could have a fixed sight of death, of the shadow itself. Therefore they had no prospect at all, but only a fear of the dusk where death supposedly hid. As they advanced in uncertainty, the dusk increased, and visibility diminished, so that death was always unseen until it was finally met.

"We who can see," Levine thought, as he tried to feel charitably towards the glowering cripple on his way past, "we have to be patient with the old gentlemen of faulty vision." He could understand, now, how their half-light made big the trivialities—the favourite arm-chair, the seemly behaviour, the low voice. "Those things can't matter to us . . . they are seen in their proper size by us who have been measured and fitted for death. As if an oculist had fixed us up with new spectacles . . ."

The club porter sat in a glass box at the top of the stairs, guarding a second pair of swing-doors, glass panelled. Expecting no letters or messages, Levine did not stop.

"Excuse me, sir," the man called. "Who did you wish to see?"

"Nobody." Levine opened the doors ahead of him. It was, of course, a new man in the box; but it was not pleasant to be unrecognised.

"Excuse me, sir—are you a member?"

Standing between the swing-doors, with his foot holding them half open, Levine said: "I've been a member for thirty years." He passed on, letting the door swing behind him.

But the little man, in his green-liveried coat and striped waistcoat, was persistent. Coming out of his box, he followed Levine through the doors and into the hall where members gathered before meals or waited for guests. "Excuse me, sir . . . what name, sir?"

"Levine."

"Beg pardon, sir?"

"Dammit—you can take my word!"

"It's the secretary's orders, sir . . ."

"Good God!"

182

Levine stood still, his great height seeming to be folded up as he felt the compression in his chest, his hearing punctured by a massive resonance, a low beat, as if a sounding-board, a drum-skin, had been brought within reach of his heart. He tried to take a slow, easy breath. As he exhaled, his chest quivered, and his vision of the room tilted. He heard his own voice, almost falsetto, clutching his breath: "What . . . damned . . . impertinence!" Losing his balance and his sight, he seemed to be supported by hands which lowered him into a chair.

"What's up, Danny?" The very comfort of the voice that asked the question put Levine back into infancy. "Whatever's the matter, old chap?"

"That . . . damned . . . porter," Levine said with effort. And with his eyes still dark, managed to move his body until it seemed to be almost upright in the chair. "Wouldn't let me into . . . my own club." He felt like weeping about it.

"Terribly irritating, old chap."

Quite speedily the light returned and infancy receded. Levine saw Guy Bredon and the porter standing on either side of him. "You were only doing your duty," Levine said to the porter.

"That's better, Danny. The porter'll get you a glass of water."

"No, no—I'm all right, Guy."

"Take it easy for a moment. Do you think—a doctor?"

"Lord, no! This happens occasionally."

The poor little porter stood unhappily by the chair, his body inclined deferentially towards the two members, and his hands clasped.

★　　★　　★

Guy nodded to the porter. He could not, of course, give the man a wink; but he tried to convey to him that he was blameless, and that he should go away.

"You were only doing your duty," Levine repeated.

Sitting carelessly on the arm of his friend's chair, Guy looked down on him and smiled at this insistence on the porter's blame-lessness. There was no one who lost his temper so easily as Danny, and who was so ashamed of it so quickly afterwards. "Very irritating all the same," he said, and felt it to be true. "But hardly enough . . . Have you had this sort of turn before?"

Danny shook his head. "Not exactly," he answered; "not so foolishly. Lately . . . I haven't been too well, you know."

"I didn't know, old chap."

It became a queer, strained conversation until Guy looked at the clock on the wall above Danny's head, wondering if he could now catch his train.

Danny must have noticed. In a curiously formal voice, as if he were still ashamed, he said: "Don't let me keep you, Guy. I'm quite all right."

"I've nothing to do, nothing at all," Guy said. "Just take it easy for a few minutes."

"Is it very late?"

"Lord, no!" Guy adjusted his considerable weight so as to get at his gold watch in a waistcoat pocket. "Blow!" he said to himself, remembering how, when he was a child, his grandfather used to make him blow on to this very watch before he opened it, and blow again before he flicked with his thumbnail a second time, making it strike. "The quarter," he said.

"Quarter-past nine, Guy? You'll miss your train."

"I'm not going back to-night." It was another of his habits to allow himself to prevaricate, but not to lie direct. "Not hungry, are you?"

Levine shook his head. "But you—you were going to eat on the train."

"You couldn't do with a drink?"

"I could, but I mustn't. Little Mac says . . . ." He did not finish it.

"Is this something new? Not just the old trouble with that lump of lead?"

"I guessed I should find you here, Guy. I expected to."

"A pretty safe guess if I was in town at all."

For some time they talked in this manner, until Guy felt that he had the outline of the situation. Content to let the picture develop in its own time, his only concern was to render whatever service his friend required of him. "D'ye like this place?" he asked, looking round the rather dreary hall, noting with a distant nod the few acquaintances who were passing through.

"I can't say I do."

"Let's make a move, then. Where do you fancy?" He put his hand under Danny's arm, to help him from his chair and then along the passage to the smoking-room, a long and narrow place, now almost empty. An old, old gentleman was writing at one of the tables, but the sofa beneath the far window was isolated and private. The curtains were drawn, heavy and crimson; and before sitting down, Danny twitched them aside to look into the clear night. "I'm going to visit Anne," he said.

Nobody took longer than Guy to settle himself in comfort. "Does she want you?" he asked at last.

"She sent me a Christmas card last year—*joyeux Noel*, you know, and the Virgin in relief."

"She did that to all of us. Queer—after five years' silence!"

"I sent her a telegram a few weeks ago. She answered that she'd like to have me."

"Did she, Danny? Did she?" He repeated the phrase several times, not as a question, nor in surprise, but as cover for his explanations. "We were all so fond of her, so fond of her . . . And then—this!"

"I never understood what happened. I could never find out."

"Nor me, Danny."

"Harry wouldn't tell you? And you must be his closest friend."

"Wouldn't even discuss it . . . I had my guess, of course, like every one else."

"You think she couldn't stick Neapcaster after . . . after . . ."

"I doubt if it was that." Guy was filling his pipe. "It's my belief, my feeling, that he turned her out. Though why . . . though how . . . But maybe you'll find that out." He spent several matches getting his pipe alight. "But I don't suppose that's why you're visiting her, is it?"

"Not exactly."

"You're goin' alone, Danny?"

"Quite alone." They were sitting side by side on the sofa, very contented together.

"Are you trying to . . . forget Dorothy?"

"Does every one know about that?"

Smiling, Guy put his hand on Danny's knee. "Most of 'em talk about it, y'know."

"I suppose so," Levine said. But it seemed important, for the sake of Dorothy, or perhaps for the sake of little Mac, that Guy should know the truth. "I ought . . . I ought to tell you that we've never made love together."

185

"I shouldn't think the worse of you if you had."

"But we haven't."

"Then you've been . . . somewhat indiscreet." There seemed to be no criticism, but only warmth and friendship in this comment. "And to so little purpose!" Guy added, so that they both laughed.

"She wouldn't have me," Levine said lightly, conventionally, so that he could change direction and ask: "You've heard, I suppose, that Anne's been ringing up Harry? About a girl, it seems, a relative . . . coming to Neapcaster."

"I hadn't heard . . ." But Guy, after some thought, nodded. "It'll be that child, I dare say . . . Alex, I think she's called . . . Raoul Seytoun's girl. He might have drunk himself to death at last."

"That'll please Harry," Levine said. "He has her picture on his desk, hasn't he?"

"Used to, anyway . . . I should say he's thought a lot about that child, almost set his heart on her since . . . since Anne left him." He had got up from the sofa and was going towards the bell. "Talkin' of Raoul, I've just got to have a drink! And you mayn't join me?"

"I shall all the same."

"What would little Mac say about it?"

"It doesn't matter." Danny laughed at the memory of his own remark to the doctor in that context. "He told me not to make a burden of it."

"Danny—did he tell you something . . . pretty bad?"

"That's why I wanted to see you, Guy. The will and everything is being seen to—Barry has got it all. I wanted to put you in the usual place . . ."

"Danny—what did he tell you?"

"Could we talk about the will first? As my executor, Guy, and David's trustee, I rather hoped . . ."

"Of course, Danny, of course . . ." He seemed to speak with relief as he now let his mind loose along the channels where it ran with its greatest precision and certainty, detached from all other parts of himself, such as his heart. It was almost curtly that he asked, when Danny had done explaining his affairs: "It's all tied up tight, I trust?"

"I wanted to talk to you first."

"I should, Danny, I should! David's a sensible chap—but young, heartfree."

"You know, Guy, times may change. It may be for the best, one day, to let him get at his capital."

"Don't you believe it, Danny! Times won't change as much as that!"

"*You* know best," Levine said submissively. "That waiter's taking his time!"

"He is, isn't he?" Heavily, ponderously, Guy got himself off the sofa and rolled across the room to the bell beside the fireplace. When he returned and was again seated, he put his hand on Danny's knee. "Well, old chap . . . let's have it!"

"Nobody else knows," Levine said, glad to have been drawn at last, "but Mac told me that I have a very short time to live."

Guy was back on the sofa. His hands were on his knees, and he was leaning forward, so far forward that his head was bowed. When he spoke, his voice was sorely strained. "How short . . . Danny?"

"A few months, perhaps. Certainly no more than that. That's why I'm going to France . . . I'm not coming back."

Guy spoke quickly, as if he dared not let a silence be established. "Doesn't even Dorothy know?" he asked.

"Mac has probably told her."

"Not even David? He's in the States, isn't he?"

"Not David. He'll be back in a fortnight. I've left him a letter."

"Danny—is there no doubt about it?" Guy's voice was low and full of pain.

"No doubt—so they say."

"And you're running away from us? Away from all your friends, from all your past . . ."

"I'm not running away."

"Danny!" It was as if Guy did not know what he wanted to say, except to express a love for which no words existed. But the waiter had come into the room, in answer to the bell, and had come soundlessly to the sofa across the deep carpet.

"Two large whiskies-and-soda," Guy said.

When the waiter had gone, Danny said: "Tell me more about Alex. Try to remember." Then, without waiting for an answer, he said: "I wonder what Anne's made of Edith's villa?

187

You knew it, didn't you, in the old days? You remember, don't you . . ." He was thinking of that lovely terrace, that lovely view across the harbour to the Esterelle, that view of the sunset when the red rocks lost their colour as the sun fell behind the mountains, as the shadows spread over the sea.

*   *   *

At half-past eleven on the morning of Levine's arrival at the villa, there was only a strange young man—unshaven, wearing pale blue bathing shorts—lying in a long chair on the terrace. He got up slowly and without much courtesy. "I cannot understand where Anne has gone," he said. "I think she knew you were to come. In all cases, some days ago she knew it." His accent was scarcely foreign, but only the phrasing of his speech. Very fair, sunburnt, muscular and good-looking, he made faces as he spoke, representing surprise, perplexity, and so on. "I am sure she knew it . . ."

Levine nodded and sat down on the edge of the sunlight. He lay back, letting the sun rest on his tired face. Then he tilted his hat forward over his forehead. "I suppose there's a man here or something? He'll bring down my bags? There's no hurry."

"There must be Vincent. Did you ring the bell at the door?"

Levine nodded again and closed his eyes, and it was no surprise, but indeed a fulfilment of expectation, when Anne was not at the station and when, in spite of his request by telegram the previous day, no car had been sent to meet him; and again, when the Customs were locked and there was a long wait before they could find the *douanier* to check his registered baggage; and again, after the taxi had stopped at the decorative gates of wrought-iron on the uphill side of the villa, and Levine had descended the steps into the courtyard and rung the bell, that there was no answer.

He had asked the driver to put his baggage inside the gates, at the top of the steps. It was pleasant to hear fluent French coming from one's own tongue, to pay the man in French currency, and to feel again the heat of the sunlight and the crisp contrast when one entered and emerged from shadow. It was not even unpleasant, but simply to be expected, to find this rather offensive, effeminate but muscular young man reading a book on Anne's terrace.

"If I'm not expected," Levine said, "I can always go to the Carlton."

The young man shrugged. "They may have a room there. It is possible." He raised his arms and let them fall again. Turning away, he walked to the edge of the terrace and looked down upon the path between the cacti and upon the pines that enclosed the bathing pool. Levine, lying back in his chair, looked only on to the calm and bright sea with the red mountains behind it. From the edge of the terrace, the young man asked: "You know this villa?"

"I used to—years ago, when Lady Parkes was here."

"Lady Parkes?" The young man shook his head. "I have not the pleasure . . ." He smiled; he flashed and flickered his face as he shook his head again. "Alex should be here," he said.

"Is she staying here?"

"She sleeps here."

With his eyes closed, Levine asked: "Is her father dead?"

"Happily, yes; since last Monday. And they say that she behaved perfectly at the funeral, very correct, very . . . surprising."

Shifting in his chair, Levine felt the sun already too hot for the clothes he was wearing. "My baggage," he said; "I'm not allowed to carry anything heavy. The bags are not very heavy, but too heavy . . ." He looked expectantly at the young man.

Still peering over the edge of the terrace, the young man shook his head. "Vincent . . . I cannot understand it. He may of course have taken a cocktail to Alex . . . Alex may be at the pool . . ." Now he seemed quite upset about this lack of hospitality. "What can one do?"

It seemed quite an effort for Levine to get out of his chair and move into the shade. The effort was uncompleted when he heard Anne's voice, calling for Vincent. In the pleasant, imperious and almost husky note of her call, his memory was so perfectly restored that he found his back straightened and his vigour recovered as he turned towards the house and waited for her to come out to him. She must be running down the steps, passing the fountain in the courtyard, crossing the big hall towards the archway of iron and glass that looked on to the sea, coming through the archway and on to the terrace. Levine faced her, and she was there. She ran like a child into his arms.

"Danny, Danny my sweet!"

Holding her in his arms, he was astounded to feel a pulse of love, almost of passion, making him laugh and kiss her and laugh again, as there had always been laughter in her presence. In the restoration of the years, he felt the quickness of himself that he had forgotten. "Not a pound heavier," he cried, lifting her by the elbows, "not a wrinkle, not an eyelash new . . ." An intimacy, surely a love, that they had never expressed, never even known before, was renewed. While he talked carelessly and quickly and kissed her again, he thought: "The past is being re-established. I had forgotten the joy of being alive." And even behind or below this thought, current below current, he acknowledged that the past which he was now experiencing was fiction, had never existed. And at the bottom of the deep pool, he remembered clearly, but without pain, his precise circumstances. "But time is only a fiction," he declared finally, as he said to her: "How good this is . . . Oh, how good! Hadn't you forgotten?" While he spoke, he wondered if this was what he had been seeking when, for reasons that he had not been able to establish in his own mind, he had decided to visit her. "What fun, what fun!"

As soon as he released her, she started to pat her hair and to search vaguely for her bag, her powder and lipstick. "I don't understand it . . ." she said slowly. And then, in a voice increasingly sharp, becoming almost shrill: "Those were your bags inside the door? Why didn't Vincent, why didn't some one . . . didn't Alex meet you?"

"I took a taxi," he said; "it was all perfectly simple."

She was angry. She stamped on the terrace. "Oh, that girl, that girl!" She looked around and saw the young man, sitting with his back to her, gazing out to sea. "And you, Fritz! What were you doing? Why didn't you bring down his baggage? Why are you here?" She gave him no chance to reply. He turned to face her, spreading out his golden arms, appealing, while she stamped her foot, clenched her fists and threw words, questions, abusive questions into his face. "I thought you were going out for the day? Didn't I tell you to go out? Didn't I tell you to be out to lunch? Didn't I tell you to get away from me, to get out?"

"Chérie," he said appealingly, "chérie . . ."

"I told you to get out."

"My dear Anne . . ."

"I told you . . ."

"You told me nothing." Suddenly he lost his temper. "You asked me nothing. You gave me nothing." He spoke in a high, harsh voice. "Nothing at all!"

" Oh . . ." she cried. It was a shudder of rage, a terrible gesture. Her face and manner were terrible. The whole exchange, the whole scene—concocted out of the sunlight, stabbing like a red and black explosion out of the sunlight—was terrible with unreality. She swung herself round towards the villa and went into the archway. " Come here! " she called in a voice that was almost masculine. " Come here! "

Obediently Fritz followed her into the villa. As he passed Levine, he shrugged, spread out his hands and smiled. In a moment Anne returned. " Danny—please, please lend me some money." She was quivering. " Please . . . please! "

" Of course, of course . . ." He tried to soothe her, to beseech her. He held out his note-case. " Anything . . . anything you like."

When she took the note-case, her fingers trembled so much that the money fell and drifted in the warm wind all over the terrace. Levine found it difficult to stoop to retrieve the notes. When he was on his knees he felt weak and dizzy.

" Danny, Danny . . ." she cried. She was kneeling beside him, and there were tears in her eyes. There was already a tear on her cheek.

" Give him that," Levine said, holding out a bundle of notes. He had to breathe deeply when he spoke. " Give him that lot."

" No, no—that's ridiculous. That's much too much." She was laughing and crying. " Absurd, idiotic, Danny dear! "

He got to his feet, feeling that it needed all the rest of his life's energy to do so and to cross the terrace to the archway. Inside the hall, Fritz was waiting. Obviously he had been looking out and watching them, but now he turned his back.

" Here, you! " Levine said. " Mrs. Meredith asked me to give you this." It was a large sum of money.

Taking the money and running his fingers through the notes, counting them approximately, Fritz smiled. He looked up and winked. " In settlement? " he asked.

" I hope so."

" As you say, *Monsieur*."

Levine turned away. When he got back to the end of the terrace where he had left Anne, she was not there. Sitting down again, he was surprised to find his breathing calm and his heart quiet. He felt perfectly well, and he was surprised, also, that he was enjoying himself. People were living again; this was living;

this was human life. He laughed as he got up from his chair, because Alex was coming up the path from the bathing pool. There had never been a more beautiful creature. He watched her coming up the path. In fact she was not beautiful, but only fascinating.

The path was steep and ended in a flight of steps that led to the terrace. Alex was coming up the steps between the cactus plants, the geraniums and the early mimosa. Levine could hear her voice, rather deep and liquid, talking in French to the man who followed. He wore a bow tie and a white coat, and he carried a tray with a cocktail shaker and a glass on it. Over his free arm he had her bathing wrap. Still in her bathing things and sandals, she threw her wet hair over her shoulder as she laughed and talked to the servant, Vincent. Her very dark hair reached just to the shoulder blades.

★   ★   ★

At some distance away, she waved; and as she came closer, she waved again and said " Hallo " with a warm drawl, as if she were an American, one of the Southerners. " Isn't Anne back? Isn't Fritz here? " She stood swinging her bathing cap.

" Anne is back," he answered, " but she went into the house, I think, but not through the hall; it must have been through that room we used to call the library. Though why we did—when there wasn't ever a book in it, but only picture papers . . ."

" It's still the same . . . The *Tatler* mostly."

Levine thought: " So here I am, right back again! " He was hugely happy. It was the perfectly inconsequential world, rootless, superficial, in which one had no obligations to oneself or anybody else or any other thing, except to one's pleasures and passions. One chose and acted a part to be gay, witty, amusing, irrelevant, until one's passions clamoured for a fling, and then one let them go for a romp and a ravage, and gathered them up again later without the least embarrassment. She was asking: " And where's Fritz? "

" Oh, he's gone," Levine answered.

" Has somebody sent him packing? It was high time, wasn't it? " Her English expression and accent were normally faultless; yet one would have known that she had not been brought up in England. Her idiomatic phrases, especially, seemed to disclose a hesitation, a time for translation, between thought and speech.

And with some words—*Tatler*, for instance—the stress slipped back to the final syllable.

" Anne did tell him . . ." he started to say.

" Oh—she's always telling him to . . . clear out. She'll soon want him back again . . . Have *you* come to lunch, because I don't know if . . ."

" I've come to stay. I've only been here a little time."

" I was thinking your clothes were rather curious."

" Yes—I must change."

Then she put her hand to her mouth. " Oh . . . oh . . . oh . . . You aren't Mr. Levine? "

" I am, as a matter of fact."

She repeated her cry. " I had forgotten . . . how *could* I forget? I was to meet you . . ." She went up to him and gave him both her hands. " Not for anything would I have forgotten . . ."

" It didn't matter in the least."

" I was to take Anne's car. She will be furious . . ."

But Anne, returning to the terrace, only said: " You really are a naughty and thoughtless child! Poor Danny! And there was I, spending all the morning at the Consul at Nice . . . so stupid, he was, over your passport . . . such a tiresome little man . . . and then, seeing about the sale of your father's things . . ."

" And I couldn't remember even the one thing that I promised . . . Can you ever forgive me? Can Mr. Levine? "

" You must be very nice to him."

*   *   *

The girl entertained him charmingly when Anne went out for dinner. On the terrace the three of them had watched nightfall, from its stages when the sun was low above the red mountains whose seaward slopes, with all the raw-sienna coast to the west of Cannes, had already gone colourless, lightless, dissolving into dusk, to the very end of the day when a peak cut into the sun's circumference and, a few minutes later, the stretching shadows reached the villa like a chill tide. On the greater heights behind the villa, and on the equal heights to the east, there was still sunlight. Those people there had a longer day. And as Levine thought: " No, even here, I have not escaped! " Anne shrugged and rose from her chair, saying that she found it cold and wanted a jersey.

" I'll get it," Alex said.

"No . . . I want to go up anyway, because . . ." There was perhaps a moment of hesitation, even embarrassment, before she said: "Danny—you wouldn't, I suppose, like to go to a party to-night; a party on a man's yacht?"

"Whatever you say, Anne."

"You don't sound very enthusiastic . . ." She was awkward, unsure. "But if you don't feel inclined, Danny, you won't be letting me down, because I can always get, you see . . ."

Levine said quickly: "You go without me. I'll be quite happy here alone."

"Oh, you won't be alone," she said. "Alex won't want to come, not on her last night, and with an early start and all that travelling to-morrow. . . ."

When Anne had left them, Alex said: "She's gone to ring up Fritz. It is terrible to get old. I suppose one day I shall have need of a Fritz myself." Even with this reminder, Levine found it hard to believe that she was only seventeen.

"There she goes!" Alex said an hour later, when they heard a car arrive on the road above and behind the villa, then voices, then a car door slam, then the car driving off.

Thoughtlessly Levine said: "She never came to say good night!"

"She's ashamed, you see," said Alex, combing her hair, as they sat with a table and cocktails between them. "I don't suppose I shall see her again—not ever, perhaps. I don't suppose she'll be back before lunch-time to-morrow."

*　　　*　　　*

Alex was able to talk without the impediment of thought. "Anne said I ought to cut my hair. She said it was too long for England, for the country, for Neapcaster; either too long or not long enough. But I said: 'One doesn't cut one's hair for a country'; and she said: 'Jeanne d'Arc did.' But then *she* heard voices, didn't she?"

"I suppose so," Levine said, and thus put a silence on her chatter. "I wonder," he thought, "what she's going to try next? We've had the sophistication; we've had the pretence of childishness. *Now* will she get down to it? And down to *what*?"

But she only looked at him steadily with those very large, dark eyes. Then she picked up her *crème de menthe*, threw away the straw and tipped the liquid into her mouth out of its crushed ice. It was some time since dinner, but still some time till they could go to bed.

"You don't want to go to Neapcaster, do you?" he asked suddenly.

"The idea is detestable," she answered at once. "I'm to be sent there—like to prison." He recognised fear in her laugh.

They were sitting on a large balcony, a miniature terrace, that projected out of the dining-room. High overhead there was hung a very bright light to attract the mosquitoes away from human flesh. Danny and Alex faced eastwards, and there was a moon rising and reflected below them on the utterly calm sea. Too much wine, too much moonlight, and faintly there was music! On a wisp of breeze there came the scent of pines. "All the conventions of the coast!" With this bitter touch Levine tried to suppress the conventional response. "But I can't hide from myself that, underneath everything else, I am a conventionalist!" He had not spoken; but he almost murmured aloud, as he looked at the girl: "If I could be lent a week of my youth!" For what she needed was love.

"What a swine, what a hypocrite I am!" And he remembered faintly what he had written about love in his letter to David. Yet the conclusion was true: it was love that she needed; and love she had never had. "But could I ever, in my youth, have given her anything more than embellished lust?" He writhed: "And now what a cynic!" Thus, in an orgy of self-contempt, he struggled with his mind and heart, twisting them like the knobs of a radio set to get them together in tune. "What can I say to her to kill fear?" Knowing the worthlessness of reassurance—for none knew more about fear than he himself—knowing that negations could never penetrate, he started to talk. She seemed to be listening.

*　　　*　　　*

She waited for the destination that, sooner or later, would be reached by him, as by every other man: the distant suggestion or offer of help, the plea, the plan, the start of the track that led inevitably to the same place: "We could hire a car for that week," or perhaps "You can have the spare bunk in the after-cabin; my wife left most of her things behind when she finally cleared out . . ."

Levine was saying: "Three hundred years ago, or very nearly, that's the earliest record my family have got . . ."

Old and sick and subtle, he led her a twisting path. "We who are apt to be homeless . . ." he had said at the start, meaning herself also, putting him and her together, similarly placed; it was a familiar trick. For the time being, he lay slumped in his chair, an enormous man, with his chin on his chest. She waited for the moment when he would lean forward to find with a quick gesture, a happy thought, the way out of her homeless predicament, the way he proposed to help her.

For the third time since coffee had been served after dinner, Vincent came in with the bottles. From her glass he threw the melted ice into the night, having brought her a fresh supply in a little silver bucket. Levine interrupted himself to put his hand over his own glass and to say lazily: "Do you really want that? It's pernicious stuff." And the question was so unexpected—for they always wanted you to drink—that she answered: "No, I don't want it," even though she did.

He waited for Vincent to leave before he went on talking. "That was my mother's family, in the seventeenth century. They came from Spain. And I have a photostat copy of a minute of the Privy Council, about 1680, if I remember right . . ."

"What is the Privy Council?" She had asked the question, and he had answered it and had continued talking for some time, before she knew why she needed that other drink. It was that deep voice which lapped her like the wash of a ship. And as her mistrust dissolved and her watchfulness abated, she felt her helplessness. "What does he want?" But that was not the question. "Why do I care what he wants?" But the big voice carried more than words and seemed to have fingers stroking her. "Some people must have fathers who are like this!" She was terribly ashamed of this notion. Indignantly she thought: "I might be a child, an orphan, frightened, helpless, homeless . . ." For without reason she felt an emptiness that she wanted to fill with tears, with love. To resist this feeling she wanted more *crème de menthe*.

But nothing that he was saying could have reasonably caused these reactions of hers nor have matched her thoughts. He was talking about himself. "So this ancestor of ours, a man called Moses Pachico, was thrown into gaol for practising the Jewish faith and petitioned the King to let him out. His petition went to the Privy Council—and let him out they did! And with several pretty harsh words for the people who'd put him in! And amongst those present with the King that day was the Lord Viscount Neap. And he was a Meredith . . ."

" Not one of our Merediths? " she asked, and again thought it the strangest question to have come from herself.

" Oh, yes—from Neapcaster Park, though it wasn't exactly the same house." It was then that he hoisted himself up and leant forward, making that quick gesture that she had anticipated. " Your prison, my dear, where you say they're sending you . . ."

" You seem to think I'm a child," she said.

" I rather did . . . And I thought you were frightened of going home! "

" It isn't my home."

" But it's *mine*! " he said. " That's what I meant. That's what I tried to tell you because . . ." He clasped his hands as if he was a priest. " *There* one can live without losing oneself. *There* one's self increases. Because there, in England, there are patterns for everything except its people. And its people . . . they hide their diversities behind all sorts of masks, like your own pretty face . . . but are more diverse than anywhere else in the world . . ." Suddenly he had brewed such a passion inside himself that it tumbled her over like a wave and seemed to force him to his feet. " Preciously diverse, and therefore free, and therefore of such strength . . ." He was standing, she thought, like a camel, with his head poked out towards the moonlight as if it was suspended from the air, rather than supported on his body. She almost said: " I like camels." But he was already laughing. " I just don't know how to talk to you, my dear."

" But you do, you do! " she cried.

" I'm too old and sorry for myself . . ." And this remark seemed meaningless to her. " You must forgive me."

" You're not old," she said. " Lots are older than you and they . . ." But what she had in mind did not seem to fit either his aspect or her heart.

* * *

When he was seeing her off at the station, she asked: " Won't you come with me? Won't you take me home? "

" No, I can't do that. I must see Anne again, and I must . . ." He gave her no real reason; and when she was well on her journey she came to believe either that he did not know his reasons himself,

197

or that he feared they would give her some fresh cause for mistrusting her destination. As she approached Neapcaster on the train from Paddington, the latter conclusion seemed the more probable. Now that the deep voice had faded beyond recollection, she was again frightened. Therefore she opened her bag and made up her face as vividly as she could, thus increasing her age and restoring sophistication. " If I am to go to prison . . ." Once more it was prison to which they were sending her. Suspicious and watchful, she stood up as the train halted at a platform that was almost empty. A single passenger got out and took the only porter. There seemed to be no one looking for herself.

" Can I anywhere get a taxi ? "

It was an elderly man with braid on his peaked cap whom she was asking. " A taxi, Miss ? Where do you want to go to ? "

" To Neapcaster Park."

" The General, Miss ? Oh yes, I expect we can find you somebody." He took her suitcase. " Is this all your luggage ? " It was all she had, this one, large case: all that she owned, except for a few clothes, so unsuitable for England—so Anne had said—that she had left them in France. Her lack of luggage now seemed to increase her helplessness.

On the telephone, the stationmaster had tried several garages. " We're out of luck, Miss," he said.

" What about Frank ? " the man in the booking office suggested.

" I hadn't thought of Frank."

A car arrived in a few minutes. " Bit of luck for you, Frank," the stationmaster said to him.

" You're right," Frank said. He meant only that he was glad of the fare. When he saw his passenger, he repeated the words in the same tone as before but, for his own private pleasure, with additional meaning. Alex saw him as a tall, strong, cheery fellow with red hair and a freckled face, but perhaps rascally.

" A young lady for the Park," the stationmaster said.

" If she's for the Park, we'll look after her." With his back to the elderly man, he winked at her. " Will you sit in front, Miss ? "

" As you wish," she answered, regretting it almost at once.

He rattled her along, talking all the time, asking questions that she could scarcely refuse to answer. As soon as he learnt where she had come from, he said: " So you've come from France, Miss,

198

have you? You don't happen to be French?" When she answered that she had lived there all her life, he said: "A real French Mademoiselle, come to Neapcaster Park!" and he turned towards her so that she could see him wink. Then he cried: "I know, I know! I thought I'd seen your face! I've got a wonderful memory for a likeness, but I couldn't put a name to it. But now I can!" He paused to give her the chance to join in the fun, but when she remained silent, he said: "It's Alex, isn't it? Miss Alex?"

"How do you know?" She tried to express a coldness that she scarcely felt.

"I know your picture—that's how! The General put it on his desk—oh, ever so many years ago. You were only a kid, of course, but there's no mistaking it." He laughed, he was gay, frankly enjoying himself with this exciting girl from France. She was rather pleased by it. "What's more, I can remember the very day that picture came. What a day it was! What a coincidence!" He was not at all restrained by her silence. "That day!" he said. "It lost me a job. It got me a wife. And it got me two hundred quid from the General to buy a taxi." He waited, he looked round at her, he gave her every chance to join in. "Not this taxi," he said, "nor the one before that, for that matter; but the first I ever had . . . the one that's going to be the first of my fleet . . . One day I'm going to have a fleet of taxis. One day I'm going to be rich; I'm going to be big. You'll see, Miss! You watch me!"

"Certainly I'll watch you." She couldn't help answering at last, she couldn't help laughing.

"You'll see me getting there!" he cried. "And all my friends —I'll never forget my friends—I'm a chap that'll do anything for my friends—I'll take them with me." Without slowing sufficiently, he turned the car into the drive, so that she was swung against him. She cried out, but he accelerated and rattled the car over the many potholes so that it swerved from side to side, and he and she were bounced about on their seats. "In a moment you'll see the house," he cried, laughing again and getting her laughing also at their boisterous passage. "It's not what it was, of course . . . not by a long chalk . . . but it looks the same outside."

The drive steepened suddenly, dropping away in front of the car, and he put on the brakes. "There it is, Miss! Beautiful, isn't it? It's historic." He let the car roll slowly down the drive into the courtyard. "But it's a pity to see it breaking up. There *ought* to be places like this. Things *ought* to have stayed like they was . . ." Taking off the brake, and blowing his horn, he brought the car round the courtyard, as Victor used to do, and pulled up by the pillars. "Here," he said. "Before they come . . . shove my card in your bag. It may be of use to you."

"Why?" she said. "Why should it?"

"You never know, Miss. I'll always be glad to help."

He took a card from the cubby-hole in the dashboard, and pressed it on her. Automatically she put it into her bag, but she was looking away from him, into the house, into the dark hall beyond the front door which stood open. There was no one about. Frank sounded his horn again, but nobody appeared. "Oh no —they can't know you're coming," he said, "that's clear as day-light. I'll take you in, Miss." He led her into the hall to the foot of the staircase. There was still no one about. "I don't know what to do, Miss. Do you want to go upstairs, or what?"

"You seem . . . very familiar with the house."

"I should think I was, Miss!" He laughed, but he turned as they heard a door open. "That's the library door, Miss. Here's the General himself!"

*　　　*　　　*

"What?" the old man called from the library door. "What's that? That's you, Frank, is it?" His coat and waistcoat were un-done, and he wore slippers which made him shuffle his way into the hall. It seemed as if he had just woken from sleep. "Who's this?" he asked, unable to see very clearly in the dim, evening light. "A lady, is it? Who is it, Frank?"

"It's Miss Alex, sir."

"Alex," he said. "Alex . . ." It was not with surprise that he spoke, but in a dreamlike bewilderment, as if he was not sure of his state of woken-ness. "Not Alex, not Alex to-day . . . surely not?" But now he was close enough to see her. "My dear . . . my dear," he cried. His voice had a content of desire, entreaty, fatigue, and even pain. "You're here to-day! But we didn't expect you till to-morrow." Taking one of her hands between his own, he kissed her cheek with dry lips, with a short, stiff moustache, with the smell of cigar smoke just touched with eau-de-Cologne.

"I'm so sorry," she said. "They promised to send a telegram."

"Oh, there was a telegram," he answered. "It came this

200

morning and it said—*demain*." He had kept hold of her hand and seemed to be leading her back along the passage, presumably to the library. "'*Demain*,' it said . . . 'to-morrow,' you know. That's how we took it. And young Geoff—he was going to London to meet you."

"It's of no importance," she said.

"Indeed it is! You weren't even met at the station. And it should have been such a reception, such a homecoming." He stopped and turned back towards the hall, and saw Frank still standing there, still holding her suitcase. "But you found Frank," he said. "That's something."

"Oh yes, I found Frank."

"And it's Draper's afternoon out—he's the butler. Not even a cup of tea, unless Nanny . . ." He looked about him uncertainly. "I wonder, now, where she'd be? And the boys . . . they're out: I know that much."

"I never drink tea," she said.

"Oh, but you must, my dear. You have to drink tea in England, doesn't she, Frank?"

"I should reckon so," Frank said.

"Be a good feller, then," the General said, "and get us a cup of tea, will you? You know your way about."

Frank's mouth opened and shut, as if an answer had started its journey and had been arrested. He appeared to blush and to swallow. "It's six years since I've been in that pantry," he said.

"That's all right, Frank," the General said. "There's nothing changed there that I've heard about . . ." He nodded—a conclusion, a dismissal. "Nicely, Frank—*you* know what's what for a young lady?"

"All right," Frank said. "I suppose . . . if there's no one else."

"There's a good chap!" The General nodded again, nodding his head several times, a gesture that seemed an habitual part of his conversation, serving many purposes. He saw then that Frank was still holding the suitcase. "And if you wouldn't mind just taking up her bag," he added; "they won't let me lift a weight these days. They say I mustn't."

"Which room?" Frank asked, speaking with as much obvious surliness as he could manage.

"It was to have been the Lilac Room," the General said. "But that wouldn't be ready to-night. It'll have to be . . ." He paused, before saying curtly, as if he was giving an order: "The one over the library."

When they were in the library, he closed the door carefully and said: "I almost forgot that the feller isn't still my footman. Rotten bad footman he was too, when I come to think of it."

"And now he's a taxi-driver?"

"Oh, he's grander than that, I think. Got a couple of lorries now and a feller working for him." The General shuffled across the room to the fireplace. "He's up in the world; goin' up and up, I imagine."

"He told me that," she said. "He told me to watch him."

"Did he? Did he so?" The General winked. "Well, I shouldn't, if I was you. He's a gay lad, is Frank—from all accounts."

"So I should imagine."

"He was that way inclined when he was here," the General said, "got my wife's maid in the family way and had to marry the girl. Worked out very well, they tell me."

They stood side by side by the fireplace. Age seemed no longer a burden to the General; perhaps it was only on waking from sleep that its weight was insupportable. "To tell you the truth," he said, "I was just dying for a cup of tea myself. It won't do young Frank a bit o' harm to do a bit of skivvying again." His face twitched as if, underneath the white skin, the muscles restrained his laughter. She had the impression that it was a fresh joke that had now occurred to him. "It's funny when you come to think of it, y'know. . . ." He pointed to the ceiling. "Up there," he said, "where young Frank's taking your bags at this moment . . . that's where we caught him at it—him and his young lady! On that very bed! And he won't have been there since . . . because, of course, we had to send him packing in a day or so."

By the time she had realised that this was the joke of it, by the time she had smiled in reply, the General's laughter was finished. "He told me you had given him money," she said.

"He told you that, did he?" the General said sharply. "By the way he acts, I'd have thought he'd forgotten it. I hope he behaved himself with you? I hope he was respectful?"

"He was correct enough." But as she said it, she felt guilty, disloyal, as if she owed more than that to the young man who had whirled her round corners and bounced her down the drive, making her laugh at last.

202

"Correct, was he?" the General said. "Well, that's the main thing, isn't it? It was a very nice girl he got into trouble; an excellent maid, my wife told us. But the baby died, so it didn't work out too badly."

Now he seemed such a sturdy, rock-like person, standing by his fireplace, sitting down beside the fireplace to change his slippers for his shoes, looking up at her from his chair and letting the corner of one eye twitch into a sort of wink, intentional or unintentional, so affectionate, so safe as he said: "These damn shoes, getting too tight . . . and at my age"—that she found her hands pressed together, palm to palm, beneath her chin, and her voice crying: "Oh . . . what do I call you? How should I speak to you?"

"Well . . ." he said, crouched over his shoe, with the end of a shoelace in each hand, "that's a teaser, isn't it?" Squinting up at her, he said: "Cousin . . . uncle? They sound damn silly to me. But I can't think of anything else." The shoelaces were tied now, and when he stood up, the extra inch made him a great deal taller, his head higher than her own. Taking her elbow in his hand, he led her across to the window, where they stood together beside the desk. "This is your home, you know?" he said. "This isn't just a place you're visiting. It's your home." He picked up from his desk a photograph, her own photograph, in a silver frame. "Look!" he said. "This has stood here for six years—waiting for you to come to it."

"I was only a child . . ."

"Of course you were. And now you're a very lovely young lady . . ."

She shrugged, she smiled.

"But you know that, my dear. All the lads must tell it you—in one way or another—the same as your own looking-glass."

She laughed. She was happy. "Not lovely," she said, "certainly not lovely. Perhaps there is something else, but . . ." She pressed the tip of a finger to her nose. "That nose . . . my God, it's terrible!"

He clapped his hands and rubbed them together with tremendous pleasure. "Poor child," he said, shaking his head, grinning, "it's a Meredith nose—that's all there is to it. Like it or not, you're a Meredith. That's why . . ." Taking her elbow again, he led her right up to the window. "This *is* your home," he said, in a sort of conclusion.

Frank came in with the tea. Without his chauffeur's dustcoat or hat, and in the blue serge suit that he had been wearing underneath, he seemed to be appropriately employed. "The silver wasn't cleaned," he said. "That's the best I can do—kitchen things." He spoke with a touch of disgust, a sense of impropriety, as he put down, on the table by the fireplace, the wooden tray, brown teapot and plain china cups.

"Thank 'ee," the General said. "I'm much obliged to you, Frank." Going to his desk, he asked: "And what do I owe you?"

"The journey?" Frank said. "I can put it on the bill."

"Best settle on the spot. There's too many bills already."

"The journey would be five shillings, sir."

The General pulled a bunch of keys out of his pocket and unlocked a drawer. "Young Master Geoff—he still lets me keep the keys," he said to Frank. There was a bundle of new notes contained by an elastic band. "One of these, shall we say?" And he gave Frank a pound.

"I'd rather only take the five bob."

"Get along with you!" the General said. "Don't you try to be proud with me—or I'll tell Miss Alex all about you."

Frank grinned. "That's all right, sir," he said. "You tell her what you like." But when he took the note, he touched his forehead.

When Frank had gone out, and the door was closed behind him, the General said: "Did him a power of good, you know, to be a footman again for twenty minutes. But it isn't always the case—not always."

He pulled up a chair for her and started to pour out tea. "I'll pour out the tea to-day," he said. "But to-morrow . . . It'll be *your* job, my dear; to-morrow—and thereafter." Handing her the cup, he returned to his previous thought. "Funny," he said, "how these young lads take a lift in life. A fellow like Frank—he can do with a jolt now and again, a little reminder. But not all of 'em. Not by any means!"

Sipping his tea, lying back in his chair with pleasure, he said thoughtfully, trying to recollect the circumstances: "There was a little chap here in the pantry, nervous little fellow, Walter by name—Walter Wallis. We sent him to school, I remember, and he got on to Oxford . . ." The General shook his head. The details had escaped him. "And now . . . and now . . . a sort of professor,

204

I think, research student, a sort of don or something. A feller like that now—he wouldn't want reminding. He'd want to forget. He'd want to be looking to the future . . ." Nodding his head, confirming his conclusion, he said: " One handles a fellow like that quite differently."

Putting down her cup, she rose and walked to the window. She stood up quickly, nervously, as if in haste, and then paused as if in uncertainty or fear, and then let her feet take her towards the view of the river and the valley. The book-lined walls of this beautiful room allowed her little space. The door seemed to have disappeared, as if it had been sealed up in a dream as here they handled you, set you upon a path and made you travel it, gave you your duties and made you perform them—to-morrow and here-after. This or that was good for you. This way you should be handled. This was your home.

The General had followed her to the window and stood silently beside her and a little behind her. Her left hand rested upon the desk, close to the photograph of herself in its silver frame. It marked, it monumented his claim upon her. Even Frank had known of it.

" I like to stand here, too," the General said. " One thing we *can* say—we've got this view left to us. Everything we can see from here . . . it's still all right. It's still our property." He grunted; it was a rumble of consolation. " What do you say, my dear ? "

She could not have replied, and she did not have to reply, because two young men were coming along the terrace outside the window. One of them had a gun, and the other a walking stick, and a spaniel followed. They stopped by the window and waved. One of them signed to the General to lift the window and let them in. " Here they are—both of them," the General said. Stooping to raise the window, he looked up at her. " Shall we let 'em in on us ? "

*　　　*　　　*

" I told you," Ralph said to Geoff, " to-morrow might mean to-day."

" I rang up, as soon as the telegram came. I couldn't get a confirmation."

" Well ! " said Ralph. " I ask you ! Poor Alex ! " He turned to her—a short solid young man but wonderfully light in his movements. " How can we apologise ? "

"The post office said it *must* have been sent this morning." Geoff was still distressed. "I really thought . . ." He was a big, ugly, awkward young man, anxious, like a dog, and in the same way affectionate. He smiled humbly. "Blotted my copy-book again," he said. "I ought to have known . . . but *demain*, you see . . ."

"*Mon dieu!*" Alex said under her breath. The joke, the discussion on the subject of this telegram, seemed to be prolonged for ever.

"Ralph—your dog!" the General cried. "Just look at him!"

"He's been in the river." The dog was now rolling in an arm-chair by the fireplace. "After a duck I shot. I got a duck, a partridge and a couple of rabbits." He went across to the fireplace. "Get out of it, you brute!" He turned the dog out of the chair and smacked it on the rump, hard enough to make it yelp, but then pulled its ear and gave it a lump of sugar from the tea-tray. "Hallo!" he said, "the pot's still hot! You had your tea pretty late!"

"When Alex came," the General said.

"*Demain* instead of to-morrow . . . And every one was out . . . so who got it for you, who . . ."

"Frank got it for me," the General said. "He brought Alex in his taxi, and I asked him . . ."

"Of course! Poor Alex—she wasn't even met at the station."

"She'd have been met *demain*—wouldn't she, Geoff?"

"It did young Frank a bit of good," said the General. "Surly at first, but he took it well in the end, well enough."

"As Nanny's back now, and Draper for that matter, and I dare say the girls also, I'd better go and see . . ."

"Good old Geoff! They won't know about to-day and to-morrow."

It was like an endless road through the plains, running between the poplars, stretching without a bend or turning for as far as you could see.

"We sent every one out to-day," Geoff explained, "all the servants, what there are of them, so that they'd all be here when you arrived to-morrow . . ."

"*Demain*," said Ralph.

*　　*　　*

206

"I'm very sorry, sir," the butler said. "If we'd known it was to-day . . . But the Lilac Room—it's still in dust-sheets."

"The morning-room *is* ready," Geoff said. "They got that cleared yesterday."

"It's to be your sitting-room, your private sitting-room," the General said. "It's been shut up for . . . a considerable period."

"We used to use it in the evenings," Ralph said. "Another of the fads of this household—mornings and evenings mixed up, like to-morrow and to-day . . . *Voilà!*" he said, throwing open the door. "All yours, Alex!"

"And this desk," the General said. "This is where you'll do your writing."

"My writing?"

"Letters and things," the General said vaguely. "Letters, invitations, accounts . . . you know how it is?"

"I'm afraid, sir," Draper said, "they haven't filled the inkpot." He had just opened it, to make sure. "I'll have it seen to, directly."

"I write so little . . ."

"Anne always seemed to find a lot of writing to do," the General said. "She was at it for hours on end."

"But not me," Alex answered.

"There are always invitations," the General said. "They have to be written by some one."

"Invitations to what?" Ralph asked.

"Well . . . there'd be dinners and things, wouldn't there? You'd remember it, Draper?"

"We had a cook in those days, sir."

"What's wrong with Millie?"

"She's still very young, Master Ralph."

"We had a wonderful cook at one time," the General said. "Mrs. Carr could put us up a splendid meal."

"She had a great deal of experience, sir."

"I'm afraid this light doesn't work," Geoff said. He had been trying it, following the flex to the wall-plug, looking for the fault. "It's probably the bulb. I'll get Watts to see to it in the morning."

"I'm very sorry, Master Geoff. The girls must have over-looked it."

"That's all right, Draper. I don't suppose Miss Alex will want to write to-night."

"Never," she cried, "never!" Her voice high, almost hysterical.

"There's always invitations and accounts," the General said. "And I think Anne would write out the *menus*. When you take over the ordering . . ."

"Me! The *menus*!"

"Give the girl a chance, Dad!"

"Oh, there's no hurry, no hurry at all. But as for the invitations . . ." He looked worried, as if something had been lost, forgotten. "Invitations to shoot," he said suddenly.

"It's a wonderful year," Geoff said.

"We shall have a record bag," said Ralph.

"It's a possibility."

"If God gives us the weather."

"God?" she asked. She could not always stay silent while this dream, this nightmare of chatter, flowed over and around her, sweeping her on into mornings that were to be spent here, in this room, at this desk, writing, writing . . . "God?" she repeated.

"A foolish figure of speech," the General said. "But if we're to do justice to the partridges, we do depend on Providence."

"You haven't decided the date," Geoff said. "Or have you decided on the twentieth?"

"I hope not," Ralph said. "I shan't have an eye to see out of. Not by the twentieth."

"Is the Albert Hall before the twentieth?" the General asked. "I thought it was the twenty-first."

"The seventeenth."

"The seventeenth? Then that fixes the date," the General said to Geoff. "We shoot the previous Saturday . . . It's boxing," he said to Alex. "You know—the amateur finals. Ralph boxes." He was proud of it—that was clear—but trying to conceal his pride. "He's quite good, you know. Bit of a tiger."

"*Un tigre?*" She had to say something; she had to speak; as if speech was a passing lifebelt to be clutched for salvation.

"Another of these figures of speech," Ralph said. "And again —foolish."

"I wonder who's got the keys to these drawers?" Geoff was trying the drawers of the desk, her desk. "There's a couple of them locked."

"I'll inquire, Master Geoff."

"From whom, Draper?" Ralph asked. "From whom will you inquire?"

" Nanny, Master Ralph. Nanny might know."

" I can't think why she should."

" Will that be all, sir, for the moment? "

" Yes, thank you, Draper," the General said.

" Very good, sir. I'll send Kate along to the end bedroom. She can unpack for Miss Alex."

" Unpack? Unpack what? " Alex asked. Then she started laughing. It began quite quietly. It was at first well controlled.

" Your luggage, Miss Alex."

" My luggage! " The laughter was swelling inside her, like an inrush of water that had to have an outlet. " I have one little case. I have no clothes—nothing."

" Anne left a lot of things behind her," said the General. " Beautiful things, some of them. I don't know whether they'd be out of date, out of fashion? I don't know whether they'd fit? "

" Anne . . . Anne . . . Anne . . ." Her laughter streamed out like a jet, higher and higher, drowned her, choked her, depriving her of words, thoughts and even feelings. But she heard the General say: " Forgive me, my dear! Foolish of me, stupid of me, thoughtless of me. You must be tired, of course." Then she heard him say to the butler: " Best send Kate along to her, anyway." And she felt the General's hard fingers gripping her arm tightly, lifting her up on her toes, leading her away from that desk and out of the room. " Anyway," he said, " now you've seen where you'll do your writing, I'll take you to your bedroom. It's a nice bedroom . . . You must be tired . . . You'll like it."

She was being led, almost carried, up the stairs by this strong hand, immensely, amazingly strong, of the old gentleman. Through her laughter, through her weeping, she struggled against his strength and was able to arrest their ascent for a moment. " Never! I will never write! " she cried. " And I am *not* tired, *not* tired at all."

" Of course not," he said. " You shall do just what you like . . . just what you like. This is your home."

As they reached the head of the stairs, a young girl came bustling down the corridor. " Oh, Kate," the General said, " look after Miss Alex, will you? She's a little upset, a little tired, I expect."

" And no wonder," Kate said, " after all that journey, and no one to meet her, no one at home. What she wants is a nice lie down and a nice bath. And the water is hot! Though it *was* to-morrow we were all to expect her . . ."

*　　　*　　　*

They had lit a fire in her bedroom. "Not that the evening isn't warm enough," Kate said; "but it's more cheerful."

"You are kind," Alex said sleepily.

"'Course I'm kind, Miss," Kate answered. "That's what I'm paid for; that's my nature." She had put Alex to bed some time ago and was now bringing her dinner. As she fixed the bed-table, she said: "Don't you go trying to hide you've been crying from me. What's wrong with crying, Miss? Now and again I have a cry myself."

"How old are you?" Alex asked. She thought the girl pretty, attractive, if a little plump.

"I'm twenty-one next month. You're only seventeen, aren't you? You look more."

"How long have you been here?"

"Since I left school, Miss; since I was fourteen."

"Are you happy here?"

"As much as I'd be happy anywhere."

"Will you stay here long, do you think? Will you stay here always?"

"So long as I don't get married. So long as nothing better turns up. So long as they pay my wages."

Later she came to take away the dinner things and to bring a few books which she put down beside the bed. "Mr. Ralph thought you might like to have a read." She looked at some of the titles. "Queer stuff he's chosen! Poetry some of it!"

"Does he read poetry?"

"Oh, he likes to do everything different from any one else! If there's nothing more you want, Miss . . ." She twitched the curtains, patted the cushions on the sofa and said good night.

When Kate had gone, Alex took up each of the books in turn, but without opening any of them. "I cannot see him at boxing," she thought. "Not with blood on the lips, and not able to see out of his eyes, not even to shoot." She could see him only as he turned the dog out of the chair, smacking it so that it whined and then pulling its ear and giving it sugar. "I can perhaps see him boxing like that!" She let the pictures develop and distort themselves into fantasies until she felt ready to cry again, and so turned out the light. But now her tears seemed to be great waves, carrying her, like a bottle up the beach, to a state that was almost sleep.

Hearing the tap on her door, hearing it repeated several times, she turned her head away and closed her eyes as tight as she could. His tread was heavy but gentle. A board creaked, and the smell of cigar smoke, with the touch of eau-de-Cologne, came on the draught from the doorway. With the door open, the peculiar odour of the house overbore the lavender and woodsmoke of the bedroom. The General bent above her bed, and she feared that he would see her eyelids tremble. He could not fail to see the firelight in her tears. But he only took her hand which was thrown beside her hair on the pillow and he touched it with his short moustache. He murmured: "God bless you." The door closed, and she was completely asleep.

When Kate came into her room in the morning, waking her with the rasp of drawn curtains, Alex sat up quickly, surprised to find herself happy.

* * *

The General was only just walking along the corridor from the library—and the deep, majestic hum, provoked by Draper with his beating and stroking of the gong, was only just dead—when Alex, wearing Anne's coat and suit, came down the staircase. The General's face was without expression, and he did not look directly at the girl. " I hope you slept well ? " he said.

" I did. I slept all night."

He had walked past her, not pausing, but speaking over his shoulder. At the door to the morning-room, which was open, he paused. It was a light room, and its brightness escaped into the darker corridor. With a slight nod he moved on to the dining-room, at the door of which he waited, with a stolid, almost grim appearance, for Alex to pass him and enter first. " You're old enough to precede me," he said. " You're a young lady, aren't you? I mustn't think of you as a child." There was no smile behind his words. Indeed, one had the feeling that the night had been an ordeal from which he had not yet quite escaped. Going straight to the sideboard with his solid, indifferent, almost nautical gait, he said: " Usually we all help ourselves—even the ladies. But to-day I shall give you . . ." One by one, he took the covers off the dishes that stood on the copper hot-plates. " Porridge, a little Neap trout, fried eggs, sausages . . ."

" I like just toast."

" Oh no! " he said. " We can't allow such Gallic habits. They'd never do."

Sitting down with her porridge, Alex said: " Is there no one else? Is it just us two? "

The General ate very slowly, even porridge, as if his teeth were difficult. When his mouth was empty, he said: " Geoff has his breakfast at home. He's too early a bird for me."

" At home? "

" He lives at the Lodge. His father died a year ago, and he lives there alone." He took another spoonful of porridge, and his conversation was reluctant, as if speech was inappropriate. " I've told him again and again it's not good for him," the General said crossly. " A young feller shouldn't be living alone. He should be living here." His porridge finished, the General returned to the sideboard. " But he won't have it," the General said. " He can be very obstinate, young Geoff, most obstinate."

She had put down her spoon, and the General rolled across the room to take her plate. " Another morning," he said, " you can do this for yourself . . . Young Geoff—he usually comes in to see us about this time; and Ralph . . . you can't tell when *he'll* put in an appearance." Back at the sideboard, he said: " I see you don't care for porridge, not yet . . . I shall give you a small trout."

" Please—just toast."

" You try the trout. The Neap trout, you know . . . they *are* trout. Ralph got these yesterday morning." He took the plate across to her. " But it's getting late in the season. This'll be the last of 'em."

Geoff came in a little later, looking anxiously towards the General, as if at a barometer. " She hasn't done calving," he said. " I've sent for the vet."

" Dammit," the General said, " the vet's no use. You want four men and a rope."

It was then that they heard Ralph's footsteps coming down the stairs at speed, hurrying along the corridor and into the dining-room. " Shut the door," the General said, " there's a good fellow."

" Sorry, Dad." He was wearing uniform, riding breeches and field boots, and he was a neat, hard figure, his buttons and his boots full of reflections. From the sideboard, he said: "Hallo, Geoff—more worries? Dad difficult?" And then: "Hallo, Alex—sleep all right, did you?"

"You'll be late," his father said.

"The parade isn't till eleven o'clock."

The General's stubby fingers followed the course of his watch-chain. "You've got an hour and forty minutes."

"That leaves me ten for breakfast."

"You can't do it in an hour and a half."

"Can't I? You just ask the police!" He winked at Alex. Everything that he did was objectionable, and yet it did not displease her. It made her angry only with herself, because she ought to be displeased but, instead, felt stimulated. Geoff had got himself a cup of coffee.

"Did you see Flower?" Ralph asked Geoff; "did you tell him about the seventeenth?" He spoke with his mouth full of sausage and egg.

"I did. He said there's a wonderful show of birds."

"We know that for ourselves. We're going to get a record bag."

"If every one shoots straight," Geoff said.

"Tommy will hit 'em . . . Guy will hit a few . . . Betts won't hit a lot . . ."

"*I* shan't hit 'em," the General said. "I can't see straight any longer. And young David—he won't hit 'em." The General grinned. "But he does enjoy himself, that chap."

"David isn't coming," Ralph said.

"Why? Is he away?" The General spoke sharply.

"Yes."

"He'll be back next week," Geoff said. "But he *can* be a terrible shot."

"Never mind—he enjoys himself."

"I doubt if he does," Geoff said. "Not when he's shooting as badly as he *can* shoot. Nobody *could* enjoy it."

"I want him asked," the General said.

"If we have David," Ralph said, "we shan't get our hundred brace. Every partridge in the county always flies straight over his head . . . And straight *on* over his head."

The General did not speak until he had finished the toast and marmalade that he had prepared for himself. Then he said: "He's to be asked. His father's my oldest friend—one of them."

Nobody spoke until Ralph got up quickly, saying that he must go. "On the seventeenth," he said to Alex, "we'll show you something. You'll enjoy it."

"Will I?"

"It's quite an experience," said Ralph.

"To see the birds killed?" She said it with anger.

"It must sound horrible," the General said. "I can understand that. But when you see it for yourself . . ."

"I have seen it at Monaco—the pigeons."

"It's not in the least like that," the General said sharply. "Not in the least. These are partridges. These are wild birds."

"It is better to be killed if one is wild?"

The General almost laughed. "We'll have you as keen as any of us—before we've done with you." His eyes smiled at her now; they appealed to her.

Ralph came round to her chair and primly kissed her cheek. "Good-bye, Cousin . . . I shan't be back for some time; shan't be worrying you again for a few weeks."

"Oh, you don't worry me!" she said. But by then, he had gone out of the room, the house. He had gone away for a few weeks. In his absence, the place seemed to settle itself down into a monotonous rhythm, like a machine. "But all the machine makes"—she thought, after a number of days had gone—"is old age."

$$* \qquad * \qquad *$$

Almost at once her duties in the household began to accumulate; and soon the days had become so nearly identical that they got linked together and gathered speed, so that at the end of a fortnight she said suddenly: "And two weeks have gone! And nothing, no event that can even be remembered, has happened in all that time!" She felt as if a scum was settling over herself, and that she resembled in her own mind a stagnant pool. As soon as this thought started, a fear of stagnation, of compliance with what *they* wanted, began to grow and to follow her about, as if it was looking over her shoulder. "Does nothing, nothing ever happen here?"

"Oh, I don't know . . ." Geoff answered, but he was smiling. "I think Freddy Betts is coming to tea . . ."

He came in mid-afternoon and spent an hour with the General in the library. When they came out together, Draper was serving tea in the hall and they were talking about the seventeenth, the forthcoming shoot. "A really remarkable year . . ." the General was saying.

"You've never seen a partridge shoot?" Sir Frederick asked Alex. "A treat in store!" He was the first person, since her arrival in the house, whose manner and technique were perfectly intelligible to her. By the way his eyes contemplated her, obviously conveying some sort of satisfaction or pleasurable stimulus to his heavy body, his red face, she recognised him as the ordinary sort of man to whom she was accustomed. He and the General started to explain to her the principles of killing partridges.

"Nothing short of an art," the General said, "drivin' him where he doesn't want to go . . ."

"Where should he want to go?"

"Usually, my dear, where you least want him."

"No," said Sir Frederick, leaning forward, using a finger to fix her attention, to hook her towards him. "He wants to go away from you, because you frighten him." In spite of the interest of his eyes, he spoke as if she were a child. "And he wants to go home, because home seems to be safe. And he wants to go with the wind behind him, because that gets him home more quickly. And he wants to go and hide in cover—in roots or kale or mustard or buckwheat—because that's what you do when you're frightened; you run and hide . . ."

Sir Frederick seemed to be enjoying his explanation. "All that?" she asked.

"And more, Miss Seytoun. And these various wants of the partridge are usually conflicting. They have to be reconciled, balanced, so that the partridge in the air finds the answer that suits *us* . . ."

"Us?"

"The guns," said the General. "We wait behind the hedge. It's the keeper has to get them over the hedge. That's the art of it."

She looked round the hall at the Reynolds over the fireplace, the Van Dyck on the stairs. "Art!"

"You're going too fast," Sir Frederick said to the General. "Look!" he said to Alex, as he drew out of his waistcoat pocket a gold pencil attached to a gold chain. "To reduce it to first principles . . ." He had found an envelope and was drawing a diagram. "The keeper brings the beaters in a line or a crescent, driving the coveys into, let us say, a field of roots . . ."

While Sir Frederick continued to talk, her brain was seeking a way of escape. " On the other side of the roots," said the General, " there's us! A line of guns lickin' their lips . . ."

" *Into* the roots from the country all round," said Sir Frederick, " they come as coveys, flocks—perhaps ten or a dozen in each, perhaps more . . . And *out* of the roots, they come singly, in twos and threes, over the line of guns . . ."

" Half the art's in the flankin' . . . fellers with flags . . ."

" Oh yes," Sir Frederick agreed, " to stop them slipping away to either side, out of the beat . . ."

She rose from the tea table. " I had forgotten . . ." she said; " I have this moment remembered . . ."

" You're not leaving us, Miss Seytoun! "

" But I must. I have to . . ." She made for the nearest room, the morning-room, which she scarcely ever entered. As soon as she had shut the door behind her, she halted in the alcove, surrounded by the gallery of water-colour paintings. For some moments she directed her eyes towards the pictures, but then she clenched her fists and thumped her breasts. " This—this room—this is where they want me! " She went out of the room and ran upstairs, having to pass them in the hall, hearing their conversation cut off by her reappearance, hearing the silence that followed, and knowing that they were watching her with surprise and curiosity as she made her escape.

*   *   *

Ralph did not return until the early evening of October 16th, the day before the shoot. Alex heard his voice as he came through the series of stone-floored rooms that led from the outer hall to the gunroom. " Rain, you'll see . . . Rain! The wind's gone to the west." He must be talking to Geoff.

Although she had been sitting in the gunroom, working at the table under the window, she had not heard the car arrive in the courtyard outside. When her mind was occupied, sounds vanished, her power of hearing diminishing to such an extent that sometimes she seemed to be deaf. But now, having finished the page of accounts—the total of the household books—she wrote in the result and heard his voice. " A nice stormy day will just about bitch the party."

The door behind her opened, and Ralph came in alone. " Hallo,

hallo!" he said. "Ladies in the gunroom! What next!" He was smiling nicely enough, but she knew that it was not altogether a joke. Turning round in her chair, so as to face him, she looked for Geoff. But Geoff must have gone back to the hall; he was not with Ralph.

"I apologise for the intrusion," she said.

"A welcome intrusion . . ." Just like his father—as she could now recognise—he had these phrases handy. His father and the others—Mr. Bredon, for instance—whenever they had nothing that they particularly wanted to say, or whenever they were not sure what it was that they wished to express, they made these conventional moves, these sayings, that were indications or approximations, no more, to what they meant. The conventions had to be learnt before the meanings of these people could be detected. Only Geoff —he said what he meant. But what he meant—it was never of great consequence. "Oh yes," Ralph said; "a welcome intrusion indeed."

"But an intrusion?"

"Well . . ." he said agreeably, "only an intrusion in principle —on a custom of the house."

"But that is serious."

"An obsolete custom belonging to . . . better days."

"Better days? When there was no girl? Thank you!"

"Don't tick me off," Ralph said. "I didn't mean it like that. I've just driven like the wind from barracks."

"And now the wind is in the west. How tiresome!"

Ralph looked directly at her, his face being expressionless like his father's and his eyes not precisely focused. "Don't you like it here?" he asked. He spoke quite seriously.

"I like it as much as I should like anywhere," she said. It was not true; but as she did not know the truth—as the truth changed with the hour—it was an approximation; it was their own way of talking.

"Have they got you doing accounts? They shouldn't." He was still serious, very serious, and she had now to acknowledge that he minded, or pretended to mind, about her happiness.

"Geoff is so slow," she said. "He takes hours to add."

"Don't you dislike it?" he asked, tapping the account book, leaning over her shoulder, as if he was a teacher and she a pupil, to look at her work. He put his hand on her shoulder, and she

217

did not move. For perhaps five seconds they remained, both of them, unmoving. Then he had taken her pencil away from her. "Wrong!" he said, and altered the total. It was one of his tricks that everybody talked about—this ability to read figures, as a musician reads music.

"I would have got it right myself," she said.

He ignored the assertion. "Don't you like your desk in the morning-room?" he asked. But there was no meaning in his voice, no emphasis, to help her answer the question. "Don't you like the room?"

She said: "I should be doing my adding up in there? You mean *that*?"

"I didn't mean that at all." He spoke quickly and crisply. "I was just interested."

"But not unquiet . . . concerned?" Her perplexity and embarrassment made her once more resort to translation. For some days now—for some weeks—there had been nothing to be said of sufficient importance to cause her this difficulty.

"I am very much concerned," he said gravely.

She laughed. "You are very serious to-day."

He did not laugh in reply. He said: "Am I? Can't we all have our moods?"

"Not the Merediths!" she said. "Not a Meredith *man*. He can only have his moods at breakfast."

"I dare say you're right." He was looking out of the window thoughtfully and still not laughing. "Here's Flower," he said. "Here's the most important *man* on the place to-night. You've met him, I suppose?"

"Met him!" she cried, her voice rising. "I've added up his rabbits. Hundreds and hundreds of his rabbits; hundreds and hundreds of his fourpences . . ."

The door opened, and Draper stood there, saying that Flower had arrived. "Will you see him now, Master Ralph?"

"If you don't mind." Ralph said to Alex. "If you'll excuse us."

"Naturally," she answered, getting up from the table.

"Don't go unless you want to."

"But I do."

* * *

218

"It's going to be . . . fine till lunch," Black said.

Alex turned round quickly. Standing in the courtyard, where the guests were assembling for the shoot, she recognised the voice instantly. Quiet and very distinct, it pierced all her protections, plucking the nerve-string of fear with which it was associated from early memory. And now, as Alex could not help looking at him, he turned away and stooped to clip a lead on his dog's collar; and though, as he turned, his eyes passed across her face, they seemed to ignore her. The act of ignoring her was deliberate.

"You don't know all these people?" Guy Bredon said to her. "You don't know Mr. Trant over there? You don't know David Levine? You don't know Tommy Black?"

Colonel Black took off his hat. He smiled, he bowed, but he said nothing.

"I know Colonel Black," she said.

"Do you?" said Guy. "Do you now? What a desperate pity."

"She's young enough to be . . . my daughter," Black answered.

"Younger than that," Guy said, and he took a shooting-stick from his chauffeur and handed it to Alex. "Now are you going to help me?" he asked her. "I like to make a fuss, a great deal of fuss, over getting myself ready . . . arming myself, you know . . . like a knight . . . a knight for a foray." He smiled; he was immeasurably benevolent and protective. "That's right, Charles, isn't it?"

"Yes, sir," the chauffeur said.

"Rather an impertinent answer . . . But I like, I do like a young lady to help me. Charles . . ." The chauffeur took his overcoat and handed him a tweed hat.

"Only this morning, Miss," the chauffeur said, "the Major was saying . . ."

"That's quite enough, Charles!" Guy said. "Now where's Phipps?" He pulled a cartridge bag out of the car, before Charles could get it for him; and because it was not fastened properly, the cartridges started to spill on to the wet gravel. "Phipps must be talking to Flower. These keepers . . ." He and Charles and Alex were stooping together, collecting cartridges. "A lot of old women, these keepers are, when they get together." It was almost impossible that any one could be so clumsy. "If Phipps doesn't come back soon," said Guy, "we're sunk."

"A loader and a . . . chauffeur and two guns and . . ." Black said, returning to them from his own car, "and I don't believe for a moment . . ."

"That my gun is any straighter than yours, Tommy?"

"And here's just such another," Tommy said, "and late at that!" The big car rolled slowly into the courtyard amongst the dogs and people.

"But you know Sir Frederick Betts," Guy said. "Oh, Susan, Susan . . ." For a fat labrador bitch, whose lead was somewhere caught in the car, was encircling his legs.

"If you left all that to . . . Charles and Phipps . . ."

"I don't know where the devil Phipps has got to . . ."

"I'm here, sir," the keeper said from the other side of the car. He had now fitted together the pair of guns, and, with one under each arm, came round to Guy.

"And this is David Levine. It was his father, you know . . ."

At once she felt in this young man, tall, dark and thin, a tension and strain similar to her own. Guy had hold of his arm. "Tell me, David, have you heard from your father?"

David shook his head. "Only a telegram, telling me not to follow him . . . He was moving about . . . he was on a yacht."

"He left you a letter, didn't he?"

"Yes."

"I'm glad you came out shooting just the same. It's what he'd want, of course; what he'd expect of you."

"I nearly didn't. I only got back last week. I didn't know till then."

"You were right to come—perfectly right."

"It would have upset their numbers; it would have let them down."

"He was very kind," Alex said, "Mr. Levine—he was very kind to me."

"I'm glad, I'm so glad, Miss Seytoun."

"He would be," Guy said to both of them. "He always was."

"How's your father?" the General asked. He carried a shooting-stick, holding it like a lowered sword. Dumpy and benevolent, he entered the circle. "A wonderful show of birds, they tell me, a wonderful year."

"It's the same all round," said Guy; "the same everywhere."

"Your father," said the General to David, " under the weather, I thought. How's he finding it down there?"

"I haven't heard," David said.

"He was lookin' a bit seedy before he left. The trip'll do him good." The General turned away. " Ah, Trant," he said, "but you look fit enough!"

"Gentlemen!" Ralph called, "if you'd all get into the bus . . ."

"This is always funny," Black said. "Old Harry—he sacks his footman, sells him his . . . brake, and hires it back!"

And now she saw Frank, sitting in the driver's seat of the brake, looking in her direction with an unformed grin, a secret, flickering on his face. "He's a bit of a character, that lad!" said Tommy Black.

"And you haven't met Mr. Trant?"

"The most . . . deadly of us all, Miss Seytoun."

"Ah, Colonel," the farmer said. "You know that's flattering me." He had a hammer-gun under his arm, and a black and white spaniel on a string. He was a big, red man, and he took off his cap with great dignity, bowing gravely, as he shook her hand. "I go back with the beaters," he said. "Often enough I get the best of it."

"When they won't come forward," Black said.

"That's right, Colonel, when they won't face the music."

"Gentlemen, gentlemen, will you please get into the bus?"

"We'd better get into the bus," Geoff said.

"Well, Alex," Ralph said. "This is what you came for, isn't it?" He was beside her, helping her up the step of the brake. His fingers on her elbow were hard, not merely supporting her weight, but gripping the bone. "This is the true glory," he said, "the remaining glory of the house." Presumably he was teasing her, but his eyes were quite serious. Looking directly at her face, he almost smiled, as if he was appealing to her, saying to her: "Please enjoy this; please understand what it means to us; please . . ."

From the lorry that was drawn up behind the brake there was an outburst of laughter, quickly and respectfully stopped. One of the loaders or keepers—one of the men who had been brought by their masters—had slipped off the tailboard and fallen on his back.

"It's a great day for them," said the General. "It's as much to them as it is to us."

"It's a nice thought, anyway," said Tommy Black. He was looking at Alex.

Last of all, Geoff got into the brake. "All right, Frank," he said; and followed by the lorry, the brake drove off.

*   *   *

"Oh yes," Sir Frederick was explaining to Alex in a low voice, "I own it all and farm it all . . ." Standing in the road, turning his back to Slender Ladies and the valley, he swept his shooting-stick in an arc, indicating his possessions. "But I let them keep the shooting for . . ." His voice was lower still: "For old Harry's lifetime. Naturally they ask me . . ."

"Will you draw your number, Sir Frederick?" Ralph was holding out a silver box containing ivory pegs, each peg being engraved with a number.

Drawing a number, his place in the line, Sir Frederick looked at it and said: "Number seven . . . we're the left-hand gun for a start."

Ralph was looking steadily at Alex's face. "We're seven guns in all," he said, and he kept his eyes fixed on hers. "We number from the right. After each drive, move up two places; number one becoming number three for instance; number seven becoming number two. . . ."

His absolutely serious face was meant to make her giggle; and while she answered: "Like a dance, isn't it?" Sir Frederick said pompously: "We can both of us add." This made her giggle more; and when Ralph turned away, she felt as if he had put a ticket on her, reserving her, even though he said: "Staying with Sir Frederick? He'll show you how to do it!"

The air was light, and the ground unsubstantial. She was separate from the scene and yet its nucleus; and the reaction of each of the others to his neighbour was readjusted because of her central attraction.

Now they had all drawn their numbers, and Ralph was saying: "Sir Frederick on the left for the start, then Tommy, then . . ."

"Me," said David unhappily. She could hear his unhappiness in the single word of his reply.

"Then myself," Ralph said, "then Geoff . . ."

She could feel David shrink from his right-hand neighbour.

"And the two old gentlemen holding the right of the line."

"Insolent puppy!" said the boisterous voice of Guy. "Old gentlemen indeed! What I have to put up with! Freddy steals Alex out of my pocket. Alex jilts me . . ."

"Oh no!" Alex said.

"Come now, give me my due!" said Sir Frederick with ponderous fun. "From all this fine company, you did choose . . ."

"I chose Mr. Trant."

"Since you couldn't have Farmer Trant, you took Farmer Betts."

"Mr. Trant is a proper farmer."

*　　　*　　　*

When Ralph gave the signal, firing both barrels of his gun into the air, as quickly as his finger could shift from the front trigger to the back, Sir Frederick said to Alex: "Nevertheless, there'll be a long wait before anything happens." He and the girl, followed by Parsons and a dog, were approaching their place which was marked by a stick, bearing a number, some twenty yards back from a high, ragged hedge. "Over the hedge, I've a field of roots. So I didn't let them trim the hedge—at Harry's request . . ."

The General and Guy were coming at a leisurely pace down the line of guns and were now approaching Sir Frederick on the extreme left. It was a sort of inspection that the General liked to make—happily, peacefully, as if he was sipping a delicate wine— at the start of a day's sport.

"Well, Freddy . . ." he said benignly. "A proper old gentleman's day, it's goin' to be! No walkin' to speak of! Here we shall bide in peace, while the beaters bring us the birds over here, and there, and there . . ." He pointed in turn to the hedges which enclosed three sides of the field. On the fourth side was the wall which adjoined the road. "Nice hedge, this!" said the General, pointing to their front. "High, they'll come high over the top . . ." He winked, he jerked his head. "Bad farmin' sometimes pays, Freddy! A good thing you left that hedge. Of course it wants cutting."

"You asked me not to trim it, so of course . . ."

"My dear fellow—I'd never ask any such thing!"

"Your agent, at least . . ."

"Young Geoff, was it? That'll be Ralph's doing. I wouldn't have put you to the inconvenience."

" Oh, it won't hurt till after Christmas."

" That's the right time to cut it, isn't it? "

" It should have been done *last* Christmas, if Geoff hadn't . . ."

" Well, well," said Guy, " what's a year, one way or the other? It won't make a ha'porth of difference." Both nodding together, he and the General started their return journey to their places at the other end of the line, on the right. Forty yards off, they stopped for a word with the next gun, Tommy Black.

" Always I'm somehow in the wrong! " Sir Frederick said. He was trying to make a joke of it, but the remark had a certain childish bewilderment and was pathetic.

The pathos reached Alex. " When they talk to you," she said, " it is another language, beyond English. To know English . . . it is not sufficient."

" I don't understand them." He responded at once to her indirect confidence. " Sometimes I think they're crazy, suicidal . . . This field of mine . . ." He dug his toe into it. " Times aren't too good for farming. They never are, for that matter, till somebody starts a war. But *I* can make it pay. Even now it pays; and I can show them how to do it; I can help them; I want to . . ." He had taken out a cigar and his big red hands were busy cutting the end of it. " I like buying land." He repeated the words with great force. " I . . . like . . . buying . . . land! " His voice was a function of power. " But I don't like getting their land just because they've got to sell it. I don't like profiting out of their inefficiency." He put the cigar between his teeth and was searching for matches when Parsons came forward with a box. He nodded, and Parsons withdrew. With a match held ready to strike, Sir Frederick said in a low voice: " That sort of thing . . . it doesn't do my reputation a bit of good." And later, as he blew out the first, slow mouthful of smoke: " It makes them hate me."

" Hate? " She lifted her shoulders, thinking the word so far beyond the range of feelings at Neapcaster Park, so great an extension and distortion, that it was meaningless. " They don't hate anything."

" You're right! " he answered quickly. " They don't know how to hate any more than they know how to farm in a world of science, a modern world . . . any more than they know how to learn, to listen . . . But they won't listen to any one, except their great-grandfathers—and to that boy they call an agent . . ."

224

"Geoff!" she cried. "But he is a good farmer; he is nothing else."

"He's a charity!" Sir Frederick turned away deliberately, making a deliberate gesture out of it. "I think I can be as charitable as any one else. But you can't mix it with business—not if you want to survive. Survival, nowadays, is a business by itself . . . No, no—they ought to let me find another job for that young man. They ought to send him away from here—right out of it."

"No . . . no . . ."

"It's the sensible thing. In the end . . . the kindest." He must have noticed her distress, but he could not know that she was shaking her head, and compressing her lips with evident emotion, not on Geoff's account, but for herself. "He's only a kind of servant," Sir Frederick said gently. "After all—he's no more than that."

"He's kind."

"They're all kind; they're all good and kind. Too good and kind to live."

It might be true, but she could not explain that it was incomprehensible. Kindness and goodness! These words, when applied to Ralph, or even to the General, were as irrelevant as hate. In that household, only Geoff could be good or kind. The others were only possessive; they claimed people, reserving them, asserting ownership. Only Geoff, like herself, was amongst the things owned, the belongings. "They'd never send him away!" she cried, as if this declaration, by itself, was an act of retention. "Never . . . never!"

"I've done my best," Sir Frederick said heavily. "With all the persuasion, all the logic at my command, all the experience—I've warned them."

They heard a whistle sounded, a long way off, from the direction of the Wold.

* * *

"That'll be your Mr. Trant," Sir Frederick said. "It might be a hare, of course; or it might be that a covey has broken back."

"Why should it break back?" But then she was able to answer the question herself. "Oh yes—it wants to go home. Of all its wants, that is the first."

"So you remember!" he said. "And I didn't think you were paying attention!"

" But certainly ! " As the shadow of alarm touched her—she knew not why—her speech became translation. " He wants to go home. But what . . . but where is his home ? "

" Oh . . . they belong to certain fields," Sir Frederick said. " Usually where they've been hatched. They never like to go far; and if they're driven far, they like to get back again."

" Naturally."

" A covey's a family, you know. A partridge is very much of a family bird—marries for life, no such thing as divorce . . ." He held out his cigar and let a long ash fall on to the stubble. " Admirable little fellow . . . chooses his wife for keeps, and he loves children. Do you know, if a couple loses its nest—from a fox, a stoat, a cat—they'll join up with their neighbours to help look after the kids. Like uncles and aunts ! "

" Admirable little . . ." She started to repeat his words, in order to hear them spoken in her own voice.

" Oh yes ! They keep their family together, teach them the rules, right through, almost, till the following spring. Then off they go, the children, to find husband or wife."

" So when . . ." Her eye travelled down the line of guns, each holding his weapon over his shoulder or under his arm or with the butt resting on hip or thigh, and each (except Tommy Black) with his loader behind him, and his dog sitting either beside him or in front. They were brave in the sunlight. And behind her, where the ground fell gently, rose and fell again, the autumn haze subdued the colours of the country with a monochrome tint, a wash of water-colour, like the pictures that hung in the morning-room.

All this assembly ! Her glance returned to the hedge in front. " So when they come there . . . since they marry for ever . . . it will be a man, his wife, his children ? "

" I hope not," Sir Frederick said. " Indeed I hope not. There's a field of turnips over there, a piece of buckwheat . . ."

" Where they go to hide . . . because they are frightened, because it seems safe ? "

" That's right," he said, with the satisfaction of a teacher whose pupil responds. " But it's thick and confusing in the turnips. They get split up."

" The family—it gets split up ? The husband and wife ? The children ? "

"You've got the hang of it," he said. " Then they come singly, or in twos or threes. That's when we kill 'em . . . That's when we get a bag."

Before she could answer, they heard the whistle again, now much closer. It was repeated. The line of guns and loaders stirred, as if a bow had been strung, or the string of an instrument tuned tight. Sir Frederick's labrador sat up and started to shiver.

"Is it . . ." she started to ask.

"You must be quiet now," he said, " very quiet. Quiet as a little 'mouse." Again the whistle, and at the far end of the line, from Guy Bredon and the General, they heard three shots. You could see the stir of movement as the loaders changed guns with their masters. Then a second covey came swiftly over Ralph, and she saw a bird crumple in the air, and then another; and she saw the loader, Ted Foster, whip round as he changed Ralph's guns; and she heard the click of the ejector as the loader opened the gun; and the fluttering of wings, like crumpled paper, as a bird beat its way to death on the stubble behind them.

"Was that . . ."

" Quiet as a little mouse," Sir Frederick repeated, throwing his cigar on to the stubble and the clean earth.

*   *   *

"Good God—I've hit it!" said David after his second shot.

"You've killed it nicely, nicely," said Victor. He had taken the empty gun from David's hand and replaced it with the second. As he turned to open and reload the gun, ejecting the spent cartridges in a parabola on to the stubble, and letting into the sunlight the sharp whiff of explosive, Victor said: " You can hit 'em all right, Mr. David, if you'll only take it easy. You worry yourself."

" I know, I know . . ." But now he felt that he could hit anything, that he couldn't miss. Even Ralph had waved, had taken off his hat. " But he isn't dead! " David cried; for the bird, that had been falling limp, seemed to recover himself in the air. The feathers were falling in the sunlight over the head of Tommy Black, who raised his gun towards it but lowered it without a shot.

"He's dead all right," said Victor. " The Colonel—he doesn't think him worth a cartridge." And indeed the bird, now behind the line of guns, was tilting himself sharply upwards in that curious

227

twist that means death. It was then that Sir Frederick, standing beyond Tommy Black, gave it both barrels. "Got it!" he said to Alex.

The drive was almost over. When the beaters reached the hedge, Sir Frederick said to Parsons: "That's fourteen partridges, a couple of hares and that pheasant." He had already sent off his dog, who was now returning with the first of the partridges in his mouth. "You go and get the pheasant," he said to his man.

Parsons looked at him. "Wouldn't that be Mr. Levine's bird?"

"Certainly not. You go and get it."

They could see that David, also, was walking back to pick up the bird. Victor had gathered the only brace of partridges that David had hit, out of the many that he had missed. "Hurry up!" Sir Frederick shouted to Parsons.

The two men converged upon the bird, with Parsons leading. It was not until they were within a few paces of each other that David realised what was happening. Then he halted and turned about and went back to Victor.

The pheasant was laid beside the row of partridges at Sir Frederick's feet. "There's still two more to pick," he said; "one may be a runner. The dog's on to it." They stood watching the dog at work. Then suddenly, Sir Frederick threw out his hand with a curious gesture. It was almost despair. "It *was* my bird," he said, but he stooped ponderously and picked up the pheasant and walked off with it. He passed Tommy Black without a word and went up to David. "Your bird," he said, holding it out.

"Oh, thanks," David said. He sounded surprised.

Victor took the bird from Sir Frederick and carried it to Flower, who was directing the man with the game-cart. Already it was filling up nicely.

*   *   *

"What a damn . . . silly incident!" said Tommy Black to Alex. "I can't understand that fellow Betts. If he wasn't so . . . devilish rich, I'd say he was off his chump."

Alex remained silent. Of all the incomprehensibles at Neapcaster, the one thing she did understand was Sir Frederick—the way he looked at her, and especially his attitude to the pheasant, his pettiness and then his awkward shame, contrition. She understood him like this, as she understood Fritz or Anne Meredith.

When people were childish, they were understandable. Otherwise, except for Geoff, all these people were a mystery, inhuman, invulnerable behind their armour of words, habits, jokes and correctness.

" Do *you* understand him, Alex ? "

She did not understand even herself; nor why she had said " yes " to Tommy Black and so had come to stand with him behind this hedge for this, the second drive; nor why she was standing behind *any* hedge, waiting for more birds to be driven over, to be killed, to thump and flutter on the earth.

" There'll be some time to wait," said Tommy Black.

He was watching her—she knew—but able to see only her neck, her half-profile and the back of her head. As she felt his regard, the shadow of fear began again to spread. In her memory, he brought fear with him. " Number One," she said—in order to say something—as she took from its cleft in the stick by which they were standing the card thus printed with the number of their stand. She started to fold and twist it.

" You're a damn pretty girl," said Tommy Black. In his voice there was an intensity that was absent altogether from his usual speech.

She ought to have been disgusted, but found that she had turned quickly towards him and smiled. " In England," she said, " men don't say that."

" Don't they? Don't they now! " Facing into the sun, he leant his head slightly towards her. The sun showed the wrinkles at the edges of his eyes, not old but mature, experienced. He was a man to whom one was not opposed. By his regard, his smile, his admiration, he could delete the past: it was only this moment— the present—that was of account. " So men don't talk to you like that? " He tilted his head. " Come, come . . ."

" Certainly they don't at Neapcaster."

" I've never had the chance to listen. I couldn't tell."

" Certainly they shouldn't, when they are shooting . . . *partridges*." She stressed the word, meaning it sarcastically.

" That comes next," he said.

" Next, the partridges! " And very distantly they heard the first, the warning whistle. " The partridges, the dear little birds, as all agree . . ." Her voice was rising. " The beautiful little creatures . . . the husbands so faithful, so fond of their children

. . . Of course they have to be shot!" she cried, " but later . . . but *next*."

" If you feel like that," he said softly, " I won't shoot them."

" That is . . . a stupid joke. How can you *not* shoot them? You can't stand here while they come, and not, not . . . You wouldn't dare! "

" Wouldn't I ? " He looked at her quite steadily, assessing or calculating. " Have you any cause to think me so timid ? "

His words made her cry out. He had opened her memory, as if it was a book, at the particular page, the illustration, that she tried always to pass by, never, never to look at. She had lifted a hand, the knuckles to her lips.

" My dear—what, what is the matter ? " But it was clear he understood. " I didn't mean that, honestly . . . And it was so long ago, you were so small a girl, scarcely eleven, twelve years old, you can hardly remember, surely . . ."

Especially she remembered the blood that was left on her own cheek when it was all over.

" So little—such a little girl," said Tommy Black, " that I picked you up, I carried you out."

Also she remembered the scent of his hair, of whatever it was that he put on his hair, as he held her against his shirt—a crimson shirt that he wore in the hot evening. It was because of its colour that the blood on it was invisible until it smeared her cheek.

" I never meant to do it," he said. " I couldn't help myself."

It was true. She never would forget the shout, the fear that struck her with the shout, her father's shout of rage that was awful as an unexpected blow. " I've had enough of this! " And then in French, as he raised his hands, his fists clenched towards Tommy Black: " *Fiches moi le camp! Vas t'en . . . vas t'en!* " He was so much taller than Tommy, and when he lowered his hands they gripped the back of a chair. He raised the chair above his head; and then he and Tommy Black had together fallen on top of her. She heard her own shrieks, repeated and repeated.

" I didn't want to hit your father," Tommy said.

Unaccountably, her fear had, for the moment, diminished. Indeed she laughed. " My father! " she cried. " Why not hit him ? Why not ? "

He said: " I've never hit anybody else—not in anger, not in all my life." But he seemed puzzled by her laughter, and he could not know how she had hated her father, and how she had hated his blood that was left on her cheek. "Don't laugh!" he said sharply. "Don't do that!"

"It was something to laugh about!"

"Stop it! Stop it!" And it did check her laughter, making her take a deep breath against which she felt her ribs shuddering. "Of course," he said, "you couldn't have understood. You were too young, weren't you? You couldn't have known why we quarrelled."

"Every one knew," she said. "Every one knew about Anne— about Mrs. Meredith." She felt most calm about it. The thing no longer afflicted her, but had become reasonable. The page might have been turned, hiding the picture, while the book remained open at two sheets of calm, reasonable print. "Then you went away," she said, "and she, Mrs. Meredith, she was *enceinte*."

"That isn't true." He said it in a very low voice, and there was no doubt that his surprise and protest were real. "She wasn't, she couldn't have been . . . pregnant."

"But certainly," she said. "Some said it was my father; some said it was you."

"It isn't true."

"First she went to Neapcaster, then she came back to Cannes, and then to Neapcaster, and then to Cannes—and then a doctor was found in Nice. So it was all right."

"She would never speak to me, never see me," he said.

"No?" She shrugged her shoulders. Her voice was quite hard. "People are like that."

The whistles were sounding again, now closer. Again the line of guns stirred, becoming alert. She saw Sir Frederick, a cigar in his mouth, stretch out his right hand, not bothering to look round as Parsons put a gun into it. She heard the click as the General— on the far side of Sir Frederick—opened his gun and shut it again. On the far left of the line they were shooting already.

There was more whistling, and closer; and also a sudden rush and scuttling and twittering in the air, with the sky between herself and the hedge filled with partridges, low and bright, curling and splitting their pattern, and gone far behind her before she had realised that Tommy had raised his gun and lowered it again without shooting. "A nice, strong covey," he said.

"But you—you didn't shoot!"

"I promised you I wouldn't."

"That is ridiculous . . ."

Again the whistle. Sir Frederick also was whistling softly, trying to attract their attention, and at last calling: "To you . . . to you, Black!" The hedge was thinner down there, and through it he could see the flight of the birds.

"Shoot! You *must* shoot," she cried.

"Do you *want* me to shoot?" he asked. Not teasing her, not making fun of her, he was quite serious.

"You must! You can't *not* shoot." The whistle, again the whistle.

"I can do just . . . what you want." The sound of birds, the wash of their flight, was in the air ahead.

"Oh, shoot, shoot . . ."

"As you say." As he spoke, he shot. Before she had recognised the covey, she had seen the leading bird, as it crossed the hedge, crumple, collapse, contract. The force of its flight carried it on, close to her head, as it fell on to the stubble just behind her, thumped as it hit the earth, bounced, rolled, and lay with its pale breast upmost.

Tommy had turned and was almost knocking her over. Because she was in the way, he was not able to fire his second barrel. "Dammit!" he said. "You must duck!"

"I'm sorry . . . oh, I'm sorry," she cried.

Because of the angry smell of the spent cartridge, the whistles renewed in front, the air broken overhead by the twittering fear of birds, the tenseness, excitement, she found she had clasped her hands and was crying: "They're coming, coming to us! Oh, shoot . . . shoot!"

"The father, the mother and all the little babies!" he said, as he dropped one almost at her feet.

"Oh . . . oh . . . oh . . ." She clapped her hands to her face, not knowing whether to cover her ears, her eyes or her mouth.

*　　　*　　　*

"But that," said Guy Bredon to Alex, when the second drive was done, "was a show of birds such as you wouldn't expect . . ."

She was standing where Tommy had left her when he went to search for a wounded bird that had fallen across the field. At her feet lay the game already gathered; on her shoe a splash of blood.

"What a day!" said Guy Bredon, as he and the General joined her. "Nice horse that!" he said, as the game-cart approached.

The horse was glossy and smart, his mane plaited and ribboned, the long hair of his legs brushed into silken locks. The man at his head was a scruffy, shrivelled wretch, whose hairs of reddish grey escaped from a soiled cap. His chin was unshaven, his boots too big. To each person in turn, he lifted a finger, submissively touching his forehead, but never raising his eyes from their prospect of his feet.

It was just a dung-cart, scrubbed for the day and fitted with laths, so that rows and rows of birds could be hung by their heads to dance a swinging jig and spatter the floorboards with drops of blood. "And very nice too!" said Guy, looking into the cart. "A record in sight, I think."

"Not a bad beginning," the General said.

"Get along with you, Harry!" said Guy, as he took Alex's arm. "You know, my dear, he's as pleased, if the truth were told, as a dog with two tails . . . as this old lady here!" For the General's bitch, an old labrador, had wandered astray and now came waddling up, with her fat flanks rippling, and her broad tail waving her pride and delight. "And look what she's brought you!" Guy said.

"So she has! So she has!" said the General, seeing the bird in her mouth. "Must be a runner she's found us!" He stooped to take it; and the old dog lowered her head like a bashful child, and convulsed her body with love. "Oh, what have you brought your master—you clever old lady, clever old poppet, old sweet . . ."

Rising, the General held out the bird to Alex. Its eyes were wide and liquid; its heart had a visible beat. "What a tender mouth she has—that dear old dog!" He showed her the breast, moist from the dog's grip. "See—not a mark of a tooth . . . a mother's clasp!" Then he stretched out one of the wings, at the root of which was a trace of blood. "A runner all right; the wing just broken . . . And see what fettle he's in! Plump . . ." With finger and thumb he felt the breastbone. "Plump as a pillow!" he said. The wing, released, slowly refolded itself.

"A young bird," said Guy.

"Oh yes," the General agreed, and showed it again to Alex. "You can tell by his legs . . ." As he stretched one of them out, the claw twitched and closed on his finger. "Bright and smooth and yellow, you see, whereas . . ." he pointed to the cart, "if you look at an old bird there, you'll see how his legs are scaly and white."

"And you can tell by this . . ." said the General. And she had to watch while he took the head of the bird between finger and thumb. She had to see the broad thumb broaden, the thumbnail white, as the General pressed on the bird's head until the skull collapsed.

"You can't do that with an old 'un," Guy Bredon explained. "The skull's too tough. You have to hit it on the head."

"Hit its head on the side of your boot," said Sir Frederick, joining the party. They were all gathering at this spot.

"On the butt of your gun," said Ralph.

"Furthermore," continued the General, "you can tell by this . . ." With the thumb that had crushed the skull, he forced open the beak. Holding the lower beak only, which then took the weight of the carcass, he watched the beak bend and break.

"With an old 'un," said Guy, "the beak's too tough."

"But you," said the General to Alex, "you'll very soon learn for yourself." And he threw the corpse into the cart. Then, brushing together the palms of his hands, he asked: "And now, my dear, who will you favour? Who will you stand with next?"

With her breath caught, her voice impeded, she tried not to turn away, but found she had done so and was facing Ralph. Turning again, she met Tommy Black. He had found his bird, which he now swung by the neck. "Got it!" he said.

"Who's to be favourite?" the General asked.

Shaking her head, she managed to say: "I'm going home."

"Home! Not now—with the best of the day to come!" And when she nodded, he asked: "You're not feelin' ill, I trust?"

"Only, only . . ." Gulping, she drew her breath, feeling it catch at her ribs. She got out the words: "Slight . . . headache."

"The guns and the noise and all that—that's what it is." The General reviewed the party gathered about him. "Who shall it be? Where's Geoff?" But Geoff was the only one absent. "There's Frank and the brake . . ."

"Not here," said Ralph. "It's taking the beaters round to drive-in Lampitt's . . . *I'll* take her back."

"Certainly not!" said his father, with evident sacrifice. "*I'll* take her home myself."

"No, no . . ." she cried, finding her breath released. "Alone . . . alone . . ."

" If you insist . . ." said Ralph. " You know the shortest way, the track? "

She heard the General say: " She knows it well enough. *She'll* be all right," as she walked away from them, down the hedge. Behind her, the game-cart rumbled and creaked along the same route.

Passing David Levine, she found she was shaking her head. " Not you," she might have said. " But your father, if he had been here, if he had come back . . ." And she wanted Geoff. " But they've sent him away! " she cried, she wailed aloud, as she reached the road alone. " They're sending him away, as Sir Frederick said . . ."

Climbing the wall on to the road, she turned towards Adam's cottage and the start of the track. But there the old man stood, his legs planted apart; and the hands that ripped out a rabbit's guts were now holding a flag.

She turned from the flag, and down the road she went, till she came to the end of the mustard, and then climbed the low, stone wall and started to run across the rough grass. She seemed to be running in the rhythm of the General's voice. " You can tell by this . . ." and he crushed the skull. " Or by this . . ." and he pulled out a leg. " Or this . . ." and the beak broke. " Plump as a pillow! " said the General's voice.

She tripped and recovered as the hill steepened, as she ran into the valley, over the brow of the hill towards the hidden stream. At last, where the tussocks of grass were long and matted, she lay down to hide and listen. There seemed to be no pursuit.

★   ★   ★

Here, in this sector of the valley, the hillside was at its steepest. Moulded into the shape of female breasts—the woman reclining and facing the opposite crest—it held between these two hillocks the usual channel, a re-entrant or fissure whose sides were almost precipitous but gentle, graceful and flowing like flesh. This channel had once held a tributary to the Neap; and the springs of the uplands still bubbled and ran this way in a wet winter; but now they were dry, and the diminutive valley, into which Alex stumbled and slithered, carried only a faint track leading to the nearby stream. Alex followed this track, making for the shade of the willows and the bright water.

She was panting; but as she brushed the hair from her forehead and the tears from her face, she became aware of the quietness and stillness of the place to which her flight had brought her. It was enclosed by the hillsides, and within the enclosure the sunshine collected, and no wind penetrated. Nor any sound from outside. The sounds here were all private and peculiar to the place itself: the creaks and whisperings of birds and insects, the fall of a hoof, the beating of the air by a late butterfly who had lingered into the autumn, and the cluck and rustle of the stream itself. And all these events made noise, the noise being silence.

Listening to this silence, she heard, somewhere close at hand, the call of a partridge and the answers, the plaint and the reassurance in reply, the rebuke, the summons, the calling on various notes and with various inflections of anxious voices. A covey, or what was left of it, must have come here in flight, seeking the same harbour as herself. Here they were safe, as she was safe, in this place of fugitives, where the warm, moist stillness smelt of mint.

She drew into her heart the compassionate breath of silence, and started to walk through the hip-high weeds and tussocks of the meadow, not knowing where or why she was moving, but transported by a sort of blissfulness that made her stretch out her arms as if she wanted to answer the anxious partridges, to gather them to herself. " Nobody shall hurt you . . . nobody shall make you afraid." The words were breathed from her heart with such force that she felt in her eyelids new tears that were tears of love.

But, at her step, the calling of the partridges ceased. She herself could feel and suffer their silent apprehension. " I wouldn't hurt you," she said from the agony of her heart. " I love you, don't you see ? " With a flurry and clatter of fear they rose, almost at her feet, and fled. They followed the breast of the hillside, curling along the valley, out of her sight. " But I wouldn't, I wouldn't have hurt you . . ." How could the heart speak and be understood ?

She stopped and stood still. In a tussock nearby, the tall grasses were beaten in panic by a fluttering of wings. The tremors of fear reached her as she moved towards the place and stooped to part the grasses. " It's hurt ! " she cried aloud, as she saw the wounded bird lie still, its brown feathers pressed between the grasses, seeking a rigid safety, seeking to enter the earth. At her touch, when she sought to stroke it, when she murmured to it love and comfort, it fluttered desperately, beating the ground, striving with all of the life that was left in it for a last flight. It crawled and fluttered a few inches through the thick stems of grass and thistle, burrowing into their darkness; and then, exhausted, done with living, it again lay still. When she touched it, it scarcely stirred. When her hand enclosed it, her fingertips felt its heart.

She knew that she had to kill it. The love that she felt for it had, somehow, to be turned into death. With her thumb she felt the hard curve of its skull. The heat of its body filled her two hands which were cupped about its breast. Shutting her eyes, drawing a breath that quivered and sobbed, she put all the strength of her heart into her hands, and from her hands into the thumb that pressed upon the bird's head. It fluttered feebly. Nothing else. And the heart continued to beat under her fingertips.

Gasping, she tried to imitate the men, turning the bird on to its back and swinging its head against the side of her foot. Again and again she swung it with all her might. But the bird held itself rigid, its head stretched forward, away from the blows, and its claws struggling and scratching against her wrist. Shuddering, sobbing, she let the creature drop.

Regaining the earth, the bird started once more to flutter and beat with its wings upon the grass, smearing the grass with blood. She stamped at it with her foot, grinding her heel into its feathers, while the sickness rose in her throat. She threw herself upon the bird, seizing it, clasping it to her blouse, smearing its blood upon herself, feeling the desperate flutter against her breast, feeling its warmth against her heart.

* * *

"It's all right," the man said.

"Kill it . . . kill it!" She held out to him, in her two hands, the warm partridge. "You're a man . . . a man . . . a *man*," she cried. "*You* kill it!"

He took it from her. "See!" he said, "it's quite, quite dead."

The thing lay limp and still in his hand, the eyes shut and the head hanging free. He folded the head against the breast, drawing the wings about the head, and putting the bundle into his pocket. Now it was only a bundle, a packet of feathers. Then he stooped to wipe his hands upon the grass. "Let me get you up," he said to her, lifting her by the armpits and transferring his hands to her waist, taking her weight. He held her on her feet while a younger man brought a handkerchief, soaked and cold from the river. Gently they wiped her face. "Don't worry," he said, as he drew the handkerchief over her forehead. "I'm a doctor. You've no need to worry, no need to worry at all."

"Give me a hand, Walter," the doctor said to the young man, his companion, and they led her to the river bank, setting her with her back against a willow whose branches hung into the stream. As her tears fell, the doctor wiped them away with his handkerchief. "That's better," he said; "you're all right now. You'll soon be all right." The young man took off his coat, and the doctor rolled it up and put it under her head. As her eyelids closed, she heard the young man say, astonished: "Good God, she's asleep."

The doctor continued to stroke her forehead and to smooth the hair on her brow. She felt him take her wrist. Entering, then, upon a spell of complete tranquillity, she heard him say: "Rather a slow pulse." His voice was far off. "Nothing to worry about," he said. And this was happiness.

*　　*　　*

Briefly she rested, aware of the man and the boy talking together quietly. Then she recalled herself. At her invitation, the glow of noon returned to her eyes, growing red and bright, until she let the lids quiver and lift. "Better?" the doctor asked.

"I've been asleep."

"Only for a little while—half an hour . . ." He had a hairless face, smooth and pale, with nothing but a touch of red for eyebrows. The hair of his head was thick, coarse and red, cut short and slightly curly. He was surprisingly small and insignificant for his immense authority. "Better . . . better . . ." he said. It was a comment that became a command. Obediently she smiled. "That's fine," he said; "you're all right now." And so she was. "It's all over," he said, "all over." And it was. "You've nothing to be afraid of, nothing at all." She was no longer afraid.

They sat beneath the willow in a world enclosed by the hillsides. Between its weed-beds, swift in its course over limestone gravel, the water rustled and clicked, whispered, sucked, sending a tributary flow to stray into the roots of the willow and to lie there in a deep pool, almost directly beneath her, almost as dark and still as her new heart. He rose and stood looking down on

238

her, a scraggy little ginger man with feet apart and hands on his hips. His tie was out of place, and the sunlight through the willow caught the tip of his brass stud. Since he was standing, she also rose to her feet.

Having got upright, she found that the newness of the world was still more evident, the earth having no stability, but being all alive and in motion, beating and trembling to the rhythm of herself, as if she grew out of it. The feeling was pleasant and exciting, but uncertain. Taking the arm of the young man, the silent companion of the doctor, she found that he was big and tall. " You and your son are most kind," she said to the doctor. But at the sound of these words she felt that a stranger had spoken from somewhere behind her.

The doctor answered her with a little laugh. " Not my son," he said, " but a friend, a young man from Oxford, Mr. Walter Wallis."

A man on either side of her, they started to walk slowly up the banks of the stream. Very soon, the slight track narrowed, and while the doctor went ahead, Walter stepped aside into the willow-herb and tussocks to let her pass. He had a large pink face, with long hair, the colour of dark tow, falling across his forehead. Over his shoulder he carried a haversack; over his wrist he had her handbag. She recognised this article but did not trouble to take it. It did not even seem necessary to powder her face after her tears and the water from the stream.

Soon the river split into two arms, divided by a bed of withies which reached to within a foot of the bank they chose to follow. In several places the bank had fallen away, leaving indentations which were spanned by slippery planks. The young man gave her a hand until she reached the centre of each plank; and then the doctor, who had gone ahead, turned to help her for the remainder of the passage. Thus they passed her from one to the other. And at length, like a convoy of ships, they rounded the point of the withy bed and came in sight of a great ruin and two stone bridges which carried a cart-track over the two arms of the stream.

"Hence this mill," said the doctor; and she was then aware that he had been speaking about it for some minutes. His words had even been lodged in her mind, like a page of print that has been absently read. " Centuries after the forests went, there were sheep instead of trees. Great flocks of sheep made this the richest part of England. Look ! " And he held out his hand towards the derelict buildings beside which they were now standing. "The merchants who bought and sold the wool returned their wealth in churches and barns and mills—built like this."

"Some village mason," the doctor said wistfully, "some villager with the genius . . ." He waved at the noble proportions and the fine and graceful stonework. "And nobody counted the cost. Nobody had to."

"Whose is it?" she asked. It was a long, long time since she had last spoken.

"It's part of Neapcaster Park," the doctor said.

"It still belongs to the Merediths," said Walter Wallis; "at least, it did yesterday." He spoke with a queer kind of bitterness and a half-laugh which made the doctor look up at him—she thought with reproof—but without raising his head. She and the doctor had seated themselves on the parapet of the bridge, and Walter stood in front of them.

"Please—my handbag!" When he had given it to her, she started to powder her face. "What a terrible sight!"

"You must tell me who you are," the doctor said, letting his hand rest on her knee for reassurance. "Are you, perhaps, the young lady from France who's come to the Park?"

She shrugged. "As you like," she said. To herself it seemed a sincere answer.

"And all this shooting going on, up at the top? Shouldn't you be there, with them?"

"I left it; it didn't please me." Again the answer seemed to herself to be complete.

"I am their doctor—I ought to tell you. And Mr. Wallis—when he comes for the night from Oxford, I try, if I can, to spare a few hours from my patients, to walk, perhaps, through this valley and . . . lunch. But we're late for lunch!"

Walter unslung the haversack which he was carrying.

"There'll be enough for three," the doctor said. "Let's see what Dorothy has done for us."

*　　　*　　　*

"Why did you say 'yesterday'?" she was asking Walter. And although he pretended to be perplexed, it was clear that he knew what she meant. She persisted. "Why did you say that the Merediths, they owned this . . . 'at least they did yesterday'?"

Evidently uncomfortable, he answered at last: "It was just a way of speaking."

They were eating sandwiches; and after another bite, she returned to her question. "But why *yesterday*?" And after another bite: "Don't they own it to-day, for example? Won't they own it to-morrow?"

"Of course, of course ..." He laughed; he mentioned the sunshine, the season, the stream over which they were sitting. But at last, when her questions continued—because, somewhere in her mind, there lodged the notion that yesterday was significant—he had to admit: "It was only, I suppose, because yesterday I met Ralph ..."

"Yesterday!" Her cry interrupted his explanation. "But Ralph ... only yesterday he came from his soldiers, came like the wind, as he said ..." She thought of the strange mood in which he had entered the gunroom. "But you ... you met him? But where?"

"As a matter of fact," he said, with a touch of impatience, "I met him with Sir Frederick Betts."

So the doctor intervened then. "Walter, you see, works for Sir Frederick."

"I certainly don't!" Walter said. "He's paying for my research."

"But you will in due course," the doctor insisted.

"That remains to be seen."

"Sir Frederick!" she said. "It is *he* who wishes to send away Geoff!" And when she saw Walter's face become again distressed, she was quite determined to catch the truth, some truth which concerned herself, from behind what he said. Her brain felt quick and nimble, as one's feet when they leapt and scrambled from boulder to boulder across some stream in the Esterelle hills. Quickly she asked: "Was it that thing, about Geoff, that he said to Ralph?" Nimbly she added: "He wants to send away Geoff, because ... because ... But no, they would *not*!" And she put into her voice a laugh, a disbelief, that she wanted to feel in her heart. "How could they send away Geoff? What could they do without Geoff? Because ... because ... everything, it is everything, that Geoff does in that house."

"We know, we know," the doctor said. "We are all devoted to Geoff."

"More—more than that! He is wise, clever ... a good

241

farmer . . ." This she was telling herself. " Sir Frederick says— *no*! But he *is*, he must be! "

" Well, well—there's an argument there," the doctor said. He was filling his pipe. " Between the clever folk, the chemists like Walter, and the wise old folk—like Geoff. Walter will tell you to feed your land from a sack; that you don't need stock . . ."

" That's not a fair statement," Walter said. And at once, at speed, the argument started as, obviously, it had often started before. " The golden hoof—at present-day prices! " He laughed sarcastically. " Rather, let us say, the figures in red—on a bank statement! "

" Any one," said the doctor, in a good-natured manner, " even you and Betts, can sell for cash the stored fertility of a few generations."

" And any one, even Geoff, dear Geoff, can throw away money on cattle and sheep."

It was nothing, all this! She had risen and walked away: a few paces across the track to the verge of the ruined barn and mill, to the nettles and seeded thistles and docks, as high as her hip; then back and over the farther bridge and up the track that became, at once, a ledge in the hillside; then back again to the sound and ripple of their dispute. While they talked, she clasped her hands, as if she was holding her heart, commanding her heart: " Be still! "

" He's a century, a couple of centuries, out of date."

" Supposing he is, Walter? What then? Were the yields of a Cotswold ground so very much less? I fancy—quite the reverse! "

" Times change, and science . . ."

" This? " The doctor picked up a handful of earth from the rut of the track between his feet. " Has *this* changed much? "

" A doctor, you! It's a matter of chemical fact . . ."

" Sometimes I give an old lady a bottle," the doctor said. " A bottle with a nasty taste. But these—these fingers . . ." He spread them out, and the handful of earth crumbled and dropped. " And these, these eyes . . ." He touched his eyelids, his forehead. " This brain . . . You can keep your bottle on its shelf! "

Back up the track, she was out of hearing. Again her heart, in her clasped hands, was asking: " What do they care about Geoff? " And again she commanded: " Be still! " Their voices were lowered now, their dispute quicker, their anger, impatience rising. Because of this, her ears were alert to a wayward current of speech.

Walter's voice: " Be that as it may, if Ralph wants help from Sir Frederick—he's got to get rid of Geoff."

As she turned quickly, the doctor asked in amazement: " And you told *that* to Betts! "

" Never, never, never in my life! " Walter was crying, with agony in his voice. " But I had to agree . . . I couldn't argue . . . I couldn't . . ."

Angry and scornful, she reached them. " Never, never, would they send away Geoff! " She saw their surprise and dismay. " My ears heard you! But never . . ." Yet her hands were still clasped.

" I think that's right," the doctor said. " They'd rather go bankrupt first. Loyalty, fondness . . ."

" It isn't *that*! " she said with tremendous disdain. " Quite the contrary! It is . . . that they are too clever, too sensible at least, to do so stupid a thing."

" Nevertheless," said Walter, speaking like a sulky child, " bankrupt they'll go! " He pointed to the ruin. " See for yourself! "

★   ★   ★

" I do think you must let me ring them up."

The doctor made this remark for the third or fourth time that evening; but Alex, sitting in the chair by the window of his sitting-room, again shook her head. She had spoken very little since they had left the valley and driven to his house; she had answered scarcely any of the arguments that he had put to her or the pleas he had made; she had withdrawn herself into a distant obstinacy, a state of negation, having nothing positive that she did want to do, but only a certainty of what she did *not* want to do.

" I wish Dorothy was here," he said again. " I wish I knew where Dorothy had got to." Once more he went out into the hall and looked in a futile manner up the stairs; he went to the front door, which stood open to the mild night, and looked into the drive where his own car stood, and into the garage where Dorothy's car was in its usual place; then he returned to the girl. " If only Dorothy was here . . ." He put a hand to the telephone. " Really, I'm going to ring them up."

At once she stood up. " Then I am going."

" Where to? " he asked angrily, as he had asked the question many times before during the last few hours.

"It is of no consequence," she answered as usual. "I am just going."

"But you can't . . . just go—in the middle of the night, in the middle of the country."

"It is quite early."

"It's quite dark."

"It is not yet eight o'clock."

"Sit down, sit down," he said wearily. "Listen," he said, "will you please, please listen?" He walked up and down the room, finally standing beside her and looking out of the window into the darkness. Then he pulled the curtains, shutting the room. "I only want to tell them you're safe. I needn't tell them anything more than that. I needn't even tell them you're here." She was still shaking her head. "They'll be searching the countryside. They'll be ringing me up anyway. I can't think why the police haven't rung me up already. But they're certain, quite certain to ring up soon, the police or the General, certainly the General, because, after all, I am his doctor, and after all, I do owe him some consideration . . ." He had sat on the arm of her chair and had taken hold of her shoulder, speaking to her in a soothing, reasonable voice, and trying to send the force of his reason, and of his doctor's persuasion, through his fingers and into her consciousness.

Then the telephone did ring. It stood on a small table beneath the window, beside the chair in which she was sitting. As he took up the instrument, she got to her feet; but he pushed her back into the chair, and put out a hand to take hold of her wrist. She moved it away from him, pressing her arm against her breast, holding her hands clasped together on the shoulder that was farthest from the telephone. He smiled to reassure her, but she looked back at him steadily, without any expression. Those big eyes were opened at their widest, to their most liquid depths.

"This is Dr. Macdonald."

Her eyes were fastened upon his own while he listened. So as to reassure her, he put his hand over the mouthpiece and said: "It's only a patient," and then, speaking into the instrument: "Say that again, Nurse, please!"

When he had finished the conversation, he got up and said: "Now I'm entirely at your mercy. I have to go out. I may be away an hour, an hour and a half, perhaps even longer . . ."

She stayed motionless and silent, with her eyes fixed on his face.

"You won't go away, will you?" He waited for her to answer, but he had to repeat the question several times before she finally shook her head. "Do you promise me that? Will you promise me that much?" At last she nodded.

She remained sitting in the chair while he got his bag and a coat. "I wish you'd just eat something," he said. "There's plenty of food in the kitchen. You ought to eat something." Again she shook her head. "If only, if only Dorothy was here," he said as he left her. "If only I knew where she'd gone . . ."

*　　　*　　　*

When the sound of the doctor's car was lost in the rustle of the night breeze, Alex took her handbag from the corner of the chair in which she had been sitting. The only money it contained was a ten-shilling note. Alongside this note was the business card given her by Frank. Picking up the telephone, she asked for his number.

A woman answered. "Who's that speaking, please?"

"I want a taxi to take me to the train."

"There's no more trains from Neapcaster, not to-night." The woman had a pleasant and gentle voice, but she spoke quite sharply. "Who is it speaking?"

"This is Dr. Macdonald's house . . ."

"Oh, Mrs. Macdonald, this is May here . . . But it isn't Mrs. Macdonald speaking? It doesn't sound . . ."

"No, but it's her house. Please may I talk to Frank?"

"This is his wife. Perhaps I can help you?"

"I have to catch a train; a train quickly; away from here."

"Oh, you'd much better speak to my husband, hadn't you?" The woman spoke in a good-natured, jolly sort of way. "Here— hold on a jiffy while I try to find him."

After a short delay, Alex heard his voice saying breezily: "Hallo, hallo!"

"Is that Frank? Is that the driver?"

"It's you, is it?" he said. "I thought it might be. The wife said it sounded foreign . . . And what are you doing at the doctor's house?" Before she had to answer, he said: "Hang on, while I shut the door!" And when he came back, he asked: "Where do you want to get to? Bit of trouble, is it?"

"Away from here. Away from Neapcaster."

"Running away, Miss?" She thought he was laughing. "It's no concern of mine."

"Will you please take me . . . somewhere?"

"I've been out all day, Miss, as you know yourself. And I've been to the station this evening. And I've been out your way once already—to Colonel Levine's house. I've only just got in, as a matter of fact, and wanting a bite to eat."

"You can't take me?"

"I wouldn't—not in the ordinary course of trade. I've had about enough for one day. But if it's to oblige a lady . . ."

"Please!" She was annoyed to hear her voice tremble.

"I'll come when I've had a bite to eat."

"Please come at once!"

There was a pause before he said: "But, mind you, I'm not fetching any more pots of tea for the General or any one else . . . unless, that is, it's to oblige yourself . . . 'less it's to oblige a lady."

"Please—when will you come?"

"About twenty minutes."

*　　*　　*

When he had rung off, she felt hungry and went into the kitchen. On the dresser she saw a neat row of papers and little notebooks, with money placed on each. She saw that they were bills from Neapcaster tradesmen, mostly from the same shops whose books and bills she herself had to check and record each week and pay each month. For this purpose, they had put her into the morning-room and given her the desk.

The bills on the kitchen dresser were for October—right up to date, for two and a half weeks. It was curious that they should be paid at such an odd time of the month, on October 17th, as if the doctor was going away and was settling up his affairs before he left. Going into the sitting-room to fetch her bag and returning to the kitchen, she picked up the money, all along the row, and put it into her purse. It amounted to very little—only three pounds and a few shillings.

Really, she had a practical mind and a sense of money that was precise. She was aware that she still had insufficient to get anywhere at all; so she looked into the kitchen drawer, but found nothing, and then returned to the sitting-room to search the desk.

There were only a postal order and a few stamps. The door to the surgery was locked.

She cried out aloud with fear when the telephone rang and went on ringing, ringing. " Stop it! " she cried, and then found herself running into the hall, opening the front door, and standing in the drive.

A radiance lit the horizon and grew as she watched it. While the car approached, the telephone continued to ring. It seemed determined never to stop.

*   *   *

" Aren't you going to answer that thing? " Frank asked.

She shook her head violently. " I want to go at once."

" Just as you say, Miss. Where do you want to go? "

" London," she said, for no particular reason, except that she would, thereby, be retracing her steps.

" That's a tidy step! " he said. " Where's your luggage? "

She shook her head again.

" Not even that little bag you came with? "

She opened the rear door of the car, but he shut it again, saying: " You'd best sit in front. If I'm going to drive you to London . . ." He was putting into his voice a meaning that was familiar and unmistakable. " You in a bit o' trouble? You kept my card, I dare say? " He got in beside her and drove off, accelerating quickly. " Those cards come in handy. I give them around—not to just any one, of course . . . I'm choosey about it . . . and one of these days, there's a lady in a spot of trouble . . . and she thinks of Frank! "

They were coasting down a steepish hill at the foot of which there was a bridge with a hump. The jolt sent her nearly to the roof. " Hold on! " Frank said. " You got to hold on along this road if I'm going to drive you fast . . . What's all the hurry about? "

" I must get to London."

" By rights I oughtn't to do it," he said. " If I'd told my wife what was up, do y'know what she'd have said? She'd ha' said: ' You take her right back where she belongs. You take her straight back to Neapcaster Park.' But I didn't tell her. She doesn't know what's up."

" What *did* you tell her? " She knew, almost before she had spoken, that the question was a mistake.

" I told her a bit of a tale," Frank said. " I told her I'd be back

I didn't know when . . . Oh, she's used to it! Before now I've been away two or three nights—and no questions asked when I get back. I won't have questions."

After a while he said: "If you're in a bit o' trouble you better tell Frankie about it. Frankie's your man if there's any trouble about."

When she remained silent, he seemed to drive more slowly. Then he tried it another way round. "This little trip," he said. "It's going to cost you a bit. You've reckoned on that?"

"How much?"

"It's all of ninety miles," he said. "Twice that, for there an' back, makes a hundred an' eighty. Call it a tanner a mile, makes four pun' ten. An' a quid for night work . . ."

"You can put it on the General's account."

"Oh no, I can't! There'll be none o' that." He was driving very slowly now. "Either this is a job, or it's something else." Although the car had almost stopped, he was still looking straight to his front. "Maybe I could help you," he said. And without looking at him, she could see, or she could hear, or she just knew, that the muscles of his throat were tight, that the blood would be rising to the base of his ears, that the top of the jawbone would be trembling. "I might maybe get you to London. I might get you farther'n that . . ."

He accelerated sharply, simply in order to skid round a turning and to put his arm round her when she was thrown against him. She caught at his wrist with both hands and tried to disentangle herself, but she said nothing. Since she held her body rigid, his grip slowly relaxed until he quickly withdrew his arm in order to change gear. He did not replace it.

"Listen!" he said. "I'm all right with girls. I know what I'm about." Again he took the car round a turning, but this time slowly, and into a narrow lane. After a few yards he drew up. "Listen!" he said. "I've got what you want. I've got this car. I've got a bit of cash with me. I've got my savings book in my pocket—and it's good for plenty in the morning." His voice was now strained and had become higher and thicker. "I've nothing to do but send a telegram, and tell 'em I'm on a job . . . and they don't expect me, not till they see me. Easy as that! I can put you on your road, y'see, wherever that road may be. I can put you right . . ." He waited for an answer. "You can trust me," he said.

She drew in her breath, knowing perfectly well what she was doing. " Won't you help me ? " she asked.

" 'Course I'll help you. But you've got to help *me* a little—haven't you ? "

" Please drive me to London."

Then he put his arm round her again. " Don't you want me to drive you farther than that ? " He bent down his head, but he made no determined effort to kiss her when she turned her face away, and he did not resist at all when she tried to remove his arm.

" Please drive on," she said. " Please help me."

He sat quite still for a few moments, and then he said: " All right, Miss." After he had driven a little way, he said: " I owe your people a tidy bit. I'm not so black as I try to paint myself." He turned the car again and gradually accelerated until they were once more going quite fast, but without danger or excitement. Once again, at the foot of a hill, there was a bridge with a hump to it; but this time he took it gently. Without recovering his speed, he drove on for a mile or so in silence. Then he slowed down and stopped in a fairly narrow lane. It was very dark outside the car's headlights.

" Oh, please go on," she said wearily. She was not frightened of him; she understood him too well to be frightened.

" No, Miss," he said. " You got to forget this evening."

" Of course, of course," she said. " Please take me to London."

" You get out here, Miss," he said gently. " This is where I fetched you."

" You wouldn't dare ! " she cried.

" I wouldn't dare anything else," he said. He opened the car door, leaning across her to do so. " The gate's just behind us. You slip into the house quick and quiet—and no one will know you ever left it." Getting his hand behind her shoulders, he levered them up from the back of the seat and pushed her away from him towards the door. " Get your legs out slippy," he said, " or you'll fall on your face."

*   *   *

It was funny—and it ever afterwards made her laugh, in spite of its tragic context—that as soon as she re-entered the house, she went straight to the kitchen dresser and started to replace, on the

249

tradesmen's books and bills, the moneys she had stolen. It was, of course, an easy task until she came to the last two or three reckonings; and then, although she was solvent in the whole transaction, she was left without the correct change to complete it. She was making various adjustments—exchanging a half-crown from one book for two single shillings and a sixpence from another —and was finding it an absorbing puzzle of the kind which engaged completely all her senses, so that she was quite deaf and almost unaware of her surroundings, when she heard him calling from close behind her.

"Dorothy, Dorothy . . ." It was a tragic cry; not the doctor's voice, but another, much more resonant, that was also known to her.

Utterly weary, and seeming desperately ill, Daniel Levine followed the light and came into the kitchen. "You!" he said. "Oh, Alex, Alex . . . where is she?"

He sat down heavily on a small upright chair that stood by the door. His bulk and the skirts of his overcoat completely hid the chair, and the spectacle was ludicrous. But this made it only the more pathetic. "I've had such a journey!" he said. "No sleeper. I couldn't get a seat on the boat. And the Customs . . ."

"You've come from Cannes!" she cried. And in her voice there was almost the same appeal as when he had called for Dorothy.

"The weather had broken. It rained and rained. At Théoule there was an avalanche."

"So you came home?"

"Oh, not because of the weather." He managed a little laugh. "A wet shirt isn't, even now, enough . . ." But the conclusion was not worth the effort of speech. "Are they all out?" he asked. "Little Mac . . . Dorothy?"

"The telephone rang, and he had to go. But she . . . she hasn't been here at all."

"So every one is out!" He smiled in that very tired way. "All day it's been the same. I tried to telephone . . . from Cannes, from Paris, Dover, London . . ." The record of his journey teased her. She drew in her breath; she was standing on her toes. "But there was always something . . . Either I couldn't get through at all . . . or no reply from my house . . . or so they said . . . or else . . ." Again, he found the effort not worth it.

"David was shooting to-day," she said.

" Was he? And I suppose Victor . . ."

" Yes—he was loading."

" And now they've gone to London. David—they tell me—had a bath, and then he took the car, the little car, and Victor with him." His voice had a very calm quality. " I had to get Frank to fetch me from the station."

" I've run away," she said suddenly. " I'm going back to Cannes. Will you give me some money?"

" Of course—if it seems sensible."

" Sensible, sensible!" Her voice rose, and she put a hand on her breast. " It is a question not of sense, but of the heart."

" But we mustn't be too French—not in Neapcaster!" He smiled at her, and she was not at all angry. In a few moments she smiled in return; and they looked and smiled at each other for quite a while, as if they were creatures with their own speech that needed no words.

He started to get up from his chair. When she held out her hand to help him, he took her arm; and her arm trembled at the fraction of his weight which it carried. With both hands he held on to her and asked: " Will you come home with me . . . *my* home . . . please, my dear . . . ?"

For some reason she was almost crying. Not wanting to speak, she just nodded her head. And when he asked: " Coat . . . hat?" she held up her handbag to show that she had it already. They went out together, and he bowed his head under the doorway. He was saying: " I didn't expect, didn't hope to find you here . . . Or any one at all . . . But I had to come to see for myself, though the telephone . . . no answer, none . . . though I made them keep on ringing."

He held open the door of the long black car. And when he had gone round and got into the driving-seat, he said: " Please, don't tell on me! I'm not supposed, you know, to drive myself about, but only . . . to sit and be driven."

As he started the engine, they heard the telephone ringing yet again through the open window. He listened to it for a moment and then said: " If we were to answer it, now, whatever should we tell a patient?" She knew that he was smiling in the darkness as he drove through the gates and took her home.

* * *

"No, no!" she cried. So he withdrew his hand from the telephone which stood within reach of his arm-chair by the fireplace. But he did protest patiently: "Poor Harry will be very worried. The clock says half-past ten. Why won't you let me?"

"Always you ask for reasons! And when *I* ask *you* for reasons —why you have come back to your home—there is no reason."

"It is such a difficult thing to explain."

"For me, also."

"Then you make me try." He tried to smile at her across the fireplace, towards the arm-chair where she was sitting facing him. "I came back to all the things that belong to me and that I belong to. I did think they were a kind of prison from which I had to escape . . ."

"But it is true!" she cried. "The prison from which I also must escape!"

"But now I know differently." He was lying back in his chair and was too tired to be diverted. "I know that my pattern of my life here—the things I own and the privileges that are mine—is also my responsibility, as so often, as always . . ." She was sitting upright now; she seemed at last to be listening. "Ownership, privilege, brings this sense of responsibility, of belonging as well as owning, of accepting rules, laws, obligations . . ."

"So detestable!" she said in a whisper.

But he only thrust out his legs towards her and folded his hands on his stomach. "And while history shows that those who reject their responsibility will, in time, forfeit their privilege, their ownership—the reverse may likewise be the case. You see . . . those who reject their privilege, or are deprived of it, lose also their responsibility. And so . . ."

"You do not care what the Christ said?" she cried.

"I care very much what Jesus said. But sometimes He said things—as Moses also said them—relevant to certain people at certain times, but not, in their literal sense, relevant to us all to-day. We can't all be Apostles. Somebody must make bread . . ."

"So—who is one to believe, if not Him? And who should want this . . . this *responsibility* . . . if she need not have it?"

"Every one, I fear," he said heavily; "because, without this responsibility, one is not inside the law. Without the law, one cannot be human. The human capacities—great, divine—they cannot operate." She saw that he had closed his eyes and joined together his hands, fingertip to fingertip. "It is only the law that knits people together. Until they are knitted together, they are not . . . People."

She threw herself back in her chair. She could no longer listen; she could only hear. But the words did make her tremble, and did later return, like the memory of a view that one has scarcely noticed at the time, or a snatch of scent or song or loveliness that has gone straight from the senses to the heart. "Without being knitted together by the law—without accepting responsibilities, privilege, and the rest—we can't see vision, can't hear prophecy, can't believe promise, because . . . because there is no love."

But at the time when he said it, she heard only the word "love," which she grasped quickly as something that meant something, and was at least understandable. "The people here," she said, "they do not love at all. They do not know *how* to love."

He opened his eyes then and smiled again. "Our languages," he said, "are all very tiresome and inadequate. They have only the one word for love."

This much she could understand completely. "There should be hundreds of words!" she cried.

"We could do with several."

"But none here—at Neapcaster. There is no love here!"

"Within the human entanglement — I think there is great love."

"That entanglement—tight and cruel!"

"But full of love."

"*That* isn't why you came home!" she cried. "To be again entangled . . . like me . . . like this, from which I escape. That isn't why?"

"Partly," he answered.

* * *

Again he was listening through the telephone to the clicks made by the operator—the bell ringing in the emptiness of the doctor's house. Seeing his lips move, she thought that he whispered the name—"Dorothy." And she asked: "Was it for *that* that you came home?"

Again he answered: "Partly . . . Perhaps I had many reasons . . ."

"Me also!" She was shaking her head like a child, making her hair swing to and fro. "Yet it is not reason at all; not even the heart; not even . . . *dedans*." She had put her hand on her breast. " It is the things outside . . . beyond, above."

" The Greeks said the fates. But we, perhaps, say design—the law. But, either way, we cannot escape it."

" But the people," she said, " all the people—they are with the fates. One is alone; against them alone! One cannot choose this or that. One may think there is choice, but one finds, after all . . ." Closing her eyes, pressing her fingers against her eyelids, she struggled to transmit her feelings into thought, and her thought into speech. " One has wanted the one thing, and when one has got it—one finds it is the other. One is driven . . ."

" Or drawn," he said quietly.

" Driven, not drawn . . ."

" Ah—that's the difference between us. I—I am drawn, not driven."

She had found, at last, her answer; but she spoke calmly and in a low voice. " Like the partridge," she said. " Like the partridge, one is driven. He is frightened, the partridge, by the line of men. He is frightened and flies away. He wants to fly with the wind. He wants to hide from his fear—perhaps in the turnips. You see? One is the partridge." She was scarcely aware of her words. " In the turnips," she said, " there he is lost, the partridge. He loses his friends, his family; he calls them; they answer." So clearly she heard the creaks, the plaints, the alarm and fear, of the birds calling to each other, up and down the scale of their hearts, calling in the meadow.

" Then he is frightened again, the partridge. He flies up into the air . . ." It was as if she was telling a story to a child, one child to another. " He wants to go home, but there are men, a line of men, and so he turns away. He wants to go with the wind, more quickly . . . it is safer to go more quickly, more quickly home. But there is a flag, a white flag, an old man with a white flag and blood on his fingers. So he turns again, the partridge, and there is a hedge. And over the hedge, there is Ralph and Sir Frederick Betts, and even David and Geoff. There is Colonel Black! " She leant forward. " But me—they will not turn! I will go home! "

Very quietly he said: " My dear, you have no home anywhere but here, with us. Not Cannes, for instance, where Anne . . ."

" They drove her out from her home which is here! And they drive me out from my home which is there! "

254

Slowly he shook his head. "She drove herself out, and now . . . oh, but she wishes to return! And I . . . I have to tell this to her husband."

"That, also, is why you have come home?"

This time, when he nodded and scarcely whispered "Partly," there was no smile at all. The flesh of his face seemed to have fallen away from the bone, as he stretched out his hands. "Stay with us, dear! Please let me take you home." And when she would not respond, not quite, but hesitated still, he said: "I'm not one of the beaters; not the man with a flag; not with a gun, behind the hedge. Only another partridge, perhaps, older, wiser."

"An old one!" Her voice was high and strained. "And when they press your head with their thumb, it won't break! Did you know that? Also the beak! And your legs—they are not yellow and bright, but scaly and white . . ." She had started laughing.

Sharply he asked: "May I take you home?"

The laughter stopped at once. "What can I tell them?" she asked, like a child who has suddenly surrendered.

He answered her as if she were a child. "I shall do all the telling. I shall come."

Desolate, crumpled, she collapsed. There seemed to be tears. "You promise?"

"I promise." But he did not stretch out his hand to the telephone until, as the tears fell, she nodded her head.

"You will see," she said as she wept, "we are both—you and I—like the partridge. In the turnips we shall be apart."

*   *   *

"Ought you to go out, sir, to-night?" Hicks was asking. "Ought you to drive yourself?"

"I'm keeping a promise," Levine answered.

"That you won't go away?" Alex whispered.

He was too tired, too uncertain in his movements, to bother much with speech; but he put his arm about her shoulders, and she found it heavy as darkness. She rested her hand on his.

"So long as you are here," she said, "so long as you don't leave me . . ." Feeling his hand move under her own, feeling the pressure on her shoulder increased and relaxed, as his fingers answered her, she was comforted.

When he put her into the car, she still had hold of the hand that was on her shoulder. When she was seated, he drew it away. Reluctant to let it go, her fingers caught at his fingers; and as if they were lovers, they spoke to each other through their loving hands.

She saw him go very slowly round the front of the car, leaning on the bonnet as he went, and then returning to her, hauling himself into the seat beside her. He switched on the lights, as Hicks shut the door of the car and stepped back. Surrounded by light, they sat in darkness, in a private tent where her love and sadness were complete.

"It's not very far," he said; but he seemed to enjoy the power of the car as he let it loose. Where the road forked, he hesitated, before swinging the car to the left and then decreasing speed while they passed the doctor's house. It seemed to be still empty, and he said: " Still no lights! "

Later he slowed right down to enter a lane, narrow and rough. Even this great car bumped and skidded, recovering speed on the broken surface. "You know where we are? " he said. " We come out not very far from Slender Ladies . . . not very far from where old Adam lives. But first . . . you know who lives here? " In the darkness she shook her head. " This is Tommy Black—and lights, plenty of lights! " It was a small place, but now bright; and on the other side of the gates, a little car was standing with its lamps lit. " Activity! " he said.

For a very short while he drove in silence, and then said: " You know, there are some very good and wonderful people here, as some who are . . . sometimes bad." He uttered a number of names, as if—she thought—he was remembering in his prayers the people he loved. " Dorothy . . . dear old Guy . . . Watts and Victor, and Draper even . . . my own son, David, perhaps . . . and Geoff, Geoff . . ."

He gave a strange sort of cry, as if he had forgotten something or lost it. The tyres screamed, and she was thrown up against the roof and then thrown against him, on top of him, as the car seemed to settle at a steep angle, partly in the ditch, with its headlights throwing beams skywards, striking the treetops. She clutched at his shoulder and then started to shake it, shake it, savagely, with passion, with anger, with love.

She must have climbed out on to the road, because she was

256

standing there when the lights of a car approached. This car slowed down and stopped, and two people got out.

*　　　*　　　*

The argument went on and on, as they stood in the lane between the two cars. Alex was held in the arms of a tall woman, cheek against coat. Alex could feel on her forehead this woman's tears.

"You're sure—absolutely sure of it?" Tommy was asking.

"I'm perfectly sure," the woman said. Her voice was deep, calm and dry, quite divorced from her tears.

"Poor, poor Danny," Tommy said. "I can't understand it."

"His heart," the woman said. "He knew he oughtn't to drive."

Their voices continued, thrown against each other, then joining together, then separating again, then drowned in the pressure of darkness that covered Alex, smothering her against the woman's coat until, suddenly, that darkness parted, and words or fragments of vision could dart through.

"I tell you," the woman was saying, "*I* shall stay with him. Do you think I'd leave him alone?" She spoke scornfully.

"But what possible good . . . what possible point . . ."

"Do you think I'd leave him alone?" the woman repeated. There was fury, now, in her voice. "Alone up there!"

Alex said: "If you're the one he called Dorothy, he tried and he tried, again and again he tried, to find you, to speak to you."

The woman whispered in her ear: "Please, please don't!" And at last her voice trembled.

Tommy said: "Alex, I must take you home."

Alex heard her own voice shuddering and wailing into the woman's breast. "No . . . no . . . no . . ." and she clung to the woman with her utmost strength. The woman's arms tightened, and the voices joined and conflicted, and were lost in each other, somewhere above the head of Alex, who was still crying: "I won't . . . not alone with *him* . . . not alone . . ."

"What a pickle this is!" Tommy said.

A new voice entered then, a rough and blurred voice that emerged from shuffling feet.

"And who may you be?" she heard Tommy ask.

The voice answered inaudibly, and the feet shuffled. "He's just a tramp," Tommy said; "but he'll do, won't he?" And all the argument started again, joined like the branches of a tree.

"No!" the girl cried, as she felt herself drawn across the road towards the new car. But the woman's arm remained fast and secure, and her voice said: "It's all right, dear, I'm coming with you."

Tommy was saying: "Since we've got to go to the Park, we can't very well . . ." And then Alex, opening her eyes, saw him taking luggage from the back seat of the car and stowing it into the boot. It made her giggle and say: "What a lot you're taking!"

The woman answered in a soothing way: "It is, isn't it?"

"She *would*!" Tommy said. "That girl . . . she *would*!"

The woman said to him: "Shut up!"

When they were all pressed together into the front seat of the car, Tommy leant out of the window and spoke loudly, clearly, crisply to the tramp. "There'll be a quid note for your pains."

"A quid, Mister?"

"I said a quid . . . But don't you touch him, don't you touch anything, d'ye hear? You just stand there and wait—and I'll be back."

Quite clearly, in the uptilted lights of the wrecked car, Alex saw the face of the tramp, surprisingly young, with bristles on his chin shining red or golden in the queer light.

"You can trust me, Mister," the tramp said.

* * *

Tommy sounded his horn as the small car rolled down the steepening drive into the courtyard, and he sounded it again as he came round in a sweep to draw up by the front door of the house. All along the house the windows were lit. The door stood open, and there were people waiting, standing against and under the various lights.

"Wait here a moment," Tommy said to the two women, and he went out quickly and joined the men who were standing in the doorway.

Alex lay against the woman, clinging to the hand that held her, wanting only to remain quite still, quite untouched, until there was no more of anything, no more movement, no more voices, no more light. But there was no harm about the faint smell of cigar, the touch of eau-de-Cologne, as she was led or lifted into the house.

"Poor, poor thing," the General was saying. "Oh, you poor,

258

poor thing." It was his arms that were now about her, but there was no harm in them, and no harm in the strong hands, much stronger than those of the woman, that were now gripping her elbow and her waist. The woman receded. "All right, Dorothy —*I've* got her," the General said.

In the hall she was standing on her own feet; her own limbs were supporting her. But the General's arm remained firmly placed until he said: "Take her, my boy! Take her, Ralph! Gently, gently . . ."

In his two arms Ralph picked her up. Her head lay back against his shoulder, her cheek folding itself against his chest, while he carried her up the staircase. She heard Kate's voice, and Kate's feet running, running down the stairs to meet her. "You bring her gently—you take care of her, Master Ralph!"

As she lay in Ralph's arms she was weeping freely. His voice was only a whisper: "My sweet, my pretty . . . it's all right, it's all right . . ." His own voice was trembling, quivering, only a breath.

"Carefully!" said Kate sharply. "You bring her carefully, Master Ralph! You mind her head against that staircase!"

"*I'll* bring her carefully," he said; but it was no answer to Kate; it was a whisper to Alex.

As they reached the top of the staircase, she asked: "Where's Geoff?"

"He's gone home long ago—in bed, I expect."

"You haven't sent him away."

"Of course not." He laid her on the bed. "Nor shall we— I can promise you that!" Then he stooped down and kissed her on the cheek.

"You'd much better leave her to me," Kate said. "Poor thing —she's altogether worn herself out."

259

BOOK THREE

September, 1938
At the Time of the Munich Crisis

It was the early morning of September 28th 1938—
the time of the Munich crisis

THE knocking on the door of Geoff's house, the Lodge at Neapcaster Park, was loud and prolonged. Because this sudden racket came from directly beneath his bedroom window, and at three o'clock in the morning, waking was even more unpleasant than usual. It always hurt.

Sitting up quickly, Geoff lit the candle that stood on the table beside his bed and saw there, close to his head, the letter from David. And while he was driven out of sleep—like Adam, deprived of his Eve and evicted from the garden—he found himself trying to fasten together the urgent knocking from below and this letter's contents. No such fastening was possible, except that his love for the remote, inexplicable person that was David seemed to have been identified, quite recently, with the formless thing, the loveliness, that had been snatched away from him when his sleep was broken by this clamour. By this queer, half-made identification, the letter and its request became imperative. Something that David wanted, and asked in the name of love, had to be done urgently. This was Geoff's legacy from sleep.

Yet as Geoff awoke, seized hold of the letter and started out of bed, the extension of this letter backwards into his sleep became first irrelevant, and then entirely obscured; and its extension forwards, into this world of ominous knocking, became the new puzzle. He could not solve it. Just as if the hook and eyelet of a woman's dress were refusing to be fastened, so the urgency of the noise and the appeal of David's letter declined any sort of association.

For a single second, Geoff's fingers trembled, as if he was again committed to his kneeling posture on the carpet of Alex's bedroom, to the terrible force and longing that he had had to suffer from her voice, her scent and emanating warmth, and from her dress tickling his cheek. "Geoff darling—do this up for me!" When he knelt, she said: "If you stood, it would surely be easier? But then I suppose you'd have to stoop so . . ." And when he remained kneeling, she laughed, partly in affection but partly with irritation, as his fingers fumbled, trembling, with the hook and eye.

Now, when Geoff reached his bedroom window, he was clutching David's letter, as if it was a gift from Alex. And his forehead was already damp from her warmth, scent and nearness. And as he called from the open window, his ears that were still no part of himself heard his voice that was even more alien asking in calm and level tones: "What is it, then? Is it war? Has war been declared?" While these words were still escaping, he himself thought it an astonishing question.

"War, Mr. Geoff? I'm sure I couldn't say, not having heard the midnight news. It's Draper, Mr. Geoff. It's the General. He's very bad and he's asking for you."

"I'll come at once," Geoff said. And now he was quite awake: General Meredith wanted him.

*   *   *

Geoff dressed very quickly and, at the end of the drive, overtook the butler. He saw the red button at the back of Draper's bicycle wobbling from side to side and progressing slowly. But when he drew level, neither of them spoke; when he drew ahead, Draper accelerated enough to keep in company behind him; and when he braked slightly, Draper braked also, unwilling to catch Geoff up. In this moment of personal crisis, the butler depended for strength upon precise stations, precisely defined and recognised. It was this insistence on Draper's part that made Geoff aware that the General was believed to be dying. It was as bad as that.

In this solemn order, Geoff and Draper reached the house, coming out of the night and into harbour where the lights from the windows rested in the courtyard. Geoff turned to Draper: "You've seen him of course?"

"Not to-night, Mr. Geoff. It's you he asked for. I shall be in the pantry if I'm wanted."

Geoff stood uncertainly and unhappily in the hall. The butler took a pace towards him, as if he was offering strength. He said: "Watts has mended the bell in the General's room. He's got it ringing again in the pantry." He was not yet ready to withdraw. "There will be coffee and sandwiches," he added; "should I serve them in the gunroom?" It was a question that Geoff answered with a nod. "In the gunroom then," the butler said, "whenever you ring for them."

"Mr. Ralph . . ." Geoff started to ask.

"The Captain should be here shortly."

"You've rung him up?"

"I spoke to the Mess sergeant. One of the other young officers telephoned back to say that the Captain had left already."

"And Miss Alex . . ."

"Mrs. Ralph is asleep. The doctor said not to wake her—unless the General wanted it. Her condition . . ." The butler deliberately suspended the explanation. The pregnancy of Alex, which had only recently been announced and was not yet obvious, was an almost holy subject. After five barren years it was miraculous.

The two men stood together at the foot of the staircase, unable to separate. For the first time the butler appeared old to Geoff, the greyness of his thin hair becoming assertive, and the dark folds beneath his eyes becoming a feature of his solemnity. Draper was able to say: "Hadn't you better go up, Mr. Geoff?" But he did not turn away until Geoff had reached the bend in the stairs and had looked back to give him a nod, a queer sort of smile of excitement, a dismissal.

And still it was impossible for Geoff to get a sense of calamity, or even of sadness, out of the occasion; or to ignore the shameful excitement caused by the General's dying as it was caused, equally, by the approach of war. The prospects of war and death were both wrongful excitements—twin liberations.

The staircase had grown in size to the proportions of a child's climb to bed. At the head of the stairs Geoff glanced to his right, along the shorter corridor of the west wing, towards the door at the end that had once been Mrs. Meredith's bedroom. It now belonged to Alex and Ralph: it was still Mrs. Meredith's bedroom.

Dr. Macdonald came quietly from the General's room. He

smiled at Geoff as they stood by the open door, and he spoke gravely, almost in a whisper. "He insists on seeing you. I had to have you fetched."

"Is it . . . the end?"

"I think so. But his mind is perfectly clear. He knows what he's doing."

"Do you mean . . ." Geoff started to ask, but the General's voice interrupted him, calling his name in clear, normal tones that had their usual authority. Only their volume was diminished. "Is that Geoff?"

"Go along in," the doctor said.

"He's got a precious litter of papers," Nanny said from the doctor's elbow. "You take his mind off them, Master Geoff, and he'll be the easier for it."

"Is that Geoff?" the General's call was repeated.

The doctor had hold of Geoff's elbow and he led him to the door and pushed him through it.

"Shut the door," the General said; but the doctor had already done so, remaining outside it.

*   *   *

"Come round to this . . . side of me, Geoff. Here, by the . . . lamp." The General's spasmodic speech was breathless; as if, in a way, it was Tommy Black speaking.

In the small room a fire was burning; and a single lamp, very heavily shaded, was beside the bed. The lamp and the fire being both on the same side, the farther half of the General's face was thrown into unnatural darkness, while the nearer half was scooped with shadow where the flesh, in advance of more general dissolution, had already shrunk away. From seeing the old man constantly, Geoff had not previously observed or acknowledged the steady enfeeblement that had taken place. But to-night the muscles had surrendered, leaving the skin of face and hands as flimsy as paper.

Geoff did not immediately recognise that twitching of the lips, withdrawn from the pale gums, as the old man's attempt to muster his grin. "Nanny wanted to . . . take out my teeth," he said. "This damned plate . . . hurts me more every day. But I . . . wouldn't have it!" His voice came out jerkily, creaking with his breath, no longer like Tommy Black's affectation, but rather the noise made by some inanimate thing swinging in the wind.

" Y'know, Geoff, when I was . . . small boy . . . this was . . . my room. My grandfather's day, before even . . . my father inherited . . . we . . ."

Around the room there still hung his pictures of school groups and of Sandhurst, and a sepia print of a young and lovely lady, his mother. There were also bad paintings, as well as photographs, of horses and dogs. But Geoff had forgotten them. Like most of the house, this room had for years been disused, its furniture covered with dust-sheets, until now it had been reopened for the General to end his life a little closer to his beginnings. "We used to . . . come here for . . . partridges," the General said. "Those days, always . . . at the end of the summer holidays . . . and again . . . Christmas . . ."

The General's eyes moved to the plush curtains, then slowly to the upright arm-chair of worn leather, to the heavy mahogany furniture that crowded the bed and reflected the firelight many times from piece to piece.

Some terrible fate had fallen upon Geoff. At this solemn and tragic moment, he could feel only a nervous excitement that made his own lips twitch as if they were trying to imitate the General's grin. The muscles of his mouth struggled and pulsed, in an effort to get control, until the General's voice said suddenly—" These papers! " And the General's hand made a definite gesture towards a small pile of documents on the table beside his bed. Then Geoff found that he had approached more closely the brass bedstead, had left the safety of shadows, and was standing in the light with his hand resting on a long envelope. " These? " he asked stupidly, and he could see the old man trying to frown with impatience.

The voice said: " You know . . . I'm dying? " It sounded disbelieving, but Geoff had the impression that his head had given a nod. " Times are . . . bad," said the voice. " Bankrupt? " it asked. Really, it was making a statement, but it was owed an answer. Geoff shrugged his shoulders. On this side of the family's affairs he had insufficient knowledge to answer a question so precise.

" Geoff . . ." The struggle with the breath went on for a while. " What will you, *you* . . . what will *you* do? "

" Oh, I shall be all right." Geoff had started to speak almost gaily, as if the impending event would be not only a negative release, but a positive freedom and, more, a vast opportunity. But before the words came, a feeling of shame and sorrow got hold of him from behind and touched his throat, so that the answer came out of his mouth distorted with misgivings: "Oh, I shall be . . . all right . . ." as if it was his voice, now, as well as his lips, that was imitating the General's distress.

"I'm seeing to . . . that, Geoff. At least . . . *that*."

The protest that Geoff wanted to make was stopped low in his throat. The dismay that he felt at this new threat to freedom, this new seal of dependence and obligation, never got as far as thought. "Geoff . . . when you were a little boy . . ." said the voice. And so the hateful love returned and was forced upon Geoff's limbs, through his bowels, his heart, his throat, to his eyeballs, until he was looking at the tired and beloved face through tears. When he put his hands upon the General's hands, he found them cold and he felt them stir protestingly. "Papers . . . take 'em . . . shove 'em in your . . . pocket!" And Geoff's hand moved to take hold of the documents: a few letters, lists of figures, long envelopes. "Money there, Geoff! Bearer bonds."

With anxiety and even appeal, the General's eyes watched Geoff until the papers had been put away in a breast pocket. Then the eyes closed, and the General said: "Nobody else knows . . . nobody."

At these words, Geoff's brain started to work, telling him that something wrongful, perhaps even a crime, had its source in this speech. In the long silence he tried to object, knowing that unless he spoke now, unless he withdrew the papers from his pocket, he was committed to the General's intention. But no objection got expressed, and the General's eyes reopened as he asked: "Promise? Your . . . promise?" And those eyes watched him until he nodded his head.

When next the General spoke, his speech was continuous, as if pressure had been found from somewhere to keep the words issuing from his mouth. "Get up to London, y'see, Geoff? To-morrow, to-day, this morning—get it in the bank! Half is for you, Geoff; and half for Alex. Not Ralph, you understand, but Alex. You and Alex . . ."

"Half for me and half for Alex," Geoff said, like a child repeating instructions.

"That will . . . see you all right . . . both of you," the General said with the last breath of his endeavour. "That's . . . definite . . ." His lips closed, and suddenly he appeared to be in great distress, struggling and fighting in a moment of indignity that was shocking and unthinkable. He opened his mouth, and it stayed open, the jaws moving very slightly as if they were driven by a small pulse like an engine.

Going to the door, Geoff called in a whisper: "Mac... Mac!"

The doctor and Nanny were standing together by the baize door, one on each side of it, the doctor leaning against the wall. He pushed quickly past Geoff and from inside the room called for Nanny. When the old lady had joined the doctor, they closed the door, not fully shut but ajar, and Geoff was left alone in the long corridor. It was dimly lit now, with only two or three lights burning along the whole length of the house—from the end of the nursery wing on one side, to the door of Alex's bedroom on the other. It was rather horrible that, even at this moment, some part of his mind or imagination fastened itself upon Alex and upon his own fingers fumbling with the hooks of her dress. There was no lust about his thought, but only fear and guilt.

A pale, unearthly light of daybreak was coming now from the hall, diluting the electric lamps: and quite clearly Geoff remembered, with physical remembrance, the short, evil finger of old Adam pointing to the swollen belly of the girl, Judy, at the cottage gate. He felt overladen with guilt. Under his armpit there was the pressure of the documents in his pocket. But in the side pocket of his coat his fingers were twisting and tearing the edge of David's letter. Although he had seen the General, he had not got an answer for his friend, David. Again he had failed.

Despair flooded the corridor with the growing light. It was easy for that old man in there! He had only to give up the struggle, to slip away out of it.

*   *   *

The doctor came out with his shoulders hunched. While he rubbed the palms of his hands together, his shoulders slowly straightened themselves; and while he took out a cigarette, played with it between his fingers and tapped it on his case, he breathed heavily through his nose, keeping his lips tight shut.

Geoff struck a match and held it to the doctor's cigarette. In the end the doctor said: "I must say, Geoff—you're taking it magnificently." He put his hands in his pocket, letting the cigarette

267

dangle from his lips and be rolled by his tongue while he talked jerkily. "I didn't quite mean it like that, old chap . . . I know how you feel it. You don't show anything—never did; not since you were a boy; not since I've known you." He seemed to want a response and he persisted. "This'll mean a good deal to you, won't it?" He looked so anxiously at Geoff's face that at last he got a nod. "You know . . . it won't be altogether a bad thing. It'll be the end of this place, I take it?"

Geoff shrugged his shoulders.

"You know," the doctor continued, "you might be better off away from here? There are plenty of people would be glad to have you. The Bredons, for instance. Or even Betts—now that it isn't all quite so easy as he'd thought it."

Again Geoff shrugged.

The doctor gave it up. He said: "If those papers in your pocket are of any value, you shouldn't clutch them like that. Someone will have them off you."

Geoff's hand had been holding his tie, as if his forearm was protecting the contents of his breast pocket. "They *are* valuable," he said.

The doctor nodded.

"He made me promise," Geoff said. "I had to promise him something."

"That usually happens."

"Is that promise binding?" As he asked the question, Geoff moved to the switches by the baize door and turned them off, leaving this part of the corridor lit only by the growing daylight.

"I assume it's something that you don't want to do?" Geoff nodded slightly; and the doctor, fingering his chin where the red bristles of morning were visible, said: "Weren't you, perhaps, just humouring a dying man who will never know whether or not you keep that promise?"

"Can that make any difference?"

The doctor looked away, making the decision easier. "If the General doesn't die," he said, "if he recovers—I expect you could make him change his mind about it?"

"No, Mac—I doubt it."

"Anyway, I'm pretty sure he won't recover."

The matter was really concluded, but Geoff had to get it arranged in an orderly manner. "Supposing the promise is wrong?" he asked. "A wrong thing to do."

"Unwise or *wrong*? Inexpedient or *wrong*?"

"Wrong," Geoff answered; "morally, legally, criminally wrong."

"Did you tell him that at the time?"

"I meant to; but I didn't."

The doctor was scratching his head. The hair was thin but still curly, and not yet sufficiently grey to hide that it had once been very red. "You're making this awfully complicated," he said. Wanting to get rid of his cigarette, and finding nowhere to put it, he walked to the baize door where the carpet ended and the linoleum began. While he was walking away, while he was putting out the cigarette on the linoleum floor, and while he was returning, he continued the analysis. "If the General were to recover . . . or, rather, if he had never been ill but had asked you to make the same promise, and if you had told him that the thing was wrong, perhaps criminal, would he have expected you to do it?"

"No. He'd have done it himself."

"There you are!" said the doctor. "It can't be your job to commit a crime—just because he can't commit it for himself. That isn't your obligation."

"That's just what it is," Geoff said; "an inescapable promise." The doctor threw out his hands, then turned away, putting his hands back in his trouser pockets. Geoff asked: "Do you think he'll want me again?"

"No. I don't think he'll talk again. I don't think he'll want any one."

"Well, I've got to get to London."

"You'd better be on your way; I'm going home myself, as soon as Ralph gets here."

"Thanks very much, Mac."

"Well, go on," the doctor said; but since Geoff seemed unable or unwilling to move, the doctor went back into the General's room and closed the door after him.

* * *

Geoff observed his feet overtaking each other down the precise centre of the corridor carpet, as when Nanny, on a wet afternoon, had let the boys through the baize door to play quietly. " Let me hear one sound from you, Master Ralph, and back you come! To the top of the staircase, Master Geoff, and not one step farther! "

Standing at the top of the stairs, with a foot dangling, Ralph said: " I'm going down. I'm going down one step, two steps, three steps . . ."

" She'll see you," said Geoff, meaning of course Nanny who, from the other side of the baize door, was all-seeing, all-knowing.

" She won't! You can come down one step behind me, then if she *does* see us . . ."

" I'm going along."

" Anybody can go along. Why do you want to go along? There's nothing along, except Mum's bedroom. You don't want to go there. Anyway, you mustn't." Ralph meant that the prohibition was his own, not only Nanny's. Ralph meant, without saying it, that behind the bedroom door there was *his* mother resting.

" I'm going along," Geoff repeated. The warmth, scent, flimsiness, loveliness of that room and of Mrs. Meredith's belongings seemed to suck him down the corridor.

" You're not to go along," Ralph said. " You're just not to."

One could never escape either the childhood at the beginning or the dissolution at the end. Childhood chased one all along the corridor, in the pale light of dawn, until one was stopped at the end of it—at dissolution. In between the beginning and the end there was no time, no pause of satisfaction, but only this dumb progress.

" Why do you want to go along? " Ralph asked.

" I don't know," he had answered then. Nor did he know now, even now, when he was twenty-eight years of age, a fair way along the road to dissolution where hands were reduced to paper, movement to a fluttering of paper; even now he did not know—or, at least, he could not produce his knowledge and express it—what was the force that drew him with such longing towards the door of that end bedroom.

Of course, Ralph walked in and out of that bedroom as he pleased. Ralph need not even knock. Once Ralph had called to him to enter, and Geoff had stood by the door, with Ralph barring the way between the end of the bed and the fireplace, while the scent and the steam from the bath floated with Alex's voice through the open door of the bathroom. "Geoff's here," Ralph had called over his shoulder to Alex. "Geoff says the car won't start."

"Geoff—dear Geoff!" she cried, speaking directly to him out of the steam and the scent. "Geoff—*you* can make anything start, can't you?" And she had come into the room and had stood there, wrapped only in a long bath-towel, shaking back her hair, laughing, letting the bath-towel slip a bit, as if he didn't count, as if he was another woman, as if he was a eunuch.

On the other side of that door there was not only the cause of shame, but its cure also, just as a chemist kept on his shelf both poison and antidote. On the other side of that door there was not only the source of longing, but also its destination; there was a world, half-recognised as the world of sleep, where man got manhood, and from manhood his fulfilment, and where things that seemed to conflict were reconciled, or even identified with each other, and where all beloved people were the act of loving. And now, as Geoff walked along the corridor to the staircase which he had to descend, he was in fact—until he reached the head of the staircase—walking towards that bedroom door.

From some part of the house some other door banged. In the stillness of morning dusk, this banging caused trembling through a house even as massive and great as this. When one heard the movement of a door it meant that Nanny was watching: shame and guilt. Thus Geoff approached the staircase, the door, with prayer and fear—the two joining hands—that the door would open. "Please God, let the door open! Oh, God—if the door should open, what then?"

By the time that door did open, the light of a grey morning, coming through the tall windows of the hall, had dissolved every shadow and had rendered the top of the staircase more bright than the hall below, more bright than the corridor. Behind him, as he stood at the top of the staircase, the corridor darkened towards the door of the General's dying; and in front, the corridor darkened towards the door where Alex slept. She must sleep with her windows uncurtained, for a flow of light escaped into the dark corridor when her door opened.

As if she was still asleep, she approached slowly but not uncertainly. He stood quite still while she approached him as if she was unobserved, as if he was there but neither more nor less accountable than the balustrade of the staircase, the panels of the corridor, the corridor carpet. Below the blue dressing-gown, the flimsy stuff of her nightdress hung to the carpet about her bare feet. With one hand she held the blue dressing-gown tight about her. The other hand rested on her belly. He could now see—or perhaps only imagine, believe—that she was pregnant. She was not visibly big with child, but visibly carrying treasure, and complacent.

The hot scent of her sleep preceded her. She was almost touching him when she said, in a low, sleepy voice: "I heard you; you woke me, Geoff dear. Didn't David come?"

In his astonishment he could not possibly answer. She pushed him gently aside so that she could stand at the top of the staircase, looking down it to the empty hall. When she rested her hand on his arm, it was her prayer to him to remain absent and not to awake her. "I thought I heard David," she said in the same absent voice. "I thought I heard David coming." Then she returned to her bedroom.

"I think I shook my head," he said aloud, as he descended the staircase. "I think I shook my head, and she turned away and went back and closed the door after her." He descended the stairs very slowly, talking aloud. "I can't remember, it's very queer that I can't remember, but I didn't hear my voice, and she went away." He was almost at the foot of the stairs. "I must have shaken my head . . ." He did not dare be silent and to let his heart, in the silence, expand with joy that it was not Ralph's child that she was carrying, not his child at all, not another Ralph. His love for Alex was his love for David. "She told *me* . . . It was *me* she told . . ." And in the side pocket of his coat, his fingers turned and tore the edge of David's letter. "I must have shaken my head. Or I must have nodded . . ."

He had to be silent when he reached the outer hall, because Ralph drove into the courtyard.

★   ★   ★

Although the morning was chilly, and Ralph had driven through much of the night, he had the hood of his car open, and he was bareheaded. His hair was cut short, and its fine texture let it be ruffled and blown across the top of his forehead, giving him an adolescent and impertinent appearance.

As Ralph pulled up the car quietly, switched off the engine, and stepped over the car door without opening it, he saw, as he had expected, that Geoff was coming out of the house to meet him. "Good old Geoff!" he said, meaning only that although he had not been thinking of Geoff—his mind being occupied with his job, as adjutant, preparing to mobilise his cavalry regiment—he had been conscious that Geoff, in spite of the hour, would be at hand, controlling the crisis.

Geoff said: "Hallo—so you didn't stop to change!" He must have noticed, beneath Ralph's long, tweed overcoat, the Mess overalls, blue with a yellow stripe, fitting tight about Ralph's legs and strapped beneath his patent-leather boots.

"No, old boy, I didn't wait." When Ralph came round the car to the house, his body moved quickly, smoothly, like a sailor on board his ship.

"You've been quick," Geoff said. "It's a long drive from Catterick."

"All of two hundred." Ralph looked at his wrist-watch. "Twenty past five. I had a puncture. Held me up a bit." He was bending his knees to get the stiffness out of them. "What's the news, old chap? How's Dad?"

"Unconscious. Mac's still here."

"Does he think . . ."

"There's not much hope that he'll be conscious again."

Ralph stamped and shuffled his feet, feeling the gravel of the courtyard through the thin soles of his Wellington boots. Raising his head and looking up the drive, up the hill towards the Park where the huge elms were still dark in partial silhouette, he drew on to himself, as if it were a garment, that characteristic state of Meredith repose: nothing human was of much consequence, except a man's armour of self-sufficiency; all the rest was entertainment; the gods of the elm trees and of daybreak could do no more to a man than take away his life. "Half an hour to sunrise," he said. "Sunrise is at five fifty-seven, or thereabouts. And this . . ." The stillness of his body and the low, plain voice in which he was speaking made emphatic the slight, skyward gesture. "The sailors call this 'nautical twilight.' And did you know, Geoff, the duration of nautical twilight varies according to the latitude and the season? Did you know—like the tides, it's very precisely measured and tabulated?" The breeze lifted his hair. "And Alex?" he asked.

"She's asleep."

273

" You haven't seen her this morning ? "

Geoff shook his head. He could never lie; it was hard enough to prevaricate; but on this occasion it was impossible to be truthful.

" But you've seen Dad ? "

" Just before he became unconscious. I've just left him."

" I'm glad of that," Ralph said. He was thinking that if his father had seen Geoff, he would be easier in his mind. Even Geoff's defects—his narrowness, his dependence, his unimaginative slowness—seemed sometimes to add up to his great heart which would reassure anybody, any time. " Was Dad in pain ? "

" He didn't seem to be."

" Easy in his mind ? "

" I think so . . ." Geoff hesitated. Ralph almost smiled at the hesitation. Geoff was such a stickler for accuracy, for his own fumbling precision, as if he knew that his unrevealing, inscrutable face and voice gave no one any help in interpretation, and that his words, by themselves, had to be adequate. " I do think he was easier when he'd seen me," Geoff said. " He sent for me, you know. He had some papers that I've got to take to London."

" Poor old Geoff ! " Ralph knew how Geoff hated a city and disliked spending even a day away from Neapcaster. " But while you're in town, old chap, you might drop into the Dairy Show at Earl's Court. There's a couple of Ayrshire cows we might . . ."

" Ralph ! "

" Yes, old boy ? "

" These papers he gave me . . ." Geoff tapped his breast pocket. " You ought to know . . ."

" I shouldn't worry overmuch about them. They can't make a lot of difference, can they ? "

" Ralph—they're bearer bonds, they're cash."

Ralph's lips twitched slightly, just like his father's. " I suppose it all goes into the maw of the overdraft, the mortgages ? "

" This doesn't." Geoff's voice was almost tragic. " Not if I do what he made me promise."

" Don't *worry* so much, old chap."

" This is supposed to be for me and for Alex."

" Thank God for that ! "

" Ralph—it's a lot of money, I think."

" So much the better, Geoff. And while we're on the sub-

274

ject . . ." He swung round on his heel, a complete turn and half a turn, making a little hole in the gravel and ending up with his back to Geoff and his face towards the stables, the sunrise. "It seems rather awful to be talking about it just now, but whatever happens . . . however we end up . . . I do guarantee one thing. I'll see *you're* all right. Somehow or other, I will—*that* I promise." Getting no reply from Geoff, he swung back towards him. "You won't, you wouldn't worry on that account?"

Geoff shook his head.

"Of course you wouldn't! That's just your trouble! You won't worry about yourself." Geoff still remained silent, and Ralph took hold of his arm. Geoff was so much taller and bigger than him, yet so much more vulnerable, so dependent. "You only worry about *us*, about Father, me, Alex . . . You're too good to us." Watching his friend closely, he saw a rare sign of emotion, the muscles of his throat working. "Poor old Geoff! It's worse for you than it is for me. You know . . ." Ralph was biting his lip, trying to think closely and to reduce this thing to reason, to calculation. "I just can't feel very badly about it myself, I can't make it mean to me what it must mean to the rest of you—to you, Draper, Watts and even Nanny."

"Draper is up," Geoff said. "He's got sandwiches and coffee when you want them. I said to serve them in the gun-room."

*   *   *

Instead of the shining row of guns in the long cupboard, there were now only a couple. Instead of the orderly litter of masculine kit, there were Alex's things everywhere. The old desk which she had taken for herself was pulled away from the window and now seemed to occupy half the room. There were Chinese screens in front of the two opposite doors, to stop the direct draught, and there were curtains, cushion covers and tablecloths, all made out of the same material. There was even a carpet on the stone floor. In Ralph's mind the real token of his household's downfall was the debasement of this room. "This place, Geoff . . . I mean the estate . . . One thing's certain, I suppose. Whatever does happen to it, *we* can't keep it."

Geoff took another sandwich but said nothing, made no gesture.

"I dare say it's time, Geoff, that somebody else had a crack at it." Ralph spoke without wistfulness or self-pity. Somewhere in his depths he had his family's mystical sense of property, but reduced to figures, calculations. "Do you remember here, this room, where we made young David come climbing, and he took a tumble? You did think me a swine, didn't you?"

"Yes."

"But in the sum total of a lifetime, it didn't hurt him, you know. I dare say it even did him good." He saw that Geoff had taken a letter out of the side pocket of his coat, was drawing the folded sheet from its envelope, and was holding it out like an offering. The movement was suddenly pathetic, so much a token of the humble, devoted, loving servant. One had to be gentle with such humility.

"Ralph—I don't know how you'd feel about this?" But when Ralph took David's letter, Geoff said quickly: "I don't suppose you'll want to bother to read it now—not at this moment."

"I may as well, mayn't I?"

"Little Mac's waiting to see you."

"That's his job, isn't it?" While Ralph spoke, he was reading the letter. He had the gift of getting the content of a document by just running his eye over it. "Refugees, is it? I don't see why those poor devils shouldn't be here, as much as any one else," he said. "They're all Huns, I take it?"

"Austrians, Czechs, Prussians, Danzig—everything, I think; mostly professors, musicians, doctors, scientists—to judge from David's lot."

"He's got a packet of 'em, has he?"

"He's got the house full; he's only got one room to himself."

"If he can do it," Ralph said, "I don't see why we shouldn't here."

"No . . . Except . . ." Geoff seemed to be weighing the matter in his two big hands, though those hands had not really moved. "They are Jews, aren't they?"

"Are they?"

"They wouldn't have been kicked out otherwise."

"I don't see that it makes much difference," Ralph said. "I suppose they're clean about the house? It seems to me that if we hadn't been such a chicken-livered lot, and if those loud-voiced Yanks hadn't sat so smug an' pretty, these poor sods of David's wouldn't be out of a job."

"I don't think they could pay a lot of rent," Geoff said. "From what David writes . . ."

"We couldn't very well charge 'em rent. I wouldn't do that."

"If there's a war, we could get a decent rent for a place like this; quite a sum, I should think. After all, we need it."

"Dad's creditors need it!" Again the lips twitched. "Nor will there be a war, as I see it . . . You let him have it, Geoff! Though chaps like that will find it a bit dull here, I should think."

"Thanks, Ralph."

There seemed to be a great deal of gratitude in Geoff's voice, as if he had badly wanted the request to be granted, although he had spoken against it. Of course—Ralph thought—Geoff had always been fond of David; a rum sort of friendship! And another thing, if a man was a friend of Geoff's, he must be a decent sort of chap—whatever one, personally, might think of him. "Fix it up, Geoff, as quick as you can. Before the creditors get to work on us."

★　　　★　　　★

When Ralph went upstairs, Geoff got his bicycle and pushed it up the steep part of the drive. On the crest he mounted and rode slowly towards the Lodge. He had plenty of time to get shaved and dressed for London, to ring up Frank's garage for a car, to have breakfast, to go to the farm and give his orders for the day, as usual, at seven o'clock, and still to catch the nine-five express from Neapcaster station. There was relief and perhaps security in fastening his mind on the details of this programme, allotting the time and testing the allotment: there was a dry path there, in such calculations, leading him between forces that curled over, above his head, as if they might very easily fall and smother him. In the Bible on his dressing-table there was an apt picture of God parting the waters for Moses and the Israelites to pass through them.

The driver whom Frank sent was a young, cheerful lad with an unfamiliar face; but it was the old Austin saloon, and Geoff sat in front. "You're new, aren't you?" he asked the boy.

"Started last month, sir; me and another learner."

"Learner?" Even now it was not easy to understand that any one could learn anything reputable from Frank.

"There's five of us learners in the workshops," the boy

said. "You know we got the yard next door—back of the Plough?"

"I hadn't heard that."

"There's a lot doesn't know about that." The boy was very proud of his employment, proud of working for Frank. "We're patching one shed and putting up another; that's for farm machinery and spare parts; that's for Sir Frederick Betts."

"Sir Frederick!" Geoff was astonished, not at the news itself, but because he had not already heard of it. Only a little while ago, all such news would have speedily reached the Park. "I didn't know that!" It was as if the General was already dead, and the Park of no more account.

"Oh yes," the boy said. "Sir Frederick—he's got money in the business. They say he's putting in more. They say we're going to have a proper factory when the war starts. He was round there himself yesterday."

"So he reckons there'll be war?"

"Oh yes, he says there'll be war all right. He made no secret of it. But he says *we* don't have to worry—*we'll* be kept where we are."

They were approaching the station by the southern road which by-passed Neapcaster Town. "Plenty of time," the boy said. "I like taxi work meself; it gets you about. But we'll be giving it up when the war gets started." A horn sounded behind them— a deep, arrogant note—and the boy pulled quickly into the side of the road. "There she goes!" he said with pride. "I'd know that horn anywhere. They let me drive her on test." The large car went past, full of people, Sir Frederick sitting in the back with one other man, two more on the collapsible seats, and a fifth passenger beside the driver, Victor, in the front. Victor, groom, then chauffeur, first to the Merediths and afterwards to Daniel Levine, had, on the latter's death, been passed to the Betts' establishment.

The boy had touched his cap to the car that overtook them. "When *he* comes round the factory he has a word with all of us," the boy explained to Geoff. "He's a friendly chap."

After passing the taxi, the car drew up in the station yard, exactly opposite the entrance. "There's the boss!" the boy said, giving Geoff a nudge. "He must be wanting a word with Sir Frederick." And Geoff saw Frank waiting there, hatless, not touching his forehead, but smiling and lifting his hand as an equal, a half-subordinate, when the car drew up beside him.

Victor had slipped from the seat, as soon as the car halted; but before he could get round the back of the car, Frank had opened the door beside Sir Frederick. All the occupants of the car, except Sir Frederick, dismounted and grouped themselves with Frank around the open door. One of them was taking notes; one of them carried two brief-cases; and one of them, pressing against Frank, was edged half in and half out of the car in an ungainly, obsequious attitude. They were all smartly dressed in London suits, with striped trousers, spats, umbrellas. Sir Frederick himself wore rough tweeds and an old hat with a new confidence that did not seem at all incongruous. It was as if the world had at last caught up with its new governors.

Sir Frederick lay back in the car, talking seriously and smoking a pipe. It was clearly the job of these others to see that he caught his train and was put into a rightful seat. A porter, Phil Brent, who had been born on the Meredith estates, had already hurried to the car, touched his cap and got his orders from Victor. And Sir Frederick, interrupting himself, turned to nod to Brent, then turned back to his companions. He took his pipe from his mouth to stab it emphatically towards Frank, and every one nodded. The man with the two cases of papers had some difficulty in getting out a gold pencil and making a note on an envelope.

Putting his hand under Sir Frederick's elbow, Frank helped him out of the car. Still talking, and preceded by Victor and the porter, the group moved towards the platform. Geoff followed. The stationmaster touched his cap, first to Sir Frederick and then, more slightly, to Geoff. But he came to Geoff's side and asked: " How's the General, Mr. Greenley? They've been saying he's bad."

"He's very bad," Geoff said, and the stationmaster shook his head.

As he got on board the train, Geoff felt the packet in the breast of his coat. He understood then what a terrible thing it was. What the General was giving by dying, he was taking back again by this other gift. "I'll see you're all right," he had said; and so had Ralph. They would not let him be defenceless or unprivileged: he could never be free.

* * *

The train ran non-stop to Paddington; but when it was past Swindon, and the first-class passengers had finished breakfast, Sir

Frederick came along the corridor looking for Geoff. When he found him, he tapped on the glass of the carriage door and beckoned with a crook of his finger. Geoff rose obediently.

"Well, Geoff," Sir Frederick said, "I've been wanting to see you. I heard the General . . ." He shook his head. "Of course it's not sudden—but none the less sad for that. All the same . . ." Sir Frederick propped himself in the corridor alongside Geoff. "If the old boy does go now—he'll be spared something."

"You think . . ."

"Oh, there'll be war all right. We might put it off for a few months, but we've poked our noses too deeply into other people's business to drag 'em back." He was smoking his pipe. He had become a sturdy, confident and censorious personage, looking a little like Guy Bredon, and even talking like him. "There are two things, three things . . ." said Sir Frederick. "First yourself. How are you going to find yourself situated?"

"I shall be all right," Geoff said quickly.

"I wonder . . . I very much wonder . . ." Sir Frederick played with his pipe, poking his finger into the bowl, to avoid concluding the sentence. "I'm projecting quite a few developments—agricultural, industrial—around these parts. I've been impressed lately by the way you've pulled up those farms. Latterly you've done a fine job considering the hard times we've had. And I don't mind admitting that my own operations haven't altogether . . ." Again he left it in the air. "I'd have plenty of room for a useful chap like yourself."

"I should be in the Army," Geoff said.

"Just a soldier? Just a junior officer, I suppose?" Sir Frederick said. "Wouldn't that be rather a pity? It certainly wouldn't be in your own interests. Would it, I wonder, be even in the national interests? As always, in a war, agriculture becomes a first, a major line of defence; and with your knowledge . . ."

"I should be in the Army," Geoff repeated. He felt now that the decision was taken. It was not a question of duty, but of liberation. The Army would be escape.

"Anyway," Sir Frederick said, "I thought that might be your answer. I just mentioned the thing in case. But, being as it is, I wonder if young Ralph . . ." Sir Frederick looked at Geoff as if he expected an answer to the unasked question. The question was obvious to Geoff but he said: "What, sir?" making Sir

Frederick speak it. "Somebody'll have to farm the place," Sir Frederick said. "I could make young Ralph a proposition that he might find . . . not unattractive."

"I'll mention it to him."

"I want you to do rather more than that. I hoped you'd see that it's the only sensible solution—from his point of view."

Geoff remained silent. There was no obvious comment to be made, because Sir Frederick was probably right.

"Leave it for the moment then," Sir Frederick said. "The third question was about the house. What's to happen to it? We shall want a house like that—several, I expect—for our London offices. I don't reckon myself that London will be a healthy place. We should pay a handsome rent."

"I'll mention it to Ralph."

"We should pay a good deal more than the Government, if *they* take over the place."

"I'll tell Ralph."

"*He* hasn't been in a war—not yet. I'd like to give him and you—all of you—a little piece of advice." Sir Frederick was speaking in a very kind and friendly manner. "When war starts, you'll find that every one gets carried away for a bit. But . . . but you've got to look after yourself! If you don't, and if you don't get killed, you'll spend the rest of your lives regretting it . . . Mind you," he concluded, "nobody else looks after you, if you don't do it yourself."

"Thanks," Geoff said.

"That's that," said Sir Frederick, rubbing his hands, as if he was a surgeon washing them at the end of an operation. "It's not often *you* go to London, is it? I don't ever remember seeing you on this train of ours . . ."

"Business," Geoff said vaguely, feeling that it was a dark enough answer to make further questions impossible.

"Going to Barry's, I dare say?" said Sir Frederick. "I know Harry Meredith used them. They're a very good firm of solicitors. I use 'em myself."

"Yes," Geoff answered, "I shall be going to Barry's." Now that Sir Frederick had made the suggestion, it seemed as good a place to go as anywhere else.

*   *   *

Mr. Dick Barry, who rose as Geoff entered, was a tall, thin young man with an Old Etonian tie. "This is where they put me to work! Disgusting, isn't it?" He let *The Times* drop from his fingers and fall on to the floor. He held out his limp fingers for Geoff to take. "I see they've launched the *Queen Elizabeth*. I see Jack Doyle was knocked through the ropes; I don't think that fellow's any good. Did you hear the Prime Minister last night?"

"I didn't know he was talking."

"My dear chap!" Mr. Dick picked up *The Times* again. "Our Mr. Chamberlain . . ." Opening the newspaper, he started to read. "*'To-day there is a lull for a brief time, and I want to say a few words to you . . .'*" He looked round the edge of the paper. "The gentleman was speaking to the nation, *and* the Empire. He was translated into German *and* Italian. Listen to this! *'However much we may sympathise with a small nation confronted by a big and powerful neighbour, we cannot in all circumstances undertake to involve the whole British Empire in war simply on her account . . .'* So much for the Czechs!"

There was no point in trying to find a reply. The performance was deliberate, but in a way natural, and not embarrassing to Geoff. He assumed that the pose was defensive.

"Do sit down," Mr. Dick said quietly, and he picked up a heavy pile of documents from the only spare chair which stood beside his table. Opening his hands, he let the documents drop on to the floor. "You're the Merediths' agent, aren't you? It's funny we've never met. I always deal with Ralph."

As Geoff sat down he said: "I never took over that side of it. My father . . ."

"Oh yes! Your father and my father used to do a lot of work together. At one time they were rather friends."

"The General is dying," Geoff said.

"I'm sorry, I'm so sorry." Young Mr. Barry looked over his shoulder through the grimy window. This was the back of the house, and his view was only of the neighbouring rooftops. "It wasn't altogether unexpected, was it?"

"I suppose it wasn't." And yet Geoff had not actually foreseen it or considered its effects, until the process of death had confronted him in the dark night.

"Funny you should come, Mr. Greenley! Only this morning I had a letter from Ralph . . . written from Catterick."

As soon as Mr. Dick said it, Geoff knew that he had seen and recognised, but not acknowledged, the edge of the letter showing itself amongst the papers on the solicitor's desk. Two or three words in the familiar handwriting must have been just visible. Mr. Dick pushed the letter across to Geoff.

Ralph's handwriting was small, very mature and neat. "*I have reason to believe that my father has some shares or something in his safe. I have written to him about them . . .*" It was an unusually long letter for Ralph to write, and Geoff dutifully turned the pages. While his eyes did not miss a word of it, the channel between his vision and his mind was either blocked or dislocated. He could not comprehend the contents until the very last paragraph. And then, because it was the last sentence that he read before handing the letter back across the desk, the thing was unforgettable. "*My main concern will have to be for the dependants, not more than a dozen of the old ones left in the house, stables, gardens and farms, and of course especially Geoff.*"

"There *were* shares in the safe," Geoff said. "That's why I've come to see you."

Young Mr. Barry was tearing up the letter into very small pieces. "Assets," he said, "are either disclosed, or they don't exist." When he had dropped the pieces into the waste-paper basket, he added: "We can start from there, if you like."

Geoff took the documents out of his breast pocket and laid them on the table. Young Mr. Barry gave them a delicate little prod with his pencil. "Those do rather stink!" he said.

*　　　*　　　*

"I take it that you haven't given a full and thorough study to the Bankruptcy Act?"

"I'm afraid not," Geoff said.

A girl forced the door half open and looked in over Geoff's shoulder; her hair which was lank touched his cheek. "Yes, Mr. Dick?"

"I want the Bankruptcy Act—of 1914, I think it is."

When she had gone, he said: "I do wish she'd go to a hair-dresser. Perhaps we don't pay her enough. I do wish she'd powder her face; she does so sweat." Tapping his teeth with a pencil, he examined Geoff and thought that he had never worked on any one so unresponsive. Most people reacted quickly, one way or the other, to his technique of effeminacy and flippancy, which hid both his own shyness and his love of friendliness—of which he was ashamed. Most people came out of their own defences to meet him. If they had been similarly educated, they, also, had learnt that a contempt for competence—if the competence was unconcealed—was a first principle of good manners, and they replied with flippancies of their own. If they were uncouth, they were outraged by the unseemliness, and one got at them through their outrage. But Geoff just sat on the other side of the table, perfectly composed, quite friendly and apparently self-sufficient.

When the girl came back and got herself wedged between the half-open door and Geoff's chair, Geoff took the booklet from her and handed it across the table. "Thanks," said young Mr. Dick, "I fancy it's section 156." He looked it up quickly, holding his pencil suspended like a plumbline over the page. Then, letting the pencil drop and making a small dot in the margin against the relevant passage, he pushed the booklet across to Geoff. "But it's really rather pointless, Mr. Greenley. Didn't we know it already?" Watching Geoff's face, which directed itself on to the page but remained quite expressionless, he diagnosed the pose at last as pretended stupidity. Then he began to wonder how much of it was pretence.

"I've got to turn these things into cash," Geoff said, putting his hand on the documents, "whether it's a criminal offence, or whether it isn't."

"It *will* be a criminal offence, won't it, if the estate isn't solvent?"

"But I've still got to turn them into cash."

"You know this is the wrong shop, of course?"

"I suppose it is."

"If you care to come round the corner for a glass of ale, I'll do you a friendly act." Mr. Dick looked at his watch. "They're open now. I could do with a drink."

"I only want advice."

"In my family, advice constitutes a friendly act." He smiled; he sniggered; then suddenly, changing altogether his attitude and posture, he smacked his hand down on the table. "You know," he said, "we're being rather silly about all this! This isn't true—all this—is it? This is a highly respectable firm of solicitors, you know, the most respectable in the country. In fact we're nothing much else *but* respectable."

"I don't question your respectability," Geoff said; and Mr. Dick wished that he would just give a suggestion of a smile when he made a joke. "The General is very respectable. I'm pretty respectable myself."

"And this sort of thing," said Mr. Dick, speaking very seriously as he tapped the documents with distaste, "it doesn't happen to respectable people, does it? Not to people like you and me and the General. It's just melodrama, isn't it?"

"Something of the sort."

They went briskly downstairs, but when they got to the first of the spacious landings, young Mr. Barry said: "Would you care to have a word with my father? Would you care for a second opinion?"

"All right."

They had stopped outside a tall and ornate doorway. "You leave the talking to me," Mr. Dick said. He knocked on the door, but there was no reply. "You know, the old boy's pretty distinguished. You know it's pretty distinguished, in this racket, to get a knighthood out of it?" He knocked again. "The old boy's a bit deaf and a bit blind, but quick as a whippet." He knocked for the third time. "Of course, he knows all about the Neapcaster business—insists on it." Before he could knock again the door had swung open.

*　　　*　　　*

The door was hung, on its inner side, with a curtain which rustled on the thick carpet. When the door had opened, Geoff saw, standing in the entrance to a large and handsome room, a very tall, thin, stooping old gentleman who was holding a copy of *The Times* and whose pince-nez dangled on a black ribbon against a buff waistcoat. "Is that you, Richard?" he said. "Don't hang about the passages—there's a good fellow." He sniffed between the phrases of his speech, as if he were taking snuff. "And who is *this* you've got with you?"

"Mr. Greenley, Father. He's General Meredith's agent."

Sir Godfrey held out a hand as limp as his son's. "I knew your father very well; a capital old fellow. Come in, won't you?" He shuffled his way across the thick carpet to his desk under the windows. "Sit down, if you please." He pointed to a huge Gothic chair, discordant with the otherwise pleasant furniture of the room. "What is it?"

"The General is very ill," Geoff said.

The old man nodded to the foliage of the plane trees in the square outside. "We seldom met latterly, Harry Meredith and I. He was a very old friend."

"The General is dying, Father."

After a considerable silence, Sir Godfrey said: "Within this office, Richard, a client is either alive or dead."

"Father—the General made Mr. Greenley promise to cash some bearer bonds for a specific purpose . . ."

The old man grunted, interrupting his son. "I hope he told him to keep his mouth shut?"

"He did, Father."

"Then what . . ." Sir Godfrey pointed a finger at Geoff. His arm was supported on the desk, but the finger trembled and the skin, like the skin of the General, was already half-way to paper. "Then what's he doing here?"

"He asked my advice."

Sir Godfrey grunted. It would scarcely have been possible to put more scorn into so brief an exclamation. "Why so?" he asked.

"He doesn't know the ropes."

The old gentleman never withdrew his finger which still trembled but still pointed at Geoff's stomach; but with his other hand he put on his pince-nez. Watching Geoff, he asked his questions quickly, and without waiting for an answer, as if Geoff's face—or perhaps the mere sound of the questions—was sufficient reply in itself. "Where had Harry Meredith got these things? Hidden away in a safe? Sensible chap!" Each question or observation was concluded with a sniff. "Have they been there some time? Are the interest coupons uncashed? Does any one else know about 'em?"

"Only Ralph," Geoff said, when he gathered that, this time, an answer was wanted.

"He's a silent sort of fellow, isn't he? I suppose he's safe enough. Where are these things at the moment?"

"In my pocket," Geoff said, putting his hand to them.

"Don't you take 'em out in here!" The old man sat in silence for some moments looking away, looking at the trees, but stabbing his finger at Geoff until, finally, he said: " Some do, you know . . . some don't."

"So you think, sir . . ."

"Certainly not!" Calling in his authoritative finger, Sir Godfrey clasped his hands and edged his body round so that it was completely facing the window and turned away from Geoff. Following his regard, Geoff was suddenly informed that the day was bright and peaceful in autumn stillness. It made him desire greatly the simplicities and authority of Neapcaster, as if it was a distant country, from which he had been exiled.

"There's a point . . ." Sir Godfrey said at last. He let his voice trail away into the treetops as he turned back to the room and pulled himself slowly to his feet. When he started to shuffle his way back towards the door, Geoff had to follow. The old man stopped at the door and turned to face Geoff. "As far as I am aware, Greenley, the only material creditor of the estates is likely to be the Bredon Trust. I wonder what Guy Bredon would have said if you'd thought of asking him?"

Before opening the door, Sir Godfrey held out his free hand— which happened to be his left—and let it dangle for Geoff to shake. As he withdrew it again, he said: "A promise is a promise, isn't it?" Opening the door he waved them out like a policeman directing traffic. "Richard—show this wise and sensible young man off the premises. I hope he's as wise and sensible as his father . . . as wise and sensible as he looks."

"Oh, I think so," young Mr. Barry said; but the curtain of the oracle had already rustled, and the door was shut.

"You didn't expect that!" Geoff said when they were half-way down the first flight of stairs.

"Not exactly. But you got your answer. Lay your head on Guy Bredon's bosom . . . You know him, I expect?"

"Very well indeed."

"It was fun while it lasted," Mr. Dick said, when they got to the hall. He shook Geoff's hand warmly. "So sorry I can't give you lunch."

★ ★ ★

From a telephone box Geoff rang up Bredon & Co. "Mr. Bredon won't be back till after lunch. You might try again at three o'clock."

He rang up the firm of publishers of which David was a partner. "Mr. Levine isn't coming into the office to-day. You might be able to get him at his home, if it's urgent. He lives at Neapcaster."

"It's all right; it isn't urgent."

But as soon as Geoff had left the telephone box, it was again urgent that he should find someone, some inhabitant, to relieve the hatred of a city. Men in herds, like beasts, like cattle or fowls or pigs, were hostile to the stranger, hating him.

"Excuse me!" Two girls pushed past to get to the telephone box. As they closed the door on themselves they were giggling. "'Course he owns the place!"

He waited a long time for them to finish their telephone conversation; but when they had at last finished, they started to ring up another number. And all this time they were sliding glances at him through the glass door and then turning to each other to giggle. They were no more and no less intelligent than a bunch of heifers, ready to be turned into a field with a young bull.

He had to walk down three streets before he found another box at which to wait; and when at length he got into it, he forestalled a man with a brief-case arriving in a hurry. Impatiently the man waited while Geoff sought in his pockets for coppers. But he had no coppers, not even a silver coin, but only notes. So he smiled at the waiting man as he surrendered the box and said: "I'd forgotten—no change!" Unsmiling, the man stared back for an instant, as if Geoff was mad.

Geoff bought an early edition of an evening paper. "What's this?" the man asked. "I'm not a bank, governor. And if I was, you wouldn't want nineteen and elevenpence in coppers." He had to give the man back his newspaper.

Not so much as a silver coin, but only a few treasury notes and thousands of pounds of bearer bonds: how did a man in such a state get twopence for the telephone? "Could you change me a pound note? I'm awfully sorry to trouble you—could you change me a quid?"

Once he had started to walk in this way—movement becoming flight—it was very difficult to stop. He wanted only twopence. From one year to the next, he never wanted twopence at Neapcaster. In a city, twopence was unobtainable. When he had bought a packet of cigarettes—he never smoked cigarettes—he had again to look for a telephone. He rounded each corner with hope, but found no box, or else a box already possessed: a voluble man with a note-book, a laughing girl exchanging jokes with the telephone, a girl and a man laughing together. If ever he caught their glances, the laughter, the smile, was at once covered, like a blind drawn down over a lit window. Instead of a smile there was a look of enmity or distaste. At last he had both twopence and a telephone and was through to Betts' office. "Mr. Wallis, Mr. Walter Wallis . . ."

"I don't think I know the name, sir. Do you know which department?"

"Agricultural research."

"He's probably at Slough, isn't he?"

"I know he has an office in London."

"He must be one of that Barbicon lot. You might try Moorgate double-five-four-three."

When he got through to Barbicon House, the girl put him on to a man with a young and pleasant voice. "I haven't seen Walter to-day. He'll be in this afternoon, I expect—he's sure to."

"Thanks—I'll try after lunch."

Whose lunch? It wasn't so easy even to get lunch. There seemed to be no eating-place that invited the solitary stranger, the alien to the city. "I'm afraid, sir, I haven't a table. All are booked."

"Excuse me, old chap," said the little man in the black hat as he pushed Geoff aside with a kindly hand on his arm. "Ah, André—a table down below?"

"Excuse me!" All three of the women walked round Geoff, as if he was a lamp-post, as they went, laughing and chattering over their shoulders, into the restaurant. Geoff followed.

"Good morning, Emile," they said. "Can we have the one in the corner?"

"Whichever you wish, madam."

"*That* corner, perhaps?"

"That or the other, madam. Just as you please."

When the man returned from showing them to their seats, Geoff asked him for a table.

"Alas—they are all taken!"

"Those over there, by the wall?"

"They are all reserved, Monsieur. What can I do?"

At the corner of the street a foreign little man, a waiter with a napkin, stood in an open doorway, wistfully, sadly regarding the people who hurried past. He smiled, he beckoned to Geoff with a timid, floating hand. Geoff turned away his head and quickened his step. "Why did I do that? Why didn't I go in and eat?" Through the glass window he had seen that the restaurant was empty. One couldn't eat by oneself in an empty room; one had to be suspicious of the man who beckoned and invited, of a place which the herd shunned. One could trust only a place which the herd favoured.

He walked more quickly now, because it was easier to increase one's pace than to reduce it. Here, on the left, was a glimpse of a man in a chef's cap; and here a visionary instant—a hand lifted like a blessing while the two waiters exchanged reproach. Incongruous lights conflicted with the sunshine; the music started and stopped as the man in uniform opened and shut the door, the tongues were foreign—*niente, niente* . . . and aromatic steam came in a wisp into the street round the edge of a palm in a pot. If one could only be inside, secure and hidden in the herd, belonging to the place! If one could only be back at Neapcaster, where there were no strangers, where every tree and stack and shed, and every man and beast, belonged to the place! One ought never to leave Neapcaster; it was madness to leave such a harbour, secure and safe; madness to come to a city where one became friendless, unwanted, a tramp.

★　　　★　　　★

"Hallo!" She called in a friendly voice; and she seemed quite a nice and neat sort of girl to Geoff in his first astonishment at being spoken to. "Won't you stop and talk to me?"

He did stop and raise his hat.

"Are you all alone—lonely?" she asked.

"I'm alone at the moment." He saw now that she was a woman of his own age or more, and quite smartly dressed in a dark red frock.

"It isn't nice to be lonely, dear. It isn't nice, is it?"

"No!" The sound of this one syllable, drawn with so much of his breath and from such depths, shocked him. When he had recognised her as a prostitute, and found that he had stopped and spoken to her instead of hurrying past, and when this recognition had been endorsed by the hardening of his innards, by the feeling of a lump embedded in his stomach, at once his strength was taken away and his chest contracted.

" Wouldn't you like to come with me, dear ? "

Even his mind denied that he would like it, while his body was trembling with fear; but he had the courage to nod his head. Only his voice was less courageous. " I wanted lunch," he said. " Have you had lunch ? "

" I don't bother much about lunch, dear. You can come home with me, dear, and I'll give you something better than lunch." Her voice was gentler, responding to his fear. " You're a stranger here, aren't you ? Stranger to London ? You're not a foreigner ? You don't look like a foreign gentleman."

" I'm a countryman."

" I thought you were from the country." They were walking side by side. " This way, dear."

" Where are we going ? "

" It's not very far, dear—just a step."

" How far ? "

" Only a step." He kept his eyes lowered and he walked quickly, so that she had almost to run beside him, her legs being restricted by the narrow, dark red skirt. " Not so fast, dear! I haven't got your long legs, you know. You're a big boy, aren't you ? Ever so big ! "

This made him laugh—a nervous, breathless sound—and she put her hand into his arm, pulling him back to her. When they had turned into a short and narrow street, she said: " You've got a little money, haven't you, dear ? We've all got to live, you know."

" I've got some money."

" How much are you going to give me, dear ? " When he didn't answer she asked: " Are you going to give me five pounds, dear ? " And after a pause: " You're going to give me three pounds anyway, aren't you ? " And finally: " I couldn't do it for less than two pounds, you know. I don't ever do it for less than that. It wouldn't be right, would it ? "

He looked at her, and he found that he was actually smiling.

" I believe you're going to give me three pounds, aren't you ? "

" All right."

" I believe you're going to give me five pounds, dear. I'll give you a lovely time, you know." They had stopped at a small door beside a greengrocer's shop which had an open window and baskets of produce standing in the street. The shopkeeper had come out to talk to a customer. "Here we are, dear." She was getting a key out of her handbag.

He knew by now that this incident was quite unrelated to the shut door of the bedroom at the end of the passage. He was sweating. He could feel it on the forehead, under the brim of his hat. The palms of his hands were damp. Whatever he was to do now would require courage. He looked at his watch while she was putting the key into the lock. "I'd forgotten," he cried; "good lord, I'd forgotten! I've got an appointment." At last his memory provided him with inspiration. "I've got to go to Earl's Court. I'd forgotten it."

"Earl's Court, dear? Well, you needn't stay with me very long."

"I can't come in," he said breathlessly. "I can't possibly come in. It's the Dairy Show."

"I'm just as good as a dairy show, dear." She giggled and tucked her hand back into his arm. "You're joking, aren't you?"

"No, no—I can't . . ." He pulled his arm free, turning abruptly and seeing that the greengrocer and customer were both watching this scene on their doorstep.

"The Dairy Show!" She spoke sharply now. "But you promised me, didn't you? Think of all the time I've wasted! I can't afford to waste time like that. Time's money, dear, isn't it?"

Under the eye of the greengrocer, he took out his note-case. "Here!" He gave her a couple of pounds.

"You promised me more than that, dear."

He gave her another note.

"You promised me five, you know."

He gave her the rest and ran a few paces down the street before dropping into a brisk and purposeful walk.

* * *

Soon he had reached a telephone box, but he did not dare stop at the first one in case she should come past it. Later he did stop and, although it was not yet three o'clock, got through to Guy Bredon.

"He's just back," the girl said, "earlier than we'd expected. I'll put you through to him."

"Look here, old boy," Guy said, "I'm afraid I'm absolutely full up until late, until nearly eight o'clock. Could you pick me up here for dinner? Have you got to get back to-night?"

"I ought to. The General . . ."

"I know, I know, old boy. I telephoned Draper before lunch. He's still unconscious; there's been no change."

"I can take the late train back," Geoff said.

"It's a beastly journey that way, isn't it?"

"I don't mind it."

"All right then—eight o'clock."

Since there was a long time to be consumed, and it was now too late for lunch, he went into a cinema where they showed the news, where at least there was darkness into which the people melted, so that there was no crowd to jostle him and hate him as a stranger, an alien. In the darkness of the cinema he slipped into the herd before they had detected his strangeness.

As he got into his seat he heard the foreign voice that had become familiar on the wireless. The words were spat into the darkness on a rising note. Higher and higher the phrases were strung together up a ladder of passion that reached at last the final scream. A million voices answered: "Sieg heil . . . sieg heil," and the chant continued, "Sieg heil . . . sieg heil . . . sieg heil," precise and rhythmical as the beat of a piston. Thus, in long, meticulous ranks the men marched through the darkness. With their chant unbroken, and bearing their similar banners, they were an all-consuming host, a single beast, consuming man. Man was eaten up by the beast of the host; and man was excreted in this terrible chant: "Sieg heil!"

The crowd from the screen continued into the street when Geoff left the cinema. But it was not yet a host. As the people jostled Geoff, crossed his path, blocked his way or hurried past, their eyes were friendless, their faces were blank, but they were still people, not yet consumed, not yet turned into the excreta of that chant.

In the first telephone box that he came to, he got through to Walter. The voice was blessedness. "Geoff—whatever are you doing in London? Are you up for the night? At least we can have a drink."

"I'd like to very much."

"What a shame! If only I'd known . . ." Walter was talking with such warmth! "Couldn't you have let me know, Geoff, that you were coming up? I'd have loved to have taken you . . . I've only just got back . . . we could have gone together . . ."

"Gone where?"

" To Earl's Court—to the Dairy Show."

" I'd like to have gone to the Dairy Show," Geoff said. " Only I couldn't fit it in; I had too much to do."

*   *   *

" What were *you* doing at the Dairy Show, Walter? What do *you* know about cattle? Why don't you stick to your stinks? "

There was no one else with whom Geoff was so comfortably intimate as Walter. The affection that he had for him was not tangled up in the sort of admiration and respect that he felt for David, nor complicated by the range of different and conflicting emotions inspired by Ralph. With Walter, Geoff had a simple and trustful friendship in which, with unusual self-confidence, he became the dominant partner.

" I was told to go there," Walter said.

" By the big boss? "

" By Betts. He's going in for milk."

" Is it that, Walter? Be truthful with yourself! It isn't by any chance that he's seen the red light? That the corn yields are getting a little less? "

" They're not, Geoff. They're satisfactory enough."

" But each year they're needing a few more hundredweight of stinks? "

" You've got a phobia," Walter said. " You're becoming a crank. You use our stuff yourself."

" Only in moderation, Walter; and only after the muck."

" You and your dust-bowls! You and your blessed muck! "

" Blessed it is, Walter! Can I ring up Frank? "

They got through to Frank almost at once, and without stating the number, as if the office exchange was well accustomed to making this connection. When Geoff asked for a car to meet him on the train arriving at midnight, Frank said: " We don't like it, you know. We've rather given up this late work. But to oblige a friend . . . to oblige *you*, Geoff . . ."

" Come on! " Walter said, as soon as Geoff had rung off. " Let's get out of here! I know you want a drink." They hurried out of the bright and dust-free office, whose windows looked high over the city roofs to the great dome itself, and they clattered along the airy corridors to the bronze doors of the lifts. They pressed all the buttons, calling all the lifts at once.

" Is this all Betts'? " Geoff asked. " All these offices? Whatever do they all do? "

" You'd be surprised! " Walter said. " We share the two top floors with the legal chaps."

" Legal? How do *they* come into it? "

" You'd be surprised! " Walter repeated.

While they waited for a lift, they laughed; they were immensely happy together. Walter's pink face lost its anxious and responsible look when it turned upwards to Geoff. Although he was quite a big man himself, he was not Geoff's height; and though he was a year younger, he looked easily the elder, and his hair was already thin at the top of his forehead.

" Walter—you're getting fat and bald! You've got too good a wife . . ."

" I'm putting on a lot of weight. I'm wearing a bit thin on top—it's true enough."

While they were going down in the lift, Walter said: " But you look tired, Geoff. You hate London, don't you? I should have thought you'd have liked it."

Geoff found the answer easy. " It's all right when I'm with a friend," he said; " then it's fun. But to be alone, alone in a crowd, a city . . ." His feelings became so easily disentangled, were so easily seen and distinguished, and seemed to be so simple, in Walter's company. " I hate crowds. I hate to be a stranger amongst a crowd. . . ."

On the ground floor the lift opened into a huge hall or lobby which, being a passage-way right through the whole block of offices, was full of people. " Like beasts they are," Geoff said, as they jostled him. " Like beasts, they make a set against a stranger."

" I always thought you rather liked people."

" Not strange people, not in crowds. What is there to like about them? "

" They're people." They were parted by a bunch of girls and they came together again when the girls had been passed.

" They might as well be anything else," said Geoff.

" I love people." Walter was smiling, not from amusement but in the happiness of friendship. He took hold of Geoff's arm as they got through the crowd in the vast doorway and came into the street. " I love them just for being people," Walter said.

★　　　★　　　★

They had gone to a bar just round the corner, but Walter had ordered only lemonade for himself. " Still teetotal? " Geoff asked him. " Won't you relax for once? "

" I don't suppose I'd like it."

" Try it, anyway."

" My nonconformist conscience wouldn't let me."

Carrying their drinks—the glass of lemonade and a glass of gin—they got a seat against the wall. On the marble-topped table there was a fern in a pot. Geoff asked: " And how does the nonconformist conscience get along with Betts? "

Geoff had been laughing, but Walter answered gravely, too gravely perhaps: " That's just what I'm asking myself."

Geoff couldn't take him very seriously. " Nothing really criminal, I hope? "

" Oh, we never break the law, of course. We never go near breaking it. On the contrary, we live by the law—literally live by it." He spoke with a bitterness that Geoff had never heard from him before. " We have whole departments to find out the most we can do and tell us how to do it. We lend money, for instance . . ."

Since he seemed to have finished, Geoff said: " Well, that sounds fair enough! "

" So it is, of course. We lend money on land—more money on land than anybody else—at very low interest."

" You sound like public benefactors."

" We do, don't we? " He pulled some bits off the fern and dropped them on to the table. " But somehow or other . . . we always seem to get hold of the land . . . it always seems to be ours in a year or two."

" What sort of land, Walter? "

" Any sort of land that's agricultural. Anywhere in England; all over the place."

" I don't know what you want with so much land," Geoff said, drinking his gin. " It's not worth much nowadays. It doesn't make sense."

" We look a long way ahead."

" Can any one see ahead? "

" Betts thinks he can."

" And what does he see when he looks into his crystal? War, of course? "

"Oh yes—he sees war all right. And agricultural expansion, and shortages—shortages of everything we make—that we do make now, or could turn to making . . . Shortages of feeding-stuffs and fertilisers and implements . . . Shortages and high prices for crops and stock . . ." Walter was playing with his glass of lemonade, tilting it and stirring it with his straw, avoiding Geoff's eyes while he talked.

"Well," Geoff said, "I don't like the chap myself, but I don't see what your conscience has against him."

"It can't exist," Walter answered. "That's all there is to it." He had spoken very bitterly before, but now his voice dropped as if he minded about it very deeply, too deeply even for bitterness. "Conscience doesn't come into it, when it's a question of that man's vision. That man's vision has to be Holy Writ. He sees me in politics now. He wants me to go into politics."

Geoff laughed at this tremendous joke. "I can't see *you* in politics, Walter boy!"

"Can't you, Geoff? I think I'd be rather good at it."

"All right then!" Geoff cried, emptying his glass and waving his hand towards Walter. "If you like to take the gamble—be a politician! Go right ahead!"

"But it wouldn't be a gamble," Walter answered in a low voice. "He says I can keep my job with him. He says he'll put up my salary—whether I get into Parliament or whether I don't."

"He couldn't be fairer than that."

"He couldn't—could he?" Walter answered. But the bitterness was back in his voice. "And now, Geoff—another drink?"

"Oh yes. I need it after that." They took some time getting to the bar and getting back again. Then Geoff asked: "And what would little Mac have to say about it?" He asked the question gently. "How would the doctor view his friend, Walter, a respectable Conservative politician?"

Of course he was still laughing, and Walter was very serious, so that the gap between the mockery of the one and the gravity of the other was all the time getting wider. So far, the bridge of their friendship was adequate to reach across it.

"Mac likes the idea very much," Walter said slowly. "You see . . ." He was playing with the bits of fern that he had pulled off the plant, and he arranged and rearranged them into several different patterns before he said: "Betts doesn't care what party I belong to; he just wants me . . . in Parliament."

Geoff had no answer to make, but he emptied his glass and put it down with a very deliberate clink on the stone table. Walter said: "Betts thinks it would be easier to get in as a Socialist. He wants me to stand at the first suitable by-election . . . So I suppose . . . that's what I shall do . . . But whether there's a *quid pro quo* to it, Geoff, and what it's likely to be . . ."

They both of them got up together and went slowly towards the door. It was as if their friendship had been temporarily expended by this conversation. There was no enmity or even discomfort between them; but the well of friendship would need some little time of absence to fill itself up again.

"How are the wife and children?" Geoff asked. And the thought that impinged like lightning on the dark view was: "Even Walter, even the boy, has his wife, his woman, his closed door of a bedroom, closed against me!"

They shook hands solemnly. Geoff felt rather ridiculous doing so: they never did shake hands—he and Walter—their friendship being too close and easy for that. As they parted, Geoff asked the way to Guy's office. It was only ten minutes' walk, and the time was now nearly half-past seven. He would not be much too early, but he could have stayed with Walter a little longer if he had wanted to.

"Guy Bredon—now there's a good man, really good!"

* * *

The big, respectable, old-fashioned building of the Bredon Trust was, of course, closed for the night, but there was an old porter on duty at a side entrance.

"Mr. Greenley?" He already had his instructions, and he took Geoff through a night-room, where a couple of clerks were working, into a long, narrow passage. A very small lift from the lobby at the end of the passage took them up to a top storey whose walls were darkly panelled to head-height and finished, from the panelling to the ceiling, in deep red paper. There were still gas brackets on these walls, but the light came from unshaded bulbs, sparsely stationed, hanging from short lengths of flex.

"You've never been here before, Mr. Greenley? Your father— he used to come often. He used to have dinner here with Mr. Guy, and with old Mr. Guy before that." The porter was a short man with a big grey moustache and gold spectacles. The coat of his dark blue suit was open showing the medal ribbons stitched to his waistcoat and the heavy watch-chain with a Masonic emblem.

In an angle of the building at the end of the passage, Guy had a very big room, reached through a small ante-chamber and furnished like a private study, with heavy things, with deep, sober and soft things, and with things deposited casually at some time or other in odd places, and never moved afterwards except to be dusted. It smelt richly of cigars. The lights were rosy and soft. "My dear Geoff . . ." Guy got up from his enormous desk and came towards the doorway. "How nice of you to come!" Like the odour of incense, swelling with the organ music, the scent of cigar swept comfortingly ahead of Guy's approach. Geoff felt his hat and coat taken from his hand by the porter. "I expect Jack told you that he knew your father?"

"I was telling him, Mr. Guy. Will you be having something up here?"

"Shall we eat up here, Geoff? I don't do it often these days, but it's rather nice."

Geoff thought that he hadn't replied, but it seemed settled that they should each have a steak. "Do you like it on the raw side, sir?"

"Yes, please," Geoff answered.

"And two pints of stout," said Guy, returning to his desk.

"Do you like stout, Mr. Greenley?" the porter asked. "Some people don't; but Mr. Guy, he never thinks to ask. He likes stout himself, so he takes it that every one else . . ."

"I like stout," said Geoff, as he followed Guy across the room, watching sideways for the porter to be gone, and then, as soon as the door had closed, pulling from his pocket the bundle of papers and putting them on the desk. "The General gave me these last night," he said. "At least it was early this morning—just before he went unconscious."

"Did he . . . did he?" There was no surprise in Guy's voice as he picked up the papers and looked through them. His words were just an acknowledgment, soothing to Geoff, while the big red hands played with the papers as if they were glad to have this occupation. "Did he know what he was doing all right?"

"I thought so. The doctor thought so."

"Little Mac was there, was he?" The question didn't need an answer. It was just a comment, an accompaniment, while Guy pointed to the deep arm-chair beside the desk, waited for Geoff to be seated, and then leant back in his own chair—as if he was leaning back in the saddle, always the Master—and drew his spectacle-case out of his pocket as he might have drawn the horn from between the buttons of his pink coat. The spectacles were steel, plebeian articles, and they slid a little way down his nose so that he could look over their tops. "Tell me, Geoff, where did these bonds come from? Out of a safe or something?"

"Yes—it was out of a safe."

"D'ye know, Geoff, all these years—and I never knew old Harry had a private safe in the house! Where did he keep it? In the study, was it? Somewhere behind all those books?"

"In his dressing-room, I think. I believe Ralph knew, but I've never seen it."

"Your father would have known. You can bet your life on it!"

"I've got to ask your advice," Geoff said. There was weariness in his voice, a great weariness in his body, but now less weariness in his heart. "He made me promise, you see . . . I know it's a wrong thing to do . . . but I couldn't refuse to promise, could I?"

"No, no, old Geoff—I'm sure you did the right thing; sure of it."

"He was so ill, you see, so feeble. He said he was dying, and I couldn't do anything but promise."

"You did the right thing, of course."

"It can't be right to promise to do wrong."

"I shouldn't put too fine a point on it. You hadn't much choice. And after all . . . a promise of that sort . . ."

"It's still a promise."

"Well . . . yes . . . so it may be . . ." Guy pulled his chair closer to the desk. "Let's have a better look . . ."

It was a deep and comforting silence, while Guy drew out of a drawer a large white pamphlet, searched through its pages and started to make notes on a slip of paper. He wrote with a gold pencil attached to one end of his watch-chain. Watching him, one could see the watertight doors closing between his personalities, as one whole set of characteristics was shut away, and the other exposed and brought into action. "This is going to be quite a sum of money," he said as he went through the bonds. "Quite a sum at that! Quite a sum . . . a nice sum . . . a tidy bit . . ." His voice rumbled into silence while he finished his task.

At length he lay back in his chair, playing with the pencil, following the watch-chain up to his pocket and back again. "Have you any idea of it, Geoff?"

Geoff shook his head.

"The best part of twenty thousand pounds—at present prices."

"As much as that?" Geoff was not surprised, either one way or the other. He had not even bothered to look at the face value of the stock, since the matter of value had seemed irrelevant.

"Yes—it's pretty good stuff, most of it."

The silence continued just as comfortably as before until Guy drew out his watch, blew on it and snapped open the lid, blew on it again and made it strike the half-hour. "It doesn't really surprise me," he said at last. "Harry was . . . is . . . an old peasant at heart. A passion for a little something hidden away . . . the hole in the hearth."

The door opened without a knock, and the porter, Jack, returned with a wheeled trolley covered with plates and dishes. From the corner by the door he got a folding table which he set up by the fireplace. From a cupboard he got a tablecloth. "You haven't given yourselves a glass of sherry!" he said.

"Nor we have, Jack!" Guy rolled across the room to the top part of the cupboard, which was locked. His keys were on another chain that led to his trouser pocket. While he got out the decanter, Jack put glasses on a tray and set the tray upon Guy's desk.

*   *   *

"So it's to be half for you and half for Alex? Does any one else know about it?"

"Only Ralph. It may have been his suggestion."

Guy got up from the table by the fireplace and wandered to the tall windows whose deep red curtains hung to the floor. Standing some paces back from them, with his legs apart and his hands in his trouser pockets, he seemed as grave and solid and seasoned as anything else in this immensely respectable chamber. You felt that this was his own world—just as the hunting field was his other kingdom—so familiar, so much under his mastery, that he could look right through the curtains over the city rooftops. You wondered if it was a clear night and if there was a moon above the chimneys. There was a waning moon, of course; it would not yet have risen. "These Merediths!" Guy said. "What a pity there aren't more of them!"

Slowly he made his way round the room, returning to his desk, rumbling out his thoughts as he went. "You and Alex, you see? Two of the family—but the two they had imported, so to speak, the two who might find themselves . . ." He sat down at his desk, settling himself with pleasure as if that station suited his thought. "Come over here, old Geoff. It's the best arm-chair in the room. Shall we give ourselves a cigar apiece?" He got the box from a drawer in his desk, opened it, parted the paper flaps, all with such evident enjoyment of the slow and deliberate movements. "You know, Geoff, I'm not altogether a disinterested party myself? Had you realised that?"

"Sir Godfrey said something about it."

"Godfrey Barry? You've seen him, have you? The old devil sent you on to me, did he? That was a wicked notion!" But it made Guy chuckle as he leant right back in his chair and very deliberately cut his cigar with a penknife. "Well, Geoff, what did he tell you?"

"He said: ' A promise is a promise, isn't it?'"

"And a shocking remark too—from an eminent lawyer!"

"It was rather what I'd felt myself."

"That's as maybe, Geoff!" But Guy was smiling to himself, with his chin tucked into his rucked-up waistcoat. "After all . . ." He tapped with his penknife on the desk, reaching as close to Geoff's papers as he could manage without stirring himself. "This is a useful sum of cash . . . and—you an' I—we've both got a claim to it! Have you thought what it means to yourself?"

"I'd as soon not have it."

After a considerable pause, Guy said: "I wouldn't believe it from anybody else! But from you—I believe it!" He lit his cigar while he thought it out. "I wonder, now, why you feel like that?" Rather dexterously, without leaning forward, he threw the matchbox on to the desk, and with his penknife flipped it across to within Geoff's reach. "In a way, I suppose, you want to be shot of the Merediths? Shot of the lot of us? You feel like standing on your own feet?"

" Something like that, I think."

" But you don't reckon that a tidy sum like this would do the trick? You'd feel there were too many conditions attached to it? Obligations? "

" Obligations for life."

" I wonder . . . I very much wonder if you're right? "

" I've thought it all out—all that part of it," Geoff said; and it was not until he heard the words spoken that he knew how false they were. " But I've got to think of Alex. From her point of view, you see . . . what is it *right* for me to do? "

" *Right . . . right . . . right* . . . It's a very difficult word, isn't it? "

" There's a right and a wrong to everything," Geoff said, as Nanny had taught him. " In each case, one's got to find it."

" Does the case come into it? " Guy smacked his hand down on Geoff's documents. " This is just fraud, stealing—whatever the case! We have a law about that, to evade this sort of question, to reduce the strain on our consciences."

" So has Betts! " Geoff had spoken as soon as the thought developed. " Betts shelters behind the law; he doesn't have to have a conscience."

" That's his concern, isn't it? " Guy spoke briskly. " You can make the law your maximum or your minimum; you can add to it, to satisfy your conscience; but you can't subtract from it, to meet your convenience. And if you do—if you break up the law to suit yourself—you break up society."

The door had opened, and Jack was saying that the car was downstairs to take Geoff to the station.

" All right, Jack; he won't be long. There's plenty of time, as yet." As he spoke, he looked at his watch, giving it again that idiotic little puff. A wild skitter of irritation, shaking Geoff, made him want to strike the watch, knocking it out of the great red hand that held it. " Keep your money! " he cried.

" In any event," said Guy equably, " it's not mine." He showed no surprise at the outburst, so rare a phenomenon from Geoff. " It may belong to the Meredith creditors, and I may be amongst them. Or it may belong to you and Alex. The choice is yours, Geoff. You must make it with your usual calmness." With his hands back in his pockets, and his feet apart, he stood facing Geoff directly. His face and his voice were kind, and even benevolent, but somehow severe. " It's your choice, Geoff—all your choice.

303

You can put those things back in your pocket, or you can leave them where they lie. If you leave 'em, they'll go into my safe for to-night. And to-morrow . . . to Harry's executors, to Barry's offices."

Geoff had taken a pace towards the door when the telephone rang. He said: "I shall leave them on your desk!" before Guy had spoken down the instrument.

"It's Neapcaster," Guy said. "You'd better wait." He sat himself heavily on the edge of his desk. "Yes, Bowling, I see . . . I see . . ." He was talking to his butler at Neapcaster. "You had it from Dr. Macdonald? No . . . I've nothing else." Very slowly he put back the instrument, saying: "Harry has, unexpectedly, recovered consciousness. They don't think he'll live. But they don't think he'll die—not just yet." He nodded rather curtly. "So put those things back in your pocket! You can have it out with Harry yourself."

Geoff was shaking his head. "Either it's wrong or it's right, whether he's dead or whether he's living. It makes no difference."

"Of course it does!" At last Guy spoke with impatience. "If he were dead, it would be owed to his estate. While he's alive, the same liability exists—but it doesn't have to be met."

"Just the same—I'll leave those things with you."

"Will you indeed! And how will you explain it to Harry Meredith?"

"I rather thought *you'd* do the explaining," Geoff said; and he hurried out of the room, time being short. Outside the door, in the little ante-room, Jack was holding his hat and coat. While he put them on, he heard a great outburst of laughter behind him. Then, as the door opened again, Guy, struggling with his laughter, cried: "Geoff, I take off my hat . . . to you, I take off my hat! There's just one thing to be said . . ." He subdued his laughter very quickly, took Geoff's arm and led him down the corridor towards the lift, out of Jack's hearing. "You and I, Geoff, it's our job in the world, I think, to stick to the rules, letter and spirit. A little better than the rules perhaps . . . Because, besides our integrity, we may not have a lot else." He nodded a cheerful good-bye, but then added: "Others can be crooks, old Geoff, maybe admirable crooks, but we . . . we daren't!" He patted Geoff's shoulder, pushed him down the passage and shut the door again.

Before Geoff had reached the lift, the door opened once more while Guy called: " Send back the car when you've done with it. I shall want it later myself."

*　　*　　*

When Geoff dismounted at Neapcaster he saw, under the lamp of the exit, the solitary porter talking and laughing with a man who, for just a moment, was a stranger, a gentleman in a tweed cap and long, loose-fitting tweed overcoat. As he swung on his heel and gestured with his pipe, this gentleman had the assurance of Ralph or of Tommy Black.

" I thought I'd come myself," Frank said. " I wanted the chance of a chat." They walked across to his car, which was long and black and looked expensive. " Recognise the old bus? 'Spite of her age, she'll still touch ninety."

" It's Mr. Levine's, isn't it? " Geoff thought it was the car in which Danny had died.

" Sure enough! I got her off Levine last month. I reckon that chap's feeling the pinch—filling up his house with all those foreigners." He got into the driver's seat, leaving Geoff to climb in beside him. He continued to talk. " I thought I'd best come myself. With the hours they're doing, I don't like sending the boys out late. An' when the war starts . . ."

" I thought the war was off. Chamberlain goes to Munich to-morrow."

" Him! Hitler knows the ropes! I take off my hat to that chap, Hitler; knows what he wants and goes after it. We could do with a bit of Hitler over here, Geoff."

It was not these common sentiments that shocked Geoff, but Frank's use of his first name, without prefix. When the footman called him " Geoff," then they were right; society was dead, finished.

" I hear the General's conscious again," Frank said. " I hear it can't last."

" How did you hear that? "

" From some one in the house." Frank answered vaguely and perhaps provocatively, evidently hoping to be pressed. But when Geoff remained silent, he added: " If you must know, Geoff, I got it from Kate. She's a nice girl that! She's learning her way about, learning her stuff. I give you that tip, for what it's worth."

305

On the straight piece of road at the top of the town, they could have driven fast. But instead, Frank slowed right down, taking his time over the short journey, and choosing the slightly longer route, past Slender Ladies, and down and up the steep hill, into and out of the valley. "I've another tip for you, Geoff. Didn't you have a word in the train with Sir Frederick? You didn't know it was me as suggested it? You said 'no' to him, didn't you?"

"You seem to know a lot."

"He rung me this afternoon, like he usually does. And all he'd got for me was *Mister* Colonel Black!" He might have spat out of the side of the car, the way he said it. "I don't want that chap in my lot! But I want you, Geoff! I want you to come right in on top of me, as my boss. Because that's how May says it ought to be, when I tell her that it frightens me, the way we're going, and the pace of it . . ."

"Frightens you, Frank?"

"Listen, Geoff! You haven't heard him talk, Sir Frederick! You haven't heard what he's going to make of it, right here in Neapcaster! That's why May says it's *you* we want, with your head screwed on the way it is, and . . . May thinks ever such a lot of you, Geoff. But you know what she says? She says: 'Geoff's got to look after himself.' She says: 'Geoff's got to ask himself if his wages are in the till all right.' She says: 'What about the till at Neapcaster Park?'"

"You're talking a lot of rot, you know."

"Am I, Geoff? If ever I saw a place that's falling to bits—*that's* it!" He was very earnest indeed, almost passionate. "I don't mean only the General, the Park, but the whole lot of them, Geoff! All of it!" He waved his hand through the window of the car towards the dark countryside. "You've seen plenty of barns a-tumble in your time, Geoff. You've seen the walls bulging and the timbers giving up. Then the crack in the wall starts reaching up from the roof; and with the first fall of snow . . . there's mighty little left."

There was a sort of fire in the man's voice, as if this was the urgency inside himself, his force; as if the fire was his vision of this disintegration. His accent now was rougher and more natural, so that Geoff remembered that, in his youth, he had come from the slums of the North. "It's on the totter," he said, "all *that*! An' what's more, Geoff, I wouldn't mind giving it a push."

"I don't doubt it for a moment," Geoff said rudely, foolishly, like a schoolboy.

"But I don't want *you* to go down with them, Geoff. You were always decent to me, Geoff. More'n that—I respect you, Geoff. You got it hidden away where you want it . . ." He tapped his forehead. "That's why I'm telling you to get yourself out."

"There's such a thing as loyalty," Geoff said; but the remark sounded stupid, pointless and unconvincing even to himself.

"Loyalty to what? To a dead man . . . 'cos it'll soon be that? To a place that's broken up? To a lot o' memories? To Mrs. Meredith—who ran off with her fancy boy and never came back? To Ralph—who doesn't want you and couldn't pay you if he did? Or is it to Alex?" He changed down his gears and accelerated quickly. "She's a smart enough skirt—I'll allow you that." He raised his voice with the power of the car up the hill. "But most any one can have his dip there, can't he? Most any one—by all accounts."

"That's enough!" Geoff snapped it out as quickly as he could, but the smack of Frank's words had unbalanced him. He hadn't spoken soon enough; he was too late. "How do you dare . . ."

"How do I *dare*, Geoff?" Frank spoke gently and with astonishment. "I've said no more—not as much—as the whole of Neapcaster. They all know as the outfit's rotten. You'd as well hear it for yourself. Whose child is it that Alex is carrying? The Jew's, isn't it?"

"Shut up!" But Geoff couldn't stop him. He could only feel a fool repeating: "Shut up, shut up!"

"Why did Ralph marry her? He thought he had to."

"God blast you—shut up!"

"Why did the General kick out his own wife? 'Cos she was going to have a baby—Black's baby—and wouldn't go through with it."

"That isn't true!"

"Oh yes, it is! You ask May for yourself! You ask my wife! The General said . . . do you know what the General said? He said the kid was to be born in the house. He said the kid was to be a Meredith. His own son, he said. He said if she had it taken away, she could get out an' keep out . . . An' that's what she did!"

They had reached the drive gates, by the side of Geoff's house,

307

and Frank pulled up the car. He had more to say yet, and he switched off the headlights; but Geoff got out quickly. When he was standing in the road, he said: "You'd better choose your words more carefully when you're talking to any one else." It sounded feeble, and he tried to speak more sternly. "Everything you've said—it's lies, damn lies, and it's slanderous. You'd better watch your step!"

"Don't you worry about me, Mr. Geoff! You worry about yourself." He hesitated, as if he had more to say, but then he switched on the headlights and started to drive off. But at once he stopped again and called back: "Geoff . . . Geoff . . . Mr. Geoff!" He had to scramble out of the car and run back, to seize hold of his arm and make him listen.

"What do you want?"

"Maybe I laid it on too thick," Frank said. "Maybe I shouldn't ha' said as much as I did."

"You're too damn right, you shouldn't!"

"You know I wouldn't harm them up at the House? Ask any one you like, Mr. Geoff! I'm the one who always has a word in their favour."

"They don't need it."

"That's just what they do, Geoff. That's where you make your mistake. That's why I came to meet you to-night. That's why I came myself. I want you to see Sir Frederick, Mr. Geoff."

"I've seen him already."

"See him again, Mr. Geoff . . . I don't forget a kindness, you know . . . you were kind to me, Mr. Geoff . . ."

Geoff made no reply, and awkwardly Frank said: "Well . . . good night," and walked up the lane to his car.

Geoff stood for some time outside the Lodge, at the entrance to the drive where the great iron gates were fastened permanently open by the growth of weeds in the gravel.

*   *   *

Frank took a long time to vanish. From the drive gates, Geoff watched the headlights sliding along the treetops, dissolving into an aurora, diminishing slowly, and at last becoming extinguished but leaving behind them the sound of Frank's voice and the wickedness that it had uttered. Lies? Lies! Yet their mere statement breathed a tarnish over truth—whatever the truth might be; if truth there was in anything; if truth existed. Then the full weariness descended, so that the few steps needed to get into the chill and sorry house seemed not worth taking.

Homecoming here had never been joyful, for this house was without those happier memories of childhood—such as they were —which belonged to the nurseries at the Park. There had never been happiness at the Lodge, but only custom; never love, but only veneration, obedience, timidity. Weary and hopeless, therefore, and without any pleasant prospect, Geoff dragged himself through the garden gate and shut it behind him. With his back against it, he rested for a moment. Something about the house seemed odd and notable.

There was no obvious explanation of why the curtains were drawn over the hall windows: Mrs. Beach would have finished the housework by lunch-time, and nobody should have been there since; nobody but Geoff himself ever drew those curtains. But though this oddity was unexplained, it made no particular impact on Geoff's weakened attention. Even when his eyes recorded a very faint fringe or suggestion of light round the edge of the curtains, his interest remained dormant. He was so far submerged in fatigue that he even fumbled at the latch, as if it were strange to him, and stumbled on the step that had been familiar for a lifetime.

When he saw that on the far side of the sofa the fire was burning —though now reduced to embers which laid a steady glow on the curtains and walls—and when he heard Alex's voice, slow and deep, asking: " Are you back, Geoff? " he felt no astonishment. Her presence was astonishing enough; but he felt nothing, nothing at all, except the need to be allowed to crumple up, to enter into dissolution. Feeling nothing, he asked: " What are you doing here, Alex? "

The sofa—an immense and deep piece of furniture—had always stood where it was now, across the fireplace, with its back to the front door and to the staircase. And when you came downstairs in the very early morning, if the embers of the fire were not completely dead, you saw the dark line of the sofa in silhouette. You crept down the stairs in your socks, while the silhouette of the sofa rose out of the carpet and ascended the shiny walls, and you crept across the hall to sit on the sofa and to put on your boots. It was important to escape the sleepless watchfulness of your father, and not to attract his voice, his questions, demands, advice.

The same board in the floor of the hall still creaked. It was still a guilty sound, making Geoff halt some paces from the sofa itself. He and Alex talked in whispers. "I came because . . ." Her voice dwelt on the two long vowels and then paused. She must have shrugged her shoulders in the darkness. "What else could I do? I couldn't stay up there. Why should I have to?" Her voice was low and quiet. "Even Kate was out; it was even *her* night out. I couldn't stay there with a corpse."

"A corpse!" It was not till he repeated the word that the shock of it reached him.

"You see . . . Ralph had to go away. It was something to do with the war." In the darkness, her slow speech, with its pauses upon the long vowels and its precise pronunciation of the consonants, sounded as correct and foreign as when she had first come to Neapcaster. "It was a telephone message. He expects to return for the funeral . . . So, I came here."

"And you lit the fire, and you drew the curtains? But . . . but . . ." He had not yet detected the real cause of his bewilderment. He had been so drowned in fatigue, and in the horror of Frank's speech, that the values of information had been all muddled up. "A corpse? A funeral? But he isn't dead!" He had found the bewilderment at last. "He's better. He's recovered consciousness."

"Only for a little . . . after Ralph had left . . ." Her voice shuddered. "I had to see him, I had to speak . . . I had to see him, Geoff!" Her words choked on his name. "I had to . . . I had to . . . And then he was dead!" She was crying, and he went quickly to the back of the sofa. "Geoff, dear Geoff . . ." As he came to her, she stretched up from the depths of the sofa and took his hand. She pulled his hand down to her cheek and rubbed it in her tears.

He saw first the light splash on the hearthrug, caught in the firelight. Then he saw that it was her clothes thrown on the floor. When she pulled him towards her, so that he had to stoop over the back of the sofa, he felt his own dressing-gown that she was wearing, rough against his face.

"But you've undressed!"

"It was easier to sleep undressed."

"All in the dark."

"It was easier to sleep on your sofa in the dark."

"You've been asleep? You're wearing *my* dressing-gown!"

" Come beside me, Geoff! "

It was only then that he started to tremble. His whole body quivered so violently that he had to press his knees against the back of the sofa to steady himself as he stooped over it. He stopped trembling only when she pulled at his hand so violently that he lost his balance and tumbled, very nearly somersaulting, over the back of the sofa and almost on top of her. Then they were both laughing and clinging to each other in a combined wave of laughter.

The laughter was very quickly finished.

" Geoff, dear, I was so frightened."

Suddenly he knew what he was doing. He tugged at the cord which fastened her dressing-gown. It was his own dressing-gown, wasn't it? He tugged; and when the knot came undone and the dressing-gown fell open, he hid his face in her flesh. With his arms round her, he pulled her flesh into his face as if he could suffocate himself. He heard her voice: " That's so beautiful, Geoff," and she went on repeating his name: " Geoff . . . Geoff . . ."

Her hands were round his neck, his shoulders, his throat. " It is such a terrible thing," she said, " to get off a man's tie and to get the collar unbuttoned . . . A man is all, all buttons . . ."

That started them laughing again, but the laughter trembled with their breath. But his limbs now, at last, were not trembling. They were immensely strong.

It was just at the moment when she had got off all his clothes, and had herself slipped out of the dressing-gown, that they heard the footsteps. Then the knocking on his door started—just the same knocking that there had been the previous night.

Maybe it was still the previous night? Maybe this was just sleep, with sleep's accustomed manliness? He had all the terror of waking up, and he started to cry out: " Who is it? "

The word " who " came out in a strained sort of squeak before she got her hand tight on his mouth. She drew in her breath sharply, but was perfectly composed. She whispered in his ear: " Quick, quick . . ." and she pushed his arms into the dressing-gown. Then she got up from the sofa quite naked—the first naked woman he had seen in all his life—and walked about the hearth-rug in the firelight, stooping and collecting her clothes. It was a black, woolly hearthrug which buried her feet.

She had all her clothes in her arms, and her handbag and shoes in her hands, when she stooped to kiss him on the forehead as she went past the sofa. "Now answer!" she whispered, "now go to the door—sensible, quick!"

He heard the soft thud behind him, as the swing-door between the hall and the kitchen swung shut.

*　　　*　　　*

It was Draper again. "Thank God you've come, Mr. Geoff! Thank God you're back."

"Yes, I'm back."

"You wouldn't know, Mr. Geoff—the General . . . He died at ten o'clock. He was so much better, Mr. Geoff. He spoke to Mrs. Ralph . . . and then he was dead."

There was nothing that Geoff could safely do or say. His weariness had gone for the moment; but so had reason, and any powers of calculation or contrivance. "Oh, Mr. Geoff—I know you'll feel it more than any of us. It's a sad and terrible thing, Mr. Geoff."

"A sad and terrible thing," Geoff said.

"It isn't that, Mr. Geoff; it isn't *that* that I've come for. It's Mr. Ralph."

"Ralph!" The word was torn out of him, igniting wild apprehension, terror, almost a wild flash of joy and hope. "He isn't . . . isn't hurt?"

"No, no, Mr. Geoff! No, that would be too much. I had to ring him up."

"Yes?" Geoff had suddenly got hold of himself and he spoke curtly. It was the only thing to do, with Draper in this distressed, incapable state. "You told him about the General?"

"Yes, Mr. Geoff. But it was after that. I had to ring him *again*—about Mrs. Meredith."

"Miss Alex!" The real terror had now been lit in Geoff. They had found Alex gone and had rung up Ralph.

"No, no, Mr. Geoff! Not Mrs. Ralph . . . Mrs. Meredith! She arrives to-morrow. She's coming back."

"Coming back?" It was almost a foreign language that Draper was talking.

"From France, Mr. Geoff. From where she lives. Coming back because of the war, Mr. Geoff."

"The war! Has the war started?"

312

"No, no, Mr. Geoff. But it might start, mightn't it? It might start at any minute."

"Mr. Chamberlain is going to Munich."

"Perhaps he'll stop it . . . let's hope he'll stop it, Mr. Geoff."

Geoff was shaking his head. "I still don't see why she's coming back."

"Mr. Ralph—he wants you to go to Croydon to meet her. The aeroplane, it gets there at ten o'clock."

"Then I can't catch the nine-five train."

"No, Mr. Geoff. That's why I had to wake you. You'll have to catch the 6.56 in the morning . . . there's nothing else. And after last night and everything, Mr. Geoff, you won't have had very much sleep."

"I still can't think why she wants to come back."

"It's only natural, Mr. Geoff, with a war coming on; it's natural, isn't it, that she'll want to be at home; at Neapcaster, that is. Wouldn't you yourself, Mr. Geoff?"

"No, not especially," Geoff answered.

"What a terrible, terrible thing it all is, Mr. Geoff. And the doctor—he wouldn't stop . . ."

"There wouldn't be any need for him, would there?"

"And Mr. Baker, Mr. Geoff—he says he won't come about the coffin till the morning. And you'll be away, Mr. Geoff. And Mr. Ralph—he'll be away. There'll only be Mrs. Ralph. . . ."

"Well, that's all right, Draper."

"But who's to say about the coffin, Mr. Geoff?"

"I'm sure you can do that, Draper. Nobody better."

"Thank you, Mr. Geoff. I didn't want to disturb Miss Alex—Mrs. Ralph, that is—not in her condition."

★   ★   ★

Geoff went back into the house, but the hall was empty; and through the swing-door, the kitchen and scullery were empty also. She must have been very, very quick about it; she had left the back door open; but though it was a still night and he listened carefully, he could hear no sound of her flight.

Back in the kitchen, he found on the dresser a large sheet of paper, taken from one of the drawers, with a message scribbled in thick, red letters, presumably with a lipstick: "*Lie in your bed.*

I lay in mine before I left. So if I am seen, it is all right. Here is—letter from Ralph."

It took him a moment or two to puzzle it out, and then he went straight upstairs to disturb his bedclothes so that they should look as if he had slept there. He came down again, put on his trousers and returned to the kitchen, knowing immediately that his sequence of actions was quite foolish. Carefully folding her note, he put it in his pocket, but at once took it out again and pushed it into the embers of the fire in the hall. *She* had lit that fire! From the sofa he had seen her standing in front of that fire, collecting her clothes. When the note had blackened and curled, he kicked it to ashes.

He was now too tired to dare to sit down on the sofa until he had planned his duties. He was too tired to bicycle up to the house to use the telephone and try to get a car. He could not take the farm lorry, even if he could find the key and start it, because it would be needed for lifting potatoes, and he could get hold of nobody to drive it back from the station. He rubbed his knuckles in his hair, trying to keep awake while he made himself think; he straightened his knees which were bending and dropping him on to the sofa. Moving clear of the sofa, he stood in the very middle of the room where the board creaked, and decided that he would have to bicycle to the station. The alarm clock usually worked. Taking off his trousers again, he carried all his clothes upstairs and went to bed. Since it was just on three o'clock, he would have three hours' sleep.

Out of the first tide of sleep, he dragged himself up, remembering that she had said there was a letter from Ralph. " She really ought to have given it to me," he said crossly, speaking aloud. " She ought to have given it to me, the moment I got back. It might be important."

He found it on the floor of the kitchen, where it must have fallen from the dresser. It was sealed, so that Alex would not have read it. The writing was as neat, and the expression as precise as it always was, but it started: " *In great haste . . .*

" *I don't expect to see Father again; he is still unconscious. Meanwhile I am recalled urgently to Catterick. Alex seems very upset, and if Father dies, may want to get away from the house. If so, I know you'll give her a bed, or whatever she wants.*

" *About David's refugees: if Father dies, they can move in as soon as they like. Rent-free, of course. Betts rang me up and said he had spoken*

314

to you about the house, but his proposition is uninteresting. Reserve us three or four rooms somewhere in the place. Consult Alex, of course.—Ralph."

After reading the letter twice, he saw that it was of no immediate importance, and he returned to bed. It was an hour before he was able to sleep, and when the alarm clock went two hours later, he was quite unrefreshed; and in an almost empty train, carrying mostly milk and mail, he slept all the way to Paddington.

*   *   *

" The funeral is on October 1st. Yes, I've got that, Draper. Yes, yes—at eleven o'clock." Geoff was telephoning from Croydon aerodrome. " I've got all that, Draper, but Mrs. Meredith . . ."

" Mrs. Ralph, sir ? "

" No, no—Mrs. Meredith."

" Will she be coming down here, Mr. Geoff ? "

" I can't find her; she's not on the aeroplane. You haven't had a message ? "

" We've had nothing here, Mr. Geoff. When do you expect her ? "

" I've no idea where she is or when she'll be coming. I'll ring again later."

" You understand the arrangements for the funeral, Mr. Geoff ? "

Geoff hung up the telephone and sat down again in the airport waiting-room. It was by now the middle of the afternoon, and during much of the day he had slept. One of the Airways officers who seemed to like the look of him came across to Geoff. " We've done everything we can—though it isn't much. They know nothing about her in Le Bourget or in the Paris offices. But they never do know much. Have you tried Cook's ? "

" Both at Paris and Cannes," Geoff said. " And I've tried her villa. She left a couple of days ago for Paris—but no address."

He had collected quite a few evening papers. The officer picked up one of them, and read aloud: " Before leaving, the Prime Minister said: ' When I was a little boy I used to repeat—*If at first you don't succeed, try, try, try again.* That is what I am doing.' Can you make rude noises ? " the officer asked.

" I'm out of practice."

" Women can be the devil, can't they ? This one of yours—is she a peach ? "

" She's a fair age, you know."

" They're usually less trouble, aren't they ? "

315

" I suppose so."

The Airways officer started to read again. "Duce and Führer journeyed to Munich together and received a great ovation at the Station Square. Signor Mussolini wore the uniform of a corporal in the Fascist Militia. Herr Hitler, in his usual brown, looked grave but had a charming smile for two little girls who brought him and the Duce bouquets of flowers."

" Is there *no* other aerodrome she might have come to? "

" Not to-day, old boy. Heston's for statesmen only."

" If she came by boat . . ."

" You might leave a message at the Customs."

" Is Chamberlain there yet? "

" Oh yes—he's been arguing since lunch."

There was another plane from Paris coming in, and they went out together to meet it; but Mrs. Meredith was not on board. At six o'clock he rang up Neapcaster again.

" Oh yes, Mr. Geoff," Draper said. "Just after you rang up last time the message came. But we didn't know where to get you. She's coming to-morrow, Mr. Geoff, arriving at two o'clock."

" In the morning? "

" Oh no, in the afternoon, Mr. Geoff."

" Did they finish the potatoes to-day? "

" I haven't heard, Mr. Geoff. Mr. Ralph rang up; he expects you'll be meeting Mrs. Meredith to-morrow. And Mrs. Ralph has gone to London . . ."

" To London! Why has she done that? "

" I think she was rather distressed in the house, all by herself, Mr. Geoff. She'd be staying at Claridge's as usual, so she said."

" If there's any more news, Draper . . . I don't know where I'll be staying. I haven't thought about it yet."

" If there should happen to be anything, should we leave a message for Mrs. Ralph? "

" Yes, Draper, please do that."

" At Claridge's then, Mr. Geoff."

He asked his friend, the Airways officer, where he should stay for the night. "Which hotel? " he asked.

" There's nothing to choose between 'em, old boy. They none of them look too closely, so long as you book a double room—and pay for it."

★   ★   ★

316

"I must have walked five miles, I must have walked six miles at least. I must be mad."

Alex was not at Claridge's. She had been there and left her suitcase and gone out again. There was no message left.

"I must have walked six miles, I must have walked seven miles. I've been walking for the best part of two hours, but never very fast." He was looking for the greengrocer's shop and the woman in the dark red dress.

He had gone right down the street—and then he realised that he had gone right down this same street twice within the hour—before he recognised it. The greengrocer's shop, like all the other shops, was of course shut, which made all the difference to the street's appearance. He had never known the name of the street; he had never noticed it. But finally he recognised the faded blue door, with the smear right down it, although previously he had not been consciously aware of either the smear or the colour. And then he saw the shop next door, all shuttered up, and without the baskets of produce outside it, but bearing an Italian name and declaring that it sold fruit and vegetables.

He rang the bell several times, but he heard nothing, and he had the idea that it was not working. He tapped, softly at first, then louder and louder. "She shall have five pounds, she shall have six, seven, eight, nine, ten pounds . . . Please God, let her come to the door and open it!" He was sweating again, but now it was out of eager, not timid, anticipation.

It was true that there was no light in any of the three windows that faced the street. But there must be other windows facing the back. Louder and louder he knocked. "She shall have ten pounds . . . She shall have all I've got." He tried to calculate what that would amount to. Not so very much. But more than she'd asked.

* * *

At eleven o'clock at night, when he returned for the third time, there was still no light in the windows facing the street. Of course he might have missed her; she might have come in and gone out again during one of his absences. He had gone away to have a drink and some sandwiches, to go to a news cinema, to ring up Claridge's again. And now he knocked once more and without much hope on the faded blue door beside the greengrocer's shop.

He knocked louder, and at length a door did open, not the one that he wanted, but the door of the greengrocer's shop itself. A man and a voice came out; the voice sounding from a wireless somewhere inside the house. He recognised the man, although now he was without his apron and was smartly dressed with a pearl tiepin. His shop might have a foreign name, but he was altogether English. "That's not much good, old man," he said.

"Is she out?"

"Out? They don't use it much—none of 'em. Must be a dead loss, I reckon. It's not the right district."

"Doesn't she live here?"

"Who, old man?"

"The lady in the red dress?"

"I never notice their dresses, to tell you the truth. If I ever notice anything very much, it's the fellows they come with. They can give you a quiet laugh—some of 'em."

"Nobody lives here?"

"There's a fellow rents it. Nasty bit o' work."

"A man?"

"Of course it's a man. I s'pose he charges 'em so much a time for the use of it. Or perhaps they give him so much of their takings. I don't know how they work it."

"Thank you, thank you," Geoff said.

"That's all right." He nodded to Geoff and then nodded several times up and down the empty street. He made a clicking noise with his tongue against his teeth. "No news yet!" He jerked his thumb backwards through the open doorway from which they could hear the voice on the wireless. "We'll be up all night if we're going to wait for that lot! They'll argue for days, I expect." He listened for a moment, and somebody inside the house was making the instrument louder.

"There is still no news from Munich. The latest session at the Führerhaus began at ten o'clock, after a short interval for dinner during which Mr. Chamberlain and the British delegation were escorted back to their hotel by Baron von Neurath, Chairman of the Secret Cabinet Council for Foreign Policy. After dinner, at which . . ."

Somebody inside the house had turned it off.

"Well, I'm going to bed," the greengrocer said.

" Good idea," said Geoff. " Thanks again. Thanks very much."
" Not at all, old man. Good night."

＊　　　＊　　　＊

Back at Claridge's again, at midnight, it all became rather complicated: the usual muddle of impulse and incompetence of Alex's passage. At the porter's desk, they were quite sure that no message had been left for a Mr. Greenley; and at the hotel exchange they were sure, also, that she had received no calls from the country. But a gentleman had left a message that he was calling for her late. " Oh yes," the Head Porter agreed, " a gentleman called for her all right!"

Neither the Head Porter, nor any of his assistants, nor the doorman, had taken much notice of the gentleman or could give a description. The doorman said: " I wouldn't know Mrs. Meredith, not if she was standing here this moment."

" A lady in a red dress," said Geoff, now so perilously tired that he wanted only to be between sheets, and had forgotten, in numb fatigue, why it was urgent to find Alex. His doggedness made him continue, though the motive had vanished. " A dark red dress . . ."

" There was a gentleman with a lady in a black dress . . ."

" That might be her," Geoff said. " I remember the red dress was another one."

" You wouldn't be Mr. Greenley?" the man asked suddenly. " I was to look out for a very big gentleman who might be looking as if he was lost . . ." It was evidently not the end of the description given him.

" That's me," Geoff said; " was there a message?"

" I thought there was a message left inside, sir."

But inside, there was still no message. " Lady in black," said the doorman, who had followed Geoff in, " she must have gone out about an hour back. There was a gentleman with her."

" That was Mrs. Meredith," said the Head Porter. " She came to the desk and she went away again, but she left no message."

" They took a taxi," said the doorman. " I heard the gentleman say the Palm Tree. They might be there yet."

Geoff's taxi went only a few hundred yards, and round a couple of corners, before it stopped, and the driver said: " Down those steps. The door's at the bottom."

319

But the doorman here was big and unpleasant. He soon got tired of it. "There isn't any 'must' about it. Not unless you're with a member, you can't come in here." He was watching Geoff closely, ready for trouble; but although he, himself, was of a size nearly to fill the small doorway, he must have realised that Geoff was a tough customer, and the balance of power delicate. "You can have a word with the boss . . ."

Just inside the door, the Manager, a sharp little man with a white face, sat in evening dress at a long table. "Mrs. Meredith?" He looked her up, but neither she nor Ralph was a member. "You can't think who the gentleman might be?"

The thought came suddenly: "It wouldn't be Colonel Black?"

There were several "Blacks" in the card index; but the doorman, who was standing tactically close behind Geoff, said: "The Colonel's not been here to-night; not for a week."

"It's the police," the Manager explained. "They were here the other evening. We daren't risk it."

"I only want to look inside the door . . ." And Geoff found that his feet had taken a couple of steps onwards. By now, he was quite ready to hit somebody hard and quick.

"Take him to the door, Charlie," said the Manager immediately, "but don't let him get any farther. I daren't take the risk."

*   *   *

The lights were heavily shaded, and the music was soft and insignificant until the little man with the violin came down from the platform and started to walk between the tables. Although the room was small, the dancing space in the centre was so filled with people that, in the dim light, it was not easy to distinguish anybody. A rose-coloured spotlight followed the violinist in his slow progress. He was a little gipsy kind of chap. He seemed to go straight to Alex, and she turned round lazily towards him. As she turned, her body overlapped David's, because he had drawn his chair round the table, very close to her.

Geoff wondered why he had thought of Tommy instead of David. Hadn't she told him herself? She had told him it was David in the very early morning, at the head of the staircase. And he was glad to see them together; together, they were beautiful.

"I've seen them," he said to the doorman. "I'll leave a message."

He went back to the Manager, who seemed more friendly, but the doorman stayed close behind. "Not there?" the Manager asked cheerfully.

"Yes—they're there. Can I leave a message?"

"If he's a member, you can go and talk to him."

"Is Mr. Levine a member?"

"Oh yes, he's a member. He used to be here a lot; but not very often just lately."

"I'll leave him a message."

"Why don't you go and talk to him? He'd like to see you. He's a very pleasant gentleman."

"I know he is. I'll leave him this letter." He took out of his pocket the letter from Ralph, the letter that Alex had left in his kitchen at the Lodge. "May I borrow your pen?" But when he had taken the Manager's pen, he did not know what note he could add to the message. Finally, he drew a line alongside the passage referring to David and to the refugees, and he wrote at the top in his large, adolescent writing: "*My love to you and Alex. I'll ring you both up in the morning.*" There was no need to sign it. "May I have an envelope?"

"I'll see he gets it," the Manager said to Geoff when he had taken the sealed and addressed envelope. "You're sure you won't have a word with him? I dare say he'll be sorry to miss you."

Geoff shook his head. "No, I don't think he will. I don't think so."

The Manager walked with Geoff to the door, and was now very affable. "Where can I get a room?" Geoff asked him.

"You ought to have asked Mr. Levine. There's any number of places." He had come with Geoff all the way up the steps, and they were standing in the street, which was quite deserted. "Any of the places just round here. Of course it's getting late. You're not alone, are you?" He looked up and down the street, as if he was searching for Geoff's companion. "Of course it's not so easy if you're alone. Still you might try any of them." The man gave him a friendly nod and ran briskly down the steps again. "I'll see Mr. Levine gets your note," he called behind him.

Geoff walked very slowly and sadly down the street. So he had found Alex in the end! So he had found the lady in the dark red dress! Only . . . he had found her too late.

Yet he was not jealous of David. David was too fine, too

splendid, too far above him, for there to be jealousy between them.

*   *   *

Every nerve was tormented. David looked down at his fingers which twisted and turned a teaspoon; his eyes slid across the table to her own hands, with the rings and the bracelet, placed side by side on the tablecloth. He did not dare to look at her. " But you love me, Alex. You say so."

" Love? It can mean so many things, can't it? " She didn't know that she was quoting his own father. " This or that, it can mean. This can be love, but not only this, and not always."

" You don't know what you do mean," he said crossly. He kept his eyes away from her, but he was pretty sure she was looking at him directly. " You just let words take hold of you. You just take hold of words and serve them out in any sort of a jumble that happens to occur to you."

" That's true," she admitted. " I'm not clever. David dear, you know I'm not clever."

" Dear God—I don't want a clever woman! "

" What do you want, David? "

" You know what I want. You know that I want to make love to you."

" Making love—that's nothing, nothing! " She said it very scornfully. " Like that—animals can make love."

" If it means so little to you as that, why, why don't you give it to me? " He was quite exasperated. " If it's so little that I'm asking, why, why do you refuse it? "

" If I said . . . that it didn't please me? "

" It wouldn't be true, would it? " He lifted his eyes and looked straight at her and saw her shake her head. " It *would* please you, then . . . It doesn't mean much to you . . . You think nothing of it . . ." He counted out the arguments. " I want it so badly . . . And you love me, don't you? "

" I love you more than anybody else."

" More than Ralph? "

" Oh yes, more than Ralph."

" More than you've ever loved Ralph? "

She thought for a moment before she said: " More than that. But quite differently."

"In what way differently?" He had become patient now; he was making his voice strained, patient and forbearing. "Is it that I don't attract you? Is it that physically you don't want me?"

"Physically I do want you. Very much I do." All the time she kept her voice on the same level note and tone, low, soft and almost husky. "Very much . . . you attract me."

"Like Ralph attracts you? Like Ralph did once attract you?"

"As much, only different. He was strong and attractive. You are not strong in that way; you are weak in that way; strong in another way altogether."

"What does it all mean?" he cried. "Do *you* know what you mean? Do *you* know what you're trying to say, what you're really feeling?"

"I don't think so," she answered.

The band played very softly and unobtrusively, matching the shaded lights. They were so heavily shaded that each of these tables by the wall, each with its own lamp, was in its own island of lamplight, entirely surrounded by shadow. The tune was sentimental, an old and familiar tune revived, full of distant and forgotten associations. "Oh, this music! Oh, Alex . . ."

"Poor, poor David!"

"Look here!" he said, suddenly furious. "Do you get a hell of a kick out of sitting there pitying me, saying that you love me, that you find me attractive, that you don't give a damn who you go to bed with, so long as you don't go to bed with me, *me*, who you say you love better than anybody else . . ."

"I do mind who I go to bed with. I only said it was nothing. I said going to bed with people was nothing at all."

"Then what are we waiting for?" He tried laughing; he tried being forceful and breezy and merry. "Then for God's sake let's get down to it! What's keeping us?"

But she only said: "That doesn't suit you, David." And he answered bitterly: "No, it doesn't, does it?" Then they both drummed with their fingers on the table in time to the music. They watched each other's fingers, and when one lifted the little finger, so did the other; when one lifted the thumb, the other also.

"Would you have married me?" he asked.

"Yes," she answered. "And would *you* have married *me*?" He did not answer. "David—you wouldn't have married me,

323

would you?" She watched him closely. "Why not, David?"

"You know perfectly well, don't you?"

"If you love me like you say you love me, why must I be a Jewess?"

"There isn't any reason," he said. "There are dozens of reasons, but I don't believe in any of them. I could say you're a heathen, but I'd marry a Jewish heathen without blinking. I could say it was something to do with race; but it isn't. Anthropologically, I'm more nearly related to you than I am to . . . to . . . that little Slav over there."

"No reason, David? It's the same with me . . . It's why I wouldn't want to make love to you."

It went round and round and round, without entrance or exit. He said: "But with any one, any one else . . . it would be quite, quite different!"

"David!" He was humming the tune and again drumming with his fingers. "David!"

"Well—what is it this time?" He was smiling at her.

"David—I haven't ever been to bed with any one else, you know; not in all my life. Not except Ralph."

"Is that true, Alex?"

"It's not quite, quite true," she said slowly. "But so nearly true. There was only one other, and that wasn't anything."

"Just light-hearted?"

"It stopped in the middle . . ." It sounded so obscene that he couldn't help laughing. She said: "Truly it *was* rather funny. We were interrupted."

"And you didn't love *him*, I suppose?" It was asked very bitterly.

"Very, very fond of him," she said. "I was lonely."

The band was playing a nondescript sort of thing that seemed to have no real tune but to be mainly an accompaniment. They heard the violin single itself out, and the little violinist started to come down from the dais. He had no coat, but wore a crimson blouse and a sash. He had a rather remarkable face—Slav or Croat or Pole or Czech or something.

"Truly," she said, "truly, David, I was so, so fond of him. But not love. Not like I do . . . I do love you, David."

The violinist came towards her, stepping daintily in the little spot of rose-red light that seemed to precede and direct him. He

324

stopped and leant towards her as he played. His notes soared and hovered so that, in the sentiment of the encounter, she and David seemed to take hands together and to climb up the music as if they were climbing up love, and love was a straight staircase. She turned her body slightly so as to face the violinist.

When the man had passed on, taking his pool of light with him, she said: "When I don't want to make love to you, David, it's because I'm frightened. I'm frightened it would be too much; so much more than anything else. I couldn't . . . David, I couldn't hurt myself like that, could I?"

His physical desires and anxieties were too strong for any other thought or compassion. "I don't see that you'd need to," he answered.

"You wouldn't mind, David, if I kept myself safe from you? If I could do it like that—like an animal?"

"I wouldn't mind a damn thing—if I once got you into bed with me." He spoke as coarsely as he could, and she didn't mind in the least. Indeed her lips quivered or slightly twitched, while her eyes dropped, as if there was something to laugh about, or to smile about with pleasure or anticipation. She had clearly assented. "Alex, darling! You've promised!"

She was pulling at his sleeve. "David, he wants you."

"Who does?" He turned and saw the Manager. "Oh, hallo, Mr. Heron!"

"A gentleman left this note for you, Mr. Levine. I asked him to come and see you, but he wouldn't. He saw you from the door and wrote this note."

"Nobody knows I'm here." David had opened the envelope quickly. "It's Geoff!" He asked the Manager: "Do you know where he went to?"

"He was looking for a room; for somewhere to sleep."

"Oh, God! Poor old Geoff looking for a room in London!"
Alex said: "Oh, he'll find somewhere."

"He'll find somewhere. But I could so easily have had him in my flat. I've got a spare room and everything."

"He's only just left, just this very minute," the Manager said. "Perhaps I could stop him."

"Try, try quickly!" David was already on his feet. "I won't be a second," he said to Alex, and he followed the Manager. They ran up the steps, and from the top they could see, at the very end of the street, a solitary figure. David whistled as best he could, and the doorman whistled expertly through his fingers; but the figure took no notice. Then David started to run; and at the sound of running feet, Geoff turned and saw him.

They all went back down the steps together, and the Manager bowed them past him. As David took Geoff up to Alex, he said to her: "And he was actually going to sneak away—he was actually sneaking away—with nowhere to sleep, and without a word to us!"

Geoff seemed shy, bashful, almost sheepish. "Well," he said, "well . . . after all . . . two's company, isn't it?"

"My dear Geoff, not when you're the third!"

"When *any one's* the third," he said, looking at Alex.

But while David continued to protest, she said nothing.

★   ★   ★

They had another bottle of champagne. It was against the law to serve it at this hour, but the wine-waiter smuggled it under his black apron, the Manager shielding him. They needed it; they needed something to crack the surface of gloom that spread itself over them like a film of oil upon water.

"Cheer up, Geoff!"

"I haven't had any sleep, David. For two nights . . ." He looked at his watch, and it was nearly two o'clock. At this time a day ago he had been in his house with Alex. He could not now look at her, he didn't dare to; but he looked affectionately at David, feeling pleasure and pride that he and David shared this same privilege of her naked loveliness.

"Drink up, Geoff! Come on, Alex!" But she put her hand over her glass, preventing David from filling it. "Here's to us all!" cried David.

But then the drums rolled and the cymbals clashed.

The Manager was standing up on the platform, talking to the leader of the band, the violinist. The violinist shrugged his shoulders, but the Manager came to the front of the dais, his arms spread wide, as if he was blessing them.

"Ladies and gentlemen!"

Nobody took much notice, and he looked behind him for the drums to give him another roll, and the cymbals to clash for silence. "Ladies and gentlemen! We have just heard an announcement on the wireless . . ." There was immediate silence. "The announcement is from Munich!" The hush became a tremendous, over-whelming force, against which nobody could have spoken. He was reading from a slip of paper. "It was announced at 1.30 in Munich that, an hour earlier, the Führer, the Duce, the British Prime Minister and the French Prime Minister had all four signed an agreement as to the methods to be adopted in the transfer of Sudeten territory."

For a few moments of silence, his arms remained aloft, while the purport of the news developed. By then, every one in the room knew that, in exchange for a broken promise—a guarantee torn up, the surrender to the Germans of a small strip of Czech territory, an odd million Czech citizens—a World War had been averted.

As the Manager dropped his hands, the cheering started. They all rose from their chairs. They all cried: "Peace . . . peace . . ." They started dancing together, stranger with stranger, any one with any one, while the piano and a saxophone and the drum played some kind of music. At once the Manager decided that the law could be broken, and champagne was carried to every table.

Thoughtlessly, joining with the rest, Geoff had jumped to his feet and started cheering. Then he saw the violinist. "Look . . . look!" he said to Alex. Taking her by the shoulder, he pointed to the platform where the little musician had thrown his fiddle on the ground and was stamping it to pieces. Turning away, the little man hid his face and shook with weeping. "Look at him, Alex!"

She said nothing. But her eyes turned towards David, who had covered his face with his hands.

*　　*　　*

So then the piano bore the burden of the music; the drum and the saxophones accompanying the pianist who, now that he was free from the violin's authority, tinkled out the tunes with virtuosity and abandon. Now, one knew that all through the earlier part of the evening there had been a humid, heavy atmosphere of apprehension which had suddenly been dispelled, leaving the air of the room lighter, more people talking, more laughter, a sort of continental charm, pleasure, irresponsibility. Geoff, feeling himself buoyant with the pianist and with the crowd, said: "That chap's good, isn't he?"

David had tilted back his chair and was playing with his cigarette case; and when Alex said: "For God's sake give me a cigarette!"

he took one out and threw it on the table. Geoff was able to strike a match and hold it for her, a service which gave him satisfaction. But as soon as it was completed, she stood up abruptly and said: " I'm going home." Then, as quickly as she could get between the dancers and the tables, she went out of the room.

As Alex went, David stood up also, but slowly. Taking out his note-case, he put something on the table for the waiter. Looking away, he said something to Geoff which Geoff could not hear and then went, without haste, after Alex. At the door, the Manager bowed, and David said something like: " On my account, please . . ." and, when he got outside, ran quickly up the steps into the street. The doorman was about to close the door of Alex's taxi when David and Geoff caught her up and got in beside her. Geoff said: " We seem in a great hurry!" but neither of the others spoke, all three sitting squashed together on the back seat, silent. And when the taxi stopped, Alex went straight into the hotel while David paid the driver. The doorman said to Geoff: " So you found them, sir!"

When they got inside, they could not see Alex anywhere; and the porter told them that she had gone straight to the lift and upstairs. Geoff said: " She's in an awful hurry to get to bed!" and David nodded. When they had turned towards the door and were walking slowly away, Geoff said: " I rather feel, Dave, I've rather broken up the party . . . You're not worrying about me, are you? If you were wanting to . . . to have a word with her or anything, I can fix myself up on my own . . . quite easily."

David said: " It's about a mile and three-quarters to my flat. Wouldn't the walk do us good?"

Weariness had been striking Geoff and abating, like irregular gusts of wind. A gust at this moment was approaching, and it was nearly three o'clock in the morning, but he said: " I'd like a walk."

* * *

It was utterly unfair and unreasonable to blame Geoff for any of it; and when Geoff said: " I'm awfully sorry to have butted in like that . . ." David answered: " My dear old Geoff, you didn't butt in! We were only too glad to get hold of you."

" I'm afraid I spoilt your evening. But . . . well . . . anyway, we've been spared a war. I suppose we can thank God for that."

" Not my God, if you don't mind."

"No—I suppose not." They had reached Park Lane and now turned southwards. There was only one other person in the whole visible length of the street. "Anyway, you saw in Ralph's letter, you can send your chaps to Neapcaster Park."

"It's exceedingly good of Ralph."

"He feels like that about it. Most people do, I think. They want to help."

"But not to fight, Geoff?"

"Well, you can't fight about a thing like that, can you?"

"Just a little matter of the human spirit? The triviality of a guarantee, a promise, a promise to a little, foreign people?"

"But really, Dave! The whole British Empire! It can't go to war simply on that account."

"Oh no—of course not."

For a long way they walked in silence, keeping to a military step, perfectly together—left, right, left . . . Then Geoff started asking his question. "Dave—if there was a man you had always loved and respected, regarded as a father, a person who never did anything dishonourable or wrong, and then one day, suddenly, that person behaved in a way that you wouldn't have thought possible, committed a crime . . ."

While Geoff's words stumbled into the empty street, accompanied by severe footsteps, David's thoughts and passions were on flights of their own. His ears heard what Geoff was saying; but his mind, supposing the words to be some hypothetical tangle coming out of Geoff's usual mental awkwardness, made no attempt to relate the question that was imminent to any special circumstance or person. And when Geoff concluded: "Dave, how would you regard that person, the person you had respected and loved?" David answered casually: "As dead, Geoff!"

"But you had loved him, Dave."

"You can go on loving a dead man." And as he answered, David thought: "How apt! I go on loving England!"

The streets and squares and crescents between Hyde Park Corner and Sloane Street were empty, but people were still awake in these grand houses. But the lights were at last going out. The wireless was switched off. In these mansions they had heard the news and rejoiced, and now they could go to bed and sleep in peace.

"Dave—supposing that person got you to promise something, to do something wicked and wrong . . ."

"I suppose a promise is a promise."

"But if, on balance, it seemed more wrong to keep that promise than to break it, does loyalty demand . . ."

"Loyalty demands loyalty; love demands love; a promise is a promise . . . One can go on saying that sort of thing for ever and ever, like your old Nanny up at the Park."

"Don't I know it, Dave!"

"I'm not a lot of help to you, Geoff, am I?" For it was not much use, David thought, to say to Geoff: "Oh, put your fiddle on the floor and put your foot through it!" or again: "Jump into bed with Alex, and forget, forget about anything else in the world! But jump in quick—before you lose the chance! Forget, sleep, be still, be at peace!"

They turned down Sloane Street, which stretched a long way in front of them, straight and depressing. Quite savagely, Geoff said: "And to-morrow, I suppose, I've got to spend another day waiting at that bloody aerodrome!"

*　　　*　　　*

Geoff's friend on the Airways staff came along and said: "There's another plane due in five minutes; they're all haywire to-day."

Geoff got up from his seat to go and meet it; but David said: "I'm not meeting any more planes. I'm going to ring up."

"We've only just finished ringing up."

"I'm not going to ring up the hotel; I don't think they're interested. I'm going to ring up the Park."

When he had got through, the line was indistinct and Draper seemed confused. It took some time to make him understand who was speaking.

"No, no, Draper, it's me. It's Mr. Levine."

"Mr. David?"

"That's right. I'm speaking from Croydon aerodrome. I'm here with Mr. Geoff, but there isn't any sign of Mrs. Meredith."

"There wouldn't be, Mr. David. Not after she sent that message."

"What message?"

"We told them at Claridge's, Mr. David. They were going to tell Mrs. Ralph . . ."

"What message was it, anyway?"

"That Mrs. Meredith isn't coming, of course." Draper spoke

330

quite sharply. "She's staying in France, Mr. David, now that everything's all right."

"What's all right?"

"Well, the war, Mr. David, isn't it? After what Mr. Chamberlain did for us in Munich! Mrs. Meredith, she wouldn't have to return now, would she, as it would be quite safe to remain in France?"

"I see what you mean," David said.

"It's a wonderful thing, Mr. David, a truly wonderful thing Mr. Chamberlain did for us!" He had spoken with fervour, but now he corrected his voice. "But we oughtn't to talk like this, ought we, with the General lying upstairs like that?"

"We oughtn't to talk like that," David said.

"Is Mr. Geoff there, Mr. David?"

"He's just outside—waiting for the next plane to come in."

"You'll make sure he knows about the funeral, Mr. David? To-morrow morning at eleven o'clock."

David found Geoff and told him the news. "Come on, Geoff! Now we can get back to the bright lights and both of us get drunk."

*   *   *

The policeman in the Mall said: "You won't be able to get through, sir. You can try if you like." His black cape was shiny with the rain.

"What's it all about?" David asked.

The policeman looked at him as if he belonged to another world or another generation. "Mr. Chamberlain," he said, "the Prime Minister."

"I did know he was the Prime Minister."

The policeman smiled in return. "Back from Munich . . . You can *try* and get through, sir. It's quite certain you can't get back; not now, not the way you've come."

At the same pace as the crowd on foot, they progressed in the car towards Buckingham Palace. "We ought to have gone right round," David said.

"Oh, I don't know," Geoff answered. "This is rather fun, isn't it?"

Outside Buckingham Palace it was impossible to move any farther. "You'll have to pull right in," the police sergeant said; "right in to the side, sir."

The cheering had started, away down the Mall, in the direction from which David had driven. The police had at last got the road clear, and a car came through slowly. Inside it there was only a tired-looking woman with pathetic eyes. "That's his wife! That's her!" the crowd was saying, as the cheering was passed along, slightly ahead of the car's progress. The car drove into the forecourt of Buckingham Palace.

The crowd grew. A man, pressed against the car, explained to David: "She'll have come on ahead of him, see? *He'll* be coming straight off the aeroplane."

The rain increased, and a few in the crowd had umbrellas, but most of them pulled their coats over their heads. It was dusk, on the very verge of nightfall, and all the lights were coming up, thickening the darkness beyond their immediate zones. The police sergeant said: "If you wouldn't mind, sir, you could get into the side another couple of feet." And he went round to the front of the car to clear the crowd so that David could obey his instruction. The police had now been reinforced, and the mounted men walked their good-natured animals slowly along the verge of the road. Soon the road was clear, and the cordon of policemen established. The rain diminished and later stopped, and over the rooftops there was fashioned a rainbow out of the last evening light.

"And God made a covenant!" said David.

Geoff was getting tired of his bitterness. "How are you so sure you're right, Dave, and everybody else so wrong?"

"God made a covenant," David repeated. He wound up the window slowly. A plump woman had got on to the step of the car for a better view, and the rising window caught the projection of her rump, as it was meant to do. She got down indignantly and turned to thump on the pane, shouting at David through the glass, but the policeman urged her gently away. He grinned at David.

The distant commotion began again, as Chamberlain himself approached. The crowd, breaking through the police and flowing round the car, as if it was a rock projecting out of water, spread right across the road. The floodlights were switched on, all up the front of the Palace, touching at their crest the Royal Standard. At a steady trot, a couple of mounted policemen preceded the car, and the cheering spread like a wave of wind, a sudden storm, tearing away a voice as soon as it was issued. The other cars which were drawn up in front of, and behind, David were sounding their horns, and Geoff leant across and pressed the button on David's steering-wheel. David struck at Geoff's hand, hitting it quite hard; but then he pressed the button himself and shouted, so as to be heard above the cheering: " Go on, Geoff—play the bloody thing as much as you like. Play it for all you're bloody well worth! " The old gentleman in the back of the passing car, following the mounted police, sat bareheaded, smiling and waving to either side of him.

As soon as the Prime Minister had gone into the Palace, the crowd started to call for him. The individual shouts became a chant: " We want Neville . . . We want Chamberlain . . ."

David pulled open the sliding roof of the car. " All right, Geoff," he said, as if he was talking to a child, " stand up and enjoy yourself! " Geoff did so, standing on the seat and then sitting on the car roof, joining in the chant: " We want Neville . . . We want Chamberlain . . ." Later he stooped down and said: " Come on, David! Come on up and join in the fun."

David said: " Do you ever go to a news cinema? Ever hear them chanting ' Sieg heil ' in that other country? Ever see them ' joining in the fun ' in a Berlin street? "

" To hell with you! " Geoff said, laughing; " it's utterly different." But when Geoff was standing up again, David tried it for himself, his voice being carried away and quite inaudible. As far as he could tell, without hearing his own voice, there was not really much difference. You could shout " Sieg heil " twice, while the crowd shouted " We want Neville."

The roar of the crowd suddenly increased as the curtains were drawn apart from a tall window of the Palace. You could see the figures moving about inside the lit room like men in a fiery furnace. Then the King and Queen and Mr. Chamberlain and his wife came out on to the central balcony: four tiny figures standing in the white floodlights. All of them waved in answer to the cheering. The singing started and crowned the cheering until there was nothing but the song everywhere. *For he's a jolly good fellow, for he's a jolly good fellow* . . . David banged his fist on the button of the horn, but he could not tell whether or not it was sounding, because all sound was singing. When the little figures from the balcony went back into the Palace, the singing gradually changed back into cheering. The cheering diminished and changed back into song. This time it was the National Anthem. Feeling foolish about it,

David stood up and pushed himself through the roof of the car beside Geoff. His lips moved; breath came up his throat and into his mouth, and he himself sang, slightly ashamed of himself, of being one with the crowd, but still with fervour: " God Save our King . . ."

While the singing continued, the police started to clear the way for the Prime Minister's return; but as his car left the Palace forecourt and drew level with David and Geoff, it was entirely surrounded by people and came to a halt. Quite close to David, the people tapped on the windows of the Prime Minister's car and cried " God bless you, sir . . . God bless you! " The man and his wife, now united in the one car, smiled and waved in return. A woman was weeping. " God bless you—you've saved my son, my baby son—you've saved him! " The Prime Minister smiled and waved back at her. The woman stepped back against David's car. " I'm ever so sorry, sir," she said to David. She was still weeping. " Last time they took my dad, my brothers and my man. They wanted to take my son. Now they wanted my son . . . " She choked and sobbed. " But he wouldn't let them . . . God bless him—he wouldn't let them! "

* * *

" I don't know," David said, " I don't know anything at all." He and Geoff were in the train on their way to Neapcaster for the funeral. They were talking about the weeping woman. Although they were in a third-class carriage, only the four corner seats were occupied, and David and Geoff were sitting opposite to each other. For a while, each read his newspaper privately. Then David tapped Geoff's knee and leant forward to read to him from *The Times*:

" ' *No conqueror returning from a victory on the battlefield has come home adorned with nobler laurels than Mr. Chamberlain from Munich yesterday . . . The terms of settlement in the Czech-German dispute, reached in the small hours of the morning . . . had been seen to deliver the world from a menace of extreme horror . . . Yet even this great service to humanity was already beginning to appear as the lesser half of the Prime Minister's work in Munich . . . He had not only relegated an agonising episode to the past; he had found for the nations a new hope for the future. The joint declaration made by Herr Hitler and Mr. Chamberlain proclaims that " the desire of the two peoples never to go to war with each other again " shall henceforth govern the whole of their relationships.*

"It isn't that."

"You're afraid of getting caught, getting prosecuted; newspaper headlines." And when she shook her head, he added: "You're afraid of the headlines, because of your father." And then finally: "We shan't be found out, not with Frank. And if we are, we shall be in good enough company—the whole County."

She took hold of his arm and said quietly: "Please, not Frank!" He walked out of the house to get the car, and she came with him, still holding on to his arm, twisting herself to follow him through the doorways without letting go of him. Smiling up at him, she said: "Don't be so unhappy, darling, please don't! *I'm* not—you see?" He made himself smile at her in return; but all the strength of his love for her was not enough to dissolve the hopelessness. Yet, because she had so contrived it that they were both smiling together before they parted, he was now momentarily happy. Releasing his arm, she watched him go to the garage. "Please, Dave, please not Frank!" she called after him.

"For God's sake don't nag me so," he answered, but not crossly, still smiling. "If you want anything in London, I shall be at the club for lunch. I'm lunching with Guy Bredon, just to see . . . to try . . . in case there's a hope . . ."

"I shan't ring you up in London; it's much too extravagant."

He was in comfortable time to drive to the station, leave the car there, and catch the nine o'clock train to Paddington. It started five minutes earlier, and got in ten minutes later, than before the war. But then, in the intervening period, there had of course been a revolution.

*   *   *

"Rum world they've made of it!" Guy said. "I don't fancy I shall have to live in it a lot longer." Yet once he was seated in the dining-room of this club where he and Daniel Levine had met so often, and where he and David were now lunching, and once his rubber-shod sticks had been taken and put in a corner by a waiter, he was not notably infirm.

"I didn't know you'd been bad again," David said.

"I didn't *want* any one to know. And nowadays, people don't ask like they used to. Doubtless they're all too busy, poor devils, tryin' to get along on their own account, without havin' to bother

. . . Rum world!" he repeated. "But there's still a glass of port in it. I insist, David; your office can wait for you."

Many of the older members, on their way out of the room after lunch, stopped to speak to Guy Bredon sitting at the head of the long table. He answered them with a vitality that he seemed to draw from his surroundings. "At least we still do things decently here; that much, at least. The waiters . . . cheerful fellows, anxious to do one well . . ." He had signalled the wine-waiter, who now came and took his order for the port. "Though the doctor," Guy said to David, "tells me I shouldn't drink it."

While he sipped the port with great pleasure, he said: "Yes, I get little Mac up to London from time to time. He doesn't like it very much; says he's too occupied with this new business of giving every Tom, Dick and Harry his something for nothing. But I tell him it won't be for long; I tell him I mean to be helped on my way by familiar faces."

Later he said: "You look a bit pinched yourself, David. Things a bit of a trial, I shouldn't wonder? It's the very devil, isn't it?"

"It's not too easy."

"That father-in-law of yours . . ." Guy lit a cigar, saving himself the labour of defamation. In between the preliminary puffs, he added: "By all accounts, a desperate fellow!" And then: "But that girl of his you married . . . a dear little thing, I thought her . . ."

Knowing that Guy was watching him closely, David answered: "I'm very fortunate, very happy."

"A bit of a pinch, nevertheless?" It was obvious that, as Danny Levine's executor and David's trustee, he was now referring to money. "I don't really know how you fellers manage at all. I live modestly enough myself, but I've had to give up a lot that I've always reckoned to be near-necessities. But you chaps with children . . ."

"It's just not possible," David said, and there was almost despair in his voice, "without spending capital. That's how they all manage it."

"I know they do, David. But I won't! I'd as soon deny Holy Writ as spend a penny of *that*—though I've no one much to leave it to, and the Government'll collar, I suppose, some eighty per cent . . . It's the way I've been brought up, David; the way I've lived my days; the way I mean to end 'em!" With port and cigar he sat, grumbling but adamant, secure in friendship, and still insulated by what was left of his wealth from all threats except those of mortality. "D'ye know, David, when I was a young man— and not so very young either—it was thought to be bad manners to talk about money? You'd remember it yourself, I dare say? But nowadays . . . see what we're reduced to! Money's become everything—now that it's taken away from us."

The people at the table were thinning rapidly but Guy and David sat on, mostly in silence, while the servants cleared away the remnants of meals from vacated places. Waiting for the room to empty, bringing them privacy, Guy rumbled along in speech that was not much more conscious than his digestive processes. " Rum world, isn't it?" he repeated for the third time. " Oh, most odd! Upside down and inside out . . . a feller like Betts, a feller like Frank, a feller like that little Walter Wallis out of old Harry's pantry . . ." Examining his cigar, he said: " Walter Wallis! That's a queer thing, if ever there was one! What is he now—something in the Government? Junior Minister or Parliamentary Secretary or something of the sort . . . ridiculous business. . . ."

But now the two men were left alone at the end of a long stretch of tablecloth; and Guy, twisting himself in his chair so as to face David, said: " There was something I wanted to ask you; there was a thing about your father's Will . . ."

" That wretched trust? There's no hope of breaking it? No hope of getting at the capital?"

" None, I'm afraid. They're wicked things, these days, these trusts, for a feller like yourself, preserving a man's money for no other purpose but to let the State steal it. What do they tax you —sixteen or seventeen bob in the pound . . . Eighty per cent, I suppose?" The hand holding the cigar was shaking as he spoke of it. " Me, myself . . . ninety-seven an' a half per cent, I have to pay 'em! And when I die . . ." The difficulties of digestion overtook him and stopped his speech.

David said: " It means I can't earn anything . . . they take nearly all of it. If you could find some way to break the trust . . ."

But Guy shook his head. " D'ye know, if I'd had children, I'd have doubtless done the same as Danny myself?" Yet he spoke absently, with his body slumped back in the chair, and his chin lodged on his chest. " I know what it was!" he said suddenly.

" Those arrangements your father made . . . annuities . . . a lot of millstones round your neck, I should imagine? "

David said: " Well, there it is! He did make provision for rather a lot of people and institutions."

" Some of those want looking at," Guy said; " some might be stopped. I've got certain discretions in that respect." With slow, almost painful movements which nevertheless seemed enjoyable, he took out of his pocket a sheet of paper, out of another pocket his steel spectacles, out of his waistcoat pocket a gold pencil. There were few other members who would dare to give so close an imitation of conducting business in this club where any kind of business was prohibited. " What a lot of charities! " he said. And David saw the full list of all those Anglo-Jewish institutions which his family had helped to found, and had supported for so many generations, and to which he was still reluctantly attached. " These meant a lot to your father, didn't they? "

David kept quite still and silent. It was true that these were his father's cherished causes, and that, before the war, they had appealed equally to himself. But in those days, he thought, the world of Anglo-Jewry was a little, live community, like a fruit, with a core of old and established families such as his own. And the fruit seemed then to be part of the whole, splendid yield of the country which was as precious as the faith, and of the people of that country who were as much his kinsmen as the people of his religion. But now, he felt, the core was rejected and left to wither. The fruit had fallen and decayed and been eaten by the pests of nationalism, zionism, fanaticism—just as all the fruit in the world seemed to have gone rotten with the " isms " that buzzed, burrowed and consumed until only their own excreta and their own corpses were left to enrich the earth.

All the same, turning to Guy Bredon, he tapped the list of charities, brushing aside the gold pencil that was poised ready for deletions, and said: " I'll leave that lot as it is! "

Looking over the top of his steel spectacles, Guy said: " They amount to a sizeable sum, but it's your choice." And then, when he got no response, he added: " But there's one, quite a large one, which at least . . ." And he made a cross against a name at the foot of the list. " A girl, a granddaughter of that old fellow of Harry Meredith's, old Adam Rogers, a bastard child . . . Some said . . ." He made a slight gesture of his hands, now pale and unsteady, turning the palms upwards. "But then again, others denied it."

"You mean Ralph's child? There wasn't much doubt about that! That little girl Judy Rogers . . . she died giving birth."

"I never really knew," Guy said, "how your father came into it. It was about the last thing he did, before he went to France. There was a bit about it in the Will, but I really forget what."

"He said he'd seen the child uncared for, on the road, I think. He said . . . that since nobody else was providing for it, he would."

"By which he meant yourself!" said Guy, crossing the name off the list. "By now she's a young lady who's . . . very well able to care for herself. I've had it looked into, as a matter of fact."

David said: "It'll all help."

"I'll have it stopped at once." While he spoke, Guy had begun the laborious exercise of getting to his feet. "They've been waitin' to clear this place these ten minutes past. Won't hurt 'em!" A waiter brought his sticks and supported his elbow until he was vertical. "Tell 'em . . . send my bill to the card-room. My lunch and Mr. Levine's . . . both together . . . and the port." He spoke in puffs and grunts as he progressed painfully to the door.

* * *

So that they should not have to conduct this slow and embarrassing exit in silence, David asked: "You don't ever go to Neapcaster nowadays, do you?"

Guy shook his head, but got through the door before he halted and then leant on his sticks, in order to answer. "Hardly ever. Nowhere to put up, if I was to go. I don't fancy that little cottage that Madge would keep. Life in a cottage, like poor little Alex . . . though I dare say she's well enough placed in the Lodge . . . not my fancy, you know; not at my time of life." He puffed and grunted his way back on to his line of thought. "And the house . . . as you know, *my* house . . . a pack of giggling schoolgirls."

"It makes a good school, I gather."

"Oh, it would, it would! But somebody ought to be down there—I know that well enough. Those two farms of mine—I've still got 'em in hand; and I haven't a doubt that they're not being run as they should. I hoped . . . I'd had at the back of my mind . . ."

Out of the silence, into which Guy had let his words wander, the conclusion seemed to emerge under its own power. David said: "You were hoping that Geoff . . ."

"Exactly! It's self-evident, isn't it?"

"I suppose so," David answered, but there was doubt in his voice. "He was rather a changed man, when I saw him last."

"Would be," Guy said; "natural, isn't it? That would have been in Burma, I suppose?"

"Yes. He'd just been made Brigadier—just before I came back, and he decided to stay on."

"Wasn't there some row or other with young Ralph?"

"In Tunisia," David said; "just before Ralph was killed. Geoff was his Brigade Major." David paused, as if he disliked the conversation, but he finally added: "Ralph sacked him."

Guy nodded his head several times before saying: "I had heard something of the sort. It sounded strange. Was it warranted?"

David hesitated. "I rather doubt it. But one can't tell, can one? Ralph was very exacting, a very good soldier." Dissatisfied with his own answer, David sought for the truth out of the dark stream of recollection. The truth was difficult to find amongst the currents of conversation, so many conversations in so many strange places, that had joined together himself and Geoff and their common past whenever they had met, often, but sometimes at long intervals, through the weary years. "I think, judging by Geoff's subsequent achievement, Ralph must have been wrong."

"It must have been a knock for Geoff at the time."

"It was."

"Yet he stayed on in the Army . . . voluntarily, when it was all over. And in Malaya, of all places!" The effort of bewilderment, of not understanding anything, seemed to be too much for Guy. His voice was becoming fainter and less certain. "But now . . . now he *is* coming home, isn't he?"

"Very soon, I believe."

"Oh, sooner than that, I think," Guy said vaguely. "I gather he landed last night . . . or was it this morning . . . There was a telegram . . . or was it a telephone message . . ." Shaking his head, he sighed, presumably at his own uncertainties. "Y'know, David, there's nobody in the world has got my respect and affection like young Geoff. What a fine feller! What a remarkably fine feller!"

"He is," David said. "He did a wonderful job one time in Burma. There was chaos—you know how it is . . ."

But Guy was not listening. His lips were moving, and he eventually said: "But I wonder what he'll make of the way he'll find it at home? I wonder what he'll make of our splendid new world, our revolution? I wonder . . . Lettin' Geoff loose on this lot . . on the country as it is to-day!" He chuckled; but the sound that came from his lips seemed to be expelled by effort or even pain. "Like loosing a young bull into a bunch of heifers . . ." He held out his hand vaguely, as if David was scarcely more than an acquaintance. "So nice to have seen you. . . ."

*   *   *

It was a little before three o'clock when Guy left the card-room and returned by bus to his office in the City. At this hour the journey was not unpleasant, the bus being fairly empty and the people unhurried and, therefore, considerate of his rubber-shod sticks. It was not until he approached his office that his spirit became impregnated with a loathing and dread of the comfortable room upstairs in which he had worked for the greater part of his life. Here his energies had been slowly expended whilst his powers declined.

When he had worked his way into his chair behind the great desk, with the silver appointments introduced by his father and grandfather, and after a decent interval had been allowed him by his staff for recovery from his journey, Miss Budge entered. "Mr. Geoffrey Greenley has telephoned again."

"He's on the telephone?" Guy stretched out a hand uncertainly towards the instrument on the desk.

"No, no, Mr. Bredon. He rang up while you were at lunch. He'd like to see you this afternoon, but I told him that I didn't really think . . ."

"Capital fellow! Splendid chap!" In Guy's unstable memory, oscillating now after his exertions, Geoff Greenley was not clearly placed, nor distinct from the old man, Richard; but Guy continued to seek for suitable and descriptive tributes. "A splendid chap, Miss Budge. He's what I call 'a whole chap' . . . 'a whole fellow' . . ." A warmth of delicious affection, like a current of wine, confused him but made him happy. "One of the best, Miss Budge. Rides straight at his fences . . . Chases the ball to the boundary . . ."

"Then you'll see him, Mr. Bredon?" Miss Budge asked the question very patiently. "He wondered if half-past four . . ."

"Most certainly, Miss Budge," Guy said with great decision.

Then she went out of the room and left him alone. He was glad to see the last of her: she was such a stupid woman, so slow to grasp his intention, even his simplest instructions.

*   *   *

Much later she came in to say: "Mr. Greenley is here, Mr. Bredon."

He scarcely heard her with his mind and was only aware of an added endurance. He said: "But I'm just going home."

"Well, shall I tell him that you can't . . . ?"

But then the name came through like a far shout. "He must come in at once," Guy said. And as the door opened, he made the effort of a gesture, supporting his weight on the arms of his chair, half-rising to say: "My dear Richard!" aching for the sight of the square, aggressive little figure bustling in. He corrected himself quickly. "My dear Geoffrey! What an age it is! You've been a long time coming back to us."

Guy was watching Geoff's face closely, as he nowadays watched all faces, to see what it recorded of his own age and infirmity. He dreaded the signs of pity. "You'll find things very changed." Geoffrey nodded, but said nothing. The silence of this boy, and his expressionless face, restored the past with a rare clarity. "Tell me, Geoff . . ." And the boy didn't try to prompt him, as they all did nowadays, but just waited until he had forgotten altogether what the question was to have been, and asked instead: "Is it gone the half-hour? I can't very well see the clock."

"Nearly twenty to five," Geoff told him.

Guy gave a great sigh, as if all the breath that had been collecting itself inside his body during the whole of this long hour could at last be expelled. He put both hands on the arms of his chair and started to heave himself to his feet.

*   *   *

Without any actual feelings of pity or disgust, Geoff watched the old man edge himself along the desk, reaching for his sticks, breathing heavily. When Geoff made a gesture of assistance, the old man said: "No, no . . . I'd rather you left me to it." When he was standing upright and had recovered his breath, he said: "I usually make for home about now."

" I'm sorry to have come so late."

" It isn't that. I hoped you'd come back with me for a drink or a little supper. Madge would be so pleased to see you."

It was not what Geoff had wanted, but he answered: " I should like it very much," hiding his reluctance, watching, with a shameful but irrepressible distaste, the old man dragging himself across the room to the curtained door of his lavatory. " I'm going in here for a moment. What about you?"

" I'm all right."

The old man took a long time. While he was gone, Geoff waited with irritation, seeking to extract from the empty room what secret quality it possessed—or had once possessed—that made its memory so impressive. Words hung in the air, here, with the remnants of cigar smoke. Words, just words, gathered truth. " You and I, Geoff, it's our job in the world to stick to the rules, letter and spirit. Others can be crooks . . . but we daren't." The sort of truth that those words had gathered was like a flower made of wax that remained unchanged, under its little glass dome, long after its season was spent: it could die only by fire, not by autumn. But there had been fire; and there had been a great melting, from which there was nothing left of that sort of truth but a stain on the Tunisian hillside where Ralph had said: " Will you please get the hell out of my sight?"

     *   *   *

" Unusual sort of place," Guy said, " but it suits us admirably." It was a Queen Anne house with Georgian additions, situated off Covent Garden; one of a small row which had been largely destroyed in the blitz. " Happily for us . . ." but now his shortage of breath was more evident, " they've repaired only the bottom couple of floors; few stairs, and we have it all to ourselves." As he turned the key, he added: " I must say, Madge has made it very decent."

When the door was opened, the birds sang and the air blew sweet. The singing came from a cage of budgerigars, and the sweetness from a bowl of pinks. But the singing and the sweetness transcended these origins. They were legendary. When the door was opened a legend was restored, and the place inside it was calm and beautiful. " Dead as a dodo!" Geoff had said to his dead life: dead dependants, dead loyalties, dead affections. " Dead

347

as a legend!" he had said. But now he found that the legend was alive. He had not so easily escaped from the past.

"Madge!" the old man called. In his voice was almost anguish, and she came at once with the calmness and grace of an old lady into the long hall. The light that shone from behind her had the green radiance of a country house, and it flowed from a far window that looked on to trees whose foliage was reflected in the polished floor. It was a french window opening on to a tiny garden, and beside it there was a great bowl of lupins and delphiniums, a background for the budgerigars. Geoff had forgotten that it was June. He had forgotten the strength of the legend; and when Mrs. Bredon put her hands upon his arms and with joy cried "Geoff, dear Geoff," he almost wept. He was struggling to keep his heart hard, as an antagonist.

She said: "I've always been wondering when you would walk in." She might have been quite a young girl, slim and pretty, with the green light behind her. But it shone upon white hair. She put a duster down upon the table. She wore a check apron. "I shall have to stand on my toes to kiss you." He could not remember that she had ever kissed him before although, when he bent his head for her to do so now, it seemed like an old custom.

"Madge, could we find Geoff some supper?" The old man's voice was now serene. With the anguish of his cry, when he had first entered the house, he had expelled the self-pity.

"It was to have been corned beef," Madge said. "But I wouldn't give corned beef to Geoff."

"Have those girls gone?" Guy asked.

"Oh yes. I only have them for the mornings nowadays. Once the house is clean, I always say, it's much less trouble to do the rest myself."

"I didn't know of the arrangement."

"Why should you know, my dear? So long as you get fed . . ."

"Not corned beef," Guy said.

"Certainly not corned beef, but we did eat our meat last night."

"'Twouldn't have been a day's rations for Madge's dogs," Guy said. "The snippet they give you!"

"Well, dear, it's dollars, isn't it?"

"Fiddlesticks! It's mismanagement!"

They did not include Geoff in the conversation. They talked

together in front of him as if he were a child. The terrace at Neap-caster must be through the french window at the far side of this hall; that bowl on the table must hold the lavender and the rose petals from the walled garden. The past survived, in spite of the death of the past; and he, Geoff, was once more overtaken. When they went into the sitting-room, she left them for a moment and returned carrying a bag and scarf. "You're not going out like that," Guy said, "not without a hat?"

"I certainly am. I'm just going round to Mr. Scarletti. Geoff shan't eat corned beef in this house."

"But not without a hat; not Mr. Scarletti! He's black market."

"Mr. Scarletti is a very nice person indeed, especially with old ladies. He has a *penchant* for old ladies . . . We live here in Covent Garden," she said to Geoff, "because his Lordship's club is a couple of minutes in one direction, and his Lordship's bus a couple of minutes in the other. And he expects me still to shop in Knights-bridge! He brings home an honoured guest, and he expects me not to go to the black market for something to eat!"

"And to wear a hat," Guy said.

Hatless, she went out, and they followed her on to the door-step and stood there to watch her walk briskly, lightly down the street. Except for an unattended horse and cart, the street was empty in the sunlight of a June afternoon.

* * *

"That's a decent sort of horse," Guy said. "Those fellows look after them extremely well, considering the difficulties." A little breeze, a warm touch of air blew up the street, stirring the dust. "You can almost smell the hay," Guy said. He was standing quite comfortably now without his sticks. "What are you going to do with yourself?" he asked suddenly.

"I'm not absolutely sure," Geoff said, deciding to be forthright. "I wanted to ask your advice."

An elderly man in a leather apron was coming down the street with heavy footsteps. When Guy nodded he raised his hand half-way to a salute, but then pushed back his cap as he crossed the road and spoke to his horse. Running his hand along the loins, he picked up the reins, climbed into his seat and started to turn his dray away. He was a solid, decent sort of chap, dependable.

Guy said: " A fellow like that ought to be on the land, oughtn't he? I don't know how he sticks it in a city. I'd gamble my shirt that he's a countryman by birth."

" You mean . . ." Geoff began to speak with the force of his indignation, which he was still restraining. " You think he ought to be making hay? You think because he was a countryman, he must always work on a farm, tied to the past, to old services, servilities . . ." Surprised at his own fluency, Geoff recognised that he was quoting David. " You think that he mustn't escape, because once . . ." But the protest seemed quite pointless. And it died in the quiet street with the footfalls of the departing horse.

Guy said: " You know I have Redbarrow in hand? I get back Woodbridge, also, next Michaelmas. There'll be over three thousand acres."

Geoff said " Yes? " in a voice as dull and disinterested as he could make it.

But Guy persisted. " I want a chap like yourself to farm it," he said bluntly.

Of course, this sort of proposition was bound to have been made by Guy or by somebody. It had to be rejected, but Geoff said, speaking out of his instinct: " It's a good farm, Woodbridge, isn't it? " He remembered the deep valley, over a mile long, that cut the farm in half. " You could winter a lot of cattle down there, if you laid on water."

" I always thought so."

" Those banks . . ." Geoff could see so clearly the deep banks, the walls of the valley, easy at the top and getting suddenly steep towards the foot, very rarely grazed and growing nothing but weed grasses, squitch and bent. " Too steep to plough, I suppose, but half a ton to the acre of basic slag. . . ."

" I dare say you're right." Guy was still looking down the street towards the horse and cart which was just vanishing round the corner. " There's no mistaking the cut of 'em."

Geoff said suddenly, in a voice that was too loud for the empty street: " You mean he almost touched his cap to us? You mean there's no mistaking the deference? Oh, he's a countryman all right! "

" I think I understand you," Guy said in a level, neutral voice, without looking at Geoff. " You wouldn't have said that five years ago."

"No, sir."

"And perhaps you won't say it a year hence. So many of you chaps who've been too long abroad . . . it was the same with some of us last time . . . Here's Madge coming back again!"

Mrs. Bredon was coming round the corner, spry and brisk, with a parcel wrapped in newspaper under her arm. "I've got you such a supper!" she cried. "Mr. Scarletti's mixed grill, wrapped in the *Daily Express*!" She never stopped talking while they followed her into the house. "When we're alone, sometimes we call it tea, and sometimes supper; and once a week, or sometimes twice, we plan it all out and call it dinner again and get in Draper to help. He lives in Chiswick now, does Draper. But why Chiswick, why on earth Chiswick . . . and when he comes, he polishes the silver, and sets the table, just like it used to be, and still should . . ."

"Now pause for breath," said Guy, and he pushed Geoff ahead of him into the sitting-room, a lovely room around which Mrs. Bredon now drifted, shaking a cushion, putting straight the newspapers. "It's time you sat down," she said to Guy and took his hand, supporting his weight, while he sank into a chair. "And now the men must drink, and the woman must cook." And she went to get a great silver salver, with decanters and glasses, which she set upon a table, moving a bowl of flowers to do so, and then readjusting a book, cigarette box, ashtrays and such, patting the room as if it was her hair before a glass.

Guy sat back with his eyelids drooping. "Would ye do the drinks, Geoff. Mine's . . . to hell with Mac . . . a stiffish whisky."

"So stupid a husband!" Mrs. Bredon cried. "And all the pills that Dr. Macdonald gives him, after coming such a way to do it—he won't even open the box! But whisky and port that he mustn't touch . . ."

"Never would take drugs; never will," Guy said. "The Almighty must mean us to be hurt; and if I can't stand pain at my time of life . . . But whisky—Geoff, if you'd be so good . . ."

"And the siphon empty, or almost!" Madge cried. "And the new one . . . Draper must have put . . . If only it were one of Draper's evenings, if only he was here to-night! Like old times, it would be, with Draper and Geoff."

Taking his own whisky neat, Geoff squirted the rest of the

siphon into Guy's glass. A fine, old-time couple, he thought: Draper and Geoff!

*　　　*　　　*

Mrs. Bredon had gone to the kitchen. And each time that Geoff refilled his glass, he rejected once again the queer appeal of that mile-long valley where the cattle ought to be wintered. " I was told to get to hell out of all that. I got to hell out of all that! I'm not, not, *not* going back! " Recently he had become accustomed to taking drink to strengthen his resolution.

Preceded by her voice, her chatter, Mrs. Bredon returned. " Now I wonder what time my two fine gentlemen will want to be fed? Such a lovely meal it's to be, but not just yet, I suppose? And in the old days, when one used to say ' Dinner at eight,' but now . . ." She had opened the dividing doors that led to the dining-room. Evidently she was laying the table, for they could hear the sounds of cutlery and glass alongside her voice.

Drink put Geoff afloat, as if he was in a ship at sea, with enough of a swell to reduce his control of limbs making tentative moves and of senses, no longer selective, receiving haphazard emissions from this room or that, from the street, and from all the near and distant kingdoms of memory, all mingled, and mostly irrelevant to what was being said or what was emotionally developing. When Guy spoke, there was a dog barking somewhere in the street; the high, incessant yelp of a mangy, flea-ridden brute chained in the Tunisian farmhouse beside the vineyard. Guy said . . . But Guy was carrying a glass of wine across to Mrs. Bredon, who sat down saying: " Meanwhile, I think I've earned myself a glass, just a very small glass of sherry, if dear Geoff would perhaps . . ." when Guy said: " By the way, Madge, I've spoken to Geoff."

" Oh, but isn't that splendid! " she cried. " Redbarrow, I suppose, and of course Woodbridge? So suitable, it would be, for Geoff, and for all of us."

Heavily Guy said: " It seems it's not to be. It seems—he doesn't care for the notion of farming again, at least not on our account."

" Doesn't care! Doesn't want to! " She was shocked, insulted, incredulous.

" He doesn't want to go back."

" Doesn't want to go back! Back where? Back to Neapcaster? "

Guy's hands moved uncertainly on the arms of his chair. "Back to . . . everything, I suppose it must be."

Their explanations and cries of astonishment passed by Geoff like orderlies in the ward of a hospital. When he said: "I don't want to go back," they both looked at him together, as if they were surprised that he had come out of his anæsthetic. So he repeated: "I don't want to go back."

"But my dear boy . . ." Sympathetic but firm, she spoke like the ward sister. "Whatever else will you do? Because, surely, Geoff dear, farming . . . it's what you're so good at, isn't it? And after all the hard times you've had, and that terrible wound, surely, you've earned yourself . . . And every one—Harry, Ralph—has always said that farming was so much your *métier* . . . And surely," she said to her husband, "surely, Guy, one must do what one's good at?"

"I should have thought so," Guy said. But he started to explain to her that, though he could not, for his part, understand Geoff's attitude, he could see that perhaps, in a way, there might be a feeling . . . And Geoff listened to them from his own detached world of the hospital bed, remote from the doctor and the nurse who were talking by the door, himself insensitive to what was said, until suddenly Guy's voice came through: "I don't know, Madge, that I understand what I'm trying to say myself. And I dare say we, anyway, couldn't understand how he feels. Because you and I, Madge, we would belong to an old world which—I take it—these young people would be tired of."

"But who's talking about the old world?" she was asking. "That's altogether gone, hasn't it? And whatever it is that's come instead. . . . A fine world it is!" she cried with fiercest contempt. "One wouldn't expect Geoff to get mixed up with a thing like that!"

But Guy answered wearily: "When you're young—thank God —you can't help hoping for something better to come; hoping that the past is the worst of it."

"Good heavens!" she cried with intense irritation. "He isn't as young as all that!"

"He may still be young enough to hope. Evidently we're not. To go on hoping for the past—like you and I, Madge, that isn't really to hope at all. But only to dream . . . One can hope only for possibilities . . ." He sounded so tired and near to death.

" These young people, they won't be, shouldn't be, content with making do . . . as you and I, Madge, make do with the present. They mustn't make do; they must *make*! They must make something new, new pattern, new design altogether. And they might feel, as Geoff may feel, that they can't make new worlds from the middle of an old entanglement."

She said: " I think you're talking just so much nonsense."

" I dare say I am. I'm only trying, trying . . ."

" Why can't Geoff speak for himself? "

" I don't know," Guy said. " Perhaps he can. But I doubt it."

That seemed to put the room into silence, like putting a child to bed. They seemed to be listening—the old man and the old lady—to make sure that Geoff didn't dare to speak.

" I won't ever go back! " he said. And then, to reinforce himself: " If I did go back, I shouldn't ever leave again. I shouldn't ever be able to." But he knew, even while he was speaking, that his declaration had taken him right out of the drift of understanding, where Guy had begun to lead him, and right into the thickest of the fog, into Mrs. Bredon's own country.

" But why . . . why do you want to leave? " she cried. " Farming *is* your job, isn't it? You're born to it, bred to it, like . . . like . . ."

" Like a horse to pull a plough, a cow to be milked," Geoff said and laughed. The laugh did not sound pleasant even to himself; but he had somehow to make fun of himself, this being the only licence that seemed left to him.

" Well! " she said, " well! *I* shouldn't have likened you to a cart-horse or a cow! " She gave a hard little laugh. " I should have said, perhaps, like . . . like a thoroughbred, you know, bred to race . . ." But it did not sound convincing.

" But Geoff may believe," Guy said, " that a cow can race if she wants to, and a mare can breed meat." He did not laugh nor even smile, but he added with a sigh: " And so they both can—in their own class, and after a fashion."

" No! " Geoff spoke violently. " I once read genetics, you know. I don't fool myself with any nonsense about equality. I don't believe I'm as good as you . . ."

" My dear boy! " They had both protested at once.

" I haven't much of an opinion of myself," he said fiercely. " I haven't anything of an opinion of myself. I don't know what

354

to believe about the new world and the old, except that we certainly haven't come to any new world yet, and that the old world certainly isn't good enough." He felt like a child choking back its tears, but not daring to pause for breath, for fear of being halted. " I don't know what to believe about anything, I don't . . . But I just *don't* believe . . . I just don't *have* to believe that I have to be dependent on the old world, on Neapcaster, not for the rest of my life."

"Yet you came to see me," Guy said, speaking very gently. " You know that I'm glad you did?"

" I wanted you to help me to get a job."

" But you didn't want the job I offered you . . ."

" No!" Geoff cried. " No, no!" He leaned his head on his hand; his forehead in the palm of his hand. " Of course," he thought, " of course I've drunk a lot; but not a real lot, not too much, only enough to have forgotten the argument." Through his forgetfulness, he could hear David's voice and see his face with remarkable clarity; he could so distinctly recall the conviction with which he had listened to David's words, that the listening might have been a current experience. But the words themselves were gone as were the argument that he had lost. While he was remembering, while the palm of his hand felt the dampness of his forehead, while he made the effort to turn his memory the right way up, he knew that the old lady had raised her eyebrows and that the old man had made her some sort of signal, because he heard her chair scrape back from the parquet floor and then there was no further movement. The room was quiet.

David had said: " Personally, I'm not going back!" He said it quite violently. " Oh no! Not back! Not to the old racket, the old hypocrisies, the old set-up of privilege and poverty. Not to the old gang of Munich!" Later he said: " I don't know what star there is ahead of us—but it's got to be a new one. We've got to have something—we've got to *be* something—new."

They must both have been rather drunk—just as he was rather drunk now, only more so—because it was in Algiers, at a restaurant right at the top of the hill, when the news that Ralph had been killed had just reached them. The tables had been set in the open, beneath fruit trees; and some sort of fruit—figs, wasn't it—kept on falling upon them, falling on to the table and into the soup.

★　　★　　★

355

Geoff remembered that Mrs. Bredon had scraped back her chair on the parquet floor, beyond the edge of the rug, and he, Geoff, must have been laughing, because when the thing fell into the soup, David said: " Stop giggling. It isn't really funny."

" But it is—damn funny! " Geoff had answered.

" You haven't said what happened."

" It was in that damned vineyard."

" The vineyard where I visited Ralph? It was the last time I saw him."

" That very same vineyard," Geoff said.

Beyond the vineyard the hills rose fairly steeply, enclosing the farm on three sides. Beyond the farmyard there was a brief olive grove on a shelf of the hill, and then only the twisted scrub that ran up to the long curving crest. But so far as Geoff was concerned, there was nothing beyond the vineyard except a hill which stopped the wireless from working in a forward direction—and also too much space. If there had been less space, if the farmhouse had been closer to the crest, it would have been in safe ground. By standing back where it did, it got the shellfire directed at the crossroads below it. So they had tried to move their headquarters up to the olive grove; but there was too much mud up there for the vehicles, when winter springs came out of the hillside, met dust and wheels, and created a quagmire. The wheels increased the mud until a walk to the hole in the ground on the far side of the track was nothing but blasphemy.

For the first day or so, a new headquarters had always a certain fascination; and from this farmhouse you could look down the steep hill to the looping road taken by the sparse forward traffic, the infantry trucks, or you could look up the hill, lifting your eyes to the crest that curled like the wind itself. The wind was bitter. Yet the change, even into the bitterness of this wind, and even into the domestic inconveniences and tactical chances of this new headquarters, was in a way refreshing, because it was in fact new. " A couple of weeks' holiday in the mountains," Ralph said. But almost at once, almost after the first day, a new place with its new outlooks became too familiar. And then, soon afterwards, it became imprisonment. This phenomenon was not, of course, specific to warfare: it was just life. But, as David said, all warfare was just life put through a sieve. And every day the Brigadier—that was Ralph—went out for the day; and every day the position of the farmhouse seemed more deplorable. "Again . . . just life, don't you think? Let me fill up your glass." It was David's voice.

A couple of Hurricanes came over the headquarters, flaunted their British markings, and dropped a few bombs on the hillside, just wide of the Brigade vehicles. On that particular morning there had been a good deal of mortaring and general disturbance, coming in a muffled sort of way from over the hill in front. When the aircraft had gone, the Staff Captain got out of his slit-trench and said: "You'd think those silly bastards could learn to read a map! I could have sworn I heard tanks." The shelling stopped for a bit and it was exceedingly quiet. They could indeed hear tanks.

All this had happened—as it now seemed—with great elegance. There was a nice formality to introduce to the vineyard the few hours of war. It was like an old-fashioned dance. "More of this yellow stuff?" David asked, as he filled Geoff's glass with the local liqueur. "I didn't realise at the time that it was *you*, your lot, mixed up in that mess. We got quite a turn in Algiers, we turned in our sleep."

"It was us all right."

"Did they shoot up that filthy farmhouse?"

"The tanks never got to the farmhouse," Geoff said. "Ralph was out on the left, visiting the yeomanry, and the tanks came through on the right. Ralph had to leave his jeep and come back on foot."

Ralph had got back to his headquarters in the early afternoon. He was, by then, alone. His driver, who had been walking with him, had been killed; and his Intelligence Officer, also with him, had got wounded or lost. When Ralph walked in, the headquarters was having a little battle of its own, clerks and all, with a few German infantry. The farmhouse was now under mortar-fire, heavy and accurate.

"Extremely unpleasant," David said.

"And yet—just when Ralph got back—I'd even stopped being frightened. It was almost fun. You know how one does?"

"Not me."

"It was very exciting," Geoff said. "I was just taking some chaps with a Bren up the hill. I thought they could get a shoot through the olives from the left flank."

You had to remember the noise, by comparison with which

the bullets and fragments were of no importance; not the noise of explosion so much as the noise of approach; the shriek that grew and rose and drove you to fasten yourself exclusively to one job. The only alternative to an exclusive job was to get into a hole. " I fastened myself to the wrong job," said Geoff.

" Where do you think you're going ? " Ralph asked the moment he got in. And when Geoff told him, he said: " That's a sergeant's job. You're supposed to be a Brigade Major. When are the Rifles going to counter-attack ? "

" He meant," Geoff said to David, " that I ought to have ordered it. And so I should . . ."

" But you couldn't get through," David said.

" Earlier I might have."

Ralph had said: " I walked back myself. It's not very difficult." He then sent two men independently with messages. One got through, but the other didn't.

" I can never remember," Geoff said to David, " just what Ralph said to me then, or I to him. Some sort of silly row started —bang in the middle of the battle. Then he turned round and walked away; just ignored me; just went on giving orders in that quiet, contemptuous voice of his, until something landed pretty close—too damn close! "

It had more or less hit the office truck which was camouflaged with branches, their foliage wilted, making a sort of tent under the edge of which there were several people collected. Ralph was handing round cigarettes and giving them orders. When the sun came out it was suddenly quite hot, and very peaceful. It was still more peaceful, because Geoff was left out of the pattern of light and shade and the sound of Ralph's voice; but slightly embarrassing, as if he had to show that he didn't mind not being included in a tennis four at the vicarage. The battle seemed to have stopped or drifted away, and it was quiet.

The thing landed then, and every one went flat. If they failed to throw themselves down, the solid hammer of air beat them into the young vines. The bits of stuff went whipping through the vines and clanged against the truck, and about half a tree fell from nowhere. When the stillness was restored, Ralph was still standing up. There was a mess of blood on one side of his face, all down his cheek beneath his eye, down from beneath his eye to the edge of his mouth. It was probably a superficial cut. He had lost his hat, but he still carried his small stick. He looked like a devil.

He walked through the men on the ground towards Geoff. The worst of the devil approaching was the lack of expression on his face; even when he hit Geoff across the buttocks with his stick, while Geoff still lay on the ground with his cheek in the mud, his head turned sideways to watch Ralph, there was no expression on the devil's face. He said: "Get up and get out!"

Geoff must have asked where he was to go, because he remembered that Ralph said next: "I don't care where the hell you go, but get the hell out of my sight!" He said: "You're no bloody use to me, frigging about with a Bren-gun instead of doing your job." He said: "Get some other job where your childish pranks can't ball things up." He said: "You can spend the next hour or so packing your kit; and when you get to Division, tell them you're out of work. Tell them I'll talk to them about it later when I'm not so busy. And send back your truck."

"That was it," Geoff said to David. "That was the last thing he ever said to me: 'Send back your truck.'"

David and Geoff walked back together through the Algerian night in spring-time. It was soft and warm at the top of the hill, but not hot. The breeze was just cool, but not chilly, and the stars swept down to the sea.

"So they promoted you?" David said. "But a lousy job? How would you feel about jumping out of aeroplanes? When I tried it myself, I knocked out a tooth. But if you don't mind that, there's some interesting stuff . . ."

Geoff said: "I'd like it very much." And then the bell went.

The last thing that had happened was the scrape on the parquet floor when Mrs. Bredon pushed her chair off the edge of the rug. And now they could hear the bell ringing faintly, somewhere at the back of the house. If Mrs. Bredon had left the room, she had now come back again for she was saying: "Whoever can that be? How tiresome!"

"But somebody has to answer it!" Guy gave his grunt, his laugh, down in the belly. "The butler, the footman, the pantry maid . . . shall the old man go?"

She put her hand on his shoulder, restraining him. The bell rang again. "I'll go," Geoff said. Everything that had happened, in the memory and emotion between his own arrival at this house and the present ringing of the bell, was enclosed, isolated, as a single incident. "I'm the one to go," he said; and he was back at Neapcaster, back in his youth, when Guy crooked a finger at the side of Slender Ladies Covert and sent him on a message for Craddock, the huntsman.

"Oh dear me, *you* mustn't go!" Mrs. Bredon cried; "not the guest!" And now she passed from her husband to Geoff, moving her hand from the old man's shoulder to the boy's hair. He was back, right back, in the most distant captivity of a most distant past. "It's me to go," she said.

They sat very quietly, listening, playing a game, while she went into the hall. They heard the front door open. Then they heard the voice crying: "Madge! My dear old Madge! Lovely as . . . ever!" They could hear the shuffle of feet in the hall while, of course, he kissed her. "Years, isn't it? Years! A couple of weeks at least."

"Isn't that Tommy Black?" Geoff asked.

"Tommy, it is," Guy said. He was grinning happily. Everybody had always grinned when Tommy Black came into the house.

$$\star \qquad \star \qquad \star$$

"And there this feller, Geoff, was sittin', all . . . glorious in a red hat an' tabs; and there was me, a poor dug-out Major sent to command one of . . . his transit camps! 'The Brigadier will see you now,' says the young chap outside. An' when I get . . . inside the holy of holies an' start to . . . unhitch my salute an' see . . . it's none other than young Geoff . . ." Ripples of laughter, like a gay breeze on a lake, transformed the room with ruffs and reflections. Every one now, as always and always before, was two persons—himself for one, and the " himself " presented to Tommy, for the other. With age he did not decline like the rest of them, but became only greyer, more wrinkled, more simian. One day— you felt—the translation would be complete, and he would have slipped right into his own monkey world, with no more human pretences, and with you following, as Madge had followed, and Anne, and all the rest. And once again there was the old, shameful desire to follow, to surrender, to be a creature or even a woman who could decently and reasonably surrender to that light tread of feet, their balance and poise unimpaired, to the knowingness of those eyes, to the breathless voice, and to the electric fingers that took hold of Geoff's shoulder, as he said: "My dear . . . old Brigadier! Don't you get up from that deep an' comfortable . . . chair, but . . . my word, but I am glad to see you!"

"Not for a week," Guy was saying. "You haven't been near us for a week."

"Your old friend, Guy, has been a . . . pretty busy man. He's off! Makin' a strategic withdrawal! Pullin' out!"

"Where to—this time?"

"The land of the free, old chap, what they . . . call Kenya. But there isn't any . . . 'this time' about it, because . . . your old friend is off for keeps!"

"Alone, Tommy?"

"Madge—what a notion! How are you . . . fixed? Can you get packed in a couple of days? How's your . . . technique with white ants?"

"Beating a retreat, are you?" said Guy through the laughter. "You're chucking it up?"

"Fair enough, Guy! The old world's gone . . . sour on us. The new world beckons with its . . . pretty face."

"It's Geoff you'd better take," said Guy. "He feels much the same, I think."

At the prick of these words, just sharp enough to inject reproof, Geoff raised his eyes to look steadily at Guy Bredon. He thought: "I'm not any longer to be brought to heel by the first rebuke!" And he heard Tommy saying: "That's quite an idea, Geoff! With your . . . brains, and my low cunning, and Guy's . . . capital, we could make . . . quite a go of it."

Geoff heard himself answering thoughtfully: "I'm not sure we mightn't."

"I suppose," Tommy was saying, "that what I . . . really want, Guy, is no more an' no less than an . . . introduction to the feller behind the grill, the chap at the bank. Unless, of course, you'd care . . . strictly as a business venture . . ."

When Guy nodded his head, he was looking not at Tommy, but at Geoff. And the nod was not in assent, but in recognition of the precise nature of Tommy's request. And it was Geoff whom Guy now asked: "Well, do you intend to go with him?"

"I think so, Mr. Bredon. I think it's just what I want."

Tommy said: "I'm very glad to hear it, Geoff. I think it's a . . . very wise decision."

Guy replied: "I wouldn't even pretend to understand the issue."

"Clear as daylight," said Tommy. "Never stay where . . . they don't want you."

"Do you really think," Guy asked—and it seemed a genuine question—"that this country doesn't any longer want people like Geoff?"

"Not if he wants to . . . think for himself; not if he has a fancy to be shown a job an' . . . left alone to do it; not if he wants any more than to . . . come and go with the hooter; not if he isn't content with . . . pay-packet every Friday an' a pension at the end of it an' . . . free false teeth . . ."

As Geoff sat listening, but detached, he thought: "The little monkey man, alone of them all, knows what he's after."

The world had had to halt until he caught it up, to slow down until it fell into step with him. And suddenly he saw the thing in the clear light of battle when an object, emerging from the fog of war, was isolated, distinct, and not any longer blurred by normal lights. "For now we are living in a monkey age of toys and gadgets, bombs, speed, racket—so what more sensible than to wait for the monkey man and fall into step?" Aloud he said to them, interrupting their voices: "Oh yes, I'm going with Tommy!"

In a steady, expressionless voice, Guy said: "If your mind's made up, Geoff, I'll see if I can help in the way Tommy suggests."

"Capital feller!" Tommy cried to both of them at once. "Come out to dinner, Geoff, an' . . . we'll sign an' seal it, over the port."

"Thanks—I'd like to," Geoff said.

It was Mrs. Bredon's voice that cried: "Oh no, not dinner, not to-night! To-morrow will be time enough!"

It was Geoff's voice that Geoff heard answering: "I'm afraid to-morrow I have to go back to Colchester. I'm not a civilian for another fortnight." And he was adding silently: "At least I'm sober enough to remember *that*!" while Tommy was saying: "So it has to be to-night, and . . . Madge, my sweet, you'll understand it, won't you?"

"But my dinner, such a lovely dinner, and enough for both of you." It was a tragic wail.

"Madge dear, I only wish . . . that I could. But a feller is coming to the club, a feller who . . . has a ship . . ."

"But, Geoff," she said, "you anyway . . ."

362

Guy said: "I think perhaps he'd best go along with Tommy."

And Mrs. Bredon—as if she really didn't mind in the least, as if it was all really rather a joke—said: "Then I can't interest any of you gentlemen in my mixed grill, my *Mister Scarletti*?"

"For to-night," said Guy, "only your husband." And when he made some sort of effort to rise, for the party was obviously at an end, Tommy said: "Don't trouble to bestir yourself, Guy, old chap," and somehow managed by these words to confer a favour. Then he went to kiss Madge, putting an arm round her waist. Pathetically she turned her face towards him. And it was impossible to believe that they were of the same generation; that this man, still young on his feet, still sure, had made love with this grey-haired old lady.

When Tommy withdrew his arm from Mrs. Bredon and took hold of Geoff's elbow, pushing him in front of him out of the room, the old lady remained standing in the same place and attitude in which he had left her, pathetic and graceful amongst her flowers in her pretty room, left behind by everything, like an indifferent picture painted in a style that has long gone out of fashion, comic. Guy also had not moved. His hands were still on the arms of his chair, ready to take his weight, as when he had started to rise to say farewell.

From the hall Geoff heard his name called, almost sharply, like an order. He returned quickly to the doorway, pushing himself past Tommy. There, when he had seen these two old people fixed in their places where he had left them, as if they were enchanted, he heard Guy say: "Well, Geoff, if you go—I'll help you. But in case you decide, after all, to stay amongst us—I shall do nothing about Redbarrow and Woodbridge for a couple of months." He nodded, but it was not quite a dismissal; and in a moment he added: "An' if you don't feel quite like rattin' it out of the country, not yet . . . and still don't want to be tied to any of us old 'uns in any shape or manner, you might do worse than—go an' see Freddy Betts."

"Sir Frederick Betts!"

"Well, Geoff—he's what you might call the new world, y'know." From the depths of his chair, the old gentleman seemed to be marshalling all his strength to puzzle it out correctly. "It's a thing you must figure out for yourself; but, as I see it . . ." Yet the vision, whatever it was, seemed reluctant to take to speech.

" What you an' I knew as England, Geoff . . . though you an' I, we don't like talkin' about it overmuch . . . but it's still here, Geoff! It's not so easy to find, perhaps; it's not . . ." He shook his head; it was all too difficult. " But that fellow, Betts," he said. " Betts isn't England—and you mustn't, you wouldn't, make the mistake of thinkin' that he is. He isn't even the gang that's got hold of England for the time bein'—and *they* aren't England either! But England . . . but Betts . . ." He couldn't continue. " Our England! " he said loudly before he almost choked. The colour had come back to his face, not healthily but from embarrassment, as if he had committed some shameful indiscretion, an emotional outburst, by talking of his country by name. " Oh, go an' find out for yourself! " he said crossly. And then: " Blast ye, Geoff, for making an old feller like me go talking like that! " Obviously he thought that something he felt deeply had actually been said, and at last he nodded dismissal.

" Well, good night, Mr. Bredon," Geoff said. He had to walk carefully across the polished floor of the hall—going towards the open door of the house where Tommy was waiting—because of the slight unsteadiness of his feet. The budgerigars in their cage were still twittering and singing complacently.

* * *

" Haven't we got to go to your club? " Geoff asked.

" As a matter of fact, no. But nowadays I find that . . . half an hour of Madge's company, bless her, is more than enough." They were walking through the streets on a quiet evening in June when all good folk were finishing haymaking for the night. You could feel it like that. Or you could feel that you were walking with a lighter step, and with the burden less heavy on the hump of your shoulders, because you had now, again, a clear destination, a glow in the sky for which you were making—a purpose. A man became again a man, his circuit being re-connected, when he had a purpose restored to him: they were going to Kenya. " They know me here," Tommy said as they came to the outskirts of Soho and to a doorway with an awning, outside which a commissionaire touched the peak of his hat. " Good evening, Colonel," the commissionaire said.

Inside the door, the man in the white waistcoat and the man in the black waistcoat both said: " Good evening, Colonel," and then repeated, one after the other: "For two . . . for two . . ."

"As usual," Tommy answered; and a card marked "Reserved" was whipped off a corner table as they sat down at it.

"A little melon?" the head-waiter suggested. "*Truite au bleu?* And then a little spring chicken?"

At the top of the menu there was printed a notice saying that the cost of a meal must not, by law, exceed five shillings. "That doesn't mean you and me," Tommy said; "nor, for that matter . . . anybody else."

"Certainly not, Colonel," said the head-waiter. "Would you, perhaps, prefer a steak?"

"Poor old Guy," Tommy said, when the meal was ordered, "ploddin' along a lap behind the . . . rest of the field. And doesn't know it." He opened the wine list. "And poor old Madge, bless her heart! And her little . . . sallies into the black market! Rather pathetic!"

$\star$ $\qquad$ $\star$ $\qquad$ $\star$

"This steak—wouldn't it be a ration for a week?"

"My dear fellow—you've been a . . . long way off. Ration for a week? For a family of six perhaps."

Geoff looked around him. "I don't see any tables for six," he said inconsequentially.

"You know," Tommy said, "there are still a few chaps like Guy who . . . won't come to a place like this."

The room was full and people were crowded at the doorway waiting their turn for a table. As each couple or group was led forward and became, for a few moments, detached and distinct, it was seen to be surprisingly ordinary before it slipped into its place in the room amongst the low and pleasant voices, and the faces that emerged and receded, that became swollen and then deflated like a trick of the camera. They were such ordinary people, not of a type, but just people. Yet they could not be The People. "Somewhere, one supposes," Geoff said, "there are hives of honest workers turning out the goods." For one had to imagine some saving factor that put a meaning into the world's revolutions and orbit.

"My dear old Geoff—keep your illusions. It's only a . . . question of which door to open. When you get inside, the house is different, and the racket is different, but it's . . . always a racket."

Yet somewhere there was the brave company; not just the individual craftsman, the ploughman, the blacksmith, the welder; but the company behind the band, marching in step, arms swinging together, marching down the street. One listened for the music and the tramp of feet. One listened for this reassurance, but one heard only the shuffle and twitter, clatter and clink, of uniformed men who were lost, stranded, forgotten, waiting for somebody with three stripes on his arm to call in ringing encouragement: " Here, my merry lads . . . here, you so-and-so's . . . get a hold of this . . . of that . . ."

" It's got to be one-pound notes," Tommy was saying; " that's the only . . . racket that counts. You've got to gamble, you see. Without gambling, one can . . . scarcely eat. Gambling isn't taxed."

" I couldn't gamble," Geoff said, meaning only that to live would be intolerable unless one could rely on the average: that one year there would be a late spring; the next year, a drought; the next, a wet harvest; but over the years, a balance would be struck, bringing a reward small but dependable.

" All these chaps in this room," said Tommy, waving his hand at them, " they . . . all must gamble. If not, they'd be . . . sitting at home waiting for Sunday—and their five ounces of meat."

The very word " gamble " had images exotic beside a ploughed furrow or a plant of young wheat. Vaguely, Geoff said: " The horses, the dogs, I suppose; the dirt-track, the football pools . . ."

" Nowadays, any one gambles on . . . anything: on houses or . . . scrap-iron or second-hand cars or bicycles or eggs. You can always gamble on . . . anything that's short. How else do you think we live ? "

Geoff laughed. Tommy was an elevating companion, increasing your stature—whether you were a man or a woman—as he singled you, selected you, so that you looked down with pity upon the remainder, those who were culled and rejected, while you dwelt for the period of his companionship in the most confident world that you had in your heart. Geoff laughed very thoroughly, an act of evacuation. But when the laughter was all done Tommy said: " You know, I . . . mean it, old boy ! " He called the wine-waiter over to him and said: " We'll drink Armagnac, and leave the bottle." He put his hand on Geoff's wrist, saying: " Look at myself, old chap ! All my life I've never . . . had any money;

366

I've been a sponge. And now it's other people who sponge on me. They find me . . . pretty resistant."

Now Tommy laughed; Geoff laughed; the waiter smiled and almost laughed himself. There seemed to be an enormous company, all of it specially selected for an exclusive membership, all laughing. "This brave new world of Britain," said Tommy on the flow of his laughter, "has lifted me from . . . penury to comparative affluence."

"Then why leave it?"

"Oh," said Tommy, "that's an easy one, isn't it? You see . . . it won't last."

"What won't last?"

"This brave Britain, old chap. One day it'll find itself tired of me and . . . my likes."

"There's a familiar face!" Geoff said it as a joke, because, of course, the man who had just come into the room was old, an intimate friend. Yet the pink, plump face had lost its name for the moment. "Surely, surely . . ."

The plump young man was wearing horn-rimmed glasses. The chin and forehead were large, the hair rather thin. Although this person was not tall, he seemed to stoop when he spoke to the head-waiter; stooped perhaps intellectually, as if he had high qualities which needed to be depressed on this sort of occasion like the muzzle of a gun. The face had the familiarity of a press photograph. "Bless my soul!" said Tommy, "what a place for the . . . non-conformist conscience."

"So it's Walter!" Geoff said.

"Walter it is! Apart from . . . old Guy, the only incorruptible of my acquaintance."

"Isn't he a politician or something?"

"Very much so, old chap. He's in the Government." Tommy was waving his hand, trying to catch Walter's attention. It seemed as if Walter noticed him, but did not want to engage himself until, suddenly, his eyes were caught upon Geoff, his eyebrows raised themselves with an air of enlarged delight, and he came between the tables with his arms outstretched. He took Geoff's hand between both of his and held it without shaking it.

"My dear Geoff! You've not been long home?"

"Too long already," Geoff said.

"No, no—you've been in Burma, haven't you?"

"Till three days ago. I flew back."

Out of the sea of wine and well-being, the face of Walter bobbed like an antediluvian survivor. "What are you doing, Walter, in a place like this?"

Perhaps uneasily Walter answered: "As a matter of fact, I'm supposed to be dining with Sir Frederick Betts."

"Oh yes," said Tommy, "this is one of . . . Freddy's favourite haunts."

The heads of Walter and Betts, fantastically incongruous, floated and bobbed together on the wavelets, bumped and drifted apart. "Of course," Geoff said, "you used to work for him, didn't you?"

"Still does, old boy," Tommy said, "like the . . . rest of the Government."

Walter's face seemed to swell, inflated, but perhaps it was only that he flushed in saying: "Apart from the quite unwarranted innuendo of that remark, I think it in pretty poor taste."

"Don't misunderstand me, Walter." Tommy spoke lightly and without discomfort. "I was only stating a . . . natural law. Physics, wasn't it, in . . . my schooldays? For every one of your regulations there's an equal and . . . opposite racket. For every racket there's a profit for a chap like Freddy."

*   *   *

Filling Geoff's glass, Tommy said: "Mustn't let the bottle stand . . . idle, like the British workman." He held it towards Walter, who again shook his head. "Fine sort of revolution you've worked on us, Walter boy; puts money in the . . . pocket of a chap like myself; leaves a chap like Geoff looking for a job."

"That's not exactly the whole of it," said Walter pleasantly.

"Go on then, Walter, balance the account. Put all your little knick-knacks on to one . . . side of the ledger; load it with your free spectacles and wigs, your few shillings saved on food, your uneconomic rents for houses that haven't been built. And on . . . the other side put the rackets you've created; put the impossibility of saving a penny, an honest . . . penny, against your old age; of gettin' any reward for bright ideas or hard work . . ." Mistrustfully he sipped his Armagnac as if it was not very good. "Balance it up, Walter, and what . . . do you get?"

Walter said: "Progress, slow progress; but it's a start. There has to be a start."

"And now," said Tommy, "tell us about the . . . babies fed by the Government on T.T. milk. And all about the . . . men who used to be queuein' for work and are now queuein' for a gamble on the dogs. And their wives who have to queue for six-pennorth of meat!" Again he pushed the bottle across the table. "Be a man, Walter. Take a drink, Walter, an' tell us about the . . . great equality of the queues, puttin' the big ones in their place! And all the little Civil Servants seein' to it that you don't get anything unless you do queue! And then, Walter, and then what? Do *I* queue? Do I, my foot!"

"There's a way round every queue," Walter said.

"Profound remark!" said Tommy. "Walter, I wish you'd drink. Way round the queue? Of course there is. There always has been. All you've done, old boy, is to . . . change the queues and change the people who find the way round them. It used to be chaps like Guy Bredon and Harry Meredith who skipped the queues, because they . . . hadn't the time to stand and wait; bein' too busy helpin' chaps like you an' me an' Geoff." He laughed and pointed his finger at Walter and waggled it. "And now they have to . . . take their turn with the rest, don't they, Walter, while you and I, Walter, we . . . walk round to the top. Now it's we who . . . haven't the time to wait; bein' . . . too busy helpin' ourselves to . . . what little there is of anything knockin' about . . . Do you want a car?" Tommy asked.

"I've been on a waiting list for three years," Walter answered. "I suppose I shall get it sometime."

"I can get it for you to-morrow. A new one—marked 'for export.'"

"But at what price?"

"If you're going to talk technicalities," said Tommy, "it depends on what kind of car you want. If you want a cheap . . . one, you can have it at the regular price—with a hundred quid for the boys, of course."

"The boys!" Geoff said sharply, as if he had suddenly woken up.

"My dear old Geoff! The R.A.F., an' the Americans, an' the Control Commission weren't the only boys at work. They're just beginners. For every . . . Civil Servant makin' and enforcin' regulations, there's a couple of boys on the side gettin' round them." Tommy was playing with his cigarette case. "Getting round them for . . . cash, Walter. Getting round them for one-pound notes."

A waiter had come to Walter's chair. "You're wanted on the telephone, Mr. Wallis. It's Sir Frederick Betts."

As soon as Walter had left them, Tommy leant across to Geoff. "I'll tell you a . . . thing, Geoff . . ." Tommy was crouched over the table, but his eyes were raised to watch Walter's progress towards the entrance and the telephone. "Believe it or not, Walter lives in a house that's . . . owned by Freddy Betts. Interestin', don't you think?"

"Not especially," Geoff said. "Don't most people live in a house that's owned by somebody else?"

"Quite, quite, old boy. But houses being scarce, it will be . . . handy to be a landlord."

*   *   *

"Crisis?" Tommy asked when Walter returned. "Or only no dinner? Have something here?"

"My wife . . ." Walter murmured, but he sat down again at their table. To Geoff, he said: "Betts was most interested to hear you were back. He'd very much like to see you. In fact . . ." Walter seemed an uneasy messenger. "He rather wondered if, by chance, for a few minutes, to-night even . . ."

Geoff said: "I'm not interested." But Tommy was already saying: "I should, Geoff, if I were you! Freddy's a useful feller."

"You forget—we're going to Kenya."

In a pained voice, Walter said: "No, no, Geoff—you mustn't feel like that, not so soon! You must give us a chance to show you . . ."

Out of Walter's protest, Tommy was saying: "Hold hard, old chap! This thing—you must give . . . adequate thought to it!"

"I've done so," Geoff said. For all through the evening he had burnt the fuel of purpose; and all through the chatter and argument he had felt himself committed—as he tried always to be committed in battle—to this exclusive plan which had made everything else as irrelevant as distant gunfire. The shocks and disgust he had suffered from time to time had only been able to strengthen the wine in strengthening his decision. He said: "We'll take out a pedigree bull."

"Steady, Geoff. There remains much . . . to be thought about."

"Does there? With Guy's offer, I thought . . ."

"There's a 'but' to it, Geoff. You see . . ." When Tommy paused, and the pause continued, Geoff leant forward and said sharply: "But what, Tommy?" As if a man's heart was a motor, propelled by a man's purpose, its power was already lagging, as the purpose diminished. So Geoff made the question come sharply, as if he was speaking to a soldier in a crisis, a mess; or as if it was Ralph's voice speaking to himself. "But what? Isn't it all fixed?"

"A slight complication, Geoff . . ." It was rare to see Tommy unsure of himself. "A while ago . . . before you were back, I had, I did . . . mention the thing to somebody else. They haven't, of course, made up their minds, or I wouldn't have put it . . . to you. But if they should . . ."

"I'd be out?"

"No, not so fast, not that . . . because . . . three of us might be . . . very good company. Or they might be . . ."

"A bloody mess!" As Geoff rose to his feet, the scrape of his own chair somehow gave him the anger to substitute for purpose. He asked Walter: "Where does Betts live?"

Walter, in a voice almost scared of Geoff's anger, said: "Geoff, not in too much of a hurry, Geoff . . ."

"Where does he live?"

"In Albany. You know—off Piccadilly, only a few steps from here."

"I don't know. But I'll damn soon find out!" As he went, he heard Tommy's protest in pursuit. "Geoff . . . there's nothing yet fixed." And a timid plaint from Walter: "Geoff . . . Geoff."

To a handy waiter, Geoff said: "I think Mr. Wallis wants something to eat."

*　　　*　　　*

"I'm glad you came, Geoff—and so quickly. I imagine that Walter gave you my message? Conveniently enough, I have with me at the moment another old friend with whom I hope, if we can come to some sort of working arrangement, you'll agree to associate yourself."

As if he was the butler, Sir Frederick had taken Geoff's hat and was pointing the way from the small hall along a narrow passage. Neither time nor words had to be wasted by Sir Frederick. Like a good general of an army, he said only what had to be said and what was meant.

One had known Sir Frederick all one's life, hearing him laughed about and despised, but not always positively disliked. "Poor old Freddy!" they said; "he's got nothing in the world except a few millions in the bank." But people could change; or the environment could change, so that people's endowments became newly appropriate; and to such changes one must not oppose oneself. Nor could one escape the affection which belonged to an old acquaintanceship, even if that acquaintanceship had never before been affectionate. All those traversed years of common, if interrupted, associations pushed one into a sort of friendship, loyalty or trust which made the reunion enthusiastic.

Indeed, Sir Frederick now put his hand on Geoff's arm, saying: "I'm so glad you're back at last. Perhaps you and I could work together now? As you may remember, I've had it in my mind for many years."

Looking complacently at Sir Frederick's face, so very little changed—although the man was scarcely any younger than Guy Bredon—Geoff answered: "I think we might."

"Good! Come along then."

Sir Frederick now preceded Geoff, as if the latter's declaration or admission had immediately deprived him of the privilege of a guest. Opening a door, Sir Frederick said into the room: "Do you know who's joined us?"

A voice that was not unfamiliar, but not at once identified, answered: "I heard a voice, Sir Frederick; I can make a guess."

"Quite right," Sir Frederick said and turned back to Geoff, waving him through the doorway. "Of course you remember Frank?"

*   *   *

Sir Frederick talked in a low, comfortable voice, reassuringly precise. "There you have it, Geoff. We touch nothing that doesn't fit; we reject nothing that does fit. Provided you keep the rhythm right, the rhythm of the whole, there's nothing that can't be made profitable. Don't you agree, Frank?"

"I do, Sir Frederick."

Geoff, without movement, had both men in his zone of vision,

372

Sir Frederick on the opposite side of the fireplace in a chair as deep as his own, and Frank in a hard chair between them. It was a small and pleasant room furnished, except for the comfortable chairs, in its own Regency style. Although it was not yet night, the curtains were drawn; although it was warm outside, there was a small fire burning, its incongruity giving to this interview a pleasant and luxurious sense of security. The lamps were deeply enough shaded for the reflections of firelight in the furniture and glass to catch the wandering eye and pass it on to the two faces, both of them firm and confident, both of them having a distinction which seemed not acquired but inherent. Frank's boldness of eye was still roguish, but the lines of shadow in his face that were new to Geoff produced a kindly shrewdness mixed with gallantry. It was not easy to trace the translation of this man from the awkward footman; and one might have thought him a country gentleman, of sporting tastes, turned to commerce. And Sir Frederick—surely an aristocrat whose ease and air of calm command were marked at birth?

"As Frank will explain to you when he takes you around, we are self-supporting, independent." On the extended fingers of one hand, Sir Frederick made his points with the forefinger of the other. "First and foremost, our groups of farms all over the country. For each county group, a pool of major implements, common warehouses for seed and fertilisers, common mills, driers, silos and so on." It was a catalogue without embellishments. "Of course we make our own fertilisers; grow our own seed; market, through to the consumer himself, our own produce. We build our own barns, sheds, poultry and pig houses; we manufacture some of our own implements, and repair and maintain all of them. When any complementary business comes on the market—a corn merchant, for instance, or an agricultural engineer—we buy him up." Pausing for emphasis, Sir Frederick said suddenly and bluntly: "You will see there is unlimited scope at the top for a man like yourself."

Sir Frederick waited for Geoff to give the slightest nod of concurrence before continuing in the same low and level tones. "I must make it clear that what we want is men of ways and means. I must make quite clear what I mean by that."

The immobility of the man in his not untidy bulk and his comfortable age made his least movement significant. Now he joined his fingertips together. "Our object is to grow and sell food and maintain or increase the fertility of our soil. One might think it to be in the national interests. The Government do not appear to regard it as such. Indeed, if we were to keep one-tenth of their rules and regulations, we could not remain in business."

The note and emphasis of his voice never varied in the least—its invariability becoming, in time, almost sinister—even when he said: "We have to find our way past, through, over or under most of those regulations. Of course we keep men in London whose job it is to contact, on our behalf, the various Ministries. That, Geoff, is one of the new professions. We do not inquire about the means they employ, we do not quibble about their expense accounts, so long as they get what has to be got. But for the man on the spot, the man on the farms and in the provincial towns . . ." And now Sir Frederick did shift his weight slowly in his chair, drawing himself more upright. "Their only rules are the rules of fair trade and good husbandry, with the overriding proviso, of course, that . . . they must not be caught."

The wine that Geoff had drunk, acting on all the back-happenings of the evening, had seemed to encase Geoff with a thick, protective skin when he first reached Sir Frederick. Penetrating this skin, advancing like a drill, the steady recital had cut its own path straight to Geoff's visual and calculating brain. And now, when Sir Frederick paused for many seconds and then asked: "Any use to you? Would you care to work with us?" Geoff answered immediately: "Very much indeed."

Replying with a single, deep grunt of consolidation, Sir Frederick said: "Frank, get us something to drink."

While they each had a mild glass of whisky, Sir Frederick said in the same easy way of a general giving orders to his senior commanders: "You tell me you'll be free in a fortnight? I suggest, for a start, that you let Frank take you round his Neapcaster area. Since those are your native parts, and you know their ways and husbandry, we shall get your immediate reactions to what we are doing. After that . . ." He emptied his glass before concluding: "You must tell me what you fancy; where you think you can best fit in with us."

"And now," Sir Frederick said, "it's past the time that I usually get to bed. Where are you staying?"

Geoff answered: "I hadn't thought of it. Is it difficult in London at the moment?"

"Not for us. I expect Frank can arrange it. Mr. Spry, for instance . . ."

Frank said: "Easy as winking."

"Well, wink on it," said Sir Frederick, holding out his hand, smiling, dismissing them.

*   *   *

Mr. Spry was neither in his office nor at the reception desk, just inside the entrance of Mayfair Mansions, a large modern building in a small Mayfair street. Mr. Spry's assistant, a young man, said that Mr. Spry himself would be back in a few minutes. Frank said: "It doesn't matter in the least. Brigadier Greenley wants a room; as near mine as possible."

Flicking through his register, the young man said: "On the account, I presume? We're full, of course." But he put two keys on the desk, one of them Frank's and the other of a room on the same floor and a few doors distant.

The whole place in white stone gave an impression of Perpendicular splendour, but on a miniature scale. As they went up in the lift, Frank said: "They call them flatlets, but they're just rather decent rooms; very handy, we find them."

The corridor and the rooms themselves were deeply carpeted and seemed taller than was architecturally necessary or economically desirable. It was probably an illusion. The whole plan, the whole evening that was not yet ended, was a masterful illusion leading to this triumphant climax.

Very soon Geoff was alone in a bright room of meticulous contrivance, like the luxury cabin of a ship, only larger, and with all furniture of unstained, polished wood built and fitted as part of the structure. The only movable objects were a writing-table and two chairs, one for sitting upright, and the other for reclining on pearl-grey cushions, the colour of all the hangings and of the carpet, both inside the room and along the corridor outside it. This consistency increased the illusion of being in a synchronous world, obedient to some regular beat that was not the natural pulses. This pearl-grey orb spun on its own account, independent of the elemental controls with their complex syncopations, and of the cycles of life and dissolution, and of the laws that related matter to matter and one human heart to the next. One abandoned such laws, with their attendant obediences, loyalties and ethics, when one trod this pearly way; while the other world, where these things belonged, became as distant and detached as somebody else's music.

On the wall hung a single print of an elegant person holding an implement like a hockey-stick: "The Royal and Ancient Game of Golf." Across the carpet whose pile sucked at the toes of one's feet, a door led into the bathroom, a very shiny place, almost as big as the bedroom itself. At one end, it had a partitioned cabin appointed as a tiny kitchen. After this exploration, one sat in an unworldly way upon the deep and comfortable bed, too big for one human, too small for two, as if the creatures of this world had sizes, shapes, habits and appetites different from those of ordinary, terrestrial inhabitants.

After a little while the telephone rang, and it was of course Frank. "You weren't asleep, Geoff? Got everything you want?" Frank's voice on the telephone was a very different and lowlier manifestation than Frank sitting at Sir Frederick's fireside. "You know, if you want a bit of comfort, you've only got to ask Spry. He has them on tap in the ballroom. Decent kids, too, decent class—not just the street tarts. Give Spry a tinkle when you're feeling ripe. . . ."

Geoff said: "Not to-night, thanks." Then he asked: "What exactly *is* this place? Does Spry run it? Does Betts own it?"

"I suppose indirectly Freddy owns it. There's not much he doesn't, you know. Could you do with a drink? I've got a bottle of Scotch . . ." Geoff protested. "Oh, it's no trouble," Frank said. "We're almost next door."

In his dressing-gown and slippers, but still wearing his shirt and trousers, Geoff sat on the bed while Frank, beside him, poured whisky into Geoff's tooth-glass. "Say when."

"I don't really want this. I've had enough to-night."

Frank's red and hairy chest, displayed by the yellow and blue silk jacket, glistened slightly as if it were damp. He was younger and more scamp-like, he was much less distinguished and responsible, than when he had been wearing a dark suit, subtly concealing the pattern of a check, with a white, long-pointed collar and splendidly polished shoes. Now he wriggled his toes as a slipper dropped on the carpet; now one could almost trace the imprint, back through the years, of his remarkable progress; and now he was again, mostly, a strong, clean, jolly sort of rogue, pleasant and only just ageing. And yet, when he handed Geoff the tooth-glass, then took it back again, he drinking from one side, and Geoff from the other, there was all the time in Geoff's mind a thought, a recollection—the sound of the strange, hoarse cry that had come out of his own throat when he had gone into Mrs. Meredith's bedroom and had then returned to the boy, Walter, who was quivering, gasping and sobbing in the corridor. This—which had not even yet become a comic episode—still brought back into his stomach that original feeling of sickness. Of all the obscenities with which war had presented him, there were none that still touched the nerves of his stomach like the redness and hairiness of the footman's loins. From that night to this, an awful fascination had been exercised upon his bowels by men like Frank and Tommy.

He took a drink, cleaning away the disgust that was really a disgust of himself, and the shame that was only a shame of his own envious admiration and attraction. He said: "We're getting old, Frank."

"Forty's not old—and you're a bit younger than that."

"Three years," Geoff said. Looking away from his own body, and carefully away from Frank's, Geoff fixed his eyes upon the picture of the old-fashioned gentleman with the broad-brimmed hat and the old-fashioned golf club. He said: "All this and heaven too—Betts owns it?"

"More or less," Frank answered. "It's a useful enough investment, and no end of a convenience. Besides . . . we do rather collect properties where people can live, or even just sleep." He took another drink from the glass, upturning it until it was empty and he was looking through its base at the ceiling light. "We collect anything that's short or scarce. There's nothing shorter or scarcer than places to live or sleep." Rolling himself forward in a feline manner, he refilled the glass from the bottle. They were drinking the whisky neat. "Houses are short as whisky. Give a chap a house, give him a roof, and you've got him where you want him."

"Like Walter," Geoff said suddenly; but the remark seemed to himself to have not much significance.

"What do you know about Walter?" Frank spoke sharply, almost as if he were alarmed. "*I* don't know anything about

Walter, nothing at all that I've heard about . . ." But it was obvious to Geoff that he was not speaking the truth.

Geoff said: " I wouldn't care to live in one of Betts' tied cottages."

" You probably will," Frank said. " I do myself. We all do. There's nowhere else. Besides, there's nothing to worry about, so long as one keeps in step: what Freddy calls ' the rhythm of the outfit.' "

Such words as these to-night fell slowly, like non-buoyant objects of war dropped into a deep pool, languidly descending but dangerous. Later they would come explosively to rest. One knew of their delayed fuse, but ignored it, even while one listened and spoke. " And here," Frank said, " we keep just a few rooms for country chaps like us. The rest, of course, are let—with no end of a waiting list . . . so, if ever you want a room, any time you like, for as long as you like, just phone Mr. Spry. I'll give him the tip."

For some time they sat in silence on the bed, passing the glass from one to the other. " About ready to get unconscious?" Frank asked. " Nothing to do myself but say my prayers and hop into bed. " He stood up slowly, stretching himself on the way to sleep. " I'll leave you the bottle—what's left of it."

" No, thanks."

" It's quite all right; I've got another . . . So we go to Neapcaster together next week . . . the week after that? My May will like that." He gave a little affectionate laugh, deep in his chest, at the thought of his wife. " She's never stopped talking about you, you know, Geoff. It's my belief she's always been sweet on you." He smiled with the pleasure that he got from thinking of his wife's fondness for Geoff. " You'll stay with me and May, won't you, Geoff?"

Geoff nodded and said: " Thank you very much." It would be queer to stay in a house as a guest of Miss May and Frank.

" Well . . . bed!" Frank stood in the open doorway. " I think maybe I will give Spry a tinkle and get up some kid or other from his basement shop." He was now entirely Frank the merry lad, Frank the scamp, almost Frank the footman; wholly incompatible with himself as Sir Frederick's shrewd and smooth assistant. " If ever . . ." he winked, " you're feeling that way yourself—just a word down the phone. It's easy as that!" Rubbing his knuckles in his hair, he said: " There's one called Celia—very ripe . . .

378

mention my name, of course." He yawned, he stretched from his toes to his lifted fists. "She puts you sweetly to sleep. . . ."

When Frank had been gone for some minutes, Geoff got up and made himself ready for bed. It was a very comfortable bed, but when he was inside it, he felt a long, long way from sleep.

* * *

Alone in his bed, he suffered the internal concussion, as all the delayed despair of the day at last ignited, blew up.

This was now the night, and in retrospect the most recent events were no longer the clearest, all having become a flat swamp through which he had floundered, and in which he was still stuck. "All the parts of man, fighting between themselves, betray him . . ." There was no person or thing more despicable than a man betrayed by himself.

In search of relief, he turned his mind to the periods of his achievement, recalling the astonishment with which he had heard his own lips giving orders that were right orders, and had seen men obeying him, respecting him, following him and seeming to draw their courage and success out of himself. But then there had been a power motivating his mind and body, issuing his voice. And when he burrowed inside himself to regain that power, or at least that self-respect which was part of that power's manifestation, it seemed not to be there, or ever to have been there, but to have been always extraneous to himself, he being only its agent.

Trying to pray "O Lord, make me again your agent!" he heard only the level and logical words of Sir Frederick showing how futile were commandments that came between a man and his purpose, between a plan and its accomplishment. Shutting his ears to Sir Frederick, he heard only Tommy Black. Turning from Tommy, he met Walter Wallis, living in Sir Frederick's house. From Walter to the Bredons, who pointed the way back to the old loyalties and captivities of a lifetime which, in league with his own sinful parts, had finally betrayed him. When Ralph had struck him, it was the blow of his own guilt, his own sinfulness. All the sinful deeds and imaginings of his whole life had now completed his encirclement. When again he tried to pray, this time for the least ray of forgiveness, his prayers, even from their start, had no destination.

In anger, then, he laughed at his guilt, and it vanished. Ceasing to struggle in the swamp, he found it was firm under his feet.

Raising his head to the cool certitudes of Frank and Sir Frederick Betts, he found the horizon was again glowing with an evident purpose. Again an agent, he put out his hand to the telephone. But the operator told him that Mr. Spry was not in his office.

Trembling with relief, because he still had to doubt the obedience of his own body, he switched out the light and turned again towards sleep. But when he tried to bury his misery in the pillow, he was again as sleepless, as restless, as vividly and painfully conscious as when only the mosquito-net separated him from the clatter of palm trees in the hot wind. This sound declared with unbearable insistence the appetite of his aching limbs.

Then the telephone rang. "Did you still want Mr. Spry?" the operator asked. "He's back."

Mr. Spry met him three-quarters of the way; there was scarcely need to formulate the question. Mr. Spry concluded: "And, Brigadier, if you should ever want me again, and you happen to find me out of my office, don't hesitate to ask my assistant. He's fully competent to deal with these matters in my absence."

*   *   *

When he had spoken to Mr. Spry, Geoff lay in his bed waiting for a long time, trembling slightly. He had to watch the door. When he tried to look at the picture, his eyes were recalled to the door handle which would have to turn before the door was opened. He suffered a fear more intense and enfeebling than the fear of waiting for battle.

He heard footsteps. The carpet of the corridor was thick, but he heard or felt the slight vibrations. Heavy and slow, they passed from end to end of the passage: a man had passed. Later he lay on his bed, sweating only slightly, desire having receded. The act of picking up the telephone seemed now to have been the act of an imbecile. Again he heard footsteps, this time a woman's footsteps, but they too passed, paused beyond his door and went on, dwindled, finished. And now his trembling and sickness began to abate, so that he was able to lie quietly and resignedly, like a patient in a hospital cot. Soon, the nurse and the orderly would be coming with the screens and the surgical dressings. He wanted a cup of tea. In some hospitals they brought you a cup of tea before they came through with the dressings.

It must have been much more than half an hour before the

door opened; and by the time she came, his perception was quietened and indeed he was so nearly asleep that her footsteps were observed only by his deeper, disinterested consciousness, which noted her approach only as if she were a passer in the street. Thus, he was almost surprised when the door did open and she stood in the room with an expression of uncertainty, like a girl entering a shop, not knowing what counter she wanted. She was remarkably young, fresh, slight, pretty, and had a little bag in one hand, black with sequins, and in the other hand a handkerchief, a piece of lace. It was the hand holding the handkerchief which she raised to touch her brown hair. " Oh—I must have mistaken my room," she said. It was an educated voice, and curiously but very, very distantly familiar in some indirect way, as if there was a path already connecting him to her, but a path hidden in a maze.

Her eyes were surprised—they were blue, but she was neither dark nor fair—and her whole expression, her nose which was small, too small and impertinent, all of her face expressed this surprise as if it was an emotion that belonged less to this particular episode than to her general experience. " Silly of me . . ." She murmured the words and, turning to look at the number on the outside of the door, which was still half open, added: " Mr. Spry told me . . ."

She had let the words trail away, but they were of course the password; and Geoff was about to say " I did ring up Mr. Spry," when he recognised that the tightness of his throat would make speech difficult, and so instead pushed out from his chest a sort of grunt, and violently nodded his head.

" That's all right then ! " From each of her movements, deliberate and sure, but light—as she closed the door, and went to the dressing-table to look in the mirror and pat her hair—and especially from the curious stillness and concentration which she applied to her image in the glass, he got the same sense of familiarity that had first been stirred by her voice. When she picked up the bottle of whisky that Frank had left behind him she made a face.

" Would you like a drink ? " His voice slipped out naturally.

" There's only one thing in the world I'd really like—a cup of tea."

" Me too." He reached towards the telephone.

" Oh, I shouldn't do that." She held her hand to him. " Look.

I'll show you." When he took her hand and jumped up, she said: "You're light on your feet for such a big chap, aren't you?" She led him through into the bathroom that had, in one corner, its kitchenette with an electric kettle. "These are *good* flats, you know: everything provided." She sniggered, but opened the little cupboard at the side of the kettle, showing him the packets of tea, sugar, coffee and a half-pint bottle of milk. "All off-the-ration; only for very special guests; friends of Mr. Spry!"

"I've never met Mr. Spry in my life."

"He's a very nice man." She had filled the kettle and switched it on. "While it's boiling," she said, "I'll wash my face."

"Will you? Why?"

"Well, we're not going to drink tea all night, I suppose." She had turned on the tap at the basin; now she picked up his sponge and sniffed at it before dropping it into the water. While she rubbed her face, she spluttered and giggled like a child. "*I* wouldn't like lipstick either, if I was the management. It makes hell of the sheets."

He stood behind her, looking down upon her bowed neck as finally she dipped her face right into the water. This caused her hair to flop forward, making her still more childish. "You're not very old," he said, "are you?"

"Too young—by a lot." She threw up her head and threw back her hair and started to scrub her face, in an angry sort of way, with his face-towel. She spoke crossly: "But I dare say I'll be old enough, when the next war starts, to register as a 'common prostitute' . . . You know, if you say you're a common prostitute, they can't conscript you? Last time, I got into the Wrens."

He was surprised. "You're as old as that, then?"

"Oh yes—I was old enough even to be sent overseas. I was sent overseas in 1944." She giggled a little. "If you call New York overseas, that is."

"You were lucky to go to New York," he said.

"Was I—hell? Still . . . they taught me my job."

"What job?"

"This, of course." She had dried her face now, and when she had shaken back her hair, went up to the dressing-table to pick up his comb. But after trying it, she threw it away and got her own from her handbag. "They teach you pretty quick in a place like New York."

She knew of a cupboard in the bathroom from which she got out a tray and crockery. Very neat and quick in her movements, she laid the tray and made the tea, and then bringing it to the bed, set it down between them. They sat together on either side of the tea-tray, without the least uneasiness now and no silence, because she kept on talking, chattering away lightly and laughing. "When you spoke to Mr. Spry, what did you ask for?" She didn't wait for his answer. "Some men are awfully discreet; they ask for a nurse or a typist or a masseuse. That's what they do in New York . . ."

"Always New York!"

"Well, I shan't ever forget it! You try living on Navy pay in New York—a few dollars a day . . . I forget how much exactly, but not enough to eat anyway. We had to live in rooms, you see." She was drinking her tea, talking in between sips, and raising her eyebrows to look at him over the rim of her cup. "You just try to find a room in New York—on Navy pay! Give me a cigarette!" When she had taken it, she said: "Of course, I ought to have lived with my special friend, but they wouldn't let me. We volunteered together, you see, and we went over together in the same detachment. But she was an officer, and I was only a rating, and an officer couldn't share a room with a rating, because it was bad for discipline . . . Can't you give me a light?" For the first time her voice sounded querulous.

When he had lit her cigarette she said: "So we had to go to an agency that found you rooms and people to share them with. They found me a girl from Iowa . . . please, another light!" Her cigarette had gone out, and when he lit it again for her, it went out again almost at once. "I don't know why I'm telling you this," she said. "I don't usually; very rarely in fact."

"Please do."

"You seem like wanting to put it off, don't you? I expect you've been a prisoner of war or something? Perhaps you were in Burma?" She stretched out her hands across the tea-tray and touched his hair. "You're a nice kid," she said. "Why don't you lie back and relax? You can trust me, you know . . . It'll be all right."

He leant back against the end of the bed, while she leant across the tea-tray stroking his hair. "Tell me about the girl from Iowa," he said.

" All right. What's your name? Your *first* name," she added quickly. Then she said: " It's Geoff, isn't it?"

" How do you know?"

" Never mind," she said. " Perhaps I just guessed it . . . The girl from Iowa was a very nice girl. She was a stranger like me, you see. So the agency put us together and found us a room. It was a very good agency." She continued to stroke his hair. " Feeling better?" she asked. And when he nodded, she said: " Do you know, you wouldn't believe it, but it's true, but when the agency had found us a room, the Navy had to come and inspect it. Do you know what they had to inspect?" When he had shaken his head, she said: " They came to see if there was a man on the door downstairs, and then if we'd got a fire-escape. D'you know why?" She waited for him to shake his head again. " So as if anything happened to us, the Navy wouldn't be to blame for it."

He poured out some more tea, but she wouldn't have any. " What else about the girl from Iowa?" he asked.

" Funny kid, aren't you?" She ruffled his hair and then started to smooth it back. " She was a stenographer, the girl I shared with. And they didn't pay their stenographers enough to live on in New York—any more than they did in the Navy, the British Navy . . . So this girl, you see, she was dual purpose—stenographer by day, tart by night. They have to be in New York. She showed me how . . ." She jumped to her feet, smoothing her skirts. " How old are you?"

" Nearly thirty-eight."

" As much as that? Some of my men are over sixty. They get tiresome when they get as old as that." She stubbed out her cigarette, and he offered her another, but she said: " You can't put it off any longer. Why can't you trust me? I know my job." Then she said: " Business is business, though . . . In case you don't know the terms, it's five pounds—and no arguments, now or later."

" My note-case—it's on the dressing-table . . . Please take what you want."

She threw it on to the bed. " *You* give it to me. I don't want to see what you've got." She held out her hand while he gave her five one-pound notes. She counted them and put them into her bag and then took the bag across to the chair by the door. When

384

she came back, she picked up his note-case and took it to the dressing-table. "Look—I'm putting your note-case in the left-hand drawer—look!" She did so, and then undressed neatly and quickly, laying her frock over the chair which had her bag, and her stockings on top of her frock. He had half sat up in bed, propping his head up against the back of the bed; but although his limbs felt that they were trembling, he was stiff and rigid as if he was dead. He had to close his eyes to try to stop his trembling, but he heard her voice in his ear: "Lie back, silly, relax . . ." She was as skilful and competent as a nurse in a hospital, and soon he was almost asleep, with a great load of soft sleep hanging above his closed eyelids. He heard her in the bathroom with the taps running and then moving about the room as she dressed again. She said: "You're feeling better, aren't you? Sleepy? You'll sleep all right!"

"Very sleepy." And his voice seemed to come from as far away as the night-nursery.

"That's right." He felt her sitting on the bed, and he just opened his eyes sufficiently to see that she was fully dressed and doing her face. "Don't wake up," she said, "but I'll take another of your cigarettes."

"I'd like to wake up a little." He struggled up and lit the cigarette for her, but the match almost burnt his fingers before she blew it out; and even then she had to take the burnt match away from him, because his eyelids would not keep open.

"Were you just feeling lonely?" she asked. "Or did you have a row at home?"

"I haven't a home," he said. "I haven't a wife."

"Don't ask me to marry you," she said quickly.

"Why not?" He really meant it at the moment. It would have been wonderful if she would have married him.

She sighed. "People are always asking me to marry them. That's the worst of this job."

"Why don't you?"

"I have enough troubles with my little girl—without a husband as well."

"You've not got a child?"

"Why else do you think I'm doing this? It's the only way to keep a child these days. No taxes to pay at this job!"

"I'd never have thought you had a child."

"It got me out of the Navy," she said; "and she's very sweet."
He felt her standing up again and going away from his bed. She
came back and pushed him gently on to the pillow because he
had been half propped up on one elbow. While she tucked the
sheet round him, she said: "You've got far too many bedclothes
for such a warm night," and he felt her stripping off the eiderdown
and some of the blankets. "I'll leave you just the one blanket."
She smoothed the pillow round his head. "Now go to sleep."

Then he heard her whispering in his ear: "Don't get me
wrong, will you?" He was not very sure of what she said, but
that much was certain. The rest was something like: "You know
I'm not a nice girl, don't you? You know that? You wouldn't
think of me like that, would you?" She sounded anxious. "I
can be coarse as hell when I like."

She said something horrible about men, as if she was trying to
shock him, but he hardly heard the words and, if he did, he forgot
them immediately afterwards. And then finally: "But you . . .
you can come here any night you like and ask for Mr. Spry . . .
You ask Mr. Spry for *Celia*." She was speaking very distinctly,
close to his ear. "Have you got that, dear? Celia! The name's
hell, isn't it? As bad as Geoff! But there it is." He knew she
was going then. He said: "But you haven't kissed me." But
the door was shut and he was asleep.

*   *   *

He was not able to see her again in London, for he had to drive
down to Neapcaster with Frank. Frank knew a short-cut out of
town, avoiding most of the traffic lights.

They were working their way through side streets, west and
north towards Lisson Grove, threading the horrible slums where
children were playing and paddling in the gutter. "This would
have been paradise to me when I was a kid," Frank said. He
steered the big car, a Bentley, with a couple of fingers. "Our
street in Newcastle was too narrow for us kids to play in—used
to block up the traffic, so the coppers stopped it." He sounded
the loud, deep horn, sending the children scattering in front of him.

The streets soon got wider, and the houses more ornate and
respectable but no less dingy. There was a lot of bomb damage
left, and Frank said: "Messy, isn't it? But those flats where we
stayed the other night, they're pretty well bomb-proof, you know,

unless it's atomic. Steel and concrete. And don't forget, will you, any time you want a bed—just give Mr. Spry a tinkle. Any time you're feeling lonesome—that's where you go, see? Mr. Spry'll fix you up. He'll fix up anything."

They were passing the gaol at Wormwood Scrubs and Frank said: "I've kept out of *that*, so far!" When he laughed, Geoff had to laugh too. Frank said: "Old Spry—he's got one or two real good 'uns, down in his ballroom. You ought to go down there some time and look them over. There's the one I told you about..."

After the roundabout at the bottom of the hill, Frank took the car into the middle of the one-way road and went roaring past the traffic up Western Avenue. "She's a smart one, that one; she's a smart little kid, is Celia. Hard as nails, of course, tough as sin; she has to be . . . but she's not greedy, not as they go; and she knows her stuff. You get your money's worth."

"A funny thing," Frank said, "the way these girls take to it. Some of them are ladies, you know; educated and all that. They do it for fun or pin-money or something at the start. My one—the one they call Celia—she's not one of them. Not her! She does it for hard cash. She's got a kid to keep. Lots of them have kids . . . I've given the matter some research." A policeman was holding up the traffic while a troop of school children crossed the road, walking two by two, herded by some nuns and older girls. "Celia's rather a rum case," Frank said. "She's one of us." Geoff kept silent. He had to do something, so he lit a cigarette. With a cigarette between his lips, he thought he could risk a question. "One of us?"

"She comes from Neapcaster," Frank said. "As a matter of fact, I helped her to a job with Spry. I fixed her up." They were driving on again fast, between the long ribbon-rows of cheap houses. "She had this kid, you see, and got chucked out of the Wrens and came along to me for a job—at Neapcaster that was. She wanted to work in our factory. I told her she was too good for that."

Geoff's cigarette had gone out. It was not often that a man let a cigarette go out between his lips; it was a woman's trick. Geoff lit it again before he asked—he had to ask: "Who was she?" But when he heard the answer, it seemed as if he had known it all the time.

"Well, it's rather a joke," Frank said. "You remember old Rogers, I expect? Up at the cottage by Slender Ladies?"

"Of course I do."

"She's one of his brood," Frank said, laughing. "One of the many. He's still alive and kicking, by the way. He's an official rat-catcher. Do you know what they call him nowadays? 'Pests Officer'! He's an Assistant County Pests Officer. What do you think of that?"

"It seems appropriate."

Frank said: "Light me a cigarette, old boy, will you? No lipstick!" Then he went on about Adam Rogers. "Of course old Adam goes on just the same as before—poaching what there's left to poach. Now he gets paid for it—by the Government . . . You ask Celia what her granddad is, and she'd tell you he's a Civil Servant!"

Geoff drew on the cigarette and handed it alight to Frank. He spoke with a certain amount of cunning: "This girl . . . what name did you say? Celia? She's one of the granddaughters? But surely . . ." He checked himself just quickly enough. He was just about to say: "Surely she's too young for that?"

"And I'll tell you which she was," Frank said. "There was a bit of a fuss about her birth."

Geoff knew which one it was. He listened to Frank's words with only enough attention to confirm his knowledge, because he could feel, he would always be able to feel, the General's hand on his shoulder as they stood at midnight by the french window, looking across the valley at the bright star, far brighter than all the other stars, where the doctor and the nurse and the little girl, Judy, battled their way into birth and death.

How clear and unforgettable were the voices of the dead! And all the General could find to say as he pointed his stubby finger into the night, at the bright star of the cottage: "They've got it lit up all right . . ." And he said: "There's a child being born over there . . . with no great prospects."

"I remember it now," Frank said. "Judy was the girl's name, and she was a bastard herself, and Celia was a bastard too; and Celia's baby—she's another of them, another bastard. Funny, isn't it?" The road was almost empty, and they were heading for High Wycombe at eighty miles an hour. "Of course, *we* all knew who the father was," Frank said. "You knew, didn't you?

His first shot in the dark . . . Not bad for a youngster of fifteen! At that age, I hadn't started myself!"

Geoff had counted up the years and knew all this to be true. But he could not bear to believe that whatever Ralph had left behind him in Celia's face, bearing or manner was the cause of that queer, strong feeling of familiarity that had made him, in retrospect, think of this new love as predestined, inevitable. He would not believe that Ralph, through Celia, had got himself back into Geoff's life; that Ralph's power was not dead with his body, but still malignantly lived.

"Now let's see what this old lady can do," Frank said, stepping on the accelerator. The car looked shiny and new, but Frank said it was a 1940 model: "Before they switched production . . . It belonged to the firm—cost them three thousand quid—but I have the sole use of it. They'll give you one, I expect. All the boys get a car—all of us top chaps, that is."

It was all concluded: Geoff was one of the boys, with the privileges and duties, mutual obligations and loyalties, of their order. He and Frank were fellow-members, somewhere or other in that hierarchy, each with a house, a car, a room ready with Mr. Spry, a girl ready with Mr. Spry, anything that they wanted. "Just ring Mr. Spry, old chap; he'll fix you."

"Ninety!" Frank said, tapping the speedometer. The road was wide and straight. Perhaps he would content himself with speed and suspend the chatter. But he insisted: "You really ought to try that girl some time, don't forget the name. As a matter of fact, Geoff . . . I hope you don't mind . . . but I did tell her about you . . . told her to be ready with the red carpet . . . just in case . . ."

The road went on wide and straight for a long, long way. "Ninety-eight! As a matter of fact, to tell you a secret, Geoff, I had old Celia up the other night. . . . After I'd left you, you know. After I'd left you with the bottle and the tooth-glass. I had her along for about twenty minutes. . . ."

"A hundred!" Geoff said quickly, watching the speedometer. He was not going to hear Frank's last statement, not acknowledge it, nor add twenty and ten and ten and so on, and put the result alongside himself, himself reading the evening paper and smoking a cigarette, switching out the lights, feeling his limbs go hard with sleeplessness, picking up the telephone, hearing of the absence of

Mr. Spry, and then the bell ringing later, the long wait and then footsteps. "A hundred and six!" Geoff said.

"That's what I like about Celia," Frank said. "Twenty minutes or half the night—it's all the same to Celia."

"Oh, shut up!" Geoff said. The words came with great force out of his heart, but quite mildly out of his mouth. "Shut up about your *prostitute*!"

"I've never done a hundred and ten before!" Frank said. "It's power, it's the feel of it . . ." His voice had dropped down the scale, as if he was talking to himself almost with awe. "The power of chaps, the power of just men . . . to invent a thing like this, to make it, to be able to drive it . . ."

Geoff heard only his own voice, his last remark to Frank. "I didn't say that!" he cried silently. "I never said that; I never meant it; I never said that about Celia!" It was as if the cock had crowed thrice all at once, in one breath out of his body. It was cock-crow.

*　　　*　　　*

Nearly all these farms through which they were now passing were familiar; not just generally familiar, but intimately known by riding across them or shooting over them, or walking with the farmer across the field to look at a bunch of cattle, to lend or borrow a boar or a bull, to sell or buy a horse.

"To put you wise . . ." Frank said, and started to catalogue the farms that had fallen in Betts' ownership. "The Brides, Draper's, Beechwoods, the Wold, Swire's, Plinny, Westford, Sheepbrook . . ." As Geoff heard the names, the pictures slipped into place. In the centre of the pattern was an ugly gap, an island of independence entirely surrounded by Betts' property. "The Home Farm," said Frank, "you've heard all about it, of course?"

"I wasn't in the least interested." And it was a perfectly fair answer. Because—when you got the hell out of it, you didn't, like Lot's wife, stop to look back. And when you got the hell out of it, you read only with your eyes, and listened only with your ears, on getting a letter from David or Mac, or giving a pilot a drink in the Mess by the airstrip, or meeting a Neapcaster lad in a transit camp.

"You must have heard anyway," said Frank, "that Betts got the Home Farm and the Lodge when Ralph was killed and the

Government took the house? You probably know that she moved to the Lodge, and Betts was soft—the only time he's ever been soft —letting her keep the farm, not kicking her out when he could— and now he can't! Because of the new Act . . . You know about the new Act?"

"I wasn't interested," Geoff repeated.

Frank gave a disbelieving sigh, obviously meaning Geoff to hear it. "Surely you know that you can't, any longer, get a tenant out? Not unless you can prove the greater hardship, or his bad husbandry? And though we may serve her with notice to quit . . ."

With some satisfaction Geoff said: "You'll hardly fiddle your way through that Act!"

"Of course she may not appeal. The thing's new, and it's not every one that knows of it, not yet, and she's only got a month to do it . . ." One could feel Frank's eyes sliding sideways to get at one's face. "But of course she'll be getting Trant's advice. She couldn't run the farm the way she does, not without his help . . ." He was driving very slowly now, on the last stage of their journey, sort of feeling his way with the car, as he was with his voice. "What do you think, Geoff?"

But all Geoff answered was: "You won't get her out, not for bad husbandry, not if she's taking Trant's advice."

"There may be other ways," said Frank. "Only, you see . . . we couldn't be sure how *you* might be feeling about it."

"I feel nothing at all about it," Geoff said. And the answer was strictly true when the words came to his lips, but wholly false when they were issued with his breath. "Why should I?" he asked.

"Frank's my name and frank's my nature," Frank said. "It was pretty obvious, wasn't it?"

"What was?" asked Geoff, though he had to know perfectly well what Frank meant.

"That you and Alex . . . when you came back . . . that, at least you'd want to help her, look after her, if nothing more than that."

"Ridiculous!" Geoff said. But when he heard the word uttered in his own voice, he heard also the second cock-crow of his journey home.

"We'll all be glad of that," Frank said. "A great relief!"

The July afternoon had slipped into a sultry evening. The

clouds had gathered and darkened. Frank said: " Rain, I think; perhaps thunder."

And Geoff found himself answering: " I'm afraid so. It'll mess up haymaking. They're late, anyway, with the end of it." All around him he had been smelling the hay. His ears had heard the purr of tractors pulling trailers or wagons, or pushing a hay-sweep; a baler at work, and men strung out from it like wheel-spokes.

" A storm . . ." A drop or two of rain, heavy drops, had already struck the windscreen. But the clouds were moving fast, and Geoff said: " It might blow over."

Frank said: " I think we're driving into it."

★   ★   ★

Darker grew the afternoon before the storm.

" We're home! " Frank said, driving into the market-place. " I do like to get home! " He waved to the policeman, who touched his helmet in answer. " I must send that chap some butter; his wife's been ill now for months." He waved to a gentleman who was walking down the street with a gun-dog at heel; the gentleman gestured back. " He's a pretty fine shot," said Frank; " he usually shoots with us. You know, our shooting's about as good as any there is to be had? "

In the queer, theatrical light and gloom preceding the thunder, they turned down Brewer's Lane, twisting round the noble church and the Town Hall, and coming at length to a wide and handsome street called Duke's Walk. " I do like getting home! " Frank said once more, as he stopped by a weeping ash that drooped above a wrought-iron gate. Inside the gate, a paved walk led to the house, to fluted pillars and a porch. On either side of the walk there were lawns and formal beds, all bright and beautifully neat. " They say it's Queen Anne," said Frank. And the door had opened before they reached it: a young man, a servant, in black trousers and a white coat, coming down the path to meet them. " Evening, Jack; it's good to be home! " said Frank. The man, smiling, went down the path to get the luggage—everything that Geoff possessed—which was stowed on the back seats of Frank's car and in the boot. The rain started to come down hard as they reached the house. " Come in quick! " said a woman's voice. " So Geoff's come to see us at last! " And over Geoff's shoulder,

Frank called: "Hallo, ducks!" as the rain ripped and tore the air behind him. The rain struck the path, with huge, bouncing drops. "Almost a cloudburst!" the woman cried. "What a greeting for Geoff!"

There were pillars in the hall and a curved staircase with white bannisters and duck-egg painted walls; and beyond the pillars, a window into a garden, a lawn sloping up the panes where the ground rose on the far side of the house. Against this window the rain, turning to hail, clattered and cracked. Jack, with his white coat soaked, came in with a couple of bags. "Leave them for a bit," said Frank, "I don't see the point of your getting soaked." The rain had plastered a forelock against Jack's forehead. Rising from the rain, a gust of wind slammed the front door shut. And then, in the new gloom, a whiplash of lightning cut across the garden window and into the trees around the rising lawn. Some dreadful doom seemed heralded, or a prophecy imminent. But the only voice that spoke was the woman's, and all it said was: "Lord! What's Frankie brought with him! A real bust up!"

When she turned from her husband to greet Geoff, he found her soft and generous, not fat, not even plump, but robust and pink and sparkling, so that he could almost trace how the deft and correct Miss May had got, through the years, this generosity and brightness, with the big blue eyes, laughing and content. "I'm going to kiss you, Geoff! And, after all, didn't I use to kiss you, once? But then I had to stoop to do it. But now . . ." She laughed and trilled, and cried in a loud but pleasant voice: "Tiptoe it has to be! Come on, Geoff, and make Frankie jealous! Not that he'd care! Just let him try it!"

So Geoff stooped down and kissed her, while Frank said: "What a woman!"

"You've got a cold nose, like Frankie, like Dora!" May said. For Dora, a spaniel bitch, had come galloping in from the rain, was greeting Frank, leaving paw-marks on his coat. She threw herself into a chair and there rotated on her own circuit. "Get out! Get out, you horrible brute!" said Frank. He scolded and smacked it lightly, with the gestures and voice that used to be Ralph's.

Another door banged in the wind, somewhere upstairs in the house, and a girl, pretty and light, came running down. "Oh, M'm, did you ever see such a storm!"

"Have you shut all the windows?" May asked. "It'll all be drenched if you don't."

"I've been round the bedrooms," the girl said. "Am I to unpack for . . ." She nodded her head towards Geoff.

"That's Mr. Geoff," May said.

"A Brigadier," said Frank. "It ought to be Jack to do it . . ."

"I expect they'll do it between them," May said. "Most things they do between them, I've noticed lately." She giggled, and the girl giggled too; mistress and maid chattering and giggling to overcome Frank's voice saying: "Stop it, you two! Let Geoff give her his keys . . ."

There was so much noise, with every one laughing and talking, and the dog circling the hall in a scamper of welcome, skidding on the polished floor, and Jack bumping the bags on his way upstairs, that the wind and the rain outside, distantly and comfortably noted for their harshness but impotence, only made obvious the benefits of this homeliness.

"About time we got down to it," said Frank. "A decent wife would be mixing her husband a little liquid refreshment."

*　　　*　　　*

The noise never abated, and they never stopped laughing, all three of them and sometimes the servants as well, before dinner, during dinner, after dinner—except for the one incident—before they went to bed. Everything seemed to be tremendously funny.

"But Geoff was too little a boy," said May, "when I was the sort of girl that men ran after—before Frankie caught me. But I never passed him by without wanting to rub my knuckles in his hair." She had not entirely lost her country ways and soft, local inflections. "Such a little chap he was . . ."

They were all laughing. "And now I dare say he'd be glad of it," Frank said. Then he clapped his hands. "Do you know what? I think we'll buy some greengrocers' shops—and grow the stuff to sell in them! Those chaps—they make too much cash . . ."

"He will, too!" May said.

"Here and Cheltenham and Stow—to begin with. To tell you the truth, I've made a start."

"He has too—if he says it!" What a joke it was! "He's like that—the man I went and married."

"She caught me," said Frank. "I got in ahead of Ralph."

" Oh, Ralph—he was an awful one, even in those days! Though perhaps we oughtn't to say such things about him, now that he can't answer."

" Not that he'd care," said Frank.

" Not that he ever cared about anything or any one! Not that he got a thing out of me! Till I fell properly, I was the cautious sort. But he *did* out of others."

" Judy Rogers," said Frank, with rather less laughter than before. He was sitting in the window at a writing-table which also had a telephone on it. He had his back to the room when May said: " That kid of hers, Frankie. Didn't she come to you for a job?"

" I got her a job in London." Frank did not look round to answer. " But I don't remember that I told you anything about it."

" I dare say you didn't," May said, restoring the laughter to its proper spate; " but, my goodness, I hear a heap more than you tell me about! To-day, this morning, they were talking about Alex . . ."

" Were they, ducks?" Frank was busy writing. " There's plenty of *that* going round."

" Poor thing! You know, I *admire* her!" She stressed the verb, as if it was a surprising or unusual reaction. " The way she carries on out there, without a single servant in the house, and the farm and everything to look after, and young Ralph . . ." This got her laughing again. " He's a kid, that one! He's going to be like his dad!"

" Is he? Is he?" Geoff asked. He was surprised at his own question which came out of a foolish grin, a general compliance which he let appear on his face, to indulge their mirth.

" And why shouldn't a kid be like his dad? It isn't all kids, you know, that are born the wrong side of the blanket!"

" No reason at all," Geoff said. For no buoyant mood of indiscretion—the general air of this household—would let him discuss the paternity of Alex's son. " And anyway," he said, explaining the thing to himself, " Alex is partly Meredith, and used to look it."

" Still does," said Frank. " She hasn't changed a bit—not that I've noticed."

" You've chance enough to notice!" It was a queer, bitter outburst from May. It cut off the general merriment, whose tremors had never subsided the whole evening, as if a series of soundproof doors had been shut upon them. The silence remained, like a hard, indigestible lump, until Frank, rising and licking his envelope, came across the room to put an arm round his wife. There were no denials. Geoff couldn't help noticing even then, even that evening, that Frank denied nothing. He just said: " Now, now, ducks . . . I'm sleepy. What about a little nightcap, and then a little bed ? "

" You and your nightcaps! This is the fourth, isn't it ? " And over their last drink, the happiness was quite restored, with greater warmth even than before. Laughing in harmony, they all climbed the staircase to bed. " It's supposed to be a fine staircase, very antique," said Frank.

" Who cares ? " said May to Geoff, " so long as it gets us to the right place." She managed to make the remark sound suggestive.

" If you want anything in the night," Frank called in the same vein, from the door of their bedroom, " you'll have to do without! It's not the least good ringing, 'cos we shan't hear you . . ." This, also, was able to make them snigger.

Over her husband's shoulder, with her chin on his shoulder, May added: " And the servants—that boy and that girl—they sleep out. Not together, mind you, not that we know of. They're supposed to be respectable kids."

" But who is ? " said Frank.

On a last ripple of common laughter, Geoff shut himself into his bedroom. The happiness had got hold of him. He laughed to himself that the return to Neapcaster, foreseen with so much foreboding, had been so ridiculously pleasant. Moreover, he was surprised, and enjoyably shocked, to find that all sorts of nerves and senses in his body were feeling quite openly and shamelessly provoked by the impact of a woman, not Celia any longer, but Mrs. Meredith's maid, Frank's wife. So infectious were the merry bacteria of this house, that he presented himself to the looking-glass, grinned at himself, and said aloud: " A bit late in the day, Geoff, old chap ! "

*　　　*　　　*

There was no morning disillusionment: the household woke as brightly and carelessly as it had gone to sleep, although it parted its curtains to one of those grey Cotswold days, with a soft mist or drizzle which would later be dissolved in sunshine—" Pride of the morning," it is called—common in that countryside. Though not depressing, these mists did tend to limit and confine: a household to its own domesticity; a farm to its territorial frontiers; a man's mood to his immediate purpose; his road to his immediate destination. The road that they took to Swire's farm did not have to be regarded as the road that ran on to the Lodge, and on after that, down and up again, to loop round the Home Farm, Slender Ladies, the house and the garden—all that section of the Neap Valley which had once been the heart of the Meredith kingdom. Through the kind and concealing mist, the road ran to Swire's; and that was enough.

Swire's farm, also, did not have to be regarded, not at first, as the property which marched with the Home Farm, all along its eastern frontiers. It was an agricultural proposition on its own account. Thus it was registered in Geoff's slow, steady, calculating and precise brain, which became extraordinarily penetrating and critical the moment it was re-employed on an agricultural project; the moment, that is, that he stepped out of the van which they had taken instead of the car; the moment that the toe of his boot was stubbing itself into starved earth that had grown three white-straw crops in succession, and his voice was saying: " This ground needs stock."

" You're telling me! " was Frank's answer. " There's plenty of stock up top, on the other side of the road. But this side . . . no buildings, no water."

" It would pay to build. It would pay to pipe water from the river."

" So it would—if we aren't ever to get . . ." And in conclusion, Frank pointed across the eastern boundary.

At once it became evident—as it had been evident during the whole of Geoff's life, but forgotten—that the Home Farm and this ought to be run as the one unit. The superfluous buildings of the former would serve both properties; and the water supply of the one could easily be extended to serve the other. " Stands out a mile! " Frank said.

Recalling how often the General had talked about buying back Swire's, if ever times should improve, and finding not even irony in the new notion of Swire's acquiring the Home Farm instead, Geoff just nodded.

"Plain silly, isn't it? I thought we'd go and see her when we've done here." When Geoff just nodded again, Frank said: "I thought you'd say so. I rang her up and, as a matter of fact, she was very keen on seeing you."

For the third time Geoff nodded, not for a moment doubting it.

*   *   *

They had not gone to the farmhouse which lay on the farther side of the farm, but straight from their van into the fields. When Frank had pulled his van on the grass verge, he had given some reason or other for this procedure; but Geoff had the impression that visits such as these were normally unannounced—surprise inspections. And now Ted Foster, the farmer, the former under-groom in the Meredith stables, came down the hill to meet them. "Which one was it he married?" Geoff asked, remembering only that it was one of the girls out of the kitchen.

"The little apple-faced one, called Lizz."

"I scarcely remember them," Geoff said. "She left a long time back. I remember Kate, of course, because she stayed on . . . what happened to Kate?"

"Not so good," Frank said.

"Does that mean . . ." But Ted had reached them and was shaking Geoff's hand, but not with the warmth that should have been natural. He had changed a great deal, perhaps more than any of them, and had become a big, sturdy chap with a flat and red face which ought to have been jolly but was somehow furtive.

As they all walked back up the hill to cross the road and get to the fields where the pigs and poultry were kept, Geoff said: "Before the war, as I remember, they didn't keep much in the way of poultry and pigs on Swire's. . . ." He was thinking of the regulations that only those farms which had previously had these classes of stock could now get rations to feed them. It was a quite ridiculous condition, meaning that no farm could legally change its character for the better, recovering its fertility and health from dung dropped in the fields. A law such as this would not, of course, command the obedience of a competent farmer. So he said: "I suppose you grow your own foodstuffs? I suppose you transfer them from farm to farm?"

"We wouldn't do a wicked thing like that!" said Frank, winking. "Do you take us for a bunch of crooks?" But when they had finished laughing, he said seriously and bitterly: "If you'll tell me how to grow animal protein . . . or if you'll tell me how to make hens lay eggs without it . . ."

"Is that so short?"

"Short? It doesn't exist! The Ministry of Food . . ." He spoke with the hatred and scorn which, Geoff imagined, must be the normal emotion of any farmer. "They tell the trawlers to throw their fish-heads into the sea. Then they buy eggs for dollars —and wonder why dollars are short."

Crossing the road and entering a long field covered with poultry units and pigs tethered in harness, Geoff said: "But you seem to do all right."

"They're after us, of course," Frank said; "all over the country. But they'll never prove it."

Ted Foster seemed uneasy. "They have their men round here a sight too much. The inspector was here last week, and again the night before last. We're tired of his face."

"Snoopers!" Frank said, with a sound like a spit.

*   *   *

A woman was coming across the field towards them. "Lizz, isn't it?" Frank asked. And Ted, nodding, planted his stick in the ground and stood with his feet apart, waiting for his wife to approach them.

It was extraordinary how much she had aged, by comparison with May, although she was seven or eight years the younger. She had been hurrying, half running, but stopped some paces away from her husband, her breast heaving and her head tilted up. As they faced each other, they seemed, in some curious way, like a coloured picture out of an illustrated Bible. Panting, she said: "Ted—it's the Food Man again, another one, a stranger." She had no time to greet Geoff, being evidently too distressed. And he could scarcely recognise her, for her girlhood had been so completely wilted out of her face. But Ted said: "You remember Mr. Greenley, Lizzie? You remember Master Geoff?"

She did not smile; she raised her eyes to Geoff's face, and let them fall again; then, giving him a curious little bob of the head, the slightest gesture, continued breathlessly: "He got hold of Willie, the Food Man did. He found Willie hanging about the gate and he asked him . . ." The story was tumbling out in the

399

sort of way that a child unburdens itself. "He's a new one," she said. "He's different from the others, different from any of them. He asked could Willie help him to a dozen eggs."

"They all do that," Frank said. "They always go for the kids."

"His wife was sick, he said," Lizzie continued, "the doctor had said she was to have them—that's what he said. So Willie told Jenny . . ." While she told her breathless story, her eyes turned anxiously from Ted to Frank. "*I* couldn't help it, sir," she said. "Jenny let him have them, you see—his saying it was for his sick wife and all that—and then he said he was the Food Man, that's how it was . . ."

"Did he pay for them?" Frank asked sharply.

"Oh yes, sir! He paid all right." She turned then, so as to talk directly to her husband. "He asked Jenny how much, and she didn't know, of course. She's silly that way. She's silly, Ted."

"Well, what was it?" Frank asked in a hard, curt voice.

"The man said what about five shillings, you see; the man asked was that enough? She didn't know, you see, so then she said seven and six."

"Double the price, isn't it?" Geoff asked.

But Frank was speaking angrily to the woman. "Haven't they that much sense? A silly, a damn silly little thing like that!"

"They're only kids," Ted said. "You can't expect sense from a girl of nine and a lad of six."

"It can't be very serious," Geoff said. "Surely not?"

But the woman hadn't finished. "You see, he asked was that what we usually got—the seven and six, and Jenny said . . ." She stopped herself quickly. Her eyes had been on her husband's face; and though he had not moved, he was looking at her closely and his eyebrows were drawn down, as if it was some sort of signal. She moved her hand in a sudden, unintended gesture; she almost put her hand to her mouth.

"Go on!" Frank said, and he was looking hard at Ted.

The woman said: "There's nothing more to it, sir. Nothing more to it than that."

"Go on! Go on with what you were saying! What did Jenny tell him?"

"Lizz told you," Ted said to him. "The child said she didn't know, nor does she. She doesn't know anything about anything that kid doesn't. She doesn't have to know."

He and Frank stood face to face, looking at each other hard; it was quite obvious that Ted was lying and that Frank knew about it. " Come on! " Frank said, and started to walk quickly towards the house. " Is the Inspector still there? " he asked the woman.

" Waiting to see Ted," she said.

" *I'll* see him," said Frank.

" See him if you like," said Ted, " but watch your step! Once they start on you . . . Let them find one thing like this, one little thing like this to turn up, and they won't stop so easy as they start." Bitterly he added: " An' there's plenty to turn up around here, if they look in the right place."

" 'Twere a shame," the woman said, " to get hold of Willie, to get hold of just a kid."

" You tell them so, Lizz," Frank said. " You and your husband, go on and tell them so. Don't talk about anything else—only the eggs." And when they had gone on ahead, he said to Geoff: " They won't find a lot here; I'm not worrying about that. But once they start on us, once they find something to work on . . ."

Not wanting to arrive too quickly, they went across the fields into the road, and down the road so as to enter the farmhouse by the main gate. " I always thought Ted was a bit of a crook," Frank said. " She gave it away, didn't she? Seven and six for the eggs! He's been making a nice little bit for himself out of that! "

* * *

The little group—the man and his wife, and the Food Inspector —were standing in the middle of the yard. When they saw Frank and Geoff approaching, they all turned round together, and the stranger detached himself from the others and came forward. He walked with a stick and limped. Frank went briskly to meet him, while Geoff followed slowly. Frank had his hands in his pockets; and seen from behind, he was a square, burly, competent chap, with a red neck; altogether a confident figure, calling " Good morning " in a loud, cheerful voice. The stranger just nodded. He was slight and dark, with a hollow face. It was difficult to tell his age, but he was a young man. " This is Greenley," Frank said; and the stranger nodded again, his eyes, vague and distant, turning slowly in Geoff's direction. His face was unusual—apart, even, from the curious, sad eyes—sick and resolute, and with blue shadows on the pale skin.

"Good morning, Brigadier," the stranger said.

Looking at him closely, Geoff asked: "We know each other?"

The stranger shook his head. "You wouldn't know me. You've talked to me, with a hundred others, at Fourteenth Army, an officers' conference. . . ." Having nothing more to say to each other, they remained silent.

Frank said heartily: "Well, since you're old friends, what's the nonsense with those kids?" But the man's only reply was to turn his eyes from Geoff back to Frank. "The kids don't know anything," Frank said. "See for yourself!"

The man seemed to nod again, very slightly. In a low voice he said: "I have to do that." But it was not quite clear what he meant.

"It's Gestapo stuff, isn't it?" Frank said; and he waited for the man to answer, trying to draw him out. But the man declined, keeping silent, and leaving the initiative to Frank. "Not much of a game," Frank said, "spinning a tale to a couple of kids." The man still kept his silence. "Tale of a sick wife! Don't you expect a kid to have a soft heart?" With leisurely movements the man pulled out his note-book, sought in his pocket for a pencil, and started to write.

Ted and his wife stood close together, close behind the inspector, so that they could almost overlook his note-book. The two children stood beside their mother. When one of them spoke the mother told it to keep quiet, and the child took hold of her skirt. A sheep-dog had joined them, its passing backwards and forwards, with its sheepdog slink, being the only movement in the yard, except for the Inspector's pencil. "Of course, I shall take this up," Frank said. "This business with the kids—you slipped up there, I reckon."

"I have my orders." It was only the third time that the man had spoken and his words came in the same low voice as before. He did not look up from his note-book. You had the feeling that the man was winning a mastery over the rest of them, simply by his silence, and that he could not be stopped.

"Nice sort of orders," Frank said. "Nice work! Have you nothing better to do than get round to kids?" The man went on writing. "A chap who's been in Burma ought to have something better to do than badger kids."

The man stopped writing then and put the pencil back in his

pocket, but continued to read his note-book. With his free hand, he took the stick off his arm, and it happened to swing against his leg, making a dull, hard sound—wood against metal, through cloth—as it hit his knee. "You've forty-four sows in that field," the man said.

"So what?" Frank said. "You'll find our stock in the agricultural returns. They're accurate." But the man was limping across the fields towards the poultry. On his way, he stopped at one or two of the empty pig troughs, scraped them with his stick, and examined the end of it. He did not speak at all, but limped on, compelling the others to follow. On his way he picked up a handful of food from a trough and smelt it. When he had turned away and resumed his progress, Geoff did the same, wondering where the fish-meal had come from.

When the Inspector came to the end of the field, he had some trouble with the gate, which had dropped on its hinges and stuck. Nobody helped him to open it. And after they had all gone through, nobody helped him while he closed it carefully behind them. In his detachment and silence he was independent, isolated, alien, and impregnable. When he had looked into some of the poultry units, counted the hens roughly, and examined the troughs, he wrote some more in his note-book, saying at length: "If you don't mind, we'll go back to the house. I shall want to see your foodstuffs." He returned to the gate, struggled with it again, held it open for the whole party to pass through, and then closed it after them, with the same care as before. "Where do you get your meal?" he asked Ted.

"You can put your questions to me," Frank said.

"Who's farming this place?"

"I am," Ted said.

"Then where do you get your meal?"

"We're not answering any questions," Frank said. "I can't stop you looking where you like. I don't particularly want to stop you—we've nothing to hide."

"That's good," the man said. He always spoke in the same low and level voice.

"What I mind is this business with the kids," Frank said. "We shall be taking that up."

"Where do you get your meal?" the Inspector repeated. But nobody answered.

When they got back to the yard, the Inspector went to his car and took out a number of small white bags. Then he went across to the barn. This barn, a great stone building with a stone roof, occupied the whole of one side of the yard, except for the gate on to the road. Beyond the barn, at the end farthest from the gate, there were twin walnut trees that spread their branches over the small front garden of the farmhouse itself. The farmhouse and the barn, at right angles to each other, made two of the sides of the rectangular yard; and the other two sides were composed of nondescript buildings, cart-sheds and byres, all of different shapes and sizes, but all built of the same stone, with the same steep, stone-tiled roofs, fitting into each other to a design almost purposely haphazard. The whole rectangular group, it was clear, had been composed through the generations by the personal whims and methods of husbandry of successive farmers. When the sun came out, the walls and roofs, with their coating of lichens, gleamed softly, as if they were absorbing sunlight, putting it into store rather than reflecting it. But even towards noon, as it was now, with the sun directly overhead, the geometrical shadows of the various buildings made a second pattern on the white dust of the yard itself. The light rain or mist, the "pride of the morning," had not been sufficient to turn the dust dark.

When the Inspector, returning from his car, walked across the yard, you could hear his irregular footsteps, and the beat of his artificial leg. It was as quiet as that. The debate and complaint of geese, somewhere out of sight, and the bellowing of a couple of newly-weaned calves that wanted milk, had no effect on this quiet.

"I'm sure I shan't want you, Mrs. Foster," the Inspector said. He spoke in a very gentle voice; and she gave again her queer sort of bob of the head, like her greeting to Geoff, and then took her children through the low gate that divided her small front garden from the farmyard, and up the little path to her house.

The Inspector went into the barn. He opened one or two sacks, took samples and carefully re-tied them. A good many of the sacks were stitched at the top, just as they had come from the mill —so that they were evidently not home-grown food—and he had to cut the stitches with a knife. Unable to close them again, he said: "I'm sorry to leave them like that." Nobody answered him.

When the Inspector had finished with the barn, he went round all the other buildings. The door of one of them was fastened with a padlock. "I'm afraid I shall have to have this one opened," he said. Ted Foster went into the house for the key.

While they were waiting in silence, Geoff asked suddenly: "Weren't you one of Wingate's lot?"

"Yes." The man almost smiled. A touch of understanding must have travelled between him and Geoff.

Geoff said: "After the Chindits, I don't suppose you like this job a lot?"

The man gave the old answer: "It's a job."

Then Frank said: "Look here, I'm sure we can settle this business." But the man did not reply. His silence was deliberate —a positive refusal. "If we had a quiet word together . . ." There was plenty of meaning in Frank's remark, and in the way he said it, the way he looked at the Inspector. Then he gave Geoff a glance, a signal, asking him to withdraw. So Geoff wandered casually away towards the shed where the calves were bellowing. He heard the Inspector raising his voice, no doubt so that Geoff should hear, when he said: "It's quite unnecessary . . ." Then Geoff saw the Inspector turn away from Frank, so that Frank, when he persisted, had to speak to the man's back. "Shan't we go into the house? Foster will let us have a room to ourselves." But Ted was returning now with the key, and there was no need for the Inspector to answer. They entered the last remaining building which had a new concrete floor, rat-proof, and which was evidently the main food store. It was full of bins and sacks. While the man examined them, Frank said: "Look here, we've nothing to hide. What is it you want to know?"

"You've said that you've no need to answer questions," the man replied. "I should advise you not to invite them."

Frank said: "You'll find us quite willing to co-operate. I dare say I can save you trouble."

"You've not obstructed me in any way. You've done all that was necessary."

"If we could have a few minutes in the house . . ." There was a new note in Frank's voice, almost desperate.

The Inspector said very softly to Geoff: "Do tell your friend to keep his note-case to himself. This is only my job."

"A word over a glass of sherry . . ." Frank continued; "you know . . . we're a pretty reasonable lot."

405

Geoff said quietly: "Shut up, Frank!"

"That's all," the man said at last. "Thank you very much for your help." As he turned towards his car, Frank muttered: "*You* have a go at him, Geoff. He seems to be a pal of yours. No matter the cost . . ."

Geoff knew that it was useless, but he followed the Inspector to his car.

"There's nothing much wrong, is there?" he asked.

"What do *you* think?" the man said. This time he smiled outright at Geoff, making it as friendly as possible.

"I don't know," Geoff answered. "I only got down here last night. I only got back a fortnight ago."

The man nodded. "If you're like me, you'll soon be wishing you hadn't."

"Do you have to make it any worse for us?" Geoff asked. "If we've slipped up somewhere . . ."

"Somewhere!" The Inspector laughed.

"I gather it isn't so easy, these days, to stick to the rules too closely."

"It isn't easy at all," the man said.

"Do you *have* to bother us? Couldn't you just . . ." Geoff shrugged.

"Not even for *you*, Brigadier," the man said. "I'm sorry, but I just have to make my report."

"That was a dirty business with the kids."

"It was," the man said. "But we've got a start. After all, if you've got to break up a racket, you can't do it . . . in kid gloves." He climbed with some difficulty into his car. When he was in the driver's seat, he said: "After all, we're fighting real crooks . . . not so different from the Japs."

"I think you've got it wrong," Geoff said. "They're not crooks."

"It's not my business, Brigadier, but if you're not committed too deeply—I should keep clear of this little lot." He started the car and put it into gear. Then he added: "I dare say the Fosters are more or less all right." And finally he said: "Sorry, and all that . . ." He drove off.

When Geoff went back, Frank was standing apart from Ted Foster. "Any luck?" he asked softly.

"I shouldn't think you've a hope."

406

" Too bad on Foster."

" It's not Foster he's after, it's you yourself. I dare say it's even Betts. You'd better get on the phone to Whitehall, if you think it any use."

" Oh, there's plenty of time for that," Frank said cheerfully. " Don't worry, Ted," he called to the man. " It'll be quite all right. We'll fix it." He seemed remarkably unworried himself; and his demeanour was curious, after the desperate note that had at one time appeared in his voice. " Come on," he said to Geoff. " Let's go take a drink off Alex."

*   *   *

There was only a quarter of a mile of road between Swire's farm and the start of the long fringe of beeches which enclosed the northern side of the Park, and which held the entrance to the drive beside the Lodge.

It was only a matter of seconds before they would see the tops of the beeches, and a few seconds more before they would see the beech trunks themselves and the wall, what was left of the low wall of the Park—a tumble of ivy-covered stones, a ruin of stones and nettles, with a few gaps through which a tank could have driven without a check, and with many sections through which a child could peep between the tree-trunks at the cattle, and sometimes the deer, on the other side of a wire fence. In a second now they would be there.

As the van came round the curve of the lane, there was a gleaming wall of newly-quarried stone raised to a man's height. The wall swept down the lane, enclosing the Park. The Park was made as private as a prison; the privacy that it had cherished, flaunted, for so many years until the last quarter of a century, was restored. " The nation owns the place nowadays," said Frank, " so we mustn't look at it." It was a fine job of work, brave and white, although in ten years' time the stone would be weathered down to its melodious neutrality. " They had thirty men on it for six months." Frank spoke savagely, clearing away his recent uneasiness. " With half the country homeless, they go and build this . . ."

Two or three pale people were looking through the hedge on the opposite side of the lane to the wall, watching a baler at work in a cut hayfield. " Students!" Frank said. The house had, of course, become one of the Government's technical colleges. " But

407

they can't get the students to come, not enough of them—it's too far out." A young man with a beard, holding by the arm a girl in a striped dress, were laughing as they watched the baler through the hedge. " I know a few of them by sight—these are mostly the staff."

And so they were turning into the Park without noticing that they had come to the drive gates. And the Lodge, where Geoff had been born, stood back behind its privet hedge. At the low gate, a number of students or staff were gathered in a group, talking to Alex, who was selling them eggs. These people made way grudgingly as the van stopped. Through the window of the van Frank called to Alex: " There's a snooper about, a new one. You'll be run in for doing that."

One of the men said: " He won't worry us—we're the Government! " Every one laughed at the joke.

Geoff got out of the car, and Alex said: " Hallo, Geoff! " and came running to kiss him. She called out: " Shop's shut for to-day! " and took Geoff's arm, leading him through the group of people, and up the path, his own path, to his own front door, to his own house. He noticed the tide of chatter and laughter that followed him up the path, as if he was an object as comic as the machine at work in the hayfield, baling hay. But they were probably laughing at something quite unconnected with himself.

Coming into the hall, he found this part of it unchanged, with the same furniture in the same places. Alex had taken over the furniture when she had come to live here, on Ralph's death. She had not yet paid for it. And the big sofa stood where it had always been, in front of the fire, where he and Alex had lain together. He knew now—at this instant, though he later denied it—that he was, at last, really back: his return was complete.

*   *   *

But there were two quite separate and contrary versions of this reunion: the illusion at the time, and the illusion that developed very shortly afterwards—that same evening—out of the total sum of Geoff's recollection.

By the time evening came, or rather by the time it was almost dissolved into night, the affair had completely reversed itself, satisfaction turning into disgust, and love into hate. For by then Geoff had recalled—though he did not consciously note at the time—

how familiar Frank was with the ways of the house, how he acted naturally the part of host, as if he was a frequent and intimate visitor, and how he made plain to Geoff that what was left of the Meredith family had got itself new relationships.

It was Frank who went through, towards the kitchen, for the glasses, and to a cupboard under the stairs for a bottle of sherry, which he held to the light, saying: " We shall just about finish this lot, I dare say. I must bring you some more. But you don't drink a lot, do you? It must be a fortnight since we opened this one, and I must have drunk the best part of it on my own account."

She said: " Frank—what I need much more than sherry, much, much more, is something for my chickens to eat."

Bringing the bottle and the glasses, and putting them on the low table by the sofa, Frank said: " That won't be quite so easy as before. We've got to be rather specially careful, just for the moment."

" It's all very well to tell me things like that! " There was a sort of intimate mockery in her imperiousness. " But my chickens have got to eat! It's the egg-money that pays, mostly, my farm wages."

Frank pulled up a chair. " I don't know so much. I'll have to see what can be done. I could perhaps slip a few sacks into the car and bring them along after dark. But, these days, it isn't dark till so late." She did not say anything, and he held up the bottle again to see that there was a little left and then refilled their glasses, as far as it would go. " That's dead enough! At least you shall have a replacement . . . Apart from the chickens, how's the rest? "

" All right." It was her indifferent shrug which Geoff, afterwards, especially recalled. She treated Frank as if he was a husband whom she could be irritated with, in public, or could show herself tired of, in favour of a mere friend, a guest. Geoff was the guest— so it seemed afterwards—to whom she should open herself graciously, ignoring Frank. " Oh, Geoff dear, it's been such a long, long time. And so much has happened to both of us. . . ." To Frank, she said: " I'm sure I had some cigarettes left somewhere. . . ." And it was only when Frank had got up, saying: " I guess I know where they are," and had left the room to get them, that she said to Geoff: " But you don't smoke cigarettes! Or do you? " And then: " Geoff, dear Geoff, how does one forget these things? But then, as we said, so much has happened, so much . . ."

This was the structure, the outline, of the scene, as it appeared to him afterwards. It developed gradually throughout the rest of the day, becoming fully distinct only towards midnight when Frank drove off into the darkness. But at the time of the actual visit to the Lodge, so far as Geoff was concerned, Frank was scarcely acknowledged as being present until he got up to go, leaving Geoff to stay with Alex for lunch and to find his own way back to Neapcaster. "I can walk," Geoff said. "I might even borrow a bike." And Alex said: "Mr. Trant will give you a lift. He'll be coming in during the afternoon."

You know how, in a battle, you may not feel any pain from quite a grievous wound, may not even notice it, until long after the thing has hit you? If you are busy enough, and if your heart is sufficiently committed to the engagement, your senses either do not register pain, or else those senses can find no other part of you receptive to their message. At those times, it seems that all your sensitivity is tuned, like a directional receiver, towards one special beam. And everything else, every other kind of recognition, is excluded from making an immediate mark on your consciousness.

Anyway, it was only along the line of this comparison that Geoff could afterwards explain his illusion and obtuseness at the time of regaining Alex. These self-explanations began when he was again fully susceptible to pain, as Frank drove off into the night. But at the time, when Alex kissed him, it was a dawn's sunburst.

As Frank left, before lunch, he said: "Expect you when I see you. . . ." But he gave Geoff a beckon with his head, as if he wanted to speak to him privately outside the door. But Geoff stayed by the sofa, leaving Alex to see Frank off the premises.

As it seemed at the time, he had come home.

As soon as she kissed him at the gate, Geoff knew the absurdity of his earlier denials. As soon as her softness touched his cheek, he knew how ridiculous it had been—and how much a fantasy of absence—to suppose the allegiance of the heart to be a contract of service, terminable by will. Love could not be argued about by two men drinking beneath an Algerian fruit tree. No argument could identify anything that he had suffered from Ralph, any release from the Meredith yoke, however complete, with escape from love.

She was a good deal changed; but the changes were rather an acquisition than a loss of youth. Her physical and spiritual movements were just as light, but more subtle; as if so many successions of cause and effect had been coiled and compressed inside her, that she was better sprung than before to withstand impacts and bruises, made more adjustable to accidents. She had learnt how to submit without loss, even with gain; and in submission had become compassionate.

When, after Frank had left them, she returned to the sofa, and got Geoff sitting beside her again, and suddenly took his face between her hands, he let himself collapse until his forehead was resting on her knee and she was touching his hair.

They did not, of course, mention the word "love"; it never had been mentioned between them. Nor, for that matter, had this compassionate relationship existed in the past: it had been created, perhaps not by absence itself, but by the things that had happened during their long separation. In the last ten years the fates had cleared the way.

She was talking of David and his wife, saying: "And then he married her. That was before Ralph was killed. She's very sweet."

This new understanding was so close that she had no need to say, but yet had said: "If he had waited a little longer, till I was a widow . . ." She didn't even need to add: "But I think he's happier with her than he would have been with me." It was somehow plain to Geoff that her thoughts had reached that point when she said: "Of course you've never met her!" And when she asked him if, since his return, he had seen David, and he replied that he had not yet had the chance, he believed that she knew the truth: that he was unwilling, afraid, to submit himself at once to David's domination. It was as if she understood this feeling of his, and was trying to reassure him, when she said: "David's changed rather a lot, I think. He's so sorry for himself. I think it's a great mistake, don't you, to be sorry for oneself?"

"Aren't we all?" Things seemed so simple and plain, with her beside him, that it was really quite difficult to understand why every one had not previously diagnosed the sickness of the world as this same self-pity.

But she said: "I don't think, really, that I'm very sorry for myself. I don't know if I should be."

"You must have a fairly hard life . . . no servants and so on . . . couldn't you, surely, get in a daily maid?"

This descent to such practical matters made her laugh and pull at his hair, as if he was a dog. But she said: "I dare say I could, but I couldn't pay her. I haven't any money, you know. You know, a widow's pension wouldn't do more than pay a girl's wages."

"But surely Ralph's estate . . ."

"Jessie Levine does have two girls who come in daily, but then her house is a lot bigger than this." Her reluctance to talk about money was not, it seemed, out of reticence, but rather that the subject was too unimportant for this first meeting. But to Geoff the matter had some obscure, overall significance that he wanted to extract. When he pressed her, she answered: "There didn't seem to be anything left, when it was all settled. But I suppose it isn't finally settled, not after all these years, not even yet. Old Guy is still muddling along with it, still writes me letters. But really it's too much bother . . . there isn't time . . . there's too much else. . . ." Now, when she raised her hand to her hair as part of her conversation, it was not the old gesture of impatience, but a sort of assertion that this was what really mattered—her composure, her grace. "Jessie is very pretty, very *petite*. . . ." And Geoff felt that a comparison had been made, but without any rancour. "Of course, I don't see very much of her. Sometimes, she or I, we take the children to tea with each other. But not very often; we haven't the petrol." And this last, casual remark seemed to switch on the light for Geoff, who had not, till then, been able to realise that such a triviality as a petrol ration could disturb so vital a human function as friendship, and that the total of all these administrative measures had amounted to social revolution. "Really," she said, "none of us, these days, is ever able to see very much of anybody else. It isn't very easy to get away or to get about." And into the picture of this new society, disrupted and redeployed into little, independent, separated worlds, he had to fit himself.

After she had given him lunch and they had together done the washing up, they prepared to go out to the farm. "Do you know what it is that makes women so old?" she asked. "Working women like us?" She was stooping at the slow oven, hauling out of it a great cauldron of cooked potatoes. When he took it from her, he was amazed that she could even lift it. "Yes," she said, "it's not the jobs that wears people out, but the heaviness of buckets."

There was only a cut-down garden implement, a dutch hoe, with which to mash up the potatoes for the poultry and the pigs. Finding it awkward work, Geoff said: " This is a poor tool! There must be contraptions better than this."

" You try to find them! " she answered, bringing the swill-bucket across from beneath the sink. " And if you did—the price! Besides, where is the time to go searching the shops ? "

After they had fed the pigs and the poultry, and collected the eggs, they went at once to the yard at the back where, in one of the boxes that had once housed Geoff's pony—when the Park stables were full—old Watts was already milking. He stopped, but without getting up from his stool, to say: " So you're back, Master Geoff! About time, isn't it? " Then he returned to work, and the milk started again to rattle its spurts into the pail between his knees. With his old red cheek and his white hair pressed against the cow's flank, he said: " That box next door, Master Geoff, that heifer . . . I reckon she'll calve to-night? " He was really asking a question, and when Geoff had taken a look at the wild-eyed creature, blue and white, but with wide horns—perhaps a Friesian-Ayrshire cross—he answered: " She ought to calve to-night. She's got something queer about her eye. What do you want with an awkward beast like that? "

Watts muttered something, but Alex said: " We can't always be bothering Mr. Trant."

They took the eggs into the kitchen and stood together at the sink, beneath a small latticed window which had become so over-grown with ivy that it would no longer open. If somebody was to spend just ten minutes cutting back that creeper, it would make all the difference to the airiness of the room! But who was there left to do it? And that overgrowth of ivy now reproached Geoff for his absence, counting the years with its suckers, that crept and clung from one leaded pane to the next across the cobwebbed glass. That darkened window, charging him with absence, was also responsible for the pale green, placid light which formed a sort of aquarium in which the basket of eggs lay drowned. Into the wavy light they thrust their arms to wash and pack the eggs; she scrubbing them in a bucket, searching them for defects and handing them to him; and he passing them through a cloth and fitting each one into its square receptacle in the big carton.

For a time she was always ahead of him, waiting for him with her arm outstretched like a dark dancer in the dark light. But soon he had caught her rhythm, and their two pairs of arms passed smoothly, steadily to and fro, mingling and separating, as if they were saints come to life in a stained-glass window, or swimmers close together in a verdant sea. This was love.

But all he was able to say was: " You know, you're doing all your feeding and milking much too early in the afternoon ? "

She answered: " Mr. Trant says the same thing. But if we did it any later, it would mean paying overtime to Watts."

One could scarcely recall a memory of Watts that was not at night, with the smell of the stables enlarged in the dark; the old groom getting from his bed for a last look at his horses; and back with them again some hours before a winter dawn.

But she was explaining. " Now he's an agricultural worker, and not just a worker, you see, the rules are quite strict. They sometimes prosecute . . ." Their task continued steadily while she talked. " And of course, he doesn't want to work overtime at all, not here, not for me. He'd much rather go next door to Ted Foster or any one else. Because they can pay him in cash, you see, as casual labour—so they needn't deduct his tax. . . ." And all the time, in the pool of light, their hands continued to join and to draw apart, weaving their love. " Overtime apart," she was saying, " if I made myself any later, I wouldn't be ready for Ralph. He'll be wanting his tea in an hour from now, when he's back from school . . . then he has to be read to . . . then put to bed . . . then my supper to get. And if I'm not early in bed myself, I'd oversleep. . . . And to-morrow I wouldn't get the chickens done before I got Ralph off to school. And if that should happen . . ." Having finished the eggs, she was swiftly drying her hands and emptying the bucket. " I'd be caught with the housework. And once you're behind with *that* . . . then lunch. . . ."

She was bustling across the kitchen, and he turned with his back to the dark window and held out his arms wide, as if it was some ritual gesture; the priest of protection crying " Here, my dearest! " But she was much too busy to notice him.

The actual words that he spoke were: " This is too damn ridiculous! Here's me, here's you! And if, and if . . ." But she was clattering the buckets and heard only a word or two. She answered: " Ridiculous, Geoff dear? But it's all got to be done, hasn't it ? "

He had started to cry: "Alex, Alex . . ." when a deep and powerful voice from behind him said: "It's just about time you got back to us, young Geoff!" And the big, slow figure of Mr. Trant was standing in the kitchen doorway. "I see, Miss Alex, you're all dolled up to-day," he said.

"I put on a dress," she answered, "in honour of Geoff."

"You should see her as she usually is," said Trant to Geoff, "a regular farm lad, a regular scamp, in her corduroy trousers and shirt."

*   *   *

"Just look at this lot," said Trant; "it's not more'n three or four days since I was here last, and see how they've collected!" The table, at which Geoff's father used to write his personal letters, was still standing under the window. Here Trant was seated, dealing with the many official forms that had become a formidable part of any farmer's work; all the typewritten envelopes that Alex had left unopened. As he sat stolidly writing, pinning together and enveloping documents, sorting and filing, with broad fingers that were made for quite different occupations, he grumbled partly to Geoff and partly to himself. "Permit for a bit o' barbed wire . . . permit for a scrap o' netting . . . three sheets o' corrugated iron . . . twenty foot of galvanised pipe . . . What my dad would ha' said of it! Or yours, Geoff!"

Since the old days, the face of Mr. Trant had steadily extended itself at top and bottom into a higher forehead and more jagged chin, until it had become definitely a long and stubborn face, indicating that his habits of mind and self-regard had not been modified from those of his youth, but rather reinforced. For him, the old fealties had survived new times, and he was glad of the chance nowadays to demonstrate them.

Alex was clattering the tea-things in the kitchen, passing backwards and forwards between that place and the sitting-room, racing to keep ahead of young Ralph's return. "We want some more calf-nuts," she said to Trant.

"I don't know if we can have'n," he answered, partly teasing her. "We could try pitchin' 'em some sort of a tale." To Geoff he explained: "She's given her calf food to the pigs, an' her pig food to the fowls. . . ." With an obvious effort he returned laboriously to his writing. "Return of stock for one Ministry . . .

same thing for another. . . . Return of cereal crops. . . . Return of carrots and 'taters still in the ground . . . only the A'mighty knows that. . . ."

As she re-entered the room, Alex said: "Frank is bringing me some more corn for the poultry."

"I wish you'd keep clear o' that chap," Trant answered, without looking up, but Alex had gone again. "I heard a whisper," he said to Geoff, "that they're on his track. We dursen't be mixed up with *that*. . . ." Licking an envelope, he said: "A permit to fell a tree!" Thumping a stamp on to the envelope with his fist, he said: "Permit to send a pig to Government slaughter-house! Lucky they taught us to write!" Then he whistled suddenly and stood up from his chair, holding a letter to the light, incredulously fingering it and making the paper crackle. "They blasted buggers!" he said in a furious voice.

"What is it *this* time?" Alex asked brightly, as she brought in the tea-tray. She had to repeat the question in a more serious voice. "What is it, Mr. Trant?"

"Notice to quit," he said.

She carefully put down the tray before speaking. "Notice to quit? Me? Us?"

"To clear out, Miss Alex; out of the Home Farm; out of the Lodge."

"But they can't do that." Slowly, without emotion, she clasped her hands in front of her breasts.

"So far as I know, there's nothing to stop them."

"They did promise they wouldn't. He promised." Her voice was quite level. "Personally, he promised me that."

"Promises don't mean much to that lot," Trant said. Holding the letter towards the window, shifting the steel spectacles which he wore for this sort of work and which looked incongruous and comic on his long and ruddy face, he said: "You can't read the chap who's signed it; you can't read his writing. . . . 'General Manager,' it says. . . ." He held out the letter to Geoff, who took the crisp, oblong fragment of expensive stationery on which only two or three lines were typed. In plain black letters it was embossed: BETTS AGRICULTURAL ESTATES.

"You must appeal," Geoff said. "I should think you've a very good chance."

"Appeal? Who do we appeal to?" Mr. Trant was very much

more agitated than Alex. "There's no one to appeal to—not that I know about."

"The new Act, the Agricultural Act," Geoff said. "You've surely heard about it? You must have read about it?"

"I don't get time for gossip. . . . I don't get time for reading. . . . I haven't the time for the papers. . . ." Trant mumbled his excuses like a schoolboy found at fault.

"Take it to a lawyer," Geoff said. "You've got a month to lodge an appeal, but you want to be quick. I doubt if they'll get you out."

"I will . . . I will. . . ." Trant's big fingers fumbled clumsily, folding the letter. His hand even seemed to tremble as he took out a wallet, worn black, and pushed the paper into one of its pockets. Scarcely audibly, he was repeating: "The rats, the rats . . ."

In a voice as low and clear as a summer stream, Alex said: "It's not worth the trouble, Mr. Trant; it suits me well enough."

Both men turned slowly to look at her, but her face was expressionless. Mr. Trant's great hand, holding the wallet, stopped in the air, *en route* for his breast pocket. But her face was like a portrait of herself, done by a master who had sought to contain, within the creamy texture of her skin, all the fluctuations of her passion in a single distillation. Her face was like a memorial of herself, of somebody beloved who was dead. In a perfectly ordinary voice, she said: "Anyway, it doesn't matter. I'm going away."

Since neither of the men spoke, and the silence and stillness of the room were becoming oppressive, she repeated gently, as if she was speaking to children: "I'm going away, you see; away from this." Her hands were still clasped below her breasts; her whole figure was motionless and lovely; but one felt she had gestured a surrender. "Away, away from this . . ."

"Where to?" It was Geoff who had asked the question; but he spoke for both of them; he spoke for the room itself.

"To Kenya," she said. "It's quite different there, they say. I'm going with Colonel Black."

It was some time before Geoff, speaking in a voice which he hated, was asking: "When did you settle this?"

"Weeks ago he asked me. It was only yesterday I told him ' yes.' You see . . ." She seemed to stoop her head in gentle explanation. "For all Mr. Trant's kind help, I couldn't go on living like this. At least I might myself, but Ralph . . . he needs . . . other things. He oughtn't to be brought up in this sort of way, ought he? It isn't right. Of course if . . ." But she never added, never quite said: "Of course, if there had been Geoff . . ."

Roughly Trant was saying: "You can't go over the sea, Miss Alex; you can't go and marry a razzling old rip like that; you can't . . ."

But she put her hand on his wrist. "I'm going to Kenya, to take Ralph to Kenya, with Colonel Black."

On their way out of the house, neither man spoke to the other; but Trant was talking to himself, testing his own reactions. "I'll put in an appeal for her, nevertheless. Be it as it may, I'll appeal on her behalf. I'll see that lawyer chap. She'll not be treated like that. . . ." It was clear that he had not yet digested a half of the situation, or discovered what it would mean to his own lifelong habits when there was not left, at Neapcaster, a single Meredith. When he got to the car, he asked Geoff if he wanted a lift.

"To Neapcaster town; Frank's house," Geoff said.

*   *   *

The silence in which they drove suited the temperaments of both men. The shock they had suffered made each of them with-draw behind his established defences, each face becoming entirely inscrutable, each body adopting that curious, stubborn calm which emitted a sort of smoke-screen. You could not have had the least idea what either of them was feeling or if, in fact, he was feeling anything at all. The first word spoken was ten minutes after they had left the Lodge, when Trant, drawing up at Frank's fine house, and jerking his thumb towards it, said: "You don't want to hang about with that lot, not any more than you can help."

Geoff nodded and thanked Trant for the lift. When the car had driven away, he said or thought: "I've got to hang about somewhere! Where else is left?"

His silence during the rest of that evening suited Frank's house-hold, which played its way through the hours to a music very different from that of the previous night. The whole equipoise of the orchestra had been upset by the first tremors of disaster, as if Frank had expressed anxiety after his telephone call to London, instead of resuming, as he did, his usual boisterousness. "Hark at the girl!" Frank cried, when May suggested that he put away

418

the car, or at least put on its lights, since "there isn't any sense, Frankie, in getting run in for *that*!" To which Frank said: "Any one'd think I was already half-way to jug!"

"I don't believe you'd mind if you were." To Geoff she said: "He doesn't mind anything; it's me that has to do the minding." She looked round her beautiful room, the symbol of all their efforts and success, which now seemed so precarious. "Frankie, dear, do put away that car! I don't see why you had to get it out."

But the big car remained outside the house, sinister, and a threat. And the whole house felt desperately quiet, as May seemed to feel it trembling about her. "He doesn't mind anything. But I . . . I do mind, I do mind so!" It was a wail, a choke.

Frank went across to kiss her. "Stop all these imaginings, ducks! Nothing's going to happen. Everything's going to be all right. . . . You're a bit worked up; you'd best get along to bed."

"We could both do with it."

"You go on up, ducks! I've got a little job that I've got to do first."

Sharply she cried: "You're not going out to-night, Frankie?"

"Half an hour or so; no more'n that."

"Not to-night, Frankie."

"I promised a person a few sacks of corn. If Geoff will help me load it . . ."

"Who? Who is it?" Her voice was strangely fierce.

"With things as they are," he answered, "the least known by every one, the better for all of us." He went out into the hall and came back with a cap slung comically on the back of his head. Then he went and gave his wife another kiss, although she turned away from him. Patting her back, he said: "Don't worry so! Everything's all right."

"Please . . . please, not to-night!"

He answered from the hall: "I shan't be long. And Geoff, he'll only be a few minutes. Coming, Geoff?"

Like the three monkeys, Geoff followed Frank out of the house and into the car. He allowed himself not to see, nor to hear, nor to speak about, this new evil. He allowed himself neither to think nor to feel, as they drove round the corner to the warehouse, which had two high, wooden doors painted with the name Green & Co., Ltd. "We bought up Mr. Green," Frank said, giving Geoff the key. "Do you mind opening up?" As he drove the car into the yard, he called sharply: " Shut them, please. Quick as you can, Geoff!" A man went past in the street, and Frank said: " I wonder who that was?"

As soon as the doors were shut, Frank got out of the car briskly and went to the side door of the warehouse, the key to which he had in his pocket. Inside the door, a set of wooden steps brought them to the platform of the warehouse, which was head-high above the level of the yard, so that a man could easily take a sack on his shoulders or load it direct into a truck.

All this time Geoff had followed Frank silently, obeying his requests. Now he saw the sparks from Frank's lighter which at length gave them a flame, enabling them to get between the rows of sacks to the steel shutters which, like a stage curtain, divided the platform from the yard. It needed another key to throw up a section of these shutters, and then there was enough light from a lamp in the street to show them a separate little group of sacks, left on the edge of the platform, ready for loading. " I expect this is our lot," Frank said. " But best make sure. Have you got a knife?"

Geoff cut the string at the mouth of the sack and put a hand inside to feel the grain. " Wheat," he said at once, the word being uttered by the reflex action of his lips when his fingers felt the corn.

" That's what it ought to be," Frank said. " Good stuff?"

Geoff drew out a handful, feeling it cool and hard and clean in the dark. He sniffed at it and said: " A pretty good sample."

" Seed sample, I expect," Frank said. " Does it feel like that?"

Geoff felt it clean on his fingers, and free of weed-seeds. " Yes," he said.

" I think it's a Fylgia variety. It's not dressed, is it?"

Geoff touched the grains with his tongue. The normal mercury dressing for seed-wheat was poisonous to poultry. " This is not dressed," he said.

" A bit extravagant for hens. But if the customer pays the price . . ." They got down into the yard and loaded the sacks into the back of the car. One of them had to go into the boot, which would not quite shut. Frank paid great attention to this shutting of the boot. " It won't shut," Geoff said. " It's all right like that."

" I'd rather have it shut."

" There won't be anybody about—not at this hour of the night. It's pretty late."

While he was forcing shut the door of the boot, Geoff woke up. All that evening, ever since he had left Alex, he had been in the frontier state, neither awake nor asleep, still holding on to the fringe of the beauty and triumph belonging to sleep, not yet deprived of the dream, almost forgotten, of his hours of love. The identity of the dream had long ago slipped away, leaving its glory to linger like the afterglow at dusk. It was the shock, the double shock of his meeting with Alex and his climb to the pinnacle of his life, followed by the tumble caused by the thing she had told them at the end of it, which had brought him to this state. The state was familiar. He suffered it for a few seconds, or a fraction of a second, every time that he awoke. This evening, to-night, it had been a long, long session. Or so it seemed now, when he did at last awake.

The moment before he woke, he was carrying sacks. As he had stood with his back to the platform, grasping the mouth of each sack over his shoulder, and taking the full weight of its two and a quarter hundredweight on to his back, he had felt pleasure that he could still hump a load as well as anybody else. There were few men, certainly not Frank, who could make any lighter than he could of a sack of wheat. It might have been this thought that started him awake.

When Frank had driven a little way down the street, clear of the warehouse and of the street lamp, and then had waited for Geoff to come up and give him the key, he said: "It's just as well, isn't it, that you're not interested yourself? It was a relief, I can tell you, when you said . . . what was it . . ."

As Frank drove off into the night, Geoff heard his own voice saying, not now but in the past, not that afternoon to Alex but the previous day to Frank, that treacherous word: "Ridiculous!" The cock-crow of his journey home echoed its punishment. Left alone in the street to make his way back to May, Geoff could at last detect, trace and suffer from, the wound inflicted that morning when he and Frank had entered the Lodge. And now the forgotten dream was restored, but not as he had forgotten it. He saw the reunion from its other aspect, with Frank the intimate, Frank the host, Frank making plain to Geoff that what was left of the Meredith family had got itself new entanglements. The pale green pool of the ivy-covered window had become a stinking swamp.

*   *   *

When Geoff got back, May was standing in the hall, her face and whole figure distressed, very much changed from her rosy and bright appearance, now pale and tragic, less pretty than beautiful. This pallid beauty she cast upon Geoff, as if the two of them had been put into alliance by Frank's betrayal, and as if Geoff had succeeded Frank as her natural protector. " Where's he gone, Geoff ? "

" He didn't say . . . Just to take some wheat for somebody's chickens."

" Alex's chickens ? He's gone to Alex, hasn't he ? "

" He didn't say where he was going. He didn't say whose chickens it was."

" But you know it was Alex, don't you ? "

" I don't know anything at all."

She stamped her foot and said: " I'm not a Food Inspector ! Only his wife ! " Then she smiled suddenly. " Poor Geoff ! You'd better have a drink ! "

" I think it's time for bed." But he had to turn away to prevent his eyes from showing her what feelings and appetites she had started to provoke. He was not yet in a state of sufficient internal security to let his mind consider whether her provocation was deliberate, or even conscious, or whether it was nothing to do with her at all, but just a product of his own despair and emptiness. Despair had peeled off him all his protective insulation, leaving the sensitive wire exposed to her touch that was making him quiver, to her eyes that were becoming less tragic and more languorous, and to her presence that had already, suddenly, become seductive.

" We'd better have a drink," she said, nodding her head gravely, as if it was an important decision.

" Frank said he wouldn't be long." It was a defensive answer.

" He'll be away all night. Oh, I know him—he won't be back till to-morrow." This was said quite carelessly. " I know him when he's like this," May said. " No matter what he says—he'll be away all night. He's gone to Alex, hasn't he ? "

" I don't know," he said, as he had said before in his solemn, childish way.

" I bet you do know," she said. " He's keen on her, isn't he ? You were keen on her yourself, weren't you ? "

" She was Ralph's wife."

"That's kid's stuff," May said. "Every one knew you used to be keen on her. Some said it went further than it ought." She giggled. "I bet it did, didn't it?" The debasement of her new beauty by this commonness was desperately and coarsely seductive. Geoff shook his head. He was helpless against the magnet which, at her activation, was drawing his body out of him. "I bet you're still keen on her. I don't see how you could help it. Why do you let Frankie get away with it?" She was an extraordinary woman, she was laughing now. "He's getting away with it now, at this very minute, isn't he? Him with a wife waiting at home—isn't he?"

Geoff said: "I just don't know, I tell you."

"You're the loyal sort," she said. "That's what it is."

"It certainly isn't that."

"I don't know what else it is . . . but Frankie won't be back to-night."

Geoff managed to say: "Then let's have a drink."

"All right, we *will* have a drink."

But the drink was of no assistance. Geoff poured it out for both of them, and he made it strong. Later he repeated it; and on each occasion she drank hers down very quickly, while he sipped his own. It was a mistake, perhaps, that they had sat down in two arm-chairs, facing each other across the empty fireplace, and leaving the sofa empty between them. To get up from one arm-chair and to walk across the fireplace to the other would be a gigantic operation. And yet he was sure that the slightest movement from him, the least gesture that showed her how much he shared her physical mood, would make happen all that he wanted. He was physically incapable of that gesture.

"It's a hot night," he said, wiping his forehead. When he went to the window, crossing the room, he had to pass close beside her chair; and she looked up at him with that twist of the neck which is so beautiful when the neck is beautiful. His step hesitated but, against his wish, took him past her to the window, where he parted the curtains enough for the cool air to come from the garden and touch the moisture on his face.

"Yes," she said, "it *is* time we went to bed, isn't it?" She got up from her chair briskly.

He turned from the window, startled, as if he had heard something fall and break behind him.

423

At the top of the stairs she kissed him. She said: "You're a sweet boy, Geoff," and she kissed him on both cheeks. In spite of his throbbing and trembling, he did contrive an attempt, scarcely more than a twitch of the head, to kiss her lips while she kissed him on the cheek. But she had turned her head so quickly and firmly that he could not tell whether or not his intention was detected and her evasion deliberate. "You're the nicest boy anybody could ever know," she said.

Watching her going into her room and closing the door behind her, he was angry with himself, and yet almost amused. "You're the hell of a man, aren't you, Brigadier Greenley!" And as he undressed he declared how ridiculous it was that he and she should be undressing separately, with an empty corridor between them, in an empty house. Tommy Black or Frank—either of them—would have gone along the passage and opened the door of her bedroom, as a matter of course, as if there was no alternative. Yet he could not do it. And yet, when he analysed the action into the little trivial movements that were needed to complete it, it was so simple. No doubt she was waiting for him, expecting him to come. Almost he had to go; almost he had no choice. But he knew he never would go, and he got into bed. Unexpectedly he went to sleep at once.

* * *

He looked at his watch the moment he woke up, but the night was too bright for the luminous dial to be distinct. Either there was a late moon, or the morning twilight had already started. At this time of the year, the coming day began to declare itself at about three o'clock. Then he heard the telephone ringing, and no other sound in the house. The telephone kept up its distant, rhythmical pulse, and nobody went to answer it. Without troubling to put on a dressing-gown, he went downstairs in his pyjamas and bare feet; but as he got to the hall the ringing stopped. Nevertheless he went to the telephone, which stood on the table by the window, and pulled the curtains slightly apart, letting the light from outside enter. It was still a long way from dawn, but light had started to return. There was a shred of radiant mist on the strip of garden outside the open window, but it was not chilly at first. The room was hot inside, and the air that came in from those pre-natal mists was refreshing and sweet, as if it was falling into a valley from the uplands, not dragging itself through the streets of a town.

He picked up the receiver, and after he had joggled the lever a good many times a woman asked what number he wanted. " You were ringing us," he said.

"Were you the long-distance from London? You didn't answer. Put the receiver back and I'll try to get them."

He had not heard her coming, but May was standing beside him. Before he saw her, he smelt the secret, warm smell of her body fresh from bed. Then he felt the silk nightdress touching his bare feet. " Is it Frankie? " She spoke in a whisper, as if she was afraid of disturbing the empty house.

" It's not Frank," he said. " Not unless he's in London? "

" He *could* be in London, of course." She spoke hopefully.

" Rum sort of place to be taking a sack of wheat! "

" Shall I make us some tea? "

While he hung on to the instrument, he said: " I could do with a cup of tea." She went to make it, and he was a very long time waiting on the silent line. The warm odour returned, and the silk brushed his ankle and then his face, as she put the tray down on the table beside the telephone. When she stooped to pour out the tea, not only the silk of her gown, but her hair also, touched his skin. Without the least warning, a voice said very clearly in his ear: " This is Betts speaking."

May was whispering: " It isn't Frank? "

Geoff shook his head as he answered, down the telephone: " Oh, Sir Frederick, it's Greenley here. Frank is away. Do you want to speak to . . ." May was shaking her head. " She's asleep, I expect." It was a real pleasure to tell this lie, establishing the conspiracy.

" You'll do, Geoff," Betts said. " You can get hold of Frank, I take it? "

" I expect so, in the morning."

" I hope so. I want him here by lunch. You can fix that up? "

" I expect so."

" I hope so. Tell him it's important. I wouldn't have rung up at this time of the morning if it wasn't important. Sorry to wake you, Geoff. Good night."

" Good night." But he said it into a dead instrument.

When he told May what Sir Frederick had said, she threw

herself back into tragedy, as if she enjoyed it. "If *he* says it's important, it must be a dreadful thing. He doesn't ever, ever say that. . . ." Clasping, unclasping her hands, she finally took Geoff's cup and refilled it. "I don't think I can bear it, Geoff." This was said very calmly, as she handed the cup back. "I can't, I can't bear it!" Her voice rose right up. "I can't bear the way this goes on and on, and one day it's bound to happen, bound to, there's bound to be judgment. . . ."

Geoff put his cup down carefully and fiddled with the spoon, still saying nothing, because all down his body, all through his limbs, he could feel the interior constriction, unbearable by now, and some nodal centre of himself quivering like a transmitter under his skin and flesh, transmitting to his limbs, organs and extremities these terrible waves of wanting this woman so that, while his head stayed fixed in one position, his eyes had to follow her and to keep recording the movement of her shapes under the pink satin dressing-gown.

"There has to be a judgment; oh, there has to be justice done! That man he talked about . . ." Now she was standing in the middle of the room, with her fingers twisted together, generating the necessary distress that she owed to the occasion. "Could it be that man with the limp?"

"Might be," Geoff said. He didn't care in the least. He was waiting until the fuse that had been lit burnt itself down to something explosive somewhere. Now he felt sure that the explosion was inevitable.

She came to the table, by which he was sitting on the arm of the chair, and put out her hand to take the empty cup. Instead of doing so, she dropped her head on his shoulder and started weeping, transferring her tears to his cheek. He just lifted his arm, and it was folded round her waist, with the palm of his hand on the shiny, satin curve where the gown was drawn tight about her loin. He just got to his feet, and he was carrying her across the room. On the sofa, he was not lost or taken away or oblivious. On the contrary, he was perceptive of every little thing about the room and the growing light, the shred of mist in the garden and, somewhere outside, a wood-pigeon waking for a brief call over the rooftops and then becoming silent again, a dog distantly barking and then silent, a car starting some streets away and driving off and leaving the street silent.

He found himself grinning, feeling quite hard and brutal about this business, without tenderness but with a sense—as she herself had said—of justice being done at last. But she was clinging to him and, while he kissed the back of her neck, was murmuring between sobs: "You're so sweet, Geoff. Oh, Geoff, you're so sweet to me."

Thus the murmurs continued, becoming a croon, while the adventures of his hands progressed, until suddenly she gave a whimper and cried: "No, no, Geoff!" But he went on stroking and kissing her with increasing vigour, because—so every one always said, so every one always told him—always women said "No, no!" like this, but always meaning the opposite. So now he took hold of her quite roughly, enjoying her little gasps and cries of "No, no, you mustn't!" And even when he started to use his strength, so that there was not much she could do except to stiffen her limbs and continue her protests, he was still grinning while he made his voice say hoarsely: "But I must, I must! My darling, I must!"

Then suddenly she had struggled free, and, with one quick twist, was sitting beside him on the sofa, drawing tight her dressing-gown and patting her hair. When he took hold of her again, he had no courage to use his strength, and she pushed him away with only one hand, while the other remained busy with her hair. Thus she sat primly at the far end of the sofa saying: "Behave yourself, Geoff!"

Arguing, pleading, he put passion, misery, loneliness and almost tears into his voice, while all the time she kept repeating: "You must behave yourself, Geoff," and all the time he was silently saying: "You slut, you bitch!"

No arguments were any use. It wasn't any use to remind her of Frank's infidelity, or of his own loneliness, or of his long absence. The distance between his desire and her readiness seemed all the time to be increasing; while his desire, although it became dissolved in hatred and anger, remained paramount. When he told her treacherously about all Frank's women, she said: "I know, I know . . . but it doesn't make any difference." When he told her that it was her actions, and surely her invitation, that had brought him into this terrible desire, she said: "Oh, Geoff, dear Geoff, I didn't, I didn't mean it!" And when he tried to tell her the force of this desire, she said in a voice that was suddenly quite hard and sharp: "Oh, I know all about that rubbish!" And then, as if to make the slap as hard as she could, she added: "What you'd best do is to go along the street to Kate. She's open all hours, is Kate."

"Kate, Kate . . ." he said stupidly.

"That little bitch that used to be up at the house; that Frank was keen on; that Alex had for a maid and Ralph had for what he wanted . . . She's the town tart! That's all you want—the town tart. . . ."

He got to his feet quickly, saying: "I've a bloody good mind to."

May got up from the sofa and walked straight out of the room, saying as she went: "Please yourself!"

Some time afterwards he followed her upstairs, and went straight to the door of her bedroom, trying to open it. It was locked. He rattled at the door and beat on it with his fists, but she made no sound from inside, none at all. It was quite light now in the early morning, somewhere approaching five o'clock, and he went back to his room and dressed. Then he tried her door again, softly this time. It was still locked, and the room seemed to be very silent on the other side of it; so silent that he thought or imagined he could hear her breathing deeply, asleep. Returning to his room, he packed.

A car passed in the street; then footsteps and a boy whistling; then again, silence. Two by two, Geoff carried all his bags downstairs and through the empty streets to the station yard. Each time that he returned to the house for another load, he tried the bedroom door; but there was never any change in the situation. He had to make a good many journeys, because he had brought all his baggage to Neapcaster, having nowhere else to leave it; and now nowhere at all.

The mist had turned into drizzle, another dose of "pride of the morning"; and by six o'clock, when Geoff had got the last of his bags to the station, his coat was quite damp. One or two of the porters were now coming on duty, none of whom he knew or remembered. But they told him that the early train had been discontinued since the war; and there was now nothing to London till eight o'clock: two hours to wait.

"An' that's only the slow train that won't get you up more'n twenty minutes better'n the nine o'clock." The young porter had a soft and friendly voice which filled the silence of this sad morning, but what he was saying had no meaning in this forgotten spot, forgotten by catastrophe. For there had been, one felt, some catastrophic devastation which had swept the earth, leaving only this station, an island of survival, and only Geoff and the porter, the remnants of humanity. But the porter did not know of it. The porter didn't know that no more trains would ever run along these shiny rails which, seen beyond the damp palings of the station yard, appeared to stretch to left and right along the circumference of the world, but in fact came to a stop, a skyward twist of demolition, only a little way beyond the first steep breaker of encroaching mist.

Moisture had ceased to precipitate; and the gaseous mists rolled in upon all that was left of the world: the desolate, rusted structure of this tiny station whose only surviving inhabitants were Geoff, sitting on his luggage, and the young porter propping himself against the booking-office wall. After the cataclysm, these two casualties were the survivors of humanity, and this dripping shack the only relic of human creation, a personal transit camp for the two of them to heaven or hell. But the porter didn't know of this. He was calm and bored, as they often were. A torn poster, the upper half of which had come unstuck, drooped over his left shoulder and tickled his smooth brown face. (Thus: the crawling flies on the face of a stretcher case!) He had very bright, innocent eyes, not more than half his age, and a minute particle of their blue had been caught by a drop of moisture that hung from the peak of his cap. When he shifted his feet slightly, the dangling strip of poster rustled against this tunic. " 'Tisn't much of a service from here, 'cept for the one up an' t'other down. The rest are nothing to speak of. Backwater sort of place. Dead-end sort of job. . . ."

As the young man continued to talk, Geoff was constrained to accept this lesser interpretation of their fate. The world wasn't finished; only Geoff was finished, long ago finished and become a fossilised thing struck, where it lay, by every passing boot.

If only this were true! But the punishment of life had still got a long time to go; the senses had still got a great many more pains to register; and the brain still creaked drearily in the windless morning. The feet continued their awful tramp on the treadmill of living. Thus, one could not advance or withdraw, but only stay where one was, tramping one's feet to the sergeant-major's voice, and suffering.

"Here's a chap as'd put you on your way quicker'n the train," the porter said. And a lorry came out of the mist much too fast, came round the yard with a toot of the horn, and was pulled to a halt beside them with a high-spirited skid. "'Lo, Charlie!" the porter called. "Is it Lunnon to-day?"

"Up empty this morning; down with a load to-night. Does this gentleman want a lift?" The driver had short, curly hair and a hat on the back of his head. Seeing all Geoff's luggage, he asked: "What's this? Moving house?" But he didn't expect an answer.

Geoff's voice, directed by the porter's earlier complaint, started to say: "If a quid's any use . . ."

"Forget it, chum!" said the driver. "Glad of the company." He had a strong, quick body of which he was obviously proud, and he jumped down into the station yard with a hop and a skip. He stood there, flexing his knees and pushing back his hat till it toppled off his head and he could make a grab to catch it. When the porter told him there were half a dozen cases of horticultural glass consigned to Swire's, he said: "Heaviest, cussedest load there is! Let's have it! Right up our street!"

"A couple of miles out of our way," said Geoff. And wondered why he had said it. He had not consciously noted that if they took the road by Swire's, they would have to continue past Neapcaster Park and the Lodge, past Alex.

"Let's get cracking!" said the driver. And he put his hand on the side of the lorry and vaulted up, getting rid of some of his energy by this gymnastic feat. Inside, he had a pair of planks which he set up to make a ramp along which the heavy cases could be edged into place. It was a hard job employing all three men, and they worked silently, with no need to speak, knowing just how to do it best and how to use their strength. "Tears out your guts, if you try to lift them," the driver said. "No sense in tearing out your guts for a case of glass."

Geoff climbed into the cab, and they drove off. "You're no stranger here?" the driver asked, having evidently noted Geoff's remark about the road to Swire's. But when Geoff shook his head silently, there were no more questions, the driver respecting a man's right to be uncommunicative if he wished.

As they drove through the town and up the steep hill beyond, Geoff was aware that his burden had somehow been lifted. It was as if a balloonist had jettisoned most of his ballast. He could feel the muscles of his shoulder, stomach and back, still stretched from their recent exercise, loading the crates of glass. And a merciful bridge seemed to have been slung across all intervening experience, and all purport, so that he got again some physical pleasure out of his own skill and strength at humping sacks of wheat. He had still got a strong body and a countryman's knowledge or instinct of how best to use it. He had still got a countryman's craft. He was not, as he had thought, altogether destitute.

As they got to the top of the hill up which the town nowadays straggled, the mists cleared. Other things, besides the brief suburban fringe on either side of the road, also became clear in the pearly brightness. It was true—as he had felt when he was first talking to the porter—that a world had been demolished. But another world had replaced it: a world in which a man, no lower than a beast, got happiness and peace from the craftiness of his strength and the precision of his instincts. When everything else was demolished, a man did at least remain an extremely knowledgeable beast.

*   *   *

Pulling into Swire's yard, like coming into port, the young driver put on his brakes, threw his gears into neutral, switched off his engine, uncurled his legs and got down from his lorry in one smooth, proud, vigorous sequence of movements that told the world to go to hell for so long as he had his arrogance, his cock-like virility. "Where's this chap, Ted?"

Geoff sat back in the cab of the lorry, unwilling to retrace his way through the night to the previous morning when he had last met Ted and Lizz and had found himself placed with Frank on one side of the barrier, with the Biblical pair of Ted and Lizz on the other, and the dark man with the limp, the Food Inspector, seeming to hold the barrier between them.

"Hey, Ted!" the driver shouted.

As soon as Ted Foster stuck out his head from one of the low buildings on the far side of the yard, he saw Geoff in the lorry, and at once, as if it was back in the old days, he touched his cap. "'Morning, Mr. Geoff." And only then did he acknowledge the driver. "'Lo, Charlie!"

431

" Got a load of glass for you, Ted. What's the idea of it? "

" You may well ask! "

" More of Frank's notions? "

" Frank! " They both mentioned the name with scorn and hatred.

Geoff got down from the lorry and held out his hand to Ted; but Ted, holding his own hands apart, palm upwards, said: " I'm in too much of a mess, Mr. Geoff. I was trying to get a hold of a calf."

The driver was impatient. " What d'ye want done with this glass? "

" I reckon you know! " Ted said, and all three men laughed. " I ask you, Mr. Geoff . . ." Ted waved his soiled hands in despair. " What do I want with brussels sprouts? That's the latest! I got to grow sprouts plants an' caulies under that glass! " In anger he smacked his hands on his thighs. " So as Frank . . ." he said, and he spat, " so as Frank c'n send out my plants all the way round the farms, so as each on 'em c'n raise an acre or so of caulies an' sprouts. . . . It don't make sense."

" It don't make sense on my lorry," the driver said. " We got to get on. We got to get to London—while the Government lets us."

" The Government! " They spoke of the Government with the same voice as when they spoke of Frank. . . . It would not have pleased them to know that Frank, also, spoke of the Government in tones and terms similar to their own. " I got to get going," the driver said. " I got to get on my way."

When the three men had worked the cases off the lorry, down the ramp and into the barn, they came back into the yard and found Lizz standing by the door of the building whence Ted had come to meet them. " I can't do it by myself," she said querulously. Then, seeing Geoff, she gave him a little bob of the head, an uncertain gesture, while half a smile appeared on her anxious face.

" That calf," Ted said, and he started to move towards the shed. But he paused and looked back at Geoff, reluctant to leave him. So Geoff followed.

" We got to get going," the driver said for the third time, but Geoff followed Ted Foster; and Lizz, wiping her hands on an apron that was soiled with dirt, followed Geoff.

A long, long time ago, some celestial tuning-fork had struck a note whose vibrations had never been stopped. And now some trick of the scene or the moment opened Geoff's ears to the note. It opened also his tired heart as he followed Ted and was followed by Lizz . . . Here they were, the three of them, left from the past! Hadn't he rejected the past and closed his ears, for ever, to the tremors of that note? But he called to the young driver: " Shan't be a jiffy! " as he followed Ted to the door of the box.

The calves were plunging around the box, which was dark and smelt unpleasant; the man, the woman and the half-dozen young beasts being all intermingled in the gloom and sour smell. A part of the walls and bedding of the box were smeared with white scour, the source of the smell. " Get a hold of him, girl! " Ted was saying. And she did seem to be again a girl, with her colour restored and her cheeks ripe and blooming. " Get a hold of his tail, can't you? " And as Ted made a grab at it, he also seemed again the stable-lad, having shed his burliness, flatness of face, and furtive, sidling expression. " Got the little beggar! "

But the calf escaped once more and plunged between the others against the door of the box, the whole bunch of them huddling themselves together until Geoff's entry caused them to break away and stampede past Ted and Lizz, throwing themselves into a panic for the fun of it, skipping their heels and skidding and tumbling over and under each other. " I'll give you a hand," Geoff said.

" You'll get yourself all messed up, Mr. Geoff," said Lizz. She was holding a bottle of blue medicine. Her husband had his coat off, and his shirt-sleeves rolled up. And now Geoff, getting himself into the same dress, hung his coat on a nail in the wall, and found a bit of binder-twine and an old sack, and fastened the latter like an apron round his waist.

" Thanks, Mr. Geoff," said Ted. And then to his wife: " You'd best clear out of it, Lizz . . . for all the use you been to me." But he was grinning, and so was she, as she slipped past Geoff and stood with Charlie on the far side of the shut door, the two of them leaning over the top part of it which, like the door of a stable, opened separately.

Herding the calves into a corner, Geoff could see which one they wanted by the white smear on its back-end and hocks. Grabbing its tail with his right hand, he crooked his left arm under its chin and round its neck, securing it at once. The calf stood quite still while Ted forced open its mouth and poured the half of the blue draught down its throat. "Won't you give it an egg?" Geoff asked.

"Get us an egg, girl!" Ted called to his wife. And they waited while the woman, the girl, ran across the yard to the house and back. For those moments, while they waited in silence, and almost without movement, in the dark heat and smell of the box, the feel of the calf's tail in Geoff's hand, of the calf's ribs against his knuckles as he pulled the tail forward to stop the little beast moving, and of the calf's firm neck in the crook of his other arm—the feel of himself, welded to the calf, as if they were the two components of a living statue—these feelings were, somehow, just right. At last something was right, plumb right!

When Lizz came back with the egg, Ted crushed it in the calf's mouth and pushed it down the calf's throat. "That's right—shell and all!" Geoff said.

"The little beggar's mucked you up proper, Mr. Geoff."

"That's all right, Lizz. I saw a tap . . ."

"You'll come into the house and wash, Mr. Geoff?" There was more of appeal than invitation in her voice. "You'll come into the house, Charlie? You'd like a cup of tea or a glass of wine?"

"I would, Mrs. Foster; but I dursen't wait. We've quite a road in front of us." Yet they all seemed unwilling to separate; the past incident—which was scarcely even an incident in its own right—having struck some awakening, caused some little happiness, in each of their hearts. Like children, they smiled away from each other. "Well—thanks, Ted . . . thanks, Mrs. Foster . . ." said the young driver, as he swung himself into his cab, although he had no cause at all to express gratitude.

*   *   *

"Any one c'n see you're a chap as ought to be on a farm," the young driver said. "You got the know-how, you got the way of it, you got the strength. If I was a chap like you . . ."

The driver was right! One must start with whatever one possessed, not end there; not be reduced to it, not driven back to it, as a last resort of disillusionment, failure, self-disgust and degradation. One should begin from the establishment of one's modest security, in the way that one launched an operation only from a firm base. "Show me a sick beast!" he thought. "Show me a job on a farm, any job you like, a horse or a tractor to be driven, an implement to be adjusted, a pig to be gelded or ringed or driven, a calf or a heifer. . . ." With any such task a rightness came into the world, and the world diminished into this small core of rightness. What was done, and the way it was done, would be right. And what came of it, what followed—that would be right also.

Clinging, as it were, to this last security, this last hand-hold, his last hopeful belief, he was driven along the lane approaching his home, the Lodge. The young man was naturally driving fast, so that the ordeal of apprehension would be brief.

Not really fearing to meet Alex—or so he thought—he nevertheless took the trouble to persuade himself that the encounter was unlikely. He chased away her image beneath his closed eyelids.

With his eyes closed, he had felt against his shoulder and arm the pressure of the side of the cab as the lorry swung round the bend in the lane. It was difficult not to say to the driver " Faster, faster! "; but even if he had let the words escape, they would have been superfluous, for the lorry was already driving fast, fast enough, too fast. Geoff's knees hit the front of the cab as the driver put on the brakes.

So they had come fast round the bend; and when Geoff had his knee struck by the dashboard of the cab, making him open his eyes, he saw a group of those students from the Ministry College at the House taking a walk after breakfast. As the lorry stopped in the lane, the students broke and scattered into the hedge. They were running away, he saw, not from the lorry, but from the crazy blue and white heifer that came charging out of the Park gates, her head down and her heels up, like a bucking horse. She left a trail of blood through the gate; and since it was in the white lane that one first noticed the spoor, tracing it thence backwards into the Park while the heifer continued her charge onwards, the sequence of what happened was never distinct. It was never related to a pattern of time, never a progression of incidents, but more an emotional imprint.

From the hedge alongside the lorry, one of the students giggled and said: " Oh, boys, it's a regular rodeo! " And old Watts had come through the Park gates, following the heifer and shouting, not at the students or the beast, but backwards over his shoulder. His words were inaudible when they were uttered, because they had no context; but they seemed to get a response from a child's

435

voice and from a woman's voice, the voice of Alex. Afterwards his memory, as if it was a gramophone record, repeated the sound of Watts' shouting—" You get back into the house, Master Ralph! "

Full tilt the heifer came down the lane towards the lorry. " That beast—she's had it! " said Charlie, as he switched off his engine and jumped down from the cab. They had halted about forty yards short of the drive entrance, alongside the farm gate which led from the lane into the stable-yard behind the Lodge. Facing them, the hurt animal checked, swerved from side to side, skidded, stumbled, stopped. Uncertainly she stood in the middle of the lane, dripping blood from a torn and ragged teat. A number of students, with Charlie and Geoff, were now bunched in front of the lorry, a phalanx of defence. Some of them were breaking and tearing sticks from the hedge. And one of them, with a bit of an Irish brogue, was saying: " But did you see her lep that fence? Four bloody great strands of wire with the barbs on top! That's where she tore her tit."

" That heifer's blind," said Geoff; " in one eye anyway." He recalled then the wildness of her look when he had seen her the previous afternoon in her box. And it was pretty clear to him now that here was a half-blind heifer, always a dangerous beast, deprived of her first calf; and that she was one of the sort that took it badly, turning savage, not caring for her own life or for any other life, to get back what had been taken from her, her divine amazement, her first calf.

The bunch in front of the lorry scrambled backwards on either side of the wings as the animal, roused by some new urge that overcame her uncertainty, started towards them at a trot. She skidded as she started a panicky canter. " She's crazed," said Charlie. " That bloke with the beard's got guts! " For that student or teacher—the one who, yesterday morning, had been buying eggs from Alex at the gate—had now appeared out of the hedge, waving his arms and calling " Whoa, lass, whoa! " before she swung her Ayrshire horns and tipped him back again. The wide horns missed him, going each side of him, and she caught him in the chest with the poll of her head before swerving back and coming broadside, smack into the front of the lorry, as if she hadn't seen it. The wing tore a long flap of skin out of her flank.

Now she could hear her calf calling from the yard, beyond the gate by which Geoff was standing. That was the place to put her, for she was facing the gate, drooping her head, swinging it from side to side and lowing deeply. Geoff moved warily to the latch before he had heard the voice of Watts calling crossly from the yard: " Master Ralph, will you please stay in the house! " Alex was calling also. It seemed that they had all come through the house from the front to the back.

Before he had known this, and before—long before—he had heard Watts' voice rising sharply—" Miss Alex, get a hold of that kid! "—Geoff had opened the gate and had said to the students: " Let's put her in here! "

Before Geoff had actually got a sight of young Ralph, one of the students had hit the animal a crack on the rump to start her moving, and the man with the beard was running forward across the track of the beast, calling " Sonny, sonny, here quick! " and gathering the child like a football between his hands and stumbling with it through the gate. The heifer brushed him aside, and the child whimpered. Following the heifer, the students jostled through the gate, like a crowd at a spectacle, and Charlie was saying: " Come along, chum, let's pull out of it! "

" Give me a moment," Geoff said, " I'd better just see . . ." The words which had started automatically were checked. Despair raged over Geoff's head. At the bottom of despair there was no light or breath for thought, but only the blindness and suffocation of knowing that here was some sort of trouble, here in Neapcaster Park, and that here Geoff should be by instinct, by nature. But he was rejected. Again the master had kicked away his dog. For now, surmounting all other and lesser rejections, Geoff had been shown the child's face.

" We've got to get on our road; we haven't the time to waste." The driver was touching Geoff's arm, urging him into the lorry. " I don't reckon it's to do with us. There's plenty on 'em here already; too many, if it comes to that." As mazed as the heifer, more mazed because he had no single purpose or faith left, Geoff discovered himself inside the cab. " They wouldn't want us," said the driver, shutting the door. " We'd only be in the way, with all that lot there before us."

As they drove towards London, the driver continued to excuse himself. " Mind you, I'd ha' liked to have stopped. But I reckon the kid was all right, and where was the sense of it? That chap with the beard had guts, though, acting the way he did! He took a bit of a tumble, but I guess it wasn't much. I guess there wasn't any one hurt bad."

The words added themselves to the flow of despair above Geoff's head. There was no greater depth of misery and self-contempt. In spite of all that the Merediths had done to him, his heart was still fastened to their service. Unwanted by them, he longed with animal passion to be wanted again. Freed as he was from the old servitude, the allegiance continued to tie his heart.

But they did not want his allegiance. And now it seemed as if they had never wanted it. For when he had seen the child's face, he had heard again Ralph's voice—" Get the hell out of my sight! " And when he had seen the child's face, and had been shown Ralph himself in the nursery at Neapcaster Park, he was told again that Alex had lied to him. Even as long ago as that, even in her sleep, as the General was dying at the other end of the corridor, Alex had lied. For now they had shown him that it was not David's child she had been carrying, but Ralph's.

When they got to Shepherd's Bush, the driver said: " Here's where I go south." He pulled up, and they piled Geoff's baggage in the street. Shaking Geoff's hand with an air of liking and admiration, the driver said: " Glad to have met you; glad to have helped. Same as I said, any one c'n see you're a chap as ought to be on a farm. If ever you get yourself a farm, I'm a chap as could work with a chap like yourself. You c'n find me in Neapcaster . . ." He had driven off.

At this hour of the morning it was not long before a taxi passed.

" Where to ? " the taxi-driver asked.

" Anywhere . . . Piccadilly, if you like."

" You're the fare, Mister."

" Piccadilly, then."

" Piccadilly's a big place."

" Mayfair Mansions, then," Geoff said. He would deposit the miserable relic of himself into Celia's hand: the only hand he could remember that had ever been a hand of peace. Against his closed eyelids he tried to imprint her likeness. But it had vanished. Her particular features had been dissolved into her resemblance to Ralph. Yet he wanted her.

*   *   *

"Any friend of Frank's . . ." Mr. Spry murmured, looking doubtfully through his register. He was not in his office but at the reception desk. "Any friend of Sir Frederick's, of course . . . Boy!" he called to the page. "Take Brigadier Greenley to 386."

While the boy and the porter got the luggage into the lift, Geoff leant across to the bald head and rimless glasses, the serious, austere but sympathetic face of Mr. Spry, whose aspect and outlook were ministrative—an optician's or even a dentist's—and asked him: "Could I get hold of Celia?"

"Ah, I remember now!" Mr. Spry murmured; and the faint anxiety about his customer, which had previously seemed to make tentative his search through the register, vanished in a smile, not sly, but just kind and helpful. "I thought she would suit you, Brigadier; she's such a charming child."

"Can I get hold of her?"

"At this hour of the morning? I fancy she'd be asleep."

"Where?"

Mr. Spry's hands fluttered, as if above a case of shining instruments. "One supposes at her flat, Brigadier."

"Where is her flat?"

"I couldn't tell you, Brigadier. We wouldn't have any record of the private addresses of our hostesses. And even if one had the information . . . one couldn't very well, you know. . . ." Again he found it easier to conclude with his thin lips silent, twisted into another little smile of the inevitable.

"She wouldn't mind me," Geoff said, but without conviction.

Mr. Spry smiled downwards into his chest. "We all like to think that," he whispered. "But who knows? Who of us . . ." Shaking his head, he appealed to Geoff with perfect understanding. "Wait till to-night, Brigadier! Try and wait till to-night. She'll be here at eleven o'clock."

"Tell her when she comes . . ."

"Of course, Brigadier, of course. She'll know your name?"

"Of course!" He had spoken indignantly, but then he had to correct himself. "She'll know me as Geoff."

"Then that's what we'll tell her. You can depend on us to look after you, Brigadier. I know you'll excuse me a moment..." Sliding through a door at the back of the desk, he left Geoff to the page-boy.

★   ★   ★

They went up in the lift to the country of pearl-grey carpet and shiny wood. " And only this morning, in the station yard, I felt I was at the bottom of the pit! "

" And only this morning, in the calf-shed at Swire's farm with Ted Foster and Lizz, I had found a sort of happiness, humble enough . . .

" And only this morning, as we drove from Swire's to the Lodge, I got my hands on a new hand-hold, the oldest and lowest hand-hold, my last and most modest security, my last hope: ' Show me a job on a farm, any job you like . . . a calf or a heifer . . .' So they showed me a hurt heifer; a wounded heifer—and Ralph.

" And still it's only this morning; only eleven o'clock. And there's never a bottom to the pit."

When all the luggage was in the room, the plump little page-boy with the rosy, cherubic face went round explaining the gadgets, the bells, the taps, opening the doors and cupboards, twinkling his tight little body, his little white gloves. Going to the window, he asked, he saucily chirruped: " Open or shut? "

" Leave it as it is." Geoff gave him a tip, and though the boy went quietly out of the room, he could be heard through the closed door galloping away down the passage. And Geoff, opening the window which had a low sill, leant out.

The slightest shift, only the least adjustment of a man's weight and balance, would topple the human mechanism into real silence, making reality of the two notions—the pinch of dust and the bottom of the pit. Why wait for Celia? There was this other way to peace. It was so, so easy; but of course ridiculous. He actually laughed. Of course, he never had the least intention of killing himself; he was far too contemptible for that.

Nevertheless it was easier to kill a man than to kill the hours of daylight. Lying upon his bed, he watched the door, trying to see it open softly as the girl, graceful and hesitant, entered. But the image of her face was still absent. Picking up the telephone, he asked for Mr. Spry. " I was just wondering, Mr. Spry . . . I thought perhaps . . ." But the question was impossible. " Could I perhaps . . ." He had to ask for something quickly. " Could I have some coffee sent up? "

" Of course, Brigadier. You have only to ask for ' Room Service ' . . . I'll have you put through at once . . . No, not the least trouble, Brigadier. Only, of course, it's quicker to ask direct."

The service in this place was much too efficient, the coffee coming much too quickly. The day wouldn't pass and let the night come, bringing Celia to her duties. Beyond Celia—after she had come and gone—there was nothing. She had become the whole of destiny, the only peace. It was scarcely twelve o'clock.

On the telephone again: " Oh, Mr. Spry, perhaps . . ."

" Anything we can do, Brigadier . . ." Infinitely patient and obliging, and then with a twitter: " You have only to command."

" Perhaps if I wrote her a note . . ."

" Certainly, if you wish." The shrug at the other end of the line was audible. " We shouldn't know where . . ."

" She could get it when she comes."

" Just as you like. In any event we shall give her your message." It was twenty minutes past twelve.

At a quarter to one o'clock, he asked: " Oh, Mr. Spry . . ." And in final despair: " Could I perhaps have a bottle of whisky? " And Mr. Spry answered: " I dare say a half-bottle, Brigadier. I'll give you ' Room Service.' "

It came almost at once, much too quickly, and Geoff did not want it. One o'clock!

By the end of the day, all the parts of man yearned for Celia. She had not (in Geoff's mind) recovered her likeness but had become, instead, an emblem as full of promise as the token capping a dome, a spire, a church. On the flame of this promise the day had at last burnt out. Returning to the Mansions after a late dinner at a restaurant, Geoff went straight to the office. " Mr. Spry—it's eleven o'clock! "

Mr. Spry was slightly evasive. " I haven't forgotten, Brigadier, but she hasn't come yet." His hands outlined the uncertainties of life. " She could be a little late? " He made it into a question, as if Geoff could suggest as likely an explanation as he himself. " Why not wait in the restaurant? I'll take you there at once."

The waiters came wheeling through the tables, escorting between them the master himself, opening the way but sheering off as he, square and majestic, approached Geoff. Said Mr. Spry: " A very special friend of ours, Monsieur Paul . . . if you'd do your best . . ."

Monsieur Paul dipped his heavy white face and, with his elbow clamped to his hip, offered his fingertips. His head turned like a lighthouse, casting its beam into the shadows of the coveted corners.

His hand was hurled aloft. His index finger extended itself. His fingers snapped. The selected waiter came with a rush.

With waiters wide on the flanks, and Mr. Spry as rearguard, Monsieur Paul led Geoff into the deepest shadows, far from the orchestra. All held their breaths until Geoff was seated. All dipped their heads. "Monsieur Paul will look after you," Mr. Spry said. "Perhaps I shall see you later? Perhaps not."

Mr. Spry and Monsieur Paul stood at the latter's desk by the door and talked with a serious air. Monsieur Paul returned alone. "*Mon Général* . . . you don't wish to eat? Perhaps to drink?"

"Whisky!" said Geoff.

Beckoning the waiter on his mission, with the gesture of Craddock, the huntsman, putting hounds into covert, Monsieur Paul lowered his head. "The moment she comes—I will tell her myself."

"She's sure to come?"

"One must hope so, surely?" He bowed, he went.

The time did not pass quickly. Soon it became wise to ration the occasions on which one looked at one's watch. At midnight it seemed fair to send for Monsieur Paul and to ask: "Isn't she very late?"

With his hand extended and his head drawn back, Monsieur Paul examined a platinum watch at the end of a platinum chain. "She is a little late." He smiled, bowed, and was gone.

An hour or so later, one could ask again. "Are you sure she'll come?"

Monsieur Paul's head swung like a pendulum from shoulder to shoulder. "*En principe* . . . she'll come." He folded his hands together, containing within them the world's questions. "A lady can be indisposed." The hands separated with the formal gesture of a priest. "She can have a private engagement."

"These girls—they take private engagements?"

"They come, they go, as they wish." Monsieur Paul's bulk swung on its anchor chain to Geoff's elbow. "There is nothing else suitable? Not the small, dark one over there—Miss Susan?" Turning his eyes, but not his head, he considered Geoff's face, judging his measurements. "Not the one with the little red head?"

Geoff said: "There's no substitute." He couldn't very well add: "It's not a skirt I want, but Celia—peace."

And now the music, like a surgeon's fingers, was picking the

tender places. "This hurts, when I touch you here . . . or this?"
This tune they were playing now had got into strange encampments, crackling on the wireless, scratched out of gramophones, whistled and drooled by homesick soldiers. Softly the band played the soldiers' laments, as Hicks brought the letters to be censored. Said Jones: "Hicks—tell them to turn that bloody thing off!" It was a young subaltern getting rattled. "Let it be," said Geoff. "But, Hicks . . . give Mr. Jones a drink!"

The tune came softly to the table in the corner of the restaurant. As David had said . . . What had he said? Monsieur Paul swung at anchor while the band played. The image of a fireside or a garden gate, a slum tenement at the back of the gasworks, a patch of sooty cabbages slashed with pink by a girl in a cotton frock, a cushion of sticky flesh, or a wisp of hair on the cheek—almost anything of this sort, any memorial, any damned misery or self-pity, any image of dispossession, any promise of recovery, could be got from the song in the night. So David had said.

Shaking his head to Monsieur Paul, Geoff said: "I'm afraid not. No substitute!"

Mr. Spry came hurrying towards them, threading the tables with an air of disaster. "Brigadier, Brigadier . . ." he said in a whisper, containing his dismay until he had reached the corner. In his hand he had a slip of paper. "This is a dreadful thing, Brigadier. I don't know how to apologise . . . I promise you I shall take this up . . ."

"Is Celia . . ."

"No, no, Brigadier, it's not that . . ."

To this sort of tune, to this very tune, fading then and swelling and crackling, the men had written their letters which Hicks now brought. Hicks put the letters into the zone of the lamp, and swept away the crumbs with the horn of his hand, and clattered away the tin plates and the mugs. The tune came out of the darkness.

"You know a Colonel Levine?" Mr. Spry was asking.

"Very well indeed."

"He's been trying to get you, Brigadier. All this afternoon, as I understand it. He wanted you to ring him back . . . I know it's very late . . . but I'm told he was sounding most anxious."

Looking at his watch, Geoff said: "He'll be asleep, of course. It won't hurt to wake him."

"You can ring him from here, Brigadier. They'll bring you a

telephone. . . . I can't think how they never gave you the message. I promise you I shall take it up; I shall look into it . . ."

The slip of paper gave two telephone numbers where David could be got: one in London, before five o'clock; the other at Neapcaster after eight at night. The familiar and sentimental tunes worked themselves into a crescendo while the waiters fussed around Geoff's table, fixing the telephone so that he could speak to Celia's substitute.

*   *   *

It was Jessie who heard the telephone and pulled at her husband's bedclothes, waking him from his deepest sleep, at the bottom of unconsciousness, where his troubling came to rest. As he struggled up into the air, some reminder that he had taken with him to his profundities said: " It must be Geoff ! "

" Geoff . . ." He heard her yawn. " You didn't even say he was back."

" Of course you don't even know him ! " For as David opened his eyes to the grey infiltration in his bedroom, the fact that his wife and his friend were unacquainted seemed, of all things, the queerest.

" Darling . . . why should it be Geoff ? " Her voice was slow and sleepy.

" I asked him to ring me up . . . I was worried. . . ." As he awoke he remembered the precipice. He thought of the stranger, silently writing in his note-book, and the stick swinging with a thud against the metal leg. " That Food Man, the man with a limp . . ."

" Darling . . . that's too ridiculous ! " When he switched on the light he had to agree with her. The threat remained, but had lost its grotesque horror, its ghastly distortion. " Darling . . . you can't be worrying about just that ! " He saw her roll over on her back and smile; she was full of sleep, solicitude and love. " Darling . . ."

Angry with himself, he said: " Somebody's got to do the worrying in this outfit. There's enough to worry about ! " Diverting his anger, he added: " And what about your father ? Think of the headlines, the stink, if they choose to prosecute ! "

" Darling . . . forget my father ! " She yawned, she stretched. " It's still ringing, you know . . ." He was stooping for his slippers. " Though what Geoff can do about it . . . though why you should worry *him* . . . though why you should worry at all . . ." He knew why she was smiling and shaking her head. "You've always got to worry about something or other, haven't you? But . . . but, darling . . . I did say, didn't I, not to go to Frank?"

"Nor did I," David said. "I didn't *ask* him to bring the stuff—certainly not like that, like a thief in the middle of the night. He just brought it."

As he shuffled out of the room towards the telephone, he heard her sleepily calling: "Whatever you *do* worry about, darling, please . . . please, *not* my father!"

* * *

Geoff's voice by itself was infinitely reassuring, coming through the pallid end of a short night. "Listen to this!" Geoff said. There was a silence. "Do you recognise it, Dave?"

"Recognise what?"

"The tune, of course! One of those woozy tunes we used to weep about. Can't you hear it? Perhaps it's a selective sort of microphone they give you in these places."

"What places? Where are you, Geoff?"

"A sort of haunt, a dance place . . ."

"Oh, have you got a girl with you, or something?"

"The only 'something' is a half-empty bottle of whisky."

"You aren't drunk?" But he knew that Geoff wasn't drunk. He was just Geoff. And so David could say outright: "I need your help." There was nobody else in the world to whom one could say it like that—without any pretence, without even a laugh; nor was there any one else in the world who would give that quick intake of breath, of pleasure, when he heard it said. David told him about the man with a limp.

"I know about that chap," Geoff said; "met him myself when I was going round Swire's—with Frank. He may mean business; but from what he said—you, Dave, you can't have much to worry about."

"It's my father-in-law, Geoff. And there's other things too." But with Geoff's voice in his ears, the shadows had shrunk and the threats became almost harmless.

He said: "All the same, Geoff, I would rather like to see you."

"To-night?" Aud when he heard David's laughter, Geoff asked: "What are you laughing about?"

445

"The night's almost over, Geoff. Outside your haunt, it's grey, it's twilight, an hour from sunrise . . ."

"Nautical twilight, Dave?" It was almost a catchword, a code, amongst those who had been engaged in seaborne and airborne assaults. "Just say when you want me."

"Not here, Geoff. I'm coming to town to-morrow."

"By the nine o'clock train? I'll be at your office at eleven. If there's nothing else . . ."

"Nothing else in the world, Geoff." He observed without shame a queer kind of passion in his own voice. And with that second part of his mind which shone, like a spotlight from the wings, on the things that he did or said, he matched his answer with Geoff's first cry, almost of joy, when David said at the start, "I need your help."

"If there's nothing else, Dave, I'm a shade sleepy."

"Me also, Geoff . . . See you to-morrow . . . Good night."

When he got back to Jessie, she asked drowsily: "Is it all right?"

"Quite all right," he said as he got back into bed and at once returned to sleep.

*　　　*　　　*

"A great disappointment, Brigadier, about Miss Celia."

"It's of no consequence, Mr. Spry."

"I don't know how to apologise, Brigadier, about that telephone message. I simply can't think . . ."

Geoff nodded curtly to Mr. Spry, having finished with him. Briskly he went to the lift and upstairs to bed. He could not have explained his complete change of personality, accomplished almost instantaneously when, on the telephone, David had said in that well-loved voice, worried, distressed, "I need your help." But the feeling of elation with which Geoff undressed, telling himself to get a few hours' good sleep because there was a lot to be done to-morrow, the feeling that things had taken a turn towards their resolution, that he was involved in burdensome responsibilities, and glad of it, and quite competent to discharge them, and all sorts of feelings of confidence, strength and briskness which were quite unreasonable and groundless, and quite unrelated to his circumstances as he now knew them, this whole fantastic, flashlight change from despair to joy could not be justified by a brief exchange on the telephone with a sleepy friend.

"These things just happen. People are made that way." He folded his clothes neatly, with the thought of leaving them so that he could dress economically and quickly in the morning. "One gets sorry for oneself. The whole world has got sorry for itself: that's its trouble." Vigorously he brushed his teeth. "Then suddenly one feels that one can put things right. One has felt it before —in Algiers, after that evening with David; in India, in Burma. One gets into another world, another element, where all the proportions are quite different; and what seemed huge and ghastly a little while ago is suddenly worth a shrug and a little bit of contrivance."

He was in bed and stretching himself between the clean sheets. For a moment or two he was able to regard himself with sympathy and amusement, but not with pity, and was able to say: "You'd much better just admit that you love her, and that I suppose you always have loved her, though she hasn't treated you particularly well, if it comes to that, and though you seem to be badly placed a long way down a long list . . ." Now he could shrug and smile. "I've no doubt she'll want to use you again. I've no doubt you'll enjoy it. And I've no doubt you'll get another kick in the pants when it's all over. You're the sort of chap people kick in the pants. They don't think you mind it."

Before he fell asleep, he was able to smile—and now with pity— at the spectacle of despair, a contemptible sight, that he had made of himself only an hour ago and during the lifetime of the previous day and night. "It's not altogether unlike an overloaded aircraft, having a tough time getting off the runway, but then suddenly airborne. Once it ceases to be earthbound . . ."

Burying his cheek luxuriously in the pillow, he said, almost aloud: "Roll on to-morrow!"

In a very few hours he woke crisply and was under the cold shower, a little before eight o'clock in the morning, when the telephone rang. As soon as he heard the bell, he felt as if he had been expecting it. He recognised with joy this feeling of anticipation that had been restored to him so suddenly and undeservedly. It seemed that a few unruly hounds of the mind ranged wide, exploring always the most improbable misfortunes that might befall; so that when these things occurred, or lesser ones, they were not unexpected; they were not even unfortunate, but were like puzzles, problems, tests, pleasurably exercising one's resources.

In his bath-towel Geoff went to the telephone, ready for almost any encounter with the unhappy past.

"Geoff . . . Geoff!" It was a woman's voice, troubled. "Geoff dear, it's me, it's May. I've tried everywhere to find you."

"How *did* you find me?"

"Colonel Levine—he just told me. He said he'd been talking to you last night. Oh, Geoff . . ." She began to sound desperate.

There was a question left unanswered in his mind. "Do you know how David found me?"

"Oh, Geoff, I don't . . . I think it was Sir Frederick told him; I think it must have been."

"Him! How did he know?"

"I don't know, Geoff, unless he just guessed. But it doesn't matter, does it? It doesn't matter compared with what . . . Oh, Geoff—where's Frankie?"

"I haven't the least idea." He made it sound as if he didn't care either; but when he heard his own voice he relented. "When did you see him last?"

"Not since you did, Geoff; not since that night. Two nights and a day without a word . . ."

"So he didn't come back in the morning?"

"He didn't come back."

"He's done this sort of thing before, hasn't he?"

"Yes . . . yes . . ." she said doubtfully. "But somehow it wasn't the same. Somehow it was different; he had a reason, or else . . ."

He supposed that absence would be Frank's normal form of marital retribution. Anyway, he thought the matter of no importance. "Oh, well, I shouldn't worry. Have you tried Alex?" He found that the question scarcely hurt him.

But she could not hide her pain. "Geoff—I did try Alex . . . She says she hasn't seen him."

"She must have seen him," Geoff said. "It wasn't as dark as all that!" This tasteless joke was a deliberate trial of his own security.

"She says not," May wailed. "She says he never went there. Geoff, oh, Geoff . . . do you think she's speaking the truth?"

"I haven't the least idea . . . I shouldn't think so."

"Oh, Geoff . . ." It was a whimper, a gulp, a gasp.

"All right," he said; "I'll see what I can do. If I hear any-thing, I'll ring you back."

"Geoff dear—how good you are! It will be all right now."

"I don't know whether it will or not. I'll do my best."

"It will be all right," she answered.

*　　*　　*

He did not particularly relish so quick and deliberate a re-entry into the most hurtful part of the past, but he picked up the tele-phone at once and asked for the Neapcaster number. For quite a while there was no answer to the clicks which meant the ringing of the telephone in the Lodge. At length, an ancient voice spoke over an infinite distance of years. "Who is that?" he asked.

"That's Master Geoff, isn't it?"

"Nanny!"

"Oh yes, it's me, Master Geoff. I've had to come from Congle-ton, leaving my niece without a word; she being out when the telegram came." As always she rejoiced in her complaint. "All the way from Congleton I had to come; from Cheshire, Master Geoff; change at Birmingham, change at Cheltenham, and then here." The voice was unaltered by age, still intact, still gloriously indignant, serene, soft. "Poor little mite, he's ever so brave, just like his father, just what you'd expect."

"Nanny . . ." Now that he had been given the news that young Ralph was hurt, it seemed not unexpected. Doubtless the spare-man of Geoff's mind, running over the past and checking it, had acknowledged the possibility. "Nanny, is he badly hurt?" he asked. And while she was answering, his mind had out a patrol exploring the consequences of this new development. "How bad is he?"

"It was that cow, Master Geoff. You ought to have been here; you oughtn't to have let it happen. With you away like that, the mad thing came charging in at the gate, Master Geoff, and now all we can hope for is to save the leg. He won't ever walk level again, not with the best results. And Miss Alex . . ."

"Could I speak to her, Nanny?"

"I should think not! She's wore herself out, being up the two nights. She's only just asleep."

"Nanny—I'm trying to find Frank."

"Which Frank? Not the footman chap?"

" He was once a footman."

" He never will be anything else; he's a bad lot. Don't you forget what he went and did to that girl of Mrs. Meredith's! "

" Nanny—do you know where he is? "

" He's not around here, Master Geoff. He wouldn't be, would he? Trust him to make himself scarce when there's trouble about! " The voice went faint, as if the aged head at the other end of the line had been turned away to speak into the room. A man was saying something, coming nearer as he spoke and taking the telephone from Nanny.

" Is that you, Geoff? This is Trant."

" I'm speaking from London, Mr. Trant."

" I reckoned as much." The voice was even slower, softer and more solid than usual: a sign of crisis. " Things are in a bit of a way down here. That accident to the little lad—that's only the start of it. The doctor—he's away in London, looking after Major Bredon—they say he's terrible bad; and there's only a young chap here, holding his place. And on top o' that, there's one of those snoopers been here, nosing about; I don't like the look of it; chap with a dummy leg."

" Has he! " Geoff said. " I suppose he found that wheat? "

" There's no wheat here that I know of; I wish there was. But I dare say he found plenty else."

" He's been all around, that man has," Geoff said. " I met him myself on Swire's. He's been after Colonel Levine."

" I dare say he has . . ." the voice sounded weary. " That isn't the end o't, Geoff. That notice to quit . . ."

" Yes," Geoff said, " even if she wants to go now, I suppose she can't? "

" There can't be any question of moving the lad," Trant said quite sharply.

" You put in that appeal? "

" I did. But 'twon't be a bit of use. There's a Government paper come now; they want the house."

" Who does? "

" It seems the Government."

" I dare say Betts put them on to that."

" That's about what it is, Geoff. I shouldn't be surprised if that chap, Frank, had a hand in it."

" Do you know where I can find Frank? "

"I wish I did," Mr. Trant answered. "There's one or two things I'd like to say to him myself. He hasn't been seen around for a couple of days. Hasn't been home for a couple of nights."

Geoff asked: "Wasn't he at the Lodge two nights back? I thought he took Mrs. Meredith some sacks of wheat."

"Not that I heard of. We're desperate short of wheat."

"I thought he went along late—about ten or eleven o'clock."

You could see Trant shaking his heavy head when you listened to his slow, soft voice. "I don't think he did, Geoff. I was up here myself as late and later'n that. We were having a time calving that heifer—the one all the trouble's about."

The silence was brief but full of force. "You think I ought to come down?" Geoff asked.

"We could do with you here," Trant said.

Remembering David, Geoff said: "I can't get down before to-night, maybe late. I'll go and see Betts about the notice to quit."

"The sooner the better, Geoff."

When Geoff had ordered breakfast and had gone back into the bathroom to shave, he started to fit together the information from May, from Nanny, from Trant, and to couple the result with his promise to David. There might be a lot to be done in the course of the day. As usual, the service here was remarkably good: breakfast came quickly. And it was only a little after eight o'clock.

*　　　*　　　*

"Where would Mr. Spry be now?"

"Asleep," the waiter said; "asleep perhaps till eleven, twelve o'clock. Work by night, sleep by day." The waiter was a clown exploiting his foreign diction.

"Where does he sleep? In the building?"

The waiter pointed a finger at the ceiling. "There! Nearest to the sky—he has his suite."

Since the girl on the exchange refused to disturb Mr. Spry on the telephone, Geoff went along to the lift. There was a lanky lad on duty, not unlike the young Frank, the footman at the Park. Geoff asked him: "Do you know where Mr. Spry sleeps?"

"He can't be disturbed: that's what I mostly know; not till he wakes himself up."

"Of course not. Top floor please."

"Seventh . . . His room is right at the end of the passage, turn left." The lad grinned. "You going to rout him out? I'd like to see it."

"Come along if you like."

"I'm not looking for the sack, not yet."

A lobby, a sitting-room and then a door leading, presumably, to the bedroom, all dark with drawn curtains, unnaturally warm and stale, but neat, was signposted "Mr. Spry." To a knocking on any of the doors there was no answer; and no movement when the bedroom door was opened on a slight odour that meant the windows were shut tight behind the curtains. When one pressed the switch, the white light, in evil ignorance of the sun, made the scene ridiculous: Mr. Spry lay upon his belly like an infant, head turned sideways, cheek upon hand, sweetly asleep. The bald top of his head had gone pink. Without waking or moving, he said huskily: "I'm not to be disturbed; not on any account."

"Wake up, Mr. Spry."

"No."

"I'm in a hurry." Geoff shook Mr. Spry through the bed-clothes, and Mr. Spry sat up quickly, but with his eyes till shut. "Mr. Spry—I want your help."

"Oh, it's you, Brigadier!" Mr. Spry had opened his eyes and shut them again. "Didn't she come? I could have told you as much." He was not really awake. "She's not here anyway."

"If she were here, she'd open the window." Geoff did so himself and pulled the curtains. "I don't want Celia, not at the moment; I want Frank. Do you know where he is?"

"It's funny you should ask that."

Mr. Spry seemed to be falling slowly backwards on to his pillow. Pulling him upright, Geoff kept hold of his shoulder. "Why? Do you know where he's got to?"

"He rang up last night. Very late, it was."

"Where from, Mr. Spry?"

"I don't know, Brigadier. He just wanted some bags sent somewhere and some cash."

"Did you send them?"

"Of course I did." Mr. Spry spoke quite crossly. "To Victoria Station—Victoria Continental. He often does it. I suppose he's gone to France."

"Thank you," Geoff said, still holding Mr. Spry upright.

" Now I want you please to ring up his wife and tell her where he is."

" I don't know that he'd like that, Brigadier."

" Never mind. Just you do it." Geoff picked up the telephone and asked for the Neapcaster number and then, putting the instrument into Mr. Spry's hand, folded the soft fingers around it. " Don't you go to sleep till you've spoken to her! " he said. When he released the plump shoulder, the body toppled gently backwards into the bed. " Mr. Spry—don't you go to sleep! I can't stop to talk to her myself; I've got to get along to Sir Frederick Betts."

*   *   *

" I want to see Sir Frederick." Geoff was slightly out of breath from running up the stone stairs to Sir Frederick's chambers.

" Oh, but he's still at breakfast." The manservant was an effeminate little creature with a shadowy face. In the hall there was a seat or bench which he let his hand indicate. " If you wouldn't mind sitting down for a minute . . ."

" I know the way," Geoff said, walking past the man.

When he opened the door of the breakfast-room, Geoff was expecting nothing, but nothing was unexpected; nothing could harm or hurt; not even the girl's glance of non-recognition, so obviously genuine that it repudiated the whole dream as sharply and neatly as if you had put a bullet through the bulb of an electric light.

Sir Frederick pushed back the chair, wiping his mouth, holding the napkin to his lips as if he was faintly surprised, checked. The girl turned her head slowly, unstartled, indifferent. Now that Geoff had identified the feeling of familiarity caused him by her face and manner, he saw that the likeness to Ralph was remarkable.

Sir Frederick bothered himself with no explanations. He said: " Sit down, Geoff. Have you had breakfast? Do you know Miss Rogers? "

" I think so," Geoff said.

Simultaneously she smiled out of politeness and vaguely asked: " Have we, perhaps . . ." Completing the question with her eyebrows, she rose from her chair, as the hostess of the occasion, and went to the sideboard. " Tea or coffee? " she asked. " They're both here." In her pink dressing-gown she was a very lovely child; her morning face was as fresh as when she had rubbed it

453

on Geoff's towel, coming from the bathroom into his bedroom; her air as calm and graceful as when she had sat beside him on his bed with the tea-tray between them. But these comparisons and recollections were surprisingly painless.

He said: "Thanks, but I've had breakfast."

"A cup of coffee then," Sir Frederick said.

From the sideboard Celia asked: "You wouldn't rather have tea? I always have tea myself. There isn't any time when I couldn't do with a cup of tea, even for breakfast. That's the worst of America, isn't it; they just don't know how to make it, not decently anyway."

With slight malice, Geoff said: "Tea's a fine drink in the early morning or middle of the night. But coffee for breakfast."

She still showed no recognition. "Sugar, I expect? There's plenty. I don't know where Sir Frederick gets it . . . he always has lots." When she brought the cup across, Geoff saw—as he was meant to see—that as she passed behind Sir Frederick's chair, she put her free hand on his shoulder, sliding it across the crimson silk of his dressing-gown as she went, letting her fingers touch the thick red neck and end their tender journey on the shoulder nearest to Geoff. While she made this deliberate gesture, a sort of public protestation, she looked at Geoff with an expression of sweetness: an expression which, from any one else in a similar situation, would have been defiant, defensive; but coming from her, from Ralph, was pleasantly pugnacious.

Sir Frederick said: "Well, Geoff? You're staying at Spry's place, aren't you?"

"Who told you that?"

"Frank said he thought it possible—just in case I wanted you."

Celia said: "Was that where we met? I thought perhaps we had. Do you like dancing a lot?"

Geoff said to Sir Frederick: "Frank has gone to France?" He put it more or less as a question. "I gather that's likely to be convenient."

"It couldn't be more inconvenient, as it turns out . . ." Sir Frederick spoke so straightforwardly—in a slow but irritated voice, between dabs of his napkin to his lips—that Geoff could scarcely doubt him. "A shipment of potash went wrong; it got to Brest. And there was nobody else. Jenkins is sick, and Richardson is up north."

454

Watching Sir Frederick, as you watch your opponent in a game, instinctively judging his balance, Geoff said: " I've just been on the telephone to Alex's house—the Lodge."

" I must go and dress," Celia said; " it's really rather late. And my little girl that I left with my friend . . ." Trailing the words behind like a wisp of May's nightdress, she went through the door that could lead only to Sir Frederick's bedroom. Neither man spoke until the door had very slowly shut. Provocatively it swung smoothly and without a hitch so that, until the latch finally clicked, one knew that her fingers must still be on the handle; and even then she left her image imprinted on the panels, remaining there for the rest of this interview. But meanwhile, as soon as the door was closed, and the exclusion materially complete, Sir Frederick turned to Geoff. " You were saying? "

" I've been talking to Alex, Sir Frederick. It seems to me that we . . ." It surprised himself to find the ease with which the right words came; the wrong words being arrested and corrected between their conception and their utterance so that, for instance, ' you ' became ' we.' " That *we*, Sir Frederick, are being hasty, perhaps unduly inconsiderate, in our notice to quit just at this moment."

" My dear fellow—but it can't be effective till she's well on her way to Kenya."

" Her plans have changed, you know? She isn't any longer going to Kenya." He said it casually, being in no hurry to disclose his strength, since he regarded the thing as still in the stages of deployment. " In fact, she can't go to Kenya—even if she wants to."

" Her plans hadn't changed yesterday," Sir Frederick said. " Or was it the day before yesterday that I had that fellow Black in my office? I fixed up a certain amount of help for the two of them —financial help—on some pretext or other. An experimental farm was, I think, the notion."

" You regarded it as an inducement—almost an investment— having in view . . ." He didn't finish the sentence. It was often a good move to leave a sentence hanging loose, to observe the point at which the other man drew it taut again.

" Obviously it would make our steps to get possession easier, smoother, more considerate, if you like."

" You'd better get your money back, Sir Frederick."

455

Sir Frederick didn't answer in a hurry; he was lighting a cigar. With the match lit, he said: " Can't very well do that. He sails to-morrow—I had quite a job to fix the passage. She follows him later."

" No," Geoff said. " Not now. There's been an accident."

Sir Frederick got his cigar burning satisfactorily before he asked: " I'm sorry—is she badly hurt?"

" She's not hurt at all; it's the child. He's pretty bad."

" Poor kid!" The cigar was well alight. " In such circumstances the house, the Lodge, isn't especially convenient. One could probably help her to find . . ." His servant had entered, and Sir Frederick paused to wave him out again and to watch the door shutting behind him.

To cut the matter short, the moment being now right, Geoff said: " She'll appeal, of course. I don't know how it would go."

" Who put her on to that, I wonder?" Sir Frederick's lips very nearly smiled. He had a way of assuming omniscience that was evidently useful, enabling him to speed up a conversation without the appearance of haste. " It's perhaps fortunate," he said, " that the matter is out of our hands. The Ministry is taking over the Lodge—by compulsory purchase."

" Since when, Sir Frederick?"

" A few days ago—the final decision . . . I don't know whether or not they've yet served us notice. I can find out from the office."

" You'll appeal of course?"

" There's no appeal in these cases. They want it for the Principal's house—the Principal of the College at the Park." Sir Frederick's cigar was growing a satisfactory ash which he examined as he said: " It's that young chap with a beard, you know; a clever young fellow; I got him the job . . . The whole thing," said Sir Frederick, deciding to preserve his ash a little longer, " is most unfortunate."

" Have you tried persuasion?"

" Of course I have."

But Geoff, watching closely, believed now that the outright lies had started. " You tried Walter?"

Sir Frederick hesitated. One could not tell whether the conversion of his watchfulness into an air of cogitation was genuine or a deliberate deception. " I haven't yet tried Walter," he said.

"It's rather a last resort, you know. I'll do it to-day . . . this morning."

"You own his house, I gather? I gather you've helped him quite a bit—in one way or another."

Sir Frederick tipped the ash very carefully into his saucer. "It's very silly of young Walter to go talking about a thing like that. Personally . . . I had forgotten it. In no circumstances—none whatever—would I have referred to it."

"That's very decent of you, Sir Frederick." Geoff managed to make the words sound not sarcastic. "But you'll speak to him?"

"This morning."

"Of course," said Geoff, looking out of the window, "I suppose we're not on very good grounds with that particular Ministry at the moment?"

"That's a point," Sir Frederick said. Repeating the remark—"that's certainly a point"—he let his observation of Geoff's face become open, almost aggressive. "Frank told me," he said, "about a man with a limp; a friend of yours, I fancy?"

Geoff made no signal. Knowing that his face was satisfactorily blank and unrevealing, he knew also that this was a moment that mattered. Sir Frederick was looking at his cigar, but his eyes shifted to Geoff as he asked: "I expect you know him pretty well? Can you do anything with him?"

Steadily Geoff answered: "I knew him in the war. We were in Burma together."

"Old comrades?" Geoff received the question as if it had been no more than a comment. He said nothing, made no movement of his face and, out of some ridiculous scruple, was careful not to nod his head. Sir Frederick had to ask then: "Will you do what you can with him?" And when Geoff failed for many moments to reply, Sir Frederick had to add: "I'll do what I can about the Lodge. Everything I can . . . I promise you that."

"Good!" Geoff got to his feet. He had succeeded in telling no lies and in making no promises. To reinforce Sir Frederick, he added: "Let's hope we can stop a prosecution."

Sir Frederick had not yet risen. From his chair, while Geoff moved towards the door, he said: "Of course one doesn't want to make too much—in one's mind, I mean—of this threat of prosecution. We might have to help a farmer or two with a fine: Foster, for instance."

457

"It wouldn't be imprisonment?"

"Oh no, I shouldn't think so. One usually can get a fine. You know we retain Sir Philip? We'd take it to very high up indeed before any one went to prison." Sir Frederick rose from his chair with unexpected agility. He had spoken with his usual calmness, but now he had a grip of the chair-back, and his knuckles tightened. The red of his face was increasing. "By God! It wouldn't do the country any harm to have a case like that! A few decent little farmers, technical offences, damn-fool regulations broken for the sake of good husbandry. . . . One can almost read the reports of it . . ." He let his anger be spent, and then released the chair-back, raised his hands and dropped them again. "Just technical offences. That's all there is to it."

Geoff said: "In the case of Frank?"

Sir Frederick nodded. After a while he said: "I hadn't forgotten Frank. His case might certainly be a different proposition."

"And Frank is in France?"

"It's pure coincidence."

Inclined to believe him, Geoff asked: "He'll be back soon?"

"Sooner or later," Sir Frederick said, with a smile that was really rather charming. He held out his hand to Geoff. "Good luck to you," he said. "For my part, I'll get on to young Walter." Before he released Geoff's hand, he asked: "Mr. Spry—he makes you comfortable enough? Everything you want?"

"Oh yes; almost everything."

Benevolently Sir Frederick nodded his head, nodding it several times as he turned away and drifted back across the room, back to the door where Celia had made her exquisite exit. Geoff was left to bid his farewell to a broad back of crimson silk.

* * *

The adult sun made the conspicuous markings of the street pleasant to traverse: to enter alternately brightness and shadow, warmth and coolness, was a refreshing simplification. "Black's black, and white's white, Master Geoff; wrong's wrong, and right's right, Master Geoff. And nothing can't change them." One had to answer dutifully: "Yes, Nanny"—rightness being what she commanded, and wrongness her prohibitions; goodness being obedience, and badness disobedience, to her law of the nursery. "How simple, Nanny, for there to be only goodness and badness

458

—the brightness and shadow, clear-cut, of this street—with nothing intermediate!"

Contemplating this colour bar of Nanny's—as he walked slowly eastwards towards David's Bloomsbury office—Geoff smiled compassionately at the people who thronged Piccadilly and Shaftesbury Avenue. How would the old lady have divided them—the good from the bad? Looking into their hearts, as she looked so easily into a child's wilfulness—she being only and always a child herself —would it have been: " Well, that's the law, Master Geoff; that's what I told you, isn't it, and there's to be no argument!" Or did one hear her more clearly in the fashion: " It doesn't make sense, does it, whatever you choose to call it—law, regulations, restrictions, rations or anything else. Your own conscience, Master Geoff, *that's* the best friend you've got; *that's* what you've got to go by . . ." For Nanny regarded a man's conscience as a soldier was taught to regard his rifle. And Geoff now smiled, because the modern paradox—as presented by Nanny to the people in the street—of obedience to one's conscience being nowadays disobedience to the Law, and vice-versa, made him feel compassionate. Poor little Man had wriggled himself, with his poor little banner of " Progress," into a bit of a bog!

Now that he had got rid of his burden—as if he had slung away his pack, wriggling his arms and shoulders out of the webbing equipment—he was not surprised at his lightness of step and sureness of heart. It had happened before, quite often, this sudden and glorious release. " When David and I parted at Algiers, when the figs fell into the soup, and I went back to my billets . . . And the next morning I walked into the General's office—David's General —and he looked at me and said: ' I think you're the man I want.' And from then onwards . . ." There was no time now to complete the recollection: excitement was too intense.

" When they hit the bridge behind us, and I said to my Brigade Major: ' Well, there's only one thing for it . . .' The units were trickling back in no end of a mess. But David got through on the blower; and somehow or other, after what he'd said, I sorted the thing out until, a day later, the sappers put back the bridge. We held on, all right; it wasn't difficult."

We turn up here, up Shaftesbury Avenue. " That night when I walked into Ralph's bedroom at the Park, after David had broken his leg, and I meant to smash Ralph's face, but then I understood what Ralph was . . . It was the night of Celia's birth! And when I got back to the Lodge . . ."

He looked at the faces in Cambridge Circus, crowding the crossing. He felt compassionate. All were men: none good, none bad; but all made of the same ingredients, out of the same bottle, goodness and wickedness in solution; body, mind and heart; and none not worthy of love—not Ralph, nor Tommy, nor Frank, nor Sir Frederick Betts. . . . Nanny used to say so. "You must love everybody, Master Geoff, like the good Saviour tells us. Though, heaven knows, He's made it difficult enough!"

Through brightness and shadow, each refreshing, he arrived at David's office, aware that he had reached, or approached, no conclusion with which he had not started: no conclusions, indeed, which he had not brought with him from the nursery. "It's no good my trying to reach conclusions; it's useless for a chap like me to try to turn feelings and knowledge into thought and explanation: I haven't the brain for it . . . It's clever chaps like David who know how to think. But I can only feel—the same as everybody else; I can only feel and know—not think. I can only swim in the current—the flow of love. I can't explain it."

He smiled at the fuzzy little girl behind the door marked "Enquiries." "I'm afraid I'm rather early for Mr. Levine; he told me eleven o'clock. I don't suppose he's got here yet?"

"Oh yes, he has," the girl said. "If you're Brigadier Greenley, he's waiting for you. He came up early by car."

"Did he! I wonder how he gets the petrol."

"You may well ask!"

*　　　*　　　*

If there had been another way out of the office, David would have taken it. While he waited for Geoff, shame rose like a blush, as the sound of his own voice early that morning—calling to Geoff, crying like a frightened child from the brink of some imagined catastrophe—re-echoed back to him. The recollection of his own voice became the scream issuing from the guts of a boy when the pony fell over the hedge and lay rolling on the boy's stomach. This recollection, the brand of shame, was burnt for ever upon his hearing, mortifying his ears whenever shame was merited. But when Geoff came into the room, was actually there, taking David's hand and smiling shyly, shame was silent.

Yet it was not joy that David felt: his heart was too far twisted to be at once joyful. At the first impact, it was only reassurance, resignation, even the abandon of a wounded man surrendered to the doctor. The illusion that permeated the room, like the sterile smell of the doctor's accoutrements, was of hope. The easiest hope, readily accepted, was to forget that the doctor could be at fault, that his fingers were mortal.

During the years of their separation, David had let Geoff's stature become heroic. Absence, consummating their relationship, had ground up memory, true, false or exaggerated, into an idyll of fortitude and constancy decorating Geoff with all the virtues of the past gathered into himself like a monument. When Geoff came into the room, one looked again at the monument.

"How good it is—how good to see you, Geoff!"

The greetings that David and Geoff exchanged were wordless. The words that were uttered never reached to the mind for recognition, nor to the memory for issue later. The words themselves were meaningless, except perhaps they were spread upon the lawns like dew, encouraging the heart to thrust up young shoots and to gather over itself the brightness of new growth. Words bore the same relation to their greeting as the calendar to the coming of spring. The words "How good to see you, Geoff" could have been as conventional and empty as the avowal "I love you" issued to any woman when the occasion made it expedient. The reunion itself was inexpressible, being a change of the air, a restoration, a new warmth in the sunshine, a new freshness in the heart. A shaft of sunlight lit the monument.

Geoff said: "I think that chap with the limp means business. I think we'd better see Walter Wallis."

"I don't even know him," David answered. "Though I must have seen him, I suppose, when I came to the Park."

"I'd forgotten that. It's hard to realise, isn't it, that any one from Neapcaster doesn't know Walter? Where's the telephone book?"

While Geoff was finding the number and getting through to Walter's office, David sat back in his chair watching him and listening to him and extracting from his companionship a calmness which was already starting to descend like a coverlet of sleep. Into the telephone Geoff said: "All right, I'll hang on till he's free."

Hanging on was Geoff's art, as it had been the art of Guy, of Ralph, of the General, of most of the Neapcaster people. Nowadays the art was lost: men didn't hang on; they scuttled. But Geoff's bulk slid itself into repose in the chair that stood between the desk and the bow window. Down the telephone Geoff was saying lazily: " For the second time of asking—I want either Mr. Walter Wallis, or his secretary, or his secretary's secretary, or some such person in his office."

One could understand now, again, one's own confidence on that night of alarm and chaos, when one got Geoff on the blower, the radio, and sought for riddles in which to speak. " This is David calling Geoff, calling number one, calling Geoff . . ." One could not remember the actual words, but they lifted the battlefield between them and dumped it in Neapcaster Park. They spoke of Neapcaster places.

Geoff's voice crackled with atmospherics but was clear and close, as if there were no intervening enemy divisions. " Your message understood, Dave. We'll do what we can. Over."

" Good luck, Geoff! Over and off."

When David had put down the microphone and got up from the set, his General had said: " It's not a pleasant order to have to give."

But David had heard his own voice contradicting even his own thought, reassuring his General: " Geoff 'll pull it off."

Relaxed into the chair between the desk and the window, Geoff was saying to some one on the other end of the telephone: " Well, never mind . . . Tell Mr. Wallis we'll drop in—on the chance. Have you got our names? " He spelt them both out. Putting down the instrument, stretching himself out of the chair until he stood upright by the window and looked at the trees in the Square outside and at the clouds above them, he said: " It looks like rain." Opening the window wider, he said: " Yes, rain . . . rain, I think." Then he turned into the room. " Tell me, David, do we want rain at Neapcaster? "

Before the question had made its mark, David had answered: " We could do with it; there's rarely a summer when we couldn't on the Cotswold hills." But then, recognising his own astonishment, he added: " *You* ask *me* that! "

" It does seem funny, doesn't it? "

" All our lives, as I remember . . ." But he stopped, because memory this morning was skipping across the surface in its private game of ducks and drakes. " I was thinking of Neapcaster. Always —your first remark—you wanted a shower of rain for the young wheat, or you wanted a drying wind to get the scuffles working, or a warm sun to bring on the grass, or even a sharp frost to break up the ploughing—even that, even if it stopped hunting! But always . . ."

Shyly Geoff had come to the back of David's chair. He let his hand fall on David's shoulder. " Well, Dave—whose fault is it? Who told me to clear out? An evening in Algiers, do you remember, when the figs fell into the soup? "

" I remember the evening," David said. " I remember fixing you up with a job."

" You said: ' When it's all over, we've both got to clear out, cut ourselves clear of the past.' You meant that the past was bad."

" I never said that! "

" Oh yes! You said: ' We mustn't fool ourselves that we haven't come to the end of the old era, and that we aren't starting a new era.' You meant that the new era would be good."

" I must have been very drunk."

" Not much, not really. You said: ' If we don't get killed before it's over, we're going to be handed a promise on a plate.' You said: ' But it's not a promise of the past.' And you don't remember talking about ' the age of justice and truth '? That was the new age—that was *now*—you meant! And you don't remember saying how privileged we were, as soldiers, to have walked, literally, through the valley of the shadow of death? And that if we came out of it at the end, we should be . . . we should be . . . I forget exactly what."

David shook his head. " I don't remember . . . Too many soldiers talked like that."

" We did, didn't we . . . too many of us? Or too many of us have forgotten it since." Geoff returned to the open window. " It *is* going to rain, nevertheless . . ."

Talking to his broad back, David said: " What I do remember is—suspecting that you'd had a knock; trying to get out of you what it was; trying to break down your damned, stolid indifference that you put on like a pose, as if you hadn't just been shot out on your neck by the man who'd . . . been your greatest friend . .

by the man you'd served for the whole of your life. And you didn't seem to care; you didn't seem the least put out."

Without turning round, Geoff asked: "Was I really like that? I didn't feel like that. I felt it was the end of the earth, until you said . . ."

"Don't quote any more of it," said David. "It won't sound so good when I'm up in the dock—for a fiddle in the black market."

Turning quickly from the window, Geoff said: "You aren't going to be in the dock."

As they walked together into the street, on their way to see Walter, Geoff told David about young Ralph's injury and Alex's eviction from the Lodge. "Everything, therefore, seems to depend upon little Walter Wallis!" They had to laugh.

"In the old days," David said, "if I remember rightly, you used to ring the bell for the little chap."

"You don't remember rightly. One rang for Draper or Frank. Young Walter wasn't allowed on our side of the baize door, not by himself, not on any account."

* * *

For the benefit of the uniformed messengers and custodians stationed inside the door, they each had to fill up a slip, and there was some delay on the telephone, before David and Geoff could be taken up in the lift. And in the outer office, where an elegant young man and a girl were at work, they were given a seat. "He's just on the telephone," the young man said. "I'm his private secretary: I suppose I can't help?"

"It's purely personal," Geoff told him.

"Of course." The secretary returned to the desk in the window. He had a yellow silk shirt, a distinguished tie, a pleasing deportment. Under his friendly surveillance, David and Geoff waited in necessary silence. While he waited David found, returning to his memory, the conversation recalled by Geoff. The words were restored to the moment when they were spoken, and did come from himself; but now they seemed twisted and scarred with the grotesqueness that belongs, say, to a post-anæsthetic nightmare. At the time they were uttered—he excused himself—they were common enough beliefs; common, at least, to soldiers who had been long absent. But under the casual regard of the young man in the yellow shirt they sounded especially ridiculous.

In a little while the buzzer sounded, and the young man went quickly through the dividing door, closing it quickly and quietly behind him. When he came back, he said: " And now, I'm afraid, he's gone to see the Minister. I don't think he'll be long. He has a meeting in twenty minutes." Offering them a newspaper, he added: " I'm so sorry you've got to wait."

" It's good for us; it makes us humble," David said.

" I do assure you that's not the intention." He was still a little too young to recognise a poor joke.

Soon the buzzer went again, and David and Geoff were taken through the door to Walter. Walter stood up as they entered. It was a big room with a deep carpet and a desk beneath the double windows which looked on to the trees and lake of St. James's Park. The rain had started.

Coming to meet them, Walter took Geoff's hand. He held it, squeezing it for some moments, without speaking. He had a very gentle smile which seemed entirely natural. To David, he said: " I'm so glad we've met at last. I've heard so much about you, and I used to see you up at the Park when I peeped out of the passage windows into the courtyard . . . that great big car of your father's, sliding to the door like a monster! It's funny, isn't it, how such pictures stick? " There was a chair for visitors by the desk, and he went to fetch a second from a distant wall. When the secretary tried to take it from him, he said: " Thanks, Harry, I can just about manage it." Nobody ever laughed more naturally out of a pink, open face and grey eyes. His lips were small and sensitive, rather feminine, but his forehead was high and distinguished.

" You won't forget, sir . . ." the secretary said, concluding the reminder with his eyebrows.

" Ring them and tell them I may be late." Walter put on his horn-rimmed glasses to look across the room at the clock. " In fact, I may not go at all. Tell them, of course, to start without me."

" Yes, sir." The secretary put a slip of paper into Walter's hand. Taking it up and reading it, Walter said: " I see . . . I see . . ." before screwing it up into a ball and dropping it upon his desk. While he was reading it, David had turned discreetly away; but when he heard Walter say: " Geoff . . . Colonel Levine . . . I'm so sorry to have kept you waiting, but now I'm entirely at your disposal," David turned back to the desk which

465

divided him from the Parliamentary Secretary. On the surface of the desk, otherwise empty, lay the screwed-up ball of paper, the secret, as definite a barrier as a baize door dividing linoleum from carpet.

Walter took off his glasses. "In case it might help you," he said, "I have an idea what this may be about. A man of ours who came to see you—a man with an artificial leg?" He did smile slightly, but he shook his head. Obviously he was worried; obviously on their account, in their interest.

*   *   *

In a taut attitude, Levine was sitting upright in his chair. He spoke without any movement of any part of him, except his lips; yet his whole person seemed to tremble, like a wire tightly strung, or to quiver like the flame of a candle in a draughtless place, with the syllables of his low, dry voice. "I want to tell you, Mr. Wallis, that I have never before asked a favour of any one in high places. I want to say that when I have been in a position to grant favours myself—as I no longer am—I have been very cautious about it. But I think it true, and fair to myself, to add—that I am here more on my father-in-law's behalf than on my own."

It was a formal speech, evidently uttered with pain and effort. Hoping to relieve at least the man's tension, Walter answered as lightly as possible, hiding his own anxiety. "Colonel Levine, you will have guessed, I expect, that this isn't an ordinary routine sort of business?" Stooping down and opening one of the lower drawers of his desk, he took out a file of documents. "Indeed, we don't even leave the papers hanging about; not even in this office."

Looking at his two visitors, neither of whom answered him, Walter let the smile slide away from the edges of his lips, and finally from his eyes, until there was left only the anxiety, even the distress, which his smile had covered. To Geoff he said: "As much as any one, I hate this sort of thing." But he got no acknowledgment, no smile of affection or flicker of understanding from that phlegmatic face. This was the sacrifice one made to success: the loss of sympathy, of understanding, of the wish to understand, on the part of those one respected and loved.

"That snooper of yours," Geoff said; "he's not an ordinary snooper, I take it?"

Walter sighed: one had to accept the word "snooper" which had become common usage. He let them hear his sigh, detect his pain. Coming in spasms at moments such as this, the pain was too easily forgotten as one entered the office in the morning, or left it at night, looking with wonder at the place one had reached, wondering at one's self, one's accomplishment, as one scarcely dared to whisper: "So these are the seats of the mighty where I, Walter, now sit!" But now, struggling for humility, Walter said: "Try, Geoff, try, Colonel Levine, to see it from our angle, from the angle of this office."

But Geoff, leaning back and crossing his legs, answered pleasantly: "You're dug-in snugly enough, I should have said."

Walter laughed, meaning only to acknowledge a fair thrust, but hearing the sound he made as a stage response, echoing back to him unanswered from the anti-pathetic room. As the tremors died, he said suddenly, without thought: "You know . . . at least you don't know, because you can't know . . . that if I didn't believe desperately in what we're trying to do—the Government, that is—I wouldn't be sitting in this seat?"

While he had been speaking, his eyes had been fastened upon Geoff; but they had to flick across to the face of Colonel Levine, who answered him: "I do believe that. Without the least shadow of doubt."

"Thank you, Colonel Levine." Nothing could have been said with deeper sincerity; but Walter heard his voice, coming not from himself, but from the seat behind his desk, sounding unbearably pompous. Desperately he added: "So you do, at least you do understand?"

"Oh no, I don't understand. That would be something quite different. I don't understand how any one with your intelligence can be so mistaken."

There were so many answers to be made to this sort of remark when it came, in public, from a heckler at a meeting; but none of them to be given in private to a man whose reputation one respected. Smiling automatically, Walter asked: "Is it really as bad as that?"

Leaning forward, Colonel Levine answered: "It's worse, Mr. Wallis; it's a lot worse than words can express." He spoke softly, without anger, with his sensitive lips scarcely moving and his large, dark eyes fixed on Walter's face as if it was he, Colonel Levine, and not Walter, who had to cast understanding across the barrier of that desk. "You see, Mr. Wallis, you've destroyed the law. You could do nothing worse. You've torn the law away from ethics, away from a man's conscience. You've made it so that to break the law is no longer an anti-social act."

"No, no—I can't follow you there," Walter said. The argument was too familiar, leading along a route too well known and too unacceptable, to be allowed to continue in this direction. "You would say, Colonel Levine, of yourself as a farmer, that it isn't anti-social to produce food, when food is desperately needed; that, in your case, it isn't anti-social to produce eggs?" He paused, waiting for the nod of assent that was withheld. He had to go on without it. "But it is anti-social, isn't it, to break the regulations ensuring that all farmers get a fair chance of making a fair profit?"

"Certainly not," Levine answered; "not when the regulations themselves are clearly anti-social, unjust, ridiculous."

"This," Geoff said, "is degenerating into a political argument: very instructive to an ignorant chap like myself; but not what we came about . . ."

Walter sighed. "I had hoped . . ." he began, but he gave it up. Those who were not with him were against him; and with every word exchanged with his visitors, the desk between them and himself became more impassable.

The heads of the two visitors were now turned to face the door, which had softly opened. The young man, the secretary, entered gracefully. With his eyebrows raised, he waited long enough to make sure that he was interrupting nobody. "Excuse me, sir, but you won't forget . . ."

Walter said: "I haven't forgotten, Harry. . . . I shall be even later still, because we haven't quite finished."

"There's one other thing, sir." He stepped forward to put a second slip of paper on the desk. "This is the second time he's been through in the last twenty minutes."

Screwing up the paper into a little ball, and letting it drop on to the desk beside the one with which the interview had started, Walter said: "I suppose I'd better speak to him. Get him for me, Harry." As the door shut, he said to his visitors: "It's Freddy Betts."

"Shall we withdraw?" Levine asked. His voice sounded sardonic, as if the question had been launched lightly, but had turned itself, in mid-air, into a formal gesture, almost a rebuke. It was as if—Walter felt—Levine was declaring precisely what Walter was: a little boy out of the pantry, swollen with power; swollen like the fabulous frog.

"Oh no . . ." Walter managed now to smile. He wanted so badly to escape the rebuke and to restore warmth to the room. Even the warmth of antagonism was preferable to the frigid air which seemed to have seeped into it. "We get pretty practised, you know, at speaking guardedly on the telephone when others are present." He looked from David to Geoff. "We usually manage to deceive, and sometimes to intrigue, even our intelligent visitors, even our political opponents . . ." The smile on his lips which he felt to be pathetic, rather than the slight joke, did make both Geoff and Levine laugh politely.

Geoff said: "I doubt, Walter, if you'll deceive me on this occasion. I've a pretty shrewd suspicion what this will be about."

"That's more than I have."

"Haven't you, Walter? I wouldn't mind betting it's the Lodge at Neapcaster Park. They want to get Alex out of it, don't they? You know that?"

At that moment the telephone purred softly.

*   *   *

Geoff said quickly—speaking against the purr of the telephone: "I like old Freddy well enough. I rather admire him, Walter. But I know him for a double-crossing crook."

With his hand on the telephone, whose call had not been repeated, Walter asked: "What on earth, Geoff, has that got to do with the Lodge?"

"I dare say you didn't know that he promised not to kick Alex out? He's got you to do it instead."

"To do what?"

"To kick her out."

Astonished, Walter said: "But there's no question of kicking her out, because . . ." He had spoken too quickly. He did not want to hurt Geoff; and if it was necessary to cause him pain, he wanted to do it gently. Down the telephone, he said: "Hold him for me, Harry." And then to Geoff: "Have you seen her recently? Do you know about her plans?"

"Oh yes."

He got no help from Geoff's answer, or its tone, or his face. If Geoff had been hurt already, or was going to be hurt in a moment's time, Walter could never expect to know of it. So he had to ask: "Don't you know, Geoff, that she's going away? That she has plans to emigrate?"

"Not now she isn't," Geoff said in a perfectly easy voice. "Young Ralph has been badly hurt; he can't be moved; and of course she can't leave him."

"I hadn't heard of that."

Geoff said: "I'm not in the least surprised that Betts didn't mention it. He told you, no doubt, that Alex is going to Kenya with Tommy Black? He said that this morning, I suppose? I imagine he spoke to you before we got here?"

Letting his eyes droop to the pad on which his engagements were written, then rise again to the clock, Walter had to smile. "We haven't spoken this morning. I've hardly had the chance."

"I thought he'd be on to you, the moment you opened shop." There was a brief, unusual passage of expression over Geoff's face, and even a note in his voice, of surprise or puzzlement. "As a matter of fact, Walter, I've seen him this morning myself. He told me . . . a lot of things. But I wasn't such a fool as to believe most of it. . . ." When he hesitated, Walter thought it time to move his hand towards the telephone. But Geoff, as if he had forgotten where he was, as if he was giving an order, said: "Listen, Walter! Alex has to stay in England. She must *not* be turned out of the Lodge."

Walter said: "I really think it's time I talked to him." Without knowing what feelings Geoff nowadays had for Alex, he could not judge Geoff's motives and counter his insistence. "Harry— put Sir Frederick through now, will you?"

Perplexed, Walter heard Sir Frederick saying: "The situation has altered somewhat, Wallis. I think it would be wrong, indeed folly, to misuse the Lodge in the way you are considering it . . ."

"But, Sir Frederick . . ."

"I know very well, Wallis, that I did agree to it. I was mistaken myself." The tone of his voice now seemed to be changing towards a jocular kind of persuasion. "We can all be mistaken, you know—even the wisest of us—even you and I. . . . And I was mistaken in thinking I could run the Home Farm with Swire's. I now find I can't; it isn't an economic unit, you see, for various

470

. . . well . . . technical reasons. It wouldn't be right to disturb the existing tenant."

"You mean Mrs. Meredith?"

Geoff had risen and crossed the room to the desk. "Listen!" he said. "Will you listen to me, Walter, before you commit yourself?"

Patiently, Walter said to Sir Frederick: "Would you mind holding on for a moment?" Then he covered up the mouthpiece. "Well, Geoff, what is it?"

"Betts wants possession of the Home Farm." Geoff spoke tersely. "Under the new Act, Alex will appeal. Betts hasn't a chance of getting her out unless you take over the Lodge. You're playing his game for him . . ."

Walter shook his head. He remembered now, and only now, how Geoff, in his stolid, dogged, inscrutable way, could be sometimes mistaken, and endlessly stubborn in his mistake. Amongst all his immense, immeasurable, lovable qualities, and all his competence and dependability, one forgot this defect. He said: "You must really leave this to me, Geoff. You really must let me now talk to Betts."

Betts said: "The tenant does happen to be Mrs. Meredith. She farms it impeccably. Moreover, her child has just had a serious accident, and they can't be turned out. It would be a severe hardship, and there's not the least doubt she'd appeal—and would win her appeal—under the new Agricultural Act."

Quite sure of himself, Walter said: "That can't affect *this* Ministry, you know. Our decision is quite independent."

"You couldn't ignore the Tribunal's verdict?"

"We shouldn't have to. We shouldn't even consider it. It's another Ministry altogether."

"But surely there must be some sort of co-ordination, some . . ."

The frustration in Sir Frederick's voice was amusing, refreshing. With all his staff of contact-men and of experts at getting through and round the byways of Government, he could be a very ignorant person when he came to take unadvised action on his own account. "Not in this instance," Walter answered curtly.

"Well then . . ." Betts cleared his throat, a deliberate punctuation or emphasis. "I didn't want to put it in this way, Wallis, unless I had to . . ."

When Sir Frederick paused, Walter felt himself flinching. He

471

felt the blackness welling up as if, all over again, Frank was tormenting him in the pantry. He said evenly: "Go on, Sir Frederick. Please put it in any way that seems to you suitable." And as he said it, he glanced at Geoff. Geoff was watching closely. True, they were at the moment in conflict, he and Geoff; but Geoff's eyes were reinforcements. "Please go on, Sir Frederick."

"I only want to put it," Sir Frederick said, "that the child who is hurt so badly is General Meredith's grandson. Need I go any further? Need I venture to remind you that you do perhaps owe a debt, almost beyond repayment, to that particular family?"

There should have been relief; but instead, this trial by obligation was even worse than the threat which Walter had expected. With his eyes on Geoff, he answered: "I appreciate that, Sir Frederick. . . ." He felt a great need of breath and he drew it deeply and carefully so that the shudder in his chest should not escape to his throat and be heard down the telephone or in the room. "But I can't, I can't take it into account. I'm very sorry, Sir Frederick."

When he had put down the telephone, the silence gathered about him painfully, making him wish to walk out of his office and never return to it; to return instead to any obscurity. His voice was as weary as his heart when he said at length: "I'm very sorry, Geoff, but I can't, I just can't, on personal grounds, consider reversing a policy decision."

"Policy decision!" Levine cried. "You call turning a soldier's widow and child out of a little country house . . . you call *that* a policy decision!"

But Geoff was asking very quietly: "Did he threaten you, Walter? Your . . . house, for instance?"

Walter shook his head. He wondered, but quite without alarm, how Geoff knew the circumstances of his own house in which he lived free as Sir Frederick's tenant. "No threat," he said to Geoff. "He reminded me, instead, of the debt I owe to the Meredith family."

Levine said softly: "A timely reminder, perhaps!"

In Geoff's face there was at last an open expression of bewilderment. "I don't understand," he said, "how that comes into it."

"No, Geoff," Walter answered. In a queer way, Geoff's misunderstanding eased the burden. "But you got it all wrong, Geoff, somehow or other . . . Betts was asking me not to turn

Alex out; not to take the Lodge after all; he was asking me to abandon our plan for requisition."

Geoff said: "I never, never thought he'd keep to his bargain." It was one of those very rare occasions when a remark seemed to be extracted from him rather than deliberately spoken.

"What bargain?" Walter asked. But he was not much interested; and when Geoff only shook his head, becoming again inscrutable, Walter tried to untrammel himself from the coils of his obligations, his debts to the past, by opening once more the file that lay on his desk and by saying: "We ought, I suppose, to have a word about Colonel Levine and that Inspector of ours. After all—isn't that what you both came about?"

*   *   *

When Walter said: "I want you both to understand that we all of us hate this situation, but we are—after all—trying to break up a pretty formidable racket . . ." Geoff crossed the room abruptly and stood looking out of the window.

Walter said: "A lot of comparatively innocent people may have to suffer; because, as you know, this racket of Betts—and of Frank, especially, on his own level—is practically sabotage."

With his back to Walter, Geoff said: "I think you're talking the most extraordinary nonsense. I know quite a bit about the Betts concern, and I think they're as useful a job as there is in the country."

Levine said: "Geoff—you can't honestly make a statement like that!"

"David—will you please let me speak? After all, I brought you here!" Geoff spoke pleasantly, lightly, but without moving from the window. "The Betts concern—its farms—I should say they produce as much food per man employed, and per acre under cultivation, as any in the country."

Walter, astonished to hear this defence of Betts coming from Geoff, asked: "But at what price in corruption and in law-breaking?"

"Corruption?" Levine said. "It used to be a big, wicked word, didn't it? Now it's just a rather nasty habit, like picking your nose. And lawbreaking? It used to be unthinkable, didn't it? Now it's just something, like drinking, that one doesn't do to excess."

473

"None of us has the time," Walter said, "for this sort of foolish talk. Frank has to be prosecuted. That's the point."

"You may be making a big mistake," said Geoff.

Walter wanted to ask, he wanted to understand, why Geoff was talking in this way. But he said: "I'm not prepared to discuss it."

With his back to the room, Geoff said: "I wouldn't have thought it of you, Walter: after all these years, to be still harbouring old scores against Frank. I know he treated you pretty badly when you were both children, but . . ."

"Geoff!" To anybody else Walter would have answered such imputations with ridicule or anger; but to Geoff he expressed only disbelief. "You can't believe those things you are saying, imputing . . . You don't believe them, Geoff?"

You could feel the silence at work on Geoff, until he turned round from the window and answered: "No, I don't believe it. But, all the same, you're wrong to prosecute Frank."

Quite mystified, Walter said again: "That is a matter which I'm not prepared to discuss; not with any one outside this Ministry. I am, however, prepared to talk about the case of Colonel Levine."

"The case of Colonel Levine!" It was Levine himself who spoke. Whether his scorn was directed against this office or was self-contempt, was not apparent.

"What you call ' the case against Colonel Levine,' " said Geoff, " concerns, I gather, a few sacks of wheat."

Walter had let his nervous fingers play with the two screwed-up balls of paper that were lying on his desk. Now he unfolded them. It was an idle gesture, because he knew their contents; but he dropped the slip concerning Betts on to the floor and retained the other, the first that had been handed him. Smoothing it out, he read: "Six sacks of wheat; a seed sample, cleaned for sowing but without a Mercury dressing; believed to be spring wheat, of the Fylgia variety." Without looking up, he groped for his glasses and put them on. "They were delivered to your house, Colonel Levine, by Frank in his private car at 11.50 p.m. on the night before last." Putting aside the paper, he added: "The first of it had been fed to your fowls the next morning, before our Inspector called on you."

Geoff was sauntering across the room away from the window,

474

back towards Walter. Walter had a sudden feeling, a recognition, of heightened interest or even excitement in Geoff's movements. But Geoff's voice was casual enough as he faced the desk, put a single finger on its surface and asked: "Would you mind, Walter, repeating the time and the date?"

Referring again to the scrap of paper, Walter gave the information.

"You said it was a seed sample of spring wheat, but not dressed?"

"Yes . . ." Walter thought there was a smile—or something stranger, brighter than a smile—hidden somewhere in Geoff's face. He asked: "What do you know about it, Geoff?"

"I know a good deal," Geoff said. "In fact I helped to load that wheat."

"What!" Levine's exclamation was pure astonishment. "Why?" he asked.

Geoff answered: "It's irrelevant, but I thought they were going to somebody else."

"I'm not so sure that it *is* irrelevant . . ." Walter spoke slowly. This incident—he had felt from the start—had strange ways and turnings which were beginning to be discernible, as if a morning dusk over a countryside was melting into daylight. Speaking gently, Walter said: "You know . . . we do know that Mrs. Meredith had a good deal of wheat from Frank. He used to deliver it personally at the Lodge. I wonder if, on that particular night . . ." Nothing was yet clear to him; he was still peering and puzzled when he asked: "Colonel Levine, did you actually order that wheat from Frank?"

"No," Levine answered. "He just brought it. But I was glad to have it. And, like every one else, I have had it from him before."

"I wonder . . ."

In an irritated manner, David said: "I see no point at all in beating about the bush. I've no doubt he meant that wheat for Alex. But for some reason or other it didn't get to her; and I accepted it."

Slowly, quietly, Geoff asked: "I wonder why Alex didn't."

With great scorn, so it seemed, Levine turned to Geoff to say: "I don't see how you can ask such a damn silly question! Do you think Alex would have a man like Frank in her house after dark? She'd either have been asleep when he got there, or she'd have sent him packing."

In the way that one's eyes are drawn across a picture to the heart of the artist's vision, Walter found himself watching Geoff while Levine was speaking. He saw him nod an acknowledgment to Levine's answer. There was no other visible message; the rest was conveyed on the heart's wavelength. Almost too casually Geoff said: "I presume you know, Walter, that Frank's hopped it to France? Will that affect your prosecution?"

It was important and surprising news to Walter, but somehow it seemed of very little moment. It was trivial to some much bigger issue, still undetected, which—so Walter knew or felt—had just been decided.

*   *   *

Playing with his horn-rimmed glasses, Walter said: "It does seem very difficult for we three people to confine ourselves to the comparatively simple ' case of Colonel Levine.' " This time, all three men laughed together: the room was warm again.

Levine said amicably: "It might be a laughing matter, if it wasn't for my father-in-law." And the reply made their laughter unseemly.

Walter nodded in a manner much more serious than his feelings. Seriousness seemed to have leaked out of this particular problem. It had a hole in it somewhere. But he said: "The Minister is worried about it. He's seeing your father-in-law at lunch to-day. He may see the Prime Minister afterwards."

"This thing," said Geoff, "has got out of all proportion."

And Walter said: "Things have a way of doing just that—in any Government office."

"A trivial and technical offence—if it was an offence at all."

The word "technical" seemed useful; although in what direction its usefulness lay was not quite apparent. "Technically, of course . . ." Walter started to say. Then the clouds broke. "Technically, as I see it, there was no offence committed! As I see it now, Colonel Levine neither ordered the stuff nor ordered his man to feed it to his chickens. And this man, just finding the sacks in the food store, couldn't have known that it wasn't legally acquired."

Levine said: "He'd have been a dope if he hadn't!" And

476

then, in a voice that was almost disappointed, as if he was rather sorry to be too easily acquitted: "Of course he is a pretty good dope: a chap called Ben. You may even know him."

With relief, Walter said: "We can't possibly prosecute Colonel Levine. We shouldn't even have a case for him to answer."

But that strange, ridiculous man, Levine, had risen impatiently from his chair. "Of course that's a sensible decision, Mr. Wallis—as it would be in hundreds of other such cases! But one's got to come as high as this office to get even *that* much sense out of your Ministry! And the way out of it that you've found for me . . ." He threw out his hands in anger. "It's just a technical wriggle. Technically you can say that I didn't break the law. Nor did I— because I didn't have the chance! But given the chance, I'd have broken your law, and ordered that wheat, without the least hesitation. Because I don't believe it to be a right or a just law. I don't believe that the people who make and administer that sort of law are competent to make a set of rules for a kindergarten. And I know the whole thing to be damn nonsense and, if it wasn't tragic for a great country, just a comic opera!"

"So *you* are to be the judge!" cried Walter, gathering his breath for a suitable reply.

"Oh, God—they're off again!" said Geoff. And so they were.

* * *

Geoff was yawning and stretching out his legs. "You're the queerest couple of friends," he said, "that ever a chap had! We've spent the whole morning talking of crime and politics, and ending up—of all things—with love and the prophets! And doing it— of all places—in a Government office!"

Both men laughed at Geoff, and Walter said: "Do you know, if I couldn't talk about love in a Government office, I wouldn't sit in one? I wouldn't be in the Government. . . ."

"Even, Walter boy," asked Geoff, still laughing, "even for the two or three thousand a year they give you, or whatever it is?"

"Even for that, Geoff."

"I know," Levine said. "I know that, Mr. Wallis." They were all standing now, preparing to go. As they shook hands, Levine said to Walter: "I hardly know how to apologise, Mr. Wallis, for letting you waste so much of your morning on us. I really do appreciate it."

477

Walter must have pressed some button or other hidden beneath his desk, because the door had opened, and the secretary was waiting. "All right, Harry," Walter said. "I'm ready now. I suppose you warned them at that meeting . . ." They were smiling at each other, master and man, as Geoff and David left the office. They heard Walter saying: "The case of Colonel Levine seems to be concluded, Harry. I'm glad to say—wash-out!"

*   *   *

"Rum things happen," Geoff said. "The more I think of it, the more I see one's nearly always wrong about nearly everything." For some way along the street the two men had been talking more or less idly, sometimes keeping their thoughts to themselves, and sometimes letting them float out into words on the currents of friendship.

David said: "If you like, we'll get my car out of the garage and then, after lunch, I'll drive you down to Neapcaster."

Geoff said: "You're match-making, David, I gather?"

And David answered: "Not especially. I just imagine it's inevitable." In their present mood, and in their harmony of thought and feeling, almost anything could be said between them, and almost anything could be left unsaid and yet transmitted.

Geoff said: "Either way, I ought to get down to Alex. I shall want a bag from Mayfair Mansions."

When they got to the Mansions, Geoff said that he'd take only what he'd want for a couple of nights, and the rest could stay where it was. "I shan't be five minutes, Dave, if you don't mind waiting." He walked briskly through the lounge, towards the lift, but Mr. Spry, from his reception desk, summoned him with a low call and a flutter of little white hands. "Oh, Brigadier . . ." He crooked his finger. "I have news for you at last; a telephone message!" Geoff held out his hand, expecting a piece of paper; but Mr. Spry said: "Nothing in writing . . ." and leant forward to whisper: "News of Miss Celia! She wants you to ring her up."

"Oh, her," Geoff said; "I can't spare the time, just at present."

"Oh yes, Brigadier! I can have her on the line in an instant." To his assistant he said: "Give me Celia's number." And the lad took a black address book from under the desk.

"I thought you didn't know her number," Geoff said.

"Oh, well . . ." Mr. Spry shrugged and fluttered himself out of this exposure. "Take the call in my office, Brigadier; I'll have her put through to you." And with arms outstretched, as if he was herding geese, he drove Geoff into the office and shut the door on him.

Celia said: "Oh, Geoff, is that you at last? Mr. Spry gave me your message. Such ages since we last met!"

"We met this morning."

"Oh, no . . . surely not! Where was that?"

"With Sir Frederick Betts."

"Oh . . ." she giggled. "I *thought* we'd met before! I *did* say so, didn't I?"

"I think so."

After a pause, she asked: "Do you want to see me to-night? I thought I ought to give you the chance because, if not, there's a very special friend who wants to take me out." There was more giggling and twittering, as if some one else was beside her at the instrument. "He's a friend of yours too, Geoff. He said you had first call on me. He wants to speak to you . . ."

Frank's voice said: "Hallo, Geoff! How's things? Do you want Celia to-night?"

"I thought you were in France."

"So I was, but I've come back."

"I suppose you know they're after you?" Geoff said. "They'll lock you up."

"I dare say they will. But I'd rather be in an English prison than a French hotel."

"What's the matter with the French hotels? Aren't they just the same as any other hotels, only better?"

"I don't like 'em; I don't like that onion stuff they put in their food; I don't like the country. I never did." Over the telephone he sounded like a conservative old gentleman speaking from his fireside. "The immediate point is—do you want Celia to-night, or not?"

"No, thanks. Have you rung up May? She's anxious."

"Of course I have! What do you take me for?"

When Frank had rung off, Geoff was surprised and ashamed because, while he gave thanks that he had no longer any need of Celia, her services remained and always would remain an attractive proposition. He packed a bag quickly and hurried back to David, saying: "I'm hungry. What about eating, for a change, at a reasonably decent restaurant?"

*　　*　　*

Geoff asked: "And what, Dave, did it all add up to?" They were having lunch and were still talking about the couple of hours of the nation's time they had spent in Walter's office. David answered: "God knows!" And Geoff, with his mouth full, said: "I dare say you mean that literally."

After another and bigger draft of exceedingly pleasant hock, David said profoundly: "The modern paradox!"

"That's too clever for a chap like me, Dave."

"It's too clever for anybody. I don't know what it means myself."

"Love in a Government office," said Geoff, putting the best part of a potato in his mouth. "If you and Walter had your way, everybody would rush round loving everybody else, and the world would turn into a fine place for chaps like us! And so, I suppose, it might!"

But David had the fingers of his mind on a knot at which he had to worry and pick until either it came unfastened or his thought was distracted away from it. He said: "I just can't see how men can have love as their motive; love to a neighbour, of course; but not love to their neighbours collectively; not love for the community; not unless there's a war or something, and some great leader to lift them up, and then . . ."

"It always seemed to me," said Geoff, "that when that happened, you just got a sort of dictatorship."

"That's the awful part of it. . . . There *have* been great men; and so it's easier to believe that *one* great man can be entirely obedient to his conscience, with the motive of love, than that a million little men can reconcile their separate consciences and love their own multitude. Especially," David added in a bitter descent, "especially when everybody's conscience seems to conflict with everybody else's interests; and when everybody's interests seem, nowadays, to mean somebody else's deprivation."

"Now Hitler," said Geoff, "was undoubtedly one man and a conscience!"

"But his motive wasn't love."

"I dare say he thought it was."

480

"And I dare say those crowds chanting their *Sieg heil, Sieg heil*, till they ceased to be men altogether, thought their conscience was speaking! And I dare say those crowds at Buckingham Palace, shouting *Peace, Peace!* felt much the same thing! And yet . . ." The wine helped with its gracious simplicities. "The problem is such a simple one. All you've got to do is to marry together power and love—and you've got the answer."

They were sailing, now, with the tide of recollection. Rather smugly Geoff said: "I had power once, you know, in my breast pocket." He patted that pocket as if it still held more than his note-case.

"I don't think the war counts," David said; "it was different as a soldier. It was too easy then to be powerful with reasonable decency."

"I wasn't thinking of the war," Geoff answered. "I meant before that; and I'll tell you when I meant. That time before Munich, do you remember? Late one night when I found you and Alex in a haunt? It was just before that."

"I remember something rather vaguely," David said, speaking vaguely himself, because it seemed unimportant and irrelevant, and because the restaurant was now nearly empty, and the waiter was hanging about with the obvious wish to be asked for the bill.

* * *

"I suppose I must just call in at my office," David said as they got into his car outside the restaurant. They drove there in silence, because it was a condition to which Geoff was always partial, and David's mind was still involved with a knot to be unfastened. He was thinking: "My real trouble is, I can't get rid of my father. When a man's so long buried, he ought to let himself be forgotten!"

Dying, his father had gone away to look for love. But his father had found that there was no love for those who were without the law; and had returned within the law to look for love in the very place from which he had started.

Living and dying, his father had said, so often, that the laws of the land were the Law itself only when they were ethical laws, evidently just and sane, appealing to a man's conscience, emanating from love. It seemed to be a cruel circle. Without the motive of love, man could never even make an ethical law, let alone keep it. Without an ethical law, man could never arm himself with the motive of love. Man was too little to break out of such encirclement. Something was missing.

"You've driven past it!" said Geoff.

And David had to slam on the brakes and back the car for several yards to the door of his office. He left Geoff in the car and went in quickly. His secretary said: "I don't know where you've been, but I've been trying everywhere . . . And Brigadier Greenley —in case you knew where he was—they wanted him also."

"Who does, Miss Fox?"

"I'm not sure who it was, but it's Mr. Bredon's house that you're both to go to. As soon as possible, they said; and that was lunch-time."

Returning to Geoff, David said: "He's my trustee, of course. . . . But he also wants you."

"You know he's very ill?"

"I knew he was ill."

"Trant told me this morning that it was pretty desperate. He told me that little Mac has come up to London to look after him."

It was only a short drive from Bloomsbury to the area of Covent Garden where the Bredons lived, and they got there quickly. The door opened before they had need to ring the bell. It was Draper who opened it; and from the interior of the house the first voice that they heard was the voice of Anne Meredith.

Draper said: "Yes, Mr. David, it is, it really is, Mrs. Meredith!" He was an old man now, but he felt old only because the past became increasingly distant; the back end of the tunnel a smaller and brighter circle. He himself could scarcely recognise as himself the head, bald except for a thin white tonsure, the face, hollow except where the chin had folded itself over the lean neck, and the body curved forwards except where the belly hung downwards and out. Especially he could not acknowledge the diluted pigment of the eyes, blood-red at the corners, but otherwise almost colourless. All these features belonged not to himself grown old, but to an importunacy, a threat, which he would have nothing to do with.

Mr. Geoff, as usual, took his hand too vigorously, delaying its release when he let it go limp. "Yes, Mr. Geoff, you haven't changed at all that I can see. No, Mr. Geoff, it's not really surprising to find me here." It was important that they should understand the situation; they must not suppose that any ordinary occasion could draw him out of his retirement. "From Chiswick, Mr. Geoff—oh—a very comfortable little house, very convenient. . . . I've been coming in to help Mr. Bredon for several years now —just now and again, you know; perhaps for a dinner, or a little party or something of the sort. And of course with the trouble that's come to us now . . ." In their cage by the vase of flowers the love-birds twittered.

"How is Major Bredon?"

"It's a miracle, Master Geoff! Only last evening there was no hope, none at all. I'd quite given him up. And then, late that night, very late, he took a turn for the better such as we'd no right to expect. And this morning he asked for a steak!"

"A pretty forlorn request!"

"No, Mr. David! Colonel Black went out and got him one. He said: 'Leave it to me, Draper' . . . and he came back with it! It was the very last thing he did before he went to Kenya."

Hearing some one descending the stairs, he turned himself slowly round: first his body was twisted clockwise from the waist towards his painful thigh, then the neck could turn, and finally the feet shifted. The lighting on the staircase was poor, especially by comparison with the brilliance that flowed into the hall through the garden doorway, but he knew who it would be. Hearing a whispered inquiry, he bent, and slightly turned, his head to answer: "It's Mr. Barry, Mr. Geoff—the young one, of course; young Mr. Dick Barry; you'd remember him surely?"

He scarcely moved as the solicitor came past carrying his brief-case: solicitors, like doctors, could get for themselves their hat and gloves from the table in the hall. He heard vaguely and dis-tantly—for his hearing, like his vision, ebbed and flowed to varying degrees of clarity—the words exchanged between Mr. Barry and the two visitors. But he noted, with one of those shafts of perception which pierced his senses even in their foggiest states, the special attention, amounting to respect, paid by the solicitor to Geoff. And when all other words were confused, he heard, isolated into significance, the solicitor say: "I do hope, Greenley, you won't make yourself too inaccessible. I may have to get hold of you. . . ." And the solicitor let himself out of the front door and closed it softly behind him.

The occasion, for Draper, was wrapped in a happiness as peaceful and golden as the most beautiful of sunsets. All the familiar faces

483

were gathering about him in this house which, since the death of Neapcaster Park, had been the centre of Neapcaster resistance. Only here, in exile, the royalty of his world still preserved themselves against the terrible things that were being done to their kingdom. Within his knowledge, it was only here that the flame of grace and propriety was still alight.

"Yes, Mr. Geoff. . . . Mrs. Meredith had to be sent for—oh, yesterday morning. Major Bredon was most insistent that she be fetched from the Continent. She arrived only this noon, and we got the office—Major Bredon's office—to meet her at the station. There was no one else. We couldn't find you, Mr. David. And you, Mr. Geoff, though Major Bredon kept on asking for you—you were quite lost to us . . . an unknown quantity . . . The gentleman from the office had to go first to the aerodrome and then to Victoria."

But he heard her voice, so barely changed, calling to him: "Draper—who *was* it I heard coming in some little time ago?"

He opened the sitting-room door in the old manner, in such a way that the gesture of opening it became a slight obeisance, and the doorway was left clear for them to pass through it. "Mr. David, Madam, and Mr. Geoff with him." He stooped his head as they entered.

*   *   *

David first saw Mrs. Meredith standing by the fireplace, facing the doorway. In her hand she held, crumpled up, a little lace handkerchief.

It was probably the slight stoop of her shoulders that gave her the malignant look, more shocking than the merely negative signs of collapse. While her own glance was steady, David could not prevent his eyes shifting away and his brain, in panic, resorting to calculation: "Sixty-four . . . sixty-six?" She looked much, much older than that, her ageing being of the wasted, and not the cumulative, sort. When she threw up her head at the encounter, he saw the fangs of dry skin, one on each side of her throat; and since her action attracted to her face the light of a bright summer afternoon, his flinching glance was caught by the mapwork of wrinkles round her eyes and her mouth. Of course, she had been through so much.

Her hand quivered and felt frail to David when she took hold

484

ot his and said: "You've changed just a bit, David, as we all have, I expect." But he saw Geoff stoop quite naturally to kiss her cheek. By then, David could say: "I don't know how you survived it, Mrs. Meredith. What a terrible time you must have had!"

"You mustn't exaggerate, David! There was not what I'd call much comfort, but, really . . ." When she lifted her thin, stooped shoulders, it was a gesture which David recalled as clearly as his father's impatient exclamations. "That kind of German is so often so inconsiderate. But these—all things considered—were extremely correct."

As she spoke, her eyes travelled, not smoothly but in little jerks or twitches, through an arc like a submarine periscope's. She could not help this ceaseless movement. Nor could she brush away—as she raised her hand to the hair above her forehead—the thundery feeling that always, nowadays, made her head ache. Under her feet the floor moved oceanically, as if she had spent some long time aboard ship, in unfair weather, and had recently disembarked. Within these physical sensations her mind moved insecurely through a succession of objects, memories, impressions, few of which it was ever able to register before it had passed on elsewhere. "These two young men . . .

"These two young men! How that proud, dark person has grown out of all identity with timid little David Levine! But has he, one wonders, grown into Danny as yet? Does that pride hide visions as well as doubts, doubts of his visions . . . the doubts and visions that only I, Anne, could have known about . . . for it was to me, Anne, that he came, wasn't it, at the end? And it was I, Anne, who sent him back again—to die at home." She felt her lips trembling. "I said: ' Go back, Danny, to your own people.' And he had the impertinence to ask: ' Who are my own people?'" The trembling of her lips was private laughter. "I said to him: ' You go back where you belong—to Neapcaster, of course. We don't want people dying out here; it puts a gloom on us.' I never saw any one so happy!" She watched David move to the window: David was a much, much smaller man than his father.

Geoff had been asking about the journey, and she realised what a long pause she had let elapse between his questions and her answer. "Not too bad, Geoff . . . and not too good for that matter . . ." She spoke indifferently as well as vaguely, because really, these days, one couldn't bother very much about such things as comfort, not after that German camp and, even worse, the piggy sort of *pension* in which she had since had to live. " Definitely tiresome! " she told Geoff. Nevertheless, she was glad enough to come; because Guy's sending for her could only mean, one supposed, that the dear, muddle-headed man was going to find her some money at last. He could so easily, couldn't he?

" But I travel very easily and lightly these days," she said to Geoff. And she was thinking with pride what a fine, big man had grown out of her little Geoff, that curious, secret child with the inscrutable face, still inscrutable. Even his ugliness had great charm. " Yes! " she thought. " And I bet they find him attractive! I dare say he has quite a time with the young ladies. And speaking for myself, I should have been much, much more tempted by a person of his sort than by that wizened little monkey, Tommy Black." And as she thought of Tommy, she found herself lifting her shoulders again and telling herself: " But I oughtn't to hate him so! I oughtn't to hate him at all, not any longer. I ought to have grown out of hate . . . And I did it all with my eyes wide, wide open. . . ." There was somebody far more worthy than Tommy of her hatred; and he was upstairs now, ministering to Guy. But in course of time, there was no doubt that she would have to meet him. " And I do very much wonder whether or not I can stand it."

" No, David dear, I really prefer to stand. Once I sit down . . . such an effort, you know, to get up again."

Worse even than meeting the doctor would be meeting Madge. " She, without a doubt, will see these rags as rags. And will she, one wonders, offer me a cast-off frock of her own, as one used to do to one's maid, or will she be too tactful? Indeed I hope not, because I could well do with it!

" But I do just wish . . ." She could scarcely remember ever disliking the thought of anything quite so much, as the thought of going upstairs, in this wretched frock, to visit Madge in her bedroom. " If only I could borrow, just for an hour, a little Moly-neux number such as used to hang by the dozen in my cupboard at Neapcaster, and in my lovely villa. . . ." Meeting Madge and meeting the doctor! They were twin trials, if you liked! More than enough for any one!

Her last thought must have been preceded by her vision, through the open doorway into the hall, of the little man descending very slowly the bottom few steps of the staircase. His ginger hair had gone mostly grey and was the first of his features to catch the limited light. Then, as he stepped into the pool of light in the hall, she saw that his shoulders were stooped or humped like her own. "How I cried, how I wept, how I went, literally, on my knees to him . . . of all intolerable degradations!"

The lighting of that memoried scene never diminished. "And after he had had the impertinence to examine me, there on his couch, just as if he was going to help! And the insupportable pomposity of his words: 'There is a law, Mrs. Meredith; not only a law of the land, but a human law.' And the things he said afterwards, gloating, as it were, when I wept and pleaded. 'How can I treat you differently, Mrs. Meredith, how *dare* I treat you differently, from any other girl or woman in the villages whose baby is born in bastardy?' He was thinking, one knew, of that little girl of Adam Rogers. He was paying me out, I knew, for little Judy Rogers, who had died that year of Ralph's child . . . He hid it behind his pomposity: 'Not only a law of the land, but a human law, Mrs. Meredith.'"

She looked at the doctor with a steady gaze that dared not falter. He stood in the doorway in front of her, his face still capable of perkiness and aggression, but now subdued, perhaps with weariness. He looked slightly upwards at her with his tired eyes, and she saw that his skin was not furrowed or wrinkled like her own, except for two graved lines from his nostrils to the corners of his mouth—the stripes, she thought, of a renegade visionary, become a cynic. Her gaze fastened itself directly on his eyes, bloodshot under the rims. "How does he see me? What comparison is he making? At what precise point in the incident—when I came to him first, when I undressed, when I lay on his surgery couch, when I dressed again, when I wept . . . at what point has he regained his picture?"

The doctor dropped his head. He stood in the doorway with his clasped hands rubbing themselves together, as if he was washing them. The light shone on the ginger hairs between his knuckles and shirt-cuff. Every one in the room was watching him, and every one was silent. First he turned to Draper behind him and said something in so low a voice that no one could hear it.

Draper answered: "Very good, sir, I'll telephone at once."

Then the doctor turned back into the established silence which, with his own bearing, had already conveyed his message. It was Geoff who asked: "Mac . . . do you mean he's gone?"

"I'm afraid so. Just a few minutes ago."

"But he was so much better—they told us. He . . ." Geoff shook his head in that sheepdog way, just like the little boy in the nursery. "Wasn't it very unexpected?"

"No, Geoff, not really."

"Peacefully, without pain?" It was David asking that question.

There was a long pause, while the doctor turned his head to look at Anne Meredith, giving his answer to her, and making the answer his confession. "Without any pain at all," he said. And then, so that she should have no chance of misunderstanding him: "It might have been a terrible, slow business, terribly painful. But . . ."

Anne was shaking her head in an irritated manner. She wanted no confessions made in her presence. If the doctor had been merciful to Guy, although once pitiless to herself, she was only too thankful that somebody, sometimes, learnt wisdom. "I'm so glad of that," she said. She drew breath into her tired body. "But poor, poor Madge!" She was walking towards the doorway where the doctor was still standing. But he had not made way for her, and she had to halt confronting him. "Please, Dr. Macdonald, I must go up and see her."

He was shaking his head, and she had never seen a clearer expression of pain than there was now in his eyes. "I'm afraid, Mrs. Meredith . . ."

"But I must," she said gently. "I . . . her oldest friend . . ."

He lowered his eyes to say: "She herself . . . she's very ill, you know. I don't think that she ought . . ." It seemed to take a great deal of effort for him to conclude: "She oughtn't to, she can't, see any one."

It was then that the nurse came down the stairs, very calmly and discreetly. She glided graciously down to them, like a messenger from above. She was a messenger from the upstairs bedroom. "Doctor—Mrs. Bredon is asking for Brigadier Greenley." Her glance travelled from Geoff to David, as she wondered which one of them it was that her patient wanted.

Anne said: "Really, Dr. Macdonald!" But he still stood in her way. "If she can see Geoff . . ." The doctor was shaking his

488

head, a prolonged and stupid gesture. " I don't understand . . ."

" Nor do I, Mrs. Meredith." And now the doctor raised his eyes to meet her own. " But she won't see you."

" Won't see *me*, Dr. Macdonald! But why? But what possible reason? "

" You must forgive her, Mrs. Meredith. She is a little strange . . . quite ill, you know."

Geoff had his big hand very gently on her arm. " May I go up first? May I speak to her? " And she found that, between them, the two young men had led her to an arm-chair, and that she was sitting down, and that the room was rolling like a liner. Because of that dreadful, despicable tendency to break into tears, she had to pull herself very upright, purse her lips very tight, and look straight across the room, through the doctor, through every one.

*　　*　　*

" How could Guy have asked that woman to the house, when he knew very well . . ." Her voice rattled itself into silence like an old, dilapidated engine that has petered out. Her hand shook with her voice. She seemed not to realise that her husband was dead.

" We have had this out so often, Guy and I. . . ." Her face was very heavily made up; and since she was sitting in her dressing-gown in an arm-chair close to the window, and just on the edge of the entering beams of sunlight, the brightness made it appear that there were many layers of opacity on top of her natural skin. The powder showed its rough surface, and the patches of rouge had a more shiny texture. Her lips were orange. " Sit down, Geoff."

Geoff said: " I'm terribly sorry . . . we shall all be terribly sorry . . . all the world was so fond of him."

" I shall miss him dreadfully, Geoff." Her voice was now shaken with grief. " I don't know what . . . what I shall do. I can't . . . I can't think, dear Geoff, what I shall do." Then she asked: " Is that woman still downstairs? " It was like two incompatible instruments playing alternately: a comic turn by the clowns at a circus. " Is she, Geoff? "

" Mrs. Meredith is downstairs." He was able to say it quite calmly. " She seems very tired and ill."

" How can she dare to come here? " It was a plain question,

not at all rhetorical, wanting an answer. When Geoff shook his head, she said: "You know she's a murderess?" Geoff said nothing, did nothing. He looked steadily at Mrs. Bredon while the old lady raised her chin and stared at him with arrogant eyes. "You know that, Geoff?"

He said: "No, no, Mrs. Bredon."

"Don't you know she murdered her baby? Doesn't everybody know it?" With satisfaction, she added: "But she had to go to Nice to do so!"

It was the most terrible sickness that Geoff had ever seen. He wished that the doctor or the nurse would return, but he was shut up in this room, stuffy and hot, alone with this mad woman. The afternoon sunlight blazed on the window which was closed tight. She said: "You must have heard of it!" in a hard, imperious voice. And he answered: "I heard that she had to have an operation. Whether or not it was true . . ."

"True!" After this single word uttered on so high a pitch that it was almost a yelp, Mrs. Bredon shuddered again. Then she drew a deep breath, and seemed to settle into her chair and, in the course of a few silent moments, to draw a sort of calmness over herself, as if it was a shawl or a coverlet. At last she spoke quite quietly, in reasonable, almost maternal tones. "You must understand it, Geoff, because it is very, very important. You see, I'm no prude myself. I would never pretend to have led a blameless life. But there are laws of nature, Geoff, there are God's laws, that we dare not, dare not, dare not . . ." Several times she repeated those two words, as if the needle had stuck in the scratch of a gramophone record. Then quite slowly she raised a portion of the quilt which was draping her knees and covered her face.

The minutes passed slowly. There could never be any explanation. There could only be, for the rest of one's life, this fragment of extra knowledge, beyond anything that one had learnt in the hottest furnace of fear and sorrow, of the weirdness of creation. He had been shown an inner and terrible mystery: the cruelty and wickedness and insanity of which a good soul was capable. At length she lowered the quilt and said, in quite an ordinary voice: "You must be as kind as you can to her, Geoff, now that she's here. Poor creature, she's suffered enough."

"Couldn't you see her?" he asked, but regretting at once the question. And he was relieved when she answered: "Oh no!

490

That wouldn't be possible. But anything else . . ." She seemed to cast the matter aside, as she stretched out her hand for a book that lay by itself on the table beside her. " Guy wanted you to have this." She turned the pages, showing him the ancient print, but the binding was new in calf-skin and gilt. " There was a bit marked that I think he wanted you to read . . . but otherwise why . . ." She shook her head in the tolerant, amused, half-bantering manner that she had sometimes adopted towards her husband. And when Geoff took the book, it did seem to be only distantly relevant, if at all, to himself or to Guy or to their relationship. It was a history of one of the great English families, landlords and agriculturists, of the West country, written by a John Smyth in 1630.

" I wonder why . . ." Geoff said.

" Perhaps only because he was reading it this morning, when he rallied. Perhaps only because he was thinking of you at the time."

The book opened on a slip of plain paper inserted at a page where a few lines were marked uncertainly in pencil. " *And yet the golden mettle of this English Army of eight thousand (surrounded on each side with more than threescore thousand French, better appointed, and no less experience'd warriors) sodainly levied for this journey from following the cart and sitting on the shop stall, beat this French Army out of the field.*"

The words, of course, were boastful, in the way that it was pleasant and permissible and even wise to boast on occasion. And they were stirring, too. But there was no reason apparent then, or ever afterwards, for the feeling that the heart had been lifted up, and propped up, on to a higher level. It was as if one's house had been raised out of the danger of floodwater which had not previously been noticed. Misgivings never felt, or felt and forgotten and liable to recur, had been set at rest in advance. When he spoke, he expressed the only reason that he was ever able to give for his feeling of joy and fortitude. He said: " I'm so glad that he was thinking of me at the end. It makes me proud to know it; I was so fond of him. I see that it leaves me with a sort of duty, an obligation . . ."

She was saying: " He was most certainly thinking of you, Geoff. You know of course about the will he made? "

Not greatly interested, Geoff shook his head. " Didn't they tell you? He made it only this morning, when he was so suddenly so very much better." Geoff shook his head again. She said: "I am provided for, of course. But after that, it is all to go to you, Geoff. You see, there was no one else. I think it so suitable . . ." She might have been speaking of some quite minor domestic arrangement. And as far as Geoff was concerned, the news never —either then or later, on digestion—ever managed to have any real impact or to assume anything like its proper importance.

Geoff said: "That was very good of you both. I regard it as a great honour."

The old lady now seemed to be very tired. And it was with an obvious effort that she finished her mission by drawing from the chair in which she was sitting a familiar bundle of documents. "And these . . . I really forget," she said, "but aren't they yours, and wasn't Guy keeping them for you?" She leant forward, and either her body or her chair creaked and groaned as she stretched to put them into his hands. At once, almost automatically, he put them away in their old place, his breast pocket.

"I know about those," he said. "Only I thought, a long time ago, that I'd seen the last of them."

She was lying back, exhausted, with her eyes closed. Her complexion could not show any increase of pallor, because of its heavy overlay. But all the firmness had gone out of her flesh. Her cheeks were desperately shrunken, and tears were trickling down them at last. She tried to speak, but her voice, before it broke, could not even complete the single syllable of his name. He understood then that everything that she had of spirit and will had been spent on this interview. With a little movement of her hand, she sent him away. He found the nurse waiting outside the door.

The nurse said: "She's very marvellous, isn't she? The way she's taking it."

"I'm afraid I've tired her terribly. I couldn't help it."

"Oh no, you couldn't have helped it. She's very, very stubborn. And really . . ." she lowered her voice to a whisper, "though one shouldn't say it, it can't matter very much. She can't live very long herself, you know. And with her husband gone, I don't think she'll want to. She seems to have been so fond of him."

"She was very fond of him," Geoff said. "They were very fond of each other." And he went downstairs to Anne Meredith.

*　　　*　　　*

492

Anne was waiting for him, sitting in her arm-chair, and with her gaze on the door, meeting him the moment he entered. She had broken herself away from what was being said by the doctor and David, as soon as she heard Geoff's tread at the foot of the staircase or in the hall, and now she was to have her explanation. But when the boy appeared carrying a book, and she saw his face, she felt as if a spring of joy and pride had started to run again, after a long drought. "No—they can none of them tell what he's thinking or feeling. How could they tell? But *I* can tell!" And she thought: "Quite enough pain has been caused already to quite enough people. And my Geoff is very upset about something."

At Geoff's entry, Anne rose from her chair, saying: "Well, Geoff, I must be going. I waited for you to come down to say good-bye. What a time you were!" The few seconds that she waited for his reply were long ones. "Will he say, now, that Madge wants to see me after all? Will he have some sort of explanation? Really, I can't help feeling that it's due to me!"

He looked at the clock. "I hadn't thought I'd been as long as that!" he said. "Where are you staying?"

The doctor said: "I'm almost sure that Draper has made arrangements, if Mrs. Meredith hasn't."

She saw they had rung the bell. It was really, sometimes, very difficult to perceive exactly what people were doing, the room being so unstable, and objects splitting themselves into duplicates and even triplicates and sliding up and down their replicas. Casually, she lowered her hand without lowering her eyes, felt the back of her chair and gratefully rested her weight on it, supporting herself. "No, no, David—I wouldn't dream of troubling you." For, some time ago, some minutes or seconds, or a fraction of a second, he had said something about a car outside and driving her home.

Draper had come. "Oh yes, madam," he said. "It's all arranged for you . . . Oh yes, madam, at Claridge's." He sounded quite shocked that there could be any doubt either about the arrangement or the place. Dear Draper! She rather wondered who was going to pay the Claridge's bill.

"Now, Geoff, you mustn't be tiresome!" She had not actually said it—at least she hoped not—but she was not feeling quite strong enough to dissemble a great deal longer; and Geoff was being very insistent about her plans. "Very uncertain," she said to him, "just at the moment."

"I'll telephone you to-morrow."

"I shouldn't really do that, Geoff. I'm so likely to be out, aren't I?"

"I can leave a message."

"No, no, David!" she said quite crossly. For she found herself being led to the car—just as she had been led, such a long time ago, to the arm-chair—and being urged into it. But what could one do, with two strong young men, one on either side? Leaning back in the car—such a little car, too, after the monsters that Danny always drove—she said: "This is really rather pleasant!"

The doctor and Geoff were standing on the pavement; and before David drove her away, the doctor started to ask: "Mrs. Meredith, I wonder . . . have you lately seen any one of my profession?"

This was really rather more than she was prepared to stand. And she greatly enjoyed answering: "Dr. Macdonald, if you think you're going to get another patient out of me, you're very much mistaken!"

Just as they drove off, she saw the doctor smile to Geoff. It was rather a nice smile for such a nasty little man, but it was very quickly extinguished by himself, his own thoughts or feelings, as he said (as she overheard quite distinctly): "I don't know your plans, Geoff, but I've simply got to have a word with you. It's desperately important. Desperately important to me, that is."

"That little man," she thought, "he seems to be most determined to make his confession . . . Of course, it is rather fun confessing!" Groping in her bag for the little silver box, she took two of those pills which, nowadays, were getting rather difficult to buy—since those nice American soldiers had left her part of the Continent.

* * *

"Geoff, if I can't make you understand it, there's nobody else who ever will understand it."

"Shall we go back into that drawing-room, Mac, or shall we try the garden?"

"It's immaterial."

"The garden then." And to Draper, Geoff said: "Could we have tea out there?" Then he took the doctor by the arm and led him through the hall and out, by the french window, to the

494

short slope of the lawn. "It's funny, Mac, to find a garden here, right in the middle of London—or so it seems to me. Of course it's quite tiny, I see, once one gets into it. Just a strip of lawn, a flower-bed, some shrubs and trees; not much more than a decent-sized backyard; but seeing it from the house, one might almost have been in the heart of the country." He continued to talk in this lazy sort of way, because he was shocked to find the little doctor, whose fault had always seemed to be over-confidence, too much sureness and self-sufficiency, reduced to a state which Geoff had often had to recognise amongst men suffering from too many high explosives dropped too near them, and from too many months of attrition by loss, anxiety and fear.

"Geoff, ever since I lost Dorothy, ever since that man took her away, and she never came back, I've been cursed by uncertainty. Because I couldn't understand what had happened; because it seemed to be not human. You see, if she had gone off with Danny Levine, that would have been human, wouldn't it, too human? But to throw off all her decency, sensitivity, intelligence, culture, good taste, just as she doubtless threw off her clothes with that little beast . . ."

"What are you getting at, Mac?" Geoff asked the question quite sharply, because he knew that when these sorts of things were said for too long in that over-controlled, too-quiet voice, it led to some degree of hysteria which was less easy to check.

"Only, Geoff, that when I got my certainty back again yesterday afternoon, I had no doubts whatever about what I was doing. The doubts all came afterwards."

"You want to tell me what you did? Is it wise to tell me? Is it necessary?"

"I've *got* to tell you, Geoff. So many people were affected, and you in particular, you more than any one else, that I've got to tell you what happened. I killed him, you know?"

"I guessed that. You made it pretty plain to us all, I think."

"I wanted especially to tell this to Mrs. Meredith. But she was in no state . . ."

"She certainly wasn't!"

"But she had a particular right to know because, when she once asked me to do much the same thing, to break the same unbreakable law, I refused. And this time I didn't refuse. I wasn't even asked. I took it upon myself."

495

With slight impatience, Geoff said: "You must know pretty well what Mrs. Meredith would have said? One can hear her, I think. She'd have said . . ." And while Geoff paused, thinking, he found that he also had recovered his certainty in a peculiar way; that now his brain was so clear that it had split itself into two parts, the one watching and keeping guard over the other; that he could understand people, their actions, motives, strengths and weaknesses, with a sureness that he used to feel only when things were at their worst, when there was nothing to stop disaster and panic but his own will concentrated like a beam directed through a very powerful lens. "Mrs. Meredith would have said: 'Dr. Macdonald, you killed him. You gave him a merciful escape —and who can blame you—and there's an end to it.'" He paused, wondering for an instant if he really was as right about it as he felt. But he was quite sure that he could hear her voice. "And she might have asked: 'Isn't there too little mercy in the world already?'"

The doctor was nodding his head. Whether Geoff had been right or wrong, the doctor seemed to accept what he had said. This was all that mattered. With satisfaction, Geoff looked at the flowers, the lupins nearly over, but the delphiniums in full bloom. Then he noticed that the lawn needed cutting and, being still wet after the morning's rain, made dark stains on his shoes. No doubt they had been afraid that the noise of the mower would disturb the two sick people inside the house. But Guy would have been much more disturbed at seeing from the window that his grass had missed its cut.

"But that isn't the half of it," Mac was saying. "It was so much worse than I can ever make you understand; so much worse than I understood myself—until it was too late. You see, Geoff, he was in great pain; and when he asked for the truth, so very insistently, I thought it right to tell him. I said that he might live a few months. But, really, it was a matter of a few weeks. I said we'd make it as easy as we could. And he said . . ." He had to draw a very deep breath here. "He said: 'Go easy, Mac! I want to walk through the valley on my own two feet.'"

"I can hear him saying that," Geoff said. "What's more, he would have meant it."

"But, Geoff, he couldn't have done it. He couldn't have known, as I know, as any doctor knows, how the pain would have changed him, reduced him, until, towards the end . . . ." The doctor shook his head. " I couldn't have let that happen to so old and dear a friend. And when he told me that everything was settled, that he was quite ready to go—' All signed, sealed and delivered' were the actual words he used—there seemed to be no one else involved except us two; no other issue, except between his suffering and my conscience. Out of love for him, it seemed then, I had to do something that was theoretically wicked but morally inevitable."

Geoff said: " That seems right." And the doctor, anxiously, pleadingly, said: " It did, didn't it? You see that for yourself?" But he was talking now in an easier, less tightly controlled, less toneless voice. And now, when he continued, his words came quite crisply.

" I gave him his morphia then. It was a strong dose, but not abnormal for his condition. It was three-quarters of a grain, I think, but the nurse would have a record. Then we chatted till it started to work; only a few minutes, you know, before his voice began to get slower, thicker. Then I sent nurse downstairs for hot water, any excuse . . ." The speech was becoming more and more precise; it would have been unpleasant to hear for its callousness, if the symptoms were not so very familiar. When the man had given you his report, holding on to himself, holding on to everything while he forced his mind to operate at full throttle, with full power, for the few vital minutes, you gave him a stiff drink in the Mess, and, if you could, saw that he had a quiet night's sleep before going back to his unit. " When the nurse had gone, I gave it him. A shot of insulin, a lethal dose. Then nurse came back with the hot water, and I had to think quickly what to do with it, so that she shouldn't suspect . . ."

For an instant his grip slipped. But he took hold again, with only the slightest tremor, and continued: " You see, there would be no reason at all to suspect insulin. It could never be detected. It should have worked in about eight hours; the coma first, and then . . . just quietly, death. Just a slipping away . . . And it was important perhaps that I shouldn't be there when this happened . . . the end, I mean. So I left him to nurse and went to my club. Not much of a place, you know, but one gets a meal and a rubber of bridge. I happened to be playing with . . ."

Knowing the way to deal with a man when the thread was

slipping like this, Geoff let the yawn start before stopping it quickly. Never show impatience! Let the man see that he risks the loss of your concentration by losing his own.

"Not relevant, not relevant," the doctor said quickly: "but when I got back to Guy—after the bridge, that was—this *is* relevant. He should have been dead, you see. But he wasn't. Far from it!" One could see how the recurrence of the shock, as the doctor told of it, made the corners of his mouth twitch into a nervous flick of a grin. "Far, far from it!" he repeated. "Far, far from being dead! And as soon as Draper opened the door, I knew that something had gone desperately wrong . . . or was it right? That's what we shan't ever know, you see? Because Draper was smiling, and you know how rarely he smiles, and I shall never forget his actual words, because of the shock it was. 'Excuse me, sir, it's a miracle! Nothing less!' And he said, as I went upstairs: 'It restores a person's faith, sir, if I may say so.' Because Guy was sitting up in bed; he'd put on his spectacles; he was reading one of those old books of his, agricultural, I expect. He just gave me a wink. 'No pain, Mac, nothing! I've just had a meal; I've just had a drink. Feeling chirpy as a cricket.'

"Draper called it a miracle," said the doctor, "nothing less. But I knew too well that there was no miracle about it. It was just something that I hadn't read about in the book. But I have since! Oh yes! Though I needed sleep badly enough, I went straight to the hospital and looked it up. But he slept like a child, right through the night. It was most extraordinary, most unusual, most interesting. Do you know, nurse told me . . ." He checked himself with a gasp.

Geoff saw him clasp his hands so tightly that they quivered. "Yes, Mac," he said. "I think you've got to make up your mind whether Guy was your friend or your patient."

"My friend, my friend!" the doctor said with anguish. "The next morning he was like a very old friend, as we used to know him, ten, twenty years ago, jovial, joking, almost exuberant, twenty years younger than himself. He had sent for the solicitors, and the young man came just after I did myself. 'We're going to do a new Will,' Guy told him. 'I see now we must do things different. But hurry, man, hurry! You can't trust these miracles of Mac's '—that's what he said—' you can bet they won't last!'

"I knew by then," the doctor said, "since I'd looked it up in the book, that of course it couldn't last. That dose of insulin had just got to take its last effect . . ." Again the doctor drew in a great breath. " As, in fact, it did take effect a very few minutes after he'd signed that Will; a very few minutes after the solicitor had left. You, Geoff, you were in the house then; you and David and Mrs. Meredith. And he wanted to see you one at a time. He saw Mrs. Bredon first . . . we helped her in to him, in her dressing-gown . . . and then it was to be all of you. But the insulin got him first."

The doctor turned away and contemplated with such care the neat flower-bed, that he might have been trying to identify the various blooms that stood in the mixed vases of the house. Then he said: " The insulin killed him, as it had to . . . as he had to, anyway, die. And yet and yet. . . ." He had stooped to pick a pink. He smelt it. He put it in his button-hole. If one had not known the symptoms so well, his actions would have seemed incredibly callous. But they were, of course, the symptoms of shock.

But it was Geoff who was to have the shock. For there was a queer note of power in the doctor's voice as he said: " And yet it was only that lethal dose, it was only my action, that gave him back those hours of his lost life . . . his lost youth! It wasn't Guy, it was my injection, that made that new Will, that sent for you all, that . . . that . . ." He must have turned back from the flower-bed just at that moment. In turning, he must have seen Geoff raise his hand, as if he had a stick in it. Because he clenched his hands tightly and pressed them to his forehead.

Geoff saw the start of these actions even before he had finished saying, from the horror in his heart: " Mac, have you told me all this to *confess* what you did to your friend, or to boast of it?"

*　　　*　　　*

Mac was shaking his head. " This is no confession, Geoff. And certainly—God help me—it's no boast. It's information that you have to be given. If only I knew what language to speak."

" Try your own language, Mac."

After Geoff's last cruel question, he had taken the doctor's arm, to show that cruelty was not in fact intended, and had led him the few paces down the lawn to a sort of promontory where the shrubs which confined the garden had been brought to a point of pyrhus and prunus and purple nut, all copper and olive now that the blossom was spent. On the damp lawn pale relics of blossom were still sprinkled. Here, beneath an elm tree, in the bay formed by this projection of the terminal shrubberies, a seat was placed. The two men sat down together; they were directly facing the back of the house, looking up at the two tall, adjoining windows, the one with the curtains drawn, the other not; Mrs. Bredon still living, and Guy Bredon dead.

"My own language, Geoff? But where do I start?" He was able to smile then. By some trick of the afternoon, or of the movement of himself and Geoff down the tiny garden, or of the different aspect which they were now facing, he had got a new dominance over himself and over the incident. "Do you know anything about insulin, Geoff?"

Geoff must have shaken his head, relieved that the doctor was taking the chance to talk in his technical tongue; for a man talking in his own technical language was always coherent.

"Insulin is, of course, just one of the internal secretions, like adrenalin and the rest; but the one which affects the whole sugar metabolism of a man's body. A dose of insulin will increase the sugar consumption. An overdose will increase it to such an extent as to cause immediate coma and speedy death."

The doctor cleared his throat and continued to speak as if Geoff was a student under his instruction. "But a person who has what we call an idiopathic imbalance—a slight diabetic perhaps—may sometimes, but very rarely, react differently. For a short spell of time, the dose can have, temporarily, the reverse effect, to be followed by its normal effects only later. For a short spell of time, therefore, such a person could make use of his extra sugar consumption to get extra energy—a new loan of life. It must have been a loan of this sort that I, as a doctor, was able to make to Guy Bredon." But the doctor shook his head. "Unfortunately we shall never know for certain. Never! Because, you see, I never had a sugar tolerance curve done on him. There was no point in it, since I had no reason to suspect a diabetic tendency; and even if I had, the malignant growth had overtaken it."

"I believe I understand this," Geoff said in a very level voice. "The man who sent for his solicitor this morning, the man who sent for me and David and Mrs. Meredith, was not Guy Bredon at all, but a person created by an overdose of insulin."

"It was worse than that," the doctor said. "Because Guy Bredon sent for Mrs. Meredith before I gave him that injection. And I didn't know of it. It was only you and the solicitor and David that he sent for afterwards. And because of what I did, he never saw Mrs. Meredith. And whatever he meant to do to help her . . ." At last the doctor let himself crumple up and hid his face. "For the second time . . ." That was what he seemed to be saying, choking into his hands. "For the second time—me and her . . ."

Plucking at his sleeve, and at length pulling down his hand and then shaking him by the shoulder, Geoff made the doctor straighten himself. "Stand up, Mac!" Geoff got to his feet himself and got Mac facing him. "If I understand this right," he said, " and I think I do, your action makes me, *me* responsible for dealing with Guy's property not as I think best, but as I judge Guy would have wished it." As an afterthought, he asked: "You know about the Will, I take it?"

The doctor said: "That was why I had to tell you this. I witnessed it. And then I was made to read it. And then Guy said to me and the solicitor . . . we were together . . . he said: 'I don't want any doubt about this; no nonsense about not being in my right mind or anything of the sort. I'm sane as a judge, ain't I?' And we both said yes."

With a deep sigh, as if to say "Once again they've made a muck of it!" Geoff said: "Wasn't that your moment to tell him the truth? I don't suppose he'd have believed you for a moment. Who would? I dare say the solicitor would have had you hanged. But I doubt it. But at least you would have taken the responsibility for what you did—for exercising a doctor's power in the way you thought best."

The doctor answered: "Geoff, if I hadn't known how good and wise were the contents of that Will, I might have done it. And then, Geoff, at that time . . . not till afterwards . . ."

The doctor thrust out his hands and seized Geoff's two wrists. It was an awkward, ungainly, desperate action. He shook Geoff's wrists. "Geoff—I know you so well . . . for such a long time, I've known you, I've known, I've understood. . . ." He was shaking Geoff like an old-fashioned Nanny trying to get sense into a child. "I know how, all your life, you've suffered by being somebody's agent. I do understand it. I do see that when you came back, when you'd been away and came back, you had escaped, got out of it, at last. . . . And I do see what I've done, Geoff. I do see that I've pushed you right back where you came from. But I didn't see it till afterwards, till too late. . . ."

Geoff was shaking his head. Then he just put the power of his muscles into his wrists, so that Mac was left impotently shaking two fixed and solid rods. Then Geoff said an extraordinary thing, extraordinary to himself. "Everybody is the agent, the servant, of somebody or something. Everybody has got to reconcile themselves to that. It's how you exercise your agency that matters. And you, Mac? Whose agent are you, Mac?"

Mac dropped his hands and dropped his head. Speaking to his feet in the damp grass, he said: "I suppose I ought to answer that I am the agent of Medical Science, of a doctor's power. But in what I did yesterday I was the agent of my conscience, of my love for Guy, of . . ." Eagerly, like a child, he lifted his eyes and said: "Yes, that's it, Geoff! I was the agent of my love."

Geoff answered gravely, but not severely, certainly not cruelly. "Didn't your love do something very wrong? Had you got the right to make it say one thing one year and something quite the contrary ten, fifteen years later? One thing to Mrs. Meredith, another thing to me and Guy Bredon?"

Still like a child, the doctor looked up at Geoff and said: "No, I hadn't got the right. And now it's left to you, Geoff, to do what you can. . . ."

But Geoff was already nodding his head. "Oh yes, I shall have to see what's the best thing to do, I suppose. . . . Here's Draper! He's taken rather a time getting tea, hasn't he?"

Draper was carrying the pretty china and the exquisitely polished silver on a collapsible table. As he set it up by the seat, he said: "Mr. David has been back some few minutes. He wouldn't come out, Mr. Geoff; he didn't want to interrupt. He wouldn't take tea, Mr. Geoff; he seemed rather anxious to be off."

Geoff said: "Mac, I'll leave the tea to you. David is driving me down to Neapcaster." He nodded in a friendly way and crossed the little lawn with brisk steps and went into the house. He stopped and turned at the french window, in order to call back: "I take it you'll be down yourself, Mac, some time to-night? Alex is needing you pretty badly, you know—that terrible accident to poor young Ralph."

*　　*　　*

They were driving homewards, mostly in silence. They both felt battered by the day's tides; and during the journey David said: "Anne Meredith, when I got to Claridge's . . ." But some feeling that Geoff, also, was labouring under too many burdens made him keep this one to himself. And Geoff asked no questions.

A fair way farther on, David said: "I feel like a chap who's been running or swimming in a very long race."

This time Geoff answered, saying: "I think I feel like a man who's carrying too much weight." He also felt very humble, like a little, ordinary man of whom every one is asking and expecting too much. And in this role he was neither complaining nor disposed to give in. On the contrary, he had a quite groundless feeling, and a quite unreasoned determination, that everything was going to be all right. He was just in a sullen, stupid, dogged sort of mood, ready to plod on and to carry whatever anybody chose to pile on his shoulders, but not to accept the extra obligation of giving it thought. And if he could have been asked what, of all miraculous wishes, was his greatest, and if he could have discovered the answer and given it truthfully—impossible conditions, these—he might have said: "Please, to be a small boy again for half an hour, to be able to burst into tears and to be comforted!" But the prohibition against weeping was, of course, amongst the burdens on his back.

Every quarter of an hour, every ten minutes or so, either he or David spoke; and presently he asked a question which, a long way farther on, David answered. "I'm quite sure she'll marry you," David said. It was a soft bright evening, and the wind that blew on their foreheads through the open roof and windows of the car was soft.

Geoff said: "Do you mean, Dave, that she's more or less *got* to marry me; that she hasn't much choice?"

"I didn't mean that at all," David said, taking the roundabout too fast. But when he was on the straight road again, he admitted privately that Geoff had expressed his thoughts. And when he had transformed this admission into the features and form, voice and presence, of Alex herself, it made him glad, but ashamed of his gladness.

"But it isn't really so," Geoff was saying, "because that thing I was trying to tell you about, that thing before Munich . . ." and he tapped his breast pocket as he had done after lunch, "it's cropped up again and it means she's quite rich. And that being so, Dave— and she having no need now to marry me or anybody else—do you still think . . ."

"Oh yes," David said. But they were getting into High

Wycombe, along the fast road from Beaconsfield, before he added: "I'm quite sure of it." And he was sure, now, that this answer was the truth. In spite of the sadness, and even the jealousy, that it caused him to admit that he himself could be quite replaced in Alex's heart, there was only this one feature of their whole complex pattern—this long runner of a rug into which they were all interwoven beneath the trampling feet of fate—that had the distinctive colour of truth: the threads of Alex and Geoff had surely met.

*   *   *

In a little while, when they were traversing the dismal straggle that was the outskirts of High Wycombe, David said: "These ghastly little houses!" It was probable that he was referring less to this particular district than to all the rows and rows of similar dwellings throughout the land, or perhaps throughout the civilised world, for he added: "Squalid or smug!" and then shut up. And nobody could avoid thinking of all those houses joined to each other, or almost joined, foul in the slums or trim in the suburbs, but—whichever it was—making a prison that was harsher even than their walls, separating those who lived within from their natural authority without. David said: "And we have to be governed by people who live like that!"

And Geoff knew him well enough, and was enough in agreement, to add silently: "When they themselves can't be governed by God!" For how could any one be reached by God without the freedom of air and earth? But he had Guy's book in his lap, and the marker was still inside, making it open at the same place. So he said: "This must be about the last thing that Guy ever marked as worth reading." And he read out the passage: "'And yet the golden mettle of this English Army sodainly levied for this journey from following the cart and sitting on the shop stall ....'"

David said: "We're always writing about ourselves like that. But nobody doubts they can fight—least of all the chaps like you and me who've seen too much of it. But we aren't asking them to fight any longer. We're expecting them to govern us." Some way farther on, he added: "At least, that's what Walter's expecting. And he's expecting them to do so with the motive of love!"

And although David said no more, Geoff knew that he was back on the old argument, hankering for his dictator, but of course unwilling to admit it. For David still believed that a mortal man, with the motive of love, the law of his conscience, could safely be left as a law unto himself. David had not heard, and could not be told, the doctor's story. So they drove on, pursuing in silence their separate speculations.

Then Geoff heard himself inquiring: "Why aren't we asking them to fight any longer?" The answer to which was: "Because there isn't anybody to fight against. There isn't any longer any enemy." He doubted that answer. And anybody else who had fought the Japs might equally doubt it. You couldn't always expect to be able to see or pinpoint your enemy. And when you seemed to be suffering one defeat after another, there was obviously somebody fighting you. There was obviously an enemy somewhere or other; obviously an unknown battlefield.

"I suppose," said David, "that every wretched chap is his own enemy. If he hasn't got any one else to fight, he is his own miserable battlefield."

To Geoff it seemed one of those unsatisfactory answers that belonged to the pulpit, being probably true but without a place in the ordinary person's pack of troubles. But as he dozed off under the soporific of their journey, the remark seemed a comforting thing for the mind to play with indolently, in the way the jaws of Americans occupied themselves with a stick of gum.

They drove for a great many miles without talking at all. They were well into the Cotswolds, and the evening twilight had begun, when Geoff was jolted forwards out of a doze as David put on the brakes. "What's up?" But by the time he had asked the question, he could see the fox-cub standing impertinently in the middle of the road and then flattening its body and sliding away into the cover of the verge. David had stalled the engine; and through the lovely quiet of the evening they could hear partridges calling in the standing corn: no doubt a pair of old birds and their brood of young.

"Foxes, partridges!" David said. "That's us! Chivied about by Craddock with the earths stopped; or driven by Flower and his merry men over the hedge—and finish!" His voice was calm and quiet; but it seemed that the whispers of the evening that were silence, the scents of the evening that were the earth's promise, and the dusk itself that was peace, were drawing the passion out of him like a poultice. "We're missing something or other, Geoff—benediction, grace."

" You expect too much."

" I expect very little: only to see some sense in being alive, some sense of direction."

" That's quite a bit, isn't it?"

" I shouldn't have said so. If one can't have that much, why be a man at all? Why be the only creature on God's earth that has to try to look into the future, that can't help observing cause and effect and perceiving goodness and badness, when you can't know why or to what end? It's just a chapter of hell."

" You *do* expect too much," Geoff said. " You expect things to make our sort of sense. But I've never found they ever did." He waited till they had turned into the narrower lane which climbed for a bit before it dropped into Neap St. Andrews to cross the stream. " You might as well expect people to talk logically, or to feel things by a military manual, or to think along a straight line of thought, or to have the same ideas in the morning as they do at night. They ought, by the rules, to do all those things. But if we ever found they did, we should know that they weren't people at all; and, personally, I should guess I was quietly dead."

They were starting to drop down into the village. They had got over the hump of the hill, and the Neap was at last in sight. In the dusk the willows were paler than the stream between them. Across the bridge, the stone roofs climbed upon each other at all angles and shone from their store of sunlight. The cottages, the barn, the church were all radiant, though the sun had gone from the valley an hour earlier, and even the afterglow had thickened into quiet tints. And Geoff said contentedly: " One just plugs along all right and sees what turns up."

" Like soldiers waiting to be told what next! " David's answer started scornfully out of his exasperation. For Geoff's solid presence seemed sometimes too smug, his insensitivity to misfortune too indelicate, and the way he was so often and so stubbornly mistaken too irritatingly stupid. He was suited to be a soldier, just jogging along somehow, never quite knowing what was happening, but just guessing, and usually wrong, but not finding out his mistake till long afterwards, by which time it didn't matter. That was Geoff; and yet one loved him, so that the scorn in one's voice got melted in affection; and David's words came out carrying only pity—pity not for Geoff, but for the world and for David.

" Well, we got along somehow," said Geoff cheerfully.

"We got along," said David, meaning that they had stumbled through their war, much as they stumbled through their lives afterwards. And he was thinking, and talking secretly, less of their soldiering than of his whole experience of being alive, of floundering through the human jungle, of struggling in the dark to make each foot in turn get somehow past the other, and calling this labour " progress."

"It worked out all right in the end," said Geoff.

"You think so?" And even if Geoff's conclusion was justified, and the chaos of peace was all that they had fought for, its achievement was thanks not to the great human qualities of intellect and vision, but to the honest, unselfish, unreasoning, stolid, stupid dependability and low-level contrivance of lovable people like Geoff. Bitterly, treacherously and guiltily David derided Geoff, a man whom he loved. For hadn't human existence fallen to a plane where all the brighter human attributes were only superfluous ornaments, and was not the measure of its fall its dependence on such as Geoff?

To-night, the depth of the fall of man was felt in this lovely, silent dusk that was settling calmly on the hamlet through which their lane twisted around barn, manor and church in five right-angle bends, as if it had no destination, and as if no one was meant to pass purposefully from one end of the tiny village to the other, but only to drift here like a blown seed, to lodge, take root, shoot, blossom, make seed for its own continuance and quietly perish. Here it was as quiet as a garden, as quiet as the churchyard they would soon be approaching. The quietness hung like a precipitate of nightfall. There was no one about. But in the gentle cottages, behind the leaded panes, oil-lamps were being lit.

So much beauty made David not joyful but ready to weep. For the joy had been expelled from life—just as the twilight was now being pressed out of this valley beneath the darkness—by the shadow of men's despair in their monstrous communities, the shadow of fingers that grabbed great handfuls of negligible people like himself, squeezing them together into mass slavery, mass obedience to insane plans and laws that were woven like a web and entanglement, catching men and fastening them far below, immeasurably below, the contexture of human hopes.

Up in the sunset a Man might hope and pray. But the hand of communal men dragged him out of the sky and squeezed him down into a stinking blackness. The inventions of communal fingers choked his heart. The stench of a communal prison was his only breath, its darkness his only sight, and its loveless shackles his only human attachment. His dream was the communal nightmare of greed, with no hope of awakening until the loveless grave was reached. No hope of love! But from this despair he said suddenly, astonished at his own words and at his own voice: "I will lift up my eyes to the hills!"

"For the moment," said Geoff, "I should keep them on the road in front." For they were now taking the last and trickiest of the turns round the churchyard where the more recent tombstones shone bright.

And now it seemed to David that the loveliness of the evening had a quite different declaration, prohibiting despair. It seemed, too, that he owed an act of atonement for his treachery to everything that he loved—to Geoff and to his father, to his faith, his home, his vision —and to love itself. With embarrassment he expressed his repentance, quoting his father's words outright: "Lift up your eyes to the hills, because everywhere else they will meet with too little love!"

Geoff said: "He was a great man, your father, by all accounts."

"I suppose he was."

David changed gear to get up speed for the hill which rose steeply ahead. Now he would have said that, if there was a scale of humanity, Geoff was near the top of it. David envied Alex the protection and love of Geoff.

*   *   *

A few more miles over the hills and back to the river at Neapcaster Park. Where the lane divided, Geoff said quickly: "Keep to the left, Dave. Don't take me to the Lodge."

"Changing your mind, Geoff?"

"No. But drop me at Slender Ladies. I want to go there, through the valley, on my own two feet."

David turned his head and smiled his surprise: at the words used or at the sentiments they expressed? Geoff could not bother to guess which it was; for David could never be told the source of both. David asked: "What about your bag?"

"I'll carry that."

It was getting quite dark when the car stopped at Adam's

cottage. But as Geoff got out, he could just see the ancient figure slipping through the deeper shadows round his cottage wall. The old man, as usual, had a load of rabbits.

Between David and Geoff there were several moments of silence that were not awkward. They were like two friends parting on the evening before a battle in which only one of them was going to be engaged. At last David said: "I want to say thank you for quite a lot, only somehow I can't."

"I should think not, Dave! It's quite the reverse."

"Anyway—the best of luck."

"Thanks. I'll see you to-morrow or the day after?"

"I expect so, Geoff." David drove off.

Geoff waved the hand that was not carrying the bag. Even when he saw the headlights switched on, he continued, for a moment or two, to wave at the red point on the tail of the car. For his own satisfaction, he went on waving, although he knew himself to be quite invisible to his friend.

Turning away from the road, he made at a fast pace for Slender Ladies Covert, but half-way between the cottage and the wood, old Adam was waiting. When the old monster spoke, his new false teeth shone as brightly as a negro's in the dusk; but the sounds that came from his mouth were even less easy to interpret than when, as always before, he had been toothless. " Mas'r Geoff . . ." He held out three young rabbits. " If you're going Miss Alex's way . . . she'll find'n handy."

With the rabbits in one hand, his bag in the other, and the bulky documents in his breast pocket, Geoff was heavily burdened for his familiar walk. When he got to the gate into the wood, he wanted a stick on which to carry the rabbits whose legs had already been hocked—slit and threaded through each other for carrying—by the old man. But he found that he had no knife. " I've never before been in Slender Ladies without a knife in my pocket!" It seemed of tremendous significance.

Nevertheless, he went to break a stick with his hands from a clump of ash beside the gate. It was here that the notice " TRES-PASSERS WILL BE PROSECUTED " had always been nailed and annually repainted. It was still there, and the white background to its lettering still shone bright in the darkness. But now that the covert had become Government property, the notice had changed its size and shape. The wording could not be quite deciphered without the help of a match, which in the calm evening burnt steadily enough for Geoff to read: "THIS IS YOUR PROPERTY NOW. TAKE CARE OF IT!"

When Geoff had thrown away the match, he had to plunge after it with an anxious foot. "That I, Geoff, could ever throw a burning match into Slender Ladies in the middle of a dry summer!"

When he got to the bottom of the wood and came out upon the track, he could of course see the House, now the school, with nearly all its windows, on both storeys, and some belonging to the attics, alight along its whole face. He wondered if they were not wasting electricity, but had no other conscious thought.

The downward track here steepened suddenly, and in spite of his burdens, he started to run into the valley in his old fashion. At first he stumbled and slid, almost falling on to his back, until he remembered to keep his weight well forward over his knees. Running up the opposite hill, he was quickly out of breath and had to drop to a walk a couple of hundred yards sooner than had been his old habit. "I'm unfit; I must get myself fit again!" But then he remembered that he was also older. "In a year or so I shall be forty!" And it was only a year or so ago that a man of forty had to be reckoned half dead. "But now, every year, I shall have to stop running uphill at a shorter and shorter distance from the bridge. And the day will come . . ." The unstoppable decline had started; the peak of life was passed.

There was plenty of light at the top of the hill, and without the least hesitation, he left the track and cut directly across the Park towards the Lodge. He was moving now, as always on this part of the route, at a very fast walk. There was so little time before one was dead. As he approached the Lodge, still not daring to think of Alex or to acknowledge either his joy or his fear, he realised with surprise that he had run across the footbridge over the Neap without remarking it. Thus he had slipped without pain through the valley whose mists had in solution his hopes, prayers, promises and ancient guilts. "I suppose I was too busy running with that blessed bag and these rabbits even to notice it!" But he understood now that he had chosen this way home, asking David to leave him at the top by Slender Ladies, only that this ordeal, at least, might be done with.

A trifle before he had expected it, his feet were on the gravel of the drive and he was standing by the Lodge. But for some distance he had been watching the light that burnt in the window of his old bedroom. Putting down his bag and opening the garden gate, he saw that the front door of his home was standing open. He picked up the bag again, went through on to the garden path, and kicked the gate shut behind him. He saw Alex come into the hall, carrying a tray: and at the clang of the gate she turned her head.

As soon as Geoff called, Alex put down the tray, and without any sign of surprise or any inquiry as to who it was, came straight out to him. Burdened as he was in both hands, he could make little response when she stood on her toes and put her arms round his neck and kissed him. " Geoff . . . dear Geoff! "

At once she was asking him about supper, and about his journey —how he had got there, how he had come on foot. And he was answering her, telling her of the day's events.

There seemed, after all, to be nothing momentous about this homecoming, neither a conclusion nor a beginning, but just a continuing, as the waters of the Neap continued, to some lower junction with a river which itself continued to a greater river, and thence to the sea. And the distillations of the sea came back in cloud banks to rain upon the Cotswold hills. There was never an end.

That he and Alex had nothing very much to worry about, that they were going to be quite rich, as rich as anybody else, that they had nothing between them to forgive or to forget, was extraordinarily irrelevant, if not rather tiresome. The thing was too easy. There ought to have been the cry of a trumpet, calling them to battle. But the only battle, the only enemy, was within.

Therefore, when he got into the house, he made ready for battle in the only way he knew, putting down his bags, taking off his coat and asking: " What wants carrying where? " They were both laughing at this, when suddenly tears started to trickle down his cheeks. She was not in the least shocked, or even surprised. Briskly she took his face between her hands and kissed it.

THE END